Games
of the
Hangman

Games
of the
Hangman

VICTOR O'REILLY

GROVE WEIDENFELD
New York

Published by Grove Weidenfeld
A division of Grove Press, Inc.
841 Broadway
New York, NY 10003-4793

Published in Canada by General Publishing Company, Ltd.

Library of Congress Cataloging-in-Publication Data

O'Reilly, Victor.

Games of the hangman : a novel / Victor O'Reilly.—1st ed.
p.   cm.
ISBN 0-8021-1431-8 (alk. paper)
I. Title.
PR6065.R65G3   1991
823'.914—dc20   91-2872
                                                              CIP

Manufactured in the United States of America

Printed on acid-free paper

Designed by Irving Perkins Associates

First Edition 1991

1   3   5   7   9   10   8   6   4   2

For Alma and my children, Kira, Christian, Shane, Evie, and Bruff—with much love.

For Sterling Lord, my agent—a man who is widely liked, respected, and admired for very good reason.

For Miranda Cowley (Sterling Lord Literistic) and Rose Marie Morse and Marc Romano (Grove Weidenfeld) for much hard work in the salt mines.

For Tony Summers, the best of friends when the chips are down—and the man who introduced me to Sterling.

For the Swiss in general and the people of Bern in particular, who are very far from dull, as you will see.

"From ancient times, most samurai have been of eccentric spirit, strong willed and courageous."

—YUKIO MISHIMA, *Hagakure*

"Plumb hell or heaven, what's the difference? Plumb the unknown, to find out something new!"

—CHARLES BAUDELAIRE

Games
of the
Hangman

Prologue

When he was told he was to hang, Rudi had turned pale and swayed on his feet.

Later he was more composed, and it was clear to the others that he had accepted the inevitability of what was to come. He was given no choice. Either he would accept the verdict and do what was necessary or he would be killed painfully—and so would Vreni and other members of his family. It was one life or several, and either way he would die. There was only one decision he could make. He was told that his hanging would be quick and painless.

He had reached a point where he couldn't take it anymore, where what they were doing and what they planned to do—however valid the reasons—were suddenly abhorrent. He could no longer continue. Physically his body rebelled, and he felt ill and nauseated. His mind was a morass of terrible images and memories, and hope and belief were dead. He had been warned when he joined that he could never leave alive.

He thought of fleeing or going to the authorities or fighting back in some way, but he knew—knew with absolute certainty—that they meant what they said and would do what they had threatened. It must be his life, or Vreni and Marta and Andreas would die.

In many ways he welcomed the prospect of death. Guilt engulfed him and he could see no way out. He knew he would not be forgiven for what he had done already; he could not forgive himself.

The arrangements were made by the others. He had been told where to go and what to do. The rope was already in place when he reached the old oak tree. It was thin and blue and of a type used daily around Draker for myriad tasks. It was hard to believe this mundane object would end his life. He had been told that precise calculations had been made to ensure that his death would be instantaneous.

Four of the others stood around the tree watching and waiting but making no motion to help. He must do this alone.

He climbed the tree with some difficulty because the bark was wet and slippery from recent rain. He stepped out onto the branch and slipped the noose around his neck. He nearly slipped and used the hanging rope to steady himself. His hands were shaking and his skin felt clammy.

He could see two of the watchers below him. A wave of despair and loneliness swept over him and he longed to see some friendly face. In seconds he would be dead. Nobody would truly care. Nobody would ever know the real reasons why. The man in Bern was hanging him as surely as if he had been physically present instead of fifteen hundred kilometers away from this miserable dripping forest.

Rudi suddenly thought of his father and the time when the family had all been happy together. Rudi could see him, and he was smiling. It was the way it used to be. He stepped off the branch toward him.

It wasn't over in seconds. The man in Bern had been explicit: it wasn't meant to be. It took Rudi some considerable time to die.

The watchers—appalled and excited and stimulated—waited until the spasming and jerking and sounds of choking had ceased, and then they left.

It was a small thing compared with what was to come.

BOOK ONE

The Hanging

"Irish? In truth, I would not want to be anything else. It is a state of mind as well as an actual country. It is being at odds with other nationalities, having a quite different philosophy about pleasure, about punishment, about life, and about death. . . ."

—EDNA O'BRIEN, Mother Ireland

Chapter One

Fitzduane slept uneasily that night but awoke with no conscious premonition that anything was wrong. It was raining when he climbed out onto the fighting platform of the castle keep and looked across the battlements to the dawn. He reflected that rain was something anyone brought up in Ireland had plenty of time to get used to.

More than seven hundred years earlier the first Fitzduane had stood in much the same spot for much the same reason. Inclement weather or not, the view from the castle keep brought satisfaction, even in the grim, dull month of February. The land they saw was theirs, and the Fitzduanes, whatever their personal idiosyncrasies, shared a "what I have I hold" mentality.

The rain stopped, and the sky lightened.

The castle stood on a rocky bluff, and from his vantage point Fitzduane could see much of the island. It just qualified as an island, a windswept finger of bog, heather, low hills, and rough pasture jutting out into the Atlantic and separated from the mainland by a mere twenty meters. A bridge set well into the overhanging cliff tops spanned the divide.

Farther inland was a freshwater lake by whose edge stood a small white thatched cottage. A trickle of smoke emerged from its chimney. Inside, Murrough and his wife, Oona, the couple who looked after the castle and its lands, would be having breakfast. Murrough had been Fitzduane's sergeant in the Congo nearly twenty years earlier.

The Atlantic crashed and spumed against the rocks that formed the seaward base of the castle. Fitzduane savored the familiar sound. He huddled deeper into his heavy waterproof as the gusting wind, even at this height, blew salt spray into his face.

He glanced at his watch. Half past eight. Time to go. He closed the roof door behind him and descended the circular staircase with some care. The stone steps were worn by centuries of use, and it was five flights to the storeroom and the armory below. The old names for the rooms were still used. Although sides of salt-cured bacon no longer hung from the blackened hooks of the storeroom ceiling, any self-respecting Norman knight would still have been impressed by the reserves of weaponry that were on display in the armory. If the same knight had been familiar with firearms and the matériel of modern warfare, he would have been dazzled by the collection of rifles, pistols, and automatic weapons concealed in the deeper recesses of the castle. Illegal though it was under current Irish law, Fitzduane maintained the family tradition of collecting weapons of war.

IN ITS ORIGINAL FORM the castle had been a rectangular tower of five floors topped by the fighting platform, with the entrance, accessible only by ladder, on the second story. Over the centuries the castle had been adapted, strengthened, and modernized. A three-story slate-roofed extension now nestled up to the original rectangular keep. Stone steps replaced the ladder. A curtain wall surrounded the bawn, as the castle courtyard is known in Ireland, and stables and outhouses had been built inside the enclosed perimeter. A network of concealed tunnels and storerooms had been added in the sixteenth century.

The entrance, always the weakest part of a castle, was through a small two-story tower, known as the gatehouse, or barbican, set into the curtain wall. The floor of the protruding upper story was pierced with openings—murder holes—from which missiles and boiling water could be dropped upon attackers.

The original iron portcullis, the heavy spiked gridiron gate that could be dropped into place at a second's notice like a guillotine, had long since rusted away, but it had been replaced during the Napoleonic Wars. It now hung, its windlass oiled and in working order, awaiting an attack that would never come. Externally the castle was guarded by the sea and the cliffs on two sides, and a deep ditch secured the rest.

Duncleeve, the ancestral home of the Fitzduanes for more than seven hundred years, had never been taken by direct assault. That was reassuring, Fitzduane sometimes thought, but of limited practical advantage in the late twentieth century.

HOOVES CLATTERED on the wooden bridge over the defensive ditch. Fitzduane applied a slight pressure with his knees, and Pooka turned to canter up the slope to the cliff top. The sea crashed against the rocks far below, and though the ground was wet and slippery, Fitzduane rode with confidence. Pooka was surefooted and knew her way.

The island was just over ten kilometers long and about four kilometers across at its widest point. Besides Fitzduane and Murrough and his wife, the only other inhabitants lived in the isolated school on the headland.

The school was officially called the Draker World Institute. Originally the site of a monastery destroyed by Cromwell's troops in the seventeenth century, the land had been bought by an eccentric German armaments manufacturer toward the end of the nineteenth century. With his profits from the Franco-Prussian War, he proceeded to design and build his conception of an Irish castle.

The construction lacked certain desirable features. Von Draker forgot to install either bathrooms or toilets. Not realizing his error, von Draker came to stay in his apparently completed castle. Tragedy struck. While relieving himself behind a rhododendron bush, he was drenched by a sudden squall of rain—the weather in Connemara being nothing if not fickle—and pneumonia resulted. After a short struggle for the sake of form, von Draker died. He left behind a large fortune, no children, a wife he had loathed, and the request that his Irish estate be turned into a college for students from all over the world "who will mix together, learn each other's ways, become friends, and thus preserve world peace."

Those who knew von Draker well had been somewhat taken aback at such sentiments from such an unlikely source. His actual words to his lawyer were: "Find a way to keep that hag's filthy paws off my money."

The fortune of the Von Draker Peace Foundation, derived in the main from armaments and explosives, increased and multiplied. In the fullness of time the Draker World Institute opened its doors for business. It took a select group of pupils aged sixteen to twenty from various corners of the globe and subjected them to a moderately difficult academic curriculum heavily leavened with boating, climbing, hill walking, and other physically demanding activities.

Draker was a success primarily because it was so isolated. It was a perfect out-of-sight, out-of-mind location for rich but troublesome youths. It was also coeducational. The children could be dumped there during that difficult phase. All it took to gain entrance to Draker was money and the appropriate connections. Draker parents had both in commendable quantities.

FITZDUANE SLOWED Pooka to a walk. He could feel the wind off the Atlantic in his face and a hint of salt on his lips. He was beginning to unwind. It was good to be home despite the unfortunate weather.

He was getting tired of wars and of what was arguably more unpleasant: the grinding hassle of modern travel. The older he got, the more he thought there was much to be said for peace and quiet, maybe even for settling down.

Fitzduane spent two-thirds or more of each year away from Ireland. This was something he regretted, but the action tended to be in alien climes. For nearly twenty years he had been either a soldier or a war photographer, a hunter of men with either a gun or a camera. The Congo, Vietnam, the Arab-Israeli wars, Vietnam again, Cyprus, Angola, Rhodesia, Cambodia, Lebanon, Chad, Namibia, endless South American countries. His Irish island was his haven, his place to recover, to rest his soul. It might offer little more excitement than watching the grass grow, but it was the one place he knew that was free of death and violence.

Down below, he could see the small beach, boathouse, and jetty of Draker College. The sheer cliffs had made access almost impossible until von Draker had brought over some of his company's explosive experts and had blasted and hacked a diagonal tunnel from the castle gardens down to the beach.

Fitzduane rode between the walled gardens of Draker College and the cliff edge. The gray stone of the Victorian castle loomed in the background. Gargoyles competed with crenellations; flying buttresses crash-landed against half-timbering. A structure loosely modeled on the Parthenon topped the clock tower. Irish history had been complex, but even *it* was not up to von Draker's creativity.

Ahead lay a small wood, and beyond that was the headland itself. If the weather permitted, Fitzduane liked to turn Pooka loose to nibble at the salty, windswept grass, and then he would lie down near the cliff edge, look up at the sky and the wheeling sea gulls, and think of absolutely nothing.

War and death could be forgotten for a time. Perhaps, he thought, the time had come to hang up his cameras and find a more adult occupation.

VON DRAKER HAD had a passion for trees. There had originally been only one oak tree on the spot and, nearby, a peculiarly shaped mound. The locals gave the vicinity a wide berth. They said that the oak tree was a *bille* and special, and that no man could remember when it was planted. They said that in the days before St. Patrick and Ireland's conversion to Christianity, terrible things had been done under the shadow of its twisted branches. They said that even after the Church was established throughout the rest of the land, bloody sacrifice continued on the island.

Von Draker had regarded such tales as nonsense. Since none of the Connemara men would help him level the mound and plant the wood, he had brought in a crew from his estate in Germany. He left the old oak tree, not for reasons of superstition but because he just liked trees, even gnarled and twisted specimens like this one. The mound was leveled with his explosives. His workers found pieces of bone in the debris and fragments of what appeared to be human skulls. A small wood was planted. Trees from many parts of the world were brought to the spot, and despite the keen wind off the Atlantic and the heavy rain, an adequate number prospered.

Von Draker did not live to see the success of his project. His death came one year to the day after the demolition of the peculiarly shaped mound. The wind that day around his wood sounded like laughter— or so they said.

Such tales were absurd, Fitzduane thought, yet there was no denying that the overgrown wood was a dismal, depressing place. Rain dripping from the trees made the only noise in an otherwise eerie silence. Obscured by the interlocking branches, the light was dim and gloomy.

The forest reeked of decay and corruption. Pooka had to be urged on, as always in the wood, despite the many times she had walked that path before. The sound of her iron-shod hooves was muffled by the damp mulch of rotting leaves. The place seemed deserted, and Fitzduane realized that he had seen no living soul since leaving his castle nearly an hour before. Halfway through the wood the undergrowth became particularly dense, and the path inclined upward and twisted more than usual. He could see the thick trunk of the *bille* up ahead.

Horse and rider came level with the tree. He glanced up into its labyrinth of interlocking branches. It was a fine tree, he thought, impressive in its ancient strength.

He saw the rope first, a thin pale blue rope. It hung from a protruding branch of the tree. The end of the rope had been formed into a hangman's noose, and it contained the elongated and distorted neck of a hanged man.

The long, still body formed a silhouette in the gloom. Fitzduane raised his eyebrows and stared for perhaps ten interminable seconds. He thought he'd close his eyes and then open them again because a hanging body on his own doorstep just couldn't be true.

Chapter Two

There was a context to death Fitzduane was used to. In any one of a dozen combat zones he would have reacted immediately, reflexes operating ahead of any conscious rationalization. On his own island, the one place he knew that was free of violence, his brain would not accept the evidence of his own eyes.

He urged Pooka forward.

He could smell the body. It wasn't damp earth or rotting leaves or the decaying flesh of some dead animal; it was the odor of fresh human excrement. He could see the source. The body was clad in an olive green anorak and blue jeans, and the jeans were stained around the loins.

Horse and rider walked slowly past the body, Fitzduane staring despite himself. After a dozen paces he found he was looking back over his shoulder. Ahead lay the familiar contours of the path to the headland and a lazy tranquillity; behind him hung death and a premonition that life would never be the same if he turned.

He stopped. Slowly and reluctantly he dismounted and tied Pooka to a nearby tree. He looked ahead along the empty path again. It lay there, tempting him to go away, to forget what he was seeing.

He hesitated; then he turned back.

The head was slightly twisted and angled to one side by the initial shock of the drop combined with the action of the noose. The hair was long, light brown, and wavy—almost curly. The face was that of a young man. The skin was bluish despite a golden tan. The tongue was swollen and thrust out sharply between grimacing teeth. There was a small amount of still-fresh but clotting blood under the mouth and dripping from the chin. A long, thick rope of spittle, phlegm, and mucus hung from the end of the protruding tongue to halfway down his torso. Combined with the stench, the overall impact was revolting.

He approached the body, reached up, and took one of the limp hands in his. He expected it to be cold; though he knew better, he automatically associated death with cold. The hand was cool to the touch but still retained traces of warmth. He felt for the pulse: there was none.

He looked at the hand. There were greenish black marks from the tree trunk on the palms and the insides of the fingers, and mixed in were scratches extending to the fingertips. He thought about cutting the body down but doubted that he could. The knot on the nylon rope was impacted into the dead flesh, and he had no knife. The idea of burning through the rope crossed his mind, but he had no lighter.

He forced himself to think clearly. Cutting down the body wouldn't help at this stage. It would make no difference to the corpse. There was a gust of wind, and the body swayed slightly. Fitzduane started at the unexpected movement.

He made himself react as if he were on assignment: first the story. He slid his backup camera, an Olympus XA he normally carried out of photographer's habit, from the breast pocket of his coat. His actions were automatic as he selected aperture, speed, and angle. He framed each shot, cutting it in his head before releasing the shutter and bracketing, with the old hand's innate conservatism and suspicion of built-in exposure meters.

He was conscious of the incongruity of his actions but at the same time aware of his reasons: he was buying time so that he could adjust. He brushed sweat from his forehead and began to search the corpse. It wasn't easy. The smell of feces was overpowering, and the height of the limp figure made the search awkward. He could reach only the lower pockets.

In an outside pocket of the green anorak he found an expensive morocco leather wallet. It contained Irish pounds, Swiss francs, and several credit cards. It also held a laminated student identity card complete with color photo. The dead youth was Rudolf von Graffenlaub, nineteen years of age, from Bern, Switzerland, and a pupil at Draker College. His height was listed at one meter seventy-six. Looking at the stretched neck at the end of the rope, Fitzduane reflected sadly that he would be taller now.

He walked back to where he had left Pooka. Her uneasiness showed, and he stroked her, speaking softly. As he did so, he realized he now faced the unpleasant task of telling the college authorities that one of their pupils had hanged himself. He wondered why he had automatically assumed that it was suicide. Murder by hanging seemed a complicated way to go about things—but was it possible? Was it likely? If accidental death was required, throwing the victim over a cliff seemed much more practical. It did occur to him that if it was murder, the killer could still be in the wood. It was a disturbing notion.

As they emerged from the dank atmosphere of the forest, Pooka whinnied with pleasure and made as if to break into a canter. Fitzduane let her have her head, the canter became a gallop, and they thundered along the cliff and then swung into the grounds of Draker.

Fitzduane's head cleared with the burst of exercise. He knew that the next sequence of events would not be pleasant. It had crossed his mind to keep on riding. Home wasn't too far away.

The trouble was, although he did not yet fully appreciate it, Rudolf von Graffenlaub's death had moved him deeply. His instincts were aroused. The tragedy had happened on his own ground at a time when he was reassessing his own direction in life. It was both a provocation and a challenge. His peaceful haven in the midst of a bloody world had been violated. He wanted to know why.

IT HAD BEEN years since Fitzduane had visited the college.

He entered a heavy side door that stood ajar. Inside, there was a flagstone hall, a door, and a wide wooden stairway. He climbed the stairs. There was a door off the landing at the top, and through it he could hear the sound of voices and laughter and the clinking of spoons against china. He turned the handle.

Inside the large paneled, book-lined room about two dozen

people in the mix of casual and formal clothes beloved of academics were grouped around a blazing log fire, having their morning coffee. He felt as if he were back at school and should have knocked.

An elderly gray-haired lady turned around at his entrance and looked him up and down. "Your boots," she said with a thin smile.

Fitzduane looked at her blankly.

"Your boots," she repeated.

He looked down at his muddy boots. The floor was inlaid with brass in runic patterns. Shades of the Anglo-Irish literary revival and a Celtic Ireland that never was.

"Would you mind removing your boots, sir?" said the gray-haired lady more sharply, the smile now distinctly chilly. "Everybody does. It's the floor," she added in a mollifying tone.

Fitzduane noticed a neat row of outdoor footwear by the umbrella stand at the entrance. Too taken aback to argue, he removed his muddy riding boots and stood there in his wool socks.

"Hi," said a fresh voice. He turned toward a lived-in but still attractive brunette in her mid-thirties. She was tall and slim and wore round granny glasses and had an aura of flower child of the sixties gone more or less straight. She had a delicious smile. He wondered if she had a little marijuana crop in her window box and how it—and she—endured Irish weather.

"Hi yourself," he answered. He didn't smile back. Suddenly he felt tired. "I'm afraid this isn't going to make your day," he said quietly. As he was telling her his story, he handed her Rudolf's identity card. She stared at him for what seemed to be an age, uncomprehending, and then her coffee cup crashed to the floor.

Conversation stopped, and all heads swiveled in their direction. In the silence that had fallen over the room, it took Fitzduane a moment to realize that the pool of hot coffee was slowly soaking into his socks.

IT WAS NOT necessary for Fitzduane to return to the scene of the hanging, and he knew it, yet back he went. He felt proprietorial toward Rudolf. He had found the body, so in some strange way he was now responsible for it.

Perhaps a half dozen of the faculty went with Fitzduane to the old oak tree. Rudolf still hung there. Fortunately for the nervous onlookers, the body had stopped swaying in the wind and now hung motionless.

Fitzduane was aware that in all probability some of the people present had some previous experience of death, even violent death. Yet the hanging, with all its macabre history and connotations of ritual punishment, had a very particular impact. It showed on their faces. One teacher who could not contain himself could be heard retching behind the trunk of a sycamore tree. The sound seemed to go on and on. Several others looked about ready to join him.

A long aluminum ladder was brought up at a run by two fit-looking young men. The sight of them reminded Fitzduane that pupils at Draker spent a great deal of their time in outdoor activities. In a casual conversation some years earlier, one of the lecturers, since departed, had remarked, "We try to exhaust the buggers. It's the only way we can keep them under control."

Many of the students, Fitzduane recalled, came from troubled, albeit rich backgrounds, and a good number were old enough to vote, to be conscripted, or to start a family. Doubtless some had. All in all, it seemed a thoroughly sensible precaution to keep them busy rushing up and down cliff faces and being blown around the cold waters of the Atlantic.

They waited in the gloom of the forest to one side of the old oak tree until the police and ambulance arrived. It took some time. There was no police station on the island. The nearest was at Ballyvonane on the mainland, some fifteen kilometers of potholed road away. There were attempts at conversation governed by some unspoken rule that the hanging itself should not be discussed. Fitzduane, standing slightly apart from the group as befitted the bearer of bad news, chewed on a piece of long grass and made himself comfortable against the supporting contours of a not-too-damp outcrop of rock.

He was curious to see what the police would do. A man was dead, and dead from violence. There had to be an investigation. There wouldn't be one in El Salvador, where bodies were dumped unceremoniously on rubbish dumps by death squads, or in Cambodia, where so many millions had been slaughtered by the Khmer Rouge that one extra body was of no significance. But this was home, where violence was rare and different, more caring standards prevailed.

Two guards arrived: the local sergeant—well known to Fitz-

duane—and a fresh-faced youngster not long from the training barracks in Templemore by the look of him. Their heavy blue uniform
trousers were tucked into farmers' rubber boots, and their faces were
shaded and impassive under dark blue uniform hats. The sergeant,
Tommy Keane, had his chin strap in position and was puffing
slightly.

It would be untrue to say that there was no examination of the
scene of the incident; there was. It lasted perhaps sixty seconds and
consisted of the sergeant's padding around the tree a couple of times,
staring up at the hanging body as he did so, his boots leaving a perfect
trail of cleated prints in the soft ground, obscuring with official
finality any previous marks.

Fitzduane's gaze drifted back to the body. Its feet, limp and
slightly parted, were shod in surprisingly formal dark brown shoes
polished to a military gloss. He wondered if Rudolf had spit-shined
his shoes that morning—and if so, why?

The ladder was placed against the tree. The sergeant tested it a
couple of times, placed the young guard at the foot to hold it securely, and climbed. He removed a bone-handled folding knife from
the pocket of his uniform raincoat and opened the blade.

Knife in hand, he surveyed the gathering. Silhouetted in that way
above the body, he reminded Fitzduane of a print he had seen of an
eighteenth-century execution.

"Hugo, give us a hand," said the sergeant. "Let's cut the lad
down."

Automatically Fitzduane moved forward and stood just under the
corpse. There was the brief sawing sound of the blade against taut
rope, and the body fell into his waiting arms.

He clasped it to him, suddenly more disturbed than he would have
thought possible at the absolute waste of it. The torso was still
warm. He held the broken body, the head disfigured and hideous,
flopping from the extended neck. He would often think of that
moment afterward. It seemed to him that it was the physical contact
with that once-so-promising young body that forced him into the
resolve not to be a bystander, not to treat this death as one more item
in a long catalog of observed violence, but to find out, if at all
possible, why.

Other hands joined him, and the moment when he had the dead
boy in his arms alone was over. They prepared to set the body on the
ground; a thick plastic bag had already been laid out. As Fitzduane

lowered the shoulders onto the protecting surface, a long moan emerged from the hanged boy's bloodstained mouth.

They all froze, shocked, unwilling to contemplate the same unpalatable thought: Had Rudolf von Graffenlaub been quietly strangling while they all stood around making awkward conversation and waiting for the police?

The long, low moan died away. It was a sound that Fitzduane had heard before, though it was nonetheless unsettling for that. "It's the air," he said quickly. "It's only the air being squeezed out of his lungs as we move him." He looked around at the circle of greenish white faces and hoped he was right.

HALF AN HOUR LATER he sat in front of the sergeant in the library of Draker College, which had been commandeered as an interview room for the occasion, and made his statement. He looked at the mud drying on the guard's heavy boots and the crisscrossing of muddy footprints on the inlaid floor. Standards were dropping.

"You don't look great, Hugo," said the sergeant. "I'd have thought you'd be used to this kind of thing."

Fitzduane shrugged. "So would I." He smiled slightly. "It seems that it's different on your own doorstep."

The sergeant nodded. "Or the last straw." He puffed at an old black briar pipe with a silver top over the bowl to protect it from the wind, and from it emanated the rich aroma of pipe tobacco. He was a big, heavyset man not many years from retirement.

"Tommy," said Fitzduane, "somehow I expected more of an investigation before the body was cut down. The immediate area being roped off. An examination by the forensic people. That sort of thing."

The sergeant raised a grizzled eyebrow. His reply was measured. "Hugo, if I didn't know you so well, I might be thinking there was just the faintest tincture of criticism in that remark."

Fitzduane spread his hands in a gesture of apology. "Perish the thought," he said, and fell silent. The look of inquiry remained on his face.

The sergeant knew Fitzduane well. He chuckled, but then remembered the circumstances and reverted to his professional manner. "Don't go having any strange thoughts, Hugo. The site round the tree had been well trampled by you lot before we ever showed up.

Anyway, I've had thirty-four years in the Guards, and I've seen my share of hangings. They've always been suicide. It's just about impossible to kill someone by hanging without leaving signs, and there are easier ways of committing murder."

"Was there a note?"

"No," said the sergeant, "or at least we haven't found one yet, but the absence of a note means nothing. Indeed, a note is an exception rather than the rule."

"Any idea why he might have killed himself, then?"

"Not specifically," said the sergeant. "I've quite a few people to see yet. But the ones I've spoken to so far said he was very intense, very moody. Apparently there were some difficulties with his family in Switzerland. He's from a place called Bern."

"It's the Swiss capital," said Fitzduane.

"Ever been there?" asked the sergeant.

"No, although I've changed planes in Zurich God knows how many times. My business is photographing wars, and the Swiss have this strange affection for peace."

"Well, the pathologist will conduct his examination tomorrow, I should think," declared the sergeant. "The inquest will be a day or two after that. You'll have to attend. I'll give you as much warning as I can."

"Thanks, Tommy."

They rose to their feet and shook hands briskly. It was cold in the library, and the fire had gone out. As he was about to open the door, the sergeant turned to Fitzduane. "It doesn't do to make too much fuss about these things. Best soon forgotten."

Fitzduane smiled thinly and didn't answer.

As he rode back to Duncleeve, Fitzduane realized that he had forgotten to raise the small matter of his missing goat with the policeman. A goat gone astray wasn't exactly a police matter in itself, but the discovery a few days earlier of its decapitated and eviscerated carcass at the site of an old sacrificial mound up in the hills raised a few questions.

He wondered what had happened to the animal's magnificent horned head.

Chapter Three

She looked down at him. She could feel him move inside her—the faintest caress of love. Her thighs tightened in spontaneous response. His hands stroked her breasts and then moved around to her back. She could feel a tingling along her spine as he touched her. Her head fell back, and she thrust against him, feeling him go deeper inside her.

Their bodies were damp with sweat. She licked her thumb and forefinger and then reached down to her loins and felt through their intertwined pubic hair for where his penis entered her body. She encircled the engorged organ and rotated her fingers gently.

His whole body quivered, and then he controlled himself. She removed her fingers slowly. "That's cheating," he murmured. He smiled, and there was laughter and love in his eyes as he looked at her. "That is a game two can play." She laughed, and then her laughter turned to gasps as his finger found her clitoris and stroked her in the exact place and with the rhythm and pressure she liked. She came in less than a minute, her upper body arched back and supported by her arms, her loins thrust against her lover.

He pulled her down to him, and they kissed deeply and slowly. She ran her fingers across his face and kissed his eyelids. They stayed interlocked, kissing and caressing. He remained hard inside her. He

21

had already climaxed twice in the last hour and a half, and now it was easier.

They separated and lay side by side, looking at each other, still joined together at their loins. She felt him move again. Her juices began to flow once more. She felt sensual and sore, and she wanted him. He is, she thought, the most beautiful and sexy man.

He was a big man. He didn't look it at first glance because his face was finely chiseled and sensitive and his green eyes were gentle, but as he rolled on top of her, she could feel the power and weight of his physique. She drew up her knees and wrapped her legs around him. He kissed and sucked each of her nipples in turn. He was still holding back, but she could sense his control going. Her hands dug into his back as his thrusts increased. She bit the lobe of his ear and reached down to his buttocks and pulled him into her. He raised himself slightly to increase further the friction of his penis against her clitoris. She gasped as he did so and thrust her forefinger into him. She could feel herself coming again and began to moan. He lost all semblance of control and came with frantic bursts into her body. He stayed on top of her and in her when it was over, his face nuzzled against her neck. She hugged him tightly and then stroked him like a child. Now and then she could feel the contours of the scars on his body.

They slept intertwined for several hours.

FITZDUANE WAS entertained by the contrast between a naked woman in the throes of lovemaking and the same woman in the cool, clothed image she presented to the rest of the world. The thought was not without erotic content. He wondered if women have similar thoughts. He thought it likely.

In the morning Etan was the armored career woman once again: ash blonde hair swept back and tied in a chignon; silk blouse with Russian collar, tailored suit from Wolfangel, accessories perfectly coordinated; the glint of gold on ears, neck, and wrists; a hint of Ricci.

"It's as well I know you're a natural blonde," he said. "Or rather, *how* I know it. Otherwise I'd feel distanced by that getup." He gestured at the laden table on the glassed-in veranda. "Breakfast is ready."

He had bathed and shaved but then had concentrated on preparing the meal. He was wearing only a white terry-cloth bathrobe. The name of its original—and presumably still legal—owner, faded from numerous washings, could just be discerned on the breast pocket.

In the distance, muted by the thick glass, there was the sound of a late-waking city, of traffic grinding through the expensive Dublin residential area of Ballsbridge.

"A little distance is necessary at times," she said with a smile. "I've got a professional image to maintain. I don't want to climax on camera." He raised an eyebrow. She kissed him and sat down across the table. She could see scrambled eggs and smoked salmon, and there were bubbles in the orange juice.

They had met some three years earlier when Radio Telefis Eireann, Ireland's state-owned national broadcasting organization, had sent a camera crew over to do a magazine piece on Fitzduane's exhibition of war photographs in the Shelbourne Hotel. Fitzduane had disliked being on the receiving end of a camera and had been clipped and enigmatic during the interview. Afterward he had been annoyed with himself for making the interview more difficult and less interesting than it might have been. He went over to apologize and was mildly surprised when Etan had responded by inviting him out to dinner.

They were lovers who had become friends. It might have become more, perhaps *had* become more—neither admitted it—but their careers kept them apart. Program deadlines kept Etan confined to the studios in Dublin for much of the time, and Fitzduane was out of Ireland so much. Though Etan was very fond of Fitzduane and had a growing sense that this might be more than an affair, she found it hard to understand how a man of such apparent gentleness and sensitivity engaged in such a dangerous and macabre occupation.

He had once tried to explain it. He had a beautiful, rich voice with scarcely a trace of an Irish accent—a characteristic of his class and background. It was his voice above all, she thought, that had attracted her initially. She had rejected his rationale with some vigor, but she remembered his words.

"War is about extremes," he had said, "extremes of violence and horror, but also extremes of heroism, of compassion, and of comradeship. It's the ultimate paradox. It's feeling utterly, totally alive in every molecule of your body because of—not in spite of—the presence and the threat of death. Often I hate it, and often I'm afraid, yet after it's over and I'm away from it, I want to go back. I miss that sense of being on the edge."

He had turned to her and stroked her cheek. "Besides," he had added with a grin, "it's what I know."

He decided he would take a raincheck on pointing out to her that virtually every day, she presented, from a warm, safe studio, the sort of violent news stories she criticized him for covering. But then again, maybe she wasn't being so inconsistent. Eating meat didn't automatically make you want to work in a slaughterhouse.

She remembered her temper flaring and her sense of frustration. "It's like hearing a drug addict trying to rationalize his heroin," she had said. "To me it doesn't make sense to make your living out of photographing people killing each other. It's even crazier when that puts you at risk as well. You're not immune just because you carry a press card and a camera, you know that bloody well. I miss you horribly when you go. Like a damn fool, instead of putting you out of my mind, I worry myself sick that you may be killed or maimed or just disappear."

He had kissed her gently on the lips, and despite herself she had responded. "The older I get, the less chance I have of being killed," he had said. "It's mostly the young who die in war; that's the way the system works. You mightn't be considered old enough to vote, but they'll make a paratrooper out of you."

"Bullshit," she had retorted, and then she had made love to him with tenderness and anger, sobbing when she had climaxed. Afterward she had held him in her arms, her cheeks wet, while he slept. It didn't change anything.

ETAN FINISHED her coffee and looked at her watch. She would have to leave for the studios in a few minutes. Even though RTE in Donnybrook was not far away, she would be driving in traffic.

Fitzduane had scarcely touched his breakfast. He smiled at her absentmindedly when she got up, and then he went back to staring into the middle distance. She stood behind his chair and put her arms around his neck. She pressed her cheek to his. Beneath the banter and the tenderness he was troubled.

"You're doing your thousand-yard stare," she said.

"It's the hanging."

"I know," she said.

"We cut him down, cut him open, put him in a box, and sent him airmail back to Bern; nineteen years of age, and all we seem to want to do is get rid of the scandal. Nobody cares why."

She held him tightly. "It's not that people don't care," she said. "It's just that they don't know what to do. And what's the point now? It's too late. He's dead."

"But why?" he persisted.

"Does it make a difference?"

He moved his head so he could look at her and suddenly smiled. He took her hand in his and moved her palm against his lips; it was a long kiss. She felt a rush of love, of caring.

"Maybe it's male menopause," he said, "but I think it does."

"What are you going to do about it?"

"Lay the ghost," he answered. "I'm going to find out why."

"But how?" she said, suddenly afraid. "What will you do?"

"I'll follow the advice of the King to Alice in Wonderland."

She laughed despite herself. "What was that?"

" 'Begin at the beginning, and go on till you come to the end: then stop.' "

ETAN HAD BEEN sleeping with Fitzduane for nearly a year before she discovered he had once been married. He had never mentioned it. She had assumed that his way of life was the primary reason he hadn't settled down, but what she learned was more complicated. It helped explain his reluctance to make a further commitment. It also cast some light on her lover's growing obsession with this latest tragedy. Perhaps, once again, in his mind he had been too late.

The name in the yellowed press clipping was Anne-Marie Thormann Fitzduane. Etan had been putting together a documentary on Ireland's involvements with the various United Nations peacekeeping forces when a researcher dropped a series of thick files on the Congo operation on her desk.

The Belgian Congo—now known as Zaire—had been granted independence at the beginning of the sixties but had been ill prepared by its former masters for its new role. Trained administrators were virtually nonexistent. A handful of doctors was incapable of dealing with a population of more than thirteen million. Central government authority collapsed. Civil war broke out. Massacres and pillaging and wholesale wanton destruction became the order of the day.

A United Nations force was sent in to restore order and keep the peace. Before long, to many UN troopers the peacekeeping mission seemed more like a war. Elite combat units like the Indian Gurkhas were seconded to the UN. Fitzduane was a young lieutenant in Ireland's contribution, an Airborne Rangers battalion under the leadership of Colonel Shane Kilmara.

Etan was able to piece much of the story together from the clippings files. She learned that Anne-Marie had been a nurse with the Red Cross and had met Fitzduane at a mission in the bush when he was out on long-range patrol. They had been married within weeks. There was a photo of the wedding, which had taken place in the provincial capital. The honor guard consisted of Irish troops, and the bridesmaids were Red Cross nurses. The accompanying story told of the whirlwind romance. The couple looked very young and carefree and happy. The troops in the honor guard were smiling. Only their combat uniforms and sidearms gave a hint of the bloodbath to come.

The Congo was a vast land, and the UN forces were sorely stretched. Fitzduane's unit moved on to another trouble spot, leaving the provincial capital lightly guarded and under the care of central government troops. The troops revolted and were joined by an invading column of rebels—Simbas, they were called. Hostages were taken.

Etan heard the rest of the story from Fitzduane. Holding hands, they had walked slowly from his castle to the lake nearby. They sat on a log and looked out across the lake and the intervening strip of land toward the sea and the spectacular sunset. The log had been covered with moss and damp, and the air had a chill to it. She could still vividly recall the texture of the mossy bark.

Fitzduane had looked into the setting sun, his face aglow, and had murmured, "A world of cold fire." He had been silent for some moments before continuing.

"The UN Secretary-General had been killed in a plane crash a few weeks earlier. Everything was confused. Nobody could decide what to do about the hostages. We were ordered to hold fast and do nothing. The Simbas were threatening to kill the hostages, and we knew firsthand they weren't bluffing. Kilmara decided on his own initiative to go in and asked for volunteers. Just about the whole unit stepped forward, which was no surprise. Under Kilmara we thought we could walk on water.

"Anyway, we went in—the place was called Konina—by land, water, and air. Some of us sneaked in ahead at night and set up a position in a row of houses overlooking the square where the hostages were. There were about seven hundred of them—blacks, whites, Indians, men, women, and children. The town was packed with Simbas. There were masses of them; estimates ran as high as four thousand. Most of them were looting the town, but there was a guard of several hundred around the hostages in the square.

"The Simbas had threatened to kill all the hostages if attacked, and God knows, they had had enough practice at massacres. They were often compared with the siafus, the soldier ants of Africa, destroying everything in their path. The Simbas believed they couldn't be killed. They were mainly primitive tribesmen stiffened by Force Publique deserters and led by witch doctors. Each recruit was put through a ritual that was supposed to give him *dawa*—medicine. If he then chanted, '*mai, mai*'—'water, water'—as he went into battle, enemy bullets would turn to water."

"What happened to this belief when some of them got killed?" Etan had asked.

"The witch doctors had an answer for that." Fitzduane smiled wryly. "They just said that the slain had lost face and broken one of the taboos. You had to follow the witch doctors exactly to keep your *dawa*."

He continued. "The job of my command was to lie low until the attack came and then prevent the Simbas from killing the hostages until the main force could punch its way through. There were only twelve of us, so it was vital we didn't make a move until the attack started. We knew we couldn't hope to hold out for more than a matter of minutes unless reinforcements were right on hand. There were just too many Simbas, and though quite a few still had only spears or bows and arrows, most had FALs and other automatic weaponry captured from the ANC, the Congolese Army. So our orders were crystal-clear: No matter what the provocation, unless actually detected—and we weren't—do nothing until the main force opens fire.

"For eight hours we watched the scene below. Most of the hostages were left alive under guard, just sitting or trying to sleep on the ground, but a steady trickle was taken for the amusement of the Simbas and tortured to death. The torturing took place in a small garden at one end of the square. There was a statue there commemorating some explorer, and they used the plinth to tie their victims to.

"We lay concealed no more than fifty meters away on the second floor of the house, and we could see it all clearly by the light of huge bonfires. With field glasses, it seemed close enough to touch. We couldn't do a damn thing. We had to wait; we just had to. They screamed and screamed and screamed; all goddamn night they screamed. Men, women, and children were raped. It made no difference. Then they were killed in as many disgusting ways as the Simbas could devise.

"They put one little child—she couldn't have been more than four or five—between two jeeps, tied ropes to her arms and legs, and pulled her apart like a rag doll. One guy, with a beard and longish hair, they crucified. They shouted at him: '*Jésus, Jésus, le roi des juifs.*' He was still alive after four hours, so they castrated him. After they raped them, they made some nuns drink gasoline. Then they cut their stomachs open and set fire to their intestines. That was a big favorite. We could smell them burning from where we lay. And we could do nothing, absolutely nothing to help. We lay there with our GPMGs and FNs and rocket launchers and grenades and knives and piano wire, and we didn't even move when little babies died.

"Oh, we were a well-trained outfit, the best the Irish Army had to offer. We had discipline, absolute discipline. We had our orders, and they were sensible orders. Premature action would have been military suicide.

"And then the Simbas pulled one young nurse out of the crowd. She was tall and red-haired and beautiful. She still wore her white uniform. It happened so quickly. One of the young Simbas—some were only thirteen or fourteen and among the cruelest—picked up a panga and almost casually hacked her head off. It took only a few blows. It was quite a quick death. The nurse was Anne-Marie. We'd been married just seven weeks."

Etan had not known what to say or do. What she was hearing was so truly terrible and so much beyond her experience that she just sat there motionless. Then she put both arms around her lover and drew him to her. After he'd finished speaking, Fitzduane had remained silent. The sun was now a dull semicircle vanishing into the sea. It had grown much colder. She could see the lights of the castle keep.

Fitzduane had kissed the top of her head and squeezed her tight. "This is a damp bloody climate, isn't it?" he had said. To warm themselves up, they played ducks and drakes with flat stones on the lake in the twilight. Night had fallen by the time they made it back to Duncleeve, debating furiously as to who had won the game. The last few throws had taken place in near darkness.

Chapter Four

The new Jury's Hotel in Dublin looked like nothing so much as the presidential palace of a newly emerging nation. The original Jury's had vanished except for the marble, mahogany, and brass Victorian bar that had been shipped in its entirety to Zurich by concerned Swiss bankers as a memorial to James Joyce.

Fitzduane wended his way through a visiting Japanese electronics delegation, headed toward the new bar, and ordered a Jameson. He was watching the ice melt and thinking about postmortems and life and the pursuit of happiness when Günther arrived. He still looked baby-faced, so you tended not to notice at first quite how big he was. Close up you could see lines that hadn't been there before, but he still looked fit and tough.

A wedding party slid in through the glass doors. The bride was heavily swaddled in layers of white man-made fiber. She was accompanied by either the headwaiter or the bridegroom, it was hard to tell which. The bride's train swished into the pond and began to sink. Fitzduane thought it was an unusual time of year for an Irish wedding, but then maybe not when you looked at her waistline.

The bride's escort retrieved her train and wrung it out expertly into the fountain. He did it neatly and efficiently, as if it were a routine chore or he were used to killing chickens. The train now looked like a wet diaper as it followed the bride into family life. Fitzduane ignored the symbolism and finished his Jameson.

"You're losing your puppy fat, Günther," he said. "You're either working too hard or playing too hard."

"It's the climate here, and I'm getting older. I think I'm rusting." The accent was German and pronounced, but with more than a hint of Irishness to it. He'd been in Ireland for some considerable time. The government had once borrowed him from Grenzschutzgruppe 9 (GSG-9), the West German antiterrorist force, and somehow he'd stayed.

"Doesn't it rain in Germany?"

"Only when required," replied Günther. "We're a very orderly nation."

"The colonel coming?" asked Fitzduane. He patted the airline bag slung from Günther's shoulder and then hefted it, trying to work out the weapon inside. Something Heckler & Koch at a guess. Germans liked using German products, and Heckler & Koch was state of the art. The weapon had a folding stock, and if he knew Kilmara, it was unlikely to be a nine millimeter. Kilmara had a combat-originated bias against the caliber, which he thought lacked stopping power. "The model thirty-three assault rifle?"

Günther grinned and nodded. "You keep up-to-date," he said. "Very good. But the colonel is upstairs. You're dining in a private room; these days it's wiser." He led the way out of the bar and along the glass-walled corridor to the elevator. They got out on the top floor. Günther nodded at two plainclothes security guards and opened the door with a key. There were two more men inside, automatic weapons at the ready. Günther ushered Fitzduane into the adjoining room.

Colonel Shane Kilmara, security adviser to the Taoiseach—the Irish prime minister—and commander of the Rangers, the special Irish antiterrorist force, rose to meet him. A buffet lunch was spread out on a table to one side.

"I didn't realize smoked salmon needed so much protection," said Fitzduane.

"It's the company it keeps," answered Kilmara.

WHENEVER IRELAND'S idiosyncratic climate and the Celtic mentality of many of its natives began to get him down, Kilmara had only to reflect on how he had ended up in his present position to induce a frisson of well-being.

Kilmara had been successful militarily in the Congo, and the saving of most of the hostages at Konina had been hailed as a classic surgical strike by the world press; but the bottom line had a political flavor, and back in cold, damp Ireland Kilmara was court-martialed—and found guilty. He did not dispute the finding. He had initiated the Konina strike against orders, and eighteen of his men had been killed.

On the credit side of the ledger, the operation had been a success. More than seven hundred lives had been saved, and world public opinion had been overwhelmingly favorable, so he did dispute whether charges should have been brought at all. Many others, including the officers judging him at his court-martial, felt the same way, but the verdict, once the court was convened, was inevitable. The sentence was not. It could have involved a dishonorable discharge and imprisonment or even the extreme penalty. It did not. The members of the court demonstrated their view that the institution of such proceedings against one of their own was ill judged and motivated by political malice by settling for the minimum penalty: a severe reprimand.

Kilmara could have stayed on in the army, since most of his peers regarded the verdict as technical, but a more serious shock was to follow. Under the guise of economy measures, the elite airborne battalion he had selected and trained to such a peak of perfection was disbanded.

Although both the court-martial and the disbanding of Kilmara's command were publicized as being strictly military decisions made by the chief of staff and his officers, Kilmara was under no illusions as to where they actually originated or what he could do about them. He assessed the situation pragmatically. For the moment he was outgunned. There was nothing he could do. His antagonist was none other than one Joseph Patrick Delaney, Minister for Defense.

"It's realpolitik," said Kilmara to a disappointed chief of staff when he resigned. Two days later he left Ireland.

Many in the Irish establishment—political and civil—were not unhappy at Kilmara's departure. He had been outspoken and abrasive about conditions in the army and had an unacceptably high profile in the media. His very military success had made him into a greater threat. The establishment in conservative Ireland was fiercely opposed to change. It was glad to see the back of the outspoken colonel and was confident he would never return in an official capacity. Any alternative was unthinkable.

It was assumed by his colleagues in the cabinet that the minister's active hostility toward Kilmara was merely the normal conservative's dislike of the outspoken maverick, leavened by a not-unnatural jealousy of the military man's success—and as such it was understood. They were right, up to a point. However, the real reason Joseph Patrick Delaney wanted Kilmara discredited was more serious and fundamental. Kilmara was a threat not just to the minister's professional ambitions but, if ever the soldier put certain information together, to the politician's very life.

To put it simply, Delaney was a traitor. He had passed information about the plans and activities of Irish troops in the Congo to a connection in exchange for considerable sums of money, which had resulted in the frustration of some of the Airborne Rangers battalion's operations—and in the death and wounding of a number of men.

The minister had not set out to be a traitor. He had merely put his ambitions before his integrity, and circumstances had done the rest. The minister was convinced that Kilmara suspected what he had done—though, ironically, he was wrong. Kilmara's undisguised contempt for him was based on no more than the typical soldier's dislike of a corrupt and opportunistic political master.

After his resignation from the Irish Army in the mid-sixties, Kilmara should have vanished from Irish official circles for good. But then, in the seventies, the specter of terrorism began to make itself felt. It had been largely confined to British-occupied Northern Ireland and to Continental Europe, but violence, unless checked, has a habit of spreading, and borders are notoriously leaky.

The Irish government was concerned and worried, but it was the assassination of Ambassador Ewart Biggs that made the critical difference.

In 1976 Christopher Ewart Biggs, ex-member of Britain's Secret Intelligence Service, writer of thrillers—all of them banned by the Irish censors—and wearer of a black-tinted monocle, was appointed British ambassador to the Republic of Ireland. It was a controversial choice at best, and it was to end in tragedy.

On the morning of July 21, Ewart Biggs seated himself on the left-hand side of the backseat of his chauffeur-driven 4.2-liter Jaguar. He was to be driven from his residence in the Dublin suburb of Sandy-ford to the British Embassy near Ballsbridge. Behind the Jaguar drove an escort vehicle of the Irish Special Branch containing armed detectives.

A few hundred meters from the residence, the ambassador's car passed over a culvert stuffed with one hundred kilograms of com-mercial gelignite. The culvert bomb was detonated by command wire from a hundred meters away. The Jaguar was blasted up into the air and crashed back into the smoking crater. Ambassador Ewart Biggs and his secretary, Judith Cooke, were crushed to death.

The killings sent a cold shudder through the Irish political estab-lishment. Whom might the terrorists kill next? Would the British start revenge bombings, and who might their targets be? It wasn't a cheerful scenario.

The Irish cabinet went into emergency session, and a special com-mittee was set up to overhaul Irish internal security. It was decided to appoint a special security adviser to the Taoiseach. It was an obvious prerequisite that such an adviser be familiar with counterinsurgency on both an international and a national basis.

Discreet inquiries were made throughout Europe, the United States, and places much farther afield. The replies were virtually unanimous. In the intervening decade, working with many of the West's most effective security and counterterrorist forces, Kilmara had consolidated his already formidable reputation. His contempt for most bureaucrats and politicians was well known. The cabinet committee was unhappy with the appointment, but having Kilmara around was preferable to being shredded by a terrorist mine. Just about.

Kilmara drove a hard bargain. It included an ironclad contract and a substantial—by Irish standards—budget. Ninety days after his appointment, as stipulated in his contract, Kilmara set up an elite special antiterrorist unit. He named it "the Rangers" after his now-disbanded airborne battalion. The entire unit numbered only sixty members. Some were drawn from the ranks of the army and the police. Many had been with Kilmara in the Congo. A number were seconded from other forces like the German GSG-9 and the French Gigene. There were others whose backgrounds were known only to Kilmara.

The performance of the Rangers exceeded expectations. Success did not mellow Kilmara. He remained cordially disliked—and, to an extent, feared—by much of the political establishment and, above all, by the present Taoiseach, a certain Joseph Patrick Delaney.

But he was needed.

THEY LUNCHED alone. Their relationship had been that of commanding officer and young lieutenant—mentor and disciple—during the early days of their service together in the Irish Army, but shared danger in the Congo and the passage of time had made it a relationship of equals. They had been comrades-in-arms. They had become close friends.

The cold buffet was excellent. The wine came from Kilmara's private stock, and its quality suggested that he was putting his French associations to good use. They finished with Irish coffees. They had been talking about times past and about the Ireland of the present. The matter of the hanging had been left by mutual consent until the meal was over.

Kilmara finished lighting his pipe. "Ah, it's not a bad life," he said, "even in this funny little country of ours—frustrations, betrayals, faults, and all. It's my home, and we're a young nation yet."

Fitzduane smiled. "You sound positively benign," he said. "Dare I add complacent?"

Kilmara growled. "Sound, maybe; am, no. But enough of this. Tell me about Rudolf von Graffenlaub."

Fitzduane told his story, and Kilmara listened without interrupting. He was a good listener, and he was intrigued as to why the death of a total stranger had so affected his friend.

"An unfortunate way to start the day, I'll grant you," said Kilmara, "but you're not exactly a stranger to death. You see more dead bodies in a week in your line of work than most people do in a lifetime. I don't want to sound callous, but what's one more body? You didn't know the young man, you don't know his friends or his family, and you didn't kill him"—he looked at Fitzduane—"did you?"

Fitzduane grinned and shook his head. "Not that I remember."

"Well then," said Kilmara, "what's the problem? People die. It's sort of built into the system. It's what they call the natural order of things. What is Rudi von Graffenlaub's death to you?"

Fitzduane gathered his thoughts.

Kilmara spoke again. "Of course I'll help," he said. "But I am curious about your rationale for what seems, on the face of it, a somewhat arcane project."

Fitzduane laughed. "I don't have one neat reason," he said. "More like a feeling that this is something I should stay with."

"You and your instincts," said Kilmara, shaking his head. "They are, as I remember full well from the Congo, downright spooky. So what's on your mind?"

Fitzduane refreshed his memory from his notes. "I'd like to talk to the pathologist who carried out the postmortem on our freshly dead friend. The normal pathologist for the area was away at a conference, and Harbison was tied up on some thing or other. A Dr. Buckley drove up from Cork for the occasion."

"I know Buckley," said Kilmara. "A smallish man with salt-and-pepper hair. Originally from West Cork. Now based in the South Infirmary."

"That's the boyo," said Fitzduane.

"Buckley's a good man," said Kilmara. "He's first-rate, but he's like a clam when it comes to professional matters unless there are good reasons for him to talk."

"That ball is in your court," said Fitzduane. "I tried ringing him off my own bat and got nowhere. He was affable but firm."

"Ah, the people of West Cork have great charm," said Kilmara. "It must go with the scenery. I'll see what I can do. What's next?"

"I'd like copies of all the relevant reports: police, forensic, coroner's. The lot," said Fitzduane.

"It's certainly improper and arguably illegal to give that sort of thing to a civilian. But okay. No problem."

"I need some sort of introduction to the authorities in Bern," said Fitzduane. "That's where Rudolf von Graffenlaub came from. That's where his parents and friends live. I want to go over and ask some questions, and I don't want to be politely deported on the second day."

Kilmara grinned. "This one calls for a little creative thinking."

"Finally, what do you know about Draker College?" asked Fitzduane. "And I don't mean have you got a copy of the college prospectus."

"I thought you might get to that one sometime," said Kilmara. "Now it's my turn for a question. Do you have any idea what you're looking for?"

Fitzduane smiled gently. "No," he said, "but I expect I'll know when I find it."

They were silent for a few moments. Kilmara rose and stretched and walked over to the window. He peered through the venetian blinds. "The rain isn't so bad," he said. "It's only spitting now. What about a stroll in Herbert Park?"

"It's winter and it's March and it's cold," said Fitzduane, but his movements belied his words. He shrugged into his still-damp coat. "And there are no flowers."

"There are always flowers," said Kilmara.

THEY WALKED the short distance to Herbert Park and turned onto the deserted grounds.

The four security guards moved in closer, though they were still out of earshot. They were perceptibly edgy. The light was dull, and the shrubbery provided cover for a possible assailant. It was unlike the colonel to expose himself for this length of time in what could not be made, with the manpower available, a secure area. The bodyguard commander called in to Ranger headquarters for backup. He wondered what the two men were talking about. He hoped the rain would get heavier so they'd return to bricks and mortar and a defensible perimeter.

They were talking about terrorists.

"Take our homegrown lot," said Kilmara. "We hunt them and imprison them, and occasionally we kill them, but I still have a certain sympathy for, or at least an understanding of, the Provos and other splinter groups of the IRA. They want a united Ireland. They don't want Britain hanging on to the North."

"By exploding bombs in crowded streets, by killing and maiming innocent men, women, and children, by murdering part-time policemen in front of their families?" broke in Fitzduane.

"I know, I know," said Kilmara. "I'm not defending the IRA. My point is, however, that I understand their motives."

They left the ponds and gardens of Herbert Park and crossed the road into the area of lawn and tennis courts. Wet grass squelched underfoot. Neither man noticed.

Kilmara continued. "Similarly, I understand other nationalist terrorist organizations like ETA or the various Palestinian outfits, and the Lord knows there are enough of those. But I have great difficulty in grasping the motives of what I tend to think of as the European terrorists—the Baader-Meinhof people, the 'Red Army Faction,' as they call themselves, Action Directe—or gangs like the Italian Brigate Rosse.

"What the hell are they after? Most of the members come from well-to-do families. They are normally well educated—sometimes too well. They don't have material problems. They don't have nationalistic objectives. They don't seem to have a coherent political philosophy. Yet they rob, kidnap, maim, and murder. But to what end? Why?"

"What are you leading up to?"

Kilmara stopped and turned to face Fitzduane. He shook his head. "I'm buggered if I know exactly. It's a kind of feeling I have that something else is brewing. We sit on this damp little island of ours with mildew and shamrock corroding our brains and think all we have to worry about, at least in a terrorist sense, is the IRA. I'm not sure it's that simple.

"I've no time for communism, which is self-destructing anyway, but all is far from well in Western democracies. There is a gangrene affecting our values that gives rise to terrorists like the Red Army Faction, and I'm beginning to get the smell in this country."

They started walking again. To the great relief of the bodyguard commander, the heavens opened, and rain descended in solid sheets. The colonel and his guest headed toward a Ranger car.

"Is this instinct or something harder?" asked Fitzduane. "Is this academic discussion or something that crosses what I'm up to?"

"It's not academic," said Kilmara, "but it's not hard. It's bits and pieces sifted from intelligence reports and interrogations. It's the presence of elements that shouldn't be there. It's stuff on the grapevine. It's the instinct of someone who's been a long time in this game. As for whether it affects you, I don't see how—but who knows? Suicide is about alienation. There are other ways to show society you're pissed off. And there is a lot about our society to piss people off."

Kilmara stopped as they approached the car. The sky was black, and thunder rumbled. Rain poured down and cascaded off the two men. Lightning flashed and for a moment illuminated Kilmara's face. He started to say something, then seemed to change his mind. He reverted to what they had just been discussing. "In this new modern

Ireland of ours—and for Ireland you can substitute the Western capitalist world—our idea of progress is a new shopping center or video machine. It just isn't that simple. Life can't be that hollow."

Fitzduane looked at his friend.

"I've got children," said Kilmara, "and I'm not sure I like the view in my crystal ball."

They returned to the hotel and dried off and had a hot whiskey together for the road. They drank in companionable silence. The hotel's central heating was as usual too hot, but their coats and hats, draped over the radiators and dripping onto the carpet, were drying out. The room smelled like an old sheepdog.

"I wonder what you've got into this time, Hugo," said Kilmara. "You and your fucking vibes." He swirled the clove in his hot whiskey. "Tell me," he said, "do they still call you the Irish samurai?"

"From time to time," replied Fitzduane. "The media have picked it up, and it's in the files. It livens up a story."

Kilmara laughed. "Ah," he said, "but the name fits. There you are with your ideals, your standards, your military skills, and your heritage, looking for a worthwhile cause to serve, a quest to undertake."

"The idea of a samurai," said Fitzduane, "is a warrior who already serves, one who has already found his master and has his place in the social order, a knight in the feudal system answerable to a lord but in charge of his own particular patch."

"Well," said Kilmara, "you've certainly got your own particular patch—even if it is in the middle of nowhere. As to whom you are answerable"—he grinned—"that's an interesting question."

The thunderstorm was working itself up to a climax. Rain drummed against the glass. Lightning split the sky into jagged pieces.

"It's the weather for metaphysics," said Fitzduane, "though scarcely the time."

FIFTEEN MINUTES LATER Kilmara was connected by telephone to a white-tiled room in Cork.

A smallish man with salt-and-pepper hair and the complexion of a fisherman was given the phone by the lab technician. The smallish man was wearing a green smock and trousers and rubber apron. His white rubber boots were splashed with blood.

"Michael," said Kilmara after the proprieties had been observed, "I want you to take a break from cutting the tops off Irish skulls with that electric saw of yours in a fruitless search for gray matter. I'd like you to take a friend of mine out to dinner and do a wee bit of talking."

"What about?" asked the smallish man. There was the sound of dripping from the open body into the stainless steel bucket below.

"A Bernese hanging."

"Ah," said the smallish man. "Who's paying for dinner?"

"Now, is that a fair question from a friend to a friend about a friend?"

"Yes," said the smallish man.

"The firm."

"Well now, that's very civilized of you, Shane," said the smallish man. "It will be the Arbutus, so."

He decided he would have a nice cup of tea before returning to the corpse.

Kilmara phoned Switzerland.

FITZDUANE SOAKED in the bath, watching his yellow plastic duck bob around in the suds. That was the weakness of showers. There was nowhere to float your duck.

The music of Sean O'Riada wafted through the half-open door.

Fitzduane didn't hear the phone. He was thinking about O'Riada—an outstanding composer who was dead of drink by early middle age—and Rudi von Graffenlaub and the fact that killing yourself, if you included drugs and alcohol, wasn't really such an uncommon human activity. It was just that hanging was rather more dramatic. The duck caught his eye. It was riding low in the water. He had a horrible feeling that it had sprung a leak.

He heard Etan laughing. She entered the bathroom and pulled a towel off the heated rail. "It's Shane. He asks would you mind leaving your duck for a moment. He wants to talk to you."

Fitzduane picked up the phone in a damp hand. There were bubbles in his hair. He leaned over and turned the music down lower. "Still alive?" he said into the mouthpiece.

"You're a real bundle of laughs," said Kilmara. It was late on a wet March evening, and it would take him well over an hour to get to his home in Westmeath. He was feeling grumpy, and he thought it quite probable he was coming down with a cold.

"Developments?" asked Fitzduane. "Or are you just trying to get me out of the bath?"

"Developments," said Kilmara. "The man in Cork says yes, but you'll have to drive down there. The man in Bern says well-behaved tourists are always welcome, though he gargled a bit when he heard the name von Graffenlaub. And I say, if I'm not in bed with acute pneumonia, will you take a stroll over to Shrewsbury Road in the morning? I want to talk about the dead and the living. Clear?"

"In part," said Fitzduane.

THREE HOURS LATER, Kilmara felt much improved.

Logs crackled in the big fireplace. An *omelette fines herbes*, a tomato salad, a little cheese, red wine—all sat especially well when prepared by a Frenchwoman. He heard the whir of the coffee grinder from the kitchen.

He lay back in the old leather wing chair, the twins snuggled in close. They were cozy in pajamas and matching Snoopy robes, and they smelled of soap and shampoo and freshly scrubbed six-year-old. Afterward, when the cries and the squeals and the "But, Daddy, we can't go to bed until our hair is really, really dry" had died down, he talked with Adeline. As always when he looked at her or thought about her, he felt a fortunate man.

"But why, *chéri*, does he want to do this thing?" said Adeline. She held her balloon glass of Armagnac up to the firelight and enjoyed the flickering rich color. "Why does Hugo go on this quest when nothing is suspicious, when there seems to be no reason?"

"There's nothing suspicious as far as the authorities are concerned," said Kilmara, "but Hugo marches to the beat of a different drum. The point is that it doesn't feel right to him, and that, to him, is what counts."

Adeline looked skeptical. "A feeling—is that all?"

"Oh, I think it's more than that," said Kilmara. "Hugo is something of a paradox. He's a gentle man with a hard edge—and the hard edge is where much of his talent lies. It's no accident that he's spent most of his adult life in war zones. In the Congo he was a natural master of combat while in action, though he had qualms of conscience when it was all over. Combat photography was his compromise. Well, now he's heading toward middle age, and that's a time when you tend to take stock of where you've been and where you're going. I suspect he feels a sense of guilt about having made a living for so many years out of photographing other people's suffering, and I think this one death on his doorstep is like a catalyst for his accumulated feelings. He seems to think he can prevent some future tragedy by finding out the reasons for this one."

"Do you think anything will come of all this?" said Adeline. "It seems to me he's more likely to have a series of doors slammed in his face. Nobody likes to talk about a suicide—least of all the family."

Kilmara nodded. "Well," he said, "ordinarily you'd be right, of course, but Fitzduane is a little different. He'd laugh if you mentioned them, but he's got some special qualities. People talk to him, and he feels things others do not. It's more than being simpatico. If I believed in such things, I'd call him fey."

"What is this word *fey?*" asked Adeline. Her English was excellent, and she sounded mildly indignant that Kilmara had come up with a word that she did not recognize. Her nose tilted at a pugnacious angle, and there was a glint of amusement in her eye. Kilmara thought she looked luscious. He laughed.

"Oh, it's a real word," he said, "and a good word to know if you are mixing with Celts." He pulled a Chambers dictionary from the bookshelves behind the chair. He leafed through the pages and found the entry.

" 'Fey', " he read. " 'Doomed; fated to die; under the shadow of a sudden or violent death; foreseeing the future, especially a calamity; eccentric; slightly mad; supernatural.' "

Adeline shivered and looked into the firelight. "Does all of that apply, do you think?"

Kilmara smiled. He took her hands between his. "It isn't that terrible," he said. "The son of a bitch is also lucky."

Adeline smiled, and then she was silent for a while before she spoke. Now her voice was grave. "Shane, my love," she said, "you told me once about Hugo's wife: how she died; how she was killed; how he did nothing to save her."

"He couldn't," said Kilmara. "He had orders, and his men were grossly outnumbered, and frankly, there wasn't even the time. It was quite terrible for him—hell, I knew the girl and she was quite gorgeous—but there was nothing he could do."

Adeline looked at him. "I think Anne-Marie is the reason," she said. "She is the reason he can't let this thing go."

Kilmara kissed his wife's hand. He loved her greatly, and it was a growing love as the days passed and the children grew. He thought Adeline was almost certainly right about Fitzduane, and he worried for his friend.

Chapter Five

Fitzduane drove and decided he'd better think about something more cheerful than conditions on the Dublin to Cork road, because the alternative was a heart attack. He decided to review the aftermath of the hanging.

The obvious place to start his quest was Draker College—only it wasn't that simple. The impact of the tragedy of Rudolf von Graffenlaub's death on the small, isolated community of the college had been considerable. Immediately, it had been made quite, quite clear to Fitzduane that the sooner the whole episode was forgotten, the better. Nobody in the college wished to be reminded of Rudi's death. The attitude was that these things happen. It was pointed out, as if in defense, that suicide was the most common cause of death among young people. Fitzduane, who had never thought twice about the matter in the past, found this hard to believe, but investigation showed it to be true.

"Actually, statistically speaking, it's amazing that something like this didn't happen before," said Pierre Danelle, the principal of the college and a man Fitzduane found it hard to warm to.

"All the students at Draker are normally so happy," said the deputy principal. He was a Danelle clone.

The inquest took less than an hour. Sergeant Tommy Keane drove

Fitzduane to the two-centuries-old granite courthouse where it was held. In the trunk of the sergeant's car was fishing tackle, a child's doll—and a length of thin blue rope culminating in a noose stained with brownish marks. Fitzduane found this juxtaposition of domesticity and death bizarre.

During the inquest Fitzduane was struck by the one emotion that seemed to grip everyone present: the desire to get the whole wretched business over and done with.

Fitzduane gave his evidence. The pathologist gave his evidence. Tommy Keane gave and produced his evidence. The principal of the college and some students were called. One of the students, a pretty, chubby-faced blonde with a halo of golden curls, whose name was Toni Hoffman, had been particularly close to Rudi. She cried. No one, in Fitzduane's opinion, advanced any credible reason why Rudi had killed himself, and cross-examination was minimal. Fitzduane had the feeling they were in a race to beat the clock.

The coroner found that the hanged man had been properly identified and was indeed Rudolf von Graffenlaub. He had died as a result of hanging himself from a tree. It was known he was of a serious disposition, prone to be moody, and had been upset by "world problems." His parents, who were not present, were offered the condolences of the court. The word *suicide*—for legal reasons, Fitzduane gathered— was never mentioned.

As they drove back in the car, Sergeant Keane spoke. "You expected more, didn't you, Hugo?"

"I think I did," said Fitzduane. "It was all so rushed."

"That's the way these things normally are," said Keane. "It makes the whole affair easier for all concerned. A few little white lies like saying the lad died instantly do nobody any harm."

"Didn't he?"

"Lord, no," said the sergeant. "It wasn't read out in open court, of course, but the truth is the lad strangled to death. Dr. Buckley estimated it took at least four or five minutes, but it could have been longer—quite a bit longer."

They drove on in silence. Fitzduane wondered if the blue rope was still in the trunk.

THE DUTY LIEUTENANT came into Kilmara's office. He was looking, Kilmara thought, distinctly green about the gills.

"You asked to be informed of any developments on Fitzduane's Island, Colonel?"

Kilmara nodded.

"We've had a call from the local police superintendent," said the lieutenant. "There's been another hanging at Draker." He looked down at his clipboard. "The victim was an eighteen-year-old Swiss female, one Toni Hoffman—apparently a close friend of Rudolf von Graffenlaub. No question of foul play. She left a note." He paused and swallowed.

Kilmara raised an eyebrow. "And?"

"It's sick, Colonel," said the lieutenant. "Apparently she did it in front of the whole school. They have an assembly hall. Just when all the faculty and students had gathered, there was a shout from the balcony at the back of the hall. When they turned, the girl was standing on the gallery rail with a rope round her neck. When she saw everyone was looking, she jumped. I gather it was very messy. Her head just about came off."

"Did she say anything before she jumped?" said Kilmara.

"She shouted, 'Remember Rudi,' " said the lieutenant.

Kilmara raised the other eyebrow. "I expect we shall," he said dryly. He dismissed the lieutenant. "Obviously a young lady with a theatrical bent," he said to Günther.

Günther shrugged. "Poor girl," he said. "What else can one say? It sounds like a classic copycat suicide. One suicide in a group has a tendency to spark off others. Many coroners think that's one good reason why suicides shouldn't be reported."

Kilmara gave a shudder. "Ugh," he said. "This is gloomy stuff. Until our green lieutenant came in with the tidings, I was geared to go home early and bathe the twins."

"And now?" said Günther.

Kilmara waited a beat and grinned. "I'm going to go home early and bathe the twins," he said. He put on his coat, checked his personal weapons, and slid down the specially installed fireman's pole to the underground garage. He'd tell Fitzduane about this second hanging tomorrow. Hugo would have to get by on one hanging this night.

He was unmercifully splashed by the twins.

* * *

THE CITY of Cork, Ireland's second largest, had been sacked, burned, pillaged, looted, and destroyed so often since its foundation in the sixth century by St. Finbar that it now seemed laid out with the primary objective of stopping any invader in his tracks.

Its traffic problem was impressive in its turgid complexity, and on a dark, wet March evening it had reached a pinnacle of congestion that was a tribute to the ingenuity of its corporation's planning committee.

Fitzduane had a manic private theory that the reason the city's population had expanded was that none of the inhabitants could get out, and so they stayed and became traders or lawyers or pregnant or both and conversed in a strange singsong that sounded to the uninitiated like a form of Chinese but was, in fact, the Cork accent.

Fitzduane actually quite liked Cork, but he could never understand how a city that stood astride only one river could have so many bridges—all, apparently, going the wrong way. In addition, there seemed to be more bridges than during his last visit, and some seemed to be in different locations. Maybe they were designed to move secretly in the dead of night. Maybe the reason the British had burned the city—yet again—in 1921 was just to find a parking space.

He was agreeably surprised when the South Infirmary Hospital loomed through the sleet.

FITZDUANE TRANSFERRED the slides of the hanging to the circular magazine of a Kodak Carousel projector and switched it on.

The screen was suddenly brilliant white in the small office. He pressed the advance button. There was a click and a whir and a click. The white of the screen was replaced by a blur of color. He adjusted the zoom lens and the focus, and the face of the hanged boy, much enlarged, came sharply into view.

Buckley held an illuminated pointer in his hand, and from time to time, as the slides clicked and whirred and clicked, he would point out a feature with the small arrow of light.

"Of course," said the pathologist, "I didn't see the locus—the place it actually happened—so these slides of yours help. They should really have been handed in to me before the inquest, but no matter.

"Now, under our system, the decision as to whether the pathologist sees the deceased at the locus depends on the police. If they have any reason to be suspicious, the body is not disturbed in any way until the fullest investigations are carried out. In this particular case the sergeant used his judgment. A youth was involved, and his death occurred on the grounds of his own college. A very fraught situation, and the sight of a victim of hanging can be quite traumatic, as you know. There were no signs of foul play, and the sergeant knew that hanging almost invariably means suicide. There was also the matter of determining that the lad was actually dead. All these factors encouraged the sergeant to take the view that he should cut down the deceased immediately, and I have to say that it is my belief that he acted correctly."

Fitzduane looked at the grimacing figure on the screen. He had an impulse to wipe away the blood and mucus that so disfigured the face. He tried to make his voice sound detached as he spoke. "He must have been dead, surely. I checked his pulse when I found him, and there was nothing—and just look at him."

The pathologist cleared his throat. "I must point out, Mr. Fitzduane," he said, "that given the position of the hanging body, I doubt that you could have carried out an adequate examination. The absence of a pulse alone, especially considering a normal layman's limited experience, is by no means a sufficient determination of death."

"Are you saying that he could have been alive when I found him—even without a pulse and looking like that?"

"Yes," said Buckley in a matter-of-fact voice, "it's possible. Our investigations, based upon when he was last seen in the college, when the rain stopped and so on, plus, of course, your own testimony, indicate that the hanging must have taken place between half an hour and an hour of your finding him. He could have been alive—just—in the same way that a victim of drowning can survive a period of total immersion and can be brought around by mouth-to-mouth resuscitation."

As Buckley spoke, Fitzduane tried to imagine giving mouth-to-mouth resuscitation to that bluish face. He could almost feel those distorted lips stained with spittle, mucus, and blood. Had his revulsion killed the boy? Had it really been so impossible to cut the body down?

"For what it's worth," said Buckley, "and this is not a scientific opinion, merely common sense, he was almost certainly dead when you found him. And anyway, I fail to see how you could have cut him down single-handed, since the evidence stated, as I recall, that you had no knife or similar item. In addition, there would have been the probability of further damage to the boy when the body dropped. Finally, if any trace of life did remain, the brain would have been damaged beyond repair. You would have saved a vegetable. So do not harbor any feelings of guilt. They are neither justified nor constructive."

Fitzduane smiled faintly at Buckley.

"No, I'm not a mind reader," said the pathologist. "It's just that I've been down this road many times before. If suicides realized the trauma they inflict on those who find their damaged remains, some might think twice." He turned back to the business at hand.

"Our friend here," he said, "is a classic example of a victim of asphyxial death resulting from suspension by a ligature. You will note the cyanosed complexion and the petechiae—those tiny red dots. The petechiae are more pronounced where the capillaries are least firmly supported. Externally they show here as a fine shower in the scalp, brow, and face above the level of compression. You will observe the tongue, lifted up at the base and made turgid and protruding. You will observe the prominent eyeballs. You will observe that the level of the tightening of the ligature—the blue nylon rope in this case—does not circle the neck horizontally as would tend to be the case in manual strangulation. Instead, it is set at the thyrohyoid level in front and rises to a suspension point just behind the ear. The impression on the body tissues, incidentally, conforms exactly to what you see here. Such would not be the case if he had been manually strangled beforehand or indeed hanged elsewhere. There are invariably discrepancies.

"Now, hanging normally causes death in one of three possible ways: vagal inhibition, cerebral anoxia, or asphyxia."

Fitzduane made a gesture, and Buckley paused.

"Forgive me," said Fitzduane. "I'm familiar with some of these terms, but I think it would be wiser to consider me an ignorant layman."

Buckley chuckled apologetically. He selected a pipe from a rack on his desk and began to fill it with tobacco. There was the flare of a match followed by the sounds of heavy puffing. "Rudolf died from asphyxia," continued Buckley. "He strangled himself to death, though I doubt that was his intention. The tree he chose and the branch he jumped from gave him a drop of about one meter eighty. We can't be quite sure because he may have jumped up and off the branch, thus increasing the drop.

"To use layman's terminology, I expect he intended to break his neck. He would have wanted the cervical segments to fracture, as happens, or is supposed to happen, in a judicial hanging. In reality, outside official executions, where the hangman has the advantage of training and practice, the neck rarely breaks. Rudolf was a strong, fit young man. His neck did not break.

"You will recall, of course, that I stated during the inquest that death was instantaneous. That was not the truth, merely a convention we tend to adhere to for the relatives' sake. The true facts are always in the written report given to the coroner."

"What about the marks on his hands?" asked Fitzduane. "There are scratches on the fingertips as well. They look like the signs of a struggle."

"Perhaps they do," said Buckley, "but if there was a struggle that resulted in the victim being hanged by another, it's virtually certain there would be some sign on the victim's body. In this case I examined the body with particular care for the very good reason that I was working in another man's territory and didn't want to leave any possibilities unchecked—and I had rather more time than I tend to have with the work load here. Be that as it may, there were no signs of the bruising you might expect if another party were involved. The marks on the hands and fingers are entirely consistent with two things: first, the victim's ascent of the tree, which marked the palms of his hands and the insides of his fingers." He paused to puff at his pipe.

"And second?" prompted Fitzduane.

"Second, the convulsing of the victim as he hung there and slowly asphyxiated. The distance between the trunk of the tree and the body, based now upon my observation of these slides, but originally on the sergeant's measurements, indicates that the body would indeed have brushed against the tree as it spasmed or, more specifically, that the fingertips would have rubbed against the bark of the trunk. Such convulsions can be quite violent."

"I'm sorry I asked," said Fitzduane.

Buckley smiled slightly. "In addition, I took samples from under the deceased's fingernails and subjected them to various tests and microscopic examinations. The findings were consistent with what I have just said. Also, I should point out that in the event of a struggle it is not uncommon to find traces of the assailant's skin, tissue, and blood in the nail scrapings. No such traces were found in this case." He looked toward Fitzduane. Half glasses glinted through the smoke.

Fitzduane marshaled his thoughts. "Very well. If we accept that there is no evidence of strangulation, forcible hanging, or indeed any sort of physical pressure, how about the possibility that he killed himself while drugged or even while under hypnosis?"

Buckley grinned. "Great stuff," he said. "I mentioned earlier that I had taken particular care with this fellow. The fact is that I did a number of things I wouldn't normally do on the basis of the evidence available, and it wasn't only because I was off my patch. It was also because the fellow was a foreigner and, as like as not, there would be another autopsy when his body arrived home. There would be hell to pay if our verdicts differed, as has happened before—to a colleague, in fact. Very embarrassing.

"So in this case," continued Buckley, "although there was no evidence of foul play and no suspicious circumstances, I took extensive samples of blood, hair, urine, stomach contents, and so on, and sent them for examination in Dublin. I thought there was some possibility that he might have been under the influence of some self-administered drug, and I requested the toxicological tests as an extra precaution."

"And?" said Fitzduane.

"Nothing found," said Buckley. "A very healthy young man, apart from being hanged, that is. Mind you, I'm not saying it was absolutely impossible. There are a staggering number of drugs and chemicals available today. What I am saying is that we found no evidence that he was drugged or poisoned in any way. The lab people are well practiced and expert, and it is unlikely they would have missed an alien substance in the body. A more likely possibility would be that a more remote substance might take longer to identify. But let me repeat, no alien substance was found."

"What about hypnosis?" Fitzduane wasn't sure he believed in such a possibility himself, but Buckley was the expert, and he'd seen some decidedly odd things in the Congo.

"I don't know," said Buckley in a deadpan voice. "There could have been a witch doctor hidden in the tree. All I can say is that I didn't find a shiny gold watch dangling in front of his eyes when I carried out the examination."

Fitzduane didn't feel particularly amused. He knew pathologists had a reputation for ghoulish humor, but the blown-up images of Rudolf on the screen weren't doing much for his own sense of fun.

Buckley was not insensitive to his reaction. "More seriously," he went on, "the evidence available suggests that it is most unlikely an individual will deliberately cause himself harm even when under hypnosis. The survival instinct is strong. Of course, there are recorded circumstances of quite extraordinary happenings in Africa, India, and so on, but in those cases the victim was normally preconditioned for his whole life to accept that a witch doctor or whoever had the power to put a spell on him that could result in his death."

"Preconditioned?"

"Preconditioned," said Buckley. "An unlikely happening for a young man brought up in the heartland of Western capitalism."

Fitzduane smiled. "Unlikely."

Buckley switched the projector off and allowed it to cool for a few minutes. The room was now lit only by the reflecting glow of an angle desk lamp. Fitzduane stood up and stretched. One way or another he had been sitting for most of the day, and he was tired and stiff from the long drive.

Click! The lower two-thirds of Rudolf von Graffenlaub filled the screen. Buckley pressed the button on the illuminated pointer, and the little arrow of light indicated the stained area around the crotch of the dead youth's jeans.

"You will observe," said Buckley in his lecturer's voice, "that the deceased's bowels evacuated as he was dying. You may think that this indicates poisoning or something of the sort. Such is not the case. In fact, it is reasonably common, though not inevitable, for such an occurrence to take place during the convulsions of dying. It is also not uncommon in the case of a male for ejaculation to take place. As it happens, in this case there was no evidence of ejaculation.

"Police inquiries disclosed that the deceased attended breakfast in the college refectory a couple of hours before his death. This gave me a little concern when I read the report before making my examination, since it's my experience that suicides rarely eat much in the period immediately prior to the taking of life. However, on examination of the stomach contents, I was relieved to find that he had not actually eaten at breakfast, though he had drunk some tea."

"Yet another indication of suicide," said Fitzduane.

"Well, if that was what he was contemplating, it was scarcely surprising that Mr. von Graffenlaub's mouth felt somewhat dry at the time." Buckley reverted to his lecturer's monotone. "You will observe that the zip of the jeans is fully done up and the penis is not exposed. That tends to eliminate the possibility of a sexual perversion that went wrong."

"Of what?" said Fitzduane, taken aback.

"It's part of the world of bondage, masochism, and similar perversions," said Buckley mildly, "and it's not confined to high fliers in London or Los Angeles. It happens wherever there are people, such as in this good Catholic city of Cork. You see, partial asphyxia can be a sexual stimulant. This is often discovered accidentally, such as when schoolboys are wrestling. The next thing you know some youngster is locking himself in the bathroom or lavatory and playing games with ropes or chains around his neck as an aid to masturbation. Then something goes wrong, and he slips or puts the rope in the wrong place. He just nicks the vagus, and that's it. He's work for the likes of me. His parents have forced the bathroom lock or whatever, and there is little Johnny, cyanosed, looking just like Rudolf here except for his penis hanging out and dribbling semen. And often porno magazines all over the place."

"This is all news to me," said Fitzduane, "and I never thought I lived a sheltered existence."

"Well," said Buckley, "to each his own. Your average person knows more about football than hanging."

FITZDUANE FOLLOWED the pathologist's Volvo across the city, along Macurtain Street, and turned left up the hill to the Arbutus Lodge.

The box of slides and a photocopy of the pathologist's file on the dead Bernese lay on the seat beside him. There seemed to be little doubt that the hanging had, in fact, been suicide. The matter of the motive was as obscure as before.

It never seemed to be easy to park in Cork. The cramped hotel forecourt jammed full of cars made maneuvering difficult, and it took

some minutes and rather more frustration before they were able to
squeeze through to the hotel's lower parking lot, where a corner was
still free.

The sleet had stopped, though the wind was viciously cold. For a
brief moment, after they had locked their cars, Fitzduane and Buckley stood side by side and looked across to where the River Lee rolled
by below them. Its route was outlined by streetlights on its banks.
There was the occasional glint of reflected light on the black, oily
surface of the river, and below and to their right they could see the
lights of merchant ships tied up at the quays.

"Many of my customers are fished out of that river," said Buckley. "Cork people do so love to drown themselves. We had so many
drownings last year that one of the mortuary attendants suggested
building a special quay for suicides and supplying them with marker
buoys and anchors."

"I guess it's the parking problem," said Fitzduane.

BUCKLEY LOOKED at the last morsel of carefully aged Irish beef with
a slight hint of sadness. With due ceremony he matched it with the
remaining sliver of buttered baked potato. The carefully loaded fork
made its final journey.

"There is an end to everything," he said as he pushed his plate
away. He looked across the table at Fitzduane and grinned benevo-
lently.

"What I'm saying," said Buckley, "is that it doesn't do to make
too much of a suicide. In the small patch of Cork I cover, I dealt with
about a hanging a fortnight last year. There is some poor sod making
his greatest gesture to the rest of mankind, and all it adds up to is a
few hours' work for us employees of the state."

Fitzduane smiled. "An interesting perspective."

"But you're not persuaded?"

Fitzduane sipped his port and took his time answering. "I have a
tight focus," he said, "and it isn't how Rudolf killed himself that
primarily concerns me. It's where and why. He did it on my doorstep."

Buckley shrugged. For the next few minutes the cheese board
became his primary concern; then he returned to the subject of
suicide. "It's a funny business," he said, "and we know nothing like
enough about the reasons." He grinned. "Dead people don't talk a

lot. One survey in London in the fifties analyzed nearly four hundred suicides and estimated that either physical or mental illness was the principal cause in about half the cases. Well, I can tell you that Rudolf was in excellent health, there was no evidence of early cancer or venereal disease or anything like that, and the reports I received would tend to rule out mental illness. So, according to the researchers, that leaves what they term social and personal factors."

"And what exactly does that mean?"

"Hanged if I know."

"Jesus!" groaned Fitzduane.

"Suicide statistics," continued Buckley, "leave a lot to be desired. For instance, if I am to believe what I read, Ireland has a suicide rate so low as to be almost irrelevant. So where, I ask myself, do all those bodies I work on come from? Or is Cork unusually suicide-prone?" He shook his head. "The reality is that people are embarrassed by suicide, so they fudge the figures. A suicide in the family is considered a disgrace. As recently as 1823, for example, a London suicide was buried at a crossroads in Chelsea with a stake through his body. Now, there is a nice example of social disapproval."

Fitzduane put down his glass. "Let's get back to Rudi. Is there anything—anything at all—that you noticed about him or the circumstances of his death?"

"Anything?" said Buckley.

Fitzduane nodded.

The port decanter was finished. They left the now-empty dining room and retired to have a final brandy by the log fire in the annex to the bar. Fitzduane was glad that he was staying the night. How Buckley remained upright with so much alcohol inside him was a minor mystery. The pathologist's face was more flushed, and he was in high good humor; otherwise there was little overt sign that he had been drinking. His diction was still perfect. "Anything at all?" he repeated.

"Think of it as the classic piece in the jigsaw," said Fitzduane.

Buckley picked up a fire iron and began poking the fire. Fitzduane waited, his brandy virtually untasted. Suddenly Buckley stood up, removed his jacket, rolled up his left sleeve, and thrust out his arm. For a moment, Fitzduane thought that the pathologist was going to hit him and that he was unlucky enough to be spending an evening with someone whom drink turns violent.

"Look at this," said Buckley.

Fitzduane looked at the proffered arm. A snarling bulldog's head wearing a crushed military cap was tattooed on the forearm; under it were the words "USMC 1945."

"The Marine mascot," said Fitzduane. "I saw it often enough in Vietnam."

"You don't have any tattoos?"

"Not that I've noticed," said Fitzduane.

"Do you know the significance of the bulldog to the Marines?"

"Never gave it much thought," said Fitzduane.

Buckley smiled. "The choice of a bulldog as their mascot goes back to the name the Germans gave the Marines in France in 1918. They were called *Teufelhunden*, devil dogs. It was a tribute to their fighting qualities. Well, jobs were scarce in Ireland when I was a young lad, so I ended up serving a hitch in the U.S. Navy as a medic and being attached to the Marines. The tattoo was a present from my unit. It means more to me than a Navy Cross."

"Rudolf had a tattoo?" asked Fitzduane.

Buckley rebuttoned his shirtsleeve. "If you've ever been tattooed yourself, you tend to be more interested in such things. They often have great significance. For a time I used to collect photos of unusual tattoos off the cadavers as they paraded through. I built up quite a collection. Gave it up years ago, though. Well, Rudolf had a tattoo, a very small one but unlike any I've seen before. It was more like a love token or a unit badge or some such thing, and it was positioned where it couldn't be seen unless the wearer wished."

"The mind boggles," said Fitzduane.

Buckley smiled. "Not that dramatic but clever all the same. It was on his outer wrist, just under where you would wear a watch. It was very small, about a centimeter and a half across, and it showed a capital 'A' with a circle of what looked like flowers around it."

"So maybe Rudi had a girlfriend whose name or nickname began with 'A,' " said Fitzduane.

"Could be," said Buckley, "but you had better widen your horizon to include boyfriend in your search. Rudolf may have swung both ways, but he had the unmistakable physical characteristics of someone who engaged regularly in homosexual activities."

"You'd better explain," said Fitzduane.

Buckley drained his brandy and replaced his jacket. He remained standing. "The small matter of a somewhat dilated and keratinized anal orifice. There isn't much privacy on a pathologist's slab."

Fitzduane raised his eyebrows. "I'll keep that in mind."

"By the way," said Buckley, "there was a second postmortem in Bern, and the Bernese agreed with my findings. Suicide, no question."

"Looks like it," said Fitzduane, "but if I run across something, would it be practicable to exhume the body and run more tests? How long has one got in this kind of situation?"

Buckley laughed. "You're back to witch doctors," he said, "because conventional pathologists won't be much use to you. The remains were cremated."

Chapter Six

Fitzduane's Land Rover splashed through the town of Portlaoise. A few miles farther on he stopped at a hotel to stretch his legs and phone Murrough on the island. He heard the news about the second hanging with a sense of shock and foreboding. He remembered Toni Hoffman from the inquest. She had been a close friend of Rudi's and had been summoned to give evidence about his state of mind. When she had been called by the coroner, she hadn't been able to speak. She had just stood there, ashen-faced, shaking her head, tears streaming silently down her cheeks.

The coroner had been sympathetic and had dismissed her after a brief, abortive effort at questioning. Fitzduane had thought at the time that she looked as much petrified with fear as grief-struck, but then they had moved on to another witness with more to say, and he had put the incident out of his mind.

He tried to avoid thinking what she must have looked like at the end of a rope with her head half off. He wasn't successful.

PIERRE DANELLE, principal of Draker College, was not pleased. It was a not uncommon state with him, since he could not, even charitably, be described as a happy man. The word *misanthrope* would be closer to the mark. He was, in the view of most of his students, a miserable son of a bitch.

On this particular day Danelle was even more miserable than normal, and he was also annoyed. He read the school charter again. It incorporated various clauses taken from von Draker's will, and unfortunately the founder had been quite specific in his instructions, which for greater clarity were expressed in French, German, and English.

The trouble lay with the tree. Common sense dictated that it should be cut down. A tree from which one of your students had hanged himself was not the sort of thing one wanted to keep on the school grounds. It would provoke memories and impinge on school activities, and it would be a no-no on parents' day. And it might tempt someone else to experiment with the blue rope and a short jump. Danelle shuddered at the thought. One hanging was a tragedy. Two hangings were a major headache. Three hangings would knock hell out of his budget. The Draker tuition was not small. Three sets of fees would be missed.

The hanging tree had to go—but then again it couldn't. Von Draker had gone to the most elaborate lengths to establish his little forest in the first place, and he had clearly stated in his will that under no circumstances whatsoever were any trees on the estate to be cut down. The whole clause was then repeated in more extreme language to make sure that the trustees of the Von Draker Peace Foundation got the point, and to demonstrate the founder's faith in human nature, a relationship with their remuneration was referred to. Danelle got the point. Even in his grave, von Draker liked trees. It was infuriating. He was being dictated to by a dead man.

Danelle decided that he would write to the trustees in Basel. Surely they would understand that you just can't have a freshly used gallows hanging—growing—on campus.

Like fuck they'd understand. Those hollowheads in Switzerland weren't going to put their stipends at risk to save a not madly popular principal from embarrassment. He racked his brains, and then an idea blossomed, an idea that was dazzling in its scope and simplicity. An accident. Lightning, a forest fire; a maverick with a chain saw; a pyromaniac Boy Scout. The mind boggled. The possibilities were endless.

He decided he would take a walk over to the old oak tree to see
what could be arranged. He pulled on his Wellington boots and
waterproofs. It was raining.

"ST. PATRICK'S DAY APART," said Kilmara idly, "people tend to
forget about March in this country. I mean, everyone knows about
January. It's the month when the first bank statement arrives after
Christmas and bank managers decide to cut off your overdraft.
Everyone remembers February. It's the Toulouse-Lautrec of
months, and all the tennis club set go skiing with each other's wives.
Everyone likes April. People skip around and procreate like mad and
pick daffodils and eat chocolate Easter eggs. But March—March sort
of sneaks in and hangs around and confuses the issue. I'm not sure I
approve of March. It's a month with a lot of cold puddles—and it's
too bloody long."

He switched off the computer terminal and the screen went dull.
Elsewhere, in air-conditioned, dust-free isolation, the mainframe's
brain was still actively following its instructions, fine-tuning the
duty roster and carrying out the myriad other tasks of an operational
unit. "Günther," said Kilmara, who had been thinking laterally
about his manpower problems and then about Fitzduane's proposed
trip to Switzerland, "why didn't you join the Swiss Guards at the
Vatican instead of the French Foreign Legion? The pay would have
been better, the uniform more colorful, and no one shoots at you—
though anything is possible in Rome."

"Ah, but I'm not Swiss," said Günther, "and I am not celibate."

"You amaze me," said Kilmara, "but what has celibacy got to do
with it?"

"Well," said Günther, "to qualify as a Swiss Guard, you have to
be Swiss, have received Swiss military training, be Catholic, be of
good health, be under thirty, be at least one hundred and seventy-
four centimeters in height—and be celibate and of irreproachable
character."

"I can see your problem," said Kilmara.

PIERRE DANELLE decided—too late—that the waning afternoon was
the wrong time to be wandering around in a forest. He should have
postponed his little expedition until the morning despite the fact that

it was blindingly clear that the sooner that damned oak tree met with an accident, the better.

He cursed von Draker for choosing to build his eccentric construction in such an out-of-the-way location as the west of Ireland. Marvelous scenery, it was true, if you liked a fickle and eerie landscape, but the weather! It was enough to choke the Valkyries. When an Irishman said it was a nice soft morning, he meant you didn't actually need an aqualung to keep from drowning in the rain.

And apart from the weather—not that you could ever get apart from the weather in Ireland—there were the Irish, an odd lot who didn't seem to speak English properly and their own tongue not at all. Irish English seldom seemed to mean the same thing as English English. So often there seemed to be nuances and subtleties and shades of meaning he failed to grasp, most of which seemed to end up to his financial disadvantage.

Thinking of financial disadvantage reminded him of the alimony he'd been saddled with, and then of his mother-in-law in Alsace. On reflection, perhaps he was better off in Ireland after all.

"Do you ever miss the mercenary life, Günther?" asked Kilmara. He decided to light his pipe. It was that hour of day, and he was in that sort of mood.

"I'm not sure the Legion qualified as mercenary," replied Günther. "The pay was terrible."

"I wasn't referring to the Legion," said Kilmara. "I was thinking of that little interlude just afterward."

"Ah," said Günther, "we don't talk about that."

"I merely asked you if you missed it."

"I've matured, Colonel," said Günther. "Before, I fought purely for money. Now I have higher ideals. I fight for democracy and money."

Kilmara was busy for a few moments with pipe cleaners and other gadgets. Pipe smoking is not an impetuous activity. "What does democracy mean to you?" he asked when order was restored.

"Freedom to make more money," said Günther with a smile.

"I like a committed idealist," said Kilmara dryly. "Pearse would have been proud of you."

"Who was Pearse?"

"Padraig Pearse," said Kilmara, "Irish hero, poet, romantic, and dreamer. He was one of the leaders of the 1916 uprising against the British that led to independence in 1922. Of course, he didn't live to see the day. He surrendered after some bloody fighting and was put up against a wall and shot. He had company."

"Romantics and dreamers tend to get shot," said Günther.

"Good evening," Fitzduane broke in from the doorway.

"Speak of the devil," said Kilmara.

DANELLE DID NOT like to admit, even to himself, that he felt uneasy. There was no good reason for a highly educated, rational, cosmopolitan twentieth-century man to be prey to such a feeling so close to home on land he knew well. Nonetheless, there was a certain atmosphere in the wood that was, at best, unsettling. Oddly, there were no bird sounds, and indeed, everything was quite remarkably silent. His boots made no noise on the thick mulch. It was ridiculous, of course, but it was as if he could hear his heart beating.

There was, from time to time, a sudden rustling of what must have been a large animal—either a fox or a badger—but otherwise the oppressive silence continued.

Danelle wished he had brought a colleague. He was not fond of his fellow faculty members, but they had their uses, and on this occasion even the most obnoxious of his fellows would have been welcome. Slowly he recognized the unsettling sensation that gripped him. It was an old ailment of humankind and could be smelled as well as felt. Fear.

It was darker in the wood than he expected. These short, gloomy March evenings of Ireland. He wished that he were somewhere farther south, somewhere warm and sunny and dry—especially dry. A raindrop slithered down the back of his neck, and soon there were others. He began to feel cold and shivery.

The feeling he had was changing. It was no longer fear. He stumbled on through the gloom and gathering darkness, branches and briars whipping and dragging at his face and body. The feeling identified itself. There remained little doubt about it. It bore a distinct resemblance to absolute, all-encompassing, mind-dominating, blind panic.

He stopped and tried to get his nerves under control. With great deliberation, his hand shaking as if he had malaria, he removed a white handkerchief from his pocket and wiped away the cold sweat and rain and streaks of dirt from where the branches had whipped him. The action, calmly carried out, made him feel better. He felt more in control. He told himself that he was being ridiculous and that there was no rational reason for this extraordinary terror.

He walked on. The undergrowth became particularly dense, and the twisty path began to incline upward. He realized he was near the old oak tree, God rot it, the source of all his trouble. His feeling of relief was canceled abruptly when his foot caught on a protruding root and he tumbled headlong into the dank mulch. He rose slowly, his heart pounding from the shock.

A sudden vile stench assailed his nostrils, and he gagged. It was like rotting flesh mixed with the acrid smell of sulfur, the tang of hell.

There seemed to be light coming from behind the old oak tree. He thought at first that it was the last gesture of the setting sun, but he realized now that it was too late for the sun, and anyway, this was different, a strange glow, and its source was from below, not from the sky. He wanted to turn and run, but he felt compelled to move forward. He walked as if in a trance, his steps slow and faltering.

What he saw, as he rounded the thick trunk of the old oak tree, was more than his brain could—or wanted to—grasp. In the clearing ahead, a large circle had been made out of stones, and the spaces between the stones were filled with greenery and flowers. Inside the circle of stones and flowers was another shape. It looked like a vast letter "A," its extremities touching the inside of the circle at three points. In the center of the circle a fire burned and flickered and slowly devoured something that had once been living. Entrails spilled in yellowing coils from the ripped-open stomach. The small, hot flame of the fire hissed and spit—and close up, the smell was nauseating.

There was a flash and a sudden, sharp smell of sulfur from the fire, and the lower branches of the oak tree were lit up in the glow. Danelle raised his eyes. It was the last conscious vision of his life, and it was utterly horrible. Through the smoke of burning flesh and sulfur, he beheld the horned head of the devil.

He was still unconscious when they threw him off the edge of the cliff onto the rocks and the waters of the Atlantic far below.

FITZDUANE SLEPT a sound, dreamless sleep and woke up the following morning feeling cheerful and rested.

After Etan had left for the studios, he made himself a large pot of black coffee, put his feet up in front of the crackling fire, and began reviewing what he had learned so far. It came to him that if you're the kind of person who turns over stones—and most people learn not to early in life—what comes crawling out can be disconcerting.

He started with his meeting with Kilmara the previous evening. A computer search had thrown up the fact that Draker was more than a select school for the children of the rich and powerful. Out of a full complement of sixty pupils—now fifty-eight—no fewer than seventeen were designated "PT" on the Ranger computer printout.

"Computer people prefer to talk in bits and bytes," Kilmara had said, "but one of the advantages of getting in at the start of the Rangers was that I was able to twist the buggers' arms to make them take some cognizance of the English language. 'PT' stands for 'possible target.' It's not a high-level classification, but it means that, in theory, you take some precautions and you think twice when some incident occurs involving someone with 'PT' after his or her name."

"Tell me more," said Fitzduane.

"Do I detect a flutter of interest, Hugo?" said Kilmara. "Relax, my son. Thousands of people in Ireland have a designation of 'PT' or higher: politicians, businessmen, diplomats, visiting absentee landlords of the English variety, and God and the computer only know who else."

"But why these particular seventeen students?" asked Fitzduane.

"Oh, it has nothing to do with them as such," said Kilmara. "It has to do with families and backgrounds and the like. For instance, included in the Draker seventeen at present are a minor Saudi princeling—and there're thousands of those knocking around—a cousin of the Kennedy clan, two children of the Italian Minister of Foreign Affairs, the son of a Japanese automobile tycoon. . . . Well, you get the drift."

"How about Rudolf von Graffenlaub and the girl, Toni Hoffman?"

"In our baby computer system, *nada*," said Kilmara. "But that doesn't mean there shouldn't have been. It's a rough-and-ready classification. Deciding who might be a terrorist or criminal target is very much a matter of judgment. To make life more confusing, fashions change in the terrorist business. It's politicians during one phase and businessmen the next. For all I know, it will be garbage collectors after that—or pregnant mothers. It's all show biz in this game. It's the media impact that counts."

"So what do you do about these PTs, apart from giving them a couple of initials on computer input?"

"Well," said Kilmara, "if one of them drowns in the municipal swimming pool, we drain it a bit faster, but that's about the size of it. Basically it's the government contribution to the media game. It's called taking every reasonable precaution. It helps to cover the official ass if something does happen."

"Were you always so cynical," said Fitzduane, "or did someone salt your baby food?"

Kilmara turned his cigarette lighter into a small flamethrower to work on his pipe. Success achieved, he stood up from his chair and walked across to a whiteboard screwed to the wall. He picked up a black dry-wipe felt pen and started to write.

"You find it odd, Hugo, that we don't do much more? Well, let me throw a few figures at you. They're a little rough, but they're accurate enough to make the point, and the same situation applies to most other Western European countries.

"We have about ten thousand police in this country to deal with about three and a half million people. Police work is a twenty-four-hour-a-day business and involves a great many things other than guarding against terrorism, so at any one time the force would be stretched to the extreme to free up from routine duties any more than a thousand, and even that would mean drawing manpower from all over Ireland. In the wee hours manpower resources are even more limited. At such times it's an interesting thought that the entire country's internal security is looked after by a mere few hundred.

"Now, to set against the resources I've described—and I have left the army out of the equation to keep things simple—we have more than eight thousand names classified 'PT' or higher, and remember 'PT' is only a judgment. We could probably triple that number if we did our homework. Now, it takes at least six trained personnel to provide reasonable security for one target. That means we would need a minimum total of forty-eight thousand trained bodyguards.

"We don't have them. We can't afford them. And we really don't need them. As I have mentioned before, there just aren't that many terrorist incidents—just enough to keep the likes of Günther and me in reading and drinking money."

"Amen to that," said Günther. He closed his copy of the book he had been reading, *Winnie-the-Pooh*, with a snap. "Great book," he said. "No sex and no violence. I'd be out of a job in Pooh Corner."

"Shut up and have a drink," said Kilmara, "and let's see if we can make some sense out of our Wiesbaden friends' enigmatic communication."

"Wiesbaden?" asked Fitzduane. "How does Wiesbaden enter the picture?"

Kilmara slid open the top drawer of his desk and removed his service automatic. Fitzduane noticed with some relief that the safety catch was on.

Kilmara gestured with his pistol. "People think this is how we fight terrorism. Not so." He tossed the weapon back into the drawer and closed it with a flourish. "Firepower plays a part, of course, but the real secret is intelligence, and the key to that, these days, is the computer."

He looked across at Günther. "You tell him, Günther. It's your *Heimat*, and you like the things."

"Wiesbaden is the headquarters of the BKA, the Bundeskriminalamt," said Günther. "The BKA is, very roughly, the German equivalent of the FBI. It has primary responsibility for counterterrorism, with my old outfit, GSG-9, providing muscle when terrorists have been identified and located. The BKA has been very successful at hunting down terrorists, and one of the secrets of this success is the Wiesbaden computer"—he grinned—"better known as the Kommissar."

"It's quite an installation," interjected Kilmara. "I was there a year or so ago. It's all glass and concrete and sits on a hill that, appropriately enough, used to be a place of execution. More than three thousand acolytes feed the beast in Wiesbaden alone, and the budget runs to hundreds of millions of deutsche marks. They don't just record information. They positively vacuum it up. Names, descriptions, addresses, relatives, ancestors, contacts, personal habits, food preferences, sexual idiosyncrasies, speech patterns—you name it, anything that might in some way contribute to the hunt gets entered."

"Twelve million constantly updated files, and the number is climbing," said Günther with pride.

George Orwell's 1984 has arrived, thought Fitzduane. It just hasn't been noticed. He took the whiskey Kilmara had poured him.

"Very interesting," he said, "but what has the Kommissar got to do with my modest investigation?"

Kilmara held up his glass. "*Sláinte!*"

"*Prosit!*" said Günther, similarly equipped.

"*Olé!*" said Fitzduane a little sourly. Games were being played.

Kilmara slid a file across the desk. "One of the twelve million," he said. "Reads kind of sanitized."

Fitzduane picked up the thin file. It was labeled: RUDOLF VON GRAFFENLAUB (DECEASED).

Chapter Seven

The young German tourist and his pretty Italian girlfriend had flown into Dublin the night before on the direct Swissair flight from Zurich. The German checked his Japanese watch when they landed. In the predictable, boring way of the Swiss, the flight had been on time.

At the Avis desk in the arrivals area they rented a small, navy blue Ford Escort for a period of one week at the off-season rate. They opted for unlimited mileage and full insurance. They identified themselves as Dieter Kretz, aged twenty-four, from Hamburg, and Tina Brugnoli, aged nineteen, from Milan. They paid their deposit in cash.

Armed with maps, guidebooks, and copious directions, Dieter and Tina drove into the center of Dublin and checked into a double room at the Royal Dublin Hotel on O'Connell Street. They ate in the hotel restaurant and retired early. A fly on the wall would have noticed that they spoke little as they undressed, and though they slept together naked in the large double bed, they did not make love.

When Dieter awoke in the morning, he could hear Tina in the bathroom. Its door was open, and light spilled into the curtained bedroom. He threw back the bedclothes and stretched like a cat, his body lithe and strong, his chest covered with curly black hair. A thick black mustache drooped above shining white teeth. He looked with pleasure at his penis jutting hard and erect. Moisture gleamed at the tip of his organ, and it was throbbing, crying out for relief.

He rose from the bed and walked the few paces to the bathroom. Tina's hair was tied loosely on top of her head, and she was bent over the basin. Her young body was olive gold in color, and she was naked except for skimpy black panties. He could see the down on the back of her neck. He rested his fingers on the top of the cleft of her buttocks and slowly moved them down, taking the black panties with them. He pushed the thin panties down to just above her knees.

Tina scarcely stirred. She gripped the sides of the basin with long, slim hands as he slowly parted the cheeks of her buttocks, and then there was the sweet smell and cool, smooth touch of hand cream. She gave a muffled cry when he entered her constricted passage, and her knuckles turned white as she gripped the basin. She sucked on his finger. There was so much pain and so much pleasure. It was the way of the Circle. It was so ordained in The Grimoire.

It was so enforced by the Leader.

THE PACKAGE WAS somewhat longer than a shoe box, and it was heavy. Its outer wrapping was of several layers of thick brown paper held securely in place with shiny brown adhesive tape. The contents didn't move or rattle. Whatever was inside was well padded.

The package was addressed to Mr. Dieter Kretz and had been left at the reception desk of the Royal Dublin Hotel just a little after eight in the morning. The messenger was dressed like a Dublin taxi driver and was unremarkable in appearance. Afterward nobody could remember much about him except that he spoke like "a typical Dub."

The young couple had breakfast in their room, hung the "Do Not Disturb" sign on the door, and, as was common enough with young couples, did not emerge until nearly midday. The receptionist handed them the package when they checked out. She had almost forgotten about it until she was gently reminded by the young German. He smiled at her when he received it and made a remark about there not being that much time for reading. He had his right arm around his girlfriend's shoulders and was relaxed and confident—satiated even.

The porter carried their bags to the car, though the German kept the package tucked firmly under his left arm. He placed it in the trunk of the car. The porter wondered why anyone would want to take a holiday in Ireland in March. He returned to his desk in the warm hotel with relief.

DIETER, WHO NORMALLY HAD the German's belief that accelerators exist to be kept pressed to the floor, this time drove cautiously. It was his first visit to Ireland, and he was unused to driving on the left-hand side of the road. Fortunately he had been well briefed on Dublin's inconsistent signposting system and relied instead on Tina's map-reading skills. Despite the random one-way systems that were not shown on the map, they became lost only once before they found the road to Galway and the west of Ireland. It was also a route that led toward the home of Colonel Shane Kilmara.

On the outskirts of Dublin they entered the sprawling green acres of Phoenix Park, the largest enclosed urban parkland in Europe. Hundreds of deer roamed the rolling, tree-dotted landscape, and the sheer scale of the area ensured relative privacy for its few visitors.

Dieter left the main through road and turned onto a side road, where he stopped the car and switched off the engine. For a few minutes they sat quietly, took stock of their surroundings, and watched the deer grazing under the trees. Then, satisfied they were not observed, he opened the trunk, removed the heavy package, and climbed into the backseat of the car. Using a short, thin-bladed knife he had taken from his suitcase, he cut through the layers of tape and outer wrappings of the package, then removed the layers of corrugated paper and the final layer of oiled cloth. There lay two compact Czech-made machine pistols—the model known as the Skorpion VZ-61. There were also eight twenty-round magazines of 7.65 mm ammunition, cleaning materials, and a copy of the Automobile Association's *Touring Guide to Ireland*.

Tina switched on the radio, and to a background of traditional Irish music the pair began to clean the weapons and prepare them for action.

AFTER THEY LEFT Phoenix Park, Tina drove.

She was a better driver than Dieter, and as she became used to the narrow potholed road that passed for a main highway, she gradually increased her speed almost to the legal limit—whenever, that is, road conditions permitted. They wanted to arrive close to their destination during daylight. It was their experience that darkness brought an increase in police patrols.

Dieter, his Skorpion ready for action at the flick of the fire selector lever but concealed under a newspaper, lay across the backseat and dozed. Tina's weapon rested in a plastic shopping bag under her seat.

She rounded a long curve in the road and slowed when she saw the cars stopped up ahead. At first she thought there might have been an accident, but then, as the traffic moved forward in a series of stops and starts, a large orange sign came into view. It read, unambiguously: STOP! POLICE CHECKPOINT.

Almost at the same time she saw the two policemen in their heavy navy blue greatcoats standing back to back in the middle of the road, desultorily checking the traffic flowing from either direction. A muddy police car was parked by the side of the road, and its blue light flashed intermittently. Just behind it was a long-wheelbase Land Rover painted a dull army green. A soldier wearing earphones sat by a radio in the back. Another soldier leaned against the door, his rifle held casually, his bored eyes scanning the long lines of cars and trucks.

A brief feeling of alarm came over Tina before training and common sense came to her aid. They were innocent tourists. They had committed no crime in Ireland. This was just a routine check that could not affect them. She tried not to think of the concealed Skorpions but had already noted that the majority of cars and trucks were being waved through unsearched.

She turned around and shook Dieter. He woke instantly.

"You think . . .?" she began, pointing ahead to the roadblock.

Dieter watched the policemen. In most cases there was no more than a brief discussion through the window and now and then the producing of documents. The policeman covering their side of the road was young, with an open, friendly face tanned a reddish brown by the wind. Sometimes he laughed. There was no urgency in his manner, no tension.

"A routine check, no more," said Dieter. "It is of no concern." He grinned sardonically at Tina. "Remember, we are harmless young lovers."

Tina looked at him coolly for a moment. "We may fuck," she said. "We are not lovers." She let out the clutch, and the Ford moved forward again.

THE BULLETIN HAD stipulated a black or navy blue Ford Escort, and this was Quirke's ninth navy blue Ford Escort of the day. The first two or three had set the adrenaline going, but now he was only marginally interested in the car. He was considerably more interested in the pretty girl driving it.

Tina rolled down the window and smiled up at the large policeman. "Good afternoon, Officer," she said. Her accent was Italian, her tone friendly and just slightly provocative. She was the most exciting thing he'd seen all day, and if there was one thing he was sure of, it was that under normal circumstances she would have been too exotic to have anything to do with the likes of Liam Quirke. But there were some consolations to checkpoint duty.

"Afternoon, miss," said Quirke. He peered into the front and then the back of the car, trying not to stare too hard at the Italian girl and being irrationally disappointed that she had a companion in the back. He felt a pang of loss, the knowledge of a beauty that could never be his. "Afternoon, sir," he added. "Nothing to worry about. Just a routine check."

"We thought at first that there was an accident," said Tina. She smiled directly at him.

"No accident, miss," said the young policeman, his cheeks pink under her gaze. "A bank robbery in Dublin. One of them got away. It's not too likely that he'd come in this direction, but you never know."

"I suppose not," interjected Dieter from the back of the car. His voice broke the spell that for a few seconds had bound the Italian girl and the policeman together.

"Could you tell me where you've come from and where you're going?" asked Quirke, his official manner partially restored. "And I'd like to look at your driver's license and insurance."

Tina removed the car rental documents from the glove compartment and passed them, together with both their driver's licenses, through the window.

"We have only just arrived in your country," she said. "Last night we stayed in Dublin. Now we go to the west of Ireland for a few days. We would like to be away from crowds and people, to be alone together, you understand."

As she finished her remark, Tina looked directly into Liam Quirke's eyes—and saw in them a slight flicker of doubt. Something had him puzzled; something was out of place. There was the faintest hint of something wrong. She thought quickly, but her words were reasonable and innocent. It wasn't something she had said. Something else had aroused his suspicions, but what on earth could it be? The weapons were well concealed. There was nothing else to attract attention.

Quirke looked at the line of half a dozen cars behind the Escort. He didn't want a major traffic jam on his hands. He began to hand the documents back, and then he caught that smell again. His mind flashed back for a split second to his firearms training in Templemore.

The police mightn't carry guns, but they had to be prepared. Forty-two practice rounds and the same again for the proficiency test. The sharp cracks as the line of police fired. Man-shaped targets ripped and torn. The routine of cleaning weapons afterward. The unique smell of preservative grease in the armory and the faint aroma of gun oil as they checked in their Smith & Wesson .38s. Back to relying on the uniform, a pair of fists, and, on the rarest of occasions, a wooden truncheon to enforce the law.

The odor of gun oil remained in his nostrils. He hefted the documents and licenses in his hand, half thinking that he was just being overimaginative. The documentation seemed to be in order. Still, he wouldn't mind getting a closer look at the girl.

"Please, miss," he said pleasantly, "would you mind stepping out of the car and opening the boot?"

"Certainly," said Tina. She removed the keys from the ignition and let them drop from her hand. As she felt for them on the floor, she slipped her hand under her seat and moved the fire selector from safe to automatic, then she sat up, keys in hand, and smiled apologetically. She unbuckled her seat belt, opened the door, and walked to the back of the car. The policeman watched her. Thirty meters away the two soldiers eyed her nylon-clad legs and gave Quirke ten out of ten for judgment.

Dieter remained lolling back on the rear seat of the car. His hand reached under the newspaper to the concealed Skorpion. He couldn't think why the policeman had decided to search the trunk. It could be just a whim, because they had done nothing suspicious—and yet something had changed in the policeman's manner. Of that Dieter, his senses refined, was sure. His skin prickled with the sense of approaching danger. He willed himself to be calm but ready.

In an exercise of willpower, he withdrew his hand from the actuated machine pistol. He glanced down at the airline bag containing the spare magazines, which just protruded from under the passenger seat. It was zippered shut. Nothing suspicious showed.

The sense of danger became more acute, and it became impossible to do nothing but wait. He carefully removed the short-bladed hunting knife from the sheath on his belt and placed it out of sight in his right sleeve, ready to drop into his hand in a much-practiced maneuver.

Quirke completed his examination of the trunk. He had not really expected to find anything, and with a rental car God knows who had used the vehicle in the past. Probably some hunter had spilled gun oil months ago. It was the kind of smell that tended to linger.

Quirke laughed silently at himself. He closed the trunk, rested an arm on the back of the car, and relaxed. He tried not to stare too openly at Tina's long, shapely legs. The breeze whipped at her skirt, and he caught a brief glimpse of inner thigh.

"Well, that's it then," he said. "Now I'll have a quick look inside and you can be about your business."

He opened the rear door of the car. "Would you mind stepping out for just a moment, sir?" he said to Dieter, who had been lazing back as if half asleep.

The German stretched lazily. "I expect a bit of fresh air will do me good."

He got out of the car by the left-side door and closed it behind him with his left hand. His right hand hung at his side. He walked to the driver's side of the car and stood with Tina to the rear of the policeman.

"Thank you, sir," said Quirke. He bent his head and began a cursory search at the rear of the car.

There was nothing on the back shelf apart from guidebooks and a book by some war photographer. The rear seat was empty except for a newspaper. Almost absentmindedly he turned it over to check the football scores—and screamed in pure agony as Dieter's hunting knife ripped open his stomach.

The young policeman sagged back into the road, his two hands gripping his abdomen, vainly trying to hold his intestines in place. Blood soaked his fingers and his uniform and bubbled from his lips. Still conscious, he collapsed in the middle of the road, and the tarmac began to turn crimson. Gurgling sounds like those of some dying animal came from his mouth.

Tina snatched her Skorpion from under the driver's seat. Her first burst caught the rifle-carrying trooper as he stood, stunned, his eyes rooted on the dying policeman. Rounds ricocheted off the magazine of his FN and tore into his groin and thigh. A second burst smashed his rib cage. He collapsed against the Land Rover and rolled face-down onto the muddy road.

Dieter plunged his knife into the back of the second policeman and, without waiting to withdraw it, grabbed his Skorpion from the rear seat, extended the collapsible butt, and with great speed but practiced accuracy began to pump three-round bursts into the rear of the Land Rover, at the radio and the shadowy figure of the operator.

The corporal manning the radio back-rolled out of the Land Rover just as a burst of fire from Dieter blew the high-powered transceiver apart in a shower of sparks and disintegrating electronics. The canvas cover of the Land Rover caught fire, and flames licked along the vehicle.

The corporal crawled behind the empty patrol car as the combined fire of the two terrorists tore through the thin metal of the bodywork and shattered its windows in a cascade of glittering fragments. Blood began to stream from cuts on his face. A bullet ripped open the calf of his right leg, sending a spasm of agony through his body and paralyzing him with shock for several precious seconds.

In stark desperation, scarcely believing what was happening, the soldier unslung the Carl Gustav submachine gun from his shoulder and worked the cocking handle. A high-power nine-millimeter round slid into the breech.

Bullets pierced the fuel tank of the police car, and gasoline drained into a spreading pool across the road.

There was a lull in the firing.

Dieter changed magazines. Tina waited. The collapsible butt of her machine pistol was now fully extended and nestled into her shoulder. She steadied herself against the rented Ford. As the corporal raised his pain-racked body into firing position from behind the police car, she fired twice on single shot. His neck pumping blood and his collarbone smashed, the corporal spun backward and slid into the ditch. Tina changed magazines.

For a few moments there was silence. Then the two terrorists became aware of the crackle of the flames from the burning Land Rover and the gurgling and intermittent screams of the dying Liam Quirke. Tina walked across to where he lay. His agonized moans were getting on her nerves. She pointed her machine pistol at his head and blew away his jaw. She saw that he was still alive, but the noise had ceased.

"Fool," she said quietly, and walked away.

Dieter removed his hunting knife from the back of the other policeman. The body did not stir. He paused reflectively, then, without bothering to turn the body over, he jerked back the policeman's head and cut his throat. A gout of arterial blood spread across the middle of the road and made islands of the empty cartridge cases. Dieter cleaned his knife on the corpse's blue uniform and replaced it in the sheath clipped to his belt. He shivered in the chill March wind. He felt excited and feverish, almost omnipotent. He felt the same kind of exhilaration after a particularly difficult off-piste ski jump, but this was even better. He put his right hand into the pool of blood next to the policeman and then brought it, dripping, very close to his face. It was visible proof of his power to kill. He could smell it. He could taste it. He stood mesmerized for several long seconds.

The wounded corporal could see her legs under the car from where he lay on the ground. Those long, tanned, nylon-clad limbs were unmistakable. Slowly he inched the leather ammunition case containing spare Gustav clips to his front. It seemed to take forever. The rough surface of the road caught at the thick leather, and he had little strength left. Pain dominated his every movement.

He rested the submachine gun on its side, using the ammunition case as a firing platform. It would give him a few centimeters of ground clearance. It would have to be enough.

He aimed. Blood and sweat dripped into his eyes, and his vision became blurred and uncertain. He blinked several times and sighted again. The wooden pistol grip was slippery with blood. His vision was going. He lost all track of time.

He could hear voices. He could see the long legs again. He squeezed the trigger, and the shuddering weapon leaped against his riven body. The hot brass of ejected cartridge cases scorched his face. He held the trigger until the magazine was empty. Just a moment too late he thought of the leaking gasoline. He slipped into unconsciousness before the pool of fuel, ignited by the muzzle blast of his Gustav, exploded—and patrol car and army Land Rover were engulfed in flames.

Black smoke fouled the sky.

FITZDUANE REPLACED the telephone receiver with a sense of relief. He had been working on the von Graffenlaub file for more than eleven hours almost without a break, and he was tired and hungry.

The contents of the file and related papers lay scattered across the top of the polished oak slab on trestles that Etan used as a desk. The information was helping build up a more complete picture of the von Graffenlaub family and its circumstances, but it was slow work. Despite the extensive network of sources and contacts typical of a successful working journalist and the advantage of an initial file from Kilmara, he was having a harder time putting together a comprehensive picture of Rudi's Swiss background than he had expected.

Most of his difficulties seemed to have to do with Switzerland. He had been reluctant to call Guido. His other contacts could tell him— at times in the most intimate detail—about such matters as the latest financial scandal in the Vatican or who was bribing whom in Tanzania or which ballet dancer was sleeping with which member of the Politburo in Moscow, but any question to do with any aspect of Switzerland seemed to result in a resounding yawn.

The consensus seemed to be that Switzerland was a boring bloody country full of boring bloody people who lived off their clichés: cheese, chocolate, cuckoo clocks, mountains, banks, other people, and hot money. Nobody seemed to like either Switzerland or the Swiss. As for Bern—dull, dull, dull was the general view.

Fitzduane doubted that the investigation of a hanging would be dull even if the Bernese did their worst, and he wondered whether any of his traditional contacts really knew very much about the Swiss. It was also clear that there was a palpable element of jealousy underlying many of the comments made about the country. No wars, virtually no unemployment, one of the highest standards of living in the world, and a healthy and beautiful country. It was, indeed, enough to make you sick.

He rose, stretched, and went into the kitchen to open a bottle of chilled white wine. He carried the wine and cheese and crackers into the living room, kicked the open log fire into life, and settled down in an armchair. He moved the television remote control near to hand.

In a few minutes he would watch the nine o'clock evening news and then Etan's program, "Today Tonight." It was strange watching this different, professional Etan through the cold medium of television. He drank some wine, the fire flickered and glowed, and he thought yet again about the von Graffenlaubs.

The file was thin on fact and short on explanation. The hanged boy's father was sixty-one-year-old Beat von Graffenlaub, a lawyer with extensive business interests. He lived in Junkerngasse and had offices in Marktgasse. He was a member of the old Bernese aristocracy, a Bernbürger, and a Fürsprecher (whatever that was). He was a director of various companies, including one of the big four banks, an armaments conglomerate, and a chemicals and drugs multinational. In his youth he had been a skier of Olympic caliber. He was extremely, but discreetly, rich. He seemed to be what is sometimes described as an overachiever. But what was a Bernbürger?

The Bernbürger had married another Bernbürger, a certain Claire von Tscherner—another aristocrat to judge by the "von"—in 1948, and together, after a slow start, they had produced lots of little Bernbürgers, four to be precise. Daughter Marta appeared on the scene in 1955, son Andreas followed in 1958, and then, after four years of limbering up, the Beat von Graffenlaubs really got to work and in 1962 produced twins, Rudolf (Rudi) and Verena (Vreni).

Twins. How had Vreni felt at the news of her brother's death? Had they been close? Most twins were. The probability was high that if anyone knew why Rudi had done it, she did. Fitzduane wondered if Vreni would look like her brother.

In 1976 Beat, by then aged fifty-six, had done something that wouldn't win him any brownie points for originality. He divorced Claire and married a younger woman, a much younger woman. Erika Serdorf—no "von"—was twenty-eight and his secretary. Exit Claire, duty done, to Elfenau and death two years later in a car accident. The new Mrs. Beat von Graffenlaub would now be thirty-three to Beat's sixty-one, and the couple had no children. An interesting situation. What did Erika do with her day, given Beat's work load, other than spend his money?

Fitzduane tried to figure out whether the bottle of wine was now half full or half empty. He poured himself another glass to help resolve the problem.

A great deal was going to depend on the attitude of Beat von Graffenlaub. On the face of it, a stranger's investigation into the death of the lawyer's son was unlikely to be welcome, but without his support significant progress would be problematic. It was clear that the Bernbürger was well connected. Fitzduane's knowledge of Switzerland might be limited to little more than changing planes at Zurich Airport, but he did seem to have heard somewhere about the Swiss fondness for deportation as a solution to those who made waves.

But back to Rudi. Why had he been sent to finish his secondary education at Draker? The Wiesbaden computer, in a printout that reeked of being fine-sieved prior to being issued, talked of "incipient undesirable political associations" and advised contacting the Swiss Federal Police and the Bern police. Titillating but not very helpful. The Swiss police were rumored to be about as outgoing on sensitive matters as Swiss bankers. The Bible said, "Seek and ye shall find." According to Kilmara, the authors were planning a rewrite since the invention of the Swiss.

Fitzduane picked up the television remote control. It was almost nine o'clock, and the electronic image of Etan doing the promo for her program materialized in crisp color.

He pressed the button for sound and caught her in mid-pitch. ". . . Later on, as security forces surround the house in which five hostages are being held by an unknown number of gunmen, we look at the brutal murder of four victims and ask: What are the causes of terrorism? That's 'Today Tonight' after the news at nine-thirty."

The causes of terrorism all explained in forty minutes, less commercials. Television was a neat trick. He watched an advertisement and reflected that there were times when television alone provided an adequate motive for terrorism.

It was only as he listened to the newscaster and saw film of the shocked faces of what the reporter was calling "the Kinnegad Massacre" that he realized the import of Etan's words: Kilmara and his Rangers would be busy.

He hoped Kilmara had enough sense to keep his head down. He was getting too old to lead from the front.

KILMARA WORE the dull blue-black combat uniform, black webbing, and jump boots of the Rangers. The humor was gone from his face, and his expression was controlled and intent as he took one last look at the bank of eight television monitors that dominated the end of the Mobile Command Center. "Give me a search on main screen by five," he said.

The Ranger sergeant sitting at the control panel operated the array of buttons and sliders with easy familiarity. At five-second intervals the picture on the main screen switched to images from each of the six surveillance cameras surrounding the house.

The windows of the modern two-story farmhouse were curtained. No sign of life was visible, yet inside, Kilmara knew, four children and their mother were being held hostage by two killers of singular ruthlessness. To demonstrate their seriousness and disregard for human life, the two terrorists had already killed the farmer in cold blood. His body lay where it had fallen, barely two meters from his own front door. His wife and children had been forced to watch as the young German with the drooping black mustache and gleaming white teeth had neatly cut his victim's throat.

Kilmara turned from the bank of television monitors and walked down the aisle of the command center. On each side of him combat-uniformed Rangers manned sophisticated electronic audio surveillance and communications equipment. To aid screen visibility, the overall light level was dim, with individual spot lamps providing illumination as required. There was the faint background throbbing of a powerful but sound-deadened generator.

He entered the small conference room and closed the door behind him. In contrast with the surveillance area, the room was brightly lit. "Anything?" he asked.

Major Günther Horst and a Ranger lieutenant looked up from their examination of the two terrorists' belongings, which they had found in the hastily abandoned Ford Escort.

"Personal belongings, maps, and guidebooks," said Günther. "Nothing that looks likely to help our immediate problem, though the forensic boys may find something in time." He paused and then picked up a hardback book from the table. He handed it to Kilmara. "But I think you might be interested in this."

The impact of the photo on the front cover of the book was total. In grainy black and white, against a background of swirling dust and smoke, there was the tired, strained, unshaven profile of a soldier. He held a dove in his hands very close to his face and was looking at it with obvious tenderness. Tied to his webbing belt, just next to his water bottle, were two severed human heads.

The book was entitled *The Paradox Business*. It was subtitled "A Portrait of War by One of the World's Top War Photographers— Hugo Fitzduane."

"Well, I'll be buggered," said Kilmara. He looked at Günther. "Let's find him and get him here. Perhaps he can make some connection we've missed."

"And where might he be?"

"At a guess, still in Dublin," said Kilmara. "Try Etan's flat or any good restaurant with a decent wine list in the area." He looked at his watch. It read 9:40 P.M., which without conscious thought Kilmara translated automatically into military twenty-four-hour time. "You could also try RTE. He sometimes picks up Etan there after her show."

"I'll give it a shot," said Günther.

Kilmara smiled. "I've faith," he said. He turned to the lieutenant. "Give me a shout when the house plans come."

FITZDUANE SAT against the back wall of the small control room of RTE Studio Two and watched Etan do useful damage to the self-possession, credibility, and viewpoints of an eminent churchman, the Minister for Justice, and an associate professor of sociology from UCD.

From the looks she was receiving toward the end of the program, it appeared that the assembled panel of experts on the causes of terrorism were more afraid of Etan than of terrorists. The Minister for Justice had no real answers, and it showed visibly as a thin sheen of sweat fought a winning battle with his makeup.

The program was due to be over in a few minutes. Fitzduane looked at the bank of ten monitors and listened to the producer and the production assistants plotting camera movements while the seconds ticked by. Idly he noticed that they all wore dark stockings and ate mints and chain-smoked while they stared at the monitors, controls, and running order with intense concentration. It didn't seem like the kind of occupation that would lengthen your life.

The credits rolled, there was a blast of theme music, and the show was over. Back to the commercials. For a moment the sheer disposability of the medium shook him, and he was glad he worked in print.

The monitors were still live. The studio floor cleared. The monitors featured only the image of Etan, who had remained behind alone to tidy up her notes. She bowed her head, suddenly looking tired and vulnerable. It made Fitzduane want to take her in his arms and wonder what the hell he was doing going away yet again. Perhaps the time had come to settle down. He felt tired enough himself.

The production team looked from Fitzduane to the monitors and back again. He seemed unaware of their existence. The producer put her hand on his shoulder.

"Come and have a drink," she said. "Etan will be along in a few minutes."

THE "TODAY TONIGHT" HOSPITALITY ROOM served the same general purpose as the emergency room of a hospital, except that experience had taught the editor of the program that alcohol, if administered in large quantities soon enough, guaranteed a faster recovery rate.

Interviewers on the program tended to go for the jugular, yet it was important, if the victim was to come back for more, that he have some element of self-esteem restored. The effect of the hospitality room was to ensure that many a politician or bureaucrat, whose dissemblings and incompetence had been revealed only minutes before on prime-time television, soon felt, after a couple of Vincent's gins, that he had carried off the ordeal with the aplomb of a David Frost—and was raring to come back for a second round.

This pleased the editor, who knew that in a small country like Ireland there was only a limited supply of political video fodder. Also, he was a nice man. He liked people to be happy except when being interviewed on his program.

So as not to set a bad example, Fitzduane accepted an oversize gin, a drink he normally never touched, and thought thoughts he had avoided for close on twenty years.

Etan came in freshly made up, the professional mask on again. He checked her legs. She, too, was wearing dark stockings. Full house. He maneuvered her into the corner of the small room for a minute of privacy. "I've been thinking," he said.

Etan looked at him over the top of her glass and then down at the melting ice and slice of lemon. "Of what?"

"Our future together, settling down, things like that," he said.

"Good thoughts or bad thoughts?"

"The very best thoughts," he answered. "Well, I think they are the very best thoughts, but I'm going to need a second opinion." He leaned forward and kissed her on the forehead.

"Is this a consultation?" she asked. She had gone a little pale.

Across the room, which meant no distance at all, given its size, a very drunk Minister for Justice went into shock at the sight of his erstwhile tormentor displaying human emotion. It was clear that he would have been less surprised had she breathed fire.

The telephone rang. Less than thirty seconds later Fitzduane was gone.

The minister came over to Etan and put a beefy arm around her shoulders. He was pissed as a newt. "Young lady," he said, "you should learn which side your bread is buttered. You work for a government-owned and -licensed station." He leered at her.

Etan removed his arm with two fingers as if clearing away something unpleasant. She looked him up and down and wondered, given that Ireland was not short of talent, why such scum so often floated to the top. "Fuck off, birdbrain," she said, and it coincided with a general lull in the chatter.

The editor choked on his drink.

GERONIMO GRADY HAD not acquired his name for nothing.

In his hands the modified Ranger Saab Turbo screamed through the streets of Dublin and out onto the Galway road in a blurred cocktail of flashing blue light, burning tire rubber, and wailing siren. When the traffic ahead failed to give way fast enough, Grady drove the wrong way up one-way streets, cut through the front lots of garages, or took to the sidewalks with equal ease. Fitzduane regarded him as a skilled maniac and gave thanks that Ranger regulations stipulated four-point racing harnesses and antiroll bars in pursuit vehicles. He winced as Grady roared through a set of red traffic lights and sideslipped around a double-decker bus. He kept his hand tight over the top of his gin and tonic glass and tried to retain the sloshing liquid.

They covered the thirty-eight miles to the mobile command center in half an hour. Fitzduane was glad his hair was already silver. He unclipped his safety harness and handed Grady his now-empty glass.

"You really deserve the ears and the tail," he said.

Chapter Eight

"Legs," said Günther. "They might have got away if it hadn't been for the girl's legs. The corporal in the back of the Land Rover was enthusing about them over his radio to a buddy of his stationed at another roadblock a few kilometers away. And then came gunfire and screaming for split seconds, and then silence.

"The warning was enough. The terrorists' car was intercepted in less than three kilometers, and there was an exchange of fire. The terrorists abandoned their car and made a run for it under cover of a driveway hedge. At the end of the drive they burst into a farmhouse located a few hundred meters off the main road. The army, in hot pursuit, surrounded the house and kept them pinned down until reinforcements arrived.

"So far two policemen, one soldier, and the farmer are dead. Another soldier looks likely to die, and a nurse who went to help got shot to pieces. As best we can determine, the corporal must have mistaken her for a terrorist and put a burst of Gustav fire into her legs. That makes a total of four dead—and two pending." He was silent for a moment. "That we know about," he added.

"An obvious question," said Fitzduane. "Why?"

Günther shrugged. "We are pretty sure they aren't IRA, but other

85

than that, we don't know who they are, what they were up to when they were intercepted, or anything much else about them."

Kilmara stood in the doorway. "We thought you might be able to help, Hugo," he said. He placed two plastic-covered bloodstained rectangles on the table in front of Fitzduane. "Look at them closely and think very hard."

Fitzduane picked up the first of the international driver's licenses. The face was smiling into the camera, displaying shining white teeth under a drooping mustache. He studied the photograph carefully and shook his head. He picked up the second license. This time the expression on the face looking into the camera was completely serious, almost detached. Again he shook his head.

Kilmara leaned over and placed the licenses side by side on the table. "Try looking at them together," he said, "and take your time."

Fitzduane looked down at the small photographs and racked his brain for even the slightest hint of familiarity. Mentally he ticked off the assignments he had been on during the last few years. The girl was supposed to be Italian, but she could be Arab—or Israeli, for that matter. The facial types were often very similar. For his part, the man was dark enough to be of Middle Eastern origin, but despite the mustache he looked European.

Fitzduane pushed the two licenses across the table to where Kilmara and Günther sat. "The facial types are familiar enough, so I could be tempted to say maybe I've seen them before. It's possible— but if so, it must have been in the most casual way. Certainly I don't recognize them." He shrugged.

A Ranger came in and set three mugs of coffee on the table. Wisps of steam rose in the air.

Kilmara placed a heavy book in front of Fitzduane. "Hugo," he said, "we found this in the terrorists' baggage. It could be coincidence. . . ." He smiled. "But when you're involved, I tend to believe in coincidence just a little less."

"Nice friendly reaction," said Fitzduane dryly, looking at the familiar volume. It had sold surprisingly well, and he still saw it in bookshops and in airport newsstands when he traveled. The soldier with the dove had been killed two days after the photo had been taken. He'd heard that the bird had survived. He indicated the book. "May I handle it?"

"Sure," said Kilmara. "Forensics have done their thing."

Fitzduane examined the book slowly and methodically. He turned back to the flyleaf. On it was written in pencil a price, a date, and a code: Fr 195—12/2/81—Ma 283. "A recent fan," he said.

"A recent purchase anyway, it would appear," said Kilmara.

"Francs?" asked Fitzduane.

"French, Swiss, Belgian, or indeed from a whole host of French colonies," said Kilmara. "We're looking into it."

"Any ideas," asked Günther, "why two killers should have bought your book? It's a heavy volume to carry if you're flying."

"No," said Fitzduane, "but I'll think about it."

"Hmm," said Kilmara. "Well, we've other things to worry about right now. Thanks for coming. I'll get Grady to drive you home."

Fitzduane shuddered. "I think I'll be safer here. Mind if I hang around?"

Kilmara looked at his friend for a moment and then nodded. "Günther will give you some ID," he said. "You know the form. Keep a low profile and your head down. It's going to be a bloody night."

Fitzduane expressed surprise. "I thought a waiting game was the policy in a hostage situation."

"It is," said the Ranger colonel, "when you have a choice. Here we don't have a choice. The nice young couple in the farmhouse have issued an ultimatum: a helicopter to take them to the airport at dawn and then a plane to some as yet unspecified destination—or they kill one hostage every half hour, starting with the youngest child, aged two, name of Daisy."

"A bluff?"

Kilmara shook his head. "We think they mean what they say. They killed the little girl's father for no other reason than to make a point. Well, they made it and we can't let them get away and we can't let the hostages die—so in a few hours we're going in."

A Ranger poked his head through the doorway. "Colonel," he said, "the cherry picker has arrived."

THE CHILDREN WERE asleep at last. The three younger ones were sprawled on the king-size bed under the duvet. Rory, the eldest at nearly sixteen, lay in a sleeping bag on the floor. A large bloodstained bandage on his flushed forehead marked where the German with the black mustache had struck him savagely with the butt of his machine pistol.

The master bedroom was dimly lit by one bedside lamp. Maura O'Farrell, her eyes betraying the classic symptoms of extreme shock, sat knitting in an armchair near the curtained windows. The knitting needles moved automatically with great speed, and the nearly completed double-knit scarf coiled around her knees and draped down to the floor. The scarf had been meant for Jack to keep him warm as he worked the four hundred acres of their prosperous farm. He would be so cold now. She knew they wouldn't let her, but she wanted to go out and wrap the scarf around his neck. It would at least cover the wound.

She rose and went into the bathroom, whose door opened onto the master bedroom. Everywhere there were signs of Jack. His razor lay in its accustomed place, and his dressing gown hung behind the door. She unscrewed the cap of his after-shave and smelled the familiar, intimate odor; then she replaced the cap. She brushed her hair and checked her appearance in the mirror. She was a touch pale and drawn, which was understandable, but otherwise neat and well groomed. Jack was fussy about such things. He would be pleased.

She took a roll of adhesive tape from the medicine chest and returned to her chair. The knitting needles began to flash once more, and the scarf grew ever longer.

At regular intervals the young Italian girl checked her and the room and peered out of small observation holes cut in the thick curtains. Maura O'Farrell paid her no heed. From time to time the children moaned in their sleep but did not wake. The makeshift sedative of brandy and aspirin mixed with sweetened warm milk had done its work. For a few hours they could rest, oblivious of the memory of seeing their father slaughtered like a pig.

For her part the young Italian girl felt tired but not too unhappy with their situation. They had been unlucky, but now things would work out. Those fools outside would have to give in. Killing the farmer had been a stroke of brilliance. It would cut short futile negotiations. At the agreed time of 3:30 A.M. the phone would ring and the authorities would announce their capitulation: a helicopter at dawn to the airport and then a requisitioned plane to Libya.

The Irish government would never allow a mother and her four children to be killed. Tina was looking forward to that phone call.

She could feel the warmth of the Libyan sun on her face already. Ireland had the most beautiful countryside, but the wind and the rain and the damp cold were just too much for a hot-blooded woman.

THE FINAL PREASSAULT BRIEFING took place in the twelve-meter-long Special Weapons and Equipment trailer. The walls of the mobile unit were lined with row after row of purpose-designed weaponry. Ammunition, scaling ladders, bullet-resistant clothing, and hundreds of other items of specialized combat equipment were stored in custom-built racks and cabinets. At one end of the trailer there was a giant high-resolution television screen flanked by huge pinboards covered with maps, drawings, and photographs. A long table ran for a third of the length of the trailer. On it, a scale model of the farmhouse and vicinity had been roughly constructed, using sand and children's building kits.

Kilmara stood to one side of the giant screen, which was connected to the surveillance system controlled by the separate Mobile Command Center. The twelve Rangers of the assault group sat in folding chairs facing their colonel. Army and Special Investigations Branch liaison personnel swelled their numbers to more than twenty. A digital clock flashed away the seconds. Fitzduane sat discreetly in the background, thinking of how many times before he had watched the trained, attentive faces of troops being briefed—and afterward photographed their corpses. He wondered who in the room this night was going to die.

Kilmara began the briefing. The twelve men in the assault group listened intently. "We're going in. Our objective is to release the hostages unharmed, using only such force as is necessary to achieve that objective. It is my judgment that this will entail killing or, at the minimum, very seriously wounding the terrorists. For the last two hours you have been practicing against a similar house a few miles away. What I'm telling you now incorporates the lessons learned during that exercise.

"There are five hostages in all—specifically, Mrs. Maura O'Farrell and her four children. As best we can determine from acoustic surveillance, they are being kept in the second-floor master bedroom. We believe that the windows of that room are locked and that the windows and the heavy tweed curtains have been nailed in place. Since there is a bathroom directly off the master bedroom, the terrorists can keep the hostages quite conveniently in one place under close observation and at the same time have freedom of movement themselves.

"The farmhouse, as you've discovered, is a modern two-story building with one feature of particular interest to us, the hallway. That hallway is a small atrium. It runs the full height of the house and is lit from the top by a sloping skylight—which can open, incidentally, but is kept closed and locked this time of year. The hallway contains both the stairs to the second floor and the telephone.

"Most of the time the two terrorists prowl the house and keep watch on us—and the hostages—on pretty much a random basis. However, our surveillance has shown that a pattern has developed during the negotiating sessions on the phone. During these times the German, Dieter Kretz, according to his papers, is in the hall near the front door, using the phone. He has no choice. The phone is directly wired in on that spot, and there are no other extensions in the house. Of course, the hall door and adjacent hall windows are covered with blankets nailed into place. They started to do this after O'Farrell was killed, and while they were hammering away, we used the opportunity to insert acoustic probes into all key external areas of the house. That means that while we cannot see the terrorists—with one notable exception that I'll talk about in a moment—from the sounds they make we do have a precise idea where they are at any time. I'm also pleased to be able to say that the equipment is sufficiently sensitive for us to be able to determine not only the presence of a person in a particular location but the identity of that person, provided he or she talks or moves around.

"While the telephoning is going on, the girl normally sits halfway up the stairs so that she is near enough to the hostages and yet at the same time can talk with Dieter and put her two cents' worth into the negotiations. Sometimes she actually descends the stairs and listens in on the incoming call. The crucial time is therefore during telephone contact. Not only is Dieter in a predictable location then— and Tina, too, with luck—but we can actually see him."

Kilmara spoke quietly into a miniature microphone attached to a compact earpiece. Almost immediately the picture on the screen changed from a medium shot of the whole house to a small yellow rectangle. Kilmara spoke into his microphone again, and the yellow rectangle blurred and increased in size until it filled the whole screen. There was an adjustment of focus, and suddenly the assembled men realized they were looking directly through the skylight into the hall of the besieged farmhouse. They saw Dieter come into camera view, pause, look at the phone, and then walk out of sight in the direction of the front sitting room. The long-focus lens gave the picture an unreal, ethereal quality.

Kilmara continued. "The terrorists have said that if we attempt to approach any closer than the agreed perimeter of about two hundred meters from the house, they will kill a hostage. On the terrorists' instructions, we have floodlit the area up to about ten meters from the house. This allows the terrorists to see out without being dazzled. Now, the effect of all this is that although it is exceedingly difficult for us to cross that floodlit perimeter area undetected—and we have not yet been willing to take that risk because of the hostages—at the same time our friends inside cannot see beyond the wall of light surrounding them. They look out into the perimeter, no problem. But if they look up, then they just see the glare of the wall of floodlights."

The Ranger colonel spoke into the microphone again, and the picture on the screen changed. It now showed a giant metal arm with a platform on the end, the whole device being mounted on a self-propelled chassis.

"That picture of the hall," he said, "was taken from the top of that cherry picker crane. There is enough space on the platform for at least three people; the range into the hall from the platform is about two hundred and eighty meters. The problem is that the skylight is double-glazed and made out of toughened glass set at an angle to the direction of fire. It will deflect a conventional rifle round.

"So there are the main elements of our problem—and this is exactly what we're going to do."

FITZDUANE WATCHED the assault group select and check its weapons. His profession made him more knowledgeable than most about tactical firepower. Of the three Rangers in the cherry picker, two were armed with accurized M-21 automatic rifles fitted with high-magnification image-intensifier sights. Early models of these sights had "whited out" when exposed to a sudden increase in light—say, a room light being switched on—but the current version was microprocessor-controlled and could adapt without the marksman's losing his aim. The ammunition had the lethal apple green tips of special-purpose TKD high-penetration rounds. The Teflon-coated rounds lost stopping power as a corollary of their penetrating ability, but with the massive tissue destruction effect of the high-velocity 7.62 mm bullets, that problem would be a little academic.

The third Ranger on the cherry picker team selected a semiautomatic GLX-9 grenade launcher actually custom-built in the Ranger armory. Inspired by the original single-shot M-79 launcher, this weapon held four rounds in a rotary magazine and could hurl a stream of grenades with considerable accuracy for up to four hundred meters.

The actual entry into the house would be made by a team of six Rangers under the command of Lieutenant Phil Burke. They took British-made SA-80 5.56 mm assault rifles and Dutch V-40 hand grenades. The rifle ammunition was a derivation of the Glaser safety round and had the unusual characteristic of expending virtually all its energy in the target. It inflicted the most appalling wounds on the victim and yet did not ricochet.

The task of the third group was to provide intensive fire support from the front of the house. They took grenade launchers and Belgian-made 5.56 mm belt-fed Minimi light machine guns.

The plan provided that the cherry picker team would take out Dieter first, and then Tina if she was by the phone. If she kept to her normal position on the stairs, it was calculated that the combined firepower of grenades and concentrated machine-gun fire would cut her to pieces before she could reach the hostages in the master bedroom. Meanwhile, Phil Burke's team would cross the perimeter and enter the master bedroom using lightweight scaling ladders. There three of them would pour covering fire out through the bedroom door into the hall toward the stairs while the balance of the team hurled the hostages down a chute to safety below.

The danger lay with Tina. If she climbed the stairs to the hostages without being incapacitated by the volume of fire and before Burke's team made it into the bedroom, the hostages would die in a burst of Skorpion fire. It was that simple.

In Fitzduane's opinion it was going to be very close—or as Kilmara put it to the assault group: "If at first you don't succeed, well, so much for skydiving."

THE MEN ON THE cherry picker team moved off first. They needed time to maneuver into the best firing position and to attach the rifle mounts to the platform rail. Their main fear was that a gust of wind would jar the platform ever so slightly at the crucial moment. Kilmara had requested stabilizing cables with hydraulic mounts, but the truck carrying them had suffered a double flat tire and would not arrive in time. Fortunately, the night so far had been calm.

The six men of the Ranger entry team were hideous in blackface camouflage and night-vision goggles. They wore light mat black helmets made of ballistic material and containing miniature radios. Fitzduane was reminded of the head of a deformed fly.

With twenty minutes to zero, all units had completed checking in. The digital clock in the command center flashed second by second through the remaining time.

Outside, a stiff breeze sprang up, and the waiting perimeter of security forces cursed at the effect of the windchill factor in the damp cold and huddled into their parkas.

At 3:30 A.M. the negotiator, Assistant Commissioner Brannigan, picked up the phone to tell the terrorists that the government, reluctantly, would agree to their terms. It was the signal to commence the assault. Now a series of different actions had to mesh together. Seconds were critical. A twenty-round Skorpion magazine can be fired in under two seconds.

It could take even less time to kill a defenseless woman and four young children.

"THIS IS KRETZ," said Dieter.

"He's in the hall," said Acoustic Surveillance.

"We see him," said the cherry picker team leader. "A clear shot but no sign of Tina."

"Tina is moving," said Acoustic Surveillance. "She's leaving the second-floor landing and moving down the stairs. She's stopped."

"Entry team—go!" said Kilmara into his microphone.

On the giant screen the six Rangers of the entry team could be seen sprinting across the two hundred meters of the perimeter. Each pair carried a single rubber-covered titanium alloy scaling ladder.

". . . but in exchange for our providing a helicopter at first light to take you to the airport, you must agree to release the hostages before entering the helicopter," continued Brannigan. His face was creased with strain.

"Tina's moving," said Acoustic Surveillance.

"Can't see her," said cherry picker team leader.

"Where?" said Kilmara.

"Can't tell exactly," said Acoustic Surveillance. "The noise doesn't sound right. Hell, I think she's just kicking her leg against the banister. Wait! She's definitely moving now—down the stairs."

"Dieter still a clear shot," said cherry picker team leader.

"*Du Arschloch!*" shouted Dieter. "Do you think we're idiots? You'll agree to our terms immediately, or I will kill one of the children here and now. You understand, huh?"

Brannigan waited a few seconds before replying. His face was dripping sweat, and he looked ill. "Kretz," he said, "Kretz, for God's sake, hold it. Don't touch another hostage."

"I spit on your God," said Dieter. "You'll follow our terms exactly." He gave a thumbs-up sign to Tina and beckoned for her to come over and listen.

The entry team had made it across the floodlit section of the perimeter and was now crouched in the ten meters of shadowy darkness immediately surrounding the house. The men placed the three ladders outside the rear window of the master bedroom, and the first three Rangers started to climb. The balance of the unit hunkered down in firing position, ready to give covering fire.

"She's definitely going for the phone," said Acoustic Surveillance.

"We can see the edge of her shoulder," said cherry picker team leader. "Not enough for a shot."

The first three members of the entry team reached the top of the ladders and placed a large rectangle of explosive cord on the glass. At the press of a detonator, the focused explosive charges would cut through the glass, blowing any debris into the curtains.

"Entry team ready," said Burke.

"Shit, it's really starting to blow," said cherry picker team leader.

"Stand by, front team," ordered Kilmara.

"Front team ready," said the team leader. The three Rangers facing the front door had their grenade launchers pointed at the fanlight above the door. The grenades—a mixture of blast and stun—were aimed to explode just below the top of the stairs, creating a lethal wall between Tina and the hostages.

"Hostages still in the master bedroom in same positions," said Acoustic Surveillance.

"Very well, we agree," continued Brannigan. "The helicopter will arrive at precisely eight A.M. You will have to wait till that time if it is to be able to reach us from its base. It does not have night-flying instrumentation."

"You Irish are so backward," sneered Dieter, grinning at Tina. She laughed.

"It's a German helicopter," said Brannigan inanely. It was clear he thought that he would be unable to sustain the conversation much longer. He signaled a hurry-up sign.

"We have Dieter in clear shot—and Tina's shoulder," said cherry picker team leader, "and we're steady for the moment."

"Cherry picker, fire!" ordered Kilmara.

THE APPLE GREEN BULLET ENTERED Dieter's head near the crown and exited through his upper teeth and thick black mustache. He swayed slightly, and blood gushed from his mouth. The telephone was still in his hand, and his eyes were open, but he was already dead.

The second sniper hit Tina in the upper right shoulder. The high-penetration round drilled straight through the bone, and the Skorpion dropped from her hand.

All the lights were cut.

Forty-millimeter grenades exploded on the stairs and in the front hall in a rolling series of eyeball-searing flashes. The front team switched to machine-gun fire and the three belt-fed Minimis poured 750 rounds into the confined space in fifteen seconds.

Simultaneously the entry team detonated the explosive cord, and with a sharp crack the thick glass of the double-glazed window dropped onto the bedroom floor.

The cherry picker team poured rifle fire through the skylight. After a couple of seconds, when the tough glass was adequately weakened, the sniper with the grenade launcher opened fire, his grenades punching straight through the remains of the skylight and exploding in the hall below.

Night-vision goggles in place, the entry team cut through the heavy curtains with razor-sharp fighting knives, and Rangers leaped into the darkened bedroom, covering the open doorway and spraying automatic rifle fire through it onto the landing. Then Lieutenant Burke moved forward and tossed V-40 hand grenades out onto the landing and into the hall below. Each grenade burst into 350 lethal fragments.

Meanwhile, the second three Rangers of the entry team clipped the top of an emergency escape chute to the window aperture and began sliding the four children to safety with the backup team on the ground below.

"We're in the bedroom," said Burke into the helmet microphone. "Hostages are alive and being removed now."

"Cherry picker and front teams, cease fire," said Kilmara. "Restore perimeter lighting. Entry team, secure house."

The second three Rangers of the entry team slid the last child down the chute. Burke was changing magazines and the remaining two Rangers were checking the bathroom when Tina crawled in.

No trace of the pretty young Italian girl remained. Her clothes and body were shredded. Her left cheek was gone, exposing the bone. Blood and matter streamed from dozens of wounds. Her right arm hung uselessly, and the fingers of its hand were missing. But she had the Skorpion in her left hand. Its muzzle wavered, and she fired.

Time seemed suspended. There was nothing the young Ranger lieutenant could do. There was a stab of flame and a huge blow over his heart. Burke spun around and collapsed against the wall.

The thing that had been Tina gave a gurgling cry, and the Skorpion dropped from her hand. She moved her fingers up to her throat and scrabbled uselessly at the knitting needle that emerged through it, then collapsed onto her back, her heels drumming against the floor in her agony of death.

Maura O'Farrell, her two hands clenched around the adhesive tape handle of the knitting needle, withdrew the makeshift blade and plunged it in again and again until a Ranger pulled her away.

THEY PICKED their way through the wreckage. It seemed inconceivable to Fitzduane that anyone could have survived the destruction in the hallway. There was scarcely a square centimeter of the floor, walls, and ceiling that was not scarred with shrapnel or pocked with the huge bullet holes of the modified Glaser rounds.

A Ranger technical team was meticulously photographing the scene with both video and still cameras. There was always something to be learned for the next time.

Dieter lay facedown. The pool of blood he lay in was sprinkled with fallen plaster and pieces of debris. His whole back was pitted with wounds from the salvo that had followed the initial fatal shot. Fitzduane bent down and examined first the right wrist, which bore a gold identity bracelet, and then the left, after removing a heavy gold wristwatch. The glass was intact, and the watch was still working. He dropped it on the body. "Nothing," he said to Kilmara.

The staircase had been shot almost to pieces.

"Beats me how she got up," said Kilmara. "We'll get a ladder. I'm buggered if I'm going to break my neck at this stage of the game."

Two Rangers brought one of the scaling ladders and placed it against a protruding joist of the landing.

The body of the once-pretty young Italian terrorist—if, indeed, her stated nationality was not as much a lie as her stated name—lay just inside the doorway of the master bedroom. It looked as if it had been hacked and chopped by some sort of infernal machine. The blood from a dozen or so puncture marks in her neck and throat had run together in an obscene halo around her head. Prepared though he was, Fitzduane felt the bile rise in his throat.

Kilmara emerged from the bathroom, a damp washcloth in his hand. "My turn," he said.

He lifted the corpse's right arm and wiped away the thick crust of congealing blood. The body smelled of blood, feces, and perfume. He saw that a grenade fragment or bullet had sliced into the wrist and carved a furrow in the soft surface flesh. He sponged around the rough edges. The light wasn't good. They were depending on external floodlights shining through the window. He removed a flashlight from the right thigh pocket of his combat uniform and shone the beam on the lifeless wrist.

The mark was very small and partially obliterated by the furrow. Nonetheless, most of the small tattoo could be seen: the letter "A" surrounded by what looked like a circle of flowers. He looked up at Fitzduane, and their eyes met. The Ranger colonel nodded and rose to his feet. He tossed the bloodstained washcloth through the open bathroom door and then bent down to pick up several of the small cartridge cases lying beside the corpse. He put them in his pocket.

They descended the ladder and picked their way through the organized chaos of snaking floodlight cables and departing security force vehicles. Engines roared, and vehicle after vehicle drove away.

"How do you do it?" asked Kilmara. Fitzduane smiled, spread his arms, and shrugged.

"Do you know what Carl Gustavus Jung wrote?" said Kilmara.

"I didn't know he was called Carl Gustavus."

"A rough translation," said Kilmara, "and I quote: 'There are no coincidences. We think they're coincidences because our model of the world doesn't account for them. We're tied up in cause and effect.' "

"And now you're going to tell me Jung's nationality."

"Sharp lad," said Kilmara with a smile, "so you tell me."

"Swiss."

They walked across to the Mobile Surgery trailer. Inside, an army doctor was playing cards with a Ranger lieutenant. A bottle of Irish whiskey and two glasses beside them displayed evidence of current use. Kilmara removed two more glasses from a wall rack and poured generous measures, then topped up the glasses of the doctor and the lieutenant. He removed the cartridge cases from his pocket and placed them in front of the lieutenant. "Souvenirs," he said. "How are you feeling?"

"I've got a sprained wrist, and I'm bruised as hell," said Burke. "It's no fun being shot."

"Lucky she was using a Skorpion," said Kilmara. "It uses a piss-poor underpowered pistol cartridge. It'll kill well enough, but it's got little penetrating power."

"There is a lot to be said for being dressed right for the occasion," said Burke, indicating the scarred but otherwise undamaged Kevlar bullet-resistant vest hanging on a hook on the wall. He suddenly went pale and rushed to the adjacent toilet. They could hear the sounds of retching through the door.

"He's physically okay," said the doctor, "but there may be post-traumatic stress involved. He was bloody lucky."

"Jung also wrote: 'Every process is partly or totally interfered with by chance,' " said Fitzduane. "Not everybody knows that."

"Good grief," said the doctor, and drained his glass.

As Fitzduane and Kilmara left the trailer, the two dead terrorists were carried by on stretchers on the way to the morgue. Fitzduane felt the good mood induced by the banter inside the Mobile Surgery trailer vanish. "A depressing waste," he said soberly.

"I'd feel a lot more depressed if it was us in those body bags," said Kilmara cheerfully. "You've got to see the up side in this game."

THEY ARRIVED at Kilmara's house at just after five-thirty in the morning. Inside the security perimeter all was quiet until the Saab crunched to a halt on the gravel. Then two Irish wolfhounds came bounding around the corner of the big Georgian house.

"One would wonder if they were dogs or elephants with hair," said Fitzduane. "They're enormous bloody brutes."

"You'd know if you visited more often," said Kilmara. "Now stay quiet until I identify you."

Fitzduane did not need to be told twice. He watched while Kilmara called the two hounds to heel. Each dog was well over a meter and a quarter high and, he guessed, weighed at least as much as a fully grown man. Long pink tongues lolled over sharp rows of teeth.

"Ailbe and Kilfane," said Kilmara. "Fairly recent acquisitions."

The two men entered the house through the courtyard door and made their way to the large country-house kitchen.

"Do you know the story of the original Ailbe?"

"Remind me," said Fitzduane.

"There was a renowned Irish wolfhound called Ailbe in the first century," said Kilmara, "owned by MacDatho, King of Leinster. Now Ailbe was such a remarkable dog that he could travel from one side of the kingdom to the other in a single day, and of course he was unsurpassed in hunting and war. Ailbe became so famous that both the King of Ulster and the King of Connaught coveted him, and an offer of no less than six thousand milch cows, a chariot with two fine horses, and the same again after a year was made. This was an offer MacDatho could hardly refuse. At the same time he knew he still had a problem because the king who did not get the hound would give MacDatho a most difficult time. It was a real dilemma."

"So what did MacDatho do?"

"MacDatho promised the hound to both kings," said Kilmara. "When they arrived to conclude the deal, no sooner did they see one another than they forgot all about the hound and fell to fighting. MacDatho, in the manner of a politician, watched the battle from a nearby hill, and an excellent battle it was, with heroics and bravery all over the place and regular pauses for light refreshment and harp playing. However, Ailbe, the bionic wolfhound, was no voyeur. He tossed a coin and entered the fray on the side of the King of Ulster— and had his head chopped off."

"Is there a moral to this story?"

"Pick your battles."

Kilmara gestured Fitzduane to a seat at the big kitchen table and then strode across to the cast-iron range. He poked the cooker into life and stood for a moment enjoying the waves of heat coming from the stove. He donned an apron over his combat fatigues and hummed as he cooked.

Fitzduane dozed a little. It was nearly dawn. Images flickered through his mind. He awoke with a start when Kilmara put a plate of food in front of him.

"Bacon, eggs, sausages, tomatoes, mushrooms, black pudding, white pudding, and fried bread," he said. "You won't see the likes of this in Switzerland." He poured them both coffee from an enamel pot that looked as if it had been around since MacDatho's time.

Fitzduane picked up his mug of coffee. "That book of mine you found in the terrorists' car—"

"Uh-huh," said Kilmara.

"You thought it had to do with me?"

"It's a possibility," said Kilmara. "Maybe on one of your foreign forays you photographed some local supremo from his bad side or something, and our friends were sent to teach you a permanent lesson. They didn't seem to be slap-on-the-wrist types. Well, who knows? I'll worry about reasons after I've had some sleep."

"I've got another idea," said Fitzduane. "Since you took this job, no photographs of you have been published. Right?"

"Right."

"So two things," said Fitzduane. "First, our terrorist friends were killed no more than ten miles from this house while heading in this direction. Second, my book contains a large photo of you at that reunion in Brussels. It's probably the most up-to-date picture of you that's freely available."

"You're suggesting that I could have been the target?" Kilmara had a forkful of bacon and black pudding and fried bread poised for demolition.

"You're sharp this morning," said Fitzduane.

Kilmara munched away. "Ho and hum," he said. "You really should leave such suggestions until after breakfast."

The first shading of dawn appeared through the windows. Outside, a cock began to crow.

BOOK TWO

The Hunting

"The distance is nothing; it is only the first step that is difficult."

—MARQUISE DU DEFFAND,
concerning the legend that St.
Denis, carrying his head in his
hands, walked two leagues

"Crime in Switzerland is rare. . . . And the law is clear. The traffic directions, for example, are clear enough for a blind man to read, but, as a precaution, I have heard, though I cannot consider my source reliable, they are considering writing them in braille."

—VINCENT CARTER, *The Bern Book,* 1973

Chapter Nine

A large harp, comfortably secured by its safety belt, occupied the front first-class passenger seat of the plane to Zurich. Fitzduane was curious. Eventually he asked, and was not reassured by the answer. The harp, he was informed, belonged to the pilot.

Fitzduane raised an eyebrow, then fell asleep. He hoped he would wake up. Thirty-three thousand feet up was more of a head start toward heaven than he really cared for, even without a pilot who seemed more prepared for the afterlife than made for good airline public relations. Fitzduane flew a great deal and did not like it much. In the Congo he had been shot down. In Vietnam he had been shot down. In a series of other wars he had gotten used to the idea that everybody shot at aircraft; whose side they were on seemed to have nothing to do with it.

He awoke when the BAC 111 was over the Bristol Channel, and looked out the window. The wing was still there, which made him feel better, and there were no fresh holes. There was the crackle of a microphone, and an android voice announced that they were flying at five hundred miles an hour and that it was five degrees Celsius in Zurich. Fitzduane closed his eyes and slept again.

* * *

THE MAN they soon were to call the Hangman stood naked in front of the mirror and stared at his reflection. His face and upper body were encrusted with drying blood. His chest and pubic hair were matted and sticky with it. He had fallen asleep after the sex and the killing that had accompanied their orgasms. The room smelled of blood and semen and sweat and, he liked to think, their victim's fear. The mutilated body still lay in the room, but neatly in one corner in a body-fluid-proof body bag.

The woman—she had done the actual killing this time—lay sprawled on the bed, fast asleep, exhausted after her endeavors. Her satiety, he knew, wouldn't last long.

The man smiled and stepped into the shower. He looked down at his body as the needles of pulsing water washed the last traces of the boy's life off the gridded porcelain floor and then down through the drain into the sewers of Bern. So much for beautiful Klaus.

The man—one of his many names was Kadar—dried himself and donned a light robe of silk. The activity and the sleep that had followed had done him good. He went into his study and lay back in his Charles Eames chair for his first session with Dr. Paul.

The solution had been so simple: Since he could not visit a psychiatrist without risk, he would do the job himself. He would tap into his own considerable resources. He would be his own expert. He would be able to speak absolutely frankly in a way that would otherwise be impossible. And, as always, he would be in control.

Since childhood Kadar had invented imaginary friends. The first had been Michael, who had been pale-skinned with sun-bleached golden hair. He looked the way Kadar wished to be but was not. Other creations followed.

As the years passed, Kadar refined the process of creating a new person to a ritual. Always the process started with his lying back, his eyes closed and his body relaxed. He would focus his mind in a way he could not even describe to himself. It was something akin to fine-tuning his natural life-force. When he was ready to begin, he would see a wall of thin gray mist swirling gently. The mist would have a glow as if lit from within.

Slowly a shape would appear in the mist, its details obscure. Only one factor would be clear: the height of the figure. Kadar's creations, regardless of their eventual age or sex or external appearance, always started with height.

He often thought that this first stage was the hardest. It required such an infusion of energy. Sometimes he would lie there for hours, his body drenched in sweat, and the wall of mist would stay blank. Once the basic shape had appeared, the work would be easier and more pleasurable. He would mold and paint in the details as if in an artist's studio, but use his tightly focused mind instead of brushes or tools to achieve the result. He would adjust the height and then work on the general build. Features would become defined. He would work on the posture. Clothing would be added, then texture and color. Finally the creation would be complete but lifeless. Then, in his own time, he would breathe life into it—and it could talk and move if that was his wish.

Most of the men he created had pale skin and sun-bleached hair and were beautiful. Most of the women he created were more utilitarian, although there were exceptions.

Over time he had learned to modify his ritual to mold and change real people. There wasn't the same totality of control, but there was more challenge. There was a higher wastage factor, but that in itself yielded benefits.

It was in the process of killing that he reasserted control.

FITZDUANE PATTED the harp on its little head, then left the plane. The flight had taken under two hours. It was on time. He pushed his luggage cart through the NICHTS ZU DEKLARIEREN and looked for a public telephone.

There were times when having intuition and perception could be a disadvantage, even a curse.

They had not parted well. Etan lay next to him, their sweat mingled, yet there had been a distance between them. Different people, different ways, different goals, and, for the moment, no bridge. Love and desire, but no bridge. That bridge was commitment, not just talk about marriage but the serious practical business of changing their lives so they could be together. There would be small people to nurture and care for. That meant being around, not departing yet again on another quest. It meant choices and some hard decisions. He smiled to himself. He missed her already, but hell, growing up was harder when you were an adult.

In the end Guido was the obvious man from whom to obtain

background information on the von Graffenlaubs. He and Fitzduane either had covered assignments together or had competed for them in half a dozen different countries. Since being wounded in Lebanon and subsequently contracting a severe liver infection, the Swiss journalist had been deskbound and was currently filling in the time with a research job in the records section of Ringier, the major Swiss publishing house.

And yet Fitzduane hesitated by the phone; Guido had been Etan's lover for several years. Lover—familiar with her body in the most intimate of ways. A kaleidoscope of explicit sexual images crowded his mind. Another man, his friend, in the body of the woman he loved—in the past perhaps, but in his mind now.

Life, he thought, is too short for this kind of mental shit. He began to dial.

DR. PAUL HAD pale, aristocratic features, and his blond hair was silky smooth. "Are you comfortable?" he asked. He managed to sound genuinely concerned. The tone of his voice was reassuring, and its timbre projected professional confidence.

Kadar thought he'd got Dr. Paul about right. He relaxed in the Charles Eames chair. He nodded.

"Then tell me about yourself," said Dr. Paul. "Why don't we start with your name?"

"Felix Kadar. But that's not my real name."

"I see," said Dr. Paul.

"I have many names," said Kadar. "They come and go."

Dr. Paul smiled enigmatically. He had beautiful white teeth.

"My birth certificate," said Kadar, "states that I was born in 1944. My place of birth is given as Bern. Actually I was born in a small apartment in Brunnengasse, just a couple of minutes' walk from here. My mother's name was listed as Violeta Consuela María Balart. My father was Henry Bridgenorth Lodge. She was Cuban, a secretary with the diplomatic mission. He was a citizen of the United States of America. They were not married. It was wartime. Even in Switzerland, passions were running high.

"Father worked for the OSS. He never got around to mentioning to Mother that he had a wife and young son back in the States. When Mother explained that it wasn't the high standard of Swiss wartime cuisine that was thickening her waist, Dad had himself parachuted into Italy, and by all accounts he had a very good war.

"Mother and I were shipped back to Cuba and banished to a small town called Mayarí in Oriente Province. The area has one claim to fame: the biggest hacienda for miles around—it was over ten thousand acres—was owned by a man with a singularly inappropriate name, Ángel Castro. He sired seven children, and one of them was Fidel.

"Many people say that they have no interest in politics because no matter who is in power, it seems to make no difference. Life just goes on grinding them down. Well, I can't agree with that view. The Batista government meant a great deal to me. All of a sudden—I was about eight at the time—I had new clothes to wear, shoes on my feet, and there was enough to eat. Mother had a new hairstyle and smelled of perfume. Major Altamir Ventura, the province head of Batista's secret police, had entered our lives. He wore a uniform and had shiny brown boots and smelled of sweat and whiskey and cigars and cologne. When he took off his jacket and draped his belt and holster over the chair, I could see that he had another, smaller pistol tucked into the small of his back."

"How did you feel about your mother at that time?" asked Dr. Paul.

"I didn't hate her then," said Kadar, "and of course, it's pointless to hate her now. At that time I merely despised her. She was stupid and weak—a natural victim. Whatever she did, she seemed to come out second best. She was one of life's losers. She was abandoned by my father. She was treated abominably by her family. She had to scrimp and scrape to make a living, and then she became Ventura's plaything."

"Did you love her?"

"Love, love, love," said Kadar. "What an odd word. It is almost the antithesis of being in control. I don't know whether I loved her or not. Perhaps I did when I was very small. She was all I had. But I grew up quickly."

"Did she love you?"

"I suppose," said Kadar without enthusiasm, "in her own stupid way. She used to have me sleep in her bed."

"Until Major Ventura came along?"

"Yes," said Kadar.

"Was your mother attractive?"

"Attractive?" said Kadar. "Oh, yes, she was attractive. More to the point, she was sensual. She liked to touch and be touched. She always slept naked."

"Did you miss sleeping with your mother?"

"Yes," said Kadar. "I was lonely."

"And you used to cry and cry," said Dr. Paul.

"But nobody knew," said Kadar.

"And you swore never to rely on anybody again."

"Yes," said Kadar.

"But you didn't keep your promise, did you?"

"No," Kadar whispered. "No."

FITZDUANE HAD several hours to kill before he met Guido at the close of the working day at Ringier. He took a train the short distance into the center of Zurich and left his luggage at the central station. He shrugged his camera bag over his shoulder and set off to explore. Wandering around a new city on foot was something he loved to do.

Zurich was as sleek and affluent as he had expected, but to his surprise there were signs of discord amid the banks, the expensive shops, and the high-rise office buildings. At first it looked like a few isolated cases of vandalism. Then he began to notice that the damage, albeit superficial, was widespread. There were clear signs of recent rioting on a substantial scale. Plate glass windows had been cracked and were neatly taped up pending repair. Other windows had been smashed and were boarded up, again in the same painstaking and professional manner. Shards of broken glass glittered from the gutters. Spray-painted graffiti festooned the walls. A church just off Bahnhofstrasse was smeared with red paint as if with gobbets of blood. Under the red streaks were the words EUTHANASIE = RELIGION. On another side street he found two empty tear gas canisters. He bought a map and walked to Dufourstrasse 23.

Ringier was one of the largest publishing houses in Switzerland, and its success showed in the sleek modernism of its headquarters building. The foyer was large and dominated by a bunkerlike reception module; *desk* hardly seemed the appropriate term. There was a magazine shop built into the ground floor. While Guido was being located, Fitzduane browsed idly through some of the Ringier output. A miniature television camera whirred quietly on its mobile mount, following his movements.

The last time he had seen Guido, the Swiss had been fit and noticeably handsome, with a deep, confident voice and a personality to match. The overall effect was to project credibility, and it was not a misleading impression. Over the years Guido had built up a considerable network of sources and contacts who confided in him with unusual frankness.

This time, as Guido stepped from the elevator, Fitzduane felt a sense of shock and then sadness. He knew that look all too well. Guido's face seemed to have shrunk. It was newly lined and an unhealthy yellow. His eyes were bloodshot and cloudy. He had lost weight. He walked slowly, without his normal vigor of stride. Even his voice had changed. The warmth was still there, but the assurance was lacking, replaced by pain and fatigue. Only his smile was the same.

"It's been a long time, Samurai," he said. He grasped Fitzduane's hand with both of his and shook it warmly. Fitzduane felt a rush of affection but was at a loss for words.

Guido looked at him in silence for a moment; then he spoke. "I had much the same reaction when I looked in my shaving mirror every morning. But you get used to it. Anyway, it won't be long now. I don't want to talk about it. Come on home and tell me all."

THE LAST Batista presidency, as far as Major Ventura was concerned, was an opportunity for both career advancement and the acquisition of serious wealth.

Ventura's ambitions were furthered by the international political climate of the period. The Cold War was at full chill. The Dulles brothers were in charge of the State Department and the CIA, and they did not look kindly on even the hint of communism on their doorstep. Batista's approach to upward mobility mightn't exactly be the American Way, but at least the son of a bitch couldn't be accused of being a Red.

Within two years Major Ventura was Colonel Ventura and posted back to Havana to become the deputy director of BRAC, the special anti-Communist police. He stopped wearing a uniform and instead dressed in immaculately tailored cream-colored suits cut generously under the left armpit. He was fond of alligator-skin shoes. He took vacations in Switzerland. He investigated, arrested, interrogated, tortured, and killed many people who were said to be Communists. He had close working links with the CIA, which was how Kadar met Whitney Reston, the only person Kadar truly loved, and by whom he was seduced.

"We'd been in Havana for a few years," said Kadar. "Ventura still lived with Mother, but he was getting bored with her. He had other women—many other women.

"Whitney worked for a CIA man called Kirkpatrick. He used to come to the house regularly to see Ventura. The CIA had set up BRAC with Batista, and they funded it. They liked to keep an eye on where the money was going. Ventura was their man within BRAC, probably one of many. He was paid a regular monthly retainer by the CIA on top of his BRAC salary and the money he made in other ways. One of his favorite techniques was to arrest someone from a rich family, rough him up a bit, and then have the family buy the prisoner out."

"How did you know all this?"

"Various ways," said Kadar. "The house we lived in was big and old. I had time on my hands—I had made the decision not to have any friends—and I had already discovered that I was smart, really smart. I found if I could get a book on how to do something, I only had to read it a couple of times and I could become proficient in whatever it was. In this way I learned some basic building skills and how to plant microphones and organize spy holes. I stole much of what I needed from BRAC and the CIA. I learned how to tap phones. To tell the truth, it wasn't difficult.

"I learned early that knowledge is power. I made it my business to know everything that went on in that house, and from that I learned much of what BRAC and the CIA were up to elsewhere. I learned that words such as *good* and *bad* are meaningless. You are either master or victim.

"I used to look at Ventura and my mother in bed together. That was easy to arrange because my room was over theirs and all I had to do was make a hole from my floor to their ceiling. I put in a monocular so I could see every detail, and I had the place wired, of course. He made her do some disgusting things, but she didn't seem to mind. I thought she was pathetic."

"Tell me about your affair with Whitney Reston," said Dr. Paul. "Did you have homosexual inclinations to start with?"

"I don't think I was either homosexual or heterosexual," said Kadar, "merely sexually awakening and alone. I hadn't yet mastered how to mix with people and to take what is needed without being involved. I was still vulnerable.

"When I was small, I had an imaginary friend called Michael. Whitney looked like an older version of Michael. He had the same blond hair, pale skin, and fine features. And he was nice to me and gentle, and he loved me. It lasted for a year. I was so happy.

"I spent so much time with Whitney that I stopped monitoring all the activities of the house. I still kept an eye on Ventura, but provided I knew where she was, I left Mother unsupervised. I didn't think she was important. I was wrong. Even a pathetic figure like Mother could be dangerous.

"I don't remember all of it, but I remember too much. Whitney and I had driven out to the beach at Santa María-Guanabo. As far as other people were concerned, Whitney was just being a family friend giving a lonely teenager an outing. We had been very discreet. Whitney knew he'd be in real trouble if the CIA found out. He said that the Company was obsessed with homosexuality.

"The beach, a ribbon of white sand some ten kilometers long bordered by pine trees, was only about twenty kilometers from Havana. We liked it because it was easy to get to, yet during midweek it was always possible to find a private spot. Most people used to cluster near the few bars and restaurants. Ten minutes' walk, and you'd think you had the world all to yourself.

"It was a hot, hot day—hot and humid. The sea was calm, and the sound of white-topped rollers was beautifully relaxing. I was nearly asleep in the shade of an awning we had rigged up. There was the smell of the sea and of pine from the groves behind us.

"I heard voices—not a long conversation, just a quick exchange of words. I opened my eyes a little. The glare off the sea and the white sand was dazzling. I was drowsy from drinking half a bottle of *cerveza*. Whitney used to limit me to half a bottle. He said I was too young to drink more.

"Whitney had gone for a swim to cool off, but he wasn't far out. I put my sunglasses back on to cut the glare, and as my eyes adjusted, I could see two men walking down to the water's edge. They were wearing loose cotton shirts and slacks. Both men wore wide-brimmed hats like those of cane cutters.

"One of the men called to Whitney. I couldn't hear what was said, but Whitney waved and shouted something. He swam toward shore and rose to his feet in the shallow water. He looked across at me and smiled. He ran his fingers through his hair to remove the water. His tanned, wet body gleamed in the sun.

"The two men stepped forward a few paces, and my view of Whitney was momentarily obscured. One of the men moved, and I heard two bangs very close together. The sound was muffled by the noise of the sea.

"I sat up, but I was still not seriously alarmed. What I was seeing was unreal. None of the actions I was observing seemed to have any relevance to me. They were pictures in the landscape—nothing more. Sweat trickled into my eyes, and I had to take my sunglasses off for a second to wipe it away.

"The two men separated. One was reloading a short, thick weapon. I could see the sun glinting off cartridge cases. The other man had an automatic pistol in his right hand. He stepped into the shallow surf and pointed the weapon toward Whitney but didn't fire immediately. For some moments he stared at Whitney, his weapon extended as if he were shocked into stillness by what he saw.

"Whitney's body remained upright, but where his face and the top of his head had been there was nothing. A fountain of arterial blood gushed from his head and cascaded down his torso and lower body and stained the water around his feet.

"Then the man with the pistol fired. The first shot hurled the body back into the water in a cloud of pink spray. The man went on firing shots into the bundle at his feet until the gun was empty and the slide locked back. He pulled a fresh clip from his pocket and pulled back the slide to insert a round into the breech and recock the weapon. He looked toward me. The other man said something, and the two of them walked away into the woods."

Kadar looked up at Dr. Paul. "I think I'd like a rest now," he said.

THEY TOOK a taxi from Ringier, picked up Fitzduane's bags from the station, and traveled the short distance to Guido's apartment on Limmatstrasse.

The River Limmat was a dull steel gray in the evening light. The rush-hour traffic was heavy but moved easily. Trams were filled with tired faces heading homeward.

As they turned into Guido's street, they passed a factory or warehouse that looked as if it had been involved in a minor war. It was covered with banners and graffiti. Stones and other discarded missiles littered the ground. The place was surrounded by coils of barbed wire. Police, some in uniform, some in full riot gear, occupied every strategic point. Outside the barbed wire, knots of people stood looking and talking.

"As you can see," said Guido, "my apartment is well placed. I can walk to the war zone, even in my present state of health, only a modest three hundred meters."

"What *is* this war zone?" asked Fitzduane.

"It's the highly controversial Autonomous Youth House," said Guido. "I'll tell you about it over a drink." He looked amused. "Not exactly what you expected of placid Switzerland, Hugo."

"No," said Fitzduane.

The apartment was on the second floor. As Guido was about to place his key in the lock, the door opened. A handsome but studious-looking dark-haired woman in her early thirties gave him a hug. He rested his arm around her shoulders. "This is Christina," he said. "She tries to see I behave myself; she pretends I need looking after, thinks I can't boil an egg." He kissed her on the forehead. She squeezed his hand.

The apartment was spacious and comfortable. Guido ushered Fitzduane into his study and poured them both a glass of dry white wine. "I should be hard at work, preparing the salad," he said, "but Christina knows we want to talk. I have a reprieve."

"An attractive woman," said Fitzduane. "I never thought to see you so domesticated."

"Made it by a short head," said Guido. "If I had known it was so enjoyable, I might have tried it earlier in my life."

"You did try it earlier," said Fitzduane, "or had you forgotten?"

Guido gazed at him directly and took his time before answering. "No," he said.

They were both silent for a little while; then Guido spoke. "I've been doing some work on Beat von Graffenlaub, as you asked. You have found yourself a formidable subject. Don't cross him, or you'll find yourself leaving Switzerland sooner than you might wish."

"How so?"

"Von Graffenlaub is very much an establishment figure," said Guido, "and the Swiss establishment looks after its own. You rock the boat too much, they ship you out. Very simple."

"What constitutes rocking the boat?"

"That's the random factor; you won't necessarily know," said Guido. "They make the rules. It's their country."

"Yours, too," said Fitzduane.

"So my papers say, but I don't own a big slice of it like von Graffenlaub. That makes a difference."

"To your perspective?"

"To my perspective, sure," said Guido, "but mostly I'm talking about power, real power." He smiled cheerfully. "The kind you don't want to be on the receiving end of," he added.

Fitzduane looked at him and nodded.

Guido laughed. "Don't pack yet," he said.

"I'd like to know more about the general Swiss setup," said Fitzduane, "before you go into detail on von Graffenlaub. What constitutes the establishment? How does the system work? Why has this haven of peace and prosperity got to rioting in the streets? What is an Autonomous Youth House?"

Guido lit a Brissago, a long, thin, curly cigar with a straw as a mouthpiece. It looked not unlike a piece of gnarled root. Smoke filled the air. The room was warm, and the sounds of dinner being prepared emanated from the kitchen.

"I'll start with the basics," he said. "Population, 6.3 million. Currently one of the most prosperous nations in the world. Inflation minimal, and unemployment almost nonexistent. Trains, buses, aircraft, and even joggers run on time. In many ways not a nation at all so much as a collection of diverse communities; in many cases these communities do not even like each other or, in terms of language and culture, would appear to have little in common. Yet they are linked together for mutual advantage.

"Four different languages are spoken—German, French, Italian, and Romansh—and God alone knows how many dialects. The Swiss are further divided by religion. Nearly fifty percent are Catholic, and about forty-eight percent Protestant of various shades. I'm not too sure about the balance.

"Unlike most other countries, which are strongly centralized, power in Switzerland, at least in theory and in many cases in practice, comes from the bottom up. The core unit is the Gemeinde, or community. A bunch of Gemeinden together make up a canton, and there are twenty-six cantons, or half cantons, making up what the outside world knows as Switzerland.

"Central government in Bern is kept very weak. The constitution strictly limits its powers, and the voters make sure it does not get too much of the tax revenue. Control of money is power: little money, little power."

Guido smiled cynically, yet his expression belied his tone. Guido had a certain pride in being Swiss.

"Different languages, different dialects, different religions, different geography, different neighbors, different customs," said Fitzduane. "What holds it all together?"

"Different things," said Guido, smiling. "A damn good constitution, nearly seven hundred years of precedent, a shared affluence—though not shared equally—and one very strong element in the social glue, the army."

"Tell me about the Swiss Army," said Fitzduane.

"Time to eat," said Christina, appearing in the doorway. "It's not good for Guido to eat late." She moved forward to help Guido out of his chair. The gesture was discreet but well practiced. As he grew tired, he needed assistance but still must be seen to be in command of his faculties. It was a caring action, one of love.

Fitzduane resisted the impulse to help. He stayed back and busied himself moving the wineglasses to the dining room table and, with a little encouragement from Guido, opening another bottle of wine.

KADAR WAS silent, lost in his recollections. Whitney Reston's death had been blamed on Castro and his rebels. As a CIA man helping Batista's anti-Communist police, Whitney was an obvious target.

After Whitney's death Kadar had gone back to his little world of microphones and tape recorders and spy holes. He fitted time switches and experimented with voice actuation. He made his own directional mike and experimented with using the electrical circuitry as a transmission medium. He even managed to install bugs in both Ventura's and his mother's cars.

It might have been thought that all this surveillance activity was dedicated to finding out more about who had killed Whitney. Ironically, that was not the case. At the time Kadar was in shock. He had accepted Ventura's claim that the killers had been caught and executed. Even when he learned—it was from a conversation in the car—that the people who were actually executed were innocent of that specific killing, he had still accepted that the killers were rebels.

In truth he was looking for nothing in particular. The work was an end in itself. It stopped him from thinking about what he had lost. It helped prepare him for his future on his own. It helped him feel in control.

One day Ventura called Kadar. He said that somebody wanted to see him and that he wasn't to tell his mother. He told Kadar to clean himself up and put on a suit and tie, then drove him to a house on Calle Olispo in Habana Vieja. On the way Ventura told Kadar that this man had something very important to say and that if Kadar knew what was good for him, he'd pay attention, be polite, and respond favorably to anything that was suggested.

Kadar was shown into a sparsely furnished room on the second floor, then left alone. The windows were closed, and the place had an unlived-in feel to it. A few minutes later a distinguished-looking American came in. He locked the door and motioned Kadar to take a seat.

Kadar knew immediately who he was. Mother had kept a photograph of him and had talked about him many times. Of course, he was older now, and there was gray in his hair, but he had one of those spare New England faces that age well.

He took a cigarillo out of a silver cigarette case and lit it. He wore a pale gray lightweight suit, a club tie, and a shirt of blue oxford cloth with a button-down collar. His shoes were the kind that bankers wear. He couldn't have been anything but an American of a certain privileged class.

"I think you know who I am," the man said.

"My father," Kadar answered, "Henry Bridgenorth Lodge."

"Your English is good," Lodge noted. "Your mother, I guess?"

Kadar nodded.

"I haven't got a lot of time," Lodge said, "so listen carefully to what I have to say. I know I haven't been any kind of father to you. I won't try to apologize. It would be a waste of time. These things happen—especially in wartime. That's all there is to it.

"When I met your mother, I had a wife and a small son already. When I got back to America, I didn't even want to hear about Europe for a while. It was all a bad dream. I wiped out the last few years from my mind—and that included your mother and you. I never gave you a thought.

"Peace and quiet were fun for a while, but soon the juices began to flow. There's a high you get from action, and I missed the excitement. The OSS was officially disbanded at the end of the war by Truman, who hadn't much time for spooks. After a year or so of being outmaneuvered by Stalin on every front and with country after country being grabbed by the Reds, Truman did an about-face, and the CIA was born. Because of my OSS background, I got in on the ground floor. I had field experience; I speak several languages, including Spanish. I got promoted fast.

"About seven years ago I was asked to take a look at our Cuban operations. The Company had taken over Cuba from the FBI, and there were some questions about the reliability of a number of the agents we inherited. It all got straightened out, but in the process something made me track down your mother and you.

"Now don't get me wrong. I wasn't thinking of rekindling an old passion. I was happily married. I'm one of those lucky people for whom it has worked. No, it was more like curiosity.

"I found the pair of you weren't doing too well. You were stuck in some nothing town in the toughest province in Cuba. You were barely surviving.

"I have learned to be cold-blooded over the years—this job doesn't leave you with much faith in human nature—but something pushed me into trying to help. I figured what you needed was a guardian—some kind of protector—and some money."

"Ventura," Kadar muttered.

Lodge looked at Kadar appraisingly. "Smart boy. Ventura always said you were bright. You've probably guessed the rest of it. He's been one of our people for a long time. I didn't tell him to make your mother his mistress; that was Ventura mixing business and pleasure and saving on travel time. I told him to look after the pair of you, and I paid him a retainer. It was my money—not CIA funds. He received those as well. Ventura knows how to work the angles."

"Why have you sent for me now?" Kadar said. "Do you expect thanks?"

Lodge smiled thinly. "I can see we're going to have a loving relationship. No, it's got nothing to do with my expecting gratitude, and it's not for any feeling I have for you. I don't even know whether I'm going to like you. But that's not the issue. I need you for my wife. Two years ago our son died—of meningitis, of all stupid things. She can't have any more children, and neither of us wants to adopt a complete stranger. You're a solution. She's been seriously depressed since Timmie's death. You could make all the difference."

"Does she know about me?" Kadar asked.

"Yes," Lodge said. "I told her about you a year ago. She was upset at first, but now she has come around to the idea that it would be wonderful. She's a religious lady, and she sees your filling the gap as something preordained by God. You have Bridgenorth Lodge blood of the right shade of blue flowing in your veins."

"What about my life here?" Kadar asked. "What about Mother? Does she know about this?"

"Listen, kid," Lodge said, "in a few weeks' time Castro and his Commie friends are going to take over, and Cuba is going to sink even farther into the sewers. This country isn't much now. Under the Fidelistas it's going to get a whole lot worse. They talk about democracy. They mean a one-party dictatorship controlling every second of every Cuban's life. People will remember the Batista years as the good old days.

"In contrast, if you come to the States to live with my wife and me, you're going to have a chance to really make it. You'll lose that accent. You'll go to the best schools and the best universities. You'll be able to follow whatever career you want. I ask you, which is the better deal?"

"And what about Mother?" Kadar repeated. "Does she know what you're proposing?"

"Not yet," Lodge answered. "But don't pretend you care what she thinks. Don't try to bullshit me. I know about your relationship with your mother. Don't forget Ventura's my man."

"Are you rich?" Kadar said.

"You're a sentimental young fellow, aren't you? I see you've inherited some of our family traits." Lodge smiled slightly. "Comfortable."

"How comfortable?"

"I'll give you a million dollars when you are twenty-one if you agree to my proposition. Does that help?"

"Yes, Father," Kadar said.

It had become clear to him that he was going to need a great deal of money. Lodge's million would not be enough, and there were sure to be terms and conditions. Besides, he wanted money that no one would know about. Money is power, but secret money is control.

Kadar was lying on his bed that same evening, listening to Ventura and his mother through headphones, when he heard something that determined what he had to do—and then all the little pieces would fall into place.

"Well, my sweet," Ventura was saying, "you are more stupid and more dangerous than I thought."

Kadar's mother didn't say anything.

"Last night," continued Ventura, "my men picked up a certain Miguel Rovere, an enforcer for those American friends of ours who like to support our economy by financing gambling, prostitution, drugs, and similar examples of the American Dream. Apparently he was better at inflicting pain than receiving it. By morning he was screaming for mercy. He said he had some very important information fit for my ears only. It was about a Señor Reston—the late Señor Reston.

"Rovere said that he and an imported hitman from Miami had killed Whitney Reston—and that the contract had been put out by you. You know, I'm so used to hearing lies from prisoners—people say anything to stop the pain—that I find myself quite taken aback by veracity. I find the truth extraordinary in the literal sense of the word. Because it is extraordinary, it is distinctive and immediately recognizable. Rovere's smashed, bloody lips whispered the truth."

Kadar's mother started to cry. Then she shouted at Ventura that if he had been willing to do something about Whitney in the first place, none of this would have been necessary. Was she supposed to do nothing when her only son was being turned into a woman by some perverted American? And so it went on—an outpouring of hate, frustration, and pent-up rage. Much of it was garbled. But Kadar didn't think Whitney was killed simply for what he was supposed to have done to him. No, Whitney's killing had come to symbolize for her a way of getting back at all the people who had used and discarded her over the years.

"SO SHE KNEW," Dr. Paul broke in. "Did she speak to you about it?"

"Not a word."

"I suppose she knew it wouldn't have done any good."

"I suppose she did," said Kadar. "When the significance of what was being said began to sink in, my reactions were disparate. Part of me was so stunned I had difficulty breathing. Another part of me went very calm. I was not altogether surprised at what I had heard. The two killers had dressed like campesinos, but their body language had been wrong. They had borne themselves like city people. I had trained myself to notice such things.

"Mother sniveled for a while and then spoke. She sounded frightened. She asked Ventura what he was going to do. He answered that for the moment he would do nothing except keep her out of circulation until he could figure out some answers. Then she asked if he was going to tell the CIA. He said he would have, but to be frank, he was afraid of being included in their tidying-up process.

"Mother had to go—I was sure of that. Soon it became equally inevitable that Ventura must be killed, too. I had nothing against him personally—indeed, I admired and had learned much from his single-minded ruthlessness—but he had something I needed, and with him dead I knew how to get it.

"For the next few days I considered a wide variety of plans and methods. I decided for security reasons not to involve anyone else— look at how Rovere had implicated Mother. Besides, I knew that I was going to have to kill again in the future if I was going to make my way as planned. I might as well make a good start. I was aware that I suffered from squeamishness—I disliked intensely the sight of blood—but I was determined to eliminate such weaknesses from my makeup.

"Don't get the idea that I was a total stranger to violence. Quite the contrary, it would be hard to be around Ventura for long without being exposed to one of the major realities of life. Nonetheless, seeing someone killed is not the same as doing it yourself. It was important to get hands-on experience.

"It began to dawn on me that I had picked a tough target to begin with, and of course, Mother shared in Ventura's protection. Ventura himself was a physically formidable man and was always armed. The house was heavily guarded at all times, and when Ventura traveled, he was driven in a car fitted with bulletproof glass and armor plating. In addition, heavily armed security police rode in Jeeps in front of and behind him. The same level of security was maintained at BRAC headquarters. Many people wanted Ventura dead, and he knew it. He was an intelligent man. His precautions were well thought out and implemented.

"In the final analysis I abandoned all my complex plans and high tech methods and opted for a scenario that would exploit the one major security weakness, the lack of guards indoors, and at the same time would allow me to lose my virginity and exact retribution in a most direct manner. It was a simple scheme, and it depended heavily on precise timing.

"I thought of blaming the killings on either the CIA or the Fidelistas—either would have represented a certain natural balance to the affair—but in terms of access, neither was very credible without taking out some of the perimeter guards. I would have the advantage of coming from inside, something they would not be expecting, but even so, it was a tall order for a novice.

"By a process of elimination—and yes, I did think of the Mafia, which doubtless was not too pleased by Rovere's disappearance—I came up with a traditional motive, very Cuban in its fire and passion.

"Day after day I practiced Ventura's signature. I have always had considerable artistic ability, so the results were good. Meanwhile, Ventura and Mother played into my hands. They fought in front of the guards and servants. There were long periods of icy silence between them, and both drank heavily. The tension increased as it became clear that Batista was going to be overthrown. The exodus of Batista followers had started. Mother screamed publicly that Ventura was planning to leave her to be executed by the Fidelistas. This was good stuff. It provided a credible motive. Now it was down to nerve and timing.

"The house was a large three-story building. The guards protected the gate, the walls, and the various entrances to the house itself. There were five servants, but only two lived in. Their quarters were over the garage, with an access door leading directly to the first floor. That door was padded to cut down noise. It didn't seem likely that the sound of shots would penetrate, but sound carries at night, and I had to be sure.

"I typed a note on Ventura's study typewriter, signed it with his signature, and addressed it to Mother. I placed the note in my pocket. I had already taken a small .22 caliber automatic pistol that Ventura had given my mother several years before. I checked that and placed it in the other side pocket of my robe.

"They tended to go to bed late. Through my spy hole, headphones in place, I monitored their progress. As I watched each action, I thought, there, they are doing that or that for the last time. It gave me an odd feeling, almost of omniscience.

"Ventura climbed into bed naked. He drank some brandy and leaned back against the pillows. He was smoking a cigar. His automatic pistol lay, cocked and locked, on the bedside table. Mother sat in front of the dressing table. I knew she would be there for several minutes. She no longer enjoyed sharing a bed with Ventura.

"I left my door open and descended to the floor below. I knocked tentatively on the door and announced myself. Mother let me in. 'I need to talk,' I said.

"Ventura looked both irritated and amused. His glass was nearly empty. I walked over to his side of the bed and refilled it. His chest was matted with black hair, and he was sweating. 'Thanks, kid,' he said. His voice was friendly.

"My mother had her back to us as she finished at the dressing table. I replaced the brandy bottle on the bedside table. Beside it there was a hand towel that Ventura had been using. It was damp with his sweat. I wiped my own hands with it and reached into my pocket for the .22. I shot Ventura twice in the chest.

"I turned as Mother turned and in three swift steps was in front of her. I went down on one knee. Over my shoulder she could see Ventura. She stared, mouth open, too shocked to scream. I placed the pistol in her mouth, angled toward her brain, and squeezed the trigger. There was less noise than you'd expect.

"I heard a faint gasp and walked back to Ventura. He was still alive, though his eyes were going dull. Blood mixed with brandy was staining the sheets. He was saying something. I leaned over to hear, being careful to avoid the mess. 'But why me?' he whispered. 'Why me?'

"I pulled the note from my pocket and showed him his signature. A look of understanding crept into his eyes. I recited a number to him and an amount: 'One million, three hundred and twenty-seven thousand dollars.'

" 'I was aiming for two,' he whispered, 'but that fucking Castro has screwed things up.'

"I shot him again, twice, this time in the head, then tore up the note and scattered the pieces over his body. It announced, in my best version of Ventura's style, that he was leaving Cuba and that Mother would have to look after herself. I placed the pistol in Mother's hand.

"Nobody heard a thing. I didn't have to be found screaming as if

I'd run into the room after having heard the shots. I waited ten minutes and adopted the second option. I locked their bedroom door and went upstairs to sleep. I slept like a log. In the morning the guards broke down their door, and the crashes and shouting awoke me. It was easy to drop Mother's door key where it would have been flung out of the lock as the door was burst open.

"I met my new mother three days later. Father gave me a strange look when I shook hands with him, but he didn't say anything."

"What did you feel after you had killed your mother?" asked Dr. Paul.

"I wished I'd used a shotgun."

THEY DINED simply: salad, potatoes, cheese, and fruit. There were candles on the table. Throughout the meal they talked about memories, mutual friends, food, and wine, but rarely about the future. From time to time, in unguarded moments, Fitzduane perceived a flash of sadness in Christina's eyes. Mostly she projected warmth, tenderness, and a deep, caring affection. He realized that Guido, despite his pain and approaching death, was quietly content.

They talked about the recent riots in Zurich and the youth movement.

"Consider me confused," said Fitzduane. "Apart from no unemployment, virtually no inflation, and the highest standard of living of any European nation, what other problems haven't you got? Who exactly is rioting, and what are they breaking windows about?"

"They are not just breaking windows," said Guido. "Thousands of young people also paraded through the streets of Zurich stark naked."

Fitzduane grinned.

"It's very difficult to say precisely what they are protesting about," continued Guido. "Basically it's a rather ill-defined reaction against much of the Swiss system by a certain percentage of Swiss youth. Whatever the merits of this country, there is no denying that there is tremendous social pressure to conform. Most of the rules make sense by themselves. Put them all together, and you have a free Western democracy without a lot of freedom—or at least that is what they say."

"It sounds not unlike the 1968 protests in France."

"There are similarities," said Guido, "but 1968 was much more organized and structured. There were leaders like Daniel Cohn-Bendit, and specific demands made. This is much more anarchistic and aimless. There are few precise demands. There is no one to negotiate with. The authorities don't know who to talk to or what to do, so they respond with overreaction and the riot police: clubs, tear gas, and water cannon instead of thought."

"Is the youth movement throughout Switzerland?" asked Fitzduane.

"In various forms it is throughout Europe," said Guido. "Here in Switzerland I think many of the youth are concerned, but only a small percentage riot, and that is concentrated in the cities."

"Bern, too?"

"A little," said Guido, "but not so much. The Bernese have their own ways of doing things. They don't like confrontation. I think, perhaps, the authorities in Bern are handling it better."

"I thought you were suggesting that the Bernese were a little stupid," said Fitzduane, recalling an earlier remark by Guido.

"Slow; I said the Bernese had the reputation of being slow," said Guido. "I didn't say they weren't smart. But I'd like to show you something." He smiled, then stood up and went over to a closet and removed a bulky object. He placed the assault rifle on the dining room table against a backdrop of cheese and empty wine bottles. The weapon glistened dully in the candlelight. The bipod was extended in the forward position. The slightly curved box magazine was in place.

"The SG-57," said Fitzduane. "Caliber 7.5-millimeter, magazine capacity twenty-four rounds, self-loading or fully automatic, effective range up to four hundred and fifty meters. No dinner table is complete without one."

"Always the weapons expert," said Guido.

Fitzduane shrugged.

"About six hundred thousand Swiss homes contain one of these rifles," said Guido, "together with a sealed container of twenty-four rounds of ammunition. Just about every male between the ages of twenty and fifty is in the army. Over six hundred and fifty thousand men can be fully mobilized within hours. We are prepared to fight to stay at peace. The army is the one major social organization that binds the Swiss together."

"Supposing you don't want to join?"

"Provided you are in good health," said Guido, "at twenty years of age, in you go. If you refuse, it's prison for six months or so—and afterward there can be problems in getting a federal job, and other penalties. But there are more important things to know about the army. It's not just an experience common to all Swiss males between the ages of twenty and fifty. It is also one of the main meeting grounds of the power elite.

"You start off in the army as an ordinary soldier. You do your seventeen weeks of basic training and then return to civilian life with your uniform and rifle—until next year, when you do a couple of weeks' refresher course, and so on until you are fifty.

"However, the best of the recruits are invited to become corporals and then officers, and later, conceivably, they end up on the general staff. There are about fifty thousand officers, and only two thousand of these are general staff—and it is officers of the general staff who dominate the power structure in this country. The higher you go in the Swiss Army, the more time you have to put in away from your civilian job. We call it 'paying your grade.' That's especially difficult for an ordinary worker or a self-employed businessman. As a result, the general staff and, to a lesser extent, the officer corps as a whole are dominated by senior executives of the large banks, industrial corporations, and the government."

"In Eisenhower's phrase, 'the military-industrial complex,' " said Fitzduane.

"He was talking about America," said Guido, "and collusion between the military and big business. Here it is not just collusion. The senior army officers and the senior corporate executives are the same people. They don't just make the weapons; they buy them and use them."

"But only for practice," said Fitzduane.

"That's the good part."

Later, when the exhausted Guido had retired, Christina showed Fitzduane to his room. By the window there was a huge potted plant that was making a serious attempt to reach up and strangle the light bulb.

"It's doing well," Christina said proudly. "It came from England in a milk bottle."

"A two-meter-high milk bottle?" said Fitzduane.

"It grew since then."

"What's it called?"

"It's a papyrus," said Christina. "The same thing that's at the head of your bed."

"Jesus!" exclaimed Fitzduane. "How fast do these things grow?"

KADAR DID not speak. He was remembering.

He wondered if he should have felt remorse. In truth he hadn't felt much of anything immediately after the event except an overwhelming feeling of fatigue mixed with a quiet satisfaction that he had been able to do it. He had passed the test. He had an inner strength possessed by few people. He was born to control.

He tried not to remember how he had felt one day later. From the time he had woken he had been unable to stop shaking, and the spasms had continued for most of that day. "Classic reaction to shock," the doctor had said sympathetically. Kadar had lain there in quiet despair while his body betrayed him. In later years he had undergone training in a variety of Eastern combat disciplines to fuse his mental and physical strength, and the post-action shock had not manifested itself again. Very occasionally he wondered if such stress symptoms were nonetheless there, but in a more insidious, invisible way, like the hairline cracks of metal fatigue in an aircraft.

The silence continued for several minutes. Kadar was caught up in the excitement of that time and the almost unremitting stimulation offered by his new life in the States. The greatest surprise of that period had not been the luxury of his new home, or access to all the material goods he could reasonably want, or the effect of an environment in which almost anything seemed to be possible. It had been the attitude of his father.

At their first meeting in Havana, Henry Bridgenorth Lodge had been cold, hard, and cynical—almost dispassionate. He needed a son to satisfy his wife. So be it. Subsequently, although his manner remained superficially distant and though the hardness and cynicism proved to be real enough, Lodge displayed a concern for and attention to his son's well-being that almost made Kadar drop his guard and develop an affection for him.

Kadar had to exert all his formidable sense of purpose and self-discipline to resist an emotion that threatened to overwhelm his sixteen-year-old frame. He reminded himself again and again that to be in control, truly in control, he must remain above conventional emotions. He repeated this constantly in the privacy of his room at night even while the tears trickled down his cheeks and his body was suffused by feelings he could not, or would not, begin to understand.

Shortly after he had settled into his new home—a comfortable twenty-minute drive from Langley—he was subjected to what seemed like a barrage of examinations and tests to help determine how the next phase of his education might best be carried out.

It emerged that he was unusually gifted. His IQ was in the top 0.1 percent of the population. He had an ear for languages. He showed considerable artistic promise. His physical coordination was excellent. He was an impressive if not outstanding athlete.

It was clear that a conventional school would not be adequate. For the first year he was tutored privately. Lodge tapped into the immense pool of highly qualified academics and analysts that were part of the CIA community, and Kadar was exposed to a quality of mind and a sharpness of intellect that up until then he had only read about. It was exciting. It was fun. And he flourished both intellectually and physically.

For his second academic year he was sent to a special school for the gifted, supplemented by private tutoring, a routine that was to remain constant until he left Harvard. It was during this second year that he discovered he had charm and a naturally magnetic personality—and that he could use these qualities to manipulate people to his own ends.

He was conscious that his experience in dealing with people was inadequate and that such a deficiency could be a weakness. He studied other people's reactions to him and worked hard to improve his overt personality. The public persona became further divorced from the inner reality. He became one of the most popular boys in his class.

Lodge had some instinctive understanding of the nature of the son he was nurturing. He knew there were risks, yet his perception was counterbalanced by a weakness: Lodge was excited by talent. To such a man, Kadar, who responded to intellectual and other stimuli in such an attractive, dynamic way, was irresistible. It was like having a garden where every seed germinated and flourished. Educating, training, and encouraging this astonishing young stranger who was his son became an obsession.

Henry Bridgenorth Lodge came from a family that had been so wealthy for so long that career satisfaction could not be achieved by something as mundane as making money. The Bridgenorth

Lodges did make money, a great deal of it—more than they could comfortably use, a talent that seemed to survive generation after generation—but they channeled their foremost endeavors toward higher things, principally service to their country. The Bridgenorth Lodges worked to advance the interests of the United States—as they saw them—with the zealousness and ruthlessness of Jesuits. To the Family—as they thought of themselves—the ends did justify the means.

Many people go through their lives without ever being lucky enough to come under the influence of a really great teacher. In this respect Kadar was doubly fortunate. Ventura had—unintentionally—given him a consummate grounding in the fundamentals of power grabbing, violence, manipulation, and extortion. Lodge and his colleagues taught Kadar to think in a more strategic way, set him up with a network of connections in high places, taught him the social graces, and gave him numerous specific skills from languages to project planning, cultural appreciation to combat pistol shooting.

Lodge might have had some inkling of Kadar's inner conflicts, but he had hopes that they could be channeled in the Bridgenorth Lodge tradition. His son was being groomed for a career of distinction in the CIA, followed by a suitable switch to public office.

Kadar, who in the more relaxed environment of America was surprised to discover he had an excellent sense of humor, was not unamused years later that this training for the public service was to produce one of the most dangerous criminals of the century and someone who secretly despised everything the Bridgenorth Lodges stood for. Except, it should be said, their money.

WHEN FITZDUANE AWOKE in the morning, the apartment was empty. He could hear faint sounds of traffic through the double-glazed windows. A light breakfast had been laid out. The assault rifle had been cleared away from the dining room table.

He looked for some jam in the kitchen cabinet. He found two different kinds, together with a jar of English marmalade. Behind the jam pots was a sealed container of twenty-four rounds of rifle ammunition. The container resembled a soft-drink can.

Over breakfast he skimmed idly through the notes and tapes on the von Graffenlaubs that Guido had left him. He pushed the tapes aside for the moment and concentrated on the written material. Guido's notes were clear and pointed:

The von Graffenlaub family is one of the oldest and most respected in Bern. The family has a centuries-old tradition of involvement in the government of both city and canton. The present Beat (pronounced "Bay-at," by the way, not "Beet") von Graffenlaub is a pillar of the Swiss establishment through family, business, and the army.

Apart from the natural advantages of birth, Beat laid the foundation for his distinguished career by carrying out several missions for Swiss military intelligence during the Second World War. Briefly, he acted as a courier between sources in the German high command and Swiss intelligence. Under the cover of skiing exhibitions and other sporting activities, he brought back information of the utmost importance, including details of Operation Tannenbaum, the German-Italian plan for the invasion of Switzerland.

Having risked his life in the service of his country while still only in his late teens and early twenties, Beat was rewarded with accelerated promotion in both the army and civilian life.

After the war he spent some years in business but then switched to study law. After qualifying, he established his own practice, eventually becoming an adviser to a number of major Swiss corporations. At the same time he pursued his army career, specializing in military intelligence. He officially retired in 1978 with the rank of colonel in the general staff.

Von G.'s influence in business circles is further enhanced by his role as trustee for several privately held estates. As such, his voting power considerably exceeds what his substantial personal fortune would warrant and makes him a very real power in Swiss business circles. . . .

The notes continued, page after page. Beat von Graffenlaub was Swiss establishment personified. How had Rudi reacted to such a shadow? Action and reaction. Was that enduring theme some indication of the way it had been for Rudi?

"Sod it," he said to himself quietly, as his thoughts of the dead Rudi passed on to the thought of Guido's wasting away. "Too much thinking about the dead and the dying." He missed Etan.

He packed and took the tram into the city center, where he boarded the train for Bern.

Chapter Ten

Max Buisard, the Chief of the Criminal Police (the Kriminalpolizei, or Kripo) of the city of Bern, was at his desk in police headquarters in Waisenhausplatz at six o'clock in the morning. Sometimes he started earlier.

Such work habits would indicate, even if no other evidence were available, that the Chief Kripo had no Irish blood in him whatsoever. In Ireland—at least south of the border—there was no excuse for being awake, let alone working, at such an ungodly hour, save returning from a late night's drinking, insanity, or sex. Even Irish cows slept until nearly eight; later on Sundays.

Buisard was, in fact, by origin a Swiss Romand, a French-speaking Swiss from the canton of Vaud, but he had been a resident of Bern for three out of his over four decades, and he worked hard at integrating. For instance, by the pragmatic if somewhat energetic expedient of having a wife and no fewer than two current mistresses, he had proudly succeeded in mastering Berndeutsch, the local dialect.

His dedication did not pass unnoticed. Recently he had overheard an eminent member of the Bürgergemeinde refer to him as *bodenständig*—the ultimate Bernese accolade for a sensible, practical fellow, with his feet firmly on the ground. For a brief moment Buisard wondered if rumors of his penchant for making love standing up—a by-product of his busy schedule, which combined sex with exercise—had circulated, but he dismissed the thought. He had faith in the discretion of his women and in the soundproofing of Bernese buildings.

The Chief stared at the blotter in front of him. He had a problem, a large, rather fat problem, with a heavy walrus mustache, a gruff manner, and an increasingly unpredictable temper.

He added a mustache to the doodle on the blotter and then, as an afterthought, drew a holstered gun on the ponderous figure. What do you do with a first-rate veteran detective who has turned moody, troublesome, and downright irascible, and who also happens to be an old friend?

Buisard drew a cage around the figure on his blotter, looked at it for a while, and sketched in a door with a handle on both sides. The Bear needed to be contained, not stifled. Even in Switzerland—and certainly in Bern—the rules could be bent a little for the right reasons and by the right person. But this time something had to be done. There had been a string of incidents since the death of the Bear's wife, and the latest was the most embarrassing.

The Bear normally operated as part of the drug squad. He was the most experienced sergeant in the unit and, like most Bernese policemen, was also regularly assigned to security duties guarding diplomats and visiting dignitaries. The latter was boring work but not too unpopular because the overtime pay came in handy. The presence of more than a hundred different diplomatic missions in the city also made security duties fairly regular. God alone knew what all those ambassadors, second secretaries, and cultural attachés did with their time, lurking down in the greenery of Elfenau, since all the diplomatic action was in Geneva, but that was God's problem.

The Bear had enjoyed a pretty good reputation. He had been both effective and compassionate, not the easiest combination to maintain in the drug squad. He was reliable, cheerful, diligent, and accommodating—an ideal colleague, give or take a few idiosyncrasies. For instance, he liked to carry a very large gun, most recently a Smith & Wesson .41 Magnum revolver with a six-inch barrel. Buisard shuddered at the possible consequences if the Bear ever had to fire it in a public area.

A stolen Mercedes, driven by a twenty-year-old drug addict desperate for something to sell to get a fix, had changed everything.

Tilly had finished work at Migros, done the shopping for supper, and was waiting for a tram. The Bear was about to join her. He was less than a hundred meters away when it happened. He heard the sound as the car struck her. He saw her body fly through the air and smash against a plate glass window. The glass cracked in a dozen places but did not break. Tilly lay crushed at the bottom of the window, one arm jerking spastically, her blood staining the pavement.

She remained in a coma for three months. Her brain was dead. The Bear stayed with her for days on end. He held her hand. He kissed her. He told her stories and read out loud from the papers. He brought her flowers arranged in the special way she liked. The life support system hissed and dripped and made electronic noises. People spoke to him. Occasionally he was asked to sign papers. One day they switched her off.

And the Bear's heart was broken.

BEAT VON GRAFFENLAUB HAD not slept until nearly dawn. The numbness he had experienced when he first heard of Rudi's death had gradually turned to feelings of pain and guilt and a growing emptiness.

Why had Rudi killed himself? What had happened to him in Ireland? What was Rudi thinking during that brief moment just before he jumped? Did he take long to die? Was there pain? Why had he not talked to someone first? Surely there must have been some hint of what he was contemplating, some sign, some change in behavior.

Was there anything he, Beat von Graffenlaub, wealthy, influential, acclaimed and respected by his peers, could have done—should have done—to preserve the life of his son? Anything? Somehow he knew that there was; there just had to be—but what?

The clock radio woke von Graffenlaub fully. For a few moments he lay there, his eyes still closed, listening to the news. Erika had objected to this early-morning habit, but it had been months since they had shared the same bed, longer still since they had made love. Erika now slept in the apartment she had created a few doors away. She needed space to cultivate her creativity, she had said. He had not objected. It would have been pointless. The signs of her disenchantment had been present and growing for a couple of years.

He thought back, with a pang, to those early years of closeness and sensuality, when they just had to be together and divorcing Claire was a price well worth paying; dear, stuffy, conventional Claire, now dead. Well, he had paid the price willingly and had pushed from his mind the risks of marrying a woman nearly thirty years his junior. But time had caught up with him. At sixty-one, physically trim and fit though he was, he knew that Erika was slipping away, more probably was already lost to him.

He recalled Erika's distinctive, musky odor and could feel hot wetness against his mouth. He could hear the special sounds she made when excited. He felt his erection growing, and he moved to look at the sultry features damp with the sweat of passion—and to enter her.

For the briefest of time Erika's presence remained with him even after he opened his eyes and looked around the room. Then came the full onslaught of grief and loneliness.

IVO WAS untroubled by the combined smell of fourteen unwashed bodies sleeping on grubby mattresses on the floor of the small room. One couple had woken half an hour earlier and made love quietly, but for the last ten minutes the only sounds were those of sleep.

He decided to wait a little longer. The Dutchman, van der Grijn, had drunk enough to poleax any normal man for half a day, but he had still managed to stay awake, talking and drinking, until the early hours, before collapsing with a grunt. Ivo, small and slight, was not eager to tangle with the huge heroin courier. Ivo was almost permanently high in a miasma of marijuana. Occasionally he sniffed glue or popped a few pills. He enjoyed, but could rarely afford, cocaine. But he hated heroin.

Heroin had killed the one person he had truly loved. While he was in prison for demonstrating and throwing rocks at policemen in Zurich, little Hilda, fifteen years old, had overdosed in the ladies' rest room of the Zurich Bahnhof; she was found facedown in a toilet bowl. Little Hilda had carried no papers, but she had eventually been identified as a result of the slim volume of Ivo's poems she carried, thirty-six photocopied pages.

"A short book," said the Zurich policeman after he had shown Hilda's photograph to Ivo in prison. They had been driving to the morgue for the formal identification.

"How long should a book be?" said Ivo. He was pale, but regular prison food had filled out his slight body. Curiously he felt no hostility toward those who had imprisoned him. The policemen and guards were strict but fair.

From the depths of his despair, he swore total revenge on all heroin pushers. And so, at the age of seventeen, Ivo came to live in the Autonomous Youth House in Bern. He became its unofficial guardian. Most of its inhabitants were harmless, rootless youths in search of something other than Switzerland's ordered and disciplined society—the "boredom and air-conditioned misery of capitalism," as the phrase put it. Some of the visitors were more dangerous, benefiting from official tolerance to push hard drugs and traffic in more lethal wares.

Ivo preyed upon heroin pushers. Operating with the cunning and desperation of one with nothing to lose, he stole their drugs and flushed them down the toilet in bizarre homage to his dead love. When the mood struck him, he informed to the police—in strange, elliptical messages, never in person or by phone, always in writing.

He had lubricated the zipper on his grimy sleeping bag with graphite powder. He slipped out of his bag noiselessly and crept toward the sleeping Dutchman. Within seconds the small packet of glassine envelopes had been removed, and Ivo tiptoed out of the room.

In the toilet he opened each envelope, one by one, and shook the powder into the bowl until the water was filmed with white. He replaced the heroin with powdered glucose and reassembled the packet. He put toilet paper over the powder in the toilet bowl but, worried about noise, did not flush.

He returned to the sleeping room. The Dutchman slumbered on. Ivo returned the doctored packet to the seamed leather jacket. Still no reaction. Reassured, Ivo crept out of the room again and this time risked flushing the toilet. The heroin vanished into the sewers of Bern.

Ivo went into the kitchen, made himself a pot of tea, and lit up the first roach of the day. He sat cross-legged on the kitchen table and stared out of the window into the gray light of false dawn. He hummed to himself and rocked from side to side. He felt good. Hilda would be pleased.

But what about Klaus? Beautiful Klaus, who could make money so easily from a few hours of giving pleasure, who was desired by so many men and women? There had been something about the man who picked Klaus up. It just did not feel right. No reason, just feelings. Ivo had been some little distance away. He had not seen the man clearly. It had been dark, but he remembered blond hair and a blond mustache and beard. He had heard conversation and laughter. Then they had walked away from him into the darkness, the blond man's arm around Klaus. The thunk of a car door—an expensive car by the sound—the faint whisper of an engine, then silence. Klaus had not come back in a couple of hours as he had promised. Ivo had slept alone. Klaus was Ivo's friend.

If only life was like the Lennon song "Imagine." If only life was like that. Ivo sang and rocked in time to the music. He would do something tomorrow about Klaus, or maybe the day after that, or maybe Klaus would just turn up.

Just imagine.

THE LUSTS, self-doubt, and sorrows of the night receded with the first sting of the icy cold shower.

Beat von Graffenlaub was a man of rigorous self-discipline and practiced routine. By 0630 he was having breakfast at a small Biedermeier table by a window overlooking the River Aare. He wore a charcoal gray flannel suit, a crisp white handmade shirt, and a black silk tie. His shoes were a tribute to his valet's expertise at military spit and polish: they did not just shine, they positively glowed. His socks were of light gray silk.

A solitary red rose rested in a slim Waterford crystal vase. At exactly 0655, von Graffenlaub would insert the flower into his buttonhole, don his navy blue cashmere overcoat, pick up his briefcase, and make any required farewells, and at the stroke of 0700 would leave his house on Junkerngasse to stroll toward his offices on Marktgasse. He could cover the short distance between home and office in less than ten brisk minutes, but even after a lifetime of familiarity he took pleasure in walking about the ancient city of Bern. Each morning and evening, time and weather permitting, he made a short detour, lengthening his walk to half an hour and arriving at his office at exactly 0730.

This morning, after he had left Junkerngasse, he detoured into the grounds surrounding the fifteenth-century Münster. The terrace between the church and the ramparts was known as the Plattform. It overlooked the river, flowing swiftly along below, its waters icy and swollen from the melting snows of winter.

Von Graffenlaub rested his outstretched arms on the low wall that bordered the river side of the terrace and breathed in and out deeply. The cool morning air felt pure and clean in his lungs. In the distance he could see the snowcapped mountains of the Bernese Oberland.

He looked up the river toward the Kirchenfeldbrücke, the elegant nineteenth-century iron bridge that linked the old medieval city with the more newly developed residential district of Kirchenfeld. His gaze followed the flow of the river to the old waterworks below. A flurry of activity caught his attention.

Two police cars, an ambulance, and several unmarked vehicles were parked by the water's edge. As he watched, uniformed police dragged what looked like a body from the river. He could see the pale white dot of the body's face before it was covered by a blanket. The face filled his vision. It was that of his dead son. He turned away. Nausea swept through him, and his skin felt clammy. He threw up over the parapet, and a spasm of shivering shook his body.

A NOOSE HUNG from a hook in the corner of the Chief Kripo's office. Buisard had brought it back from a police chiefs' conference in the United States. It was a souvenir, he had said, an exact replica of a hangman's noose, as used before technology—in the shape of the electric chair and gas chamber and lethal injection—took over in most of the civilized world.

Maybe next time he'll bring back an electric chair, thought the Bear. Buisard insisted that the hangman's knot had thirteen coils in it, but each time the Bear counted, he could make it only twelve. He started counting again out of the corner of his eye. According to Pierrepoint, the famous English hangman, it was an inefficient way to hang someone anyhow. More often than not, the large American knot and the standard American five-foot drop resulted in a slow death through strangulation.

Pierrepoint used a variable drop and a simple slip knot located under the angle of the left jaw by a rubber claw washer. After the fall, the knot would finish under the chin and throw the head back, fracturing the spinal column, almost always between the second and third cervical vertebrae. Instant death, or so said the hangman.

"Heini," said Buisard, "will you, for God's sake, pay attention? It's got thirteen coils, no matter what you say."

"You're the chief," said the Bear.

"And I'd like to stay that way," said Buisard.

The Bear raised his shaggy eyebrows.

"I'm not suspending you," said Buisard, "although you well deserve it. But I'm taking you off the drug squad for a month. You can keep your desk in the Bollwerk, but I'm assigning you to minor crimes—out of harm's way."

"Investigating stolen bicycles and missing pets," said the Bear. He glowered.

"Something like that," said Buisard. "Think of it as a cooling-off period."

"The son of a bitch deserved to be thumped," said the Bear. "He was drunk and throwing his weight around."

"You may well be right," said Buisard, "but he was part of the German foreign minister's party and on an official diplomatic visit to this city. He did have a diplomatic passport."

The Bear shrugged and rose to his feet.

"One moment," said Buisard. "There is an Irishman coming to Bern for a few days. I've had a letter of introduction about him from a friend of mine in Dublin. I've been asked to look after him if he wants to be shown around, a sort of professional courtesy."

"So now I'm a tourist guide."

The Chief Kripo smiled just a little meanly. "Not at all. Heini, you are one of Bern's attractions."

"Up yours," said the Bear amiably, and ambled out of the room.

The Chief went over and started counting the thirteen coils in the hangman's noose. He made it twelve. He swore and started again.

THE DAY WAS crisp and cold, the snow melted from the streets and the lowlands around. In the distance ice and snow held the higher ground. Jagged mountain peaks looked unreal against a clear blue sky.

Fitzduane was enchanted by Bern. He felt exhilarated; he just knew that somewhere in this beautiful, unspoiled, too-good-to-be-true medieval city lay the answer to his quest, the reason for a hanging.

He walked, more or less at random, for several hours. Sooner or later he always seemed to reach the River Aare. The river surrounded the old city on three sides, forming a natural moat and leaving only one side to be defended by a wall. As the city had expanded, the wall was sited farther and farther up the peninsula. The old walls were gone, but two of the distinctive towers that marked the landward entrance to the city remained.

It had been the quaint custom of the Bernese—prior to the tourist trade's taking off—to use the entrance tower as a prison.

Shortly after he arrived, Fitzduane had booked himself into a small hotel on Gerechtigkeitsgasse. Just outside the hotel entrance, an intricately carved statue, perched on top of a fluted pillar, crowned a flowing fountain. The carving was painted in red and blue and gold and other bright colors. The dominant female figure—showing a surprising amount of leg—held a sword in one hand, scales in the other, and was blindfolded: the Gerechtigkeitsbrunnen, the Fountain of Justice.

At the foot of this dangerous-looking Amazon, and well placed to look up her skirts, were the busts of four unhappy-looking individuals whom Fitzduane subsequently found out were the Emperor, Sultan, Pope, and Magistrate—the main dispensers of random justice when the fountain was erected in 1543.

At frequent intervals around the city there were fountains, all painted in exotic colors, each unique in itself. In Kramgasse the fountain was identified by a life-size bear, wearing a gold helmet with a barred visor, standing in the pose of a *Landsknecht*; at his feet was a little bear eating grapes. Everywhere there were bears: carved bears, painted bears, drawn bears, printed bears, stamped bears, wrought-iron bears, big bears, small bears, even real bears. Fitzduane had never seen so many bears.

He read that Duke Berchtold V of Zähringen, the founder of Bern, had organized a hunt and decreed that the city be named after the first animal killed. Fortunately the hunters struck it lucky with a bear; the City of Rabbit just would not have had the same cachet.

Until in-house plumbing and *Blick* became the fashion, the fountains of Bern had been where you went to fill up with water and all the latest gossip. Perhaps, thought Fitzduane, if I sit by the fountain, all will be revealed.

He tried it for a while, but his bottom got cold.

* * *

FROM HABIT the Bear checked the incident sheets when he returned from lunch. He did not expect to see much. He had once discussed the Bernese crime rate with a visiting American policeman. Confusion reigned initially when it appeared that the crime rates in their respective cities were roughly comparable. Then it dawned on them: they were comparing apples and oranges. The American was quoting daily statistics; the Bear meant annual figures.

One of the most consistently regular of the Bernese crime statistics was the murder rate. Give or take a few decimal points, the figures came out at two killings per year—year after year after year.

They say, thought the Bear, that Bern has enough of everything, but not too much. Two murders a year is just about right for a well-ordered city like Bern. Many more would create havoc with the tourist trade and would certainly upset the Bürgergemeinde. Any fewer might raise question marks about the manning levels of the Kriminalpolizei. A little fear was good for police job security.

His mind occupied with such weighty matters, the Bear almost missed the new incident sheet that had been pinned up over an elegantly lettered flyer announcing that the desk sergeant was selling his immaculately maintained five-year-old Volvo, with only ninety thousand kilometers on the clock, at a bargain price (four lies).

The bald announcement stated that the mutilated body of a twenty-year-old man had been removed from the River Aare that morning. Death appeared to be due to multiple knife wounds. An autopsy would take place immediately. Formal identification was yet to be made, but documents on the body suggested that the dead man was named Klaus Minder.

It says nothing about bicycles, thought the Bear. Maybe the murderer escaped on a stolen bicycle or stalked his victim through the six kilometers of Bernese arcades while perched inconspicuously on top of a penny-farthing. Then it would be his case, or at least the bicycle part would be.

He searched the incident sheet for signs of stolen penny-farthings, but in vain. No luck with tandems or tricycles either. He cheated a little and tried for mopeds. Nothing.

"Ho-hum," said the Bear to himself.

Chapter Eleven

A small brass plate identified the von Graffenlaub office on Markt-gasse. It bore just his name and the single word "Notar." The neat nineteenth-century facade of the building belied its earlier origins. The circular stone steps that led to the lawyer's offices on the second floor were heavily worn with use and dipped alarmingly in the center. The lighting on the stairs was dim. There was no elevator. The Bernese, Guido had said, are discreet with their wealth. The lawyer's offices internally might prove luxurious, but the access to them passed discretion and headed toward miserliness. Fitzduane thought that since he might well break his neck on the stairs on the way down, he had better make the most of the next few minutes. He should have brought a flashlight.

Von Graffenlaub's secretary had the long-established look of a faithful retainer. Clearly second wife Erika had endeavored to ensure that her man would not stray in the same way twice; to describe Frau Hunziker as hatchet-faced would be tactful. Her glasses hung from a little chain around her neck like the gorget of a Gestapo man.

Fitzduane announced himself. Frau Hunziker retrieved her glasses and looked him up and down, then pointedly looked at the wall clock. The Irishman was five minutes late—downright punctual in Ireland, and unusual at that. In Bern such tardiness was apparently grounds for a sojourn in the Prison Tower. Frau Hunziker's manner indicated that she regretted the Tower was no longer in use.

Fitzduane spread out his arms in a gesture of apology. "I'm Irish," he said. "It's a cultural problem."

Frau Hunziker nodded her head several times. *"Ja, ja,"* she said resignedly about what was clearly a lost cause, and rose to show him into von Graffenlaub's office. Fitzduane followed. He was pleased to see that the lawyer had not entirely lost his touch. She had excellent legs.

The lawyer came from behind his desk, shook Fitzduane's hand formally, and indicated some easy chairs gathered around a low table. Coffee was brought in. Fitzduane was asked about his flight. Pleasantries were exchanged with a formality alien to the Irishman.

Von Graffenlaub poured more coffee. Holding the insulated coffeepot, his hand shook slightly. It was the lawyer's only sign of emotion; otherwise he was imperturbable. Fitzduane suppressed a feeling of anger toward the immaculately dressed figure in front of him. Damn it, his son was dead. The lawyer was too controlled.

Fitzduane finished his coffee, replaced the cup and saucer on the low table, and sat back in his chair. Von Graffenlaub did the same, though slowly, as if reluctant for the conversation to enter its next phase; then he looked at the Irishman.

"You want to talk about Rudi, I think," he said.

Fitzduane nodded. "I'm afraid I must."

Von Graffenlaub bowed his head for a few moments. He did not respond immediately. When he did, there was a certain hesitation in his tone, as if he were reluctant to listen to what the Irishman had to say, yet drawn to it nonetheless.

"I would like to thank you for what you did for Rudi," he said. "The school wrote to me and described your sensitive handling of your part in this tragic affair."

"There was little enough I could do," said Fitzduane. As he spoke, his first sight of the hanging boy replayed through his mind.

"It must have been a great shock," said von Graffenlaub.

"It was," said Fitzduane. "I was surprised at my own reaction. I'm used to the sight of death but not, I guess, on my home ground. It had quite an impact."

"I can imagine," said von Graffenlaub. "We are all terribly distressed. What could have possessed Rudi to do such a thing?"

Fitzduane made no response. The question was rhetorical. He knew that the conversation was approaching the moment of truth. They were running out of polite platitudes.

"Nonetheless," said von Graffenlaub, "I am a little puzzled as to why you have come to see me. What is done is done. Nothing can bring Rudi back now. We must try to forget and get on with the business of living."

Von Graffenlaub spoke formally, yet there was a perceptible lack of conviction in his tone, as if he were troubled by some inner doubt. It was the first hint of a chink in a formidable personality. Fitzduane would have to force the issue. Reason alone was not going to work with von Graffenlaub. Indeed, reason dictated letting the whole matter drop. This wasn't about reason; it was about feelings, about a sense of something wrong, about sheer determination—and about the smell of the hunt. It was the first time that the Irishman had admitted this last point to himself, and he didn't know why this certainty had entered his mind, but there it was.

"I regret I cannot agree," said Fitzduane. "Nobody should die in that hideous way without someone attempting to find out why. Why did your son kill himself? Do you know? Do you care?"

The lawyer turned ashen, and beads of sweat broke out on his brow. He abandoned his controlled posture and leaned forward in his chair, his right hand chopping through the air in emphasis. "How dare you!" he said, outrage in his voice. "How dare you—a complete stranger—question my feelings at such a time! Damn you! You know nothing, nothing, nothing. . . ." He was shaking with rage.

The atmosphere had suddenly chilled. The pleasantries were forgotten. Von Graffenlaub quickly regained control of himself, but the two men looked at each other grimly. Fitzduane knew that if his investigation wasn't to grind to a premature halt, he must convince the Swiss to cooperate. It would be unpleasant in the short term, but there was little choice. This was a hunt that had already acquired its own momentum. It would lead where it would.

There was silence in the room. There was going to be no viable alternative to something Fitzduane would have preferred not to have had to do. He opened the large envelope he had been carrying and placed the contents facedown on the table.

"I'm sorry," said Fitzduane. "I don't want to hurt you, but I don't see any other way. A twenty-year-old kid killed himself. I found him hanging there, his bowels voided and stinking, his tongue swollen and protruding, his face blue and covered with blood and spittle and mucus. I held him when they cut him down still warm, and I heard the sound he made as the last air left his lungs. To me that sound screamed one question: Why?"

Fitzduane held the photograph of the dead boy just in front of von Graffenlaub's eyes. The remaining vestiges of color drained from the lawyer's face. He stared at the photograph, mesmerized. Fitzduane put it back on the table. Von Graffenlaub's gaze followed it down and rested on it for a minute before he looked up at the Irishman. Tears streamed from his eyes. He tried to speak but could not. He pulled a folded handkerchief from his breast pocket, dislodging the flower from his buttonhole as he did so. Without saying a word, he rose somewhat unsteadily to his feet, brushed aside Fitzduane's efforts to help him, and left the room.

Fitzduane picked up the crumpled rose and held it to his nostrils. The fragrance was gentle, soothing. He did not feel proud of himself. He looked around the silent office. Through the leather padded door he could just hear the sound of an electric typewriter.

On a low cabinet behind von Graffenlaub's desk stood several framed photographs, obviously of his family. One showed a sensual brunette in her mid-twenties with full, inviting lips and unusual sloping eyes—at a guess, Erika, some years earlier. The next photograph showed von Graffenlaub in full military uniform. His hair was less gray, and the long face, with its high forehead and deep-set eyes, projected power, confidence, and vigor—a far cry from the stumbling figure who had just left the room.

The last photograph had been taken on the veranda of an old wooden chalet. Snow-covered mountains could be seen in the background. To judge by the quality, the color print was an enlargement of a thirty-five-millimeter shot. The picture was slightly grainy, but nothing marred the energy and happiness that came through. The four von Graffenlaub children stood in a row, dressed in ski clothes and laughing, with arms around one another's shoulders: Marta, the eldest, her hair pulled back under a bright yellow ski cap and with a striking resemblance to her father; Andreas, taller, darker, and more serious, despite the smile; and then the twins, wearing the same pale blue ski suits and looking strikingly alike despite Vreni's long blonde hair and Rudi's short curls. The photograph bore the inscription

"Lenk 1979." In some ineffable way it strengthened the Irishman's resolve.

VON GRAFFENLAUB SPLASHED cold water on his face and toweled briskly. Some slight color returned to his cheeks. He felt sick and disoriented; none of his previous training seemed to have equipped him for the situation he found himself in. The Irishman, with his sympathetic manner and core of steel, had turned into the voice of his conscience. The Irishman's conviction and resolve were daunting. It was singularly upsetting.

The lawyer refolded the towel and hung it neatly on the heated towel rail. The image in the mirror was familiar again, well groomed, purposeful. He tried to imagine the effect of Fitzduane's pursuing an investigation in Bern. Consider the distress among the family; he could just hear Erika's scathing comments. He had his position in the community to think of, and there were well-established standards of behavior. Suicide in the family was tragic and best handled as discreetly as possible. It hinted at some instability in the victim's immediate circle. It could be bad for business. It was best forgotten, or at least hushed up.

Fortunately Rudi's death had taken place in another country. The impact, so far, had been minimal. Time would further dull the memory. There was no question about it: this man Fitzduane would have to be diverted from his obsession. A discreet phone call and he would no longer be welcome in Switzerland. In Ireland von Graffenlaub was not without influence at the most senior level. This Irishman could be dealt with. It would be the best solution.

Von Graffenlaub breathed in and out deeply several times. He felt better, not quite in full health, as was understandable under the circumstances, but definitely better. He left his private bathroom, then closed and locked the door. It was a pity he had to go through the general office to get to it, but that was the trouble with these old buildings.

Frau Hunziker looked up as he was about to enter his office. "Herr Doktor," she said, "the Irishman, Herr Fitzduane, has left. He has given me his address and telephone number and asked that you call him when you are ready."

Von Graffenlaub took the note she held out: the Hospiz zur Heimat, a small hotel, though centrally located. Somehow he had expected somewhere more impressive, perhaps the Bellevue or the Schweizerhof.

He sat down at his desk. Facing him were the photographs of the children at Lenk and of Rudi hanging. The living and the dead Rudi stared up at him. Beat von Graffenlaub dropped his head into his hands and wept.

GUIDO, WHO SEEMED to know everybody, had made the necessary arrangements. "There will be some people there you should meet," he had said.

Vernissage: literally varnishing day, when the artist put the final coat of varnish on his paintings—they looked better that way and commanded a higher price—and invited patrons and friends to a preview.

The gallery was on Münstergasse, within three minutes of the Irishman's hotel. He was beginning to enjoy the compact size of old Bern. He had needed neither car nor taxi since his arrival. If he got fed up walking, he could try roller skates.

At the gallery Fitzduane helped himself to a glass of wine and a catalog and started to look around. After examining three pictures in a row for several minutes each, he found himself quite at a loss, or else more than whiskey had been put into the Irish coffee he had enjoyed earlier in the day. He looked at the other ten paintings and was none the wiser. All of the thirteen paintings seemed to be virtually identical rectangles of pure black.

There were nearly thirty other people in the small gallery, circulating, looking at the exhibits, and talking animatedly. None looked obviously baffled. Maybe rectangles of solid black constituted normal art in Bern.

The catalog in German was of limited help. It told him he was in the Loeb Gallery, as Guido had directed, and that the artist was Kuno Gonschior, forty-six years of age, who had enough business acumen to charge about seven thousand francs a rectangle.

Fitzduane was about to turn away but to his surprise found the bizarre collection piquing his interest. Subtle differences of texture and shade began to evolve as he looked. Things were not what they seemed. Black was never quite black. What appeared at first as a mat flat surface was a minute, intricate, three-dimensional pattern. He began to smile to himself.

He sensed warmth, and an almost familiar sexual, musky smell teased his nostrils. The woman looked into his eyes with amusement and, for a moment, a startling physical intimacy. She was small and slender. He had no difficulty recognizing who she was. She wore a black off-the-shoulder cocktail dress, and her skin was deeply tanned. Her breasts were firm and prominent; the nipples pressed against the thin silk. She wore a narrow headband of gold cloth.

Fitzduane wanted to reach out and touch her, to slide black silk off a golden body, to take her there and then. Her physical impact was overwhelming. It was a power over men, a power that was relished, enjoyed, and used. He recognized this, but it made little difference; his desire was strong and immediate. Now he understood why von Graffenlaub had married her.

She gently seized a tall, energetic-looking man by the arm and playfully spun him around to face Fitzduane. It was obvious she was not in need of assertiveness training.

"Simon," she said, "let me introduce you to a famous combat photographer who is visiting our town for a few days. Simon Balac, meet Hugo Fitzduane. Simon is my greatest friend—when he is being nice—and a very successful painter."

"And you, my sweet Erika," said Balac, "are a treasure—at times—and always the most gorgeous woman in Bern."

"Erika von Graffenlaub," said Fitzduane.

She nodded.

"Your photographs do not do you full justice," said Fitzduane. "How did you know my name?"

Erika smiled. "Bern is a small town," she said. "Thank you for being so good about Rudi. It can't have been easy."

Fitzduane felt somewhat nonplussed. It appeared that she was talking about the finding of the body and not about the events of earlier in the day. And there was no sign of her husband.

Erika took his hand in hers and held it for a moment; then she pressed it to her face. "Thank you again," she said.

Fitzduane could still feel the heat of her body as she moved away from him and the fullness of her lips when they briefly brushed the palm of his hand. Simon Balac lifted his glass and winked. "Bern is a very small town."

"I WISH it were suicide," said the Chief Kripo into the phone. He looked at his watch. Ten past seven. A thirteen-hour-day already, and he was still in police headquarters. He was late for Colette, who did not like to be kept waiting, for anything, especially bed.

The tips of the Chief's ears turned pink at the thought. She really was gifted sexually, an unrecognized talent. In earlier centuries they would have built a fountain to celebrate her skills. Really, murders were damned inconvenient.

"You're not the only man with a sex life," said the examining magistrate, who was too smart by half. "Now cut out the wet dreaming and concentrate. There's no way that this one took his own life. Consider the following: stabbed seven times with a short, broad-bladed instrument, eyes put out, ears cut off, genitals removed—and, incidentally, not found yet. I suppose they are still bobbing around in the Aare. Then bear in mind evidence of both oral and anal intercourse prior to his death."

Buisard nodded gloomily. "Doesn't sound too much like a suicide. More like some kind of ritual."

"A bit more than wife kills husband with frying pan anyway," said the magistrate. "I don't like it at all. It smells too much of the kind of thing that could happen again."

"Don't even think things like that," said the Chief Kripo. "I guess I'd better put out an all-points bulletin for the guy's balls. How will we identify them?"

"They should be the only pair in Bern working independently," said the magistrate cheerfully. "Not too hard for one of your brighter policemen to spot."

"That's disgusting," said the Chief Kripo, "and unkind." Subconsciously he did a quick check with his right hand. All was in order but, considering his earlier thoughts of Colette, surprisingly subdued.

JUST AS FITZDUANE WAS beginning to feel pleasantly mellow after his third glass of wine and almost enjoying looking at thirteen black rectangles, the allocated time was clearly up. The crowd didn't dwindle over a period, leaving behind the harder-drinking stragglers, as would have been the case in Ireland. Instead, as if on a secret signal, there was an orderly but concerted rush for the door. Within three minutes, apart from gallery staff and Fitzduane, the place was empty. The wine was highly drinkable. He emptied his glass with some slight regret and headed for the door.

Erika was outside talking with friends. She left them and came toward him. She had donned a high-collared cloak of some golden material. She was mesmerizing and sexy. She took him by the arm.

"We must talk," she said. "You will come with me, yes?" Fitzduane did not feel inclined to refuse. He could feel the warmth of Erika's body next to his as they walked. The smell of her was in his nostrils. He felt himself growing hard.

"I have a small apartment near here," she said.

"On Junkerngasse?" said Fitzduane, remembering the address in his von Graffenlaub file. He wasn't sure the timing was right for another meeting with the lawyer—especially with the man's wife practically wrapped around him.

Erika laughed and squeezed his arm. "You are thinking of Beat's apartment," she said.

"I'm sorry, I don't quite understand," said Fitzduane. "I was under the impression that you lived with your husband."

She laughed again. "Yes and no," she said. "We have an arrangement. I need space and privacy. My apartment is close—it is indeed also on Junkerngasse—but it is separate."

"I see," said Fitzduane, who didn't.

"I will cook us a little supper, yes? We will be private, and we will talk," said Erika.

The building was old. The apartment, reached through some formidable security at its entrance, had been lavishly remodeled. It reeked of serious money.

Fitzduane had found it hard to imagine Erika sweating over a hot stove. He was not disappointed. She removed a Wedgwood casserole dish from the refrigerator and inserted it in a microwave. A scarlet-tipped finger pressed buttons. Fitzduane was asked to open the already chilled champagne and light the candles.

They sat facing each other over a small round dining table. It had already been laid for two on their arrival. It occurred to Fitzduane that he was spoiling someone else's fun and games—or had he been expected? Perhaps Erika had been a Girl Scout and just liked to be prepared.

"I can call you Hugo, yes?" said Erika, looking straight into his eyes. The casserole had something to do with rabbit. Fitzduane had had a series of pet rabbits as a child and found the juxtaposition of associations confusing. Erika ate with gusto.

Fitzduane nodded. Erika licked her lips in a manner that even a blind man would have noted as sexual. "I like this name," she said. "You want to talk about Rudi?"

"It's why I'm here," he said.

Erika gave a long, slow, knowing smile and reached over the table to brush the back of his hand with her fingers. The sexual electricity was palpable. "There is little to say," she said. "Rudi was a very troubled young man. Nobody is surprised at his suicide."

"What troubled him?" said Fitzduane.

Erika shrugged dismissively. "*Boeuf!*" she said, her arms raised in a gesture. "Everything. He hated his father, he quarreled with his family, he disapproved of our government, he was mixed up about sex." She smiled. "But is all that so unusual in a teenager?"

Fitzduane endeavored to pursue the matter of Erika's recently hanged stepson but to virtually no avail. The conversation turned to other members of the family. Here Erika was marginally more forthcoming. After coffee and liqueurs she excused herself. Fitzduane sat back on a sofa and sipped a Cointreau. Regarding Rudi, anyway, he wasn't getting very far with the von Graffenlaubs.

Erika had turned out most of the lights. The two candles on the dinner table cast a golden flickering light. Erika came back into the room. He could hear faint footfalls on the carpeted floor, and he could smell her musky perfume. She was standing behind him.

He turned his head to see her and started to speak. "It's getting late," he said. "I think I'd better . . ." The words died on his lips.

She reached down and pressed him to her and then kissed him. He could feel her nipples against his mouth and cheeks, and then her tongue was snaking to find his and she was in his lap, naked.

She licked his face and neck, and one hand moved to the bulge in his pants and unzipped him. He felt an overwhelming sexual desire. She unbuttoned his shirt and ran her tongue across his chest and down his body until she engulfed him.

Fitzduane spasmed at her touch and then stared at her bobbing head with disbelief. Her hair—though she was no blood relation—was the color of Rudi's. Desire died inside him. He tried to pull away. Her hand grasped him, and she wouldn't stop. He pulled her up forcibly. "My God, woman, what are you doing?" he said. He thought his choice of words might have been better.

"You are a very physical man, Hugo," she said. Her lips were wet, her lipstick smeared. "I want to fuck you."

Fitzduane rose to his feet unsteadily. He shook his head. There was nothing to say. He looked at her. She had risen to her feet. She looked magnificent. Her odor was viscerally sexual. She laughed. "Welcome to Bern," she said.

He hurriedly zipped himself up, said good-bye, and made his way to the street. The cool night air was refreshing. He thought it quite likely that steam was coming out of his ears. He walked back toward his hotel, on the way splashing some water from the Fountain of Justice on his face. The painted carving of the blindfolded damsel looming above him, showing a surprising amount of leg, reminded him somewhat of Erika.

DETECTIVE SERGEANT First Class Heinz Raufman, better known as the Bear, took the number three tram home to his new and very comfortable apartment in Saali, a suburb of Bern, just fifteen minutes from the city center.

If he was honest with himself, and he often was, he thought that all things considered, he had gotten off quite lightly. He had really deserved suspension. Instead, he had been given what amounted to a slap on the wrist and a sinecure. Played right, minor crimes could be turned into something very interesting indeed, a chance to do a little quiet exploring of the highways and byways of Bern's underworld, without the time constraints of a heavy caseload.

"Tilly, my love," he said as he fed Gustavus and Adolfus, his pet goldfish, "thumping the odd German can have its good side." He often talked to Tilly when he was alone in the apartment. They had bought it less than a year before her death. She had been at her happiest when cleaning and decorating it and making it ever more comfortable. "It must be snug, Heini," she used to say, "not just comfortable, but snug."

The Bear ate a light meal—for him—of veal in cream sauce with mushrooms, rösti, a side salad, just a little French bread with un- salted butter, and Camembert, all washed down with a modest liter of Viti, a Merlot of a most agreeable quality from Ticino. He debated having fruit and compromised with a pear, or two, or three. He had an espresso to fill in the cracks, and just a small Strega. All in all, quite an acceptable snack.

He watched the YBs on television; they lost. The Bear had strong doubts about the blending of the Bernese character and soccer. Later he watched the news. In Northern Ireland Bobby Sands was on a hunger strike and things did not look good.

THE MENTION OF IRELAND, albeit Northern Ireland, reminded the Bear that tomorrow he had better do something about the Irishman. He switched off the television and listened to the radio. Gustavus and Adolfus had a weakness for classical; they seemed to swim to tempo. The Bear cleaned his guns. He might be a little grumpy and a little heavy, but his paws worked just fine. Marksmanship trophies lined his sideboard. The Bear liked to shoot.

Tucked up in the large double bed, the electric blanket radiating just the right amount of warmth, his hot chocolate at hand on the bedside table, the Bear leafed through some paperwork he had picked up on the Irishman.

"Good night, little love," he murmured, as he always had to Tilly, before turning over and falling asleep.

Chapter Twelve

Fitzduane was the kind of man who examined credentials—something unusual in the Bear's experience. Most people tended to fold when an ID was waved about. In this case—Fitzduane was a connoisseur of such arcane documentation—the laminated identity card read: SICHERHEITS UND KRIMINALPOLIZEI DER STADT BERN. He handed back the identity card. "There is something unsettling about the word 'Kriminalpolizei' before breakfast," he said.

The Bear looked puzzled. "But it is nine o'clock," he said. "I thought you would have finished. I certainly did not mean to disturb you. In Switzerland we get up early. I finished breakfast over two hours ago."

Fitzduane looked sympathetic. "We all have our idiosyncrasies," he said. "You must be starving again by now. Come and join me."

The Bear did not need a second invitation. In truth he had been on the way to the Bärengraben for a small snack of coffee and pastries—the Bärengraben was famous for its pastries—when he realized that the Irishman was on his route.

"How did you find me?" asked Fitzduane.

"Your visitor's registration card," said the Bear. "That card you fill out when you check in. They are collected from every hotel and pension every day and are filed at headquarters."

"And if I'd stayed with a friend?"

"If you were in Bern, I'd have found you," said the Bear, "but maybe not so fast." He was a little distracted. He was busy putting butter and honey on his roll. Fitzduane was impressed. The Bear was demonstrating a certain mastery of construction, not to say balance. He gave the result a critical look, appeared satisfied, and began to munch.

"To what do I owe this honor?" Fitzduane beckoned for a second basket of rolls.

"Your friend Colonel Kilmara knows my chief," said the Bear. "He said you were coming to Bern and might need a little help getting to know your way around. Didn't your Colonel Kilmara tell you?"

"I guess he did," said Fitzduane, "but it was fairly casual. He gave me the name and number of a Major Buisseau to call on."

"Buisard," said the Bear. "Max Buisard. He's the Chief Kripo— that's the Chief of the Criminal Police—and my superior. Not a bad sort but a busy man, so he asked me to look after you. He sends his regards and hopes he will have a chance to meet you before you leave." He smiled. "Socially, of course."

Fitzduane smiled back politely. "Of course," he said. "Thank him for me—will you?—but tell him I don't expect to be in Bern for long."

The Bear nodded. "A pity," he said. He wrapped his paws around his steaming coffee cup as if warming them. He raised the cup to his lips and then blew on it without drinking. His eyes over the rim were shrewd and intelligent. His tone was casual.

"Tell me, Mr. Fitzduane," he said. "What exactly are you doing in Bern?"

The Irishman smiled broadly. "Sergeant Raufman, why do I think you already know the answer to that?"

The Bear was silent. He looked guilty. "Harrumph," he said, or at least it sounded like that. It was hard to tell; he was munching a croissant. "You know I once arrested young Rudi von Graffenlaub," he said.

"Tell me about it," said Fitzduane.

The Bear licked a little bit of honey off his right thumb. His normally glum expression was replaced by the most charming smile. "Only if we trade," he said. He hummed a few notes of an old Bernese march: "Pom Pom, tra-ri-di-ri, Al-li Ma-nne, stan-deni!"

Fitzduane thought for a while, and the Bear did not interrupt him but just sat there humming a little and looking content. Then Fitzduane spoke. "Why not?" he said, and following intuition rather than direct need, he told the Bear everything right from the beginning. He was surprised at himself when he had finished.

The Bear was an experienced listener. He leaned back in his chair, nodded his head from time to time, and occasionally made sounds of interest. Time passed. Around them the restaurant emptied and preparations commenced for lunch. Once, Fitzduane called for fresh coffee.

When he had concluded, Fitzduane waited for the Bear to speak. He did not at first but instead pulled his notebook out of his inside breast pocket and began to sketch. He showed the drawing to the Irishman. It featured the letter "A" surrounded by a circle of flowers. "Like that?" he said. The Irishman nodded.

"Well now," said the Bear, and he told Fitzduane about the body found in the River Aare. "What do you think?" he said.

"I don't think you're telling me everything," said Fitzduane. "You haven't suggested my passing this on officially. What's on your mind?"

It was now the Bear's turn to reveal much more than he had planned, and he, too, was relying on instinct—and so he confessed. He told of thumping a certain German visitor and Buisard's reaction and being assigned to minor crimes. He spoke of the opportunity this might offer if exploited creatively, then spoke of the advantage of two heads, of combining both an official and an unofficial approach.

There was silence between them, and then, somewhat tentatively at first, as they adjusted to this unplanned alliance, they shook hands.

"So that's settled," Fitzduane said after a moment. "Now, where can I hire a car?"

"There is a Hertz office just up the street off the Theaterplatz," said the Bear. "Come, I'll walk you up to the clock tower, and then I'll point the way. It's only a few hundred meters from there."

As they left the restaurant, a roller skater glided past. They walked up Kramgasse, passing two more of the painted fountains on the way. The day was hot, and they walked in the shade. The houses protruded over the raised pavement, forming arcades that sheltered the stroller from the weather and creating a beguiling intimacy. Restaurants and cafés with tables and chairs set up outside dotted the streets.

"Where are you thinking of driving?"

"I thought I'd see some of the surrounding countryside," said Fitzduane, "perhaps drive to Lake Thun and then up into the mountains."

"Are you used to driving on snow and ice?" asked the Bear. "The roads can be dangerous as you get higher. You will need snow tires. I use gravestones myself."

"What?"

"Gravestones," said the Bear, "broken gravestones in the trunk of my car. I have a friend who carves them. They are not so bulky, but heavy. They make a big difference to traction when driving on ice."

"Very sensible," said Fitzduane without enthusiasm.

A small crowd was waiting near the Zytgloggeturm, Bern's famous clock tower. The hands of the ornate clock were approaching midday. As they watched, the tableau came to life. A cock crowed and flapped its wings, the fool rang his bells, the cock crowed again, and then a procession of bears appeared in different guises, one carrying a fife and drum, the next a sword, followed by a knight in armor, then three more little bears, and finally a bear wearing a crown. Chronos turned the hourglass. The bell of the tower was struck by a man in gold with a hammer. The lion nodded his head to the count of the hour, and the cock crowed for the third time.

Fitzduane just stared. "Absolutely incredible," he said.

The Bear waved farewell and headed toward Marktgasse; after a few paces he turned.

"Gravestones," he shouted. "Don't forget what I said."

HERTZ DID not include gravestones—even when offered American Express—so Fitzduane compromised with a front-wheel-drive Volkswagen Golf.

Before he left Bern, Fitzduane checked with his hotel for telephone messages. Still no word from von Graffenlaub, but Fitzduane had resolved to give him a few days before proceeding to make inquiries on his own. Operating without the lawyer's support could well prove counterproductive. Close relatives and friends would quickly check with one another, and if they heard that Rudi's father was utterly opposed to any investigation, Fitzduane doubted he would receive much cooperation. It was frustrating, but the best tactic was to wait and meanwhile just see the sights. There was one exception to this plan: Rudi's twin sister, Vreni.

For reasons as yet unknown Vreni was not on speaking terms with her father. She had left her comfortable life in Bern, was estranged from most of her friends, and now was attempting to live an ecologically pure life on an old hill farm near a small village called Heiligenschwendi, in the Bernese Oberland. Living the natural life did not include celibacy. Fitzduane's notes recorded that her companion on the side of the mountain was a twenty-four-year-old ski instructor, Peter Haag. According to Erika—and what better stepmother to be up-to-date on sexual intimacy and its nuances—Peter was prone to stray, especially during the skiing season. "It goes with being a ski instructor. All that fresh air and exercise and energy. It generates sexual tension, and there are so many attractive opportunities for release. You understand, Hugo?" she had said. She had rested her hand on his arm as she spoke.

Fitzduane had called Vreni from the hotel that morning. Yes, she would see him. She would expect him after lunch. Ask anyone in the village how to get to the farm. Click. Her telephone manner was abrupt to the point of rudeness, but Fitzduane did not think that was the problem. She had sounded preoccupied and as if she had been crying.

HEILIGENSCHWENDI DID not seem to exist as far as Fitzduane's Michelin guide was concerned. He tried Baedeker with no more luck and was beginning to think that someone was pulling his leg when the Hertz girl came to his rescue. She had lived in Thun, only a few kilometers from the missing village. She produced a large-scale map of Switzerland and triumphantly circled "Heiligenschwendi" in red felt pen.

The Hertz girl had not exaggerated about the beauty of the village. After he left Thun and started to climb the twisting road, again and again, the different views were breathtaking. The sun blazed in a clear blue sky. As he drove higher, he could see the lake sparkling below.

He parked the car in Heiligenschwendi. Vreni's house was some ten minutes away at the end of a narrow track, and he was advised that it would be easier to walk than to drive. It would be difficult to turn the car around, especially when the snow still lay on the ground.

There was a newly built woodshed outside the farm. Slatted side walls allowed the wind to circulate and dry the wood. Inside, the logs were cut to a fixed length and evenly split in a way seldom seen in Ireland. They were stacked impeccably, properly spaced, edges aligned to the nearest centimeter.

The farmhouse was built into the slope of the hill and looked as if it were several centuries old. Its timbers were mottled and discolored from generations of harsh winters and hot summers. Melting snow dripped from overhanging eaves.

When Vreni opened the door, Fitzduane could smell gingerbread. He was strangely moved when he first saw her and was momentarily unable to speak. She was so like Rudi, yet somehow different. The reason came to him as he looked at her. Fitzduane had never seen Rudi except disfigured in death. Vreni was warm, young, beautiful, and very much alive. There was a smear of flour on her cheek.

Fitzduane had bought flowers in Bern. He offered them to her. She smiled and raised her hands, palms toward him. They were covered in flour.

"You're thoughtful," she said, "but keep them for a moment—will you?—until I wash my hands. I've been baking gingerbread men for my cousins for Easter."

Outdoor shoes and clogs stood in a neat row beside the door. At her request Fitzduane added his own and donned the Hüttenfinken she offered him. The thick leather-soled socks were heavily embroidered in bright colors. He padded into the warm glow of the house, then into the small kitchen, whose walls were lined with cabinets and shelves. He could see no processed foods. Instead, there were bundles of dried herbs, jars of different colored grains and pulses, and hand-labeled bottles of liquids. A wood stove radiated heat from one corner. A scrubbed wooden table bore several trays of cooling gingerbread shapes. Other baking materials were obviously still in use.

She led him through the kitchen into the next room. As he went through the door, he noticed that the wood stove connected into a two-level stone bench built into the corner of the room. Above the stone bench was a man-size circular hole in the low ceiling. Vreni saw his interest.

"It's a sort of central heating system," she said. "The stove in the kitchen can warm this room here through the stone benches. Also, if we want, we can open the circular trapdoor above the benches and the bedroom above will be warmed. It's called a choust. When it's cold, I go to bed from here through the trapdoor. It saves using the stairs outside."

Fitzduane was intrigued, Ireland traditionally being a land of romantic but inefficient open fireplaces. Vreni left him for a few minutes to finish her baking and to wash her hands. He felt the top stone bench. It was pleasantly warm. He noticed a system of baffles that could be used to adjust the flow of heat.

The room was of a comfortable size. It was furnished adequately, if sparsely, for what was obviously the main room of the house. There was a wooden table and four simple upright chairs. There was a low bed in one corner made up with cushions to serve as a sofa. Several bean bags and other huge cushions were scattered around. There was one pine bookcase. There were none of the normal electronic devices of modern living—no television, no radio, no stereo. The one incongruous note was struck by the presence of a telephone on the floor just beside the sofa.

He walked over to look at the books. Most of the titles were in German and meant little to him, but to judge by the photographs and symbols on some of them, they revealed more than a passing interest in left-wing politics. Several books were either by or about a Rudolf Steiner. The name struck a chord in Fitzduane, and then he remembered a German mercenary he had run into a few times called Rolf Steiner. Somehow he didn't think the books referred to the same man.

"Anthroposophy," Vreni said. She held a steaming coffee mug in each hand. She gave him one and then curled up on a bean bag. She wore a loose cotton blouse of Indian design and faded jeans. Her feet were bare. They were perfectly proportioned and without blemish.

"You know the teachings of Steiner," she asked, "Rudolf Steiner?"

Fitzduane shook his head.

"He was an Austrian," she said, "but he worked mainly in Switzerland. Anthroposophy is a philosophy of life he developed. It means knowledge produced by the higher self in man—as opposed to theosophy, knowledge originating from God. Anthroposophy covers all kinds of things."

"Like what?" said Fitzduane.

"Science, education, architecture, a biodynamic approach to farming, and so on," she said. "It even includes eurhythmics. He had a great-aunt of mine dancing barefoot in the morning dew when she was young."

Fitzduane smiled. "And you follow his teachings?"

"In some ways," she said. "Particularly his ideas about farming. Our farming methods here are completely natural. We use no chemicals or artificial fertilizers, no unhealthy additives. It's more work, but it's better, don't you think?"

Fitzduane sipped the hot liquid she had given him. It was a disturbing yellow-brown color and tasted bitter. "I guess it depends what you're used to," he said.

"You like it?" she said, gesturing toward his mug. "It's a special herb tea, my own recipe."

Fitzduane smiled. "I was going to blame Steiner," he said. "Anything that tastes this awful must do you good."

Vreni laughed. "My herb tea is good for everything. It cures the common cold, cleanses the insides, and promotes sexual vigor."

"They used to call that kind of thing snake oil."

"You don't know what you're missing," said Vreni. "Would you like some real coffee instead?"

While she was making the coffee, he continued his browse through the books, steering clear of Steiner. On the bottom shelf, title facing inward, and almost hidden by a row of encyclopedias, was a familiar volume: *The Paradox Business*, by Hugo Fitzduane. He flipped through its pages. A pressed flower and a small piece of printed paper slipped from it to the floor. The flower crumbled as he tried to pick it up. The paper was a ski pass. The book fell open at a full-page bleed photograph of Colonel Shane Kilmara.

He called out to her in the kitchen. "I see you've got my book," he said.

"We do?" she said, and there was amusement in her voice. "I'm afraid I didn't know. Most of those books are Peter's."

He replaced the book exactly as he had found it. He could still taste the bitterness of the herb tea on his tongue.

THERE WERE two windows in the room. Through one Lake Thun could be seen below, bright blue in the sunlight. The second window was set into the end of the room and was at right angles to the first. It looked along the track to a small barn about fifty meters away. The track seemed to end there.

There was something strange about Vreni, something he could not as yet identify. On the face of it, she was calm and self-assured—in fact, so self-assured that it was easy to forget she was only twenty. Her manner suggested experience, a certain knowingness that he had most often encountered in the young in combat zones, where maturity came fast if you were to survive. It was a lack of illusion, a loss of innocence rather than the judgment that came with full maturity. It showed most of all in her eyes.

Yet in contrast with her poise and assurance were other emotions. He could sense undercurrents of fear, sadness, and loneliness—and a great need for someone to confide in, for someone to help her. There seemed to be things she wanted to say but was afraid to.

Together with his coffee, she brought him a small glass and filled it with an almost colorless liquid. The bottle had fruit floating in it, some berries he could not identify. He tasted it with some trepidation, but it was delicious, a homemade schnapps distilled from fruit grown on the farm.

"We have a communal still in the village," she said. "You can make five liters per person per year without paying any tax, and one liter for each cow. It is used as a medicine for the cows, or at least that was the custom. Now I think the cows don't often see their share."

"And what does Mr. Steiner think of that?" he asked. She threw back her head and laughed again, and for a few moments all the undercurrents were gone. All he could see was a young, beautiful girl with no cares and her life ahead of her.

Outside, the light faded, and it began to freeze again. He helped her bring in more wood from the shed and, away from the warmth of the farmhouse, shivered in the cold of the evening. She showed him around the house. They climbed through the circular trapdoor into the master bedroom. It was sparsely furnished apart from a low handmade double bed, covered with a sheepskin rug, and an old carved wardrobe. A SIG service rifle rested on two wooden pegs on the wall. Vreni saw him glance toward it.

"That is Peter's," she said.

Fitzduane nodded.

"Peter owns this farm," she said, "but he is often away. I don't know when he will be back; it is dull for him here."

"You don't have a photograph of him by any chance, do you?" Vreni shook her head. "No. He has never liked being photographed. Some people are that way." She smiled. "They think their souls are being stolen."

Next door to the bedroom was a workshop and hobby room. There were piles of ski equipment. Several planks were removed from the inside of one of the walls.

"Woodworm," she said. "They have to be replaced."

"Why not just spray them?"

"There you go with your chemicals again," she said. "It is wrong. We are just killing nature."

"I understand your father is a director of a major chemical company," said Fitzduane, "among his many interests."

Vreni gave him a look. "That is not so widely known. You are well informed."

Fitzduane shrugged. Silently he cursed himself for breaking the mood of the conversation now that she was talking more freely.

"There is much that my father has done, and does, that I do not agree with," she said. "He supports a system in Switzerland that is wrong. He pretends to lead a respectable, upright life, to be a leading citizen in the community, to support worthy causes and to be a model for others, but it is all hypocrisy. He and a few thousand others in high positions in business, politics, the army, and banking manipulate our so-called democracy for their own selfish ends. They control the press, they are in league with the unions, and the people suffer. All over the world the people suffer."

Suddenly she grabbed him by the hand—her mood changed in a flash—and, giggling, pulled him with her out through the workroom door. "I've got a surprise for you," she said.

Because of the steep slope of the hill on which the house was perched, the second-floor workroom led to a path outside that ran around the back of the house. There, separate from the living quarters but under the same weather-beaten roof as the old house, was storage for hay. In one fenced-off corner were several lambs nestling together. They sprang to their feet when the door opened and stood blinking in the light of the single electric bulb. One lamb was smaller than the others and had a brown woolly coat. Vreni ran forward and scooped the little lamb into her arms. It nuzzled against the familiar warmth of her breasts.

"Isn't he lovely?" she said. "So soft and cuddly, and he's mine. Peter gave him to me. His mother died, and I fed him from a bottle like a baby."

Vreni stood there with the lamb in her arms, her face loving and gentle, her cares momentarily gone. He could smell hay and milk and the warmth of her body. She stood very close as she placed the lamb in his arms. Then she kissed Fitzduane just once, gently.

BACK INSIDE the house, Vreni busied herself making supper, something of rice and vegetables and herbs. They ate in the sitting room in the glow of an antique oil lamp, and they drank homemade red wine. Afterward there was more coffee and schnapps. The cows certainly weren't going to get much of a look-in.

Vreni sat on her bean bag again and began to talk about Rudi.

"When we were small, it was all so simple. Mommy was still alive then and married to Daddy. It was a happy home. It was lovely growing up in Bern. There was always so much to do. There was school and all our friends; there were dancing classes and singing classes. In the summer we went walking and swimming. In the winter there was skiing and tobogganing and ice skating. At weekends, and sometimes for longer, we'd go to Lenk. Daddy has a chalet there—a very old place, very creaky. Rudi loved it; we both did. We had a great friend who taught us skiing there. He farmed in the summer and would take his cows high up in the mountains. From time to time we would go with him. He never seemed to get tired, and he taught us all about the different wild flowers."

"What was his name?" Fitzduane felt a sense of betrayal as he asked the question. He was friend and confidant, but first he was interrogator.

Vreni was preoccupied. She answered his question almost without thinking. "Oskar," she said, "Oskar Schupbach—a lovely man. He had a face that looked as if it were carved out of polished mahogany. He was always so tanned, always outdoors, winter and summer."

"Do you still go to Lenk?"

"No!" she said. "No! Never again, never." The words snapped out with savage force. She started to cry and then wiped the tears from her eyes with the back of her hands. She sat on the floor on a cushion, back propped against the bean bag, legs stretched out, feet bare, head down. She looked about fifteen.

"Why did it all go wrong?" she said. "Why did it have to? We were so happy."

Fitzduane checked his watch. It was getting late, and unaccustomed as he was to driving on these frozen roads, it would take him a long time to get back to Bern in the darkness. Vreni looked up at him and read his mind. "You can stay here," she said, indicating the sofa. "The roads will be icy now, and I don't think you are used to such driving. Please stay; I'd like you to."

Fitzduane looked out the window. The night was dark. He could see no moon, no lights of other houses, no headlights in the distance. He let the curtain drop back into place. He smiled at her. "Fine."

Vreni unzipped one of the bean bags and rummaged inside. Her hand came out holding a small leather bag secured by a drawstring. She opened the bag and, with the contents, began to roll a joint. She looked up at Fitzduane.

"Grass," she said. "Want some?"

Fitzduane shook his head.

She smiled at him. "It's the generation gap."

He didn't disillusion her. She lit the joint and inhaled deeply, holding the smoke in her lungs for as long as possible. She repeated the exercise several times. The sweetish smell of cannabis smoke filled the air.

"That's good," she said. "That's very, very good."

She lay back against the bean bag again, her eyes closed. Faint tendrils of smoke emerged from her nostrils. She was silent for several minutes. Fitzduane drank some more schnapps and waited.

"You're easy to talk to," she said. "Simpatico. You know how to listen."

Fitzduane smiled.

"It's incredible to think of it now," said Vreni, "but we were in awe of Daddy when we were small. He was a little brusque, somewhat stern, but we loved him. He was often away on business or working late. I remember Mommy would often talk about how hard he was working. We knew he had been a hero during the war. We knew he was a lawyer. We knew about something called 'business,' but we had no idea what that word meant in terms of people and their lives.

"Mommy was idealistic. Daddy used to call her naive. She came from another one of the old Bernese families just like Daddy, but she wasn't an ostrich like so many of that group. She didn't just want to safeguard her privileges and live in the past. She wanted a more caring society in Switzerland. She wanted some kind of justice for the Third World, not to bleed it dry with high interest rates and sell it arms and chemicals it doesn't need.

"Funnily enough, I think that Daddy shared her ideas at first—or so Mommy said. But then, as he grew more successful and acquired power and influence, he became less and less liberal and increasingly right-wing and blinkered in his outlook. Too much to lose, I suppose.

"We—Rudi and I—were about twelve or thirteen when we noticed things beginning to go wrong between them. There was no one incident, just a change in the atmosphere and a kind of coldness. Daddy was away more. He came home from work later. There were arguments, the normal sort of thing, I suppose. Even so, Erika came as a complete shock. She was on the scene for about a year before the divorce took place. They were married almost immediately after.

"The reactions of us children were quite different. Marta, as the eldest daughter, was always very close to Daddy. She was a classic moody teenager, and she and Mommy had gotten on badly for a few years. So Marta took Daddy's side over the divorce and went to live with him and Erika. Andreas was of two minds. He was close to Mommy but was absolutely fascinated by Erika. He had a real crush on her. He used to get an erection when she was near."

Fitzduane remembered his own initial response to Erika's reeking sexuality. He had every sympathy for Andreas.

"Rudi and I were closest to Mommy. We were both terribly upset over the divorce. All that happy time was over. Rudi took it hardest of all. He took a real dislike to Daddy and, for a time, wouldn't even speak to him. Surprisingly he didn't blame Erika.

"Rudi was fifteen at the time and exceptionally bright. He was also unhappy, frustrated, angry. He wanted to do something, to get revenge, to teach Daddy a lesson. I suppose I felt the same way at the time, though not as strongly. He started to investigate Daddy's life and at the same time to seek out people who were opposed to the system and values Daddy supported.

"Rudi became obsessed. He began to read Daddy's files, and then he grew more daring or reckless and photocopied some of them. I wasn't too keen on that at first, but when I read some of the stuff he found, I began to wonder.

"The companies that Daddy is involved with, either as a director or a legal adviser in most cases, are really big. I mean, put together, they probably employ hundreds of thousands of people all over the world, and their combined turnover is in the billions. We found some terrible things."

"Such as?" asked Fitzduane.

"The worst cases involved a company called Vaybon Holdings. Rudi found some confidential minutes in Daddy's own handwriting. I don't remember all the details, but it was a review of their dirty tricks over many years. Many concerned bribery and illegal sales of arms to governments in Africa and the Middle East. Another concerned that tranquilizer they made—VB 19—which was found to have serious genetic side effects. It was withdrawn in the United States and Europe. Under a different name and repackaged, it continued to be sold in the Third World."

"What did Rudi do with the papers he copied?"

"He was going to keep them," said Vreni, "and release them to the press outside Switzerland. That was too much for me. The whole family would have been affected, and Rudi would have gone to prison if he had been discovered as the source. Commercial secrecy is enforceable by law in Switzerland, you know."

Fitzduane nodded.

"It wasn't just me who persuaded Rudi to burn the papers. Mommy also discovered that Rudi had them. She didn't want them released either. She talked to Rudi a lot, and eventually—reluctantly, but mainly to please her—he agreed. Shortly afterward she was killed.

"Rudi was terribly upset. He was quite distraught. He started saying that she had been killed deliberately by Vaybon because she had seen the documents. I don't think he really believed it. It was just an accident, but he was overwrought and wanted to lash out—to blame someone or something. In some strange way I think he also blamed himself."

Fitzduane remembered how Rudi's mother had died. Claire von Graffenlaub had run her Porsche into a truck loaded with spaghetti. It didn't seem the likeliest way to be murdered.

"The things that Daddy was involved in, the burning of the papers, Mommy's death, the influence of some of his new friends, all made Rudi more and more extreme. He began to experiment with drugs, not just grass, but with different things like speed and acid. We had moved back to Daddy's, but he was away from home a lot.

Rudi stopped arguing with Daddy and seemed to be getting on with him better, but really he was working on some sort of revenge. He wasn't just acting by himself anymore. He was taking advice, responding to some specific influence.

"He made friends with some people who were on the fringes of the AKO—the Anarchistische Kampforganisation. They wanted to destroy the Swiss system, the whole Western capitalist system, through revolution. It was mostly just talk, but some other people in the mainstream of the group had been involved in stealing weapons from the Swiss armories and supplying terrorists. They supplied weapons to order. Machine guns, revolvers, grenades, even panzer mines powerful enough to destroy a tank. They had links with the Baader-Meinhof gang, Carlos, the Basques, many extremist groups. The weapons-stealing group was broken up, and the active members were imprisoned before Rudi came on the scene. Still, there were many sympathizers who got away. Some of them were known to the police and watched."

"So you're saying that Rudi wasn't actively involved," said Fitzduane. "He was more of a terrorist groupie once removed."

Vreni smiled. "That's a funny way of putting it, but I suppose it's about right."

"And where were you in all this?" said Fitzduane.

She looked at him without answering, and then she turned away and stared at the floor, her hands clasped around her knees. "I prefer to be an *Aussteiger*. I don't want to hurt anyone," she said quietly.

"What's an *Aussteiger*?"

"What in English you call a dropout," said Vreni. "Actually it's funny. The German word means more like a 'climb out.' Here you can't just drop out like in America. You have to make the effort—to climb."

She yawned. It was past midnight. Her voice was beginning to slur from the combined effects of tiredness and grass. He had many other questions to ask, but most would have to wait until morning. He doubted she would speak so freely in the light of day. Few people did.

He had the sense that what he was hearing was true, but only part of the truth; it was a parallel truth. Something else had been happening at the same time, something that, perhaps, Vreni did not know—or was only partially informed about. He yawned himself. It was pieces, feelings, vibes, guesswork at this stage.

"I'm sleepy," she said. "We can talk some more in the morning."

She uncurled herself from the floor and knelt on her haunches in front of him. Her blouse was unbuttoned, and he could see the swell of her breasts and the tops of her nipples. She brought her face close to his. He could feel her breath, smell her body. She slid an arm around his neck and caressed him. She kissed him on the lips, and her tongue snaked into his mouth for a moment before he pulled back. Her hand flickered across the bulge in his trousers and then withdrew.

"You know, Irishman," she whispered as if to herself, "you know that they're going to kill you, don't you?" Then she vanished through the round hole in the ceiling. In his exhaustion Fitzduane was unsure that he'd heard her correctly.

SMALL SOUNDS WOKE him. The room was empty, and the lamp, almost out of oil, sputtered as it quietly died. He saw her legs first, then the V-shaped patch of fawn pubic hair as she slid down from her room onto the warm stone of the choust. The gold bracelet on her left wrist caught the last flickers of light. Then her naked body was shrouded in darkness.

He could hear her moving slowly across the floor toward him. She was sobbing quietly. He could feel the wetness of her cheek against his outstretched hand. Without speaking, he drew her into the bed beside him and held her in his arms. Her tears wet the hair on his chest. He kissed her gently as one would kiss a child, and after a long while she fell asleep.

He remained awake thinking for several hours until the first faint light of dawn eased its way through the curtains. Vreni slept easily, her breathing deep and even. Very slowly he unclasped the bracelet from her wrist, moving it only slightly so he could see what was there. It was hard to discern in the minimal light, but he could see enough. There was no tattoo. Vreni stirred slightly but did not waken.

ACROSS THE BREAKFAST TABLE she was silent and subdued. She did not look at him as she made him coffee and placed a bowl of muesli in front of him. To break the silence, he asked her who did the milking. The milk he was pouring was still fresh and steaming.

She looked up at him and laughed a little humorlessly. "Peter arranged it," she said. "We have a neighbor. He lives in the village, but his cow byre is close to ours. We take turns to do the milking."

"You're not completely alone then."

"Willi is good with the cows," she said, "but he's over sixty, set in his ways, and not given to much conversation."

"So you get lonely."

"Yes," she said, "I do. I really do." She sat without speaking for a few moments and then stood up and began busying herself around the kitchen. Suddenly, leaning against the sink, her back to Fitzduane, she started sobbing, a violent, unstoppable outpouring.

Fitzduane stood and went to put his hands on her shoulders to comfort her. Her back was corded with tension. He made as if to take her in his arms, but she shook him off angrily. Her hand clenched the edge of the sink, the knuckles white with the force of her grip.

"You don't know what you're dealing with," she said. "I was a fool to talk to you. It's none of your business. You don't understand, this whole thing is too complicated. It's nothing to do with you."

He started to say something, but she turned on him, screaming. Her face was distorted by anger and fear. Her voice broke as she shouted at him. "You idiot! Don't you know it's too late? It's gone too far! I can't go back, and no one can help me. No one!" Vreni rushed out of the kitchen into the main room, slamming the door behind her. A bag of brown rice balanced on one of the kitchen shelves thudded to the floor. He heard the phone ring and then Vreni answer. She did not seem to speak much. Once he heard a single word when she raised her voice; it was repeated several times. It sounded like *nay*, Swiss-German dialect for *no*. He went back to the kitchen table to finish his breakfast.

Some minutes later Vreni walked slowly back into the kitchen. Her face was ashen. He could scarcely hear her as she spoke.

"You'd better go," she said. "Now." She pressed a small package into his hand. It was wrapped in paper and was about the size of a screw-top coffee jar. She held her lips to his cheek for a few moments and clasped him tight.

"Thank you for trying," she said, "but it's too late." She turned and left the room. She had scarcely looked at him while she was speaking. Her face was streaked with tears. Fitzduane knew that to push her further would be worse than useless.

He walked back down the track to Heiligenschwendi. The snow and slush had frozen in the night and crackled underfoot. There was ice on the mountain road, too, so he drove slowly and with particular care. He checked his mirror often and several times stopped to admire the view. Once he broke out a telephoto lens and took some photographs of the twisting road and of a motorcyclist demonstrating his skill gliding around a corner. The biker accelerated when he saw Fitzduane's camera and did not acknowledge the Irishman's wave.

Fitzduane had lunch in Interlaken, did the things that tourists do, and drove back sedately to Bern. When the biker turned off at the outskirts of the city, Fitzduane was almost sorry to see him go. Still, it might be a good idea to find out who was following him. He was beginning to be sorry he had left his Kevlar vest back in Ireland. Switzerland was turning out to be rather different from what he had expected.

He thought he might just buy himself a gun.

Chapter Thirteen

Fitzduane was interested in weapons—training in them had formed part of his upbringing—and in the isolation of his castle and grounds he interpreted the restrictive Irish gun laws rather liberally. In Ireland a permit was needed for something as relatively nonlethal as an air rifle, and obtaining a license for a handgun was almost impossible. Also, there were few gun shops in Ireland, and the selection of weapons in them was limited.

He was intrigued by the Swiss approach to firearms and had already found out that the Swiss just loved guns, all kinds of guns from black-powder muskets to match-precision rifles. They also made them and shot them with impressive skill and consistent application.

Fitzduane found the gun shop by the simple expedient of following a respectable middle-aged burgher in a business suit who was carrying an assault rifle with much the same nonchalance as a Londoner might carry an umbrella. Passersby were equally unmoved by the sight. It did occur to Fitzduane that the good citizen might be returning to his office to shoot his boss or taking a midafternoon break to perforate his wife's lover. Both these options, on reflection, seemed to promise a certain entertainment value.

After only a few minutes—and it was a fine afternoon for a

stroll—the burgher led him to a shop in Aarbergasse. The facade bore the words SCHWARZ, BÜCHSENMACHER, ARMURIER, and the window was nicely decorated with a display of firepower that would have done credit to a South American dictator's personal arsenal.

"I'd like to buy a gun," said Fitzduane.

The man behind the counter nodded in agreement. Nothing could be more sensible. Fitzduane looked around the shop. There were guns everywhere, a quite astonishing variety: revolvers, automatics, muskets, shotguns, army rifles, carbines. They hung from racks, stared at him from display cabinets, leaned casually against the walls. Any unoccupied space was filled with ammunition boxes, crossbows, books on guns, even catapults. It was terrific. He wished he had come there when he was fourteen. Still, he wasn't quite sure of the ground rules for this sort of thing.

"What are the gun laws in Switzerland?" he asked.

The man behind the counter was unfazed. It was clear that the Swiss legal system was not going to stop him from making a sale.

"For a foreigner?"

Fitzduane thought that speaking in English must be a dead giveaway. "It depends where I am," he said. "I feel quite at home in Bern."

The shopkeeper seemed to have scant interest in repartee. His business was guns. He picked a Finnish Valmet assault rifle off a rack behind him and idly mowed down half a dozen passersby through the plate glass shopfront. He made a "tac-tac-tac" sound: three-round bursts, good fire control.

The Valmet was replaced. A Colt Peacemaker appeared in the man's hand. He held it, arm outstretched, in the single-handed shooting position that was all the rage for handguns before a California sheriff called Weaver started winning all the shooting competitions in the 1950s by shooting with two hands like a woman.

"The laws vary from canton to canton," he said. "In Bern, for instance, you can carry a pistol without a permit. In Zurich it is not so."

There were twenty-six cantons and half cantons in Switzerland, Fitzduane recalled. He wasn't quite sure of the difference between a canton and a half canton, but considering the gun law variations, it sounded as if it might be a good idea to carry something a little less vulnerable to local complications than a handgun.

"But it is not difficult to buy a gun," the shopkeeper continued. "It depends on what you want. There are some restrictions on automatic weapons and pistols. Otherwise it is easy."

"Without a permit?"

"Except for the restrictions I have mentioned, no permit is required," said the man. He twirled the Peacemaker expertly and returned it to the showcase. He selected a small .32 Smith & Wesson, looked at Fitzduane, and then put it back. Somehow the Irishman didn't seem the .32-caliber type.

Fitzduane reluctantly abandoned the idea of buying an M-60 machine gun and towing it around Bern on roller skates. He looked at his camera tripod case, which was resting on the counter while he talked, and little wheels started turning in his brain.

He pointed at a Remington folding shotgun in a rack behind the man. It was a short-barreled riot gun and was stamped, in large, clear letters: FOR LAW ENFORCEMENT ONLY.

"But of course," said the shopkeeper, offering the gun to Fitzduane. The weapon was a folding pump-action shotgun equipped with a pistol grip. Fitzduane had used a similar weapon on special operations in the Congo. With the appropriate ammunition, up to a maximum of forty meters, though preferably at half that distance, it was an effective killing machine with brutal stopping power. With the metal stock collapsed, the gun fit neatly into the tripod case, leaving room for spare ammunition in the zippered accessory pocket where Fitzduane normally kept his long remote extension cord.

The man behind the counter placed a box of twelve-gauge 00 shells beside the holstered gun. Each shell contained nine lead balls, any one of which could be fatal at close range. It was clear he didn't think Fitzduane might need birdshot. As an afterthought the man added a tubular magazine extension. "We take credit cards," he said. Fitzduane smiled and paid cash. The bill came to 918 francs 40.

He left the gun shop and went looking for a photography store where he could have some film developed and some enlargements made in a hurry. He was successful and arranged to make the pickup the following morning.

There was a café called the High Noon off the Bärenplatz, just next door to the prison tower. It seemed like the right place for a beer after buying a gun. Afterward Fitzduane strolled back to his hotel. As far as he could tell, he was no longer being followed, though it was difficult to be sure. The streets were crowded with evening shoppers, and the arcades made concealment by a tail easy. As he neared the Hospiz, the crowds thinned, and he noticed a keffiyeh-shrouded skater detach himself from an arcade pillar and glide after him. He changed direction and entered a small bar called the Arlequin. He had another beer and wondered what had happened to the "H."

Outside, the skater glided, twirled, and, finally fatigued, adopted a storklike position, supported on one leg with the other drawn up and looped behind the knee. So positioned, the skater watched the Arlequin door. He was gone, apparently, by the time Fitzduane left. This is all very fucking weird, thought Fitzduane.

BACK IN his hotel room, Fitzduane loaded the shotgun. With the magazine extension fitted, it held seven rounds. He checked the safety catch and replaced the weapon in its carrying case.

He had almost forgotten about the small parcel that Vreni had pressed into his hand. He borrowed a pair of scissors from reception and carefully cut open the package. Inside was a glass jar containing gingerbread. He unscrewed the top, and the rich aroma brought him back to the old farmhouse on the side of the hill and a girl with flour on her cheek. He ate one of the gingerbread men. It broke crisply as he bit into it. There was a hint of butter and spices.

Wrapped around the jar was an envelope. The letter inside was short, the handwriting round and deliberate. The letter was written on the squared paper used throughout the Continent for notepads.

> Dearest Irishman
>
> I am writing this as you lie asleep in the next room. I have lit the fire again, so it is warm, and I feel safe and cozy and loving toward you. I wish you could stay with me in Heiligenschwendi, but of course it is not possible.
>
> Please do not contact me again—at least for a few days. I need to think and decide what is best to do. I know you will want to ask me more questions when you awake. I don't think I will be able to talk to you.
>
> If you stay in Bern—and you should not, but I hope you do—Rudi and I have a friend you could talk to. His name is Klaus Minder. He is from Zurich and lives in different places in Bern with friends. When I last heard, he was staying in the Youth House at Taubenstrasse 12.

I suppose I shouldn't have talked to you at all—but I was so lonely. I miss Rudi.

Much love, Vreni

He placed the letter beside the gingerbread and the shotgun on the table. He felt like a schnapps. He sat there without moving, an ache in his heart for the mixed-up young Vreni. He reached out for the phone to call her, but then his hand fell away. If time to think was what she wanted, then maybe she should have it.

When the phone rang, it was Beat von Graffenlaub's secretary. Could Herr Fitzduane meet Herr von Graffenlaub for lunch in the Restaurant du Théâtre tomorrow at twelve-thirty precisely? She repeated the "precisely."

"I'll be there," he said. "Who's paying?"

Frau Hunziker sounded as if she were strangling. Fitzduane hoped she wasn't. Things were complex enough already.

IVO WAS still asleep when the two detectives called at the Youth House. They were courteous. They didn't barge in and roust Ivo out of his sleeping bag. They knocked gently on the back door—they had come in through the side entrance—and waited in their car outside for ten minutes until a tousled Ivo appeared.

It was obvious Ivo had not had breakfast. The two detectives bought him coffee and rolls from a stall in the Hauptbahnhof and chatted quietly between themselves while he ate. When he was finished, they put him back into their car and headed along Laupenstrasse with the serried tracks of the Bern marshaling yards on the right. After less than a kilometer they turned right onto Bühlstrasse. Part of the campus of Bern University stretched before them, and with a sinking feeling Ivo realized where he was going. At the university hospital they drove into the emergency entrance, and the large shuttered door closed behind them.

Given time, a skilled mortician can make the most unsightly cadaver appear presentable. In this case there hadn't been time. The pathologists of the Gerichtsmedizinisches Institut Bern—part of Bern University—had concentrated on the main task, determining the cause of death. The corpse had been roughly sewn together after the detailed examination, and there was almost nothing that could be done about the mutilation of the eyes and the missing ears. Fortunately only the head was shown to Ivo. The rest of the body was covered with a white cloth.

"Do you recognize him?" asked one of the detectives.

There was no response. Tears streamed down Ivo's cheeks.

The question was repeated again, twice.

The first detective pulled the sheet over the corpse's head and, with his arm around Ivo's shoulders, led him out of the room into the corridor outside. He brought Ivo into an examination room just off the corridor. His companion followed and closed the door. Ivo sat in a chair in deep shock. It was late morning before he finally confirmed his identification and signed the papers, and then the two detectives drove him back to the Youth House. They watched as he walked slowly down the side of the house, his shoulders slumped.

"If he's acting, I'm becoming a Berp again," said the first detective. He had quite enjoyed his years as a Berp, a member of the uniformed police, the Bereitschaftspolizei; the hours were predictable.

"He's not involved," said the Bear, "but he was close to Minder. He's very shaken now, but he'll recover and start digging. Who knows? He may come up with something."

"Well, Heini, thanks for helping out anyhow. Now you can go back to the quiet life again. It was just that I knew that you knew Ivo and would never turn down a quick trip to the morgue."

"Funny fucker, aren't you?"

They had lunch together in the Mövenpick. It wasn't really the Bear's sort of place, but it was quick and convenient, and he had a little unofficial chat with a friend in Interpol in mind for the afternoon.

Over lunch he learned that the investigation of Klaus Minder's death was getting precisely nowhere. He was neither surprised nor entirely displeased. He thought he might check with the Irishman later. Now there was a genuine wild card who was just sneaky enough to get results. Off to the Oberland to see the sights indeed! The Bear wasn't too old to sweet-talk a Hertz girl, and it didn't take much genius to figure out the significance of Heiligenschwendi.

THE RESTAURANT DU THÉÂTRE WAS one of Bern's more exclusive spots. Fitzduane arrived five minutes early. Von Graffenlaub was already seated.

There was something of the dandy about von Graffenlaub, thought Fitzduane. It was not so much the more flamboyant touches, such as the miniature rose in the lawyer's buttonhole or the combination of pink shirt, pale gray suit, and black knitted tie (color coordination or mourning?). No, sitting opposite Fitzduane, dipping his asparagus into the restaurant's special hollandaise sauce with practiced expertise, he had a vigor that had been missing during their previous encounter. He projected confidence and a sense of purpose. He radiated—Fitzduane searched for the right word—authority. This was more the man Fitzduane had expected—patriot, professional success, wielder of power, influence, and riches.

"Delicious," said von Graffenlaub. The last stalk of early asparagus had vanished. He dabbled his fingertips in a finger bowl and dried them on a pink napkin. Its shade did not quite match his shirt, but it was close. Fitzduane wondered if the lawyer had dressed for his surroundings. He had read that there were more than two hundred restaurants and cafés in Bern. It would be an interesting sartorial problem.

"Is the first *Spargel* of the season considered such a delicacy in Ireland?" asked von Graffenlaub.

Fitzduane cast his mind back. He could not recall early asparagus causing any Irishman of his acquaintance to eulogize: the first drink of the day, certainly; the first hunt of the season, possibly; but the first encounter with a vegetable, any vegetable—sad to say, quite impossible.

"A Frenchman of my acquaintance," said Fitzduane, "remarked that he had never realized how much hardship the English inflicted upon us Irish during seven hundred years of occupation until he sampled our food."

Von Graffenlaub smiled. "You are a little hard on your country. I have eaten very adequately in Ireland on occasion." There was the tiniest speck of hollandaise on his tie. Fitzduane felt it compensated for the rose.

After lunch Fitzduane declined the offer of cognac but accepted a Havana cigar in perfect condition.

"Mr. Fitzduane," said von Graffenlaub, "I confess to have been greatly upset by your proposal and even more shocked by the photograph of Rudi. It has taken me a little time to decide exactly what to do."

"I'm sorry," said Fitzduane. "My purpose was to convince, not to hurt. I could think of no other way that would have the same impact."

Von Graffenlaub's glance was hard. "You took a risk," he said, "but now I think your motives are sincere. I have found out a great deal about you over the past couple of days."

"And what have you decided?"

"Mr. Fitzduane," said von Graffenlaub, "if I had decided against your proposal, I assure you we would not be lunching here today. In fact, as you will already have surmised, it is my intention to help you in every practicable way to ascertain the full circumstances of Rudi's death. I have only one important condition."

"Which is?"

"That you are utterly frank with me," said von Graffenlaub. "You may well uncover matters I shall find unpalatable. Nonetheless, I want to know. I must know. Do you agree?"

Fitzduane nodded. He had a feeling of foreboding as he did so. "Frankness is a two-way road," he said. "I will have to ask questions you will not wish to answer. My inquiries may cover matters you do not consider relevant. But let me put it quite simply: If you are straight with me, I'll tell you what I find out."

"I understand what must be done," said von Graffenlaub. "However unpleasant all this may turn out to be, it will be better than doing nothing. It was destroying me. Somehow I felt responsible, but I didn't know why, or to what extent, or what I could do about it. Then you arrived, and now there is the beginning of an answer."

Von Graffenlaub seemed to relax slightly after he finished speaking, as if only at that moment had he truly made up his mind. The certain distance, indeed tension, that had been present in his manner throughout their meeting so far seemed to wane. He held out his hand to Fitzduane. "Do your best," he said.

The Irishman shook it. "I think I'll have that cognac now," he said.

A brief gesture by von Graffenlaub, a few words spoken, and two cognacs appeared in front of them. They drank a silent toast. Fitzduane drained his, although he could not shake the ominous feeling that gripped him.

Von Graffenlaub paid, then turned to Fitzduane. "How would you like a short walk? I have made some arrangements that may be helpful."

* * *

THE DAY, once again, was warm. Fitzduane decided he would have to do some shopping fairly soon. He had packed for snow, ice, wind, and rain. He hadn't expected shirtsleeve weather so early in the year.

They left the Theaterplatz, passed the Casino on their left, and walked across the elegant arches of the Kirchenfeld Bridge. They passed the Kunsthalle and the Alpine and Post Museum. They walked briskly; the lawyer was in good condition.

Just near the junction of Helvetiastrasse and Kirchenfeldstrasse, von Graffenlaub turned into a narrow cul-de-sac. Trees shaded the entrance. It would have been easy to miss from the main road. Nameplates and speakerphones on each entrance they passed denoted apartments. At the fourth entrance von Graffenlaub stopped and punched a number into the keyboard of an electronic lock.

The heavy glass door, discreetly barred with ornate wrought steel, clicked open. Von Graffenlaub ignored the elevator and led Fitzduane up two short flights of stairs. The stairs and second-floor entranceway were carpeted. Von Graffenlaub unlocked a second door, this time with a key. They entered a narrow but well-appointed hallway. Von Graffenlaub shut the door behind them. It closed with a sound that suggested more than wood in its construction.

Fitzduane found himself grabbed. With some slight difficulty he disentangled himself from a huge potted plant whose greenery was modeled on the tentacles of an octopus with thorns added. He was becoming quite annoyed with this Swiss obsession for growing rain forest undergrowth inside the home.

Von Graffenlaub showed him around the apartment with the detached professionalism of a real estate agent. Nonetheless, small actions and an ease of movement suggested he was very much at home.

The place was comfortable to the point of being luxurious, but the furnishings and decor were, for the most part, almost deliberately unostentatious. The one exception was the master bedroom, which featured a thick white carpet, a king-size bed with black silk sheets, and a mirror set into the ceiling over the bed.

"Homey," said Fitzduane.

What must originally have been the dining room had been turned into a lavishly equipped study. Laden bookshelves filled one wall. Another wall was equipped for visual aids. There was a pull-down screen, a recessed television monitor, and a hessian-covered bulletin board on which maps and other papers could be retained by magnets. Maps of Bern and Switzerland were already in place. The furniture was modern and quietly expensive in its solidity and degree of finish. A conference table made a T shape with the desk. The stainless steel and black padded leather chairs were of ergonomic design; they swiveled and tilted and were adjustable for height and lumbar support.

Full-height folding cabinet doors were pulled back to reveal a wall of state-of-the-art business communications equipment: there were several more television monitors, one of them for Reuters Financial Services; there was a telex, a high-speed facsimile transfer, a powerful radio transceiver, dictating equipment, and a photocopier. A computer terminal sat docile on a mobile cart.

"Phones?" asked Fitzduane; there had to be something missing. He was reminded of a cartoon in *The New Yorker*: "Even in a think tank, Glebov, nobody likes a smart alec."

Von Graffenlaub pressed a button on the underside of the desk. A recessed panel slid back, and with a whir of electric motors, a telephone console, complete with a plethora of ancillary equipment, slid into view. He pointed at one of the electronic boxes. "It's fitted with a tape recorder," he said.

"Naturally," said Fitzduane politely.

They moved on to the kitchen. Cabinets, double-door refrigerator, and deep freeze groaned with food. In one walk-in pantry, bottles of red wine presented their bottoms in rack upon rack. This being Switzerland, the bottles had been dusted. "The white wine is in the cellar," said von Graffenlaub, "which is also a nuclear shelter."

Fitzduane almost started to laugh. He had been checking the labels on the red wine. Most of it was château-bottled and vintage. "A nuclear shelter—there's no answer to that."

"No, really," said von Graffenlaub. "Almost all houses in Switzerland have nuclear shelters—or easy access to one. This has been a building regulation for many years."

The tour continued. The bathroom looked hygienic enough to stand in for an operating theater. Obviously a full scrub and mask and gown were required before one used the bidet. The toilet was fitted with an electronic flush mechanism. Fitzduane checked the toilet paper—soft and fluffy. Not a trick missed.

The living room was bright and airy. Double-glazed sliding doors

led onto a veranda. A long L-shaped sofa of modern design dominated the floor. It was covered in the softest leather Fitzduane had
ever felt on furniture. He sat down on the long arm and stretched out
his legs in front of him. The leather felt sensuous against his body,
warm to his hands.

Von Graffenlaub sat across from him in an arrangement of straps,
pulleys, leather, and steel that only remotely resembled a chair but
that the lawyer seemed to find comfortable. He placed a briefcase,
which had been resting out of sight on the floor, on his knees, then
spun its two combination locks. The latches sprang open with the
well-machined sound of precision engineering.

"This is a special case," he said. "You have to wait thirty seconds
after the latches are released before opening it—or all kinds of things
happen. Tear gas, dye, a siren, spring-loaded extension arms shoot
out. All quite nasty."

"Whose apartment is this?" asked Fitzduane.

"Yours."

Fitzduane raised an eyebrow. "No shit."

Von Graffenlaub laughed. It was a deep, rich sound, infectious in
its appeal. He may have been portrayed as ruthless capitalist by
Vreni, but Fitzduane was beginning to like the man—which was not
the same as trusting him.

ERIKA VON GRAFFENLAUB DREW up her knees and spread them. Her
hands clutched at the sweat-dampened sheet. She waited, eyes for the
moment closed, as his mouth and tongue came nearer the focus of her
pleasure. She could feel the warmth of his breath first, then the
faintest soft touch of his tongue on her clitoris. She waited, trying to
lie absolutely motionless as slowly, ever so slowly, the gentle caressing continued. Her breathing increased in tempo, but as the minutes
passed she managed to remain almost without moving, occasional
tremors the only other outward sign of the passion soaring within
her.

It was a game he had taught her. He liked to tease, to delay, to
titillate, until sheer physical desire was so strong it could no longer be
resisted but for an infinitely precious time was overwhelming, was all
dominant, was the very stuff of life itself.

The pressure of his tongue was increasing slightly. Now he was
into that rhythm that only he—and she—seemed to know. He

cupped her breasts with his hands, the tips of his fingers caressing her protruding nipples. Suddenly she could lie still no more. Her body arched and shook, and her thighs clamped his head to her. Her body vibrated, and her hands kneaded his arms and shoulders and then dug into the back of his neck, drawing him ever closer.

"Now!" she cried. "Hurt me now!" His fingers tightened on her breasts and nipples, and there was pain, stark agony contrasting with the waves of pleasure that coursed through every atom of her body, that excited every nerve ending, every essence. She screamed as she came, but in absolute ecstasy, and she screamed again as he abandoned his subjugation between her loins and entered her with brutal force.

Later, when it was over, she sat cross-legged on the bed and stared at her image in the tinted mirror. She held her breasts in her hands and then felt them gently. They were bruised and sore, but in the afterglow of sex the feeling was almost a pleasure.

"I have been thinking about the Irishman," she said.

"Don't worry," said the man with the golden hair. "Everything is under control."

"No," she said. "Everything never is. It doesn't work that way."

"Are you concerned?" he asked. He was standing in front of her. She thought he looked beautiful, awesome, dangerous. She reached out and cupped his male organs in her hands. His testicles felt heavy. His penis was already beginning to grow tumescent again. She touched its tip with her tongue.

"No," she said, "but he's an attractive man. I'd like to fuck him before he dies."

The man with the golden hair smiled. "Dear little Erika," he said, "such a creature of love."

She drew him into her mouth.

"I OWN this apartment," said von Graffenlaub. "It seems to me that your inquiries could well take some time, probably weeks, perhaps longer. You will need a place where you can talk to people in confidence, where you can plan and organize, where there is privacy. I am offering you this place for as long as is necessary. I think you will be more comfortable here than in your hotel, and you will have a better working base. I should add that there is a car in the garage that you may use. It is a small BMW. Do you accept?"

Fitzduane nodded. It was a qualified nod, but he didn't want to interrupt the lawyer for the moment. He sensed there was more.

"Good," said von Graffenlaub. "When I become involved with something, I like it to be done well." He smiled. "The Swiss passion for efficiency, it's bred into us." He tapped the briefcase. "In here I have assembled as much information as I could think of that may be useful to you. There are photographs, school and medical reports, the names and addresses of friends, contacts in the various police forces, letters of introduction, and money."

"Money isn't necessary," said Fitzduane.

"I know," said von Graffenlaub. "I gather from the reports I have received that you earn a most respectable income from your profession and in addition have other resources. My agents were unable to determine either the extent or the nature of this other capital. They were surprised at this, as was I. My contacts are normally successful in these matters." There was an unspoken question in his remarks.

Fitzduane grinned. "The Swiss are not the only people with a basic distrust of central government and a preference for confidentiality. But let me repeat, I do not need your money—though I do appreciate your offer."

Von Graffenlaub flushed slightly. They were not talking about money. The real issue was control. He realized that the Irishman had no intention of allowing himself to be manipulated in any way. He would be agreeable, cooperative even, but he would remain his own man. It was not a situation the lawyer was used to. Fitzduane's gaze was steady. There was steel in those green-gray eyes. Damn the man. Reluctantly von Graffenlaub nodded.

"I accept your offer of the apartment," said Fitzduane. "I find it hard to resist a good wine cellar." His tone was mollifying and friendly. "Tell me," he added, almost as an afterthought, "is the phone tapped and the place bugged?"

Fitzduane's tone and manner had lulled the lawyer. Von Graffenlaub was disconcerted and visibly embarrassed. Momentarily he was speechless.

"Yes," he said finally.

"Specially for me?" said Fitzduane, "or are bugs part of the decor—sort of companions to the house plants?"

"They were installed to record you. I gave the order before my investigations into your background were completed. I did not know with whom I was dealing."

"People in the electronics business call it a learning curve," said Fitzduane. "Tell me, who normally uses this place?"

"I have had this apartment for many years. I use it from time to time when I want to be alone, or to work on something particularly confidential."

"I see," said Fitzduane, "sort of an adult tree house."

"The recording devices will be removed immediately," said von Graffenlaub. He went to the liquor cabinet and poured two glasses of whiskey. He gave one to Fitzduane. Fitzduane tasted it. It was Irish, a twelve-year-old Jameson.

He thought he might shoot the potted plant in the hall.

Chapter Fourteen

Fitzduane had decided he would take a break from female von Graffenlaubs for a while. Vreni would answer the phone but then not speak except to say things like "Take care, Irishman," which he did not find either helpful or reassuring; Marta, the eldest, was away in Lenk for a fortnight's skiing; and Erika, on the basis of precedent, was going to give him an erection just as she did poor young Andreas. He didn't mind having the erection; it was what it might lead to that posed the problem. And that brought him back to Andreas.

Andreas wasn't straightforward either. Lieutenant Andreas von Graffenlaub was on active duty in the army camp at Sand, training a new batch of recruits. He could not leave his duties, but if Fitzduane didn't mind coming over, they could talk between maneuvers. A few minutes and a phone call from Beat von Graffenlaub later, and it had all been arranged. If Fitzduane could present himself at the General Guisan Kaserne at the ungodly hour of 0700 precisely, the army would provide transportation to Sand. He could get to the Kaserne on the number 9 tram.

IT TOOK them well over an hour to locate Andreas. After checking a series of combat groups waging their own little wars, they found him standing on top of an overgrown concrete bunker awaiting an attack by his platoon. He wore the forage dress cap of an officer with his camouflage fatigues, and there was a heavy service automatic in a holster at his waist. Hands on hips, his bearing confident to the point of cockiness, he looked down at Fitzduane.

"So, Herr Fitzduane," he said, "how do you like Swiss Army life?" He smiled politely and held out his hand to help Fitzduane up. The corporal saluted and receded into the trees.

"These are all new recruits," said Andreas, indicating the forest surrounding them. Not a figure was to be seen, although there were occasional noises as recruits, laden down with automatic rifles and blank-firing rocket launchers, crawled into firing position. "Only a few weeks ago they were university students or wine makers or mechanics or waiters. Now they are beginning to be soldiers, but there is still a long way to go. Don't judge the Swiss Army by what you see here today." Andreas smiled again. He had great charm and none of the tension and insecurity of Vreni.

Privately Fitzduane was impressed by what he was seeing at Sand. He knew from his own experience just how difficult it was to turn civilians into soldiers. In this case there was an air of seasoned professionalism about most of the officer corps he had run into so far, and the training programs seemed to be comprehensive and imaginative. Still, recruits in their earlier stages were seldom a pretty sight. Andreas winced when a dead branch broke nearby with a loud crack followed by a highly audible expletive.

"I'm sorry about your brother," said Fitzduane. He found a seat on the trunk of a fallen tree. Andreas remained standing, his eyes scanning the surrounding forest, notebook now ready to record the performance of his men.

"You ask the questions," said Andreas, "and I'll tell you what I can."

IN CONTRAST WITH Vreni, who knew more but would not tell, Andreas, having already heard about Fitzduane's involvement from his father, was helpful and forthcoming. Unfortunately he did not appear to know much, or if he did, Fitzduane was not asking the right questions. The Irishman was tempted to be discouraged, but then odd facts and details began to emerge as Andreas relaxed and devoted at least part of his mind to Fitzduane's mission.

Andreas looked at the symbol of the "A" circled with flowers. "The inner symbol I know of course," he said. "In a plain circle you see it in every city of this country. It's the badge of the protest movement, of the youth movement, of the small minority of idiots who don't know when they are well off." He looked at the photocopy in Fitzduane's hands. "What are the flowers?" he asked. "This is from a tattoo?"

Fitzduane nodded. "That photocopy is a blowup."

"The detail is not bad for such a small mark as you have indicated," said Andreas. "It is drawn well by a skilled hand. The flowers look like geraniums, but it is hard to be sure." He looked up at Fitzduane. "*Les Fleurs du Mal*," he said, "*The Flowers of Evil*. You know Baudelaire?"

"In translation for the most part," said Fitzduane. "Let me see if I remember any." He paused and then recited:

Folly and error, sin and avarice
Work on our bodies, occupy our thoughts,
And we ourselves sustain our sweet regrets
As mendicants nourish their worms and lice.

Andreas laughed. "Very good," he said, "but it sounds better in French."

"Why did you mention *The Flowers of Evil*?" said Fitzduane. "Does the symbol remind you of some organization of that name?"

"Nothing so precise," said Andreas. "It was merely an association of ideas, and I happen to like Baudelaire. The name seems apt considering what you have told me."

"Exceedingly apt," said Fitzduane. "Tell me, can you remember where you first ran across Baudelaire? Somehow, knowing the kind of stuff he wrote, I doubt that it was at primary school."

Andreas laughed but nonetheless looked mildly uncomfortable. Fitzduane could see that he was blushing. "My stepmother," he said, "Erika."

Andreas had no further chance to speak. The woods around them echoed to massed automatic-rifle fire, various objects cascaded through the air and landed on top of the bunker, and numerous camouflaged figures erupted into the clearing and assailed the position. It occurred to Fitzduane that he had almost certainly been killed, as had Andreas.

THE SECTION LEADERS FORMED a semicircle around Andreas, and in clear, measured tones he told them what they had done right and what they had done wrong. There were questions from two of the corporals. Andreas answered in the same measured manner. Salutes were exchanged, and the platoon formed up in two long files. Laden with their weapons and equipment, the men headed back to the camp and lunch. Andreas and Fitzduane walked behind and talked.

"Do you have any recollection of an incident in Lenk?" asked Fitzduane. "Something involving Vreni and, I suspect, Rudi?"

"Vreni told you about this?"

"Yes. She told me that there had been an incident, but she wouldn't say what. She seemed highly disturbed about whatever it was, and she mentioned a man named Oskar Schupbach, but it was not clear in what connection except that he was a great family friend. I think whatever it was may be important."

They walked along in silence for a few paces. The track led through pinewoods, the trees being mature and well separated. The air smelled good. The recruits were looking forward to lunch, and there were bursts of laughter. A Jeep roared down the center of the track between the two files.

"I don't know a lot about what happened in Lenk," said Andreas. "It was a sexual experience of some sort, I believe. I don't know the details. Rudi, Vreni, and Erika went up to the chalet as usual for a few weeks of skiing. I was busy studying, so I didn't go. Father was supposed to join them on the weekends, but he had to go away for several weeks on business."

"So they were there on their own?"

"I suppose," said Andreas. "I just don't know. I heard very little of what happened. All I can recall is that both Rudi and Vreni were tense and strained when they came back and somehow changed. They were more secretive and retreated increasingly into their own little world. I asked Erika if anything had happened, and she just laughed. She said it snowed too much, and she was sick of reading novels, playing cards, and being cooped up inside."

"And that was all?"

"No," said Andreas. "Rudi came into my room a few days later. He said he wanted to ask me something. He beat around the bush for quite a while, and then he started asking me about homosexuality. He asked me had I ever had a homosexual experience and did having one mean he wouldn't still want to sleep with girls. I wasn't much help to him, I fear. He wouldn't say why he was asking, and he seemed confused; he was a little high anyway."

"On what?" said Fitzduane.

"Oh, grass or something like that," said Andreas. "It was hard to know with Rudi. He liked to mix it around."

"And what had Vreni to do with all this? I got the strongest impression that she, too, was involved in whatever it was."

"You may be right," said Andreas. "She would certainly know. Those two were as thick as thieves, but she didn't say anything. I'll tell you, though, there are a couple of people in Lenk you could talk to. You know about Oskar anyway."

"Yes."

"Okay," said Andreas. "Well, there's him, and there is also a close friend of the twins who lives there. He's about their age. He's an apprentice cheesemaker, a guy called Felix Krane, a nice fellow, I've always thought."

"Is he gay?"

"Yes, he is," said Andreas, "but I don't know; somehow it doesn't seem to fit. If it was Felix, I don't see why all the fuss."

"A first sexual anything can be pretty disorienting, and it can certainly change relationships."

"Yes, it can," said Andreas. He was blushing again, or it may have been the flush of exertion from the long walk. They entered the camp. They had noodles, meat sauce, and beets for lunch in the officers' mess. They didn't have to eat out of mess tins, but the taste was the same; somehow with army food it always was.

THE BEAR PUT down his wineglass with a sigh of satisfaction. Three deciliters of wine had vanished effortlessly. Fitzduane was impressed by the idea of actually knowing how much a wineglass held. The Swiss glasses came in different sizes and were marked accordingly. In Ireland, in the spirit of the national obsession for gambling, a wine-glass could be almost any size. A few glasses of wine could make you pleasantly mellow, decidedly the worse for wear, or have you punching the barman in thirst and frustration.

"I'm not being followed anymore," said Fitzduane, "or at least I don't think so."

"Perhaps you were mistaken. Perhaps you were never being followed and it was a case of imagination."

"Perhaps." Fitzduane reached into a breast pocket of his blouson jacket and removed a photograph. He handed it to the Bear.

The Bear pursed his lips; his mustache twitched. It looked as if he were thinking. "What do you make of it?" asked Fitzduane.

The Bear was still studying the photograph. "A nice sharp photo of a motorcycle taking a corner somewhere up in the mountains." He looked up at Fitzduane. "And you want me to check the registration."

Fitzduane nodded. "It might be interesting."

A buxom waitress in a low-cut traditional blouse with white sleeves brought them fresh wine. There was a rising buzz of conversation around them as the cellar filled up. They were seated with their backs to the wall at a corner table, an arrangement that made for privacy yet allowed the entrance and most of the other tables to be surveyed. The choice had apparently been made without conscious thought. Fitzduane had been quietly amused. You get into habits, he supposed, if you spend a great deal of time watching people.

"A few centuries ago there used to be a couple of hundred places like this in Bern selling wine," said the Bear. "Many of the aristocracy had vineyards on their country estates, and the wine business was the one trade that was considered socially acceptable for the higher echelons, apart, of course, from the business of army and government. Then fashions changed, the nobility lost power, and people drank instead at inns and in cafés. There are still plenty of cellars left, but those that are used commercially are boutiques and restaurants and places like that. I think it's a pity. A wine cellar like this has great atmosphere: arched ceilings, scrubbed wooden tables, age-darkened paneling, wine barrels, a drinking song or two, and a good-looking widow in charge of it all."

"Why a widow?"

"Don't really know," said the Bear. "It's just a tradition now that the Klotzikeller is run by a widow." He looked across at Fitzduane. "My chief called me in."

"*Ja und?*" said Fitzduane. "It's about all the German I know."

"Just as well with an accent like that. Beat von Graffenlaub was in touch with him. They are old friends, or at least they know each other of old. They met in the army, and now they play golf and sit on some Bürgergemeinde committee together."

"Where would the establishment be without golf?" said Fitzduane. "Sir Francis Drake played bowls, the Egyptians built pyramids, and in Afghanistan, I hear, they play a sort of polo with a goat's head. I suppose those activities serve the same purpose."

"You're going to like this," said the Bear. "I've been ordered to give you official help, access to information and records, that sort of thing."

"Very nice," said Fitzduane. "Because of von Graffenlaub, you think?"

"Not just von Graffenlaub. There has also been a fair bit of toing and froing between the Chief and your friend Kilmara. They have decided to put their heads together over the small matter of the tattoo that keeps cropping up—what did you call it?"

"The Flowers of Evil."

"So, the Flowers of Evil symbol being found on various dead bodies in both countries," continued the Bear, "not to mention some other developments."

"Out with it," said Fitzduane.

"We put out a flier through Interpol—normal procedure—as did the authorities in Ireland. All European countries and the U.S. were notified. No reaction at first. It's always more difficult when something is visual. Most police records are geared toward names, addresses, fingerprints, things like that. A nameless symbol is hard to index and classify in a way that all parties will understand."

"But?"

"We had some luck. In some far-distant archive a penny dropped."

"This has all the makings of a shaggy dog story," said Fitzduane.

"A body bearing the tattoo was found in a burned-out car near San Francisco about eighteen months ago," said the Bear after a momentary pause. He wasn't at all sure how shaggy dogs had entered the picture. "The intention, it would appear, had been to completely destroy both car and body in the fire."

"So what went wrong?"

"Overkill," said the Bear. "In addition to the gasoline in the tank, there was C-4 plastic explosive in the car. Part of an arm was thrown clear by the blast. It was badly damaged, but they could just make out part of the circle of flowers and one line of the letter "A." Our flier didn't ring a bell at first until they searched under the name of the flower. It's a small drawing, so it's hard to be sure about the species. They tried various names and came up with nothing. Then they hit the jackpot with—"

"Geranium," said Fitzduane.

The Bear stared at him. "How did you know that?"

"I'm the seventh son of a seventh son," said Fitzduane. "In Ireland we believe that gives you special powers. And I met somebody who knows flowers."

"Who?"

"Andreas."

They looked at each other. "Means nothing," said the Bear.

"Who knows?" said Fitzduane. "Why don't you finish your story? You were at the severed arm."

"Humph," said the Bear. He glared balefully at a couple making signs of wanting to share their table. The couple scurried away.

"They don't know who the arm belonged to. No identification was possible. The hand was already severely burned when the explosion took place, and the body itself was almost completely destroyed, so no fingerprints, no dental records, no distinguishing marks or features apart from the tattoo, which was partially protected under the watch, and, of course, no face."

"Sex?"

"Female. A white Caucasian, as they like to say over there."

"Age?"

"Hard to say. The best guess was twenties."

"How about the car?"

"It was a burned-out wreck by the time it was found, and the explosion had nearly returned it to its component state. Forensics was able to trace it to its owner by its engine number."

"Who was not the body," said Fitzduane.

"No," said the Bear. "The owner was a company executive described by the FBI as being clean as a whistle."

"Why was the FBI involved? As I understand it, it has a strictly limited mandate."

"Bank robbery is federal business," said the Bear. "The FBI believes the car was involved in a raid that took place in San Clemente.

Over two million dollars was stolen and six people were killed. One of those shot was a guard. Before being cut down, he shot and wounded one of the perpetrators. The FBI says that the body had been shot not only by the guard but also with the same gun that killed the guard."

"So the bank robbers, finding one of their own people wounded and doubtless somewhat in the way, killed her?"

"It looks that way," said the Bear.

"How many were involved in the bank raid?"

"Including the woman who was killed, only three. But they had automatic weapons and were quite happy to use them. They killed the bank guard, as I mentioned, and five other people apparently for no good cause. Two were bank employees, and three were customers. All were unarmed and doing exactly what they were told when the attackers opened up."

"This has the smell of a terrorist attack rather than a straightforward bank raid," said Fitzduane. "Did any organization claim credit?"

"No."

"What kinds of weapons did they use?"

"A sawed-off shotgun and two Czech Skorpion machine pistols."

"Familiar hardware. I can see why your chief and Kilmara have been talking to each other. Were any of the terrorists caught?"

"The investigation got nowhere," said the Bear. "Then, about a year ago, a man was questioned in New York after using some of the stolen money. He was an oil industry executive. He'd picked up the money cashing a check in a bank in Libya. The Libyan bank confirmed the transaction but declined to say where it had received the money. It suggested that it was probably another visiting American."

"So what does the FBI think about all this?"

"It's keeping it's options open," said the Bear, "but the most popular theory is the obvious one: a Libyan-backed terrorist organization topping up its coffers with a little terror thrown in."

"I thought Libyan-backed terrorists had more than enough money."

"Nobody after money that way ever has enough," said the Bear. "And perhaps they don't regard Qaddafi as a reliable paymaster, or they want to be prepared for a rainy day."

"Or there is something special they want to finance," said Fitzduane.

Chapter Fifteen

It was dark when they left the Klotzikeller. Medieval Bern at night had an atmosphere all its own. Dimly lit alleys and side streets, shadowed arcades, the echoing of footsteps, pools of light and warmth from cafés, restaurants, and *Stuben* all conspired to create an illusion of timelessness and mystery, and sometimes, when it was late and the crowds were gone and the hostelries closed and shuttered, of menace.

They took the now-familiar route past the clock tower. Lorenzini's restaurant was off a small arcade that linked Marktgasse and Amthausgasse. The restaurant itself was on the first floor. Inside there was the clamor, vitality, and distinctive aroma of good Italian food and wine.

The Bear's eyes lit up. He was greeted like a long-lost son, a long-lost hungry son. Arms outstretched, a quick embrace, a flurry of salutations, quick bursts of colloquial Italian, and they were seated at a table, menus in hand, wine poured, in what seemed like seconds.

"Aagh!" said the Bear as he surveyed the menu and then swiveled his eyes toward the antipasti cart. "So many choices and so little time." He mused for a while, brows creased in an agony of alternatives. Finally the choice was made—a meal of restraint, one might almost say moderation: *antipasto misto all'italiana*, for starters, *paillarde di vitello con broccoli al limone*, to keep momentum up, and only half a liter of Chianti (each) before skipping dessert and going straight to coffee.

Fitzduane was mildly shocked. "Surely not a diet."

"Certainly not." A look of pain crossed the Bear's face. "It is just that too much food can dull the mind and we have some serious thinking to do. Now what was I talking about?"

"Terrorism and Switzerland," said Fitzduane, "and some ideas of your own on the subject."

"Ah, yes. My point is that here in Switzerland we don't have a terrorist problem as such, or at least not in the sense that we suffer to any significant extent from terrorist attacks. Oh, we have the odd incidents, to be sure, but they are few and far between."

"So if I understand you right," said Fitzduane, "you are suggesting that not only is there very little terrorist activity in Switzerland, but even such few incidents as have occurred were either accidental or directed at someone or something outside the country."

The Bear nodded. "I'm not suggesting for a moment that these few incidents are the limit of terrorist activity here. That would be naive and ridiculous. No, what I am saying is that Switzerland has much the same role in terrorism as it has in business and world affairs, except that in this case it's involuntary and mainly initiated by foreigners. I'm referring to our role as banker, head office, communications point, middleman, and haven. As far as those roles are concerned, I personally believe that there is considerable terrorist activity here. Perhaps we should spend less time on shooting practice and more on detective work because if we don't, sooner or later some terrorist will find he doesn't like commuting and then the blood will start to flow here."

"And what about the youth movement?"

"Any disillusioned kid can be manipulated," said the Bear. "I've seen it often enough on the drug squad. But to suggest that the youth movement is an embryonic terrorist grouping is going too far. Most of the kids who demonstrate on the streets go back home to Mommy and Daddy afterward and have hot Ovalmaltine in the bosom of the family before they go to bed."

Fitzduane laughed, and the Bear's resolve weakened. He ordered the *piattino di formaggio italiano*; the Gorgonzola, Taleggio, Fontina, and Bel Paese surrendered gracefully.

"I'll tell you something else," said the Bear. "I think most people have the wrong idea about terrorists. They think of terrorists as being a bunch of fanatics motivated by idealism. In other words, however reprehensible their methods, their eventual goals are pure and noble, at least if seen from their point of view. That may be true for some, but for many I think the objective is simpler and more basic: money."

"So you are saying that many so-called terrorist incidents are actually crimes committed solely for personal gain?"

" 'Solely' might be going too far," said the Bear. "Let me just say that I believe decidedly mixed emotions may be involved. I mean, do you have any idea of the sheer scale of money a terrorist can make? It's one of the fastest tax-free ways going to make a million dollars."

"And one of the most dangerous," said Fitzduane.

"I'm not so sure," said the Bear. "If you examine a list of incidents in which money was involved—money for the cause—" he added sardonically, "you'll be surprised how often the terrorist gets away with it, and you'll be surprised by the scale. After the OPEC hijack of Yamani and the other oil ministers," said the Bear, "Carlos received a personal bonus of two million dollars from Qaddafi. And that was a bonus on top of his other takings. Another small Arab group supported by Qaddafi receives five million dollars a year, but that pales in comparison with the sums raised by terrorists from kidnapping.

"Few details are available because secrecy is often part of the agreement between kidnappers and victim, but consider the activities of just one group, the ERP, the People's Revolutionary Army of Argentina. They got a million dollars for kidnapping a Fiat executive; they got two million for Charles Lockwood, an Englishman who worked for Acrow Steel; they got three million for John R. Thompson, the American president of the local subsidiary of Firestone Tires; they were paid over fourteen million for Victor Samuelson, an Exxon executive. But get this: In 1975, the Montoneros, another Argentinean group, demanded and received sixty million dollars in cash and another million plus in food and clothing for the poor in exchange for the two sons of Jorge Born, chairman of the Bunge y Born group."

"Sixty million dollars!" exclaimed Fitzduane.

"Sixty," said the Bear. "Hard to credit, isn't it? And I'm quoting only from the cases we know about. God knows how many hundreds of millions are paid each year by companies and the rich in secret. Either as ransom or else to avoid being kidnapped—in other words, protection.

"Terrorism is a business. The publicized hijackings, bombings, and killings create the required climate of fear. They form the terrorist promotional budget, if you will, and then the serious business of extracting huge sums of money goes on steadily behind the scenes. The iceberg parallel comes to mind again—one-tenth exposed, nine-tenths hidden. Terrorism is one-tenth composed of highly publicized outrages with an accompanying nine-tenths of secret extortion and terror, and a profit orientation in most cases that would put Wall Street to shame."

"You know," said Fitzduane, "the figures on terrorism in Northern Ireland make the point that Switzerland hasn't a terrorist problem worthy of the name—at least in terms of violence. Over the last decade here you seem to have had only a handful of incidents of any significance; during the same period in Northern Ireland well over two thousand people have been killed, tens of thousands have been injured, and damage to property has cost hundreds of millions."

"That isn't terrorism in the Continental sense," said the Bear. "It's a war."

BERN WAS nearly asleep. Cafés and restaurants were closed and shuttered. Windows were dark. The streets were empty. Only an occasional car disturbed the quiet.

Fitzduane leaned against the railings of the Kirchenfeld Bridge and smoked the last of his Havana. He knew he should dictate a few notes on the evening's developments, but he felt mellow from several hours' drinking with the Bear, and the miniature tape recorder remained in his pocket.

The night air was pleasantly cool. Below him the black waters of the Aare flowed invisibly except for the reflection of a car's headlights as it drove along Aarstrasse and then vanished past the Marzili. Another late reveler returning home, or perhaps a journalist retiring after putting the newspaper to bed, Fitzduane speculated idly.

To his right he could see the impressive mass of the Bellevue Hotel, with its magnificent view of the mountains during the day from both its windows and its terraces. The Bear had told him that during the Second World War the Bellevue had been the headquarters of German intelligence activities in neutral Switzerland; the Allies had been in the less grandiose but friendlier Schweizerhof only a few blocks away.

The lights were still on in several of the Bellevue's bedrooms. As he watched, the rooms went dark one by one. Fitzduane was much taken by the Kirchenfeldbrücke, though he didn't quite know why. It wasn't the highest bridge in Bern, and it certainly wasn't the oldest. It had none of the drama of the Golden Gate in San Francisco or the storybook appeal of Tower Bridge in London. But it had a quality all its own, and it was a good place to think.

The Bear had offered him a ride back to the apartment, but Fitzduane had declined, preferring to walk. He enjoyed the feeling of the city asleep, of the sense of space when the streets were empty, of the freedom of the spirit when there were no other people around to distract. The Havana was coming to an end. He consigned the remains to a watery grave. He turned from the railings and began walking along the bridge toward home. He heard laughter and a faint, familiar hissing sound. He looked back. Two lovers, arm in arm on roller skates, were gliding in perfect time along the pavement toward him. They were moving deceptively fast, scarves trailing behind, body movements blurred by loose-fitting garments. As they passed under a streetlamp, they looked at each other for a second and laughed again. Fitzduane stepped back to let them pass. For a moment he thought of Etan and felt alone.

The force of the blow to Fitzduane's chest was savage, reinforced by the momentum of the skater. The knife fell from his assailant's grasp and clattered to the ground several meters away. The assailant turned neatly on his skates, then glided forward to retrieve his weapon. He tossed it from hand to hand. Light glittered from the blade. The woman stood some distance behind the assailant, watching, but this was to be his kill; the fatal blow was already struck.

Fitzduane felt numbness and pain. The railings were at his back, the river below. The tripod case containing the shotgun had been torn off his shoulder; it lay to one side, tantalizingly close. He knew he would not have time to reach it before the man with the knife attacked again. His eyes watched the blade. With his right hand he felt his chest for blood. He found there wasn't any. He was surprised he could still stand.

The blade was still for a moment in the assailant's hand—and then it thrust forward in a blur of steel, the coup de grâce, a deft display of knife craft. Adrenaline pumped through Fitzduane's body. With a sudden effort he moved to one side, parrying the knife with his left arm. He felt a burning sensation and the warmth of blood. He thrust his right hand, fingers stiffened, into his attacker's throat. There was a choking sound, and the man fell back. He clutched at his throat with his left hand, making gasping sounds. His knife, held in the palm of his right hand, fended off a further attack.

Fitzduane saw the girl beginning to move and knew he would have to finish it quickly. He slumped against the railings as if that last effort had finished him. The man moved forward this time in a slashing attack and made a sudden rush. Fitzduane pivoted and, using the attacker's momentum, flung him over the railings. There was a short, terrified scream and a dull thud.

The girl now had a knife in her hand. Fitzduane moved fast. He threw himself in a combat roll toward the tripod case and came up with the shotgun. He pumped a round into the chamber. Blood was dripping from his arm, and he felt sick. The girl stared at him, her knife held out, weaving slightly. Slowly she backed away; then suddenly she turned and sped away into the darkness. He could hear the hissing of her skates, and she was gone.

He looked over the railings, but he could see nothing. His rib cage felt sore and bruised against the hard metal. He stood upright and examined where the knife had struck him initially. The blade had not penetrated. The blow had been absorbed by his miniature Olympus tape recorder. Small pieces of the machine fell from the rent in his jacket onto the pavement and were joined by drops of blood from his gashed arm.

IN HIS DREAM the Bear was happy. He and Tilly had gone to the little castle at Spiez to pick up some wine. There were those who said that Spiez wine was far too dry and was made out of dissolved flints, but the Bear did not agree. Anyway, they always enjoyed the whole business of actually getting the wine, the drive out by the Thunersee, lunch at a lakeside restaurant, and then going down into the cellar and joining the line to watch one's own wine bottles being filled. He wondered why the telephone was ringing so loudly in the wine cellar. Nobody else seemed to notice. He looked at Tilly and she smiled at him, and then she was gone. He felt lost.

He lifted the telephone receiver. "Sergeant Raufman," said the voice. It sounded excited.

"Yes," said the Bear, "and it's two o'clock in the fucking morning in case you're interested."

"I'm sorry to disturb you, Sergeant Raufman," said the voice, "but it is important. I am the night duty manager at the Hotel Bellevue."

"Good for you," said the Bear. "I like to sleep at night; some of us do."

"Let me explain," said the voice. "A man has come into the hotel. He is bleeding from one arm onto our carpets, and he has a gun. What should we do?"

"Haven't a clue. Try putting a bucket under the arm. Call the police. Who the fuck knows?"

"Sergeant Raufman, this man says he knows you—"

"Wait a second," said the Bear, "who is this man?"

"He says his name is Fitz something," said the voice. "I didn't want to ask him again. He looks"—there was a pause—"dangerous." There was wistfulness in the voice.

"What's your name?"

"Rolf," said the voice, "Rolfi Müller."

"Well, listen, Rolfi. I'll be over in ten minutes. Bandage his arm, get him what he wants, don't call anyone else, and don't make a pass at him, *capisce?*"

"Yes, Sergeant," said Rolfi. "Isn't it exciting?"

There was no reply from the Bear. He was already pulling his trousers over his pajama bottoms. Somehow he wasn't entirely surprised at the news.

AN HOUR LATER the Bear was letting the doctor out of Fitzduane's apartment when the phone rang. He closed and locked the door and slipped two heavy security bolts in place; then he took the call in the study. Fitzduane lay back against the pillows of the king-size bed and let the lassitude of reaction take over.

The Bear came in. He stood with his hands in his pockets and looked down at Fitzduane. The collar of his pajama top protruded above his jacket. The stubble on his cheeks made him look shaggier than ever.

"The doctor thinks you'll live," said the Bear. "The cut on your arm was bloody but not deep. On your chest you'll just have a good-size bruise, and I guess you'll need a new tape recorder."

"I'm beginning to float," said Fitzduane. "Whatever that doctor gave me, it works."

"They found him," said the Bear. "Or what we assume is him. He just missed the river. There's the body of a young male who answers your description. He's at the edge of the sports ground under the bridge."

"Dead?"

"Oh, yes, very much so. I'm afraid this is really going to complicate things."

"It was self-defense," protested Fitzduane. "He seemed keen on one of us leaving the bridge, and it was bloody close as it was."

The Bear gave a sigh. "That's not the point," he said. "You've killed someone. There are no witnesses. There will have to be an investigation. Paperwork, statements, an inquiry by an examining magistrate, the whole thing."

Fitzduane's voice was sleepy. "Better investigated than dead."

"*You* don't have to do the paperwork," was the grumpy rejoinder. "By the way, there is a Berp outside. Technically you are under arrest."

Fitzduane did not reply. His eyes were closed, and his breathing was regular and even. The top half of his body was uncovered, and his bandaged arm lay outstretched. There were signs of severe bruising on his torso just below the rib cage. The detective reached out and covered the sleeping figure with the duvet. He switched off the light and quietly closed the bedroom door.

The Berp was making coffee in the kitchen. He gave the Bear a cup, liberally laced with von Graffenlaub's brandy. The Bear knew he would have to get some sleep soon or he'd fall down.

The uniformed policeman rocked his kitchen chair back and forth on its rear legs. He was a veteran of more than twenty years on the force, and for a time before the Bear donned plain clothes, they had shared a patrol car together.

"What's it all about, Heini?"

The Bear yawned. He could see the pale light of false dawn through the kitchen window. The apartment was warm, but he shivered with the chill of fatigue. "I think our Irishman might have a tiger by the tail."

The Berp raised an eyebrow. "That doesn't tell me a lot."

"I don't know a lot."

"Why are detectives always so secretive?"

The Bear smiled. It was true. "We live off secrets," he said. "Otherwise who'd need a detective?"

The phone rang again. There was a wall extension in the kitchen. The Berp answered it and handed it to the Bear. "Yours. The duty officer at the station."

The Bear listened. He asked a few questions, and a smile crossed his face; then he replaced the phone. "Lucky bugger."

"Do you want to expand on that?"

"There was a witness," said the Bear. "It seems one of the guests staying at the Bellevue—a visiting diplomat—saw the whole thing from his bedroom window. He says he saw the attack on Fitzduane and tried to report it, but no one on duty could understand him, so eventually he got an interpreter from his embassy and made a statement. He confirms the Irishman's story."

"I thought diplomats were good at languages."

The Bear laughed. "I think the delay had more to do with his having to get rid of the woman in his room first," he said. "That's what the word is from the night staff at the hotel."

"Somebody's wife?" said the Berp.

"No," said the Bear. "That wasn't the problem. It was one of the local hookers."

"So?"

"Our visiting diplomat is from the Vatican," said the Bear. "He's a Polish priest."

The Berp grinned. His chair was tilted as far back as it would go. "Sometimes I enjoy this job."

"You'll fall," warned the Bear. He was too late.

KILMARA READ the telex from Bern a second time. He looked out the window: gray skies, rain falling in sheets, damp, cold weather.

"I hate March in Ireland," he said, "and now I'm beginning to hate April. Where are the sunny days, blue skies, and daffodils of my youth? What have I done to April for it to behave like this?"

"It isn't personal," said Günther. "It's age. As you get older, the weather seems to get worse. Older bones cry out for sun and warmth."

"Cry out in vain in this bloody country."

There was a slight click from the video machine as it ceased rewinding. "Once more?" said Günther.

Kilmara nodded, then looked again at the high-resolution conference video screen. The video had been taken by a four-man Ranger team that had been instructed to treat the whole matter as a reconnaissance exercise.

They had parachuted onto the island at night using HALO—high-altitude, low-opening—techniques. Equipped with oxygen face masks and miniature cylinders clipped to their jump harnesses, they had jumped from an army transport at 22,000 feet. They were using black steerable rectangular ramjet parachutes but had skydived for most of the distance, reaching forward speeds of up to 150 miles per hour and navigating with the aid of night-vision goggles by comparing the terrain with the map they had studied and the video made by a Ranger reconnaissance plane the night before. Electronic altimeters clipped to the tops of their reserve parachutes flashed the diminishing height on glowing red LED meters. At 800 feet the Rangers pulled their D rings and speed-opened their parachutes.

The fully flared parachutes had the properties of true airfoils and could be turned, braked, and stalled by warping the trailing edge with the control lines. Even so, this high degree of maneuverability was scarcely enough. Reports had forecast low wind for the time of year in the area, but there was heavy gusting, and it was only with great effort and not a little luck that the team landed near the drop zone on a deserted part of the island. Making use of their night-vision equipment, the men had then hiked across the island to Draker College. They had constructed two blinds and by dawn were completely concealed, with the two entrances to the main building under observation.

For five days and nights they saw nothing unusual, but on the sixth night their strained patience was rewarded. The video had been shot using a zoom lens and a second-generation image intensifier. It had been raining heavily at the time, so detail was not good, though it was reasonable given the conditions. Nevertheless, what the observation team had photographed was startling enough.

Shortly after midnight, with one more night of long and monotonous observation to go, a single figure was seen slipping out of the side entrance of the college. The image was scarcely more than a blurred silhouette at first, since the camera lens was set at normal pending a specific target. The figure reached the cover of some gorse bushes and crouched down, blending into the surroundings. One disadvantage of the image intensifier was its inability to show colors; everything showed up in contrasting shades of greenish gray.

The camera operator began to zoom in to get a closer look with the powerful telephoto lens but then paused and pulled back slightly to cover two more figures, who left the side entrance and ran, crouched down, to cover. There was a wait of perhaps half a minute before two more figures appeared. Several minutes passed. The camera zoomed in to try to get a close-up, but the bushes were in the way, and only small glimpses of human forms through gaps in the foliage indicated that they were still there.

Kilmara imagined what it was like for the Rangers waiting in the blinds. Holes had been dug in the ground, making use of any natural features that could be turned to the diggers' advantage, such as an overhang to prevent observation from the air or a fold in the ground to hide the entrance. The top sods had been removed intact, and the undersoil dug out carefully and concealed. The holes were covered with a frame of reinforced chicken wire, which in turn was surfaced with the original sods to match the surrounding terrain. The result could be stood upon without detection and would be virtually invisible from even a few yards away.

Routine observation was kept through a miniature lens mounted at the end of a fiber-optic cable that would peer periscope style through the roof of the blind. The incoming pictures could be monitored on a pocket-size television. The technology had been adapted from that used in microsurgery.

The first figure emerged from behind the clump of bushes, followed at twenty-yard intervals by the others. In single file they headed for the wood. The picture on the screen dissolved into an out-of-focus blur for a few seconds before sharpening again into close-up. Kilmara felt the same shock that had struck him at the first viewing. The face on the screen was not human. He was looking at the body of a man and the head of some monstrous, unrecognizable animal: fur and matted hair, short, curving horns, a protruding muzzle fixed in a snarl. It was an image from a nightmare.

The camera surveyed each figure in turn. Each wore a different and equally bizarre mask. They vanished into the wood.

"Two suicides by hanging and the accidental death of the headmaster," said Günther, "and now this?"

"Well, at least we now have a pretty fair idea of what happened to Fitzduane's goat," said Kilmara, "but dressing up isn't a crime."

"So you think all is in order?"

"Do pigs fly?"

THE CAMP WAS more than two hundred kilometers south of Tripoli and had been built around a small oasis, its date palms and patch of dusty greenery now submerged in a forest of prefabricated single-story barracks, concrete blockhouses, weapons ranges, parade grounds, and assault courses.

Two four-meter-high barbed-wire fences secured the perimeter. The outer fence had been electrified, and watchtowers equipped with KPV 14.5 mm Vladimirov heavy machine guns were placed at two-hundred-meter intervals. Missile batteries augmented with mobile radar-guided four-barreled ZSU-4 antiaircraft guns guarded the approaches.

The camp could hold as many as a thousand trainee freedom fighters, and over the years since its construction many times that number of members of the PLO, the Polisario, and the myriad other violent groups supported by Colonel Muammar Qaddafi had passed through its gates.

Slightly depleted by a steady drain of fatal casualties experienced in live-ammunition training, they emerged after intensive indoctrination in guerrilla tactics and terrorist techniques, including refinements such as constructing car and letter bombs, concealing weapons and explosives aboard aircraft, getting the maximum media reaction from a terrorist incident, torture, and the handling and execution of hostages. The instructors were proficient, experienced, and impersonal. They lived apart from their trainees in luxury air-conditioned accommodations outside the camp. The languages heard around their Olympic-size swimming pool amid the clinking of glasses, the laughter, and the splashing were those of East Germany, Cuba, and Russia.

There were other such camps in Libya and indeed in South Yemen, Cuba, Syria, Lebanon, East Germany, and Russia. Camp Carlos Marighella, named after the Brazilian author of one of the most famous urban terrorism handbooks, had been chosen because it was isolated and secure, and the project had the personal support of Muammar Qaddafi.

Since he overthrew Libya's senile King Idris in 1969, Qaddafi had provided money, arms, sanctuary, and training facilities for just about every terrorist organization worthy of the name. He had provided active support for the team that carried out the Olympic Games massacre in Munich. He had provided the PLO with a yearly allowance of forty million dollars. He had offered a million dollars for the assassination of Anwar Sadat of Egypt. He had invaded Tunisia. He had fought with Egypt. He had repeatedly invaded Chad. He had fomented unrest in the Sudan. He had given financial assistance to the Nicaraguan Sandinistas, Argentina's Montoneros, Uruguay's Tupamaros, the IRA Provisionals, the Spanish Basque ETA, the French Breton and Corsican separatist movements, and Muslim insurgents in Thailand, Indonesia, Malaysia, and the Philippines. He had provided military assistance to Emperor Bokassa of the Central African Republic and Idi Amin of Uganda. He had been behind the blowing up of a Pan American plane at Rome's Fiumicino Airport, in which thirty-one passengers burned to death. He had provided the SAM-7 heat-seeking missiles with which a Palestinian team planned to shoot down an El Al jet taking off from Fiumicino. He had been an active supporter of the OPEC raid in Vienna in Christmas 1975.

The man who had selected Libya as the training ground and marshaling area for his assault group felt quite satisfied that he had made the right decision. His every need was being met. Qaddafi had even offered a bonus of ten million dollars upon successful completion of the project. At the end of their private audience he had presented the man with a personally autographed copy of his *Green Book* on the Islamic Revolution—and a check for half a million dollars toward initial expenses.

In Libya the man was known as Felix Kadar. It was a name of no particular significance; in other countries he was known by other names. In the files of the CIA and the U.S. State Department's Office to Combat Terrorism he was known only by the code name Scimitar. The man had no particular political views or commitments to any specific ideology. He had been baptized a Catholic, but on occasion he wore the green turban that signified the pilgrimage to Mecca. He had indeed gone there. He had been one of the planners of the assault on the Great Mosque and had been agreeably surprised by the inability of Saudi Arabia's own forces to dislodge the intruders. In the end, the assistance of the French government was called for: the Gigene, the highly specialized National Gendarmerie Intervention Group, came on the scene—and the raiders died, leaving the Saudi royal family much shaken and the man in the green turban one million dollars richer.

The man had long since conceived the outline of the idea. It had struck him that unrest in the world presented an unparalleled opportunity for commercial exploitation. At Harvard, studying for an M.B.A., he had written, as he had been trained to, the business plan. It featured a specific financial objective: the acquisition of a personal fortune of one hundred million dollars within fifteen years.

More than twelve years had passed, and he was still only halfway to his objective: he had averaged something over four million dollars a year, taking the rough with the smooth, so a straight-line projection put him something like forty million dollars short by the close of his allocated period, May 31, 1983. Clearly something would have to be done; a bold stroke was called for. Allowing a surplus for inflation and unforeseen expenses, he would aim to clear fifty million dollars from one major action, and then he would retire. He would be two years ahead of schedule.

Felix Kadar had another motive for wishing to achieve his financial objective ahead of time. He had made a specialty of carrying out his work through different organizations and under different identities, and he was expert in modifying his appearance and personality. Nonetheless, it seemed to him that it would be only a matter of time before one of the Western antiterrorist units started putting the pieces together. And, he admitted to himself, he had allowed his ego to get the better of him recently.

He had played games with the authorities. In the knowledge that he had never been caught or even arrested and was soon to retire, he had deliberately increased the risks of living on the edge. That must stop. Mistakes would be eliminated.

THE SEVENTY-FIVE MEN and women in the attack force were all known to him either personally or by reputation. He had compiled a list of suitable candidates over the years and had made full use of the extensive files of terrorists maintained by the KGB. He kept up the friendliest of relations with Ahmed Jibril, the Palestinian ex-captain in the Syrian Army who was one of the KGB's most active agents inside the various Palestinian movements.

He used fingerprints and other personnel data accumulated in the KGB and his own files to vet each candidate rigorously. Kadar was particularly concerned about infiltration—a specialty of the Israelis, many of whom spoke Arabic and were in appearance indistinguishable from Yemenis and North Africans. The classic ploy of the Israelis was to substitute one of their own for one of the fedayeen killed or captured in action against them. It was not so difficult to do, and hard to detect when the Palestinians were scattered among a dozen countries. Today Kadar believed he had caught such a man. He was not absolutely sure, but then he didn't have to be. Within the camp Kadar's will was absolute law; he was judge, jury, and, if it so pleased him, executioner.

The assembled terrorists were drawn up in two ranks in a semicircle facing Kadar. It was night, and the dusty parade ground was brightly lit with powerful floodlights, though Kadar himself was in shadow. To one side a shapeless figure was spread-eagled against a metal frame embedded in the hard ground.

Kadar was further concealed by an Arab headdress made of camouflage material; his mouth and nose were covered, and his eyes were hidden behind sunglasses. Though some of his people had worked with him before, none had ever seen his face or knew his real name. They knew him as a hooded figure, a voice, and a consummate planner. The implementation was almost always left to others.

"Brothers and sisters," he said, "followers of the Revolution. For years you have been fighting to destroy the Jews and to free your native land. You have fought in many glorious battles and have killed many of your enemies, but always final victory has eluded you. You have been cheated of what is your due not just by the accursed Israelis but by the support they receive from godless America and the might of Western imperialism. You have been brought to this camp to train and prepare for an action directly targeted at the soft underbelly of the decadent West. Your deeds will echo around the world, and the pain and shock of the rulers of the West will be terrible."

There were shouts and applause from the guerrillas. Several fired automatic rifles in the air in a display of enthusiasm. Kadar thought he had spent enough time on the ritual condemnation of Israel and the West. It was time to deal with more practical matters. Terrorists—at least Kadar's pragmatic kind—didn't fight on idealism alone. They liked to be paid in hard currencies.

"Fellow freedom fighters," he continued, "this is not yet the time for me to tell you the precise details of our mission. For reasons of security you will all understand, that information must be withheld until shortly before the day of action. Meanwhile, though you are all experienced and battle-hardened veterans, you will be trained to a peak of even greater combat effectiveness. As you do this, you may care to reflect not only on the glory that will be attained from this mission but on the one hundred thousand American dollars you will each receive upon its successful conclusion."

This time the applause was considerably more enthusiastic. There were further bursts of Kalashnikov fire. Kadar reflected that experienced and trained by the liberation camps though his men might be, too many of them had become lax and overemotional in their reactions. The raw material was there, but it needed to be subjected to ruthless discipline if his plan was to succeed. His orders must be followed unhesitatingly; obedience must be absolute. The only way to achieve this in the limited time available was to instill a terrible fear of the alternatives. He had dangled the carrot in front of them; now was the time for the stick. He had stage-managed the demonstration for maximum impact.

He held up his hand for silence, and the cheering ceased. He spoke again. "Brothers and sisters, we are faced with implacable enemies. Our war is unceasing. Constantly they try to destroy us. They send their warplanes against us; they raid us from the sea; they fill the airwaves with their foul propaganda; they manipulate the media to distort the truth of our cause; they send spies and sowers of discord among us."

There was a ripple of reaction from the ranks of fighters: fists were shaken; weapons were raised in the air.

"Silence!" he shouted. A hush fell over the terrorists. The group was still. They were used to savage and sometimes arbitrary discipline but also to the informality and frequently free and easy life of guerrilla units that, whatever they boasted to their womenfolk, spent little of their time in actual combat. They sensed that this mission would be different.

Kadar raised his right hand. Instantly the floodlights illuminating the parade ground were extinguished. The group was gripped by fear and an awful curiosity. Something terrible was about to happen. It would concern the figure spread-eagled on the metal frame, but what it might be nobody knew. They waited.

Kadar's voice came out of the darkness, hard, ruthless, and resonant with authority. "You are about to witness the execution of a Zionist spy who foolishly attempted to infiltrate our ranks. Watch and remember!" His voice rose to a shout and echoed around the parade ground.

A single spotlight came on and illuminated the figure stretched out on the frame. He was naked and gagged; his eyes bulged with fear. A tall man in the white coat of a doctor came out of the darkness. He had a syringe in his hand. He held it up in front of him and pushed the plunger slightly to clear the needle of air; a thin spray of liquid could be clearly seen by the onlookers. Carefully he injected the contents of the syringe, then stood back and consulted his watch.

Several minutes passed. He stepped forward and examined the naked man with a stethoscope, followed by a close inspection of his eyes with the aid of an ophthalmoscope. He left the stethoscope hanging around his neck and replaced the ophthalmoscope in the pocket of his white coat. He nodded to Kadar.

Kadar's voice rang out in the darkness: "Proceed."

The man reached into the pocket of his white coat and held an object in front of him. There was a perceptible click, and the harsh light of the single spotlight glinted off the white steel of the blade. He held the knife in front of the prisoner's eyes and moved it to and fro; the panic-stricken eyes followed it as if hypnotized. The assembled terrorists waited.

Kadar's calm voice could have been describing a surgical operation. "You may care to know the significance of the substance injected into the bloodstream of the prisoner. It is a highly specialized drug obtained from our friends in the KGB. It is called Vitazain. It has the effect of heightening the sensitivity of the body's nervous system. In one situation the gentlest caress results in intense pleasure. In a situation of pain the effect is at least as extreme. It magnifies pain to a depth of horror and suffering that is almost impossible to comprehend."

The atmosphere was electric. One figure in the rear rank began to sway but was instantly gripped by his comrades on either side. The most hardened terrorists there—used to the carnage of the battlefield—were chilled by the cold, deliberate voice.

The man in the white coat stepped forward. His knife approached the eyes of the panic-stricken man again, and its tip rested just under the eyeball for several seconds. It pulled back and flashed forward again; this time the blade severed the cloth gag that had prevented the prisoner from screaming. The man in the white coat removed the gag and dropped it to the ground. He took a flask from his pocket and held it to the man's parched lips; he drank greedily. Faint hope flickered in his eyes. The flask was removed, and the prisoner was left alone in the pool of light.

A second spotlight came on, spreading an empty circle of light about thirty meters in front of the prisoner. All eyes looked at the space. They heard a faint shuffling sound, like a man struggling with a heavy burden. A shape appeared in the pool of light and came to a halt. He turned to face the prisoner. He lifted the riflelike launcher and pointed it at the condemned man. The watchers looked from one lighted area to the other. Screams of terror, unending screams, filled the air, and the prisoner's body bent and twisted as he tried in vain to get loose.

The operator of the Russian LPO-50 manpack flamethrower readied his weapon; with the thickened fuel he was using, he could blast the flaming napalm up to seventy meters. He was carrying three cylinders of fuel—enough firepower for nine seconds of firing, far more than would be necessary. He waited for Kadar's signal.

"Kill him," said the voice.

The man with the flamethrower fired.

Chapter Sixteen

Ambassador Harrison Noble, deputy director of the U.S. State Department Office to Combat Terrorism (OCT), put down the report with a gesture of disgust.

He was a tall, thin career diplomat with more than a passing physical resemblance to the economist, author, and sometime ambassador John Kenneth Galbraith. In his late fifties, his hair now thinning and silver gray, he was a distinguished-looking man. Women still found him attractive.

Before joining the State Department in the 1950s, Noble had been a much-decorated fighter pilot in Korea with eleven confirmed kills to his credit, palpable proof to his recruiters at the time—who were still smarting from the witch-hunting of the McCarthy era—that here was one man who certainly wasn't soft on communism and, by implication, anything else un-American.

The ambassador sighed at the possible implications of the report that lay on the polished surface of his otherwise empty desk. He leaned back in his soft leather swivel chair and looked at his assistant. He could just see her knees from this angle, and very pretty they were, too. At least his was a comfortable way to fight terrorism. "An execution by flamethrower," he said. "Quite revolting. What is the source of this report?"

"The Israelis have one of the instructors in the camp on their payroll," said the assistant. "Since the Israelis told us that, and since they have little respect for our security, it probably isn't true; but at least they seem to be taking the situation seriously."

"Does nobody in this business tell the truth?"

"It's about the same as diplomacy," said the assistant dryly. She was a determinedly ambitious woman in her late thirties. She had made it clear that she had a certain interest in the deputy director, who for his part was still debating the issue. A discreet affair surely qualified as quiet diplomacy. However, he was far from sure it was possible to do anything discreetly in Washington.

He eased his chair up from full tilt, and more of her elegant legs slid into view. It was proving to be a satisfyingly sexual conversation.

"So what do you make of it?" he asked, gesturing at the TOP SECRET folder in front of him. It seemed a ridiculous way to label something that was really secret. "A hijack?"

"Unlikely. There are at least seventy being trained in that camp."

"Maybe a series of hijacks?"

"Perhaps, but it doesn't seem likely. They're being trained as an integrated team. It's more like a commando raid."

"An embassy?" He hoped not. Well over a hundred million dollars had recently been spent on improving security at U.S. diplomatic missions abroad, but he knew full well that this had merely tinkered with the problem. Few of the existing buildings had been designed with security as a top priority, and modifications were difficult to implement while at the same time the staff carried out traditional diplomatic and consular duties. There was also the problem of modern firepower: bulletproof glass in windows and reception areas and armor plate on vehicles were not enough when a pocketful of explosives, properly placed, could bring down the front of a building or transform an armored vehicle and its occupants into bloody scrap.

"It's still a large group for an embassy," she said. "The normal practice is to infiltrate small picked teams. It's just not that easy to deploy seventy armed terrorists. In fact, that's one of the most puzzling aspects of this thing: how are so many people going to be put in place without being spotted at airport checks and borders? It is not as if these seventy are all new faces; on the contrary, it's a select team. We have records on many of them."

"If I weren't a diplomat," said Noble, "I'd suggest we take them out at source—a preemptive surgical strike, Israeli style."

"Bomb Libya?" said the assistant. "No way. The President would never agree."

"Not to mention the political fallout that would result. Our European allies do so much business with Libya and the rest of the Arab world that they regard a certain toleration of terrorism as an acceptable price. And they have a point: terrorism gets publicity, but it doesn't actually kill many people or cost an impossible amount. Seen on a wider scale, it is tolerable."

"Unless you're a victim," said the assistant.

Noble glanced at the report again. "I see our source thinks this thing will probably go down in May." He smiled. "Every cloud has a silver lining. If the source is right, I won't be here. The hot seat will be all yours. I'm going away from all this hassle to visit my son at school and do a little quiet fishing." He played an imaginary fishing rod back and forth and mentally landed his fly precisely on target. He could almost feel the wind on his face and hear the faint splash of an oar and the squeak of an oarlock as the gillie adjusted the drift of the boat.

"Where are you going?"

"Ireland," he said, "the west of Ireland."

"Aren't you worried about security there?"

"Not for a moment. There is major terrorist activity in Ireland all right, but it's mostly confined to the North and strictly the Irish versus the Brits, or variations thereof. Even in the North foreigners are left alone, and the rest of Ireland is peaceful. If I may draw a parallel, being worried about the crime rate in New York is no reason not to visit this country; you just steer clear of New York."

What a pity he's going away so soon, thought the assistant; he's almost hooked. The softly-softly technique was working, but a month apart could overstrain it. Well, she still had three weeks or so to land her catch. She crossed her legs slowly and with a perceptible rustle. His eyes flicked up to hers.

Good. Now she had his full attention.

ABSENTMINDEDLY IVO CIRCLED his right wrist with the fingers of his left hand and felt for the silver bracelet Klaus had given him. He twisted the bracelet backward and forward against his wrist until the skin was red. He didn't notice the pain. He was thinking about the man he had seen with Klaus, the man who had disappeared with Klaus, the man who had probably killed him.

Over the last few days he had talked to everyone he could think of who had known Klaus in the hopes of identifying the man with the golden hair, but without success. Now he sat in the Hauptbahnhof waiting for the Monkey to return from Zurich. The Monkey had worked much the same market as Klaus, and from time to time they had sold their services together when that was what the customer wanted. The Monkey had one great talent apart from those he displayed in bed: he had a photographic memory for numbers—any sort of number. Klaus used to say he could keep a telephone book in his head. His record of the license plates of all his past clients could be a gold mine when they got older and fading looks forced them to diversify into a bit of blackmail. Ivo couldn't imagine being older.

The only trouble with dealing with the Monkey was that he wasn't just stupid; he was stupid, stubborn, and a congenital liar. If he wasn't treated just right, he might clam up even if he did know something. And if he didn't, he might pretend to, and that could be just as bad. The Monkey could well need some persuading to tell the truth, thought Ivo. He didn't like violence and wasn't very good at it, but finding Klaus's killer was a special case. He stopped rubbing the silver bracelet and put his hand in his pocket. He touched the half meter of sharpened motorcycle chain nestled there snugly in a folded chamois. He would threaten to scar the Monkey for life. The Monkey would listen to that; his looks were his stock-in-trade.

Passersby gave the grubby figure sitting cross-legged on the floor a wide berth; his clothes were ragged, he looked dirty, and he smelled. Ivo didn't mind. He didn't even notice. He thought of himself as a knight-errant, a knight in shining armor on a quest for justice. He would succeed and return to Camelot.

Sir Ivo. It sounded good.

SHE KEPT her eyes closed at first; her head throbbed and she felt nauseated. She was conscious of something wet and cool on her forehead and cheeks. It gave some slight relief, though the effect was transitory. Confused and disoriented though she was, it struck her that her position was uncomfortable. She thought she was in bed, or should be in bed, but when she tried to move, she could not, and it didn't feel like bed.

A wave of fear ran over her. She tried to make herself believe it was a dream, but she knew it was not. As calmly as she could she made herself come fully to her senses. She began to accept what initially her mind had rejected as impossible: she was bound, hand, foot, and body, to an upright chair—and she was naked.

The damp cloth was removed from her face. She had expected to feel it against her throat and neck, but its cool caress was withheld. Instead, she felt something cold and hard around her neck. There was a slight noise, and it became tighter. She could still breathe, but there was some constriction; it felt rigid, like a collar of metal.

Panic gripped her. For a moment she choked, but as she fought to bring herself under control, she found she could breathe, albeit with difficulty. She tried to speak, but no words came out. Her mouth was sealed with layers of surgical tape. She recognized its faint medicinal smell. It was an odor she associated with care, with the dressing of wounds and the relief of pain; for a moment she felt reassured as she tried to believe what she did not believe: that she was safe. The seconds of sanctuary passed, and suddenly her whole being was suffused with terror. Her body shook and spasmed in panic but to no avail. Her bonds were secure, immovable in the face of her every effort. Resistance was pointless. Slowly, reluctantly, she opened her eyes.

Kadar—she knew him by another name—was sprawled in the Charles Eames chair in front of her. His legs were stretched out, feet up on the matching footstool. His hands were clasped around a brandy snifter. He lifted the glass and swirled the contents around, then sniffed the bouquet appreciatively. He sipped some of the golden liquid and returned the glass to his lap. He was wearing a black silk shirt open to the navel and Italian-cut white trousers of some soft material. His feet were bare. He looked easygoing and relaxed, the master of the house at leisure; his eyes glinted with amusement.

"I would guess," he said, "that you are about at the stage where you are wondering what's going on. You are probably backtracking and trying to recall your most recent memories. Nod if you agree."

She stared at him, her eyes large and beautiful above the mask of surgical tape. Seconds passed; then she nodded.

"We were making love," he said, "or to be quite accurate, we had just finished a rather energetic soixante-neuf with a few little variations, if you remember. You were very good, I might even say outstanding, but then you always did have a special talent for sensuality, and I believe I may say, with due modesty, that I taught you well. Don't you agree?"

She nodded again, this time quickly, eager to please. This was one of his bizarre sexual games, and he would not really hurt her. She tried to believe it. She could hear her heart pounding.

"I'm sorry about the gag," he said, "but the Swiss have this obsession about noise. I'll tell you how I first became aware of the noise issue. It gave me quite a shock at the time, as I'm sure you can imagine.

"Shortly after I first arrived in Bern—that was many years ago, my sweet, when you were still a chubby-cheeked little girl—one evening about midnight I decided in my innocence to have a bath. A rather pretty young Turkish waiter who worked in the Mövenpick was the reason, as I recall, but I could be wrong. The memory plays such tricks.

"Anyway, there I was with my loofah at hand, soaping my exhausted penis and singing the 'Song of the Volga Boatmen,' when there was a ring at the door. I tried to ignore it because there is nothing worse than leaving a relaxing bath after you've settled in, but the finger on the doorbell would not desist. I swore in several different languages and dripped across and opened the door. Lo and behold, there stood not my pretty Turkish waiter looking for an encore but, like Tweedledum and Tweedledee, two of Bern's finest Berps.

"Some anonymous neighbor, overwhelmed with civic duty and obviously not a lover of Russian music, had called the police. They informed me, to my shock, horror, amusement, and downright incredulity, that there is some law or other that actually forbids having a bath or a shower or using a washing machine or generally doing anything noisy after ten at night or before eight in the morning. So there you are. It's now nearly two in the morning, so I had to gag you. I wouldn't want you screaming and breaking the law."

Kadar drained the brandy glass. He refilled it from a cut-glass decanter that rested nearby on a low glass-topped table. There was a small stainless steel basin containing a folded cloth beside the decanter.

"But I was explaining what happened after our shared soupçon of sex. Actually there is not much to tell. You fell asleep; I dozed a bit;

then, gently, I struck you on a certain special spot on the back of your head to render you unconscious—it's an Indian technique, if you're interested, from a style of fighting known as *kalaripayit*—and then I arranged you as you now find yourself, drank a little brandy, read a Shakespeare sonnet or two, and waited for you to recover. It took longer than expected, and in the absence of the smelling salts so beloved by ladies of fashion in more civilized times, I had to make do with soothing your fevered brow with a damp cloth. That seemed to do the trick.

"You might well ask why I have gone to so much trouble—and I see from your expression that that very question has crossed your mind. Well, my dear, it's all about discipline. You did something you shouldn't have done—doubtless for the best of motives, but I really don't care—and now you have to be punished.

"You have to see it from my point of view. You may think my main preoccupation is our little band here in Switzerland. You don't realize that I have a number of such interests scattered across Europe, the Middle East, the Americas, and elsewhere, and the only way I can keep them under control—given that I must be away so much— is, in the final analysis, through absolute discipline. Discipline is the key to my running a multinational operation, and discipline has to be enforced.

"You see, I worked out my particular multinational management style, my objectives, and my strategy when I was at Harvard. It was while studying the activities of the big soap companies like Procter & Gamble and Unilever that I got the idea. They have different brands of soap and cleaning powder, all competing to some extent for different segments of the market. I decided there was a major commercial opportunity to exploit in the rapidly developing phe- nomenon of terrorism—all that hate, frustration, idealism, and sheer raw energy waiting to be tapped and manipulated—so I decided to do much the same thing as the soap companies, except with terrorist groups instead of detergent. Each little band of fanatics is tailored to a specific market. Each little band has its own rules and rituals and tokens to give it a sense of esprit de corps and identity, but each little band has only one purpose, just like all the others: to make me a profit.

"I'm very profit-oriented. I don't give a fuck about the rights of the Palestinians, the ambitions of the Basques, the overthrow of the Swiss establishment, or whatever. I care a great deal about cash flow, return on investment, and meeting financial targets. It's all about the bottom line in the end."

He paused for a moment and held his cut-glass brandy snifter up to the light. He swirled the amber liquid and watched the changing sparkle of golden light with concentration; then he turned his gaze back to the naked girl.

"Initially you were instructed to follow the Irishman and to report his movements, preferably without being detected. Later on, when it seemed that he might be becoming aware of your interest, you were ordered to keep a discreet eye on him from a distance and even then only intermittently so there would be no risk of your being discovered. You were ordered to do nothing more than that—*nothing more!*" His voice had risen, and he was almost shouting. He calmed himself and continued speaking. "My dear, I'm forgetting myself and what time it is. I certainly don't want to upset all those sleeping burghers of Bern, and as for raising my voice in a lady's presence, I do apologize.

"The truth is I can't abide indiscipline. I expect that's why I made my base in Switzerland; despite its many peculiarities, it's such a disciplined society. Lack of discipline shocks me, this casual disregard of precise instructions. In your case it was particularly shocking. I thought you understood. Then I come back from an important business trip to find that—on your own initiative—you and that fool Pierre have decided to exceed instructions and kill the Irishman merely because he looked alone and vulnerable on the Kirchenfeld Bridge; and you didn't even succeed, two of you, with surprise on your side."

He shook his head sadly. "This is not proper behavior for members of my organization. It is just as well that Pierre was killed before I could lay my hands on him. Have you not learned already what happens to those who disobey orders? Have you forgotten so soon the lesson of Klaus Minder? An overtalkative boy. I would have thought the manner of his dying would have made you painfully aware that I expect my orders to be adhered to." A thought occurred to him. "Perhaps you thought the elimination of the Irishman would please me."

She met his gaze for a moment; then her eyes dropped away. A feeling of helplessness swept over her. They had indeed thought he would be pleased if this unexpected threat to his plans were eliminated. In fact, it was the horrific example of Minder's ritual killing by

Kadar that had persuaded them to act. Now it had all backfired; it was hopeless. She tried not to think of the import of what he was saying to her. She looked down at the ground in front of her and tried to let his words wash over her. She began to writhe and struggle in a futile attempt to get free; then she saw that the carpet under and immediately around her chair was covered with a clear plastic sheet. Horror overwhelmed her when the significance of this typical example of Kadar's attention to detail sank in. Her body sagged in despair. She knew she was going to die and within minutes. How remained the only question.

"The snag is, my dear," said Kadar, "you cannot see the bigger picture. Fitzduane doesn't even know what he is looking for. He is working out some male menopausal hunch based upon his accidental finding of young von Graffenlaub. He won't discover anything significant before we are ready to strike, and then it will be too late. There isn't time for him to get into the game. He doesn't have the knowledge to make the connections. He's a watcher, not a player, unless through some stupidity we make him into one.

"I wanted to keep a loose check on what Fitzduane was up to through my various sources, but certainly not to draw his attention to the fact that he might be on to something. Now, by trying to kill him, you've begun to give him credibility. If you had succeeded, the situation would have been worse. You would have focused attention on matters we want left well alone for the next few weeks."

Kadar lit a thin cigar and blew six perfect smoke rings. He did many such things well; he was blessed with excellent physical coordination.

"Darling Esther," he said, "it is good to be able to talk things over with you. Command is a lonely business; it's rare that I get the chance to explain things to someone who will understand. You do understand, don't you?"

He didn't bother to wait for a nod of agreement but instead checked his watch. He looked up at her. "Well, it's time for the main event," he said. "I'd better explain the program; as a tribute to our past intimacy, it's only fair that you know the details. I wouldn't want you to miss something. It's all rather interesting, with plenty of historical precedent as a method of execution.

"My dear darling Esther," he said, "you are going to be garroted. It's a technique that was rather popular with the Spanish, I'm told. I think I've got the machinery right, though one cannot be sure without field testing, and, as you may imagine, that is not the easiest thing to arrange. So you are the first with this particular device; I do hope it all goes well.

"It works like this: At the back of the metal collar around your neck is a simple screw mechanism connected to a semicircle of metal that sits just inside the collar. Turning the screw clockwise, with a lever to make it easier to handle, forces the inner semicircle of metal to tighten against the back of the neck and, correspondingly, the front of the collar to constrict and then crush the throat. This can be done almost instantaneously or quite slowly; it's a matter of personal preference.

"They tell me that the physical result is similar to strangulation: your eyes will bulge, your face will turn blue, your tongue will stick out, and you will suffocate. Eventually, as the mechanism tightens further, the force exerted by the screw on the back of your neck will break it. By then, I expect, you will be unconscious and either dead or close to it, so you'll miss the final action. It's a pity, but that's just the way it is."

Kadar hauled himself out of his chair, stretched, and yawned. He patted her on the head, then walked around behind her. "It's all about discipline, my dear," he said. "And the bottom line."

He began to tighten the screw.

Chapter Seventeen

Colonel Ulrich Hoden (retired) had risen early. He had a problem. Major Tranino (retired), his old wartime companion, and over the intervening decades his chess partner—normally by post but twice a year in person—was on a winning streak. He had beaten the colonel twice in a row. Something had to be done if a hat trick was to be staved off.

Over a game of jass, the Swiss national card game, he had posed the problem to his companions. After much deliberation and several liters of Gurten beer, they had suggested that what the colonel needed was perspective: to study the chess problem from a new angle. One of his companions suggested that he work it out on one of the giant open-air chessboards scattered around Bern. He particularly recommended the board next to the Rosengarten. It was only twenty minutes from where the colonel was staying with his grandchildren in the Obstberg district, and apart from the pleasures of the garden itself, the view of Bern from the low hill on which the garden was located was spectacular.

The colonel took the steep path up to the Rosengarten instead of the longer but gentler route. At the top there was a glass-fronted café, still closed at this hour, with an outside eating area bordered by a low wall. He rested there for a few minutes, catching his breath after the steep climb and taking in the sight of old Bern laid out below. He could see the course of the River Aare, the red-tiled roofs of the old buildings, the spire of the Münster against the distant skyline of snowcapped mountains, and all around him trees and flowers were coming into full bloom as if in special haste to make up for their long sleep under the snows of winter. A robin landed on the wall beside him, peered up inquisitively, hopped around a couple of times, then flew away about its business.

The colonel decided that he had better follow the robin's example. Major Tranino's problem was a tricky one. The sooner he laid it out on the giant chessboard, the sooner inspiration might strike.

As he neared the chessboard, he was surprised to see the pieces all laid out ready to play. They were normally stacked away at night, and it now looked as if someone might have beaten him to it despite the early hour. Ah, well, he had enjoyed the walk, and there might be the chance of a game. Perhaps two heads could solve the colonel's little difficulty. But would that be ethical? Probably not. It was supposed to be strictly *mano a mano* when the colonel and the major were playing, notwithstanding the geographical separation.

Something about the chessboard looked odd, and he could see no other players. He came closer. The blue and white chess pieces were nearer to him, the tallest of them the size of a small child, reaching halfway up his thigh. He put on his glasses; there was nothing wrong with the blue and white pieces. He turned his gaze to the red and black pieces and walked forward onto the board itself to study the pieces one by one.

The pawns gleamed in their new paint, and the contrasting slashes of color reminded him of nothing so much as a file of Swiss Guards on parade in the Vatican. He knew that there was something wrong and that he should have seen what it was by now, and he admitted to himself that even with his glasses his eyes were not what they had been. He really should get a stronger pair; vanity be damned.

He stepped forward again to study the back row. The rook seemed fine; the knight and the bishop were normal; next came the queen— and it was the queen that killed him.

There was no queen. In her place, propped upright, was the upper half of the body of a young woman. She seemed to be smiling at him, then he realized that her lips had been cut away to expose her teeth.

The pain was immediate and massive. He swayed briefly and then fell back on the hard slabs of the chessboard. His last thought before the heart attack killed him was that Major Tranino (retired) looked as if he would win three times in a row, if only by default in the case of the third game—and that was a pity because Colonel Hoden (retired) thought he just might have found the answer.

FITZDUANE SUPPOSED that his ideas of what an Autonomous Youth House should look like were conditioned by his recollection of the one in Zurich. He remembered a battered and litter-strewn industrial building covered with graffiti and still freshly scarred from recent riots, and everywhere around it broken glass and empty tear gas canisters and twitchy policemen. He was almost disappointed by what he found in Bern.

Taubenstrasse 12 was a large, solid three-story construction with a distinctly nineteenth-century feel about it. Its style positively radiated probity, bourgeois values, and the merits of the Bernese establishment. In contrast with the sober image projected by the building, half a dozen spray can–inscribed sheets fluttered their calls for freedom, anarchy, and pot for all from the front of the house. In counterpoint, less than a hundred meters away was the gray, multistory, modernistic box that housed the Federal Police administration.

As Fitzduane approached, a young couple rushed from the building. The man's face was red and swollen, as if he had been on the losing side in a fight, and blood was gushing from his nose. The girl with him was crying. They pushed past Fitzduane and ran out into the small park that bordered the other side of Taubenstrasse.

The front door was open. Fitzduane called out, then knocked. No one answered. Balancing caution and curiosity, he went in. The hall was dark and cool in contrast with the glare of the sunlight. He paused while his eyes adjusted.

A hand grabbed his arm. "*Polizei?*" a voice asked nervously.

Fitzduane removed the hand. It was dirty, as was the person it belonged to. The person also smelled.

"No," said Fitzduane.

"You are English?" The voice belonged to a small, scruffy youth of about twenty. He seemed agitated.

"Irish," said Fitzduane. "I'm looking for someone called Klaus Minder. A friend told me he sometimes lives here."

The youth gave a start. He moved away from Fitzduane and examined him carefully. His eyes were red-rimmed, and he was shaking. He removed a hand-rolled cigarette from his pocket and tried to light it but was unable to hold the match steady. Fitzduane moved forward gently and held his wrist while flame and marijuana made contact. The wrist was frail and thin. The youth inhaled deeply several times, and some of the tension went from his face. He looked at Fitzduane.

"You must help us," he said. "First you must help us."

Fitzduane smiled. "If it's legal and quick, or at least quick. What's the problem?"

The youth leaned forward. He smelled terrible and looked worse, but there was something, some quality, curiously appealing about him. "There is a man upstairs, a Dutchman—his name is Jan van der Grijn—and he is creating trouble. If you go up, because you are an outsider, he will stop."

"Why's he doing this?"

The youth shrugged. He looked at the ground. "He stayed here a little while ago," he said, "and after he left, he found he was missing some stuff. He has come back to find it. He says one of us robbed him, and he's threatening everyone who was there that night."

"Why don't you go to the police?"

The youth shook his head. "We don't want the police in here," he said. "We have enough trouble with them."

The marijuana smoke diffused through the corridor. "I can't imagine why," said Fitzduane dryly. He was thinking it might be an excellent idea to leave.

The youth tugged him by the arm. "Come on," he insisted. "Afterward I will tell you about Klaus."

Reluctantly Fitzduane followed the youth up the stairs. "What's your name?" he called up after him.

"Ivo," answered the youth. He opened a door off the second-floor landing and stood aside. Muffled shouts came from inside, but Fitzduane went in anyway. An extremely bad decision. The door slammed shut behind him.

He could smell Ivo by his side. "The Dutchman has two friends with him," Ivo said. "They are the ones in the leather jackets."

"Good information," said Fitzduane, "but lousy timing." Before he knew what was happening, he felt an armlock around his neck and something sharp being pressed against his kidneys. Someone with foul breath spoke into his right ear. He didn't understand a word.

A big man in a leather jacket stopped punching a blond youth, who was held by an equally large companion, and came forward. He hit Fitzduane once very hard in the stomach. Fitzduane sagged to his knees. He felt sick, and he was getting quite angry.

DETECTIVE KURT SIEMANN of the Bern Kriminalpolizei, not one of the Chief Kripo's favorites, hence his rank—or rather lack of it at the mature age of forty-seven—was of two minds about whether to follow Fitzduane into the Youth House.

His brief was terse: "Keep an eye on him, note his movements, keep him out of trouble, but don't hassle him," which seemed to Siemann to incorporate certain self-canceling elements. Following Fitzduane into the Youth House could well be construed as "hassling." On the other hand, since the Bern police were not yet equipped to see through stone walls, the instruction "Keep an eye on him" was currently being obeyed only in the figurative sense at best. Another complication was that it was current police policy in Bern to steer clear of the Youth House as much as possible. It was a policy with which Detective Siemann did not agree; he was all in favor of donning riot gear and cracking a few heads.

Detective Siemann decided that on balance he was probably better off staying outside, staring at the tulips and counting the flies. He thought it wouldn't do any harm if he sat down on the grass and rested for a few minutes. He lay down and put his hands behind his head—it wasn't all bad being a policeman in the spring. It might not be fair to say that he fell fast asleep, but even Detective Siemann himself would admit that he dozed.

THE BEAR TRIED to maintain an orderly wallet with everything in its place, but somehow it didn't seem to work out that way. Cash, credit cards, notes, receipts, police bulletins, bills, letters, and other impedimenta of debatable origin all seemed to gravitate of their own volition in no logical order to an apparently endless series of pockets that he had discovered disgorged their contents only on whim. It was infuriating. He worried that he would be unable to find his police identity card at some crucial moment, but so far, at least, that piece of documentation seemed to be a bit less independently mobile than the others.

The Bear hadn't found a way to solve his problem, but he had discovered over the years that he could keep anarchy marginally in check by a deliberate daily ritual—weekly more like it—of emptying out his pockets on his office desk and doing a sort.

He swore violently in Berndeutsch, and then in Romansh for good measure, when he discovered in the debris the photograph of the motorcyclist the Irishman had asked him to check. He reached for the phone.

The answer from the vehicle registration computer came through almost immediately. The motorcycle was registered to a Felix Krane with an address in Lenk. He checked with the Operations Room and discovered that Fitzduane's tail had reported in by personal radio some eight minutes earlier. The Irishman was in the Youth House.

The Bear decided it might be a good idea to make up for his absentmindedness by delivering his information immediately. He looked at the chaos on his desk, swore again, extracted the minimum necessary for survival, and swept the balance into a drawer.

He headed toward the Youth House, which was only a few minutes away on foot. Most places were, in Bern.

FITZDUANE FELT a hand cup his chin, and his head was jerked painfully backward.

Van der Grijn stared down at him for a few seconds and then withdrew his hand with a grunt. "No, I don't think so."

He spoke a quick command in Dutch, and Fitzduane felt himself hauled to his feet and quickly but thoroughly frisked. The shoulder bag containing his camera equipment and the tripod case lay on the floor, ignored in the confusion.

Out of the corner of his eye Fitzduane could see Ivo to his right but slightly behind him. Fitzduane had the strong feeling that Ivo knew more than he was saying. Still, comparing the slight figure of Ivo with the three burly Dutchmen, he began to appreciate the youth's courage. He'd known what he was up against, and he could have gotten away. Instead, he had deliberately put himself in danger to try to do something about the situation.

Van der Grijn stepped back a couple of paces and stood to one side so that he could keep Fitzduane in full view while the Dutchman who had been doing the frisking came around in front of Fitzduane and started going through his pockets. He was carrying a Bundeswehrmesser, the standard West German Army fighting knife. He held it in his right hand as he emptied Fitzduane's pockets with his left. At all times he kept the point of the blade, which bore the signs of many loving encounters with a sharpening stone and glistened under a light film of oil, either under Fitzduane's neck or angled slightly upward for an easy thrust into his heart or stomach.

Fitzduane kept quite still. His wallet was removed from his inside pocket and handed to van der Grijn. The searcher stepped back and then returned to his position behind Fitzduane, by the door. Fitzduane mentally christened him Knife. He thought that Knife was about two meters behind him. He was beginning to have some potential room to maneuver.

Van der Grijn flipped open Fitzduane's wallet. He pocketed cash and credit cards and examined Fitzduane's press card and other credentials. The short pause gave Fitzduane time to get his bearings. The rectangular room was spacious but furnished only with a large, plain wooden table, two stuffed armchairs not in the prime of life, and two straight-back chairs. Every square millimeter of wall space was covered with drawings, slogans, and other graffiti. Light came from one large and two small windows at one end of the room.

There were roughly a dozen people of both sexes lined up in two irregular groups on either side of the room. They were mostly in their late teens and early twenties, but several were older. All of the smaller group—four in number—had been badly beaten. One lay on the floor, his bloody hand over his eyes and a pool of blood leaching from his head.

"So," said van der Grijn, holding up Fitzduane's press card, "you are a photographer." Like many Dutchmen, he spoke good English though the accent lingered. Each syllable was enunciated, and the voice was hard and uncompromising. Fitzduane noted that the second of van der Grijn's sidekicks was about five meters ahead and to his left, near the windows at the end of the room, and was able to monitor the whole room. He could see the butt of a large-caliber revolver protruding from a shoulder holster as the man shifted position. He seemed entertained by the situation. He was shorter than van der Grijn and Knife but had the physique of a body builder.

The prospects for doing something did not look good. Van der

Grijn and Knife aside, there was no chance of getting near the third man before he had a chance to fire. He designated the third man Gun. The others in the room looked as if they had been persuaded out of heroism. That left Ivo. Something less than a balance of power.

Van der Grijn put Fitzduane's credentials into his pocket. "All you people have to do is flash your ID and doors open," he said. "Very useful."

Fitzduane had the strong feeling that whatever he said would be pointless, but he thought he ought to go through the motions.

"Give them back," he said quietly.

Van der Grijn didn't reply immediately. His face slowly flushed with anger. It began to be clear that he was high on something and that rationality had little to do with his behavior. He rocked slightly to and fro on his feet, and Fitzduane braced himself for a blow. The Dutchman at the window grinned.

Van der Grijn reached inside his leather jacket and pulled a long-barreled 9 mm Browning automatic out of his shoulder holster. He checked the clip, cocked the weapon, and deactivated the safety catch. Suddenly he whipped up the gun and held it in a two-handed combat grip a hair's breadth from Fitzduane's nose.

Fitzduane could smell the gun oil. He was looking straight down the black pit of the muzzle; it shook in van der Grijn's hands. He didn't think van der Grijn could be crazy enough to shoot him in a room full of witnesses, for no good reason except machismo, and only a sparrow hop from the Federal Police building. Then he looked into van der Grijn's eyes and knew that things weren't in control, and that if he didn't do something soon, he would die. He moistened his lips to speak, and the gun barrel jabbed closer.

All eyes in the room were fixed on van der Grijn, Fitzduane, and that swaying gun barrel. A bearded man standing in the as-yet-uninterrogated group bent down almost imperceptibly, as if to massage an aching calf muscle, and with two fingers removed a Beretta from his boot. Nobody seemed to notice.

Fitzduane debated making an immediate move but decided against it. Van der Grijn only had to flinch and Fitzduane's skull would explode. But fuck it, he was going to have to do something. Van der Grijn and his people weren't going to lie down quietly. They were high, drunk on power—but they hadn't seen the bearded man draw the Beretta. Fitzduane could feel the sweat trickling into his eyes, but he was afraid to move to wipe it away.

Van der Grijn's eyes went empty; then he fired.

THE BEAR WAS looking down at the somnambulant form of Detective Siemann with amusement rather than anger when he heard the shot. His feelings of benevolence toward Siemann changed in one split second. "Wake up, you idiot," he snarled at him, simultaneously kicking him hard in the ribs.

The large window of the room on the second floor of the Youth House burst into shards of glass. A chair hurtled through it and smashed on the pavement below, missing the Bear as he ran toward the entrance, pistol in hand. Siemann tripped on the splintered remains, cut himself messily on the spears of broken glass, picked himself up, and, pouring blood, ran after the Bear, who had by this time vanished into the building.

FITZDUANE FELT a sharp, burning pain as the muzzle blast seared the side of his face. The bullet cracked past his right ear so close it drew blood, and it splintered the door behind him before embedding itself in the plaster of the first-floor landing.

"You stupid shit," cried Fitzduane, shock, anger, and sheer naked terror combining to pump adrenaline into his bloodstream. He grabbed van der Grijn's wrists with both hands and deflected the Dutchman's aim toward the ceiling. Van der Grijn fired again and again as they struggled, hot shell casings showering across the room and plaster falling from the ceiling as the rounds bored their way in.

Knife leaped forward to help van der Grijn. Fitzduane swiveled van der Grijn around as the blade was thrust at him. He felt van der Grijn jerk and saw the shock in his eyes as the blade cut effortlessly through his leather jacket and entered his back. He bellowed in pain.

The second Dutchman had his revolver in his hand.

"Police!" yelled the bearded man. The voice was American. "Drop it, motherfucker!" The man had dropped into a combat crouch and had his gun aimed at the second Dutchman.

Moving with unexpected speed, the second Dutchman whirled

toward the American, dropped to one knee, and fired two rounds at him, hitting him once in the stomach.

The American's first shot went over the second Dutchman's head, but then he sagged with the impact of the bullet in his stomach, and his aim dropped. The next five slugs from his little Beretta went into the Dutchman's face and neck. In a bloody parody of a knight's posture, the Dutchman stayed on one knee for several seconds, his head bowed, blood spurting from his wounds, his gun still held in his drooping hand, and then slid sideways to the ground.

The Dutchman with the knife, appalled and confused by his error, left the knife in van der Grijn's back and leaped at Fitzduane. The force of his attack separated Fitzduane from van der Grijn, who still held the automatic in his hand. Though half blinded by the plaster dust from the ceiling and groggy with pain from the knife in his back, he was still just able to function. He tried to aim at Fitzduane, who was wrestling with Knife on the floor.

Ivo, who had flung a chair out the window to attract attention, now flung a second chair at van der Grijn. It missed. He dived under the table, encountering a mass of arms and legs belonging to people who had beaten him to it. Van der Grijn, momentarily distracted from Fitzduane, fired back twice. One round gouged into the graffiti on the wall; the second drilled through the table, hitting a seventeen-year-old runaway from Geneva in the left thigh.

The door burst open. *"Polizei!"* yelled the Bear.

Van der Grijn fired. The Bear shot him four times in the chest, the rounds impacting in a textbook group and flinging van der Grijn back across the room. He staggered, still upright, and the Bear fired again, this time assisted by Detective Siemann.

Van der Grijn reeled back against the window, smashed through the remaining jagged edges of glass, and fell one story onto the pointed tops of the fleur-de-lis cast-iron railings below. His vast body arched at the impact and twitched for a few seconds; then it lay unmoving, impaled in half a dozen places.

The Bear smashed the one surviving Dutchman across the side of his face with his still-hot gun barrel. The Dutchman fell to the floor, his cheekbone broken, and lay on his back, moaning. The Bear flipped him over and pressed his gun into the back of his neck. "Don't move, asshole!" The Dutchman became quite still; intermittently he trembled, and moaning sounds came out of his mouth.

The Bear kept his gun in position and, using his left hand, hand-cuffed him.

Siemann pulled the table aside. Bodies, intertwined in a confusion of limbs, began to separate. Terrified faces looked up at him. He held out his hand to help and realized he was still holding his gun. He holstered it and tried to say something reassuring. They stared at him, and he looked down at his bloodstained body. He shook his head and tried to smile, and the tension on the faces eased. One by one they rose to their feet. One figure remained unmoving, blood gushing from her thigh. Siemann leaped forward, ripped the belt from his waist, and began to apply a tourniquet. Once the bleeding eased, he unclipped his radio and put in an emergency call. When he finished, he caught the Bear's eye. The Bear nodded his head a couple of times and smiled fleetingly. He rested his hand on Siemann's shoulder.

"That was good, Kurt, that was very good."

Siemann didn't know what to say. He looked away and stroked the injured girl's forehead with his bloody hand. After twenty-five years on the force he no longer felt he had just a job: he felt accepted; he felt like a real policeman.

The Bear reached down to help Fitzduane to his feet. "What was that all about?"

"I'm fucked if I know." Fitzduane walked across to the bearded man, who was lying on the floor surrounded by a circle of people. Someone had put a folded coat under his head. His face under the beard was very white.

Fitzduane knelt down by his side. "You'll be all right," he said gently. "That was some piece of shooting."

The man smiled weakly. "It's a paycheck," he said. His eyes were going cloudy. "The agency expects nothing less."

"CIA?"

"No, not those bozos—DEA." The man grimaced in pain.

"Help's coming," said Fitzduane. He looked down at the man's stomach. The large-caliber hollow-nosed bullet must have hit bone and ricocheted. The entire lower part of his torso seemed to have been ripped open. He had his hands folded across his intestines in a reflex attempt to keep them in. Fitzduane wanted to hold his hand or somehow comfort him, but he knew if he did so, it could add to the pressure and cause more pain.

The man closed his eyes and then opened them again. They were unfocused. "I can hear the dustoff," he whispered. Fitzduane had to bend down and put his ear to the man's mouth to hear him. "Those pilots have a lot of balls."

The man gave a little rattling sound, and for a moment Fitzduane was back in Vietnam watching another man die, the sound of the medevac chopper arriving too late. Then he knew that the sound of the helicopter was real and that it was circling somewhere outside the building.

The Bear looked down at the American. "He's dead," he said. As he had with Siemann, he put his hand on Fitzduane's shoulder, but this time he didn't say anything. Fitzduane, still kneeling, stayed there looking at the man's body, the hands already folded as if in anticipation of an olive green body bag. The blue eyes were still open; they looked faded. Fitzduane gently closed the eyelids, then rose off his knees.

From outside the Youth House, a heavily amplified voice boomed at them: "YOU INSIDE, THIS IS THE POLICE. LAY DOWN YOUR ARMS AND COME OUT WITH YOUR HANDS UP."

"Assholes," said the Bear. "It's the Federal Police from the building next door. They must be back from their coffee break."

EXAMINING MAGISTRATE Charlie von Beck—wearing a large, floppy brown velvet bow tie to go with his cream shirt and three-piece corduroy suit—was talking. The Chief thought von Beck looked like a leftover from a late-nineteenth-century artists' colony. He wore his fair hair long so it flopped over one eye. His father was an influential professor of law at Bern University, he was rich, had connections in all the right places, and he was sharp as a razor. All in all, thought the Chief, Charlie von Beck would have made an ideal person to hate. It irritated him that he liked the man.

"Well, it doesn't make the crime statistics look too good, I admit," said von Beck, "but you have to agree: it's exciting."

"Don't talk like that," said the Chief Kripo. "We haven't had this many violent deaths in Bern in such a short period since the French invasion nearly two hundred years ago—and all you can say is 'exciting.' I can see the headlines in *Blick* or some other scandal sheet: CHAIN OF KILLINGS EXCITING, QUIP BERN AUTHORITIES."

"Relax," said von Beck. "*Der Bund*, in its usual discreet way, will come out with something to balance the scales, like EXAMINING

MAGISTRATE COMMENTS ON STATISTICAL ABNORMALITY IN CRIME FIGURES."

"They don't write headlines that sensational," said the Chief. "So far, including Hoden, we have seven dead, two seriously injured, and eight or so slightly injured."

"At least there's an explanation for the fracas in the Youth House," said von Beck. "I'm still poking around, but we've interviewed most of the parties involved and had some feedback from the Amsterdam cops and the DEA."

"I wish they'd keep their cowboys off my patch," said the Chief Kripo in a grumpy voice.

"Don't be a spoilsport. Anyway, it looks fairly straightforward. Van der Grijn had some heroin stolen from him. He reckoned it had happened in the Youth House, so he came back with two heavies to try to find the culprit. The American DEA man was tailing him. Van der Grijn got out of hand when the Irishman walked in, and then all hell broke loose."

"It never used to be like this in Bern," said the Chief Kripo. "I don't care about explanations. I want it to stop."

"Well, don't hold your breath," said von Beck. "I've only been talking about the easy bits so far. We have an explanation for the Youth House deaths, and I guess Hoden's heart attack is no mystery under the circumstances."

"Poor Hoden, what a lousy way to go. You know I served under him for a while."

"So did my father," said von Beck.

"We're still left with a few questions about the Youth House," said the Chief. "For instance, who stole van der Grijn's heroin in the first place—and why? Is the thief selling it or has he some other motive? What was that Irishman doing there? Not content with flinging people off bridges, he seems to gravitate toward trouble like . . ." He paused, thinking.

"Do you want help on this one?" said von Beck politely.

The Chief shot von Beck a look. "And lastly," he continued, "is the Bear going to be in any trouble for killing van der Grijn?"

"I don't think so," said von Beck. "I don't see what else he could have done. He had seconds in which to judge the situation, he called it right, he put himself at risk—and he pulled it off. What's more, he didn't shoot a local, which always raises a stink regardless of the circumstances. It's all show biz in the end."

The Chief surveyed von Beck's sartorial splendor. The magistrate was himself no slouch when it came to show biz—and the bow tie always photographed distinctively. It was the kind of thing that photo editors left in when cropping a print.

The Chief tried to concentrate. He looked across at von Beck. "What about his using a .41 Magnum?"

"It doesn't look tactful in the media," said von Beck, "for a policeman to shoot a suspect six times with a cannon like the Magnum. On the other hand, the evidence is that van der Grijn, a large, powerful man hyped on drugs, was still a threat after being shot no less than four times." He shrugged. "In Heini's place, I'd have done the same thing—and fired again."

"Heini's talking about getting an even bigger gun," said the Chief gloomily. "He says to have to shoot someone six times before he goes down is ridiculous."

"If I was being shot at, I might feel the same way," said von Beck. "What was your first point?"

"Who stole van der Grijn's heroin?"

"The finger seems to point at Ivo."

"He's a dealer?"

"On the contrary," said von Beck. "He seems to hate the stuff. The word is that he destroys it."

The Chief raised his eyebrows. "Odd," he said. "What does he say?"

"Therein lies a problem," said von Beck. "By all accounts he was on the side of the angels during the gunfight—and then he seems to have vanished."

"Angels do that," said the Chief, "which brings us to the Irishman."

"Yes, well," said von Beck, "he may be innocent, but somehow—and don't ask me how—he's tied in with just about every phase of our little crime wave."

"Including Klaus Minder and the chessboard killing?"

"Yes, in a sense. According to the BKA, the chessboard girl was the partner of the man Fitzduane threw off the Kirchenfeld Bridge. Fitzduane identified her from a photo sent by the German authorities in Wiesbaden. She was also present when he was attacked but backed off when he threatened her with a shotgun."

"And how does Minder fit in?"

"That's more tenuous," said von Beck, "but it's what my English

police friends would call a 'hopeful line of inquiry.' " He tapped the
desk with a gold Waterman fountain pen to emphasize each point.
"Point one, forensics thinks that Minder and the chessboard girl
were sliced up by the same person. Point two, and I have no idea of
the significance of this, Minder and Ivo were close friends. Point
three—" The Chief flinched in anticipation but instead von Beck
unzipped a leather container the size of a small briefcase and perused
the row of pipes displayed within.

"Go on, go on," said the Chief impatiently. "Point three?"

"Klaus Minder was a close friend and sometime lover of the young
and recently deceased Rudi von Graffenlaub." Von Beck closed the
pipe case with a snap and zipped it up slowly.

"And our Irish friend is looking into the death of young Rudi with
the forceful backing of Beat von Graffenlaub," said the Chief.

"The rest is details," said von Beck. "It's all in the file." He made a
grandiloquent gesture.

"But you do have a theory about all this?"

"Not a one. This thing is so complicated it could go on for years."

"I thought you were supposed to be smart."

"I am, I am," said von Beck, "but who says the bad guys can't be
smart, too?"

The telephone rang, and the Chief gave a sigh. He listened to the
call, saying little, then turned to von Beck.

"They found the other half of the chessboard girl in a plastic bag
inside the Russian Embassy wall," he said. "The Russians are livid
and are complaining it's a CIA plot to embarrass them."

"Explain that we're neutral and will regard both them and the
Americans with equal suspicion." Von Beck stood up to leave.
"Now all we've got to find are Minder's balls."

"And Ivo," said the Chief.

KADAR WAS working his way through a pile of medical textbooks,
and he had a splitting headache. The telex chattered again, exacerbat-
ing the headache. He rose, washed down two Tylenol with brandy,
and decoded the message.

His headache subsided to an acceptable dull throb. He was knee-
deep in medical tracts because he thought he might be suffering from
some kind of psychiatric condition. In lay terms—he had not yet
stumbled on the correct medical diagnosis—it seemed not un-

likely that he was going mad. No, that conveyed images of Hogarthian excess, of twisted faces and dribbling idiots, of barred windows and straitjackets and padded cells. That was too much. He would not accept that he was going mad. He revised his analysis. As a result of sustained stress, he was behaving irrationally. He was doing things that were out of character, that he had not consciously planned, and of which he had scant recollection later.

It was worrying. He was glad that it would all soon be over. He would no longer have to live with the strain of a double existence—if indeed his life could be summed up in such a simple way. His existence was not merely divided into two. It was fragmented into multiple personas, and he had been sustaining this complex life for years. Really, a certain amount of aberration on the margin was to be expected, and possibly was a good thing. It was like letting off steam, a natural release of tensions, a purification through excess. That wasn't the real problem.

It was the periods of amnesia that concerned him. He was a man with an astonishing ability to manipulate and control other beings— up to and including matters of life and death—and yet his underlying fear, a fear that bordered on panic, was that he was losing his ability to control himself.

It was the incident with the girl on the chessboard that had persuaded him that he must get himself under control. Previous incidents, like his killing that beautiful boy Klaus Minder, were unpremeditated and perhaps a little excessive but could be rationalized in context of the needs of his advanced sexuality. Killing Esther was a matter of routine discipline. The killing and the manner of the killing were not the problem. But why had he suddenly taken the notion to draw attention to his presence by planting the torso in such a public place as the Rose Garden's chessboard—not to mention dumping the legs in the Russian Embassy?

Did he subconsciously want to be caught? Was this some sublimated cry for help? He hoped not. He'd put far too much effort into the last couple of decades to have some programmed element of his subconscious betray him. That was the trouble with the childhood phase. In your early years anyone and everyone has a go at programming you, from your parents to religious nuts, from corporations that bombard you with unremitting lies on TV to an educational system that trains you to conform to its values and does its level best to crush your own natural talent.

But Kadar had been lucky. From an early age he had sensed the realities of life, the lies, the corruption, the compromises. He had learned to have only one friend, one loyalty, one guide through life: himself. He had learned one key discipline: control. He had mastered one vital pattern of behavior: to live inside himself and to reveal nothing. Externally he appeared to conform; he knew how the game must be played.

He lay back in his chair and started the ritual of creating Dr. Paul. He desperately needed someone to talk to. But hours later, drenched in sweat, he admitted failure: the image of the smiling doctor wouldn't appear. His headache had escalated into the full, terrible agony of a serious migraine.

Alone in his soundproofed premises Kadar screamed.

Chapter Eighteen

The Bear sat in a private room of Bern's ultramodern Insel Hospital and waited for the Monkey to die. His once-beautiful face was wrapped in bandages from crown to neck. The Bear had seen what was left underneath and was too appalled even to feel nauseated. Best guess was that some kind of sharpened chain, possibly a motorcycle chain, had been used. His nose, teeth, and much else had been smashed, and the face flayed to the bone.

The Monkey muttered something unintelligible. The sound was picked up by a voice-activated tape recorder whose miniature microphone lead joined the tangle of tubes and wires that were only just keeping the Monkey alive. There was a harsh rattling sound from the bed, and score was kept by the electronic monitor. The uniformed Berp sitting at the other side of the bed held a notebook in his hands and tried to make sense of the sounds. He bent his ear close to the shrouded hole that was the Monkey's mouth. The edges of the bandages around the hole were stained with fresh blood, and the Berp's face was pale. He shook his head. He didn't write anything.

The rattling and sucking sounds culminated in a strangled cough. An intern and a nurse rushed into the room. They went through the motions while the Bear looked out the window, seeing nothing.

"That's it," said the intern. He went to wash his hands at the sink

in the corner of the room. The nurse pulled the sheet over the
Monkey's head. The Bear untangled the tape recorder and removed
the cassette. He broke the tabs to make sure it could not be accidentally recorded over, marked it, placed it in an envelope, addressed
and sealed the package, and gave it to the Berp.

"Did he say anything?" asked the intern. He was drying his hands.

"Something," said the Bear. "Not a lot. He hadn't a lot left to talk
with."

"But you know who did it?"

"It looks that way."

"Is it always like this?" asked the Berp. "That noise when they
die?" The young policeman had an unseasoned look about him. Not a
good choice, thought the Bear, but then you have to start sometime.

"Not always," he said, "but often enough. It's not called the death
rattle without good reason." He gestured at the cassette in the envelope. "Take it to Examining Magistrate von Beck. The fresh air will
do you good."

Afterward the Bear went to the Bärengraben for a little snack and a
think. There would be a warrant out for Ivo within the hour. This
time it would not be a matter of routine questioning. The little idiot
would be charged with murder—at least until more information was
available. Even if he ended up with a lesser charge, he was going to be
locked up for an awfully long time.

The Monkey had not actually died from having his face destroyed
but from a one-sided encounter with a delivery truck as he ran in
panic through the streets near the Hauptbahnhof. Whether that
made Ivo—the man who had wielded the chain and thus induced the
panic—guilty of murder was something for the lawyers to decide.
But what had possessed Ivo to behave so savagely? He had no track
record of violence, and the Bear would have bet modest money that
he would never do such a thing. Nonetheless, the Monkey was
undoubtedly telling the truth. Ivo had done it. Had he understood
the damage he was doing when he struck? Probably not, but such an
excuse wouldn't take him very far in court. The Bear doubted that
Ivo would survive a long stretch in prison.

The Monkey had been incoherent most of the time, but he had had
some lucid moments. The Bear remembered one in particular:
". . . and I gave them to him. I did. I did. But he wouldn't stop. He's
mad. I gave them to him." What had the Monkey been trying to say?
What did he mean by "them"?

The Bear enjoyed his meal. He made a list on his table napkin of what the Monkey might have been referring to, but then he needed it to remove the cream sauce from his mustache. He thought the Monkey's demise was one of the better things that had happened to Bern that day. He felt sorry for Ivo. He also thought that the Chief Kripo, with yet another dead body on his hands—albeit the killer identified—would be shitting bricks.

Well, rank had its privileges.

IT WAS Fitzduane's third or fourth visit to Simon Balac's studio after Erika von Graffenlaub had introduced the two men at Kuno Gonschior's vernissage. Simon didn't project the smoldering anger of so many creative artists, or the sense of insecurity heightened by years of rejection. His manner was charming and relaxed, but his conversational style was enlivened by a pointed wit. He was well informed and widely traveled. Good company, in fact.

Simon was often away at exhibitions or seeking creative inspiration, but when in Bern he kept what almost amounted to a salon. This took place every weekday between twelve and two, when the painter broke for lunch and conversation with his friends. For the rest of the day Simon was ruthless in guarding his privacy. The doors were locked and he painted.

Posters of Balac's various exhibitions held throughout Europe and America decorated one end of the converted warehouse down by Wasserwerkgasse. It was said that a Balac routinely commanded prices in excess of twenty thousand dollars. He painted fewer than a dozen or so a year, and many, after one showing, went immediately into bank vaults as investments. His corporate customers, keenly aware of his ability to market his output to maximum advantage, admired his business acumen as much as his artistic talent.

Socially he was much in demand. Balac was a good listener with the ability to draw others out and spent little time talking about himself, but Fitzduane gathered that he was an expatriate American who had originally come to the Continent to study art in Paris, Munich, and Florence and had then moved to Bern because of a woman.

"My affair with Sabine didn't last," he had said, "but with Bern, it did. Bern has been more faithful. She tolerates my little infidelities when I sample the delights of other cities because I always return. To me Bern has the attraction of an experienced woman. Innocence has novelty, but experience has performance." He laughed as if to show that he didn't want to be taken seriously. It was hard to know where Balac stood on most issues. His warm, open manner, combined with his sense of humor, tended to conceal what lay beneath, and Fitzduane did not try to dig. He was content to enjoy the painter's hospitality and his company.

Sometimes the Irishman just wanted to relax. The three weeks he'd spent in Switzerland had been busy and dangerous. Apart from the immediate family, he'd interviewed more than sixty different people about Rudi von Graffenlaub. It might all be very interesting, and it might even lead somewhere—but relaxing it was not.

There was also the matter of language. Most of the people the Irishman was dealing with seemed—seemed—to speak excellent English, but there was still a strain attached to conversation that was absent when both parties spoke a common language. As the day wore on and people got tired and drink flowed, the situation got worse. People reverted to their native tongues. Even the Bear had taken to suggesting he learn Berndeutsch. Fitzduane had replied that since most of the Irish didn't even speak their own language, such suggestions were on the foolish side of optimism.

The attendance at Balac's daily salon varied considerably from several dozen to zero depending on who knew he was back in town, other commitments, the weather, and one's appetite for basic food. Balac discouraged people who liked to treat his place as a handy location for a quick lunch, both by his manner and by minimizing the attractiveness of his table. Balac's was about talk and company—not gourmet cuisine and fine wines. There was a selection of cold meats and cheeses laid out on a table, and you drank beer. The fare never changed.

This was one of the quiet days, and since Fitzduane had come late and the others had departed early, for the first time the Irishman and Balac found themselves alone.

"You like our fair city, eh?" Balac said. He uncapped a Gurten beer and drank straight from the bottle. It seemed to Fitzduane that he cultivated the bohemian image when he was working. In the evenings, by contrast, he was polished and urbane. There was a touch of the actor about Balac.

"Well, I'm still here," said Fitzduane. He ate some Bündnerfleisch, thinly sliced beef that had been cured for many months in the mountain air.

"Are you any the wiser about Rudi?" asked Balac.

"A little, not much," said Fitzduane. He refilled his glass. He spent enough time in countries where either beer or glasses or both were lacking not to have learned to make the most of what was offered.

"Do you think you ever will find out more? Is it possible to know what truly motivates someone to take his own life—when he leaves no note? Surely all you can do is speculate, and what good does that do?"

"No," said Fitzduane, "I don't think I ever will find out the truth. I'm not sure I'll even come close to an intelligent guess. As to what good it does, I'm beginning to wonder. Perhaps all I wanted to do was bury a ghost, to put an unpleasant event in context. I don't really know." He smiled. "I guess if I can't work out my own motives, I'm not going to have much luck with Rudi. On the other hand, I have to admit that coming over here has made me feel better. I expect it is just being in a different environment."

"I'm a little surprised," said Balac. "I've read your book. You're an experienced combat photographer. Surely you've become accustomed to the sight of violent death?"

"Aren't I lucky I'm not?" said Fitzduane.

The conversation drifted on to art and then to that topic beloved by the expatriate: the peculiarities of host countries, in this case of the Swiss, and the Bernese in particular. Balac had a seemingly bottomless store of Bernese jokes and anecdotes.

Just before two o'clock Fitzduane stood up to go. He looked at the clock. "This is sort of like Cinderella in reverse," he said. "She had to leave because she switched images at midnight and didn't want to be found out. So what happens here after the doors close?"

Balac laughed. "You've got your stories mixed up," he said. "Having drunk the potion—in this case a liter of beer—I turn from Dr. Jekyll, the gregarious host, into Mr. Hyde, the obsessional painter."

Fitzduane looked at the large canvas that dominated the wall in front of him. No art expert, he would have called the style a cross between surreal and abstract—descriptions Balac rejected. The power of his imagery was immediate. It managed to convey suffering, violence, and beauty, all interrelated in the most astonishing way. Balac's talent could not be denied.

As he left, Fitzduane laughed to himself. He heard the multiple electronic locks of Balac's studio click behind him. He could see television monitors watching the entrance. Twenty thousand dollars a picture, he thought. Van Gogh, when he was alive, didn't need that kind of protection.

A little later as he window-shopped, the signs of Easter, from colored eggs to chocolate rabbits, everywhere, he thought about Etan, and he missed her.

FITZDUANE WATCHED the Learjet with Irish government markings glide to a halt.

The Lear was the Irish government's one and only executive jet, and it was supposed to be reserved for ministers and those of similar ilk. But Kilmara, he knew, liked to work the system.

"They wanted to send a reception committee," said Kilmara. "Good manners, the Swiss, but I said I'd prefer to use the time to talk to you first." He held his face up to the sky. "God, what beautiful weather," he said. "It was spitting cats and dogs when I left Baldonnel. I think I'll emigrate and become a banker."

"I take it you haven't flown over to wish me a Happy Easter," said Fitzduane.

Kilmara grinned. "An interesting Easter," he said. "Let's start with that."

They left Belpmoos, Bern's little airport, and drove to the apartment. They were followed by two unmarked police cars, and a team carrying automatic weapons guarded the building as they talked. At Belpmoos the Lear was held under armed guard and searched for explosive devices. It would be searched again prior to takeoff.

The Chief Kripo had enough embarrassing incidents piling up without adding the killing of Ireland's Commander of the Rangers to the pile.

"YOU'VE GOT to remember," said Kilmara, "that the Rangers are not mandated to be an investigation unit in Ireland." He grinned. "We're in the business of applying serious and deadly force when our nation-state requires it. We're considered a little uncouth to deal directly with the public. Detective work is the job of the police. Of course, we stretch things a bit, and we have our own contacts, but we're limited in what we can do directly." His mood changed. "It can be fucking frustrating."

"What was the reaction to the video?" said Fitzduane. It had been described to him by Kilmara after the Ranger colonel had first viewed it, but sight of the real thing added an extra dimension. People in animal masks running around his island didn't please him. It reminded him of the bloody history of the place when the first Fitzduane had moved in. What had that cult been called? The Sacrificers. They had been wiped out in fierce fighting. Stories of the conquest of the Sacrificers in the twelfth century were part of the Fitzduane family folklore.

Kilmara sighed. "I'm not too popular with our prime minister," he said, "which means his appointed flunkies, including our brain-damaged Minister for Justice, read the way the wind is blowing and think it good politics to fuck me around a little when the opportunity arises."

"Meaning?" said Fitzduane.

"Meaning that any further investigation of Draker is out," said Kilmara. "I did twist an arm or two earlier, and a couple of Special Branch friends spent a day there asking discreet questions, but to no avail—and then the minister received a phone call from the acting headmaster, and that was that. Besides, I have to say that I'm buggered if I know what we were supposed to be looking for. Sure, there have been three deaths, but there isn't a hint of foul play. Your intuition might have currency with me, but I can tell you it's a thin argument when dealing with the inertia of the average Irish politician. The parents of the Draker kids are some very important people, and the school spends good money in the area. No one wants to upset a bunch of international movers and shakers and lose jobs into the bargain. It pains me to say it, but they have a point."

Fitzduane shrugged. "Rudi and one of the terrorists you took out in Kinnegad had the same tattoo. It now looks as if Vreni's absent boyfriend, Peter Haag, is the late and unlamented Dieter Kretz. We are talking serious linkage here. Then there is the matter of a bunch of guys dressed up like a druidic sacrificial cult."

"I've been through all this ad nauseam," said Kilmara. "We have to create a distinction between facts and the interpretation of those facts. At present the party line is that the Kinnegad business should be investigated with vigor but that it has nothing to do with Draker.

Rudi's tattoo is only hearsay evidence since there is nothing actually on it in the file, and as for our animal-headed friends—so what? Dressing up in funny masks is part of every culture and certainly isn't either a crime or even suspicious. Look at Halloween or the Wren boys at Christmas. The bottom line is that Draker is off limits, but other avenues we can pursue. And are."

"The idle thought occurs to me," said Fitzduane, "that your ongoing feud with the Taoiseach is becoming no small problem. I wonder why he *does* dislike you so. This thing has been going on since the Congo. Kind of makes you think, doesn't it?"

"I took this job," said Kilmara, "because I hoped to find out who betrayed us back then. My friend the Taoiseach, Joseph Patrick Delaney, had the means, the motive, and the opportunity—but I have no proof. And meanwhile, I have to protect and work with the man."

"He has a certain Teflonlike quality," said Fitzduane. "I guess you could try tact."

"I do," said Kilmara. "I don't call him shithead to his face."

Fitzduane laughed. "Politicians," he said, and he was quoting. " 'Fuck 'em all—the long and the short and the tall.' "

Kilmara smiled. "The Congo—the dear-old-now-called-Zaire fucked-up Congo. You bring back memories. But we were naive then. You can't write off politicians that easily. Hell, everything's political. You're no mean politician yourself."

Fitzduane grunted.

Kilmara broke new ground. "Speaking of politics," he said, "remember Wiesbaden?"

"The BKA and its giant computer, the Kommissar," said Fitzduane. "Sure."

"Large organizations like the BKA are coalitions," said Kilmara, "lots of little factions pushing their own particular points of view, albeit within a common framework."

"Uh-huh," said Fitzduane.

"One of the factions within the BKA, a unit known as the Trogs—they work troglodyte fashion, underground in an air-conditioned basement—has been experimenting for some time with an expert system to work with the Kommissar. They call it the Kommissar's Nose." He smiled. "We have a special relationship with the Trogs."

Fitzduane was beginning to see the light. "A back channel?" he said. "You're not just getting the routine reports from the BKA. The Trogs give you chapter and verse."

"We trade," said Kilmara. "They wanted access to our files for a project they were working on, and then I was able to help them out through some contacts in other countries. It took off from there. We have most-favored-nation status with the Trogs."

He looked at Fitzduane and took his time continuing. "They think we may be able to help each other," he said.

"Who are they?"

"The computer guru of the unit is a Joachim Henssen. He's one of these people who work twenty-four hours at a stretch on the keyboard, live on junk food, and shave but once a month. He's a fucking genius. Administration is handled by a seconded street cop of the old school, a Chief Inspector Otto Kersdorf. Surprisingly they get on."

"An expert system," said Fitzduane, "if memory serves, is a kind of halfway house on the road to artificial intelligence—a computer thinking like a human."

Kilmara nodded. "Artificial intelligence is an aspiration. Expert systems are reality right now. Basically you figure out how humans do things and then program their approach into the computer. Human experts tend to reach conclusions through a series of intelligent guesses called heuristics. An expert system is based upon a series of heuristics."

He grinned. "Here endeth the lesson—because here endeth my knowledge. I belong to a pre–Pac-Man generation."

"So the Trogs," said Fitzduane, thinking it through, "have come up with a software package that can analyze the mass of data accumulated by the Kommissar in much the same way as a bunch of smart, experienced policemen—something no human could do because there is too much computerized data to crunch through."

"With one qualification," said Kilmara. "It's not a proven system yet. That means the BKA top brass won't go public on it in case they end up with egg on their faces—which means what the Kommissar's Nose is sniffing out isn't seeing the light of day. The Trogs are going nuts."

"But they've told you?"

"Unofficially," said Kilmara. "It could explain a lot if they are right—but there are many uncertainties involved."

"But you want to take a flier on the whole thing?"

Kilmara nodded. "They started off trawling through the Kommissar's data banks and noticed patterns," he said. "This led them to look at things on a more global basis—the U.S., the Middle East, and so on. Their findings have evolved into the hypothesis that one person has been behind a series of seemingly separate terrorist incidents over about a ten-year period. Common denominators include an excessive use of violence, a sick sense of humor, and a healthy respect for the bottom line. There is also a fondness for certain types of weaponry, including Skorpion machine pistols and Claymore directional mines.

"The Trogs call the mastermind a terrorist multinational. They say—and maybe they're not joking—that he thinks, operates, and organizes like a Harvard M.B.A. and probably has a gold American Express Card and his accounts audited by one of the Big Eight. They claim his pattern is to work globally through a variety of different subsidiary organizations."

He grinned. "Cynics in the BKA call this hypothetical master terrorist the Abominable No-Man. They say that it's a wild theory and that Henssen is spaced. The Trogs reckon the only way to vindicate themselves is to track down this mythical being, and to do that, they need to bypass the bureaucracy and be closer to the action. They think there's a chance he may be based in Bern. It's a place to start, and there are quite a few pointers in this direction, including the gentleman you threw off the Kirchenfeld Bridge and his girlfriend, the chessboard girl.

"Anyway, the Trogs have proposed setting up a small unit here. All they want is a couple of rooms, good communications, and a computer terminal or two. They'll supply the secure modems to link with the Kommissar and the rest of the gear."

He looked around Fitzduane's borrowed apartment and smiled.

"You devious son of a bitch," said Fitzduane. "Where do the Bernese cops come into all this?"

"It's an unofficial operation with unofficial blessing," said Kilmara. "Chief Max Buisard is skeptical. Examining Magistrate von Beck is enthusiastic. The deal is that von Beck heads it up with your friend the Bear. The one proviso is that we row in with an official representative. That way, if anything goes wrong, the forces of law and order of three countries—Switzerland, Germany, and Ireland—will be in the shit together and the fallout will be better dissipated. It's an old bureaucratic trick."

"So who are you assigning? Günther? He likes computers."

"A newcomer would take time to get acclimatized," said Kilmara.

"Anyway, von Beck and the Bear want you in on this thing. The Chief Kripo says you've brought a crime wave with you and is muttering about your screwing up his statistics but will support your involvement if you have official status. The Federal Police are kind of morbidly curious to find out what you're going to come up with next. A bit of terrorism does wonders for their funding, and the Feds think they're deprived if they don't have Porsches and this year's chopper to run around in.

"I want you in—officially now—because I think we're all holding on to different bits of the dragon without knowing quite what we've found. I want a man on the spot who already knows his way around and whom I can trust. Besides, I don't have anyone else who isn't gainfully employed. So what do you say? You'll have official status, which may prove handy the way the bodies are piling up."

Fitzduane sighed and spread his hands in resignation. There was a glint in his eyes.

"This all started with a morning constitutional," he said. "It's turning out like Vietnam."

"Don't complain," said Kilmara. "Vietnam was a photographer's war. Now, will you do it?"

"Why not?" said Fitzduane. "I've never worked with a bear and an intelligent computer before."

"We'll call the operation Project K," said Kilmara, "on account of your upmarket location."

He tossed Fitzduane a bulky package.

"An Easter present," he said.

The package contained a bottle of Irish whiskey, fifty rounds of custom-loaded shotgun ammunition, and a lightweight Kevlar bulletproof vest.

"It's our standard How-to-get-on-in-Switzerland kit," said Kilmara.

Fitzduane looked up at him. "How did you know about the shotgun?"

"Von Beck told me you were lugging one around in your tripod bag," said Kilmara. "Besides, I remember your taste in weapons from the Congo."

"I gather you think I'll need all this stuff."

"Haven't a clue, but it's no use running out with your Visa card when the shooting starts."

Fitzduane picked up one of the shotgun rounds. It was stenciled with the marking "XR-18."

"What's this?"

"It's an experimental round," said Kilmara, "that we've cooked up ourselves. As you know, a shotgun pattern is useless against a man above fifty yards—and if you've any sense, you'll fire at less than half that distance. A solid slug has more range but poor accuracy. Well, we ran across a new discarding-sabot slug that will enable you to hit a torso-size target at up to two hundred yards. We combined it with some of the characteristics of the Glaser slug by filling it with liquid Teflon and other material. It works"—he paused—"rather well."

"Any good against dragons?" said Fitzduane.

KADAR HELD a flower in his hands. He plucked the petals one by one and watched them flutter to the ground. Already they have begun to decompose, he thought. Soon they will be part of the earth once more, and they will feed other flowers. More likely some developer will grab the location and stop the cycle with a few tons of concrete. Even beautifully preserved Bern was being nibbled at around the edges. But the old town, he was delighted to say, maintained its charmed life.

He decided he would make a donation to ProBern. Just because he was a terrorist didn't mean he couldn't be concerned about the environment. Good grief, Europe was in danger of becoming an ecological desert—everything from mercury in the water to acid rain killing the trees. Half the men in the Ruhr Valley area were said to be sterile. There were too many people wanting too much in too small a space. Really, killing a few people was for the long-term good. Mother Earth needed some supporting firepower. He decided to send some money to Greenpeace, too. He had no desire to spend his retirement building up his radioactivity level so that he could read at night by the glow. Besides, he liked whales.

"It's tidying-up time," he said. "You know I like neat projects. Well, I want Geranium to be especially neat."

"How long do we have?" asked one of the five young people sitting in a semicircle before him. He was a Lebanese who had free-lanced for the PLO until the Mossad blew up his contact and two bodyguards and their armor-plated, totally untamperable-with Mercedes in Spain. He knew Bern well—they all did—and he traveled on a false Turkish passport. He had developed a strong bias against German cars and flinched inwardly every time a Mercedes taxi went by. He liked Bern because you could walk to most places or take a tram if time was pressing. You could kill to a schedule. Working for Kadar you soon learned to meet your deadlines.

"You each have your own timetable," said Kadar, "but the whole operation must be completed inside two weeks. Then we will rendezvous in Libya and finalize preparations for Geranium. By the end of May you will all be quite rich."

Kadar opened his rucksack and a large carryall and removed five packages. He gave one to each of the terrorists. "Each package contains your weapon, and the envelope contains details of your targets, travel arrangements, tickets, and so on. I suggest that you read these details here so that I can answer any questions."

There was the rustle of paper as the envelopes were opened. One of the two women present used a switchblade that she wore strapped in a quick-release mechanism on the inside of her left forearm. Her name was Sylvie, and she had trained with Action Directe in France. Sylvie read her operations order and looked up at Kadar. His face was expressionless. He looked at the group.

"Perhaps you would care to examine your weapons," he said.

Each terrorist bent forward and began to open the package. Inside the external wrapping was a layer of polyethylene followed by waxed paper. Sachets of silica gel had been added to absorb any surplus moisture. The weapons were free of protective grease and, though unloaded, were otherwise ready for use. Soon one Czech-made VZ-61 Skorpion lay exposed, then two more. Sylvie had a 9 mm Ingram fitted with a silencer. She clipped a magazine into place and cocked the weapon.

The remaining terrorist—a Swiss who operated under the name of Siegfried—sat looking at the jagged half-meter splinter of polished stone he had unwrapped. Letters had been cut into it. His face was ashen. He looked up at Kadar. "You're playing a joke with me?"

"Well, yes—and then again, no," said Kadar. "It's not just any piece of stone, though I admit it's not the size it should be. I couldn't carry the whole thing. Still, I'm sure you can work out the point."

Siegfried felt a fear he had never thought possible. It penetrated every fiber of his being. He knew he was shaking, but he was no longer able to control his body. His vision blurred; his mouth went dry. He thought of the people he had killed. He had always wondered what it felt like to be a victim. What did they think and feel when they looked down the barrel of his gun and knew that there was no way out, that nothing they could do or say would make any difference? Then he thought of all the work he had done for Kadar, and a wave of anger restored in him some slight ability to act.

"What—what do you mean?" The words came out in a jerky whisper so quiet they were almost drowned by the sound of buzzing insects. Shafts of sunlight penetrated the treetops and flooded the clearing. "Why?" he said. "Why, why?"

"I pay well, as you know," said Kadar, "but I do demand obedience. Absolute obedience." He stressed every syllable.

"I haven't disobeyed you," said Siegfried.

"I'm afraid you have," said Kadar. "You were questioned two days ago by the Kripos. You were held for twenty-four hours and then released. Under those circumstances you should not have come to this meeting. You might have led the police to us."

"It was only a routine interrogation. I told them nothing. They know nothing."

"You should have reported being held. You did not. A sin of omission, as Catholics would say."

"I wanted to work for you," said Siegfried. "Geranium is so close."

"Well, we can't have everything we want. Didn't they teach you that in nursery school?" Kadar looked at Sylvie. "In about thirty seconds." He looked back at Siegfried. "I thought you'd have recognized it," he said, indicating the polished stone. "It's a piece of gravestone. There wasn't time to have it properly inscribed."

The Ingram fires at the rate of twelve hundred rounds a minute—roughly twice the speed of the average hand-held automatic weapon. Sylvie blew her victim's head off with half of the thirty-two-round magazine in a fraction of a second.

Kadar was already on his feet. He pointed at the envelopes and wrapping paper that littered the ground in front of the four remaining terrorists. "As you know, I am concerned about the environment. I would take it kindly if you would remove this litter when you go."

"What about him?" asked the Lebanese, looking at Siegfried's splayed body.

"Not to worry," said Kadar, "he's biodegradable." With that Kadar vanished into the wood.

IVO WAS still in Bern, no great distance from police headquarters, in fact, but the Kripos and Berps of the City of Bern could scarcely have been blamed for failing to recognize him: plain Ivo no longer existed. He had been replaced by someone much better suited to the task at hand, a figure of legendary courage and valor who would pursue his quest to the ends of the earth. What had started as a pleasing notion while waiting for the Monkey in the Hauptbahnhof had metamorphosed, in Ivo's drug-blasted mind, into fact. He was Sir Ivo, noble knight and hero.

In keeping with his new status, Sir Ivo had adopted a new mode of dress. Since armor and other knightly accoutrements were not readily available in downtown Bern, he had to improvise with a little judicious pillaging. In place of chain mail, he wore a one-piece scarlet leather motorcycle suit festooned with enough zippers and chains to clink and clank appropriately. Over it he wore a surcoat made from a designer sheet featuring hundreds of miniature Swiss flags and a cloak fashioned from brocade curtain material. Roller skates served as his horse, and a motorcycle helmet fitted with a tinted visor did service as his helm.

Sir Ivo knew that he had enemies, so he decided to disguise himself as a harmless troubadour. He slung a Spanish guitar around his neck. It was missing most of its strings, but that was somewhat irrelevant since the sound box had been cut away to serve as a combined scabbard, arms store, and commissary. The guitar itself contained a bloodstained sharpened motorcycle chain—referred to by Sir Ivo as his mace and chain—and half a dozen painted hard-boiled eggs.

In his new outfit Sir Ivo was bulkier, taller, and—with his helmet visor down—faceless. The valiant knight raised his visor and lit up a joint. He was giving serious thought to his next move. He was getting closer to the man who had killed Klaus, but the question was what he should do with the information he had already acquired. He thought it would be nice to have some help. He missed having Klaus to talk to. Working out what one should do next was a difficult business by oneself. He liked the idea of a band of knights, the Knights of the Round Table.

He now knew quite a lot about the killer, thanks to the Monkey, and he might have found out more if the knave hadn't tried to knife him. The Monkey had thought that Ivo wouldn't know how to fight. He might have been right about mere Ivo—but *Sir Ivo* was a different story. He had blocked the knife thrust effortlessly with his shield (the much-abused guitar, whose remaining strings were lost in the encounter) and then had cut the varlet down with a few strokes of his mace and chain. He had been somewhat aghast at the effects of his weapon but had suppressed his squeamishness with the thought that a knight must be used to the sight of blood.

Still, it was unfortunate that he had been forced to cut down the Monkey so soon. He now had a jumble of facts and impressions of the killer—possibly enough to identify him—but these were mixed up with the Monkey's lies and with information on other clients. In his panic the Monkey had spewed out everything that came to mind, and sifting the useful from the irrelevant wasn't easy.

Sir Ivo knew that thoroughness was part of knightliness, so he had written everything down and had even attempted various rough sketches based on the Monkey's descriptions. He knew what the inside of the room was like where the blindfolded Klaus and the Monkey—sometimes separately, sometimes together—had been taken. He knew what the man with the golden hair wanted sexually and, in detail, what they did. He knew that the golden hair was not real, but a wig that was not only a disguise but a representation of someone called Reston. He knew that the man spoke perfect Berndeutsch but was probably not Swiss. He knew many other things. He had a list of license plates, but the Monkey had made his ill-fated move before he had explained them.

Sir Ivo reached into his guitar and removed a hard-boiled egg. This one was painted bright red, the color of blood. It reminded him of the Monkey's face after the chain had hit, but he suppressed this faintheartedness and decided instead to regard it as an omen, a good omen. He was going to get his man—but he needed help.

He thought of the Bear, one policeman who had treated him like a human being. But no, the Bear wouldn't do. A policeman might not understand about the Monkey. Questions would be asked. He couldn't waste time with the police until this was all over.

He thought about the last person who had helped him, the Irishman. That was a good idea. He'd find the Irishman again and sound him out. If he reacted as expected, he'd show him his notes on what the Monkey had said, and they could find the killer together. Two knights weren't a round tableful, but it was a start. The Irishman would be easy to find. He had seen him around before, and Bern was a small town. His Swiss upbringing coming to the fore, Sir Ivo carefully placed the handful of scarlet eggshell pieces in a nearby litter bin and skated away on his mission.

THE KRIPOS HAD questioned the old man, but he told them nothing. He had known Ivo for some time and had helped him and other dropouts with food and, occasionally, small sums of money. He had prospered in Bern, and since his wife had died and his children left, he had decided the time had come to put something back into the city that had been good to him. Quietly he had pursued a one-man campaign to help the less fortunate.

The Kripos knew what he did and respected him for it. They also knew, the way you do when you have been a policeman for some time, that he was lying when he said he hadn't seen Ivo, but there was little they could do except thank him for his time and leave, noting their reservations in their report and resolving to try again in a week or two if nothing else turned up.

Kadar's two-strong team did not suffer from the same scruples. With the lessons of Siegfried's death still clear in their minds, they didn't fold their notebooks and depart when they saw that the old man was lying. They bound him and gagged him, and for the next ten minutes of his life they inflicted more pain on him than he had experienced in all his seventy-three years.

When he wanted to talk, they wouldn't let him. They made him write out what he knew in a shaking hand, the gag still in his mouth. The apartment was small, and they wanted to make sure that he'd have no chance to cry for help. Then they tortured him again to confirm his story. It didn't change. His physique, despite his age, was strong. He endured the second bout of agony with his heart still beating but with his guilt at having betrayed Ivo almost a greater pain.

Satisfied that at least they now had a description of Ivo in his newer image and that the old man had told them all he knew, they hanged him. They didn't think it would take too long to find Ivo. Bern, after all, was a small town.

THE CHIEF KRIPO HAD been daydreaming. It was an understandable lapse given the hours he had been working recently, combined with the glow of sexual satiation resulting from a quick twenty minutes with Mathilde in her Brunnengasse apartment. He was still in a good mood when he picked up the phone. He recognized the pathologist's voice, which, he had to admit, he did not associate with good news. Cutting up corpses wasn't a very upbeat line of work.

"Ernst Kunzler," said the pathologist.

The Chief racked his brains. Then he remembered. Bern averaged about two suicides a week. This was the most recent. "The old man who hanged himself. Yes, I remember. What about him?"

"He didn't hang himself," said the pathologist. "He was helped on his way, but it's much worse than that."

His good mood suddenly vanished, the Chief Kripo began to feel sick.

FITZDUANE HAD three people to see in Lenk, and besides, he had never actually been to a real live ski resort. Lenk wasn't a jet set sort of place where you got crowded off the ski slopes by ex-kings, movie stars, Arab sheikhs, and rumbles of bodyguards; it was more of a family place for the Swiss and certain cognoscenti. It was also off season and felt like it. Fitzduane was mildly shocked when he arrived in the valley where Lenk nestled. Something normally associated with ski resorts was missing. There were cows, there was brownish grass that looked as if it still had not decided that winter was quite over, there were chalets nestling into the hillside the way chalets should, and there were alpine flowers in profusion—but no snow.

The sun blazed down. He shaded his eyes, looked around and then upward, and instantly felt reassured. All those picture postcards hadn't lied. The village might be two-thirds asleep, but as his gaze rose, he could see ski lifts still in action. Farther up, the thin lines of the cables, the grass, and the tree line blended into the white glare of snow, and higher up still, multicolored dots zigged and zagged.

He thought he'd better get some sunglasses. As he paid, he remembered that inflation came with the snow line. Or, as Erika had put it, "Why should we have to pay twenty percent more for a few thousand meters of altitude?" The air was clear, the day warm, and the thin air invigorating. On balance Fitzduane thought it was a silly question.

MARTA VON GRAFFENLAUB LOOKED the part of the firstborn. In contrast with Andreas, Vreni, and Rudi, who were still in the transition stage into full maturity, Marta had arrived. She was no longer a girl but very much a woman: poised, assured, and cautiously friendly.

It was hot two levels up, where they met by arrangement, and they sat on the veranda of the chalet-style restaurant, watching the skiing and listening to the distinctive swish and hiss of wax against snow.

The bottom half of Marta wore padded ski trousers and bright red composite material ski boots. The top half wore a designer T-shirt that consisted mainly of holes. Fitzduane wondered if one or the other half wasn't too hot or too cold. She had a creamy gold tan and an almost perfect complexion. She radiated good health and energy, and her nipples were nearly as prominent as Erika's. Funny, he'd never thought of the Swiss as sexy before.

He suppressed an impulse to nibble a nipple and looked across the snow to where a cluster of tiny skiers was making him feel inadequate. He thought they were probably still in diapers. They all wore mirrored sunglasses and skied as if they had learned how inside the womb. He cheered up when one of the supertots suddenly sat down and started to cry like a normal child. The little monster was probably a part-time major in the Swiss Army.

"You're very quiet," said Marta with a smile. She had the disconcerting ability to keep her distance while sounding intimate. "You drive from Bern and then climb a mountain to see me, and then you don't speak."

"I'm in shock," said Fitzduane. He was drinking hot Glühwein, which seemed like the right thing to do when you were surrounded by snow but unwise when sweat was dripping off your Polaroids. "Those things remind me of helicopters "—he pointed at the ski lifts clanking past quietly about a hundred meters away—"and I don't like helicopters."

"Oh, they're quite safe," said Marta. "We are very experienced in these things here." She saw that Fitzduane's Polaroids had angled to nipple height, and she blushed faintly.

"Mmm," said Fitzduane. Apparently it was true that alcohol hit harder the higher the altitude. He went into the bar to get another Glühwein and a scotch for Marta. Everybody was clumping along the wooden floor with the rolling gait of B-movie gunslingers. He seemed to be the only person not wearing ski boots. The five-year-old in front of him selected what looked like a beer. He shook his head. Sometimes he missed Ireland. He squeezed his way back through the gunslingers and gave Marta her drink. "Do you yodel?" he said.

"Oskar used to yodel," she said very quietly.

"I thought it was like riding a bicycle," said Fitzduane, "once learned, never forgotten." He had been looking at a particularly spectacular demonstration of skiing prowess by an adult of indeterminate sex. For a moment he had missed the change in Marta's tone of voice. The skier misjudged his approach to the chalet and slammed into the wooden railings.

"Olé!" exclaimed Fitzduane. He started to clap, and others on the veranda followed. A furious-looking mid-European face, dignity severely dented, surfaced from the snow. He shouldered his skis and clomped off toward the ski lift.

"I'm sorry," he said. "Oskar Schupbach, you mean."

"Yes." There were tears in her eyes. "Damn," she said, and wiped them away. A little troop of ski boppers went past, chattering like sparrows.

" 'The man with the face that looked as if it were carved out of solid mahogany,' " quoted Fitzduane. "Vreni told me about him, and so did Andreas. I'm going to see him while I'm here."

"You can't," said Marta. "Oskar is dead."

"He's dead? But I spoke to him only yesterday!" said Fitzduane, taken aback. "I arranged to meet him this evening in the Simmenfälle, the place beside the waterfall."

"He liked the Simmenfälle," said Marta. "He often went there for a glass of wine and a game of jass. He used to meet clients there. He was a guide, you know."

"I know."

Marta was pensive. She ran a long golden finger around the rim of her glass. She stared out at the skiers on the slopes. "He taught me to ski. He taught us all. He was part of our growing up here. Always while we were here in Lenk, there was Oskar. We skied with him, we climbed with him, in summer we walked with him. It's almost impossible to believe that he's gone. Just gone."

Marta was silent, and Fitzduane waited. He remembered Vreni's talking about Oskar in much the same way. What had the man known? Being so close to the von Graffenlaub family, what had he seen or surmised—and who might have been aware of his suspicions? Perhaps he was jumping to conclusions. There might be nothing irregular about the guide's death.

"How did he die?"

Marta gave a slight start as Fitzduane's question broke into her reverie. "I don't know the details. All I know is that he had gone to meet a client in the Simmenfälle. The client didn't show up, and while he was walking home, he was knocked down by a car. It was a hit and run."

"Did anyone see the accident?"

"I don't think so," said Marta, "but you'd have to ask the police."

Fitzduane watched his Glühwein getting cold. Then he went inside and called the Bear. There was a pause at the other end before the Bear spoke. "I'll check with the local canton police," he said. "When are you seeing Felix Krane?"

"Tomorrow if I can," said Fitzduane. "I haven't managed to track him down yet."

"I'll arrange for one of the local cops to go with you," said the Bear. "It may cramp your style, but I don't like what's going on. Where are you staying? I'll call you later."

"At the Simmenfälle."

There was another silence at the end of the line. Then the Bear sighed. "Don't go for any midnight walks," he said, "and keep your back to the wall."

"And don't talk to strangers," said Fitzduane.

"That's not so funny."

"No, it isn't."

THE CANTON POLICEMAN WAS a good-humored sergeant named Franze, with a tanned round face setting off an impressively red nose. He had the work-roughened hands of a farmer, which, indeed, he was in his off-duty hours. He arrived in a Volkswagen Beetle, a near twin of the antique that had transported Fitzduane to the Swiss Army base at Sand. It wheezed to a halt in front of the Simmenfälle as Fitzduane was finishing breakfast. The Irishman ordered an extra cup of coffee and, upon further reflection, a schnapps. The gesture was not unappreciated. Franze talked freely. Since Kilmara's visit, Fitzduane had official status, and the sergeant treated him like a colleague. Fitzduane found it quite odd to think of himself as a policeman.

It transpired that Oskar Schupbach had been related to Sergeant Franze. Talking about Oskar's death visibly depressed the good sergeant, and Fitzduane ordered him another schnapps for purely medicinal reasons. It crossed Fitzduane's mind that breakfasts with Swiss police sergeants were beginning to fall into a pattern.

"Oskar," said Sergeant Franze, his good humor resurrected by the second schnapps, "was a fine man. I wish you could have met him."

"So do I," said Fitzduane. He was annoyed at himself for not having come to Lenk sooner. "But accidents will happen."

"It was no accident," said Franze angrily, "unless you can be accidentally run over twice by the same car."

ON THE SHORT DRIVE to Lenk and the cheese maker's where Felix Krane was working, they passed the spot where Oskar Schupbach had been killed. Sand had been sprinkled over the bloodstains, and Franze crossed himself as he pointed out the spot where the guide had died. Fitzduane felt cold and grim and had a premonition of worse things to come. Then the mood passed, and he thought about Krane and being followed that day he had left Vreni and about the making of cheese.

Fitzduane was fond of good cheese and regarded the master cheese maker's business with more than passing interest. A compact but expensively equipped shop in front—featuring a lavish array of mostly Swiss cheeses, each one shown off by a miniature banner featuring the coat of arms of the region of origin—led through to a miniature factory in the rear. Stainless steel vats and electronic monitoring equipment contrasted with a young apprentice's portioning butter by hand, using wooden paddles shaped like rectangular Ping-Pong paddles. Each cheese was hand-stamped with the master cheese maker's mark.

The master cheese maker was a big, burly man with a luxuriant mustache to set off his smile. He was tieless, his shirtsleeves were rolled up, and he wore a long, white, crisply starched apron. Fitz-duane thought he would do nicely in a barbershop quartet. Sergeant Franze spoke to him briefly, and then he turned to Fitzduane. "His name is Hans Müller," he said. He introduced Fitzduane. Müller beamed when he heard his name mentioned and pumped Fitzduane's arm vigorously. To judge by the size of the cheese maker's muscles, he had served his apprenticeship churning butter by hand.

"I have told him you are a friend of Oskar's," said Franze— Müller's face went solemn—"and that you want to see Felix Krane on a private matter."

"Is Krane here?" asked Fitzduane, looking around.

"No," said Franze, "he no longer works here regularly but does odd jobs. Now he is in the maturing store just outside town. It's a cave excavated into the mountainside. Without any artificial air-conditioning, it keeps the cheese at exactly the right temperature and humidity. Krane turns the cheeses, among other jobs he does there."

Müller spoke again, gesturing around the building to where half a dozen workers and apprentices were carrying out different tasks. He sounded enthusiastic and beamed at Fitzduane. The sergeant turned toward Fitzduane. "He has noticed your interest in his place, and he wants to know if you would like to look around. He would be happy to explain everything."

Fitzduane nodded. "I would be most interested." Afterward Fitz-duane had good reason to recall that informative hour and to specu-late on what might have happened if they had left to find Felix Krane earlier. On balance, he decided it had probably saved his own life.

Unfortunately, in view of what he was about to find, he never felt quite the same way about cheese again.

THEY WERE on the shaded side of the valley, driving slowly up a side road set in close to the base of the mountains. Out of the sun the air was chill. Across the valley mountain peaks loomed high, causing Fitzduane to feel vaguely claustrophobic and to wonder what it must have been like before railways and mountain tunnels and roadways opened up the country. No wonder there was such a strong sense of local community in Switzerland. The terrain was such that for centu-ries you had little choice but to work with your neighbors if you were to survive.

Sergeant Franze was driving slowly. "What are we looking for?" asked Fitzduane.

"It's easy to miss," said Franze. "All you can see from the road is a gray painted iron door set into the mountain."

They could see a dark blue Ford panel truck parked up ahead. "There it is," said Franze, "about thirty meters before that truck."

Fitzduane couldn't see anything at first. The entrance was recessed and had weathered into much the same texture as the mountain. Then, when he was practically parallel and Franze was pulling in to park, he saw the iron door. It looked old, from another century, and there was a small grating set in it at eye level.

Franze walked ahead to the truck and peered inside, then walked back to where Fitzduane stood beside the iron door. "Nobody in it," he said. "Probably some deliveryman gone to have a pee."

An unlocked padlock hung from the hasp. Franze eased the door open. It was stiff and heavy but not too hard to handle. It was balanced so that it closed slowly behind them. Ahead lay a corridor long enough for the light from the door grating to get lost in the gloom. Franze looked around for a light switch. He flicked the switch, but nothing happened.

"Shit," he said, "I didn't bring a flashlight. Still, it's not far."

It was cool but dry in the corridor. Fitzduane felt something crunch underfoot. It sounded like glass from a light bulb. "What's the layout?" he asked. The corridor curved, and the last vestiges of light from the grating vanished.

"This passage runs for about another forty meters and then splits into three," said Franze. "The cheese storage is on the right, so if you hug the right-hand wall, you can't miss it."

"What about the other passages?"

"The middle cavern is empty, I think," said Franze. "The one on the left is used by the army. You know there are weapons dumps, thousands of them, concealed all over the country."

Fitzduane digested the idea of storing cheese and armaments together and decided it was a nonrunner for Ireland. "Why not give Krane a shout?" he said. "We could do with some light. There seems to be glass everywhere." He thought he could hear voices but very faintly. He paused to listen.

Suddenly there were screams, a series of screams, all the more unsettling for being muffled. The screaming abruptly terminated in a noise that brought memories jarring back into Fitzduane's brain. There was no sound quite like the chunk of a heavy blade biting into human flesh.

"*Mein Gott!*" said Franze in a whisper. There was silence apart from his breathing. "Herr Fitzduane, are you armed?"

"Yes." He slid the shotgun from its case and extended the collapsible metal stock. He pumped an XR-18 round into the chamber and wished he had had an opportunity to test-fire a few rounds first. He heard Franze, ten paces ahead of him, work the slide of his automatic.

The darkness was absolute. He tried to picture the layout in his mind. They must be close to where the passage widened and split into three. That would mean some kind of lobby first, more room to maneuver. He felt vulnerable in the narrow passage. There was a slight breeze on his face, and he heard a door opening ahead of him.

"Krane!" shouted Franze, who seemed to have moved forward another couple of paces. He shouted again, and the noise echoed from the stone walls. "Maybe he has had an accident," he said to Fitzduane. "One of those cheese racks may have fallen on him. You stay where you are. I'm going ahead to see."

Fitzduane kept silent; he did not share Franze's optimism. Every nerve ending screamed danger, and he concentrated on the elemental task of staying alive. When it happened, it would happen fast. There was the sound of fumbling. Fitzduane guessed that Franze was looking for a lighter. He moved from crouching on one knee to the prone position and began to wriggle forward in combat infantryman's fashion, using his elbows, holding his weapon ready to fire. Every two or three paces he held his weapon in one hand and with his free hand felt around him. The passage was widening. He moved toward the middle so that he could maneuver in any direction.

Franze's lighter flashed and then went out. Fitzduane could see that Franze, who was right-handed, was holding the lighter in his left hand far out from his body. His automatic was extended at eye level in his right hand. It was not the posture of a man who thought he was investigating a simple industrial accident. Fitzduane hoped that Franze had the combat sense to change positions before he tried the lighter again. As he thought this, he rolled quickly to a fresh location, painfully aware of how exposed they were. Darkness was their sole cover.

He had a sense that there was someone else in the tunnel with them. He could hear nothing, but the feeling was strong and his skin crawled. He wanted to warn Franze, but he remained silent, unwilling to reveal his position, and prayed that the policeman had detected the intruder as well. He heard the faintest sound of metal rubbing against stone. The sound was to his left, roughly parallel with Franze. His imagination was playing tricks. He heard the sound again and thought he could hear breathing. The hell with appearing a fool, he thought. He heard the sound of Franze's lighter again. The policeman hadn't moved from his original position.

"Drop right, Franze!" he shouted, rolling right as he did so. In a blur of movement he saw that Franze's lighter had flared again. For a split second its light glinted off bloodied steel before the lighter tumbled to the ground, still gripped in the fingers of the policeman's severed left arm. Franze screamed, and Fitzduane's mind went numb with shock. The sound of movement down the corridor toward the outer door snapped him back to his senses.

He pushed Franze flat on the cold stone floor as a flash of muzzle blast stabbed toward them and bullets ricocheted off stone and metal. He tried to sink himself into the solid stone. Two further bursts were fired, and he recognized the sound of an Ingram fitted with a silencer. The outer door clanged shut. His left hand was warm and sticky, and Franze was breathing in short, irregular gasps.

He felt again with his left hand. He touched inert fingers and the warm metal of the lighter top. He placed the shotgun on the ground and with his two hands removed the lighter from the severed arm. He wanted to wait; he was safe in the darkness. But he knew that Franze needed help. It seemed probable that whoever else had been there, Krane perhaps, was gone. He had thought that there had been two people, but he couldn't be sure. Christ, it was like Vietnam again, yet another fucking tunnel. Sweat broke out on his forehead, and he could feel the vibration of bombing in the distance. He fought to control himself and realized that the vibration was a heavy truck grinding up the road outside, where it was daylight and life was normal.

He flicked the lighter, and the flame caught immediately. Franze was slumped on the ground where he had been pushed, conscious but in shock. Blood was pouring from the stump of his left arm. It had been severed above the elbow.

Fitzduane removed his belt and tightened it above the stump until the flow had almost stopped. It was tricky work because he needed both hands for the tourniquet, so he had to let the lighter go out and work in darkness. His hands and clothing became saturated in blood. He spoke reassuringly to Franze, but there was no response, and the policeman's skin felt cold. He needed medical attention immediately. The wound itself wasn't fatal, but Fitzduane had seen lesser casualties go into deep shock and die after the loss of so much blood, and the sergeant was no longer young.

He helped the policeman back along the passage to the outer doorway. His spirits lifted when he saw the glimmer of light that signaled they were approaching the iron door and the road. It was difficult work. Franze was heavy. He lacked the strength to help himself, so in the end Fitzduane carried him in a fireman's lift. When he tried to open the iron door, he found with a sickened feeling that it was locked on the outside.

He moved the policeman back about ten paces and then went to retrieve his shotgun. Franze's arm lay close by. He left it where it lay and then, not sure what could be accomplished with microsurgery, took off his ski jacket, wrapped the arm in it, and, with the shotgun in his other hand, returned to Franze. "Keep your head down," he said. The policeman barely reacted.

Fitzduane had little faith that a shotgun blast would have much effect against the iron door, but it was worth trying. He stood about two meters back and pointed his weapon at the lock. He fired twice, working the slide quickly to deliver two concentrated blows in the minimum time.

The results lived up to Kilmara's promise. The brittle iron of the door shattered like a shell casing when the XR-18's 450-grain sabot rounds struck it. Shards of iron clanged onto the roadway, and light flooded into the passage. Fitzduane pushed the remains of the door open and helped Franze outside.

A few yards up the road Müller had just gotten out of his car. The master cheese maker had a presentation box in his hand. He looked at Fitzduane, shotgun still smoking, covered in blood and supporting the policeman. His brain couldn't take in the situation at first, his face registering total disbelief; then he dropped the presentation box and ran forward. Together they helped Franze into the car and covered him with a blanket.

"A flashlight?" said Fitzduane. "Have you got one?" He searched for the right word in German and cursed his lack of languages. He pantomimed what he wanted. Müller nodded, opened the trunk of his car, and extracted a powerful battery searchlight. Fitzduane grabbed it and pushed Müller into the driver's seat.

"Hospital and police—*Hospital und Polizei*—go!" shouted Fitzduane. He banged on the roof of the car, and Müller roared away, one arm extended in a wave of acknowledgment.

Fitzduane replaced the two spent cartridges and moved back into the passage. He advanced up it in combat fashion, the Remington held at the ready. He doubted that there was any remaining danger, but he could see no reason for behaving like a total fool. He knew if he had any real sense of self-preservation, he would have waited for the police, but he hadn't the patience.

He saw that every light along the passageway had been systematically broken. This served the double purpose of providing the cover of darkness for an escape and an early-warning system; any new arrival would have to crunch across the glass. The door into the cheese maturing room was open. It was a long, narrow room filled with row after row of wooden racking, each rack filled with wheels of cheese graded by type and age and size.

There was a pair of large porcelain sinks in the far corner of the room. He shone the powerful light toward them. The sinks and the tiling around them were splashed with fresh blood. He played the beam downward, following the splash marks. A body, dressed in a once-white overall now sodden with blood, lay slumped on the floor. The corpse was headless. Fitzduane moved closer to examine the body but remained several paces away. The tiled floor was sticky with blood. It looked as though the victim had been bent headfirst over the sink as if for ritual execution. Fitzduane could imagine the horror of the doomed man as his neck was pressed against the cold surface.

He looked into the sinks, but there was no sign of the head. He examined the floor, also with negative results, and began to wonder why the head been taken away. As proof of a job completed? To delay identification? Then he thought of the chessboard killing and the bizarre sense of humor displayed there, and he knew what he would find. He moved the light back to the racks of cheeses and began examining each row of impeccably aligned wheels. It didn't take long. Though he was prepared for the sight, the reality made his stomach turn. Felix Krane's head stared at him from between two maturing wheels of Müller's Finest High Pasture.

Fitzduane went back to the road and waited for the police. The parked van was gone. He didn't remember its being there when he had emerged from the tunnel with Franze. The presentation box of cheese lay on the ground where Müller had dropped it. Fitzduane left it there.

"BE PREPARED," said Kadar to no one in particular, for he was alone, and he gave a three-fingered Boy Scout salute.

The deep freeze, a catering-size chest unit over two meters long, was kept in a concealed and locked storage room in the adjoining premises, owned by Kadar but registered to a cutout. In fact, in keeping with his normal practice of having an escape route always available, Kadar owned the entire small block. By way of hidden doors, he could travel from one end of the block to the other without ever having to use the street. Kadar wasn't entirely happy having the freezer with its incriminating contents so near, but he considered his precautions reasonable, and the important point was that he could get at what he wanted without delay.

He entered the small, brightly lit room and closed and relocked the door behind him before punching in the code that would release the freezer lid. He glanced at the abundance of food inside. The top layer was sorted by category in wire baskets. He liked things neat. He removed a wire basket of frozen vegetables and then one of fish. The next contained poultry. The last basket was filled with game birds, mainly pheasant although quail and several other species were also represented. He had gone through a pheasant phase not so long ago, until he chipped a tooth on a piece of buckshot—the idiot hunter must have thought pheasants were the size of vultures because the shot was from a number four load—and was forced to visit the dentist. This boring experience had not been without its advantages, though it had put him off pheasant for a while. While lying back in the dentist's chair, he had begun to plan his own death. This exercise was not unenjoyable, despite the circumstances, for it involved the dentist's death, too.

He admitted to himself that the basic idea wasn't original, but he didn't suffer from the classic engineers' disease of NIH—"Not Invented Here," and therefore useless. In any case he had improved on the original pattern, thanks to his casual discovery—through the one-sided small talk that dentists enjoy while the victim lies gagged and helpless—that this particular dentist, the appallingly expensive but highly successful Dr. Ernst Wenger, was an unusually prudent man. Swiss to the core and Bernese from toe to toupee, he not only kept excellent dental records in his office—what else would you expect of someone who was also a supply officer, a major in fact, in the Swiss Army?—but kept a reserve set, updated weekly, in his bank. Dr. Wenger kept a substantial portfolio of bearer bonds and other securities in the same location, but considering the success of his practice, if he had been asked to choose which he would prefer to lose—dental records or financial papers—it would have been no contest. His dental records were the key to what he called his "private gold mine." Dr. Wenger enjoyed his little jokes. His patients, on average, did not.

Kadar placed the last basket on the floor beside the deep freeze, then looked back into the unit. Nothing had changed since his last inspection, which was reassuring if scarcely surprising. He didn't really expect the occupant to be found munching frozen peas or to have grown a mustache to while away the time. Frozen corpses tended to be low on the activity scale. Kadar leaned on the insulated rim of the freezer and spoke encouragingly. "Your time will come, have no fear." He smiled for good measure.

Inside the deep freeze, well frosted over, Paul Straub lay unmoving. The expression of horror, panic, despair, and downright disbelief on his face, frozen into perpetuity, indicated his general lack of enthusiasm for his fate. He had been drugged, bound into immobility, then placed alive in the deep freeze. His last sight before the lid and darkness descended was of a basket of frozen chickens. As a vegetarian he might have particularly objected to this. He had been frozen to death, his only offense being a certain similarity in height, weight, and general physiognomy to Kadar—and the fact that he had been a patient of Dr. Wenger's.

Kadar leaned farther over, reached into the freezer, and tapped the corpse. It felt reassuringly solid. The refrigeration was working fine. He had considered using supercold liquid nitrogen, which would minimize tissue destruction—it was used for semen and strawberries, to name but two critical applications—but when he considered what was going to happen to the corpse, Kadar settled for a more conventional solution.

He straightened himself and began replacing the baskets. Just before he replaced the last one, he looked at the late Paul Straub's frozen head. The eyes were frozen open but iced over. "Don't blame me," said Kadar. "Blame that damn pheasant." He dropped the basket into place. He felt quite satisfied as he left the room and heard the locks snap into place behind him. All in all, given the imperfections of the material he was working with, things were going quite well.

Chapter Nineteen

As originally conceived, Project K was to be a low-key support operation, close enough to the people at the sharp end to cut out bureaucratic delay but modest in scope and scale. The killings in Lenk changed things overnight.

Convinced that time was running out, Charlie von Beck had turned Fitzduane's apartment into an around-the-clock command center. When Fitzduane found that a Digital Equipment Corporation multiterminal minicomputer was being installed in his bedroom, he took the hint and moved into a spare room in the Bear's Saali apartment. It didn't have black silk sheets and a mirror over the bed, but the Bear's cuisine would have merited three stars from Michelin if ever its reviewer had dropped in, and besides, the Bear had bought himself a bigger gun—which, the way things were going, was comforting.

Von Beck had encountered some opposition to basing Project K in "nonofficial premises," but he had countered with the comment that if Brigadier Masson could run the Swiss intelligence service during the Second World War from a floor in Bern's Schweizerhof Hotel, the secluded apartment off Kirchenfeldstrasse was good enough for him.

The occupants of the other three apartments in the small block—wholly owned by Beat von Graffenlaub—were amicably moved out

by appeals to their patriotism and their pockets. Once the last of
them left, von Beck tightened security still further.

As FITZDUANE, the Bear, and, from time to time, other members of
the Project K team spoke, Beat von Graffenlaub began to look
increasingly disturbed. As always, the lawyer was immaculately
tailored, but the elegance of his clothes no longer seemed integrated
with the body inside. His face was pale, his eyes rimmed with red,
and he had lost weight. The arrogance of wealth was no longer so
apparent in his manner.

"And what do you call this man, this corrupter of lives?" he said in
a low, angry voice.

Henssen indicated that he would answer. "When he was nothing
more than a statistical anomaly, my cynical colleagues in the BKA
christened him the Abominable No-Man. Now that is not so funny
anymore."

"The Hangman," said the Bear. "We've given him the code name
'the Hangman.' "

Von Graffenlaub looked at Fitzduane.

"We believe the Hangman exists," said Kersdorf quietly, "but it
would be idle to pretend that our view is widely held. Conventional
investigations parallel the work we are doing. Even your own Chief
of Police is skeptical."

"In strict legal terms," said von Beck, "we have very little proof."
His rather formal tone was counterbalanced by his attire. He was
wearing a pink sweatshirt labeled SKUNKWORKS. The group of
snoozing skunks stenciled on it all wore bow ties.

"And if your heuristics—your intelligent guesses—are wrong,"
said von Graffenlaub, "you have cumulative error in your deduc-
tions increased by the massive power of your computing system."

"Those are the risks," agreed Henssen.

"The only thing is," said Chief Inspector Kersdorf, "nobody else
has come up with any coherent explanation of what has been happening."

Von Graffenlaub drank some Perrier. His hand was shaking
slightly as he drank. He put the glass down and bowed his head in
thought. The group around him remained silent, and they could hear
the faint hiss of bubbles bursting. He raised his head and looked at
each man in turn. His gaze stopped at Fitzduane.

"This man, a stranger, was concerned enough to want to know why a young man should die so horribly," he said. "Rudi was my son and, with his twin sister, Vreni, my lastborn. I can assure you that I'm not going to back out now. You'd better tell me everything—both what you know and what you suspect. Don't try to spare my feelings. You had better start with Rudi's involvement with this—this Hangman."

"And your wife's," said Fitzduane.

"Erika," said von Graffenlaub. "Yes, yes, of course." He was whispering, and there were tears running down his cheeks.

Fitzduane felt terribly, terribly sad. He was looking at a man being destroyed, and there was no way anymore to stop what would happen. He put his hand on von Graffenlaub's shoulder, but there wasn't anything he could say.

As IF by agreement, the others left Fitzduane alone with von Graffenlaub. What had to be said was unpleasant enough without the embarrassment of having the entire group present.

"I'll be as brief as I can," said Fitzduane, "and I'll concentrate on conclusions rather than reasons. We can go through the logic of our reasoning afterward if you wish. We've already told you about the Hangman, and we'll come to what we know about him—and that's quite a lot—later, but right now I want to focus on one point, the Hangman's method of operation. His objectives seem to be financial rather than ideological—mixed, I suspect, with a general desire to fuck the system and a macabre sense of humor. His method seems to be to tap into, and harness, the natural energies and causes that already exist. He doesn't need a coherent ideology. Each little group is built around its own obsession, and the Hangman creams off the financial result.

"He likes dealing with impressionable people. Many of his followers—and most of them wouldn't think of themselves as *his* followers but as members of some specific smaller group—are young and idealistic and sexually highly active. He uses what's available, and we have reason to believe that sexuality is one such tool. It has long featured in secret rites and initiations and is a classic bonding and manipulative lever. Consider, for instance, sexuality in satanic rites or pre-Christian ceremonies, or, inversely, the absence of sex in the Catholic orders.

"In addition to his use of sexuality as a manipulative tool, and perhaps as a consequence of it, we believe that the Hangman has sexual problems of his own. He seems to have both heterosexual and homosexual inclinations, and these are mixed up with pronounced sadomasochistic behavior of the most extreme sort."

"In short, he is a maniac," said von Graffenlaub, "a monster."

"Maybe," said Fitzduane, "but if we are to catch him, that's not the way to think of him. He probably looks and behaves quite normally, much like you or me."

"And who knows what unusual behavior lurks beneath our prosaic exteriors?" said von Graffenlaub thoughtfully.

"Just so," said Fitzduane.

FRAU RAEMY HAD finished her shopping and was indulging herself with a coffee and a very small pastry, or two, at an outdoor café in the Bärenplatz. She was pleased because she had been able to find on sale the pear liqueur that her husband, Gerhard, so enjoyed, and three bottles of it now reposed in the sturdy canvas shopping bag on the ground beside her.

Gerhard, fed enough liqueur after his evening meal, became quite tolerable, mellow even, and later on, in bed, he tended to fall asleep immediately and what Frau Raemy thought of as "that business" could be avoided. Really, with both of them in their late fifties, it was about time that Gerhard found another activity to amuse himself with—perhaps stamp collecting or carpentry. On the other hand, perhaps it was not so bad that after twenty-eight years of marriage her man continued to find her desirable.

She smiled to herself. Sitting in the sun in the Bärenplatz was most pleasant. She enjoyed the passing parade, all these colorful characters.

A figure wearing a large cloak, face obscured by a motorcycle helmet, and with a guitar slung from his neck, glided to a stop in front of her and glanced around. Then, with an abrupt movement, he slid off into the crowd.

Frau Raemy didn't watch him go. There was a blur, a muffled coughing sound, and then she was staring in some confusion at her shopping bag, which had suddenly sprouted a ragged cluster of bullet holes. From the shattered bottles the aroma of pear liqueur filled the air.

Her mind, quite simply, could not cope with what had happened. She didn't go to the police. She placed her shopping bag in a litter bin, holding it at arm's length and keeping her face averted as she did so. Then she bought replacements in Loeb's and took the tram home. She didn't speak for two days.

"WHY DID you choose this place?" asked the Lebanese. He glanced around Der Falken. The café was two-thirds full of characters who might have been lifted straight from the set of a Fellini film. Most of the men seemed to have beards and earrings and big black hats and tattered jeans. You could tell the girls because most of them didn't have beards. Both sexes drank beer and milk shakes and smoked hash. There was a relentless conformity to their outrageousness. Almost no one was over twenty-five, and the sunken eyes and general skin pallor suggested that few were aspiring to longevity.

"No mystery," said Sylvie. "I wanted to get you off the street but fast. For fuck's sake, you missed the bastard."

The Lebanese shrugged apologetically. "He moved just as I fired. It couldn't be helped. He moves so fast on those skates. At least no one seemed to notice anything. The Skorpion silencer is most effective."

"We haven't got much time," said Sylvie. "You know Kadar."

"Only too well," said the Lebanese grimly.

"Next time we'll get in close," said Sylvie, "and there will be no mistakes."

The Lebanese drained his beer and said nothing. He flicked a speck of dust off his lapel and then examined with pleasure his polished alligator shoes. Fuck Kadar, fuck Ivo, and fuck Sylvie, he thought. He came back to Sylvie and looked at her appraisingly.

She met his glance and shook her head. "You're the wrong sex."

"RUDI WAS an almost perfect candidate for manipulation," said Fitzduane, "an accident looking for a place to happen. Most teenagers rebel against their parents to some extent, as you well know. Adolescence is a time of great confusion, of searching for identity, of championing new causes. When teenagers reject one set of values, a need for a replacement is created. Nature abhors an ideological vacuum as much as any other kind.

"Two conflicting views are often expressed about divorce: one is that children are permanently damaged by the whole process; the other is that children are naturally adaptable and have no real problem dealing with two fathers and three mothers or whatever. I don't know what the general pattern is, but I do know that in this specific case your divorce from Claire and your marriage to Erika created chaos. All your children were affected, as best I can judge, but none more so than Rudi—with Vreni a not-so-close second. But I'll concentrate on Rudi.

"Rudi started his lonely rebellion by rejecting your establishment values. His beliefs received an initial impetus from his mother, who was interested, I'm told, in a more liberal and caring society than you."

"We used to share the same views," said von Graffenlaub wearily, "but I had to deal with the real world while Claire had the luxury—thanks to my money—to theorize and dream of Utopia. I had to fight, to do unpleasant things, to make harsh decisions, to compromise my principles because that's the way the world is. I had to deal with facts, not fantasy."

"Be that as it may," said Fitzduane, "the problem was compounded by several other factors. First, Rudi was exceptionally intelligent, energetic, and intense—the classic moody bright kid. He didn't just feel rebellious; he wanted to do something specific. That led to the next development: he started investigating you, reading your files and so on, and lo and behold, he stumbles across Daddy's interest in Vaybon—and Vaybon is just as corrupt as he imagined."

"He misunderstood what he found," said von Graffenlaub. "Vaybon is a massive organization, and most of what it does is quite aboveboard. He happened to discover a summary of wrongdoings—exceptions to the general pattern of behavior—that I was trying to clean up. Instead of appreciating that he was looking at only a small piece of the picture, he assumed that my entire world was corrupt. He wouldn't listen to reason."

"You're not at your most rational in your teens," said Fitzduane, "and you're feeding me a fair amount of bullshit about Vaybon, but I'll let it pass for the moment because I want to talk about Rudi and not a multinational whose collective executive hands are very far from clean."

Von Graffenlaub flinched perceptibly but didn't speak. He was thinking of the initial idealism he had shared with Claire and then of the seemingly inexorable series of compromises and decisions—always for the greater good—that had led to such a debasement of his original values.

Fitzduane continued. "We then come to the burning of the papers Rudi had stolen, and Claire's death. His mother's death changed the scale of Rudi's rebellion and removed a restraining influence. He blamed you, the system, and the world for his unhappiness, and he began to believe that the most extreme measures would be needed to change things. Also, he wanted more than change; he wanted revenge, and for that he needed help. He started with the AKO and other extremist elements. They don't mess about with inefficient old democracy. They cut to the heart of the matter: The existing Swiss system has to be destroyed completely, and violence is the only way.

"I don't know how deeply Rudi got involved with the AKO," continued Fitzduane, "but I suggest that he was more involved than even his twin sister suspected. I believe he was being cultivated as a sleeper. Given his position, your position, if you will, he was too valuable to lose to routine police infiltration, so it was made out that he was only a sympathizer—a terrorist groupie, as I said to Vreni. I think he was almost certainly much more, or, at least, was destined for frontline activity.

"But police action cut deep into the heart of the AKO and other terrorist organizations, and this left Rudi with a problem. He needed a framework in which to operate, and his original mentors were in prison or dead or in hiding. It was at this stage that Erika entered the scene, no doubt after a series of initial plays. In Rudi we have a mixed-up, sexually active young man reacting against conventional values, who wants revenge on his father and to destroy the system. In your wife Erika—and you're not going to like this—we have a rich, bored, amoral, and sexually voracious woman of stunning physical attractiveness, who likes to indulge her whims and is constantly looking for new thrills, fresh excitement, to satisfy an increasingly jaded appetite. In addition, we suspect that she is involved with the singularly dangerous individual we have called the Hangman."

"Are you sure of this?"

"Am I sure that your wife is rich, bored, amoral, and sexually voracious? In a word, yes. Bern is a small town, and I've talked to a lot of people. Am I sure about her connection with the Hangman? No, I have no proof. I merely have a series of linking factors which point that way."

"Please continue," said von Graffenlaub quietly.

"The next major incident was sexual," said Fitzduane. "As best I can reconstruct it, it occurred during what was officially a normal family holiday in Lenk. Erika, Rudi, Vreni, their friend Felix, and, I believe, the Hangman were involved. A seduction, an orgy, a series of orgies—I don't have the details, and they are not important except that you should know that your wife undoubtedly slept with your son, and so did one or more of the men. I don't know whether he was naturally homosexual or whether this was part of his rebellion against conventional values, but homosexuality was certainly a factor in his life-style, and physical evidence from the autopsy confirmed this. As for his sleeping with Erika, this was revenge in its sweetest form."

"Oskar must have suspected something," said von Graffenlaub. "He spoke to me, but he was embarrassed, and the subject was dropped. I didn't know what he was talking about. I never considered such a possibility in my wildest dreams. It's . . . it's incredible."

"Poor Oskar," said Fitzduane. "Imagine his dilemma. He probably suspected a great deal, but what could he know for sure? And how could he voice his suspicions without insulting you? Would you have believed him if he had been more specific?"

"No," said von Graffenlaub, "of course not. Not without proof."

"And now Oskar is dead."

"And so is Felix Krane," said von Graffenlaub heavily. "What is happening? Are there no limits to this lunacy? What is this Hangman trying to do?"

"To understand the Hangman, you've got to think in different terms," said Fitzduane. "At the present time we think he is tidying up loose ends, though we don't know why. His behavior is not consistent. One explanation for what he is doing now is his need to eliminate those who could identify him, but at the same time he is taking unnecessary chances. His behavior is marked by a combination of cold rationality and what one might describe as impetuous arrogance. This latter quality seems to extend to his people. They are willing to take extraordinary risks to accomplish their objectives. It seems clear that they are far more afraid of failing the Hangman than of being caught by us. On the basis of what we know of the Hangman, maybe they've got a point.

"One thing we are sure of: If you've crossed the Hangman's path, you're at higher risk, which is why we recommended you retain security for yourself and the rest of your family, particularly your children. What you do about Erika is something you'll have to work out for yourself. Just make sure you tell her as little as possible. Remember, her games may not be confined to sex. They could extend to violence."

"There are limits to what I can accept," said von Graffenlaub. "Since the time you called from Lenk, I have arranged for armed guards to look after every member of my family, and that includes my wife. She may be promiscuous, but she is not a killer."

Fitzduane was silent. He looked at von Graffenlaub. "Think of your children, and think carefully. You're all in greater danger than you have ever been in before. Don't try to be noble at the risk of your own flesh and blood."

Von Graffenlaub shrugged helplessly. "What else can I do? I will consider what you are saying, of course, but . . . I cannot, I cannot abandon my wife just like that."

"There will be some police protection as well," said Fitzduane, "but the police don't have the manpower to protect everyone individually without more proof than we've got."

"You have already talked to my wife?" In von Graffenlaub's tone it was half a question, half a statement.

"She hasn't told you?"

"She said you had dinner together after the vernissage," said von Graffenlaub, "nothing more."

"Hmm," said Fitzduane, feeling vaguely uncomfortable as he recalled that epic evening. He pulled himself together. "Actually we have talked together on several occasions," he continued, "and most recently she has been questioned officially by Sergeant Raufman. She is alternatively charming and dismissive, perhaps even a little cynical. She looks amused and denies everything, and she's most convincing."

Von Graffenlaub sat mute, appalled at the idea of hearing more, yet compelled by his own desperate need for the truth to stay and listen.

"The island where I live," said Fitzduane, "where Rudi's college is, has been my family seat since the twelfth century. Getting established on the island initially was a bloody business. The land was conquered by force, and the main opposition was a druidic cult known as the Sacrificers. They used to wear animal head masks while practicing their rituals. Rather like the Thugs of India, the Sacrificers preyed on innocent people, robbing and killing them, as a way of worshiping their gods. Over the centuries dozens of mass graves filled with the bones of their victims have been found, which helps to explain why the island is so deserted even now. Fitzduane's Island, even in our supposedly enlightened times, is considered cursed and no fit place for a good Christian to live."

"I read something about it," said von Graffenlaub, "in a section of a brochure put out by Draker College. But what does a long-dead cult have to do with all this? The Sacrificers were wiped out more than seven hundred years ago."

"Well, imagine the appeal of such an organization to young people like Rudi. An independent structure, secret and violent and dedicated. To a rebellious adolescent, you can see the attractiveness of it. To a man like the Hangman, such an organization would be ideal."

"Preposterous," said von Graffenlaub. "These are wild surmises."

Fitzduane nodded. "You're quite right. Much of this is guess-work. I have no proof that Rudi was a member of any cult, much less one involving the Hangman. But the fact of his tattoo, which has been associated with the Hangman, remains. Otherwise the object of all this—game playing or something more serious—is far from clear. Now let me show you something."

Fitzduane clicked the video made by the Rangers into place and pressed the play button. On its completion he placed a slim plastic folder containing letters in front of the momentarily speechless von Graffenlaub.

"That video was made after Rudi's death," said Fitzduane. "That pleasant-looking little group was observed coming from Draker. The masks, need I say, make identification impossible."

"So why do you think Rudi was involved?" Von Graffenlaub's voice was weary. "His tattoo—except for the circle of flowers, it is a common enough design. It signifies protest, nothing more. He could have picked it up anywhere."

Fitzduane opened the file of letters. He showed one to von Graffenlaub. "You recognize the writing?"

Von Graffenlaub nodded. "Rudi's," he said sadly. He rubbed the paper between his fingers as if this would somehow bring his dead son closer.

"Rudi was alienated from you," said Fitzduane, "and his mother was dead. He was almost too close to Vreni. He needed someone to confide in who had some perspective. He started writing to Marta. What he wrote is neither entirely clear nor totally incriminating, but if you put it together with what we now know through other means, a reasonable interpretation is that he joined some sort of cult, found himself involved in something he couldn't handle, tried to leave—and then found there was no way out."

"So he killed himself."

"No," said Fitzduane. "I don't think so, or at least not willingly. I think he was either murdered or forced to commit suicide, which amounts to the same thing. Probably we shall never know."

"May I have his letters?"

"Of course." Fitzduane had already made copies in anticipation of this contingency. They made depressing reading. He remembered an extract from the last letter, written less than a week before Rudi's death:

Matinka,

I wish I could tell you what is really going on, but I can't. I'm sworn to secrecy. I thought it was what should be done, but now I know more, and I'm not sure it's right anymore. I've been doing a lot of thinking. This is a good place to think. It's so empty compared with Switzerland, and there is always the noise of the sea. It's surreal, not like real life.

But I have to get away. You'll probably see me sooner than you expect. Perhaps things will look better when I'm back in Bern.

Von Graffenlaub had been scanning the letter. "Why didn't Marta show this to me?" he said.

Fitzduane sighed. "By the time that particular letter arrived, Rudi was dead," he said. "I guess she thought, what's the point?"

THE BEAR AND CHARLIE VON BECK were sitting in the next room when Fitzduane came in after his talk with von Graffenlaub. The Bear removed his headphones and switched off the tape recorder. "Has he gone?"

"Yes," said Fitzduane. "He's got a plane to catch, some negotiations in progress in New York. He'll be away for a week."

"Plenty of time to think," said von Beck.

"Yes, poor sod," said Fitzduane. "I don't like what we're doing."

"We apply pressure where we can," said the Bear, "and hope that something gives. It's crude and it isn't fair, but it's what works."

"Sometimes," said Fitzduane.

"Sometimes is enough," said the Bear.

"I don't think von Graffenlaub is involved," said von Beck.

"No," agreed the Bear, "but who is better placed to lean on Erika?"

"Aren't you afraid of what may happen?" said Fitzduane.

"Do you mean, do I think von Graffenlaub may attack her, perhaps kill her? Not really. But even if he does, do we have a choice? The Hangman isn't a single case of murder; he's a plague. He's got to be stopped."

"The greater good."

"Something like that," said the Bear. "But if it helps you any, I don't like it either."

Fitzduane poured himself a drink. He was drained after the long session with von Graffenlaub, and the whiskey felt smooth against his throat. He poured himself another and added more ice. The Bear was lighting his pipe and looking at him over the top.

" 'How often have I said to you that when you have eliminated the impossible, whatever remains, however improbable, must be the truth?' " quoted Fitzduane.

"Not once," said the Bear, "since you're asking."

"Sherlock Holmes. Don't they teach you Bernese anything apart from languages?"

"Good manners, for one," said the Bear. "Let me remind you of another Holmes dictum: 'It is a capital mistake to theorize before one has data.' "

"That was before computers," said Fitzduane, "not to mention expert systems. Anyway, the trouble with this case isn't lack of data. We're drowning in it. What we're short of are conclusions, not to mention proof."

"They also teach us patience in Bern," said the Bear.

"That's not one of Ireland's national characteristics."

"But what's this about the elusive Ivo?" von Beck broke in. "What headway is being made there?"

"Sir Ivo," said Fitzduane. "He thinks he's a knight in shining armor. I didn't recognize him at first. I was coming out of a bank on the Bärenplatz when this weird figure in cloak and crash helmet slid up on roller skates and started to talk to me. Before I could say much more than a social 'Who the hell are you?' he'd vanished again. He did much the same thing twice more as I was crossing the square and then pressed a note into my hand. I damn nearly shot him."

Von Beck shuddered. "I wish you wouldn't say things like that," he said. "Shooting people is very un-Swiss. Which reminds me—the authorities in Lenk want to know who's going to pay for the iron door you blasted. Apparently it doesn't belong to the cheese maker; it's Gemeinde property."

Fitzduane laughed. Von Beck tried to look serious and authoritarian, which wasn't so easy in his SKUNKWORKS sweatshirt.

"Wait till you see the bill," he said. "It's no laughing matter. The Gemeinde claims it was an antique door of considerable historical value. They also want to give you an award for saving Sergeant Franze's life—but that's a separate issue."

"You're kidding me."

"Certainly not," said von Beck. "In Switzerland we take the destruction of property most seriously."

"Ivo," said the Bear.

"Ah, yes," said von Beck. "What does this note say?"

"It's a typical Ivo message," said the Bear, "not straightforward. He uses drawings and poetry and so on. But the meaning is clear. He wants to meet Fitzduane tomorrow at the High Noon, the café at the corner of the Bärenplatz, at midday. He must come alone. No police. And it's about Klaus Minder. Ivo has information about his killer."

"Ivo's a screwball," said von Beck, "and he's already killed one man. Is it worth the risk? We don't want our Irishman slashed to death before he's paid for the door in Lenk—even if it would make our Chief of the Criminal Police happy."

"It's a risk," said the Bear, "but I don't think a serious one. It's clear that Ivo has taken a liking to Fitzduane, and I don't think he's essentially violent. I'll lay odds what happened to the Monkey was provoked in some way."

"Want to risk it?" said von Beck to Fitzduane. "We'll have you well covered."

"If the city pays for the door in Lenk."

Von Beck looked pained.

Henssen came in, smiling. "Progress," he announced. "We've done another run. If all our heuristics are correct, we've narrowed down the suspect list to only eight thousand."

Von Beck looked depressed. "I hate computers," he said as he left the room.

"What's up with him?" said Henssen. "I was only joking."

"Budget problems," said the Bear.

FITZDUANE PUT down his glass. The shotgun, an XR-18 round chambered, safety on, lay concealed in the tripod case beside the beer. There was no sign of Ivo. He checked his watch: three minutes to noon. He remembered what Charlie von Beck had said: "Ivo might be a screwball, but he's a Swiss screwball." Ivo would be on time.

The Bear, von Beck himself, and six detectives, including one borrowed from the Federal Police, had been allocated to back up Fitzduane, and it had seemed like overkill when they were running through the plan. Now, looking at the teeming crowds and the area to be covered, he wasn't so sure.

He ran through the plan again. The Bärenplatz was a large, rectangular open space with outdoor cafés lining the sunny side. The center of the space had been closed off to traffic and was filled with market stalls. Today seemed especially busy. There were flower stands in profusion, hucksters selling leatherwear and homemade sweets and organically grown just-about-everything. About thirty meters away a crowd had gathered to watch some jugglers and a fire-eater perform.

The Bärenplatz wasn't a nice neat shoebox with one entrance. Far from it: it was impossible to seal off without much greater manpower than was available. One end led into Spitalgasse, one of the main shopping streets, providing endless opportunities for escape; the other end of the square bordered the Bundesplatz, the even larger open area in front of the Federal Parliament building. To cap it all off, Ivo would probably be on roller skates, which meant he could move considerably faster than the police. Fitzduane had raised the matter with von Beck, who had laughed and said that an earlier suggestion that some detectives might wear skates had nearly given the Chief Kripo a heart attack.

The compromise was two detectives on motorcycles. Fitzduane

looked at the jugglers and the fire-eater and the dense crowds and had bad vibes about the whole thing. On the other hand, he admitted to himself, he was biased. He would have liked to have seen the Bear on skates.

The High Noon was in one corner of the Bärenplatz within a few yards of the Käfigturm, the Prison Tower, which divided what was essentially one street into Spitalgasse and Marktgasse.

Ivo had stipulated no police, and the Bear, who knew him well, had been adamant. If Ivo wasn't to be frightened away, the backup force would have to be well concealed. "Ivo," the Bear had said, tapping his nose, "may be odd, but he's no fool. He can smell a cop—and he's got a good sense of smell. Believe me."

They did. All of which put the onus on Fitzduane and good communications. The idea was that Ivo wouldn't be arrested until he had had a chance to say whatever was on his mind. Only then, at Fitzduane's signal, would the trap be sprung. Fitzduane drank some beer and tried to feel less uneasy with his role. He felt like a Judas. Ivo, a lonely soul who needed help more than anything else, trusted him.

The taped wires of the concealed transmitter itched, but he resisted the temptation to scratch under his shirt. He pressed the transmitter switch that was taped to his left wrist under his shirt cuff. The gesture looked as if he were consulting his watch. He heard an answering click from the Bear, who, together with the federal policeman, was sitting on the second-floor veranda of a tearoom more or less directly across from where Fitzduane sat. This gave the Bear a bird's-eye view of the operation, and it kept him out of Ivo's sight. He was, however, too far away from the High Noon to make the actual arrest. That would be the responsibility of the two detectives concealed in the kitchen of the café. The task force was linked by two radio nets. One channel was restricted to Fitzduane and the Bear. The second channel was netted between the Bear and all the other members of his team. The setup should work fine unless the Bear got his transmission buttons mixed up.

The clock in the Prison Tower struck noon.

FRAU HUNZIKER LOOKED up in surprise as the door opened.

"Herr von Graffenlaub," she said, a little flustered. "I didn't expect you until next week. I thought you were in New York. Is something wrong?"

Beat von Graffenlaub smiled at her gently. The smile was incongruous because his eyes were hollow from lack of sleep and his whole demeanor projected stress and worry. He had aged in the past few days. My God, he's an old man, she thought for the first time.

"You and I, Frau Hunziker," he said, "have some arrangements to make."

"I don't understand," said Frau Hunziker. "Everything is in order as far as I know."

"You do an excellent job, my dear Frau Hunziker, excellent, quite excellent." He stood in the doorway of his office. "No interruptions until after lunch. Then I will need you. No interruptions at all. Is that quite clear?"

"Yes, Herr von Graffenlaub." She heard the lock click in the door. She was concerned. Herr von Graffenlaub had never behaved this way before, and he was looking terrible. Perhaps she should do something. She looked up at the clock on the wall. It was just after midday, two hours until her employer would need her. But training and discipline reasserted themselves, and she returned to her work.

MOVING AT speed, Ivo emerged from behind the jugglers, side-slipped gracefully between a mother and her dallying gaggle of children, looped around a flower stall, and glissaded to a halt in front of Fitzduane. He slid his visor up with a click. Behind him the fire-eater started to do something antisocial. Fitzduane hoped the mother was keeping count of her children; the smallest looked as if he were planning to get fried.

"Hello, Irishman," said Ivo. "I'm glad you came."

"I hope I am," said Fitzduane. "The last time we met I nearly got shot."

"Nothing will happen today," said Ivo. "I am invisible to my enemies. I have special powers, you know."

"Nothing personal," said Fitzduane, "but it's not you I'm worried about. I don't have any magic skates, not even a broomstick, and there are people out there with decidedly unpleasant habits."

Ivo sat down across the table from Fitzduane and with the grace of a conjurer produced two brightly painted eggs from the depths of his guitar and began to juggle with them. His special powers obviously didn't extend to juggling, and Fitzduane waited for the accident to happen. He hoped that Ivo had used an egg timer, or he was likely to need a fresh shirt. The display was morbidly fascinating. One egg went unilateral and thudded onto the table in front of Fitzduane. There was no explosion of yellow; it just lay there cracked.

Ivo shrugged and began removing the shell. "I can never decide which color to eat first," he said.

Fitzduane pushed the salt cellar across the table. "It's one of life's great dilemmas," he said. "Something to drink?"

A waiter was standing by their table, looking at Ivo with ill-concealed distaste. He wrinkled his nose as the light breeze demonstrated the less visible aspects of knightly behavior, and he looked around to see if the other customers seemed to have noticed the smell. Fortunately it was late for morning coffee and early for lunch. The tables were nearly empty. In his own idiosyncratic way, Fitzduane decided, Ivo was a smart screwball, and polite, too. He was sitting downwind of Fitzduane.

"One of those," said Ivo, pointing at Fitzduane's beer.

Fitzduane looked up at the waiter, who seemed to be debating about accepting the order. Fitzduane was not entirely unsympathetic, but the time didn't seem right for a discussion of personal hygiene. "My eccentric but very rich and influential friend," he said, "would like a beer." He smiled and placed a hundred-franc note on the table, weighting it in place with his empty beer bottle.

The waiter's scruples vanished at much the same speed as the hundred-franc note. Fitzduane thought that with such manual dexterity the waiter would be a safer bet with the colored eggs than Ivo.

"Would the gentleman like anything else?" asked the waiter. "Perhaps something to eat?"

"The gentleman's diet permits only a certain type of egg, which, as you can see, he carries with him, but more salt would be appreciated." Fitzduane indicated the nearly empty cellar.

Ivo moved on to the second egg. "I've written a book," he said, his mouth half full, "a book of poems." He reached inside the guitar and produced a soiled but bulky package, which he pushed across the table to Fitzduane. "It's about my friend Klaus and the man who killed him."

"Klaus Minder?"

"Yes," said Ivo, "my friend Klaus." He was silent. Then he put some salt on the side of his left thumb. He drank some beer and licked the salt. "Like tequila," he said.

"You're missing the lemon," said Fitzduane.

"Klaus is dead, you know. I miss him. I need a friend. Will you be my friend? We can find out who killed Klaus together."

"I thought you knew who killed Klaus."

"I know some things—quite a lot of things—but not all things. I need help. Will you help?"

Fitzduane looked at him. Sir Ivo, he thought, was not such a bad invention. There was a noble and sturdy spirit inside that slight physique, though whether it would ever have a chance of fulfillment was a very moot point. He thought of the loaded gun on the table beside him and the police team waiting and the years in prison or in some mental institution that Ivo faced, and he hated himself for what he was doing. He held his hand out to him. "I'll do what I can," he said. "I'll be your friend."

Ivo removed his helmet. He was smiling from ear to ear. He seized Fitzduane's hand in both of his. "I knew you would help," he said, "I knew it. It will be like the Knights of the Round Table, won't it?"

Then his head exploded.

The long burst had hit him in the back of the skull, perforating and smashing the bone into fragments and blowing these and blood and brain matter out through the front of his mouth in a fountain of death. Fitzduane flung himself to the ground as a second burst of fire smashed into Ivo's back and threw him across the table. Arterial blood sprayed into the air and formed a pink, frothy puddle with the spilled beer.

The attacker, on roller skates, shrouded in a long brown robe, and with face concealed, slid forward and grabbed Ivo's package from the table, stuffed it inside his robe, and darted away into the crowd, a silencer-fitted submachine gun in his hands.

There was a spurt of flame and cries of agony as the fire-eater was brutally shouldered aside by the fleeing assassin and burning liquid spewed inadvertently over a crowd of onlookers. People screamed and scattered in every direction. Baby carriages were overturned, stalls were crushed in the press of bodies, and complete pandemonium broke out.

The Bear looked on aghast, barking instructions into the radio and trying to deploy his people but constrained by the chaos below. From his vantage point he could see what was happening, but he was temporarily powerless to intervene.

If the police deployment was hindered by the panicking crowd, the attacker was having his own problems weaving in and out of the melee. His very speed was at times a hindrance, and several times he crashed into an obstacle or fell. Frustrated in the center of the Bärenplatz, the attacker, who had been heading in a roughly diagonal line toward the Bundesplatz, cut back to cross the square at an angle that would bring him almost directly below the balcony where the Bear and the federal detective were stationed.

"He's doubled back," said the Bear into his radio. "He's going to pass under us. I think he's heading up this side toward the Bundesplatz. Mobile One, corner of the Bärenplatz and Schauplatzgasse. Go!"

Mobile One, an unmarked police BMW motorcycle ridden by a detective who did hill climbing in his spare time, roared up Amthausgasse toward the corner as instructed, only to fall foul of a diplomatic protection team that was escorting a delegation from the Upper Volta Embassy making an official visit to the Bundeshaus, the Federal Parliament.

The diplomatic protection team, seeing the unmarked motorcycle cut through the uniformed police outriders toward the official-flag-flying Upper Volta Mercedes full of diplomats in tribal robes, performed as trained. An escorting police car swung across in front of the BMW, sending it into a violent skid that culminated under the nose of the Swiss foreign minister, who was waiting, together with a retinue of officials, to greet his distinguished guests. The hill-climbing detective, clad in racing leathers, rose shakily to his feet, his pistol butt protruding from the half-open zipper of his jacket. The first reaction of the dazed man when faced by all this officialdom was to reach for identification, whereupon he was shot in the shoulder.

The Bear's side of the square, being out of the sun and gloomy, was less crowded. "I think I can get a shot at him," said the federal detective. He leaned out across the balcony, wrecking a window box, and clasped his 9 mm SIG service automatic in both hands.

"Leave it," said the Bear. "There are too many people."

He spoke into the radio again. With the aid of Mobile One it looked as if they might just be able to get the assassin. He hadn't seen Mobile One's unfortunate encounter with the Upper Voltans. His other teams were converging as directed, albeit more slowly than he would have liked. He kept Mobile Two in Spitalgasse to backstop any sudden changes in direction. Reinforcements were being rushed from police headquarters only a few blocks away in Waisen-hausplatz, but he guessed the whole affair would be over by the time they arrived.

Covered in the blood and tissue that had been Ivo, and holding the Remington at high port, Fitzduane presented a truly fear-inspiring sight. Rage pumping energy through his entire being, he ran across the square behind the killer, followed by one of the detectives who had been concealed in the High Noon's kitchen. It was no contest. No matter how fast they ran, the twisting and turning killer, seen in brief glimpses as he maneuvered through the crowd, was gaining. Once he reached the emptier part of the square, he could put on more speed and be out of sight in seconds.

Fitzduane crashed into a flower stall, spilling hundreds of impeccably arranged blooms to the ground. His breath rasping in his throat, he picked himself up and ran on. Behind him, the detective, his gun drawn, skidded on the carpet of petals and pitched into a stall selling organic bread, sending loaves cartwheeling in every direction.

"I can get him," said the federal detective on the balcony. He cursed when a crying child ran behind the killer, causing him to hold his fire for a split second. It was all the margin the killer needed. He could see the federal detective clearly outlined as he leaned out across the balcony.

He pivoted as the detective fired, the round smashing into the ground beside him, and in an extension of the same elegant movement, he brought up his weapon and fired a long burst along the balcony, causing the Bear to dive for cover and stitching a bloody counterpoint across the federal detective's diamond-pattern sweater. He slumped across the balcony, a stream of scarlet pouring from his mouth. Glass from the shattered tearoom windows tinkled to the ground. Moving at lightning speed, the killer skated toward the ground-floor doorway of the tearoom, changed magazines, and re-cocked his weapon. He was now directly under the Bear, who swore in frustration and ran for the stairs, knowing he'd be too late but forced to do something.

The killer scanned the square for pursuers and fired a wide burst over the crowds, shattering more windows and causing almost all the onlookers to fling themselves to the ground. Satisfied that he had bought himself the time he needed for his final dash to the corner of the Bärenplatz, where Sylvie waited with a motorcycle, he sprint-skated toward safety.

The killer's suppressing fire had given Fitzduane the clear shot he needed. From a range of 120 meters, using the XR-18 sabot rounds, he fired twice, blowing the killer's torso into a bloody mess all over the front of the Union Bank of Switzerland.

OBLIVIOUS OF the carnage taking place just a short distance from his Marktgasse office, Beat von Graffenlaub paused in his writing and put down his pen. Hands clasped in front of him, he sat back in his chair for several minutes without moving. So much wealth, so much power and influence, so much failure. An image of Erika, young and fresh and beautiful as he had first known her, dissolved into the distorted face of his dead son. Sweat broke out on his brow. He felt sick and alone.

His movements neat and precise despite his nausea, he took a small brass key secured by a chain from his vest pocket and unlocked the bottom drawer of his desk. Inside lay a lightweight shoulder holster and harness and a 9 mm Walther P-38 German Army service pistol. He had killed to get it and killed to keep it, but that was forty years ago, when his ideals were still fresh, before the corrosion of life had set in.

He checked the pistol, pleased to see that it was in perfect working order. He inserted a clip of ammunition and a round in the chamber and placed the weapon on the desk beside him. He picked up his pen again and continued writing. Tears stained his cheeks, but he wiped them away before they marked the paper.

Chapter Twenty

Sangster was thinking about the assassination of Aldo Moro, a classic case history of the down side of the personal protection business that had taken place some three years previously. The Moro killing was not an encouraging precedent. Granted, there were certain obvious errors. His original bulletproof Fiat had become unreliable because of the weight of its additional armor, and pending the delivery of a new armored automobile, Moro was being driven in an unarmored Fiat sedan; second, he was using the same route he had traveled for the last fifteen years, so even the most slow-witted of terrorists could have put together a reasonable strike plan; third, although the police bodyguards were carrying their personal weapons, it struck Sangster as being less than inspired to have all their heavy firepower locked away in the escort car's trunk.

Still, mistakes or not, the fact remained that Aldo Moro, ex–prime minister and senior statesman of Italy, had been protected by no fewer than five experienced bodyguards—and the entire escort had been wiped out in seconds, with only one man even getting his pistol out to fire two shots in vain. The moral of the story, thought Sangster, is that you're a sitting duck against automatic-weapons fire if you are operating from an unarmored vehicle.

Sangster looked at the Hertz symbol on the windshield of his rented Mercedes. It didn't exactly make his day to know that he was making an even worse mistake than Moro's team. At least their vehicles had been moving. He was parked at the head of the track that led to Vreni von Graffenlaub's house, semiblind with the steamed-up car windows and furious that the bitch wouldn't let him and Pierre into her home, where they could do a decent protection job.

Woodsmoke trickled from Vreni's chimney. She was a pretty little thing, he had to admit. He tried to think of Vreni naked and willing in the farmhouse under a cozy duvet. Bodyguarding sometimes worked out that way. He picked up the field glasses and tried to catch a glimpse of her through the windows. He could see nothing. He scanned the rest of the area. There was still snow on the ground though it was melting. At night it would freeze again. He raised the radio and checked with Pierre, who was doing a mobile on the other side of the farmhouse. Pierre was wet and cold, and *merde* was the politest expletive he used. The exchange cheered Sangster up a little.

Sangster doubted that Vreni von Graffenlaub was in any serious danger. Most likely it was Dad trying to put some pressure on a wayward daughter; it wouldn't be the first time a protection team had been so employed. Not that it made any difference to them. The conditions might be variable, but the money was excellent.

Moro's bodyguards had been hit with an average of seven rounds each. Funny how details like that stick in your mind. Sangster raised the field glasses again. Bloody nothing.

THE CHIEF KRIPO WAS busy fishing a fly out of his tea when he heard the news of the Bärenplatz shootings. He stopped thinking about the fly and started thinking about crucifying the Irishman. Easter was over, but it was that time of year, and three crosses on top of the Gurten would not look amiss. Fitzduane could have the place of honor, with the Bear and von Beck standing in for the thieves. There would be none of that rubbish about taking them down after three days either. They would hang there until they rotted—an example to all not to stir up trouble in the normally placid city of Bern.

The Chief Kripo spread a protective cloth on his desk and hunted through his desk drawers for some guns to clean. He found four pistols and lined them up on his left, with the cleaning kit to his right. Everything was in order. He picked up the SIG 9 mm and stripped it down. It was immaculate, but he cleaned it anyway. He liked the smell of gun oil. In fact, he liked everything about guns except people using them on people.

He did some of his best thinking while cleaning his guns. Today was no exception. Perhaps he'd better stop contemplating a triple crucifixion and have a serious look at what was happening off Kirchenfeldstrasse. Certainly his conventional investigation wasn't coming up with any answers. It could be that the time had come to take Project K seriously.

The four guns were now cleaned but still broken down into their component parts. He mingled the pieces at random, then closed his eyes and reassembled the weapons by touch. After that he strapped on the SIG and rang for a car.

AFTER FORTY-FIVE minutes with the Project K team, the Chief decided that life was too short and he was too old to have the time to get fully familiar with artificial intelligence and expert systems. The principles weren't too hard to grasp, but once Henssen got technical and started talking about inference engines and consistency checking and the virtues of Prolog as opposed to LISP, the Chief's eyeballs rolled skyward. Soon afterward, his chair being exceedingly comfortable, he fell asleep. Henssen couldn't believe what he was seeing and chose to think that the Chief's eyes were closed in deep concentration.

The Chief started to snore. It was a melodious sound with some of the cadence and lilt of Berndeutsch, and it prompted Fitzduane to wonder whether the language one spoke affected the sound produced when snoring. Did a Chinese snore like an Italian?

The Chief's eyes snapped open. He glared at Henssen, who was standing there bemused, mouth half agape, pointer in hand, flip chart at the ready. "All that stuff might be a barrel of laughs to a bunch of long-haired, unwashed, pimple-faced students," the Chief barked, "but I'm here to talk about *murder*! We've got dead bodies turning up like geraniums all over my city, and I want it stopped—or I may personally start adding to the list."

"Um," murmured Henssen, and sat down.

"Look," said von Beck in a mollifying tone, "I think it might be easier if you ask us exactly what you want to know."

The Chief leaned forward in his chair. "How close are you people to coming up with a suspect, or at least a short list?"

"Very close," said Chief Inspector Kersdorf.

"Days, minutes, hours? Give me a time frame."

Kersdorf looked at Henssen, who cleared his throat before he spoke. "Within forty-eight hours at the outside, but possibly as soon as twelve."

"What are the main holdups?" asked the Chief. "I thought your computers were ultrafast."

"Processing time isn't the problem," said Henssen. "The main delays are in three areas: getting the records we want out of people, transferring the data to a format the computers can use, and the human interface."

"What do you mean by the human interface? I thought the computer did all the thinking."

"We're not out of a job yet," said Kersdorf. "The computer does the heavy data interpretation, 'thinking,' if you will, but only within parameters we determine. The computer learns as it goes, but we have to tell it, at least the first time, what is significant."

The Chief grunted. He was having a hard time trying to assess to what extent the damn machines could actually think, but he decided that the balance, at this stage, between man and machine was not so important. What he had to decide was the effectiveness of the full package. Was Project K worth the candle and likely to deliver, or should he do a Pontius Pilate and wash his hands while the Federal Police or a cantonal task force took over the whole thing? "Let's talk specifics," he said. "Have you considered that our candidate is almost certainly known by the von Graffenlaubs?"

The Bear nodded. "We asked the von Graffenlaub family to list all friends and acquaintances, and they are now entered into the data base. There are several problems. Beat von Graffenlaub has a vast circle of acquaintances; Erika is almost certainly not telling the whole truth, if for no other reason than she doesn't want the extent of her sex life to end up on a government computer. Life being the way it is, none of the lists will be entirely comprehensive. Few people can name everyone they know."

"Have you thought of narrowing down the von Graffenlaub list by concentrating on who they know in common?"

The Bear grinned. "The computer did—but gave the result a low significance rating because of the inherent unreliability of the individual lists."

"I remember the days when you talked like a cop," said the Chief.

He looked down at his notes again. "How do we stand on the tattoo issue?"

"Good and bad," said the Bear. "The good news is that we finally traced the artist—a guy in Zurich operating under the name of Siegfried. The bad news is that he'd disappeared when the local police went to pick him up for a second round of questioning. He reappeared in walking boots, full of holes."

"The body found in the woods? I didn't know it had been identified yet."

"An hour or so ago," said the Bear. "You were probably on your way here at the time."

"Did Siegfried leave any records?"

"He had a small apartment above his shop," said the Bear. "Both were destroyed in a fire shortly after he did his vanishing act. A thorough case of arson with no attempt to make it look accidental; whoever did it was more concerned about carrying out a total destruction job. They used gasoline and incendiary devices. On the basis of an analysis of the chemicals used in the incendiaries, there is a direct link to the Hangman's group."

The Chief frowned. "What about Ivo's package?"

"That's still with forensics," said the Bear. "They hope to have something later on today, but it could be tomorrow. About eighty percent of it was destroyed by Fitzduane's shotgun blasts, and the rest of it was saturated in blood and bits of our unlamented killer. That shotgun load he's using is formidable."

"Not exactly helpful in this situation," said the Chief.

"I'm not used to shooting people wearing roller skates," said Fitzduane. "It confused my aim."

"What you need is a dose of the Swiss Army," said the Chief. "We'd teach you how to shoot."

"We're particularly strong on dealing with terrorists wearing roller skates," said Charlie von Beck.

"Which reminds me. I really would like my shotgun back," said Fitzduane. "Your people took it away after the Bärenplatz."

"Evidence," said the Chief. "Democratic legal systems are crazy about evidence. Consider yourself lucky you weren't taken away, too."

The Bear looked at Fitzduane and stopped him as he was about to reply. "Be like a bamboo," he suggested, "and bend with the wind."

"That's all I need," said Fitzduane, "a Swiss Chinese philosopher."

SANGSTER WOULD have been flattered by the meticulous planning that went into his death. Sylvie had been assigned the task of tidying up Vreni von Graffenlaub. With her were a technician of Colombian origin known as Santine and two Austrian contract assassins, both blond and blue-eyed and baby-cheeked, whom she immediately dubbed Hansel and Gretel.

She still felt sore about the Bärenplatz shootings. Certainly the target had been killed, and a policeman for good measure, and losing the Lebanese had been no loss—she had become extremely bored with his alligator shoes—but she wished she hadn't lent the incompetent idiot her Ingram. It was the weapon she was used to, and now here she was carrying out an assignment it would have been ideal for, and she was reduced to one of those dull little Czech Skorpions.

They considered bypassing the bodyguards by approaching the farmhouse cross-country. That would have worked if Kadar had ordered just a quick kill, but he wanted something more elaborate, so it became clear they'd have to take out the bodyguards prior to the main event.

The killings would have to be silent. Vreni's farmhouse was situated outside the village, but noise travels in the still air of the mountains, and although the immediate police presence might not be significant, this damned Swiss habit of every man's having an assault rifle in his home had to be considered.

In the end it wasn't too difficult to come up with an effective plan. It hinged on Santine's technical capabilities and close observation of the bodyguards' routine. For at least twenty minutes out of every hour both bodyguards were out of the car patrolling, and for at least half that time they were out of sight of the car.

The first move was to bug the bodyguards' car. The rented Mercedes was not difficult to unlock, and within seconds Santine, almost invisible in white camouflage against the snow, had concealed two audio transmitters and, under the driver's seat, a radio-activated cylinder of odorless, colorless carbon monoxide gas. Silently he relocked the car and slithered away into the tree line, cursing the cold and swearing that he would confine his talents in the future to warmer climes.

The audio surveillance was instructive. Sylvie was glad that she hadn't given in to her initial impulse to bypass the bodyguards. The farmhouse, it turned out, was bugged. Vreni von Graffenlaub might not have allowed her father's security people inside her house, but they still had the ability to monitor—if not actually see—her every movement. There were microphones, they learned, in all the main rooms.

Further surveillance revealed the bodyguards' reporting procedures, their code words, their routines, and the interesting gem that their vehicle was shortly to be replaced by an armor-plated van that was at this moment making its way to them from Milan. Sangster had learned something from the Moro experience. He had put in a requisition, and it had been approved. Beat von Graffenlaub had deep pockets, and his family was to receive the most effective protection the experts thought necessary.

The armored van could make things difficult. It would be relatively immune to Skorpion fire. There was only one conclusion: the hit would have to be made before its arrival. Just to complicate things, Sangster and Pierre reported in every hour to their headquarters by radio and were checked upon in turn on a random basis about once every three hours. The only good news about that was that radio transmission quality seemed to be poor. It should be possible for Sylvie's team, armed with knowledge of the codes and procedures, to fake it for a couple of hours.

Sylvie ran through the plan with her small force. Santine offered a few suggestions that made sense. Hansel and Gretel held hands and just nodded. They had wanted to use crossbows on the two bodyguards and were not happy at the thought of an impersonal radio-activated kill. Sylvie reminded them that Vreni would be a different proposition and that Kadar had issued certain very explicit instructions. All this cheered up Hansel and Gretel, who began to look positively enthusiastic. Sylvie, who found them nauseating, almost missed the Lebanese. Santine, who looked as if he'd be quite happy to shoot his grandmother when he wasn't peddling cocaine to three-year-olds, was a breath of fresh air in comparison.

* * *

VRENI WAS alone in the farmhouse. She sat on the floor, her feet bare, her legs drawn up, her hands clasped around her knees. She had stopped crying. She was almost numb from fear and exhaustion. Sometimes she shook uncontrollably.

She was clinging to the notion that if she didn't cooperate with the authorities—and she included her father's security guards in that group—then she would be safe. They would leave her alone. He—Kadar—would leave her alone. The presence of bodyguards in their car only a couple of hundred meters up the track increased her terror because it might be taken to suggest that she had revealed things she had sworn to keep secret. She knew there were other watchers, other forces more deadly than anything officialdom could conceive.

She stared at the telephone. The Irishman represented her only hope. His visit had affected her deeply, and as the days passed, its impact in her mind grew ever greater. He was untainted by this morass of corruption into which she had fallen. Perhaps she could, should talk to him. Her hand touched the gray plastic of the phone, then froze. What if they were listening and got to her first?

She keeled over onto her side and moaned.

THE FACADE OF Erika von Graffenlaub's apartment suggested nothing more than a conventional wooden door equipped with a good-quality security lock. The locksmith had little trouble with it but immediately was faced with a significantly more formidable barrier: the second door was of steel set into a matching steel frame embedded in the structure of the building. The door was secured by a code-activated electronic lock.

The locksmith looked at the discreetly engraved manufacturer's logo and shook his head. "Too rich for my blood," he said. "The only people who can help you are the manufacturers, Vaybon Security, and they are not too forthcoming unless they know you."

Beat von Graffenlaub smiled thinly. "You've done enough," he said to the locksmith, who had turned to admire the steel door.

The man whistled in admiration. "Great bit of work this," he said, "rarely seen in a private home. It's the kind of thing normally only banks can afford." He stretched out his hand to touch the flawless satin steel finish. There was a loud crack and a flash and a smell of burning, and the locksmith was flung across the hallway to collapse on the floor in a motionless heap.

Beat von Graffenlaub stared at the steel door. What terrible secrets was Erika concealing behind it? He knelt beside the fallen locksmith. His hand and arm were burned, but he was alive. Von Graffenlaub removed a mobile phone from his briefcase and phoned for medical assistance.

His second call was to the managing director of the Vaybon Corporation. His manner was peremptory; his instructions were specific. Yes, such a door could be opened by a specialist team. There were plans in the Vaybon Security plant in a suburb of Bern. Action would be taken immediately. Herr von Graffenlaub could expect the door to be opened within two hours. This would be exceptional service, of course, but in view of Herr von Graffenlaub's special position on the board of Vaybon . . .

"Quite so," said von Graffenlaub dryly. He terminated the call, made the locksmith comfortable, and sat down to wait. The elusive Erika might return first. He took the unconscious locksmith's pulse. It was strong. He, at least, would live to see the summer.

THE CHIEF KRIPO HAD been playing devil's advocate for more than five hours, and he wasn't scoring many points. The project team's approach was different in many ways from conventional police work, but to someone not used to working in an integrated way with an expert system, it was impressively comprehensive. Once instructed, the computer didn't forget things. It was hard to find a facet the team hadn't covered or at least considered. But there were some potential flaws.

"How do you people deal with data that aren't already computerized?" he asked. "How do you handle good old-fashioned typed or handwritten data?"

Faces turned toward Henssen. He shrugged. "It's a problem. We can input some data by hand if only a few hundred records or so are involved, and in Wiesbaden we have scanning equipment that can convert typed records directly to computer format. But for all that, if data aren't computerized, we can only nibble at them."

"So how much of the data isn't computerized?" asked the Chief.

Henssen brightened. "Not a lot. Orwell's 1984 wasn't so far out."

"What about Babel?" said the Chief.

Henssen looked confused. He looked at the Bear, who shrugged.

"The Tower of Babel," explained the Chief. "How do you cope

with records in different languages—English, French, German, Italian, whatever?"

"Ah," said Henssen. "Actually the Babel factor—as such—is not as much of a problem as you'd think. We do have computerized translation facilities that are over ninety percent accurate. On the other hand, that ten percent error factor leaves room for some elegant confusion that can be compounded by multiple meanings within any one language. Consider the word *screw* for example. That can mean 'to rotate,' as in inserting a wood screw; it can mean 'to cheat or swindle,' as in 'I was screwed on the deal'; it can mean the act of sex as in . . ." He went silent, embarrassed.

"Go on," said Kersdorf irritably. "We can perhaps work out some of the details ourselves."

"Well," continued Henssen, "fortunately most police information is held in a structured way, and so is the majority of commercial data. For example, an airline passenger list doesn't take much translation, nor do airline schedules, or subscription lists, or lists of phone calls, and so on."

"Okay," said the Chief, "structured data are held on the computer version of what we old-fashioned bureaucrats would call a form—so translate the headings and the meaning of the contents is clear."

"Much simplified, that's about it," said Henssen. "And unstructured data, to give an example, might be a statement by a witness consisting of several pages of free-form text."

"And it's with the unstructured data that you have most of the problems," said the Chief.

"Precisely. But with some human involvement linked to our expert system there is nothing we can't resolve."

"But it takes time," said the Chief, "and that's my problem."

There was silence in the room. Henssen shrugged.

"I'M SURPRISED people don't use carbon monoxide more often," said Santine. "It's a beautifully lethal substance. It works through inhalation. It's not quite as exciting as some of the nerve gases that can be absorbed through the skin. Carbon monoxide is breathed in as normal, is absorbed by the blood to form carboxyhemoglobin, and all of a sudden you haven't got enough oxygenated blood—oxyhemoglobin—and you're history. There is no smell and no color, and a couple of lungfuls will do you in. Most city dwellers have some carbon monoxide in the blood from exhaust fumes—say, one to three percent—and smokers build up to around five percent. These levels don't produce any noticeable symptoms in the short term, but at around thirty percent you start to feel drowsy, at fifty percent your coordination goes, and by between sixty and seventy percent, you're talking to Saint Peter."

"So if you're a heavy smoker and someone uses carbon monoxide on you, you'll die faster," said Sylvie.

"Absolutely," said Santine, "especially if you've been smoking in a confined space."

"Interesting," said Sylvie. "But all it has to do is buy us a little time if a casual visitor comes along, though I doubt a security check would be fooled."

Santine grimaced. "Come on, Sylvie, I'm not an amateur. Why do you think I suggested monoxide? The corpses will stand up to cursory examination. There will be no blood. Nothing's perfect, but with a little sponge work, they won't look too bad—and it'll be dark. You've got to remember that monoxide poisoning is a kind of internal strangulation, so you get some of the same symptoms. The face gets suffused, you get froth in the air passages, and the general effect isn't exactly pretty."

"I take it you brought a sponge."

Santine puffed out his chest. He tapped the bulky black attaché case in front of him. "Madame, I am fully equipped."

Pompous prick, thought Sylvie. She looked at the sky and then at her watch. They'd do it in about an hour, just after Sangster had checked in and when it was completely dark.

THE TEAM FROM Vaybon Security wore white coats and the blank expressions of people who are paid well enough not to care about reasons. One of their board directors opening his wife's apartment without her knowledge or permission wasn't the most unusual assignment they'd had, and besides, Beat von Graffenlaub's signature had been on the check that had paid for the original installation—even if he hadn't known exactly what he was buying. But then, thought the technician in charge, who knows what a wife is really up to?

"Can you open it without leaving any sign?"

The senior technician consulted the blueprint he was carrying and had a brief, whispered consultation with his colleagues. He turned back to von Graffenlaub. "There will be minute marks, Herr Direktor, but they would not be noticed unless the door was being examined by an expert."

Equipment was wheeled into the foyer outside the door. Von Graffenlaub had the feeling the technicians were going to scrub up before commencing. "Will it take long?"

"Fifteen minutes, no longer," said the senior technician.

"You are aware that the door is electrified," said von Graffenlaub.

The senior technician shot him what started off as a pitying glance but changed in mid-expression to obsequiousness when he remembered to whom he was speaking. "Thank you, Herr Direktor," he said.

He withdrew a sealed security envelope and opened it with scissors. Von Graffenlaub noticed that other instruments were laid out on a tiered cart close at hand. The senior technician removed a sheet of heavy paper from the envelope, read it, and punched a ten-digit number into a keyboard. He hit the return key. A junior technician checked the door with a long-handled instrument.

"Phase one completed," said the senior technician. From his bearing one could believe that he had just successfully completed a series of complex open-heart procedures. "The electrical power source attached to the door can be deactivated by radio if the correct code is used. Your wife provided us with such a code, which was kept in this envelope in a safe until required. The same system can also be used for the lock, but in this case, unfortunately, she has not deposited the necessary information. We shall have to activate the manufacturer's override. That requires drilling a minute hole in a specific location and connecting an optical fiber link through which a special code can be transmitted to override the locking mechanism. The optical fiber link is used to avoid the possibility of the door's being opened by anyone other than the manufacturer. The location of the link is different with each installation and—"

"Get on with it," said von Graffenlaub impatiently.

Eleven minutes later the door swung open. He waited until the Vaybon team had departed before he walked into the apartment and shut the door behind him. He found the electrification controls and reactivated the system, following the instructions given to him by the technician. Reassured by the sophisticated perimeter security of electrification, steel door, and hermetically sealed armor-plated windows—installed originally with the excuse that the construction of Erika's little apartment was an ideal opportunity to put in some really good security—Erika had made little serious attempt to conceal things inside the apartment.

Twenty minutes later Beat von Graffenlaub had completed a thorough search of the apartment. What he had found, detailed in photographs but with other quite specific evidence, was worse than anything he had—or could have—imagined. Nauseated, white-faced, and almost numb with shock, he waited for Erika to return. He was unaware of time. He was conscious only that his life, as he had known it, was over.

THE BEAR WAS drinking coffee and eating gingerbread in the kitchen when Fitzduane entered, and the sweet, sharp aroma of baked ginger reminded the Irishman of Vreni. The Bear looked up. Fitzduane sat across from him at the kitchen table, lost in thought about a scared, lonely, vulnerable girl hiding in the mountains.

"Thinking about the girl?" said the Bear. One piece of gingerbread remained. He offered it to Fitzduane, who shook his head. Instead, he spoke. "She was so bloody scared."

"As we now know, with excellent reason," said the Bear. "But she won't talk, and there's not much else we can do now except see that she has security and try to find the Hangman."

"Henssen was building in some slack when he spoke to the Chief. He now thinks he might be ready to do a final run in about four hours."

"A name," said the Bear, "at last."

"A short list anyway."

"Any candidates?" The Bear was checking through various containers. A morsel of gingerbread couldn't be termed a serious snack or even an adequate companion to a cup of coffee. His hunt was in vain, and he began to look depressed. "The people here eat too much," he said. "Kersdorf, for instance, has an appetite like a greyhound. The least he could do is bring in a cake now and then."

"He does," said Fitzduane, "and you eat it." He wrote a name on a piece of paper. "Here's my nomination," he said, handing it to the Bear, who looked at it and whistled.

"A hundred francs you're wrong."

"Done," said Fitzduane. "But I've got a proposal. Let's have one last crack at Vreni. You can come along for the ride, and maybe we can find somewhere nice to eat on the way back."

The Bear cheered up. "Why don't we eat on the way? Then we'll be fortified for some serious questioning."

"We'll talk about it," said Fitzduane. He was suddenly anxious to be on his way. "Come on, let's move."

"I'll check out a weapon for you."

"There isn't time for that," said Fitzduane. "You're armed, and that'll have to do." His voice was sharp with anxiety.

The Bear looked up at the heavens, shook his head, and followed Fitzduane out the door.

VRENI SUMMONED every last ounce of resolve.

She fetched a duvet and cocooned it around her body as if it were a tepee. She was sitting cross-legged, and the phone was in front of her. Inside her tepee of warmth she felt more secure. She waited for the warmth to build up, and as she did, she imagined that she was safe, that the Irishman had come to rescue her, and that she was far away from anything He could do. He didn't exist anymore. Like a bad dream, His image faded, leaving an uncomfortable feeling but no more actual fear.

She left her hand on the gray plastic of the phone until the handle was warm in her grasp. She imagined Fitzduane at the other end, waiting to respond, to take her to a place of safety. She lifted up the receiver and began to dial. She stopped halfway through the first digit and pressed the disconnect button furiously. It made no difference. The phone was quite dead.

Her heart pounding, she flung open the door and ran to the back of the house, to where some of the animals were housed. She seized her pet lamb, warm and groggy with sleep, and with him clutched in her arms ran back into the house and locked and bolted the door. She crawled back under the duvet with her lamb and closed her eyes.

SYLVIE FLUNG open the door on the driver's side. Eyes open, face distorted, Sangster slid toward her, his face covered in secretions. Sylvie stepped back and let the head and torso fall into the snow. Sangster's feet remained tangled in the pedals.

"Leave the door open," said Santine. He dragged Pierre's body out of the passenger seat and around to the rear of the car, then opened the trunk.

"Well, fuck me," he said. "The bastard's still alive."

He removed a sharpened ice pick from his belt and plunged it deep into Pierre's back. The body arched and was still. Santine levered it into the trunk. He closed and locked the lid. He looked at Sylvie. "Obviously a nonsmoker."

THEY WERE using Fitzduane's car, but the Bear was driving. They turned off the highway to Interlaken and headed up toward Heiligenschwendi. The road was black under the glare of the head-lights, but piles of snow and ice still lingered by the roadside. As they climbed higher, the reflections of white became more frequent. They hadn't talked much since leaving Project K, though the Bear had had a brief conversation with police headquarters.

"The Chief isn't too happy that we took off without saying good-bye," he had said when he finished.

Fitzduane had just grunted. Only when they drove into the village did Fitzduane break the silence. "Who is running security on Vreni?"

"Beat von Graffenlaub arranged it," said the Bear. "It's not Vaybon Security, as you might expect, but a very exclusive personal protection service based on Jersey. They employ ex–military per-sonnel by and large—ex-SAS, Foreign Legion, and so on."

"ME Services," said Fitzduane. "I know them. ME stands for 'Mallet 'Em'—the founder wasn't renowned for a sophisticated sense of humor, but they've got a good reputation in their field. Who's in charge of Vreni's detail?"

"Fellow by the name of Sangster," said the Bear. "Our people say he's sound, but he's fed up because he has to do his thing from outside the house. Vreni won't allow them within a hundred meters of the place."

"Consorting with the enemy," said Fitzduane under his breath. "Poor frightened little sod." He pointed at a phone booth. "Stop here a sec. I'm going to ring ahead so she doesn't have a heart attack."

Fitzduane was in the phone booth five minutes. He emerged and beckoned the Bear over. "Her phone's dead," he said. "I've checked with the operator, and there is no reported fault on the line."

They looked at each other. "I have a number for ME control," the Bear said. "The security detail checks in regularly, and there are spot checks as well. They should know if everything is okay."

"Be quick," said Fitzduane. He paced up and down in the freezing air while the Bear made the call. The detective looked happier when he had finished.

"Sangster reported in on schedule about fifteen minutes ago, and there was a spot check less than ten minutes ago. All is in order."

Fitzduane didn't look convinced. "Do you have a backup weapon for me?"

"Sure." The Bear opened the trunk and handed Fitzduane a tire iron.

"Why do I suddenly feel so much safer?" said Fitzduane.

THE ROOM WAS in almost total darkness, the light from the dim streetlamps of Junkerngasse excluded by thick purple hangings. Beat von Graffenlaub could hear nothing. The security windows and door combined with the thick walls to produce a soundproofed otherworld. He felt disoriented. He knew he should switch on the lights and try to get a grip on himself, but then he would have to look at the photographs again and face the sickness and the perversion and the graphic images of death.

He tried to imagine the mentality of someone who would torture and kill for what appeared to be no other reason than sexual gratification. It was incomprehensible. It was evil of a kind beyond his ability to grasp, let alone understand. Erika—his beautiful, sultry, sensuous Erika—a perverted, sick, sadistic killer. He retched, and his mouth filled with an unpleasant taste. He wiped his lips and clammy face with a handkerchief.

A well-shaded light clicked on, apparently activated from the outside. The steel door opened. Von Graffenlaub sat in the darkness of his corner of the room and silently watched Erika enter.

She removed her evening coat of dark green silk and tossed it over a chair. Its lining was a vivid scarlet that reminded von Graffenlaub sickeningly of the blood of her victims. Her shoulders were bare, and her skin was golden. She looked at herself in the full-length mirror strategically positioned at the entrance to the living room and with a practiced movement slipped out of her dress and threw it after the coat. She stared at the image of her body and caressed her breasts, bringing her fingers down slowly over her rib cage and taut stomach to the black bikini panties that were the only clothing she still wore.

Von Graffenlaub tried to speak. His throat was dry. Only a strangled sound emerged.

Erika tossed her head in acknowledgment but didn't turn. She continued to examine her reflection. "Whitney," she said. "Darling, dangerous, delicious Whitney. I hoped you wouldn't be late." She eased her panties down her thighs. Her fingers worked between her legs.

"Why?" repeated von Graffenlaub hoarsely. This time the word came out. She started violently at the sound of his voice but didn't turn for perhaps half a minute. Then, with a quick, animal gesture, she slipped her panties off her thighs and kicked them into a corner.

"And who is this Whitney?" said von Graffenlaub, gesturing at the pile of photographs beside him. "Who is this partner in murder?"

Erika faced him naked. She had regained some of her composure, but her face was strained under the tan. She laughed harshly before she spoke. "Whitney likes games, my darling hypocrite," she said. "And not all the players are volunteers. Look very closely at those photos. Don't you recognize that pristine body? Aren't those long, elegant fingers familiar? Beat, my darling, aren't Vaybon drugs wonderful? My companion in murder—well, in some of the photographs anyway—was you, my sweet. You must admit that does somewhat limit your options."

A dreadful cry came from von Graffenlaub. He brought the Walther up in a gesture of ultimate denial and fired until the magazine was empty. The gun dropped to the carpet. Erika lay where she had been flung, looking not unlike the blood-spattered images in her photographs.

THEY LEFT the car in the village and walked along the track toward Vreni's farmhouse. The Bear carried a flashlight. When he was about thirty meters away from the Mercedes, he focused it on the windows and flashed it half a dozen times. The front door opened on the passenger side, and a figure got out. He was carrying some kind of automatic weapon.

The Bear flashed the light again. "I don't want to scare them to death," he said in a low voice to Fitzduane. He stopped and shouted to the figure by the Mercedes. "Police," he said. "Routine check. Mind if I approach?"

"You're welcome," said the figure by the Mercedes. "Dig your ID out and come forward with your hands in the air."

"Understood," said the Bear. He moved ahead, hands in the air, the flashlight in one of them. Fitzduane walked beside him about ten meters to the right. His hands were extended also. When they were close, the Bear spoke again. "Here's my ID," he said, shining his light on it and handing it to the bodyguard. Fitzduane moved forward a shade after the detective and offered his ID as well. The bodyguard looked briefly at the Bear's papers and then pitched into the snow as Fitzduane smashed the tire iron against his head.

"No countersign, no partner backing him up from a safe fire position, and a Skorpion as a personal weapon," said the Bear. "Good reasons to take him out, but I hope we're not dealing with an absentminded security man."

"So do I," said Fitzduane. He felt the fallen man's body. "Because he's dead."

"Jesus!" exclaimed the Bear. "I thought I was keeping you out of trouble by not giving you a firearm."

Fitzduane grunted. Keeping the flashlight well shaded and with the automatically activated interior light switched off, he examined the person who was apparently asleep in the passenger seat. Almost immediately it was clear that the sleep was permanent. He went through the pockets of the corpse and compared the ID he found there with the bloated face.

"It's Sangster," he said grimly. "No obvious sign of injury, but I doubt he died of boredom; most likely either asphyxiation or poisoning, to judge by his face."

"There were supposed to be two guards on duty," said the Bear. He opened the trunk and looked at the crumpled figure inside. "There were," he said quietly. He looked at Fitzduane. "You and your damn intuition. This means the Hangman or his drones are inside the farmhouse. You'll need something a little heavier than a tire iron."

Fitzduane searched quickly through the car. He found two Browning automatic pistols and an automatic shotgun—but no ammunition. He guessed the attackers must have tossed it into the snow, but there was no time to look. He picked up the fallen terrorist's Skorpion and a spare clip of ammunition. He felt as if he were reliving a nightmare. It wasn't rational, but he blamed himself for not having saved Rudi. Now his twin sister was in mortal danger, possibly because of his actions in involving her in the investigation, and he was going to be too late again. "Let's move it," he said, a break in his voice. His body vibrated with tension. He felt a hand on his arm.

"Easy, Hugo," said the Bear. "Take it very easy. It won't do the girl any good if you get yourself killed."

The Bear's words had the desired effect. Fitzduane felt the guilt and blind rage subside. He looked at the Bear. "This is how we'll do it," he said, and he explained.

"Just so," said the Bear.

They split up and moved toward the farmhouse.

SYLVIE HAD endured the most brutal training, designed in part specifically to cauterize her feelings, and she had been through Kadar's initiation ceremonies, which were many times worse. She prided herself on being quite ruthless when carrying out an assignment—ruthless in the full sense of the word, without pity—and yet the execution of Vreni von Graffenlaub made her stomach churn.

Kadar had seemed amused when he gave the orders, as if he were enjoying some private joke. "I want you to hang the girl," he had said. "Let her die in the same way as her twin brother. Very neat, very Swiss. Perhaps we'll be establishing a new von Graffenlaub family tradition, though rather hard to perpetuate from generation to generation under the circumstances. Oh, well. Her father should appreciate the symmetry."

The locks on the farmhouse door had given them little trouble; they were inside in less than a minute. They had found Vreni cowering under a duvet in the living room that led off the small kitchen. She had a lamb clutched in her arms, and her eyes were tightly closed. She wanted to believe that it was all a horrible dream, that the sound of the door opening and the footsteps were all her imagination, that the telephone still worked, that if she opened her eyes, everything would be cozy and normal in the farmhouse.

Gretel had torn the lamb away and slapped the cowering figure until she had been forced to look at him. Then, with one vicious slash, he had cut the throat of the bleating animal, the blood gushing over the petrified girl, her fear so great that they could smell it, the screams stillborn in her paralyzed throat.

The living room ceiling was too low for their purposes. Instead they tied the rope to a beam in the bedroom ceiling and then hauled the girl up through the choust. The drop through the choust from the bedroom floor made for a natural scaffold.

Hansel had been assigned to keep a lookout while Sylvie and Gretel prepared for the hanging. He could watch the track leading from the village through the kitchen window, and he could just see the shadow where Santine was standing in for the security guards in the distance. There was some visibility thanks to a weak moon reflecting off the snow, but patches of cloud were frequent. At those times it was hard to see anything with certainty, and imagination made shadows move. Fortunately he knew he would get early warning from Santine in the Mercedes, so he gave in to the more compelling distraction of the preparations for the hanging.

The Bear's luck gave out when he tried to close in from the woodshed, which was located only about twenty meters from the farmhouse. The detective's movements, slowed by the snow that had banked up around the shed, aroused the distracted Hansel, whose first action was to snatch up his walkie-talkie and swear at Santine. He knew the gesture would be fruitless even before his reflex movement was completed, so he dropped the silent radio, shouted a warning to Sylvie and Gretel, and fired at the shadowy figure moving toward him.

Unhit but shaken by the blast of fire, the Bear rolled back into the cover of the woodshed and sank into a snowdrift. Emerging covered in snow but still crouched low, he was greeted by a second burst of fire. Rounds plowed into the snow about him and thudded into the wood. He couldn't see his attacker, but the window frame gave him a point of reference. He would be in one or other of the two lower corners unless he was an idiot or wearing stilts. At this stage of the game the Bear wouldn't have been surprised by either possibility. Further muzzle flashes located the sniper in the left lower corner. Looking like a giant snowman, the Bear moved into firing position. He fired the .44 Magnum four times.

The heavy hand-loaded slugs smashed through the wooden walls of the old farmhouse. Two rounds missed and shattered a jar of mung beans and a container of pickled cabbage. The remaining two slugs hit Hansel in the neck and lower jaw. The first round smashed his spinal column, killing him instantly. The second round nearly decapitated him.

Hearing Hansel's warning shout, followed shortly by automatic-weapons fire, Gretel, who had been holding the petrified Vreni at the edge of the choust while Sylvie adjusted the rope, immediately let go of his victim and jumped through the hole onto the stove and into the living room below. He ran into the kitchen toward Hansel, arriving just in time to see his friend's head blown off. Irrational with shock, Gretel skidded across the blood-slicked wooden floor, flung open the kitchen door, and fired a long, low, scything burst into the darkness.

Vreni, released by her captor but still bound hand and foot and blindfolded, tottered at the edge of the choust. Fascinated, Sylvie watched as her terrified victim swayed back and forth and then, too weakened from stress to recover her balance, dropped with a sickening sound into the hole.

The rope snapped taut.

THE OLD FARMHOUSE WAS set into the natural slope of the mountain. The plan was that Fitzduane, being younger and fitter than the Bear, would make his approach from the second-floor level. As he remembered it, an entrance there led into a workroom and then into the bedroom. It was possible to go from the living room to the bedroom either by going through the choust or by leaving the house through the kitchen and going up a steep path to the other entrance on the second floor.

When the firing started, Fitzduane, whose climb up the hill had taken longer than expected, was not yet in position. He debated giving supporting fire from where he was, but the overhang of the roof protected the terrorists inside the house from his line of fire, and he didn't think ineffective noise alone would do much good. The reassuring roar of the Bear's Magnum made up his mind, and he concentrated on trying to get to the second-floor door to take the terrorists from two sides. There was a lull in the terrorists' fire; then it increased. It was hard to be sure, but now there seemed to be at least two automatic weapons firing at the woodshed behind which the Bear was sheltering.

Fitzduane had misjudged his angle of approach and was too far up the slope. He slithered down inelegantly toward the workroom door. No window overlooked it, which made him feel better. He tried the handle. It was locked. He waited for the next burst of firing and opened up with the dead terrorist's Skorpion at the lock surround. The silencer killed most of the noise, but the door still held. He cursed the miserable .32 rounds.

He fired again—this time a long burst—and the lock gave way. He darted into the room and rolled to gain cover, changing the clip and recocking the weapon as soon as he stopped. He switched the fire selector from automatic to single shot. At a cyclic rate of 750 rounds a minute, he didn't think a single twenty-round magazine was going to do him much good any other way. He tried not to think of what might have happened to Vreni. The terrorists were still there, so there was a chance they hadn't finished their business. There was a chance she was alive. He had to believe she was alive.

There was more shooting from below him, and then a round smashed through the outer wall beside him, flinging splinters into his face and causing him to drop to the floor.

"Terrific," he muttered to himself. A virtually simultaneous boom identified the shooter as the Bear. That was always the risk with combining high-powered weapons and strategies of encirclement. You ended up shooting each other.

He wiped the blood from his face. The splinters stung, but the injuries weren't serious. He inched forward until he came to the bedroom door. Using the long handle of a sweeping brush he'd found in the workroom, he lifted the latch and opened the door very slowly.

He could see nothing but a faint patch of night sky through the window. He listened for any sounds of breathing or movement from the room, but there were none. He mentally tossed a coin and then flicked on the flashlight for a brief look around the bedroom.

It was as he remembered it, but none of that registered. All he could grasp was one brief glimpse of Vreni hanging—and then darkness. For long seconds Fitzduane fought to retain his sanity as one hanging face dissolved into another in an endless kaleidoscope of horror. The words of the pathologist in Cork—it seemed an age ago—came back to him: "He might still have been alive. . . ."

He moved forward instinctively, keeping under cover, and snatched one more brief look with his flashlight. Her lower body was concealed by the choust through which she had dropped. Her head and torso were still in the bedroom. Fitzduane felt the last of his hope drain out of him.

He grasped Vreni by the shoulders, hoisted her body out of the hole, and rested her legs on the bedroom floor. With some of the weight now relieved, he was able to remove the noose from her neck. Her body was limp and totally unresponsive, but he could do no more for the moment. He should try artificial respiration, but there was a gunfight going on below him, and the Bear was in harm's way. He lay on the floor and peered down through the choust into the sitting room below. He could just make out one figure silhouetted against the window. The Bear was still firing from outside, but Fitzduane knew he must be running low on ammunition.

Fitzduane considered dropping down through the choust but decided that there were easier ways of committing suicide. He'd be in a crossfire from the two terrorists and in the Bear's line of fire—and he'd have to leave Vreni. There was only one practical alternative: he'd have to fire down through the choust. The angle was awkward, but by using his left hand to balance himself, he was able to fire the Skorpion with his right hand, pistol fashion.

The silhouette at the window jerked when it was hit and then vanished below the window ledge into the darkness. Any illusions that the wound was serious were shattered when a burst of flame spat back at him the merest fraction of a second after he'd ducked back from the hole. Rounds whined off the cast iron of the stove and embedded themselves in the wooden walls and ceiling.

There was a smashing of glass and the sound of a body dropping outside, then another. Fitzduane looked out the bedroom window and saw a figure running toward the small barn located at the end of the track farthest away from the village. It had sounded as if both terrorists had jumped out of the ground-floor window when they discovered they were being fired upon from both sides—so where was the second one?

Wood splintered, and the front door was smashed off its hinges to hit the floor with a reverberating crash. There was a shout from below. Fitzduane looked down through the choust to see the Bear grinning up at him, looking pleased with himself. He held up the Magnum.

"Seems to work," he said, "but if I'm going to travel around with you, I'd better learn to carry more ammunition. I'm out."

"Your timing's off," said Fitzduane. "One's still in close; the other legged it for the barn. I don't think peace has broken out yet."

A round black object came hurtling through the broken living room window and rolled across the wooden floor. Fitzduane flung himself away from the choust.

There was a vivid flash, and a wave of heat blasted up through the hole, knocking Fitzduane backward. The hanging rope, severed by flying shrapnel, came tumbling down, engulfing him in its coils and invoking an instant feeling of revulsion, as if the rope itself were contaminated. He disentangled himself and crawled to the side of the window. He looked around the frame cautiously and could see a figure zigzagging toward the barn. He fired repeatedly, but he was still shaken from the shock of the explosion—and then the gun was empty.

He ducked down behind the windowsill as return fire coming from the barn bracketed his position. No ammunition. A bloody unhealthy situation that was heading toward terminal unless he could come up with some answers. Think.

He remembered something from his last visit: the incongruity of Peter Haag's army rifle hanging in the bedroom. He fetched it. It was a substantial weapon compared with the Skorpion, but not of much use unless he could find the ammunition. Somewhere in the house there would be twenty-four rounds in a special container, but where? Regulations said ammunition should be stored separately from the weapon. He checked the bedroom closet just in case, but in vain. Peter Haag might have been a terrorist, but he was Swiss, and he would have followed regulations.

Clasping the assault rifle, Fitzduane wriggled down through the choust to the living room below. He found the Bear lying on the floor, semiconscious and muttering in Bernese dialect. The heavy metal stove seemed to have protected him from the full force of the blast, but it hadn't done him much good either. "For the love of God, Heini," Fitzduane muttered as he searched through the living room, "this is no time to try to teach me your bloody language."

No ammunition.

Heavier-caliber fire started to rip through the farmhouse walls from the direction of the barn, and Fitzduane realized that the terrorists must have concealed some backup weaponry there. One of them had something like a heavy hunting rifle. Obviously he was no expert with bolt action, but the slowness of his fire was compensated for by the fact that the wooden walls gave no protection at all against the new weapon. It was only a matter of time before he or the Bear or Vreni got hit. The sniper was methodically quartering the

farmhouse, and it wasn't too big a building to cover. He pulled the
Bear farther behind the wood stove and tried not to think of Vreni's
frail body totally exposed to the rifle fire. The desecration of the
dead. Did it really matter?

Desperately he scoured shelves and cabinets for the ammunition.
He wondered if it would be hidden behind the marmalade, as it had
been at Guido's. Did followers of the Steiner philosophy even eat
marmalade? If he didn't strike pay dirt soon, he might get the chance
to ask the long-dead Steiner personally.

A rifle bullet plowed into a second jar of mung beans, filling the air
with organically approved food mixed with less friendly shards of
broken glass. Brown rice was blasted into the air like shrapnel. He
reached out for the lethal locally distilled spirit he remembered.
Behind the rear bottle lay the ammunition. He ripped open the sealed
container and fed in the rounds one by one, hoping that the rifle's
mechanism wasn't jammed up with brown rice or lentils or the like.
Crouched low, he went out the kitchen door. He found a firing
position by the wall facing the barn. He extended the assault rifle's
bipod and activated the night sight. His front was substantially
protected by a bag of some sort of organic manure; whatever it was,
it wasn't odorless.

The firing from the barn ceased. A single figure appeared, moving
cautiously but somehow conveying the impression that it didn't
expect any more opposition—scarcely surprising after the grenade
and the barrage of heavy-rifle fire and the lack of response from the
defenders.

Fitzduane waited. The figure was close now and moving more
confidently. Fitzduane tried to figure out where the backup sniper
would be and had just settled on the most probable location when the
barn doors opened and a powerful motorcycle emerged. They were
going to check out the farmhouse and make their getaway. The
remaining question was, were there only two of them left or were
there more surprises?

Fitzduane supposed that legally he should probably shout, "Police," or "Hands up," or some such crap, but he wasn't feeling either
legal or charitable. He shot the walking terrorist four times through
the chest, sending the body spinning off the track and then down the
mountainside like a runaway sled.

The motorcycle engine roared, and submachine-gun fire sprayed
the farmhouse. The bike's headlight blinded him. The machine

leaped toward him, but it hit a rut and flew through the air, skidding past him before the rider expertly corrected.

He shot the motorcyclist as the bike was approaching the security guards' Mercedes. The machine barreled into the car, flinging the wounded terrorist into the snow. Fitzduane fired again very carefully at the flailing figure until there was no sign of movement.

Fitzduane was holding Vreni in his arms when the villagers arrived minutes later, assault rifles at the ready. She was limp and still, and her body was cold, but the Irishman was smiling.

HE FELT his shoulder being shaken, but he didn't want to leave the warm cocoon of sleep. His shoulder was shaken again, this time less gently. "Chief," said a familiar voice. "Chief, we've got a name."

The Chief Kripo reluctantly reentered the real word. He'd already forgotten what he'd been dreaming about, but he knew it had to have been better than the maelstrom that his waking hours had turned into. On the other hand, perhaps he was being too pessimistic. He recalled being agreeably surprised at the progress being made by Project K, so much so that he had decided to hang around for a few hours in the hope that there would be some kind of breakthrough. And it was a legitimate way of avoiding the flak he knew awaited him on his return to his office.

"A name?" He opened his eyes, blinked, and then opened them wider. "My God," he said to Henssen, "you look terrible."

"My circuits are fucked," said Henssen. "After this is over, I'm going to sleep for a month."

The Chief Kripo unraveled himself from the couch and sipped at the black coffee Henssen had brought him. He could hear computer sounds in the background. He looked at his watch.

"It's tomorrow," said Henssen. "You've been out only a few hours, but there have been some developments. It's kind of good news and bad news."

The Chief remembered that something had been nagging at him before he fell asleep. "The Irishman and the Bear," he said. "Are they back?"

"Not exactly," said Henssen, and he told the Chief what they'd heard through the local canton police.

The Chief shook his head. He looked dazed. "Incredible. I must still be dreaming. Is that the good news or the bad news?"

"It depends how you look at it."

"With a jaundiced eye," said the Chief, who actually wasn't quite sure of his reaction. He put down his coffee and stood up. "You mentioned a name," he said to Henssen. "You mean your machine has stopped dithering? You've found the Hangman?"

Henssen looked mildly uncomfortable. "We've got a couple of strong possibilities. Come and see for yourself."

The Chief Kripo followed Henssen into the main computer room. Only one terminal was live, the one with a special high-resolution screen that Henssen found was a little easier on his eyes when he was tired. There was a name on the screen followed by file references. The Chief looked at it and felt he was going crazy.

The name on the screen read: VON GRAFFENLAUB, BEAT.

"You're all loopy," said the Chief. "Your fucking machine is loopy."

Henssen, Kersdorf, and the other bleary-eyed men in the room were too exhausted to argue. Henssen played with the keyboard. There was a brief pause. Then the high-speed printer started spitting back the machine's reasoning. The computer wasn't too tired to argue. It outlined a formidable case.

HE'D FORGOTTEN about the radiophone. By reflex he picked it up in answer to its electronic bleep. Erika lay there lifeless, her blood congealing. He had no idea of the time or of what he was going to do next. He merely reacted.

"Herr von Graffenlaub," said a voice, "Herr Beat von Graffenlaub?"

"Yes?" said von Graffenlaub. The voice was tense, anxious, and familiar. It was not someone he knew well but someone he had spoken to recently.

"Sir, this is Mike Findlater of ME Services. I regret to say I have some very serious news to report, very serious indeed."

Beat von Graffenlaub listened to what the security man had to say. Initial fear turned to relief and then absolute joy as he absorbed the key fact that Vreni, little Vreni, was still alive. Tears of gratitude poured down his cheeks.

He didn't hear the other entrance open.

* * *

CONVENTIONAL POLICING in Bern took a backseat as the special antiterrorist force was assembled and sent into action. The von Graffenlaub premises were surrounded within thirty minutes of his name's flashing up on the screen, but it was more than six hours later before a highly trained entry group gained access. It had taken this long as a result of the most meticulous precautions designed to prevent the kind of surprises the Hangman liked to produce. Scanning equipment of various types was used to locate possible traps, and the entire block was searched to eliminate any chance of the terrorist's escaping through another exit.

Despite protests from some of his senior officers, the Chief Kripo insisted on leading the entry team on its final push inside. Mindful of booby traps and checking frequently by radio with the Nose, the men entered Erika's apartment not through the door but through a hole cut by a shaped charge in an internal wall—having previously scanned the area with metal detectors and explosive-sniffing equipment that could identify volatile substances in even the minutest volumes. Only traces of small-arms propellant were found by the probes. A second concealed entrance was also located. It led directly into an apartment in an adjoining house.

Inside Erika's sanctum they found what they had been looking for, but not the way they had expected. Beat von Graffenlaub was present, to be sure, but in a fashion that transferred him from the suspect to the victim file of the Nose's memory banks. He lay across his wife, his blood mingled with hers, the point of a fifteenth-century halberd protruding a hand's width from his chest. The handle extended from his back as casually as a fork stuck in the ground.

The Chief was sweaty in his bulletproof armor. "Loopy," he said.

THE ONLY good news out of this latest fiasco was that they were now down to one name on the computer's primary suspect list. The Chief radioed through for a progress report on his remaining quarry. He tried not to think of the awful tragedy of Beat von Graffenlaub. Mourning would have to wait.

They were now looking for someone called Bridgenorth Lodge. The computer said he was an American citizen living in Bern, with connections to the city from his earliest days. In fact, he'd been born there—which didn't, of course, make him Swiss. One of the heuristics programmed into the computer was that the Hangman wasn't

Swiss. The Chief had asked Henssen for the basis of what seemed to him to be pure guesswork, and he'd been referred to the Bear.

The Bear had just shrugged. "He isn't Swiss," he'd repeated. He hadn't been able to give a reason, but the Chief went along with it. The whole business was crazy anyway, and in the Chief's experience, the Bear's hunches were every bit as good as any computer's.

Chapter Twenty-one

Within minutes of his name's flashing up on the Project K computer screen, Lodge's house in the exclusive Bern suburb of Muri had been surrounded by heavily armed police. Only minutes away from both Kirchenfeldstrasse and police headquarters, Muri was a quarter occupied mainly by diplomats, senior bureaucrats, and the ex-wives of successful businessmen. The houses were solidly built and expensive even by Swiss standards and in many cases were discreetly set back from the road in the seclusion of their own grounds.

Lodge's house wasn't just discreet; it was downright reclusive. It occupied a two-acre lot at the end of a leafy cul-de-sac. A thick screen of trees and shrubbery rendered it invisible from either the road or its neighbors on either side, and the grounds at the back of the house not only were similarly screened but led in turn to a private fenced-off wood and through it to the River Aare. Further privacy was ensured by a four-meter-high perimeter wall topped with razor wire—sprayed green for environmental reasons. The wire was electrified. The main gates were the same height as the wall and were made from oak-faced steel plate. There was no doorbell.

The Chief Kripo would have preferred to keep Lodge's place under observation for some days before taking more dramatic action,

319

but practical realities intervened. First, the Hangman was simply too dangerous to leave on the loose any longer than necessary, and second, they had to find out as fast as possible whether they were on the right track. After all, the computer wasn't infallible. Lodge might not be the right man. He might be a totally innocent run-of-the-mill privacy-loving billionaire.

The Chief wished that there were a better way of checking out Lodge, but he couldn't think of one. Once again he was going to lead the raid, and this time he was sweating under his body armor even before the assault team went into action. His skin felt cold and clammy, and there was an unpleasant taste in his mouth. He had a very bad feeling about what was to happen. He swallowed with difficulty and issued the command. The team started in.

HENSSEN REPLACED the receiver slowly and stared into the middle distance. "What a bloody business."

Kersdorf's legs were hurting him. "What happened?" he asked. "Is Lodge our man?"

Henssen shrugged helplessly. "The assault team lost two men going in plus another half dozen wounded. Lost as in dead. The Chief was scratched, but he's okay."

Kersdorf was silent, shocked. Then he spoke. "So Lodge is our man. Did they get him?"

"They don't even know whether he was there when the assault began," said Henssen, spreading his hands in a gesture of frustration, "but he certainly wasn't by the time they secured the house. Their best guess is that he wasn't there at all. They swear that nobody got through their cordon and that the house was empty."

"So how come the casualties?"

"A variation on a theme. Explosives concealed in the floors and ceilings were triggered by a series of independent but mutually supporting automatic sensors: heat, acoustic, and pressure. The explosives were wrapped in some material that neutralized the sniffers."

"What about Claymores?" said Kersdorf. "We warned them to expect Claymores."

"It seems that our people just weren't good enough," said Henssen, "or at least that the Hangman was better. Of course, he's had more practice, God rot him." He paused and massaged his temples. He felt acutely depressed, and light-headed from lack of sleep. He continued. "Oh, they found Claymores as expected and defused them. They followed our briefing in that respect, but then they thought they were safe—and boom."

"He's a creature of habit," said Kersdorf. "There is always a surprise within a surprise: the Chinese doll syndrome."

"Russian doll," corrected Henssen. "Those doll-within-a-doll-within-a-doll sets are Russian. They call them matrushkas; there can be three, or four, or five, or six, or even more little surprises inside."

Kersdorf sighed. There was silence in the room before he spoke. "Let's get some sleep." He gestured at the computer. "At least we now know how he operates. It won't be long before we get him."

"But at what cost?" said Henssen.

THE BEAR WAS in a private room of the Tiefenau. Ten days of first-class medical care and the special attentions of one particular ward nurse with a gleam in her eye had left him, if not as good as new, at least in excellent secondhand condition. He pushed aside his tray with a satisfied sigh and split the last of the Burgundy between them.

Fitzduane picked up the empty bottle. "Hospital issue?"

"Not exactly," said the Bear, "though I suppose you might call it medically selected."

"Ah," said Fitzduane. He looked at the label. "A 1961 Beaune. Now what does that suggest to you about the lady who bought you this? This is real wine. You don't use '61 Beaune to take the paint off your front door."

"Hmm," said the Bear, growing a little pinker. "Do you mind if we don't talk about Frau Maurer?"

Fitzduane grinned and drained his glass.

"What's been happening?" asked the Bear. "Rest and relaxation are going to be the death of me. I'm not allowed near a phone, and the news I'm fed is so scrappy that if I were a dog, I'd be chasing sheep."

"Don't exaggerate."

"Any progress with Vreni?"

"None. She's alive, she's physically almost recovered, but her mind is the problem. She talks little, sleeps a lot, and any attempt to question her has proved disastrous. It sends her into a fit each time. The doctors have insisted that she be left alone."

"Poor kid," said the Bear. "What about Lodge?"

"Vanished—not that he ever appeared, now I think about it. The house has been taken apart by the army and made safe, which was no small task itself. There were booby traps everywhere. Afterward the forensics people had a field day. There is no doubt that Lodge is the Hangman, but the question is, is Lodge really Lodge?"

"Why do you say that?"

"Questioning of the neighbors hasn't yielded much," explained Fitzduane. "He is a recluse. He comes and goes at irregular intervals. He is absent for long periods. It's consistent with what we expected. We have had some small luck in terms of physical description, though few people have seen him up close. Mostly quick glimpses through a car window."

"I thought all his various cars have tinted windows."

"Sometimes, on a hot day, a window might be wound down," said Fitzduane. "He has also been seen walking on a couple of occasions—both times while it was raining so he was huddled under an umbrella."

"Blond, bearded, medium build, et cetera," said the Bear.

"Quite so," said Fitzduane. "And that tallies with the photo and other personal details filed with the Bern Fremdenpolizei."

"So what's the problem?"

"We've traced some of Lodge's background in the States," said Fitzduane. "We haven't been able to lay our hands on a photograph—his father was a senior CIA man and apparently for security reasons didn't allow either himself or his family to be photographed—but the physical descriptions don't tally. Hair and eyes are a different color. Lodge in his youth had dark brown hair and brown eyes."

"A good wig and contact lenses are all you need to solve that problem."

Fitzduane shook his head. "Not so simple. Normal procedure for an alien coming to live in Switzerland involves the Fremdenpolizei, as you know. In Lodge's case, he was interviewed several times by an experienced sergeant who swears that the man he spoke to—for several hours in all—had naturally blond hair, was not wearing contact lenses, and is the man in the photo in his file, which in turn pretty much tallies with the neighbors' description."

"Fingerprints?"

"None," said Fitzduane. "None on file in the States anyway. The Fremdenpolizei apparently don't take them if you're a well-behaved affluent foreigner, and the jury is still out on the house in Muri. The forensics people have picked up some unidentified prints, but without a match they're not much use. I wouldn't bet on the Hangman's prints being among them. He seems to skate near the edge, but in fundamental things he's damn cautious."

"So Lodge is the Hangman," said the Bear, "but maybe Lodge isn't Lodge—and the Lodge that isn't Lodge isn't to be found."

"Hole in one," said Fitzduane.

The Bear looked out the full-length window. Despite protestations about security, he had insisted on being on the ground floor and on having direct access to the garden. The window was slightly open, and he could smell freshly cut grass. He could hear the mower in the distance. "I hate hospitals. But I'm developing a certain affection for this one. Dental records?" he added.

"Like the marriage feast at Cana, I'm saving the best for last."

"So?" the Bear said impatiently.

"The Nose has been set up to monitor any incident in Bern that might conceivably relate to the activities of the Hangman. A couple of days ago a dentist's surgery was completely destroyed by fire—as was the dentist, who had been bound into his own chair with wire."

"That sounds like the Hangman's sense of humor," said the Bear. "Though I guess there might be a few other candidates among the patients."

"Needless to say, all of the dentist's records were destroyed, and that would have been that except it turns out he kept a backup set in his bank."

"I'm sure his widow will enjoy looking through them. And I presume Mr. Lodge's full frontals are among them?"

"Exactly."

"Matrushka," said the Bear, "if I can quote Henssen's latest obsession."

"Gesundheit," said Fitzduane.

THE CHIEF KRIPO WAS contemplating the computer screen. His face had been gashed unpleasantly, if not severely, during the Muri raid, and the scars itched. The stitches had been taken out several days before, and he had been told he was healing well. He had also been told the scars would be permanent unless he had plastic surgery. He was unenthusiastic about the idea; he thought he'd prefer to remain scarred and dangerous-looking than have some quack peel skin off his bottom and try to stick it on his face. He didn't like strangers attempting to rearrange his bits—which brought him right back to the Hangman, who had damn nearly succeeded in disassembling him into his component parts.

He tapped the computer keyboard a couple of times with his forefinger. "It works," he said. "You've proved that it does. Why is it that now, when we're so close, it's of no help anymore?"

Henssen shrugged helplessly. "It has to be asked the right questions."

The Chief glared at the VDU. He had a totally irrational desire to climb inside the machine with a screwdriver and wrench and force the dumb beast to cough up some answers. Somewhere inside that electronic monster lay the solution, he was convinced of that. But what to do about it? He had no idea. He was certain he was missing something—something obvious. He walked back and forth across the room, glancing frequently at the computer. After ten minutes of this, to Henssen's great relief, he stopped and sat down.

"Tell me more," he said, "about how this machine thinks."

FITZDUANE FOUND walking in the Marzili pleasant but distracting. The Marzili was a long, thin park sandwiched between the River Aare and a well-to-do residential area of Bern, both of which were overlooked by the Bundeshaus and a plethora of government buildings, including the Interpol building and the headquarters of the Federal Police.

The Marzili's proximity to the center of things meant that even this early in the year, as the day was warm and sunny, a generous sprinkling of nearly naked women was scattered across the lawn. Topless sunbathing was the norm in the Marzili, and hundreds of secretaries and computer operators and other government workers were busy making up for a long, cold winter. Serried ranks of nipples were pointed at the sun like solar cells on an energy farm.

Fitzduane, encased in a bulletproof vest under a light cotton blouson jacket, felt overdressed. He glanced across at the Bear, who was humming. Externally the detective seemed little the worse for wear after his two weeks in the hospital, and his cheeks had the ruddy glow of good living. On second thought Fitzduane decided that more than good food and wine were reflected in the Bear's demeanor. Love and the Bear? Well, good for Frau Maurer. Her first name, he had learned, was Katia.

"Don't you find all this distracting?" he asked. Fitzduane's eyes followed a spectacular redhead as she loped across the grass in front of them and then lay down on a towel, eyes closed, face and body toward the sun, knees drawn up and slightly apart. Tendrils of pubic hair escaping from the monokini confirmed that she was the genuine article. She looked edible.

"On the contrary," said the Bear, "I find it quite riveting."

Fitzduane smiled. They walked toward the path that ran along the bank of the river. Downstream, minutes away, was the Kirchenfeld Bridge, and just below that was the spot where Klaus Minder's body had been fished out.

The Bear sat down on a bench. Suddenly he looked tired. He threw a small branch into the water, and his eyes followed it until it bobbed out of sight. He extracted a creased envelope from his pocket and smoothed it on his knee.

"Your guess as to the Hangman's identity," he said. "I found it in my pocket when I was getting dressed in the hospital this morning."

"It seems I was wrong," said Fitzduane dryly. "There doesn't seem to be much doubt that Lodge is our man, and God knows where he is now. Your people have checked every square millimeter of Bern over the last couple of weeks."

"Why did you think it was Balac?"

Fitzduane picked up a handful of pebbles and slowly tossed them one by one into the river. He liked the faint plop each stone made. He wondered how many people had sat on the riverbank over the years and done the same thing. Had a vast bed of pebbles built up in the river as a result? Would the river eventually be choked up by ruminating river watchers?

"A number of reasons. For starters, just sheer gut feeling that he is a person who is not what he seems. Next, a number of small things. He is the right age. He was an intimate of Erika's. He has the right kind of charming but dominant personality. His artist's training would give him an excellent knowledge of anatomy. His work habits allow him to travel extensively without suspicion, to have unexplained absences, and so on. He's paranoid about security. His studio is near where Klaus Minder's body was found. There are other pointers, but none conclusive, and in any case it all appears a little academic at this stage. We've identified our man, and he isn't Balac."

"Hmm," mused the Bear. He was no longer looking so tired.

"Anyway, I can't see him doing something as provocative as the chessboard girl."

"We're dealing with a player of games," said the Bear. "The Hangman isn't rational by normal standards. He has his own logic. Tweaking our collective official nose appeals to him. Actually it's not so uncommon. I once picked up a car thief who had operated freely for years until he stole a police car—and not an unmarked one, but the full painted-up job with radio and flashing lights and all the trimmings. When I asked him why he'd done such a stupid thing, he said he couldn't resist it."

Fitzduane laughed. "How are you feeling?"

"Good considering this is my first day out of the hospital, but I do get a little wobbly now and then. I'll take a good long rest when this is over."

"I'm not sure you should go to this meeting."

"You couldn't keep me away if you tried," said the Bear. "Don't forget I've a very personal interest these days. I want the Hangman dead."

"What about civil rights and due process of law?" said Fitzduane, smiling.

The Bear shook his head. "This isn't a normal case. Normal rules don't apply. This is like stamping out a plague. You destroy the source of the infection."

They walked along the Aare to the Dalmazibrücke. By crossing it and cutting up Schwellenmattstrasse, they could have made it to Project K in ten minutes, but Fitzduane took another look at the Bear and called a Berp car by radio. The Bear didn't argue. He was silent, lost in thought.

THE CHIEF SURVEYED the assembled Project K team; then his gaze fixed on the Bear.

"You shouldn't be here, Heini, as you damn well know. If you collapse, don't expect me to hold one end of the stretcher. You're too damn heavy."

The Bear nodded. "Understood, Chief. You're not a young man anymore."

"Needs his strength for other things," said Charlie von Beck.

"Shut up, the lot of you," said the Chief, "and listen carefully. A short time ago we had our first major breakthrough. We paid a heavy price, but we identified the Hangman's base in Bern, and we now have a fair idea who he is, though I admit there are some problems in that area. On the negative side, a couple of weeks after the Muri find, the investigation is virtually at a standstill. We are at an impasse in terms of the Hangman's identity, and the man himself seems to have vanished despite the fact that we now have a photograph of him— and dental records—to work with. To add insult to injury, the death of that dentist occurred after the Muri raid, so it looks very much as if the Hangman is still in Bern. We know what he looks like, yet this psychopath seems to come and go with impunity—and not just to look at the sights. He is still killing.

"I've called you all together to suggest we change the way we're approaching this investigation. Since Muri we've been concentrating on trying to find Lodge to the virtual exclusion of all else. We haven't been successful. Now I think we need a more creative approach, and I include in that our use of the computer." He nodded at Henssen.

Henssen stood up and then propped himself against a desktop. He looked as if he needed the support. He cleared his throat and spoke, his voice hoarse. "The Chief thinks that we may have the solution in the computer but that we're not asking the right questions. He may well be right, so let me explain a little more about what we have done—and can do.

"Our identification of Lodge was the result of a mixture of computer activity and human judgment. We tapped into a vast amount of data and constructed a theoretical profile of the Hangman, and then, using a technique known as forward chaining, we filtered through the data. We were lucky. One of our two prime suspects was our man."

"May I interrupt here?" the Bear broke in. "I thought it was agreed that the initial profile would look for someone who wasn't Swiss. If so, why did the machine cough up Beat von Graffenlaub? His age wasn't right either."

Henssen looked a little uncomfortable. "Well, Heini, I owe you something of an apology. I second-guessed you. The program allows parameters to be graded according to the confidence you have in them. I gave your non-Swiss hunch a low confidence rating because there wasn't a shred of hard evidence to back it up; it was outweighed by other material. The same applied to the age factor. In neither case were we dealing with hard facts, only with guesses."

"Fair enough," said the Bear, "but I would like to have been told that at the time."

"The system is totally transparent to the user," said Henssen. "Any of the parameters can be looked at whenever you wish. After this I'll show you how it's done."

"Can we get back to the original topic?" said the Chief testily.

"Certainly," said Henssen. "Where was I?"

"Forward chaining," said Kersdorf.

"Ah," said Henssen. "Well, forward chaining is essentially a way of generating conclusions by applying rules, either formal or heuristic, to a given set of facts. If the bank customer pulls a gun and demands money and there is no suggestion that this is a security test, then a reasonable deduction is that he is a bank robber."

"And who said computers couldn't think?" Charlie von Beck rolled his eyes. He was back in his bow tie and velvet suit.

Henssen ignored the interruption. "The point is, forward chaining is only one way to go about things. You can also use backward chaining. In that situation you could assume someone was a bank robber and then work back to see what facts supported that conclusion. It's an ideal way of checking out a suspect and ties in with the less rational elements of our human makeup, like intuition."

The Bear caught Fitzduane's eye and smiled.

"What it comes down to," the Chief said, "is that we have a much more flexible tool here than we seem to realize, and we're not using it to anywhere near its full potential. For instance, it can function in the abstract. Instead of asking, 'Who do we have on file who has a knowledge of plastique?' you can ask it, 'What kind of person would have a knowledge of plastique, and where might he or she be found?' The machine will then generate a profile based upon its file of data and its knowledge base." He rose to his feet. "Well, there you have it. Take off the blinkers. Try a little creative anarchy. Hit the problem from first principles. Find the fucking Hangman." After an angry look at everyone, he left the room.

"Anarchy!" exclaimed von Beck. "Creative anarchy! Is he really Swiss? It wasn't anarchy that made William Tell shoot straight or the cuckoos in our clocks pop out on time."

INSPIRED BY Katia, who believed that certain foods were good for certain parts of the anatomy, over the next three days the Bear ate a great deal of fish—a luxury in landlocked Switzerland—and, so to speak, kept himself to himself.

He wasn't so much antisocial as elusive. He went places and did things without saying exactly where or what. He made and received phone calls without comment. A series of packages arrived by courier and were unwrapped and examined only when he was alone. He was moderately talkative but only on any subject except the Hangman, and he was maddeningly cheerful.

On the morning of the fourth day Fitzduane, who had been researching variations of Swiss batzi with a little too much dedication the night before, rose at the unearthly hour the Swiss set aside for breakfast only to yawn to a halt in near-terminal shock at the sight of the Bear standing on his head, arms crossed, in the living room. His eyes were closed.

"Morning," said the Bear without stirring.

"Ugh," said Fitzduane. He turned on his heel and stood under a cold shower for five minutes. Toward the end he thought it might be a good idea to remove his robe and pajamas. When he returned to the living room, the apparition had vanished.

Over breakfast the Bear expounded on the merits of fish as a brain food. "Did you know," he said, "that the brain is essentially a fatty organ and one of its key ingredients, a free fatty acid, comes from fish?"

"Ugh," said Fitzduane, and spread butter and marmalade on his toast.

The Bear chewed enthusiastically on a raw carrot and wrinkled his nose at what Fitzduane was eating. "That's no way to start the day," he said. "I must get Katia to draw you up a diet sheet."

Fitzduane poured some batzi into his orange juice. He drank half the glass. "Ugh," he said.

LATER THAT morning, after a detour to the *Der Bund* office to pick up a bulky file stuffed with press clippings, notes, and photographs, Fitzduane found himself trailing behind the apparently supercharged Bear as the detective hummed his way through the portals, halls, rooms, corridors, and miscellaneous annexes of the City of Bern art museum. The corridor they were in was in semidarkness. Fitzduane wondered about the wisdom of this policy. Perhaps visitors were supposed to rent flashlights. His mind went back to Kuno

Gonschior's exhibition of a series of black rectangles in the Loeb Gallery. It had been the first time he had met Erika. It seemed light-years ago.

The Bear stopped his march and scratched his head. "I think I'm lost."

The pause gave Fitzduane the chance to catch up. He leaned against the wall while the Bear consulted his notebook with the aid of a match. He was thinking that if the Bear continued in this hyper-active, hypercheerful mood, it might be a good idea to slip a downer into his morning orange juice before both of them had heart attacks.

There was a long, furious burst of what sounded like automatic-weapons fire, and Fitzduane dived to the ground. The section of the wall against which he'd been leaning a split second before fell into the corridor, and a piercing white light shone through the gap in the wall. Fitzduane half expected the archangel Gabriel to make an appearance. Instead, a dust-covered figure clad in a zippered blue overall and carrying a heavy industrial hammer drill in both hands like a weapon climbed through the aperture, trailing cable behind him. He didn't appear to have wings. Head to one side, the figure surveyed the hole in the wall critically and then nodded his head in satisfaction, entirely oblivious of the 9 mm SIG automatic Fitzduane was aiming at his torso.

"Ha!" said the Bear triumphantly. "I wasn't lost after all." He looked down at Fitzduane. "Don't shoot him. This is Charlie von Beck's cousin Paulus, Paulus von Beck. He's a man of parts: the museum's expert in brush technique, a successful sculptor, and I don't know what else. He's also the reason we're here."

Fitzduane made his weapon safe and reholstered it. He still hadn't gotten his shotgun back, and it irked him. He rose to his feet, brushed dust from his clothes, and shook hands with von Beck. "Demolition or sculpture?" he asked. "Or were you just carried away screwing in a picture hook?"

PAULUS LEFT them in his office drinking coffee while he went to clean up before going to the restoration studios to examine the contents of the file the Bear had brought him. When he returned, Paulus had discarded his sculptor image. The overalls had been replaced by a charcoal gray suit of Italian cut with creases so sharp it seemed clear that the art expert kept a steam press in his closet. His silk tie was hand-painted.

Paulus was older than his cousin. He had a high-browed, delicately featured face set off by a soft mane of wavy hair, and his eyes were a curious shade of violet. He looked troubled. Fitzduane had the feeling that the Bear might have stumbled across more than he'd bargained for. Paulus's demeanor was not that of a dispassionate expert; somehow he was a player.

"Sergeant Raufman, before I answer the questions you have put to me, I would be grateful if you would answer a few points I would like to raise. They are relevant, I assure you."

The Bear's tone reflected the art expert's sober demeanor. "As you wish. We police are more accustomed to asking questions than answering, but I shall do what I can." There was the slightest emphasis on the word *police*. It was as good a way as any of warning Paulus to think carefully before he spoke, thought Fitzduane.

"Thank you," said von Beck. The warning had been understood. He took his time before he spoke. He straightened a small bronze bust on his desk while he collected his thoughts. He tidied the papers in front of him into an exact symmetrical pile. He cleared his throat. Fitzduane felt like taking a walk around the block while von Beck dithered.

"My first question: Do your inquiries have to do with the recent wave of killings in this city?"

The Bear nodded. "They do."

Von Beck exhaled slowly. "My second question: You have asked me to comment on a certain artist's work. Do you suspect the artist of being involved—centrally involved—with these killings?"

It was the Bear's turn to hesitate. "Yes," he said finally.

"You don't think that he could be involved only peripherally, an innocent victim, if you will?"

"Anything's possible," said the Bear.

"But you don't think so?"

The Bear gave a deep sigh. "No. I think our friend is involved from his toes to the tip of his paintbrush. I think he's a ruthless homicidal nut with a perverted sense of humor, who should be eliminated as fast as possible before he contaminates any more lives. I think you should stop playing verbal tiddlywinks and tell us everything you know or suspect. I'm running out of patience. This is a murder investigation, not some parlor game."

The color drained from von Beck's face, and he looked as if he were going to be sick. "My third question," he said, "and then I will tell you what you want to know: If I tell you everything, can I trust your utter discretion? No leaks to the press, no appearing in open court, no involvement at all, in fact, other than my giving you a statement?"

"This business is about priorities," said the Bear. "We have a mass killer on the loose. If I have to parade you around the streets of Bern with a rope around your neck to checkmate our friend, then that's what I'll do. On the other hand, you're a cousin of a trusted colleague. If I can help you, I will. We're after the shark, not a minnow."

Fitzduane broke in. "To be frank, Herr von Beck, I think you have already decided to tell us all you know, and we respect that. It takes courage. But there is something else to think about apart from public duty. Basic survival. Our murderous friend has a habit of cleaning up after himself. He doesn't like to leave a trail of witnesses. They seem to enjoy brief life spans after they have served their purpose. It just might be a good idea to help stop our friend before he kills you."

Von Beck now looked truly terrified. "I know," he said. "I know. You don't have to say any more." The Bear and Fitzduane waited while Paulus von Beck composed himself.

"Before I give you my professional opinion," said Paulus, "I had better explain the full extent of my relationship with Simon Balac. I am a homosexual. Bern is an intimate city where people of similar interests and persuasions almost inevitably tend to know one another. The artistic community is comparatively small. I got to know Balac—everyone calls him Balac—well. Nearly five years ago we became lovers."

"Your being homosexual or even having an affair with Simon Balac is neither here nor there to the police," said the Bear. "Your sex life is your business."

"I'm afraid that is not all there is to it," said Paulus. "You see, Balac is a strong personality with what one might call varied . . . exotic tastes. He has a strong sexual drive, and he likes diversions. In his company one finds oneself swept along, eager to please, willing to try things, to do things that normally one would not contemplate. He is a brilliant artist, and the foibles of such men must be tolerated, or at least that is what I used to tell myself. If I am to be truthful, I was swept up in the sheer sexual excitement of it all, the tasting of forbidden fruit.

"Balac enjoys women sexually as well as men. He enjoys group sex in all its variations. He likes children, sexually mature children but still way below the age of consent. He likes to initiate, to corrupt. He makes it incredibly exciting. He uses stimulants—alcohol, various drugs—and above all his own extraordinary energy and charisma."

"The von Graffenlaub twins, Rudi and Vreni?" asked Fitzduane.

"And Erika?" added the Bear.

"Yes, yes," said Paulus.

"Hmm," said the Bear. "You'd better tell us all of it. Does Charlie know any of this?"

Paulus shook his head firmly. "He knows I'm gay, of course, but nothing else. He's a good friend and a kind man. I wanted to tell him, but I couldn't."

"I'm afraid he'll have to know now," said the Bear. "You do understand that, don't you?"

Paulus nodded.

It was midafternoon before they emerged from the museum. While the Bear debated where to go to satisfy his audibly growling stomach—he had decided he was sick of fish—Fitzduane asked the one question that had been bothering him since von Beck had shown he could walk through walls. "Is it normal in Switzerland to chop up the core structure of the museum in the interests of artistic expression?"

The Bear laughed. "Living art," he said. "Actually there is an explanation. They were knocking down that section of the museum anyway to make way for a new extension, and they thought it might be fun to let artists take part in the process."

"Ah," said Fitzduane.

"No matter how bizarre the event, there is almost always a straightforward explanation. Don't you agree?"

"No," said Fitzduane.

THE CHIEF KRIPO HAD learned to regard the Project K headquarters as a haven. Only there did he have any thinking time; only there was he relatively free of interference from his political masters wanting progress reports; only there could he escape the profusion of foreign antiterrorist agencies that all wanted a piece of the Hangman, doubtless to skin and stuff and hang on their respective bureaucratic walls; only there did any serious progress seem to be made on the case itself, as opposed to the international hunt, which appeared to have become an enterprise in its own right with the objective almost incidental; only there could he avoid his wife and two mistresses, each of whom blamed his now excessively long absences on some relative advance in his affections for one of the others. It was no picnic being Chief of the Criminal Police in Bern these days.

As luck would have it, the Chief was in the main computer room when Henssen finished the computer runs the Bear had requested. He stared at Henssen's screen. Could this be it? Had they got a real answer at last? Could they ship that albatross of an Irishman back to his bogs? Could they think in terms of no Hangman and a nice steady traditional Bernese two corpses a year? Hell, it was going to be champagne time.

The Chief tried to rein in his hopes. "Are you sure? Absolutely sure?"

"Nothing is sure in this life, Chief," said the Bear, "except death, a strong Swiss franc, and that the rich get richer."

"Convince me. Convince us." The Chief included the rest of the Project K team with a sweep of his arm.

KADAR HADN'T expected Lodge to be discovered, and he had absolutely no idea how it could have happened. He had been so careful with this personality. He hadn't taken the risks that had characterized his behavior in other guises. How then could it have occurred?

Losing Lodge was worse than the death of a friend. Of course, that was only natural. After all, he *was* Lodge, wasn't he? There were times he wasn't sure. His Lodge identity represented his one true link with the past, but now he could never use it again. He felt—he searched for a word—orphaned.

Perhaps he was being too negative. His use of a stand-in during the immigration proceedings—a minor actor, now resting permanently under half a meter of concrete in the house in Muri—could give him a way out. The man whose description and photograph they had wasn't Kadar. He could reappear as Lodge and indignantly protest this usurpation of his name. He'd have to do it from another country, or things would get confusing. Still, it could be done. It might work.

No, it was too risky. Well, he'd think about it.

Only two days were left before he was due to leave Bern to commence what he thought of as the "active" phase of the operation. It might be wiser to leave immediately. Then again his plans were made, and he had taken precautions against discovery. It could even work to his advantage.

He checked the temperature probe set into Paul Straub's body. The corpse was defrosting, but too slowly. It would have been handier to have used hot water to thaw out Herr Straub, but he wasn't too sure what effect that would have. It was the kind of thing some forensic scientist might pick up. A body destroyed by fire shouldn't really be waterlogged. It shouldn't start off as a block of ice either; it wouldn't burn properly. A scorched outside and entrails cold enough to chill a martini might cause some head scratching.

He turned up the heat. He thought it was rather neat to be using his sauna for the purpose. He could tone up and sweat off some weight while keeping an eye on things. If his experiment with the frozen pig was anything to go by, Straub should be adequately thawed out in about another six to eight hours. That would be just about right. Then he'd be kept in the large Bosch refrigerator, nicely chilled but on call if required. If he wasn't needed, he could be refrozen and kept on hand for a rainy day.

"IT'S IRONIC," said the Bear, "but what pointed me in the right direction wasn't the computerized power of the Nose or old-fashioned police work; it was our Irishman's intuition." He looked across at Fitzduane. "You should have more faith, Hugo.

"Hugo suspected that the painter Simon Balac was our man. There was some circumstantial evidence, but it was far from conclusive. Then the computer identified Lodge, and the raid confirmed him, and naturally all our efforts were concentrated in that direction. I had plenty of time on my hands in the hospital, and I wasn't distracted by the details of the hunt." He glowered around him. "You people kept me starved of information."

"For your own good, Heini," said Charlie von Beck, "and on doctor's orders."

"What do doctors know?" growled the Bear. "Anyway, sparked by Hugo's candidate, I got to thinking about the nature of the Hangman and how he operates, and that led me to an intriguing hypothesis: Could Lodge and Balac be one and the same man?"

"Proof?" said the Chief. "But why be greedy? At this stage I'll settle for reasons and an hour alone with him in a police cell."

"Patience. Rubber hoses are un-Swiss. We're supposed to be a logical people. Follow my reasoning, and you'll see how it all fits together. First, let's remember the Hangman's habit of always having a way out. If the authorities hit one of his bases, two things can be virtually guaranteed: the place will be extensively booby-trapped, and an elaborate escape route will already have been planned. The Hangman doesn't fling himself through the fourth-floor window as the police come rushing through the front door and hope to work things out on the way down. No, this guy is prepared for the down side in detail. It's the way he operates. He's a compulsive planner, and he likes to think he has every contingency covered."

"He normally has," grumbled the Chief.

"Now, combine this behavior pattern with his habit of operating in a compartmentalized way through a series of apparently autonomous gangs, and you have someone who almost certainly works through two or more meticulously prepared identities. The Hangman is a perfectionist. His won't be just paper identities that will fold under investigation. No, he will have created what appear to be real living people. If one cover gets blown, he migrates to identity number two and continues on. Also, we know he likes to take risks—strictly speaking, unnecessary risks—so it is my hunch that he doesn't go away and hide under a stone when he switches identities. His new persona is right out there, most likely an upstanding member of the community, the last person you'd suspect.

"My next step was to go back to the computer and reevaluate our suspect list in a different way. Up till then we had concentrated on two prime targets, von Graffenlaub and Lodge, and had ignored the rest when we got lucky with Lodge. However, there were, in fact, several hundred other names on the 'possible' list.

"We could have slogged through the names in order of probability rating, but the banks would have given up secrecy by the time we had any results. Then it occurred to me that we should tackle things another way. Given that Lodge is part of the puzzle, we should evaluate the suspect list with him as part of the equation. His known activities should be matched with those of each of the other suspects to see who fits best. Now remember that although few people ever saw Lodge, we still managed to accumulate masses of data on the man. We have travel details, credit card usage, financial data, magazine subscriptions, and so on. That's the kind of stuff that led us to take a look at him in the first place. We had no hard evidence that he was the Hangman. It was merely that his profile fit.

"The results of our exercise under the amended program were intriguing. Simon Balac rocketed to the top of the list, and all sorts of other hot candidates dropped to the bottom. One and one started to make three."

"I take it Heini wasn't programming the computer," said the Chief to Henssen.

"Next we were able to fit a few more pieces of the—"

"Puzzle?" said Charlie von Beck.

The Bear shook his head pityingly. "Of the foundation of guilt." He raised his eyebrows. "One of the interesting things about the computer checks we ran on Balac is not so much what showed up as what didn't show up. Let me give you a few examples. First, Balac travels a great deal. His various showings and exhibitions are a matter of public record, yet his credit card records and travel arrangements don't adequately back that up."

"Maybe he likes to pay cash to avoid taxes," said Kersdorf. "That's not exactly uncommon. Maybe he just hates credit cards."

The Bear shook his head. "He has all the major credit cards, from American Express to Diners Club, from Access to Visa. He uses them freely in Bern and to some extent when he travels. Superficially it looks all right, but a statistical analysis of how he spends indicates that his pattern is out of sync with the norm. That's not significant in itself except to suggest that he is hiding something.

"The next factor has to do with his travel arrangements. Even if he is paying cash, his name should show up on the airline reservation computer. The point is, it doesn't. Balac disappears from Bern and then reappears at some known destination without leaving a trace as to how he got there. That isn't normal. Maybe he has a policy of traveling under an assumed name, but that isn't kosher either because it suggests strongly that he must be using a false passport. You have to remember that security arrangements on the airlines are now fairly thorough, and bookings are regularly cross-checked with passport holders. Balac doesn't show up."

"These are details," said the Chief. "He might be guilty of a passport offense. That doesn't mean he's the Hangman."

"Let me continue. So far we've got someone who, when dovetailed with Lodge, fits our computer profile exactly. Next, analysis shows his spending and travel patterns to be suspicious. Then, comparison of his known travel destinations and criminal incidents in which the Hangman is known or suspected to have been involved correlate to a significant statistical extent. That doesn't mean he was in the same city or even in the same country—but he was frequently within communication distance whether by plane, train, ship, or road. Next, we've had two positive identifications from Lenk that he was there when the incident with young Rudi von Graffenlaub and Erika took place. We struck out on that one at first when we just looked for a description, but when we went back with photographs of Balac, our luck improved."

"Photographs?" said Henssen. "Any chance our people could have been seen? He seems to have a highly developed sense of self-preservation."

"*Der Bund*," said the Bear. "Thank God for a newspaper of record. It may be stuffy, but it's certainly thorough. It has a file on every celebrity in town, and Balac has been here long enough and run enough exhibitions to justify a nice fat folder. We have numerous pictures of him and even more of his paintings. I'll come back to that.

"The next point is interesting. It occurred to us that given the Hangman's habit of making significant structural alterations to the buildings he uses, there might be a lead there. Some of his work may well have been carried out openly, as is the case with his reinforced door, but other work suggested a clandestine operation and a high level of skill. That indicated the possibility that he brings in small teams of experts, keeps them under wraps for the duration of the job, and then, given his penchant for tidying, disposes of them.

"To that end, using the Nose, we burrowed away and uncovered four incidents that fit our profile. In every case a highly skilled group of workmen had been killed in what looked like an accident. In one case, about eighteen months ago, a minibus of Italian workmen from Milan went over a cliff in Northern Italy after a tire blew. The carabinieri suspected the Mafia, since it is heavily into construction and related activities, and the tire had blown because of a small explosive charge, which is its style. Anyway, what made this case different was that there was one survivor out of the eight in the bus. He was badly burned, but he rambled on about a special job and the sound of a river and never getting any fresh air and the smell of turpentine making him sick."

"Lodge's house in Muri?" said the Chief. "It backs on to the Aare."

"I don't think so," said the Bear. "There's a wood between the house and the river that blankets out all sound of the water. I checked it out."

"So you think it was Balac's studio complex down by the Wasser-werk?" said von Beck.

"Near where Minder was found," added the Chief.

"That's my best guess," said the Bear.

"Can we talk to this workman?" said the Chief.

"Through a Ouija board maybe," replied the Bear. "He recovered, went home, and someone put two barrels of a lupara into him. Terminal relapse."

"Keep going," said the Chief with a sigh. "I'm sure you've got something even better up your sleeve."

"Hang in there, Chief," said the Bear. "It's coming."

"Before I forget," said Kersdorf, "have you any idea what those workmen were working on? Did the survivor say? Who recruited them?"

"They were recruited through an intermediary using a cover story—something about an eccentric Iranian general who had fled to Switzerland after Khomeini took over and now was afraid of assassination by a hit team of Revolutionary Guards."

"Good story," said von Beck. "It's happened."

"What exactly were they to do?" asked the Chief.

"Something about a sophisticated personal security system. We don't know much else except that the survivor was a hydraulics mechanic."

"I don't like the sound of this at all," said the Chief.

"Let me move on. The next point concerns blood types. We know the Hangman's blood type from the semen left in the chessboard girl. It would have embarrassed my line of reasoning if Balac hadn't matched. Well, he does."

"How in heaven's name did you find out Balac's blood type without alerting him?" said the Chief. "People tend to notice when you stick needles in them."

The Bear grinned. "I had all kinds of elaborate ideas for this one. In the end I checked with the blood bank. He's a donor."

"He's what?" exclaimed the Chief.

"A blood donor," said the Bear. "Actually Simon Balac is quite a public-spirited citizen. He is a member of a number of worthy organizations, seems to have a particular interest in the preservations of Bern, and he's a supporter of various ecology groups. He is known to be deeply concerned about the environment. He is also an avid walker and a member of the Berner Wanderwege."

"What is the Wanderwege?" asked Fitzduane.

"Hiking association," explained von Beck. "Wandering through the woods, rucksack on back, following little yellow signs. Very healthy."

"Most of the time," said the Bear, "but you may recall Siegfried, our tattooist friend."

"And not found where a body could be dumped from a car," added the Chief. "Go on, Heini. This is getting interesting."

"We have other circumstantial evidence, but you can get that off the printout. None of it is conclusive, but you'll see it all helps corroborate my thinking. I'd now like to turn to the few clues that Ivo left us, then the matter of alibis, and finally the evidence that I believe is conclusive. First of all, Ivo. He was killed before he had a chance to say much, and most of what he brought was destroyed in the gunfight, but we salvaged some intriguing scraps. There was a reference to purple rooms—note the plural. Well, both Erika's place and Lodge's house in Muri had purple rooms with black candles and sexual aids and other items that point to ritual and dabbling in black magic. In both cases we found traces of blood and semen of a number of different blood groups. They would fit the bill, but there is an additional line: 'A smell of snow—a rush of wet—a thrusting river— there it's set.' "

"Did he always write that way?" asked Henssen.

"All the time I dealt with him," said the Bear. "He liked rhymes and puzzles. I think they gave him a certain self-respect. He didn't feel he was informing when he gave us a tip in the form of a poem."

"How do you read this one?" asked the Chief.

"I'm biased," said the Bear. "I think it's another reference to the river and the location of Balac's studio, which supports what we've learned from our deceased Italian friend."

"But that's an opinion, not proof," said von Beck.

The Bear shrugged. "I'm not going to argue that point. It might be clearer if we had all of Ivo's book, but we don't. Of more interest is what it was wrapped in."

"I'm not sure I follow you," said Kersdorf.

"Ivo went to meet Hugo to see if he could enlist his support to find Klaus Minder's killer. He brought a package that outlined in his inimitable manner what he had learned to date. The package was wrapped in a piece of cloth. Clear so far?"

Kersdorf nodded his head. The rest of the team looked at the Bear expectantly. "The cloth turned out to be canvas, not the kind you camp under in the summer or sit on watching the talent in the Marzili, but the kind you use for painting. The piece that Ivo was using had already been sized and bore faint traces of paint. I'd guess it had been made up, but the stretching wasn't right, so it had been torn up and discarded."

"I thought painters bought their canvases already made up," said the Chief.

"Many do," said the Bear, "but that's more expensive. Perhaps more to the point, if you are a professional, you have more flexibility if you make up your own. You can produce in nonstandard sizes; you can use a nonstandard canvas base.

"Now *canvas* is a catchall term for a range of different materials used to paint on. The commonest are made of cotton; the more expensive grades are made from flax—linen, in other words. Most painting canvas arrives already coated and sized. In this case we are dealing with an expensive flax-based canvas bought raw and sized by the artist. Only one artist in Bern operates this particular way, and forensics has already compared the mix of size or base coating material he uses. They tally. There is no doubt about it. The piece of canvas used by Ivo as wrapping material was prepared by Balac."

There was silence in the room, then the Chief spoke. "You're making me a believer, Heini. But we still don't have a case that would stand up in court. You've already said the canvas looks like a discard, so a defense lawyer would say it could have been picked up almost anywhere. It doesn't even create a direct link between Balac and Ivo, merely the possibility of one."

"Chief," said the Bear, "I don't think we're going to have all the evidence we need before we pick Balac up. It would be nice, but the bastard is too careful for that. My modest ambition tops out at a prima facie case followed by a search of his house and some nice detailed investigation by a persistent examining magistrate."

"Which unfortunately won't be me," said von Beck. "A little matter of conflict of interest." There was an undercurrent of embarrassment in the room. All the members of the team knew something of what had transpired with Paulus von Beck, but few knew the details.

The Chief broke the silence. "It's not your fault, Charlie, and it doesn't mean you can't go on working on the investigation. Anyway, let's leave that until we've heard Heini out. I've only heard an outline of what he and Hugo found."

The Bear looked at Charlie von Beck. "Do you want to stay for this?" he said to the magistrate. "It's not too pretty."

Von Beck nodded. "I'd prefer to hear it straight."

The Bear put his hand on Charlie's shoulder for a moment. "Don't take it personally," he said. He continued after a short pause. "I'd like to say that our discovery of Paulus von Beck's involvement—marginal involvement, I may add—was the result of painstaking detective work and many long hours of investigation. Well, it wasn't. It was a pure fluke. If Paulus hadn't opened his mouth, we'd still be none the wiser.

"I originally approached Paulus because I wanted an art expert to give me an opinion on the tattoo design—the 'A' in a circle of flowers—that we've found on so many involved with the Hangman. The design is intricate and different from the usual style used in tattoos, and it seemed to me that there might be some advantage to checking it out further. The first thing I did was to get hold of some samples of the tattooist's work to see if the design might have originated with him."

"I thought Siegfried's place in Zurich had been completely destroyed," said the Chief.

"Yes, well, it had been in official report-type language, but I've been around long enough to know that there are few absolutes in this world. There is almost always something left. In this case the Zurich cops were thinking in terms of records and valuables when they filed their report. A pile of half-burned tattoo designs wasn't high on their agenda. I assembled all the samples of the tattoo together and had blowups made of its various features. I took those, samples of Siegfried's work, and a collection of photographs of Balac's work to Paulus and asked him to tell me if he thought either of the two had originated the design."

"Where did you get the photos of Balac's pictures?" asked the Chief.

"Mostly from *Der Bund*," said the Bear. "As I mentioned, it's written about him on many occasions, and there was a lot more stuff in the file than what it published. There was an added bonus of some color slides one photographer had taken in addition to the black-and-white stuff, apparently with the idea of selling them to a magazine. *Der Bund*, as you may know, doesn't run color. As it happens, I needn't have bothered. Paulus knows Balac's work intimately. He was extremely shaken by what he discovered, and that led to his" —

he paused, not wishing to use the word *confession* with all its unpleasant connotations— "desire to put us fully in the picture."

"My God," said the Chief, "do I understand you correctly? Did Paulus actually identify the tattoo found on the terrorists as having been originally designed, drawn, by Balac?"

The Bear smiled. "Indeed he did," he said. He glanced at Henssen. "There are some things even the most advanced computers miss."

Henssen grinned. "Pattern recognition. Give us another five to ten years, and you'll eat those words."

"We've got the fucker," said the Chief excitedly. "Heini, you're a genius."

"I'm not finished." The Bear removed a small piece of cardboard from a file and passed it across to the Chief. "Balac's visiting card," he said. "Take a look at the logo. He uses it on his notepaper and catalogs, too."

The Chief looked at the card and then at a blowup of the logo that had been mounted beside an enlargement of the tattoo. The resemblance was striking, the circle of flowers almost identical in conception and execution, the only difference being the letter in the center of the circle. On the tattoo it was an "A." On Balac's card, it was a "B."

"The murdering, arrogant bastard," said the Chief. "He's rubbing our noses in it."

"He's a *clever* murdering, arrogant bastard. That logo has been distributed thousands of times on brochures, catalogs, headed notepaper, and who knows what else. It has even appeared on posters. It's so much in the public domain that it proves nothing. Anyone could have copied it. Further, in Paulus's professional opinion, the letters 'A' and 'B' have been designed by different people. Balac didn't design the 'A.'"

The Chief looked depressed. "This guy doesn't miss a trick."

"Like Icarus," said the Bear, "he likes to fly close to the sun. Sooner or later, no matter how smart he is, that's going to be fatal. Thanks to Paulus, I think it's going to be sooner."

Chapter Twenty-two

Fitzduane played the tape that he'd made of the first half of their interview with Paulus. He plugged the miniature tape recorder into a battery-powered extension loudspeaker. Immediately the sound was crisp and clear, and the listeners were transported to that small office in the museum and the strained voice of Paulus von Beck. Fitzduane stopped the tape at the point previously agreed on with the Bear. There was silence in the room.

"For the first time," said the Bear, "we've actually got a live witness who can tie Balac in with some of the key elements of the case. It's no longer supposition. We now know that Balac was involved with Erika von Graffenlaub on an intense and regular basis. We know that he was the original seducer of Rudi and Vreni. We know that he made use of drugs in a manner similar to the Hangman. It's all getting closer."

"There's a difference between running orgies, even if they do involve underage kids, and killing people," said Charlie von Beck. "God knows I'd like to believe we've got a case. If you put everything together, I guess we have, but it's far from a sure thing. There could be an innocent explanation for almost everything we've got so far. You've put forward one hell of a clever hypothesis, I'll grant you, but that final firm link is still missing."

The Bear looked around the room. It was clear that most of the team agreed with the magistrate. The Chief looked indecisive. The Bear was glad he'd taken the time to build his argument point by point. Once the discussion stage was over, they would be back in harm's way. They had to avoid another Muri. They needed a united team convinced of what it was doing if they were to come up with an angle that would result in success.

"Both Hugo and I," continued the Bear, "felt that Paulus's reaction indicated rather more than that he was gay and had played around with group sex, even if some borderline minors were involved. This is a tolerant town if you're discreet, and whereas the Rudi/Vreni thing isn't the stuff fairy tales are made of, they weren't exactly prepubescent children—that would have been serious. No, Paulus was actually afraid, afraid for his life. Why? What does he know or surmise that brings him close to panic?

"Most of you here know what an interrogation is like. A good interrogator often learns more from atmosphere and body language than he does from the actual words used. After a while he gets so immersed in the mood of the whole thing that he begins to sense meanings, almost to be telepathic.

"Any successful investigation requires luck as well as man-hours. So far the tide of fortune seems again and again to have favored the Hangman. Whether by accident or design or a mixture of both, he seems to have been just ahead of us most of the time. He had Ivo killed before we could talk to him. Siegfried, the tattoo artist, went the same way. Vreni was saved, but she can't or won't talk about her experiences. Erika von Graffenlaub, who might have cracked under interrogation, is dead. Lodge either wasn't there or escaped before we arrived. And so it goes on. We're dealing with a shrewd and lucky man. But no one is lucky all the time. Very early into the questioning of Paulus, both Hugo and I had the feeling that here was the essential link we were looking for. You can decide for yourselves."

Fitzduane moved the tape recorder selector switch to "play."

"This is an edited version," began the Bear.

"Play it," said the Chief.

There was a slight hiss, and the Bear's recorded voice could be heard. "Paulus," he said, "you've stated that your relationship with Balac started about five years ago."

"Yes."

"Is it still going on?"

"Not . . . not exactly," said Paulus hesitantly.

"I don't quite understand," said the Bear, his voice gentle.

"It's not so easy to explain. The relationship, as it were, changed; it came to an end. But from time to time he calls me, and I go to him."

"Why, if it's over?"

"I . . . I have to. He has . . . he has a hold on me."

"An emotional hold?"

"No, it's not like that. He has photographs and other things he has threatened to send to the police."

"We don't care about your sex life," said the Bear. "What kind of photographs are these?"

There was silence again and then the sound of sobbing, followed by an editing break. The conversation started again in mid-sentence.

". . . embarrassing, terribly embarrassing to talk about," said Paulus in a strangled voice.

"So the von Graffenlaub twins weren't the only underage kids involved," said the Bear.

"No."

"How old were they?"

"It varied. Normally they were in their mid-teens or older—and that was all right."

"But not always?"

"No."

"What age was the youngest?"

There was silence yet again, and then an encouraging noise from the Bear could be heard. Reluctantly Paulus answered. "About twelve or thereabouts. I don't know exactly."

There was a crash as Charlie von Beck threw his coffee mug to the ground. His face was white with anger. Fitzduane stopped the tape. "The idiot, the stupid, irresponsible, disgusting idiot!" shouted the examining magistrate. "How could he?"

"Calm down, Charlie," said the Chief. "You nearly gave me a heart attack. I hope that mug was empty."

Charlie von Beck smiled in spite of himself. The Chief waited until he was sure von Beck was in control, then gave Fitzduane the signal to proceed.

"Where did these sexual encounters take place?" said the Bear's voice.

"Oh, various places."

"For instance? In your house, for example?"

"No, never in my house. Balac always likes things done his way. He likes a certain setting, and he likes to have the things he needs, his drugs and other things."

"So where did you go?"

"I didn't always know. Sometimes he would pick me up and blindfold me. He likes to play games. Sometimes he would pretend I was a stranger and we were meeting for the first time."

"Did you ever go to Erika's apartment?"

"Yes, but not so often. Mostly we went to Balac's studio down by the Wasserwerk."

"You mentioned that Balac likes a certain setting," said the Bear. "Could you describe it? Why was it important?"

"He likes rituals, different kinds of rituals," said Paulus, his voice uncertain and strained.

"What kinds of rituals?"

"Like . . . like a black mass, only not the real thing. More like a parody of a black mass but with black candles and mock human sacrifices. It was frightening."

Fitzduane broke in. "Could you describe the rooms where this happened?"

"There were several such rooms. They were all decorated the same way, with purple walls and black silk hangings and the smell of incense. Sometimes we were masked; sometimes the other people were masked."

"Tell me about the sacrifices," said the Bear. "You said mock human sacrifices?"

"The idea was that the victim should die at the moment of climax. It was something that Erika, in particular, liked. She had a knife, a thing with a wide, heavy blade, and she used to wave it. Then she brought a cat in and killed it at just that moment, and I was covered in blood." There was the sound of retching, cut off abruptly by an editing break.

The Chief signaled for Fitzduane to stop the tape. He looked shaken, the full implications of what he had been hearing beginning to sink in. "And next came people," he spat. "It's making me sick. Is there much more of this?"

"Not a lot," said the Bear. "I'll summarize it for you if you like."

The Chief steepled his hands, lost in thought. After perhaps a full minute he looked up at the Bear. "It's just hitting home. It's so incredibly sick . . . so perverted . . . so evil."

"We asked about the knife," said the Bear. "Balac told Paulus that he'd had it specially made. It was a reproduction of a ritual sacrificial knife used by a pagan cult in Ireland. He'd seen a drawing in some book and taken a fancy to it. Apparently he has a library of pornography and black magic and the sicker aspects of human behavior. He uses these books to set up his games. The more elaborate rules are written down in what he calls 'The Grimoire.' "

"A grimoire is a kind of magician's rule book, isn't it?" Kersdorf broke in. "I seem to remember running across a case involving a grimoire many years ago. Again the whole black magic thing was essentially sexually motivated."

"Who else was involved apart from Balac, Erika, and these kids?" asked the Chief. "Did he recognize anyone, or was he the only adult supporting player?"

"There were others," said the Bear, "but they were always masked. He said he thought he recognized some of the voices." The Bear gave a list of names to the Chief, who shook his head. He wasn't altogether surprised at the ambassador mentioned, but the other names were from the very core of the Bernese establishment.

"There were also some young male prostitutes involved from time to time," said the Bear. "He gave me several names, first names. One of them was Klaus. The description fits; it was Minder. Another was the Monkey. Knowing he was involved in the same games as Minder, Ivo went after the Monkey and, I guess, went too far trying to make him talk. Ivo, the poor little bastard, was trying to find Klaus Minder's killer. Sir Ivo, indeed. He found out too much, and his quest got him killed."

"Heini," said the Chief, "I really don't think I want to hear any more. The question is, how do we pick up this psycho without losing more people?"

"We've got some ideas on that score," said Fitzduane. "We thought we might take a tip from the ancient Greeks."

THEY WERE on a secluded testing range that was part of the military base at Sand. The man in combat fatigues had the deep tan of someone who spends a great deal of time in the mountains. Paler skin around the eyes indicated long periods wearing ski goggles. He was a major, a member of the Swiss Army's elite grenadiers, and a counterterrorist expert. He normally advised the Federal Police antiterrorist unit but wasn't against practicing his craft at the cantonal or indeed city level. His specialty was explosives.

"You haven't thought of blasting in, I suppose?" he said diffidently. "There would be fewer constraints in relation to the charges used, and I'm told it's quite a common technique when you want to gain access. Armies have been doing it for years when they don't feel like going through the door." He grinned cheerfully.

"Very funny," said the Bear. "If we blast in, we won't do anyone standing near the entry hole much good."

"And since one of those people is likely to be me," said Fitzduane, "I don't think a hell of a lot of your suggestion—though I'm sure it's kindly meant."

The major looked shocked. "My dear fellow, we wouldn't harm a hair of your head. We can calculate the charges required exactly. Just one little boom, and lo, an instant doorway."

"I once knew an explosives freak in the U.S. Special Forces," said Fitzduane. "He was known as No-Prob Dudzcinski because every time he was asked to do something involving explosives, no matter how complex, he would reply, 'No problem, man,' and set to work. He was very good at his job."

"Well, there you are," said the major.

"He blew himself up," said Fitzduane, "and half an A-team. I've been suspicious of explosives ever since. I don't suppose you want to hear his last words?"

"No," said the major.

"Besides," said the Bear, "our target is partial to burying Claymores and similar devices in the walls, which could be set off by an external explosion. We want a shaped charge that will blast out and at the same time muffle any concealed device."

A truck ground its way in low gear toward them. Well secured in the back was what looked like a rectangular packing case the size of a large doorway, but only about fifteen centimeters thick. The truck drew up near them and stopped. Three soldiers jumped out, unlashed the packing case, and maneuvered it against a sheet of 1.5-centimeter armor plate bolted to the brick wall of an old practice fortification.

"It's quite safe to stand in front of the packing case," said the major, "but the normal practice is to follow routine safety regulations." Fitzduane and the Bear needed little encouragment. They moved to the shelter of an observation bunker set at right angles to the packing case. They were joined by the three soldiers. The major brought up the rear, walking nonchalantly, as befitted his faith in his expertise. All in the bunker put on steel helmets. Fitzduane felt slightly foolish.

The major had a pen-shaped miniature radio transmitter in his hand. "You're familiar with the principle of a shaped charge, or focused charge, as some people call it?" he asked.

Fitzduane and the Bear nodded. The shaped charge concept was based on the discovery that the force of an explosion could be tightly focused in one direction by putting the explosive in a container of an appropriate shape and leaving a hollow for the explosion to expand into. The explosive force would initially follow the line of least resistance, and thereafter momentum would take over. The principle had been further refined to the point where explosives could be used in a strip form to cut out specific shapes.

"I'd be happier if we were cutting through one material," said the major. "Armor plate alone is no problem, but when materials are combined, funny things happen. In this case the charges are on the rear of the packing case. In the center we have Kevlar bulletproof material reinforced with ceramic plates; we can't use armor plate because it would make the whole thing too heavy. At the front we have left space for a painting, as you requested. To view the painting, you don't have to open the entire crate, which could be embarrassing. Instead we've installed hinged viewing doors."

"As a matter of interest," said Fitzduane, "will the painting be damaged by the explosion? We're going to have to put something fairly valuable in there if we are to get our target's attention, and knowing the way you Swiss operate, I'm likely to end up getting the bill if the painting is harmed."

The major sighed. "Herr Fitzduane, I assume this is your idea of a little joke, but whether it is or not, you may rest assured that your painting will be unscathed. The entire force of the explosion will be focused against the wall. The canvas won't even ripple. Watch!"

He pressed the button on the transmitter. There was a muted crack. A door-shaped portion of the steel plate and wall fell away as if sliced out of paper with a razor blade. There was no smoke. Dust rose from the rubble and was dissipated by the wind.

Fitzduane walked across to the front of the packing case and opened the viewing doors. In place of the painting there was a large poster extolling the virtues of Swissair. It was unscathed. He turned to the major, who was standing smugly, arms folded across his chest.

"You'd have been a wow in Troy." He looked at the packing case again. "I think we can improve our act. How familiar are you with stun grenades?"

"SIMON," SAID Fitzduane into the phone, "are you doing your lunchtime salon tomorrow?"

Balac laughed. "As usual. You're most welcome to drop in."

"I just want to say good-bye. I'm leaving Bern. I've done all I can, and it's time to go home."

Balac chuckled. "You've certainly seen a different side of Bern from most visitors. We'll miss you. See you tomorrow."

"*Ciao*," said Fitzduane. He put down the phone and looked across at the Bear. "Now it's up to Paulus von Beck. Will it be Plan A or Plan B?"

They left Kirchenfeldstrasse and drove to police headquarters, where they put in two hours' combat shooting on the pistol range. The Bear was a good instructor, and Fitzduane felt his old skills coming back. For the last twenty minutes of the session they used Glaser ammunition. "Your shotgun rounds are based on these," said the Bear. "In case you think nine-millimeter rounds are inadequate, as they normally are, reflect on the fact that hits with a Glaser are ninety percent fatal."

Fitzduane held up a Glaser round. "Do the good guys have a monopoly on these things?"

"Their sale is restricted," said the Bear.

Fitzduane raised an eyebrow.

"No," said the Bear.

THE CHIEF KRIPO WAS talking on a secure line to Kilmara in Ireland.

Kilmara sounded concerned. "Is there no other way? Hugo isn't twenty-two anymore. One's reflexes slow up with age."

"It's Fitzduane's idea," said the Chief. "You know what's happened when we've gone in the conventional way. We've taken casualties. Hugo believes half the battle is getting in. Then, if Balac is present, his own safety will prevent him using his gadgetry. It becomes a conventional arrest—*mano a mano*."

"Supposing Balac isn't alone?"

"Fitzduane won't move until he's blown the shaped charge," said the Chief. "We've added stun grenades to the mix. That should buy Fitzduane the time he needs and will enable us to get help to him fast. We're using our best people for this."

"I'd prefer it if you could get Balac away from his own territory," said Kilmara. "God knows what he's got in that warehouse."

"We're going to try. Paulus's picture is the bait. If Balac swallows it, then Fitzduane won't even have to be involved in the arrest. If he won't come across, then it's on to Plan B. Do you think Fitzduane can't hack it?"

Kilmara sighed. "He's a big boy, but I don't like it. I feel responsible."

"Look at it this way. What choice do we have? He'll smell a policeman no matter who we use. Fitzduane at least can get in without provoking a violent reaction. Then we just have to hope."

"What about this guy Paulus?" asked Kilmara. "He's been intimately involved with Balac. How do we know he won't blow the whistle? If he does, Hugo's dead."

"Charlie von Beck swears he can be trusted. Both the Bear and Fitzduane think he's telling the truth. And I have him accompanied by my people and his phone fitted with a tap and interrupt in case our team's judgment is off."

"There are many ways of delivering a message other than by phone," said Kilmara.

"It'll be over by this time tomorrow."

"Make sure you watch out for Balac's legal rights."

"Fuck his legal rights," said the Chief.

After hanging up, Kilmara turned around to the man sitting in the armchair in front of his desk. "You got the gist of that."

The man from the Mossad nodded.

"So how does it feel to be back in Ireland?" asked Kilmara.

The man from the Mossad smiled. "Nothing important ever changes."

"Let's talk about the U.S. Embassy. And other things," said Kilmara. "Fancy a drink?" He pulled a bottle of Irish whiskey and two glasses out of his desk drawer. It was late and dark, and the bottle was empty by the time they finished talking.

THE BOY HAD his back to him. He had thrown back the duvet as he slept, and he was naked from the waist up. Paulus couldn't remember how he had come to be there. He stroked the boy's back, trying to remember what he looked like. His hair was a golden color. There was no more than a light fuzz on his cheeks. He couldn't be more than fourteen or fifteen. Paulus felt himself hardening. He moved toward the boy and slid his hand around to the dormant penis. Skillfully he stroked. He felt the organ grow in his hand. He moved closer, feeling the boy's soft buttocks against his loins.

The boy pressed against him. He had a sudden desire to see his face. He stroked the boy's penis with one hand and with the other turned the boy's face toward him. The boy turned his head of his own volition, and now he was bigger and older and somehow he towered over Paulus and in his hand was a short, broad-bladed knife. The knife descended toward his throat and hovered there, and Paulus opened his mouth to scream, but it was too late. The pain was terrible. Blood—his blood—fountained in front of his eyes.

He felt his arm being shaken. He was afraid to look. His body stank of sweat. He could hear himself panting.

"You were screaming," said the voice. Paulus opened his eyes. The duty detective stood there. He was wearing an automatic pistol in a shoulder holster, and he had a Heckler & Koch MP-5 submachine gun in his right hand. The bedroom door was open behind him, and Paulus could see the outline of another detective.

"I'm sorry," he said. "Just a bad dream."

More than that, thought the detective. His face was impassive. "Can I get you anything?" he asked.

I can't do it, thought Paulus. He looked at the detective. "Thank you, but no."

The detective turned to leave. "What time is it?" said Paulus.

The detective looked at his watch. He'd have to log the incident. "A quarter to four," he answered before closing the door.

Paulus lay sleepless, thinking of the price of betrayal.

BALAC DRANK his orange juice and listened to the tape of his conversation with Fitzduane. The voice stress analyzer revealed nothing significant. It needed more material to work with and more relevant subject matter to come into its own. It had proved useful in the past. Supposedly a new and more sensitive model was in the works. Balac doubted it would ever replace his intuition.

Was he suspect? He rather thought not. Fitzduane had called in a number of times before, and they got on well. It would have been more suspicious if he had not dropped in to say good-bye. It was his last day in Bern. His—Balac's—last day, and now, it appeared, also the Irishman's. Such symbolism. With so much at stake it would make sense to go now, to forget this charade.

And yet seeing things right through to the end had the most enormous appeal. A climber didn't abandon his assault on the peak because the weather looked a trifle uncertain. He persevered. It was the very risk that made the reward so . . . so stimulating. I'm gambling with my life, thought Balac, and a ripple of pleasure went through him.

Later in his Jacuzzi he thought again about this, his last day in Bern, and he decided a margin of extra insurance might be in order. Gambling was all very well, but only a fool didn't lay off his bets. He made the call. They said they would leave immediately and should arrive well in advance of lunch.

FITZDUANE ROSE early, and the Bear drove him into Waisenhausplatz. He spent ninety minutes practicing unarmed combat with a remarkably humorless police instructor. Toward the end of the session, bruised and sore, Fitzduane dredged up a few moves from his time with the airbornes. They carried the instructor out on a stretcher.

The Bear looked a little shaken. "That's a side of you I haven't seen before."

Fitzduane had calmed down. "I'm not proud of it; only rarely is it a good way to fight." He smiled grimly. "Mostly you fight with your brain."

They spent a further hour on the pistol range, firing only Glaser rounds and concentrating on close-quarters reaction shooting. Fitzduane shot well. His clothes reeked of burned cartridge propellant. After he showered and changed, the smell had gone.

THE EXAMINING MAGISTRATE looked down at his cousin. Paulus was white-faced with fear and lack of sleep. A faint, sweet aroma of vomit and after-shave emanated from him, but his tailoring was as immaculate as ever. Without doubt Paulus was the weakest link in the plan. Fortunately his appearance and nervousness could be attributed to another cause: his apparent attempt to deceive both the owner and the museum over a painting. It was a good story, but whether it was good enough—well, time would tell.

Looking at Paulus with new eyes since he had heard his confession, Charlie von Beck wondered whether their contrived art fraud wasn't a rerun of the truth. Paulus had always seemed to live better than either his salary or private resources would seem to justify. But perhaps he was jumping to conclusions. He would have trusted Paulus with his life until the tape. Why should he change his mind so drastically because his cousin's sex life had gotten out of hand? He was family after all.

The radio crackled as the various units reported in. Charlie von Beck looked at his watch. Not yet quite time to make the call.

Paulus dropped his head into his hands and sobbed. He raised his tear-stained face to his cousin. "I . . . I can't do it. I'm afraid of him. You don't know how strong, how powerful, he is. He senses things. He'll know there is something wrong." Paulus's voice rose to a shriek. "You don't understand—he'll kill me!"

The Chief Kripo pushed two pills and a glass of water across to Paulus. "Valium," he said, "a strong dose. Take it."

Obediently Paulus swallowed the Valium. The Chief waited several minutes and then spoke soothingly. "Relax. Breathe in deeply a few times. Close your eyes and let your mind rest. There is nothing really to worry about. In a few hours it will all be over."

Like a docile child, Paulus did as he was told. He lay back in his swivel chair listening to the Chief chatting on inconsequentially. The sound was pleasant and reassuring. He couldn't quite make out the words, but it didn't seem to matter. He dozed. Twenty minutes later he woke refreshed. The first person he saw was the Chief, who beamed at him. He was drinking tea. There were spare cups on the table, and Charlie had a teapot in his hand. "Milk or lemon?" said the Chief.

Paulus drank his tea holding the cup with both hands. He felt calm. He knew what to do.

"Let's do a final run-through." The Chief smiled. "Practice makes perfect."

Paulus gave a half-smile back. "You needn't worry. I'm all right now."

"Let's run through it anyway."

Paulus nodded. "I'm going to call Balac and tell him that I have a picture in for evaluation on which I would like a second opinion and that I would appreciate it if he could take a look at it right away. I will tell him it's very important, and I shall imply that I have the opportunity to purchase it for much less than its real value. I shall suggest that I am bypassing the museum and dealing for myself. I shall tell him I don't want to move on this until I have my own judgment confirmed because the risks are too great. I shall tell him he can come in with me if he confirms the painting's value."

"Balac won't find anything unusual in this," said the Chief. "You've asked for his opinion before, haven't you?"

"Many times. He is a brilliant judge of technique. But this will be the first time I have suggested dealing on the side, though he has dropped hints—always as if joking."

"I think he'll swallow it," said Charlie von Beck. "We need some believable explanation for the critical time element. I think he'll be amused. He seems to enjoy corrupting people."

"I shall stress the urgency and will ask that he come around to the museum today since I daren't keep it here longer in case someone else sees it."

"Who is the owner supposed to be?" asked the Chief.

"The owner is a diplomat who has gotten a girl into trouble and needs some quick cash to hush the whole thing up. He thinks his painting is worth useful, but not big, money."

"What is the painting supposed to be?" asked Charlie von Beck.

"I'm not going to say over the phone. I want to whet Balac's appetite. He will be intrigued; he likes games."

"Don't we know it," said Charlie, looking at his watch again.

"It's a Picasso collage," said Paulus. "The question is, is it a genuine Picasso or from the school of?"

"Well, is it?" said Charlie.

"Yes."

"What's it worth?" asked the Chief.

"About half a million dollars. It's not mainstream Picasso, and not everybody likes collages."

"Half a million dollars!" exclaimed the Chief. "I hope there's no shooting or the Swiss franc gets stronger. Where did you get it?"

"I'd prefer not to say."

"And you're sure Balac has never seen it?" said Charlie.

"It's been in a vault for the past twenty years. There was a small matter of avoiding British inheritance taxes."

"Ah," said the Chief, who liked clear-cut motives. "So much

money. I used to make collages myself as a child. I've still got some, too."

"Pity your name's not Picasso," said Charlie von Beck. His watch started to beep.

"You're on," said the Chief to Paulus. Paulus lifted the phone.

THE MAN ON the third floor of the warehouse that overlooked the entrance to Balac's studio spoke into his radio. His partner emerged from the freight elevator as he completed his call. He was still tucking his shirt into his pants. "Anything?"

The man with the high-power binoculars nodded. "A Merc with Zurich license plates dropped off three men and drove away. One of them said something into the door loudspeaker, and Balac let them in. They were all carrying sports bags. I've got it on video." He pointed at the prefocused video camera mounted on a heavy-duty tripod.

"Odd," said the arrival. "I thought they told us that Balac had some special painting regimen whereby he locks himself away all day except during lunchtime."

"They did," said the watcher. His companion completed rewinding the tape. He pressed "play" and stared intently at the video images. There were impressions, but the faces could not be clearly seen. Then the last man turned and looked around before the steel door closed behind him. The arrival grunted. "What do you think?"

"Same as you," said the watcher. "The last man is Angelo Lestoni, which makes the other two his brother Pietro and his cousin—"

"Julius," said the other man. "You radioed it in?"

"Affirmative."

The other man replaced his bulletproof vest and started checking his tripod-mounted sniper rifle. It was a self-loading model from Heckler & Koch, designed for both high accuracy and rapid follow-on fire. It occurred to him that it cost about as much as a secondhand Porsche. He stroked the handmade stock and dull steel of the weapon and reflected that, on balance, he would prefer the rifle.

THE BEAR AND FITZDUANE were in the tiered conference room of the police headquarters on Waisenhausplatz. The news had just come in. Balac was too busy to leave his studio, but he'd be delighted to look at Paulus's picture if he would bring it around during lunch. They could talk when the rest of the guests had gone.

The Hangman wouldn't leave his lair. It was going to have to be Plan B. Fitzduane wasn't surprised.

The Bear was going through the details of the operation yet again with the ten-man assault team. Blueprints of Balac's studio obtained from the city planning office were pinned up on a large bulletin board. The key phases of the plan were carefully hand-lettered on a flip chart, and the Bear, pointer in hand, was talking.

"Most of you were on the Muri operation. You know what can happen if we try to blast our way in. We are likely to take casualties, and there is no guarantee we'll end up with the Hangman. In fact, the track record suggests that we won't.

"The intention here is to get a man in to immobilize the Hangman before he can activate any of his defenses. That man is Hugo Fitzduane, whom you see beside me. Take another good look at him. I don't want him shot by mistake."

He looked at Fitzduane, who smiled and said, "Neither do I." There was laughter.

"We've got the plans of Balac's warehouse, but if precedent is anything to go by, the inside of the building will have been extensively modified. God knows what surprises he's built in. It's vital, therefore, that he be neutralized before he leaves the main studio area; that's the large room on the ground floor immediately off the entrance, where he has a combined studio and reception area. Fortunately, since he runs this lunchtime open house between midday and two, we do know the geography of that room." He pointed at the scale drawing behind him.

"Balac's routine is to remain incommunicado—except by phone, and often that's connected to an answering machine—until noon. He then entertains friends who call in on a casual basis until 1400 hours, when he locks himself away again. It's a credible routine for a painter and damn handy for a terrorist.

"Herr Fitzduane, who's been to several of these buffet lunches, says that people normally don't turn up until about 1220. It's our intention, therefore, to have the whole thing wrapped up before then. We don't want any innocent burghers caught in the crossfire.

"Let's go through the sequence. One—just after 1200 hours Paulus von Beck will arrive in a delivery van with the picture in a packing case. He'll have two deliverymen with him. If we're in luck, they'll be allowed into the studio with the picture, and they'll grab Balac there and then. However, most likely—this is Balac's normal routine—they'll be asked to leave the packing case inside the first door. You will recall that he has an extensive security system that involves a three-door entrance hall. Only one door is opened at one time. It's a kind of double air lock, a classic installation in secure buildings and a bitch to overcome since all three doors are of armored steel. It was because of the entrance problem that we came up with this Trojan Horse idea.

"Two—a couple of minutes after Paulus's arrival Fitzduane will turn up. If the deliverymen aren't allowed in, as we expect, he will offer to give Paulus a hand, and together they will move the packing case into the studio and lean it against the wall. According to Paulus, there is one particular spot that Balac normally uses to hang pictures he's assessing—something to do with the right lighting—and that's marked on the diagram here.

"Three—we are now into the area of discretion, but the basic plan is for Fitzduane to neutralize Balac and blow the shaped charge. Then we come storming in as rehearsed and instantly remove Balac into custody. Any questions?"

The second-in-command of the assault unit, an intelligent-looking police lieutenant in his late twenties, spoke. "Will Paulus von Beck be armed?"

"No," said the Bear. "He has been associated with Balac in the past. We aren't suggesting serious criminal involvement, but we don't want to run any risks."

"Supposing people arrive before Herr Fitzduane can make his move?" asked the lieutenant.

The Bear grimaced. "Herr Fitzduane is going to have to use his discretion. He'll have to pick his time. It's not a perfect plan, merely the least objectionable."

The questions continued, double- and triple-checking aspects of the plan. The fact that the assault team members were intelligent and well trained gave Fitzduane some degree of comfort, but he still had to face the stark reality that they would be outside the building when he made his move, and for a vital few seconds—the calculation was somewhere between twenty and thirty—he'd be on his own with Paulus, unarmed and unproven, and a multiple killer. It didn't promise to be a fun lunch.

The question and answer session had finished. The assault unit filed past Fitzduane, the commander of the unit bringing up the rear. He held out his hand. "Herr Fitzduane, my men—and I—we wish you well."

"A drink together when it's over," said the Bear. "I'll buy."

Fitzduane smiled. "It'll cost you."

The unit commander gave a small salute and left the room.

ANXIOUSLY PAULUS VON BECK supervised the loading of the packing case containing the Picasso collage. He was less concerned about the safety of the painting itself—although that was a factor—than he was about Balac's noticing something unusual about the moving men. The overalled policemen weren't used to the finer touches involved in handling a painting worth about as much as the average policeman would earn in a lifetime. The exercise was repeated several times until they looked like trained moving men—at least to a superficial glance.

He was thinking that every job has its own visual style in addition to expertise. You'd imagine anybody in the right overalls could look like a deliveryman, but it just wasn't so. A man who carries things for a living soon works out certain ways of lifting and carrying that make even difficult jobs seem easy.

To his critical eye, the policemen didn't look quite right. They were using too much muscle and not enough brains to lift the heavy case. Well, what else would you expect from policemen? he said to himself. He walked back to his office briskly. There was barely enough time for him to get ready. My God, in a matter of a few minutes he might be dead or horribly wounded.

He could feel his heart pound, and sweat broke out on his forehead. He looked at the Valium sitting on a saucer beside a glass of water. The Chief Kripo had left it, and it was sorely tempting. He picked up the pill and held it between his thumb and forefinger. So that's how you get addicted, he thought. Physiological dependency. Was that what they would call his sexual needs? Was that at the root of his relationship with Balac?

Angrily he flung the Valium away from him. What was done was done. Now he must keep his brain as clear as possible and do what was necessary. He unlocked his briefcase and removed a compact .45-caliber Detonics automatic pistol. The weapon was closely modeled on the U.S. Army Colt .45 and fired the same effective man-stopping ammunition, but it was smaller and lighter and had been specifically designed for concealment.

He slid a round into the chamber and placed it, cocked and locked, in the small of his back, where it was held in place by a spring-clip skeleton holster. He knew from past experience that the flat weapon wouldn't show. He had carried it many times when transporting valuable works of art—art collectors liked their security to be there but discreet—and he knew how to use it. This was Switzerland. Paulus von Beck, art expert and sculptor, was also a captain in the Swiss Army and was being groomed for the general staff.

Charlie von Beck came into the room and closed the door behind him. He leaned back against it. He was remembering a time when he and Paulus had been as close as brothers. "You know, Paulus," he said, "I've been thinking some rather unkind thoughts about you recently."

Paulus smiled slightly. "I've been thinking some rather unkind thoughts about myself."

"You love somebody—you trust somebody—and then you find he's flawed in some way that offends you," said Charlie von Beck. "Suddenly you feel betrayed, and you start asking questions. The loved one becomes someone you hate—you want to hurt—to compensate for the hurt you feel."

"It's a natural reaction," said Paulus. He prepared to leave the room. Charlie still leaned against the door as if unsure what to do. "I've got to go," Paulus said. "Relax, I don't need a speech. I know what has to be done."

"You fucking idiot," said Charlie. He embraced Paulus in a bear hug and then stood back as if embarrassed. "I guess blood is thicker than—"

"An errant penis," said Paulus with a rueful smile. "Don't worry. I won't let the von Becks down."

"I know that." Charlie stepped back from the door. Through the window he watched Paulus get into his car and drive away, the delivery van containing the two policemen and the Picasso in its packing case following close behind.

He wondered if he should have done anything about Paulus's carrying a gun. The Chief's view was that Paulus should not be armed, and Fitzduane wasn't expecting him to be. And supposing he was wrong about Paulus?

He hoped Balac wasn't in the habit of embracing his guests. The gun didn't show, but in a bear hug it could certainly be felt. He looked at his watch yet again. Whatever the outcome, it should be over within the hour. He left the museum and headed toward Waisenhausplatz.

"HOW MUCH time have we got?" The Chief Kripo's nostrils flared in anger, and his whole body radiated rage, but his voice was controlled—barely. He held a message slip in his hand.

"Five or six minutes," said the Bear. "Charlie has called in. Paulus has already left. In fact, he should be almost there by now."

The Chief thrust the message at the Bear. "The Lestonis are here."

The Bear looked up in shock. "But this message came in almost an hour ago! Look at the time stamp!"

"There was a fuck-up," said the Chief. "Something about a new man in the Operations Room taking a shit and—well, this is no time for a postmortem."

The door of Fitzduane's car was open. A convoy of police cars and trucks was lined up behind, ready to seal off Balac's warehouse as soon as Fitzduane was inside. Army units were on call. Airborne surveillance was minutes away.

"Who or what are the Lestonis?" asked Fitzduane.

The Chief shook his head. "You can't go in. We'll have to do this the old-fashioned way, with the assault unit."

"The Lestonis," explained the Bear, "are professional bodyguards who tend to be hired by distinctly unpleasant people, the Libyan People's Bureaus and the Syrian Secret Service being two examples. The Lestonis' approach to their work might best be termed preventive. Nothing has been proved, but the consensus of several police forces and rather more intelligence agencies is that they have been responsible for some eleven hits that we know of."

"Pick them up for indecent exposure," said Fitzduane. "Is there a warrant out against them?"

"There's an Interpol 'Observe and Report' notice out on them," said the Chief, "but no warrant. That kind of animal we sling out of Switzerland for illegal parking, and the Israelis terminate them in some dark alley. But that's not the point. It's too late. The Lestonis are already here. They arrived at Balac's nearly an hour ago."

"They're probably art collectors," said Fitzduane wryly. His mind wasn't entirely on the conversation. He was doing a last-

minute check of his weapons and equipment. The remote detonator
for the shaped charge was strapped to his left wrist above his watch.
Another miniature transmitter would broadcast sound to the police
outside. He had his SIG 9 mm loaded with Glaser bullets in an
upside-down shoulder holster together with two spare clips of ammunition. In addition, he had a backup five-shot Smith & Wesson
.38 in a holster on his right leg, a razor-sharp Stiffelmesser knife was
clipped inside his waistband in the small of his back, and he had a
miniature of CS gas in his left jacket pocket and a set of disposable
nylon handcuffs in his right. To top it off, he wore a Kevlar bullet-
resistant vest designed to look like a T-shirt under his shirt. Everything was there where it should be. It seemed like a hell of a way to
dress for a lunchtime drink in a city that had been at peace since
Napoleonic times.

"I'm going in," he said. It was clear that some reckless moron had
hijacked his voice; he couldn't believe what he was hearing.

The Chief held up four fingers. He spaced each word.

"There—is—no—fucking—way that you can go up against four
people of the caliber of the Lestonis and Balac. Forget about getting
the drop on them. It isn't possible. You're dealing with profes-
sionals. Killing people is what they do—and they're very good at it.
They've had lots of practice. They like what they do. They've got
motivation, and the Lestonis, anyway, are younger than you.
They've got faster reflexes. It's a matter of biology."

The Chief grabbed a clipboard off a passing Berp and reversed the
printed form that lay on it. He rested the clipboard on the top of the
car and drew on the paper with a ballpoint.

"Look"—he indicated the three X's he had drawn—"if you do get
close to Balac, you'll find that you'll always have one of the Lestonis
at hand ready to intervene. The others" —he drew two more X's—
"will be so spaced that one will be at the edge of your peripheral
vision and the other will be in your blind spot. No matter how skilled
you are, and even given the diversion of blowing the wall, I don't see
how you can get out of this alive. Remember, you are also going to
be affected by the stun grenades, even if you are prepared. The best
you could hope to do would be to get two or at the most three. That
still leaves you dead. I ask, is the game worth the candle? Don't
answer. You can't win. If you say yes, it merely proves you're crazy,
or worse, stupid."

"It isn't four to one. You're forgetting Paulus."

"Paulus is irrelevant. That pederast isn't armed, and we don't know which way he'll jump anyway. The Lestonis will swat him like a fly if he even thinks of intervening. These people kill like you shave. It's a matter of mind-set; they have no scruples. That's what gives them the edge."

As Fitzduane got into his car, he was thinking, did Balac know he'd been discovered? He thought it unlikely. Outside the car the Chief was listening to a walkie-talkie. He held the small loudspeaker close to his ear. Engines were starting up all around, and hearing was difficult. He barked an acknowledgment into the radio. "The packing case has been delivered," he said. "As expected, my men didn't get inside. Two people came out and lugged it in. Paulus went with them."

"The Lestonis," said the Bear.

"Looks like it," said the Chief.

"I've got to go," said Fitzduane through the open car door. "I can't leave Paulus alone for too long. I'll think of something." He slammed the door shut.

"No," said the Chief, reaching for the handle and half opening it. "I won't have it. It's too damn dangerous. Paulus will have to take his chances." He reached across for the keys.

The Bear leaped forward and took the Chief by the arm. "For God's sake, Max," he said, "this is silly. We don't have time to argue—least of all among ourselves."

"He isn't going," repeated the Chief stubbornly.

"Compromise," said the Bear. "Fitzduane goes in, checks out the lay of the land, doesn't stay for lunch, says his good-byes quickly, and leaves. We don't blow the wall until he's out. That way we get confirmation that Balac is there and some up-to-date reconnaissance, but Fitzduane is clear before the shit starts to fly."

The Chief and Fitzduane glared at each other. "Do you agree?" asked the Chief. "No heroics. You arrive, you look around, and you get the hell out."

Fitzduane smiled. "Sounds reasonable."

The Chief closed the car door. "You're an idiot," he said. "Good luck, idiot."

"Stay close," said Fitzduane. Then he left the big police parking lot next to Waisenhausplatz and drove toward Balac's studio.

*   *   *

BALAC RATHER ENJOYED his informal lunchtime get-togethers. He was able to relax in the security of his own territory, on his own terms, and within limited time parameters. From twelve to two he was at home to a chosen few—although it looked casual, no one who had not been specifically vetted turned up—and he was able to delude himself that he was living a normal social existence. Of course, he knew he was deluding himself, but that was part of the pleasure.

It was convenient being an artist. You could behave in a somewhat eccentric way, and nobody gave a damn. If anything, it was good for business. Many people, in fact, thought his apparent obsession with security—triple steel doors, indeed, and television monitors—was a brilliant marketing ploy. It made him more mysterious. It made his paintings seem more valuable. It contributed to a sense of occasion leavened with a whiff of the dramatic. Anyway, getting the right price for his work, it seemed to Balac, had more to do with theater than with painting. Look at Picasso and Salvador Dali. How much more theatrical could you get? There was no doubt about it: art was a branch of show business. So was terrorism, on reflection.

"I am," he said to himself, "a man of parts." He was pleased with the thought. He uncapped a bottle of Gurten beer and drained half of it in true hell-raising chugalug fashion. The Lestonis were puffing across to the viewing area with Paulus's carefully cased Picasso. Paulus was hovering anxiously.

Balac half regretted having called the Lestonis in. They wouldn't do much for the tone of the gathering. Unfortunately they looked like what they were—professional killers. The Lestonis actually did wear snap-brim fedoras—incredible! They had even wanted to wear them inside, but Balac had drawn the line at that. The hats had been removed and now hung from three picture hooks like a surrealist sculpture. An aroma of perfumed hair oil filled the room. "Fuck me," said Balac to himself, and drained the rest of the beer. He was in a hell of a good mood.

The Picasso, still hidden from view in the packing case, had arrived at its destination. Paulus looked relieved and started adjusting the lighting to create the right effect. The Lestonis resumed their positions, standing well spaced out against the wall so that they could observe the entire room. Balac decided that introducing them to his guests as businessmen interested in his work wasn't going to play. The only commercial activity other than violence that they could

credibly be involved in was drug peddling or maybe pimping. Or
arms dealing—now there was an occupation the Swiss could identify
with. No, he'd say they were bodyguards hired to lend a little
pizzazz to his next show and he was rehearsing the effect. The good
burghers of Bern would love it.

The door indicator buzzed. He looked at the TV monitors set into
the wall: Fitzduane coming to pay his respects before he returned to
that dreary, wet country of his. Balac controlled the security doors
with a remote unit. He pressed the appropriate buttons in a spaced
sequence and watched Fitzduane's progress on the monitors. The
last door slid shut behind him, and he entered the room. What a
delicious irony—to entertain a man who was scouring the city looking for him. Life was full of simple pleasures.

They shook hands. "I can't stay long," said Fitzduane. "I just
wanted to say good-bye. I'm off this evening from Zurich, and I've a
hundred and one things to do before then."

Balac laughed. "Not the remark of a Swiss. A Swiss would be well
organized in advance and would now be going through his travel
checklist—for the third time—before leaving for the airport several
hours in advance in case he was delayed."

Fitzduane smiled. Once again he was struck by the magnetism of
the man's personality. Even knowing the extent of Balac's sadism
and criminality, even remembering the stomach-turning sight of
some of his victims, he found it impossible not to be affected. In
Balac's presence he easily understood how Paulus had been cor-
rupted. The Hangman was an infectious force of truly formidable
power. In his presence you wanted to please, to see that responsive
twinkle in his eyes, to bask in the aura he radiated. The man had
charisma. He was more than charming; his willpower dominated.

One of the Lestonis—he thought it was Cousin Julius, on the basis
of a quick look at the file the Bear had thrown into the car—stood to
Balac's left, slightly forward and to one side. If Fitzduane had been
left-handed, he would have stood to the right—always the side
nearer to the gun hand. It was a reflex for such a man. Fitzduane was
beginning to see the Chief's point. Even with the element of surprise,
he'd be lucky to get one of them, let alone three—not to mention
Balac.

He began to feel like a moron for suggesting such an idiotic plan. It
was looking beyond bloody dangerous. *Foolhardy* didn't even begin
to describe it. Now he knew how the twenty Greeks inside the

Trojan Horse must have felt while the Trojans discussed whether or not to bring it inside. The Trojan equivalent of the Lestonis had suggested burning the wooden horse. The Greeks inside must have felt great when those encouraging words had floated up into their hiding place.

"Let me introduce Julius," said Balac, indicating the Lestoni on his right. The gunman nodded. He made no offer to shake hands. Balac waved at the two other Lestonis. "Angelo and his brother, Pietro." They stared at Fitzduane, unblinking.

Fitzduane thought he'd have a quick glass of beer—his mouth was feeling sand dry—and fuck off very, very fast. He poured some Gurten into a glass and drank through the froth. It tasted like nectar.

Julius was whispering into Balac's ear. He had a pocket-size bug detector in his hand, and a small red light on it was flashing. Balac looked at Fitzduane and then at Paulus.

How he realized they were both involved, Fitzduane never fully understood, but from that moment there was no doubt: Balac knew.

ONE ELEMENT OF the plan that had particularly bothered the Bear was the correct functioning of the shaped charge. Certainly it had worked fine on the range at Sand, but that was a test under optimum conditions. Real life, in the Bear's experience, tended to be something less than optimal, often a lot less. A lot less in relation to the shaped charge meant either no hole or an inadequate hole, and either way that meant the assault team couldn't get in on time, which promised to be exceedingly bad news for Fitzduane and Paulus. Of course, Fitzduane was supposed to have left before the charge was blown so that he, at least, would be out of the firing line. But deal or no deal with the Chief, the Bear's insides told him that things were not going to work out that way.

All of which meant that if Fitzduane couldn't get out as planned, the assault force was going to have to go in—and that suggested a need for a king-size can opener. He tossed the problem to Henssen and Kersdorf and the Nose, and together they came up with an answer that derived from three of Switzerland's greatest assets: snow, the army, and money.

Strategically placed out of sight of the entrance to Balac's studio, the Bear waited, earphones glued to his head, and listened to Fitz-

duane drinking beer. Along with a unit of the assault force and an
army driver, he was sitting inside the army's latest and most expensive main battle tank. The sharp prow of a military specification
snowplow was mounted on the front of the huge machine. The
tank's engines were already ticking over. Both coaxial and turret
machine guns were loaded.

The Bear had decided it was time to stop pissing around with this
psycho. He stood up in the turret and pulled back the cocking handle
on the .50 caliber. One of the huge machine-gun rounds slid into the
breech. This time, he thought, he had a big enough gun.

He felt sick at what he heard coming over his earphones. "Go!" he
shouted into his throat microphone to the driver.

The huge machine rumbled forward.

EYES NARROWED, Balac stared at Fitzduane as if reading his mind.
The aura of bonhomie had vanished. Implacably Balac's face was
transformed into something vicious and malevolent. The features did
not change, but the image they projected was so altered that fear
struck Fitzduane like a knife in the guts.

Stripped of its mask, the face of the Hangman was diabolical. The
man radiated the power of evil. It assaulted Fitzduane's senses like
something physical. He could smell the stench of corruption and
depravity, of the blood of his many victims, of their flesh rotting in
disparate places.

All the Lestonis had drawn their weapons. Julius had a sawed-off
shotgun. The other Lestonis both had automatic weapons, an Ingram and a Skorpion. All the weapons pointed at Fitzduane. He
raised his hands slowly in defeat and clasped them on top of his head.
Through the light material of his jacket, with the forefinger of his
right hand, he could feel the button controlling the shaped charge in
the Picasso frame. The muzzles of three multi-projectile weapons
faced him. Stun grenades or not, they would fire as a reflex, wouldn't
they? It was an option he didn't want to check out. He relaxed his
finger but kept it in place.

"Where is the wire, Hugo?" said Balac.

"Clipped inside the front of my shirt."

Balac stepped forward and ripped the microphone from Fitzduane
and ground it under his heel. He removed the SIG from Fitzduane's
shoulder holster and gave it to Julius, who stuck it in his belt. Balac

stepped back, sat down on a sofa, and looked at Fitzduane thoughtfully. He uncapped a bottle of Gurten and drank from it, then wiped his mouth with his hand. He stood up and stretched like an animal. He was in superb physical condition. He looked at Paulus, then at Fitzduane, then at the packing case. "Beware of Greeks bearing gifts."

Paulus flinched, almost imperceptibly, but Balac noticed the reaction. "So, friend Paulus, you've sold me out. Thirty pieces of silver, thirty little boys, what was the price?"

Paulus stood there pale-faced and trembling. Balac walked toward him and stopped just in front of him. He looked into Paulus's eyes, holding his gaze even while he spoke. "Pietro," he said to one of the Lestoni brothers, "check out that packing case."

Pietro slung his submachine gun and walked across to the packing case. He opened the viewing doors. The Picasso in all its arcane beauty was exposed.

"There's a picture inside—kind of peculiar," said Pietro. "Looks like a load of crap."

Balac hadn't relaxed his gaze. "So," he said to Paulus, "you *have* brought me a Picasso. The surprise must lie elsewhere. Keep looking," he said to Pietro. "Check out the back as well as the front."

The remaining blood drained from Paulus's face. His eyes still fixed on the art dealer, Balac nodded several times.

Pietro produced a knife and started prying boards away from the front of the packing case around the picture. "Nothing here," he said after a couple of minutes. Splintered wood littered the floor.

"Look at the back," said Balac.

The packing case was heavy. It was positioned precisely against the wall, as Paulus had instructed, and Pietro had some difficulty in working it away. He contented himself with moving one side out far enough so that he could prize away a plank. The space was confined, but after a few seconds the nails at the edge were loosened and the plank pulled away. The planks were spaced at close intervals to support an inner casing of thin plywood. Pietro smashed through the plywood with his knife. He ripped away the piece at the corner.

His eyes bulged as the business edge of the shaped charge was revealed. "There's something here, some kind of explosive, I guess." He tried to wriggle back, but his coat was caught on a protruding nail at the back of the packing case.

Balac leaned forward and kissed Paulus hard on the lips. He pulled back and embraced Paulus with his left arm. "I'm sorry. No more little boys." He thrust his right hand forward. Paulus arched his body and gasped in agony. As Balac stepped back, the handle of a knife could be seen protruding from Paulus's groin. Balac reached out his hand and pulled the knife from the wound. Blood spurted, and Paulus collapsed writhing on the ground.

Balac turned to face Fitzduane, the knife in his hand. Bloody though it was, Fitzduane recognized the short, broad-bladed design. It was a reproduction scua—a Celtic sacrificial knife.

"See if you can find the detonator," Balac ordered Pietro, who was still struggling to free himself. "Give him a hand," he said to Angelo.

Despite the distractions, Julius's gun hadn't wavered off Fitzduane for a second. The Irishman felt sick at what had happened to Paulus. Now that same knife was coming toward him, and he had only seconds to make his move—but if he did, he would die. At that range the two-barreled shotgun would blow his head off. The bulletproof vest might protect his torso, but even that depended on the ammunition Julius was using.

Balac stopped some three paces away. "It's going to be worse for you, Hugo," he said. "It's going to hurt more than you can imagine, and there's going to be no relief except death. How does it feel to know that it's over?" His eyes were shining. A drop of blood fell from the knife and splashed to the floor.

Angelo screamed something in Italian. There was desperation in his voice. Julius's gaze still didn't waver. The twin barrels of the shotgun were pointed at Fitzduane.

"Julius!" shouted Balac.

Paulus von Beck had somehow risen to his knees. Blood was pouring from his groin. "*Sempach, Sempaaach!*" he shouted, and the automatic he held in both hands flamed, blowing a neat round hole through Julius Lestoni's head. His brains spattered over the wall.

Fitzduane watched the twin muzzles of the shotgun slip away from his line of sight. He didn't wait. He closed his eyes and, pressing the firing button, blew the shaped charge. Prepared though he was, the noise was shattering. Three stun grenades went off in a ripple effect, the blast completely drowning the crack of the shaped charge and filling the room with the searing light of igniting magnesium. Fitzduane's eyelids went white. There was a roaring in his ears, and he had to fight to avoid being completely disoriented. He shook his head dazedly and opened his eyes.

Pietro had been half behind the packing case when the charge went off. He had been surgically cut in two from the top of his head to the upper thigh of his right leg. The right-hand side of his body had disappeared in the rubble behind the packing case. The left-hand side still stood propped against the wall. Fitzduane's SIG automatic lay on the ground where it had fallen from Julius's belt as he collapsed. He leaped forward and grabbed it. Balac seemed to have vanished.

The shaped charge, moved away from its correct positioning against the wall and diluted by Pietro's body, had been only partially successful. One side and the top of a door-shaped aperture had been cut out of the wall, but the remaining vertical had been only half cut through, and rubble blocked the way.

Fitzduane caught a brief glimpse of Angelo Lestoni through the smoke and dust. He fired. Automatic fire scythed through the air in return. He crawled along the ground. Further bursts cut through the air above him. He could see Angelo's legs. He fired again.

The external wall of the studio seemed to implode. The noise was overwhelming—a growling metallic shrieking mixed with the crash of falling masonry and the rattle of gunfire. The muzzle of a huge machine gun poked into the room, spitting tracers. The bullets found Angelo Lestoni, who was lifted off the ground and thrown against the floor, a broken mess.

Fitzduane caught a brief glimpse of Balac at the end of the studio and fired twice rapidly.

The tank, rumbling farther forward, blocked his view. There was a string of sharp explosions as prepositioned Claymore antipersonnel mines detonated uselessly, their normally lethal ball-bearing missiles smashing harmlessly against the tank's armor.

The end of the studio erupted in a sea of flame. Members of the assault unit grabbed Fitzduane and hurried him out of the building and into a waiting ambulance. Paulus, paramedics working on him furiously, lay in the other bunk.

He heard noises, more explosions, and the sound of heavy gunfire. He felt a pinprick in his arm and had a brief glimpse of a man in a white coat standing over him and the Bear behind him wearing some kind of helmet.

And then there was nothing.

BOOK THREE

The Killing

"The Irish are loose, untamable, superstitious, execrable, whiskey swilling, frank, amorous, ireful, and gloating in war."

—GIRALDUS CAMBRENSIS (of Wales), thirteenth century

Chapter Twenty-three

Unwisely—but thinking his stay in Switzerland would be a matter of weeks rather than a couple of months—he had left the Land Rover in the Long Stay Car Park of Dublin Airport. Somewhat to his surprise it was still there on his return, though sticky with a thick deposit of unburned aviation fuel mixed with Dublin grime.

He reached out his hand to open the befouled door with reluctance. A sudden gust of chill north wind angled the rain into his face, drenching his shirt. He suppressed his squeamishness and yanked the door open, threw in his bags, and climbed into the vehicle. A rush of wet cold located around his right foot informed him he had just stepped in a puddle. He slammed the door shut, and the wind and rain were excluded from his cold, damp aluminum and glass box.

A rat biting at the nerve endings inside his skull reminded him that he had a hangover. God damn the Swiss and their going-away parties.

Why the hell did he have to live in such a miserable, wet, windswept place as Ireland? It was May, and he was bloody freezing.

"I THOUGHT you were dead," said Kilmara cheerfully, "or dying at least—surrounded by nubile nurses in the Tiefenau's intensive care unit." He rubbed his chin and added as an afterthought, "But I've

prepared dinner anyway." He led the way into the big kitchen. "I've
sent Adeline and the kids away for a while."

"There was fuck all wrong with me," said Fitzduane dryly,
"though I guess I was a bit dazed by the pyrotechnics. It was the para-
medic who put me out—determined to have his moment of glory."

"Have a drink and relax," said Kilmara, "while I fiddle with pots
and pans. You can tell me everything after you've eaten." He handed
Fitzduane a tumbler of whiskey. "I assume you're staying the night.
You'd better; you look terrible."

"Swiss hospitality," said Fitzduane. He slumped in a chair beside
the fire. "It feels weird being back, weird and depressing and anti-
climactic—and damp and cold."

"You're always going away to sunnier climates," said Kilmara,
"but still you come back; you should know what to expect by now.
What's so different this time?"

"I don't know," said Fitzduane. "Or perhaps I do." He fell
asleep. He often did in Kilmara's house.

IT WAS five hours later.

The plates had been cleared. The dishwasher had been loaded. The
perimeter alarms had been rechecked. The dogs had been let loose to
roam or shelter as they wished. Kilmara had received a brief report
over a secure line from the Ranger duty officer. The day was nearly
done.

Sheets of rain driven by an unseasonable gale-force wind lashed the
darkness. Double glazing and heavy lined curtains muted the sound
of the storm except for the occasional eerie shriek echoing down the
chimney. They sat on either side of the study fire, coffee, drinks, and
cigars at hand.

Fitzduane was still suffering from reaction to the events in Bern.
His fatigue was deep and lasting, and he felt only marginally refreshed after his sleep despite the fact that Kilmara, seeing his friend's
torpor, had delayed eating until very late.

He could hear the sound of a clock chiming midnight. "Hell of a
time for a serious discussion," he said.

Kilmara smiled. "I'm sorry about that. I'm tight for time, and it's
important I talk to you."

"Fire away."

"The Hangman," began Kilmara. "Let's start with his death."

"The Hangman," repeated Fitzduane thoughtfully. "So many different names; but it's funny, you know, I'll always think of him as Simon Balac."

"Different aliases and personas are still coming out of the woodwork," said Kilmara. "Whitney seems to have been another of them. Best guess is that that particular name was inspired by his late-lamented blond CIA boyfriend in Cuba. Still, it does look as if Lodge was his real name. The background fits, too, or at least the psychiatrists seem to think so. You read the stuff that was prized out of the CIA?"

Fitzduane nodded. He remembered the clipped sentences describing Lodge's upbringing in Cuba: a brilliant, scared, lonely little boy maturing into a psychopath of genius. Fitzduane doubted that they had been supplied with the full story. The CIA didn't like to talk too much about Cuba.

"We'll call him the Hangman," said Fitzduane. "The press seems to have picked up the name anyway. 'Death of a Master Terrorist. Major success for joint Bernese/Bundeskriminalamt task force. The Hangman slain.'"

"The Bernese cops had to say something," said Kilmara. "They couldn't turn part of the city into a war zone and then burn down a complete block and say nothing. So tell me about it. I need to get a feel of the situation. The Hangman may be dead, but do his various enterprises live on? A friend of mine in the Mossad has suggested a few things that make me uneasy."

"The Mossad?" said Fitzduane.

"You go first," said Kilmara.

Fitzduane did.

"So you didn't actually see the Hangman killed?" said Kilmara.

"No," said Fitzduane. "Things happened very fast after Paulus shouted, '*Sempach!*' and shot Julius Lestoni. It was all over in a matter of seconds. The last I saw of Balac he was headed toward the end of the studio. I got off a couple of rounds, but I don't think I hit him. Then the assault group and the Bear's fucking tank took over. When I woke up in the Tiefenau, they told me the rest. The assault team had seen the Hangman through a door at the end of the studio. They blasted him with everything short of things nuclear, and then some kind of embedded thermite bombs went off and the whole place went up in flames. The entire block was sealed off, and when things were cool enough, they went in and dug through the wreckage. They found various bodies. The Hangman was identified by his dental records. Apparently he had tried to destroy them and had succeeded, but the dentist kept a duplicate set in his bank vault.

"Anyway, that, according to the powers that be, was the end of the Hangman. I stayed on a week to answer a whole lot of questions a whole lot of times and get drunk most nights with the Bear. And now here I am."

"Why did Paulus von Beck shout, '*Sempach*'?" asked Kilmara, puzzled.

Fitzduane smiled. "Love, honor, duty. We're all motivated by something."

"I don't follow."

"The von Becks are Bernese aristocracy," said Fitzduane. "Paulus felt that he had besmirched the family honor and that he was redeeming it by facing up to the Hangman. The Battle of Sempach took place when Napoleon's troops invaded Switzerland. The defending Bernese lost, but the consensus was that they had saved their honor. One of the heroes of the battle was a von Beck."

Kilmara raised his eyebrows and then shook his head ruefully. He looked at his friend in silence for a short while before speaking. "So what's troubling you? The Hangman's dead. Isn't it over?"

Fitzduane looked at Kilmara suspiciously. "Why shouldn't it be over? The Chief Kripo says it's over. He even paid for my going-away party—and drove me to the airport. He thinks Bern is returning to normal. He'll have a seizure if I go back."

Kilmara laughed, then turned serious again. "Hugo, I've known you for twenty years. You've got instincts I have learned to listen to—and good judgment. So what's bugging you?"

Fitzduane sighed. "I'm not sure it's over, but I really can't tell you why, and I'm not sure I want to know. I'm so bloody tired. I had a bellyful of trouble in Bern. I just want to go home now, put my feet up, twiddle my thumbs, and figure out what to do with the rest of my life. I'm not going to photograph any more wars. I'm too old to get shot at and too young to die—and I don't need the money."

"What about Etan?" said Kilmara. "Does she come into the equation? You know she hauled me out to lunch a couple of times when you were away. I have the feeling I'm supposed to act as some sort of middleman. I wish you two would talk to each other directly. This habit of not communicating when you're away on an assignment is cuckoo."

"There was a reason for it," said Fitzduane. "The idea was for both of us to keep a sense of perspective, not to let things get out of hand."

"As I said," said Kilmara, "cuckoo. Here you are, crazy about each other, and you don't communicate for months. Even the Romans used to send stone tablets to each other, and now we have something called a telephone." He shook his head and relit his pipe. "But why do you think it may not be over?" he said. "Are you suggesting the Hangman didn't die in that fire?"

Fitzduane took his time answering. "The Hangman's whole pattern is one of deception," he said eventually. "And I would feel a whole lot happier if we had had a body to identify. Dental records can be switched. On the other hand I was there, and I don't see how he could have escaped. He certainly couldn't have lived through a fire of that intensity. So the guy must be dead, and I'm not going to spend my hard-earned rest in Connemara worrying about what might happen next. Almost anything *might* happen. My concern is with what probably *will* happen."

"The evidence suggests that the Hangman is dead," said Kilmara, "but that is no guarantee his various little units will vanish or take up knitting. Remember, he operated through a series of virtually autonomous groups, and it's likely that new leaders were waiting in the wings. Another thought that nags away concerns Rudi von Graffenlaub's hanging and the other peculiar happenings on your island. There are a lot of rich kids there, and the Hangman never seems to do anything without a reason. He has a track record of kidnapping. Were Rudi and his oddly dressed friends being psyched up to provide some inside support for a kidnapping, maybe of the whole school? The place is isolated, and the parents are richer than you and I can imagine."

"Geraniums," said Fitzduane sleepily.

"What?" said Kilmara.

"Geraniums keep on popping up," said Fitzduane, "on the tattoos and in Ivo's notes, and the word was actually written down in Erika's apartment—but I'm fucked if I know what it means."

Kilmara drained his brandy and wondered if there was any point in talking to Fitzduane when he was this tired. He decided he'd better make the effort since time seemed to be a commodity in distinctly short supply.

"Leaving flowers out of the equation," he said dryly, "I've got some other problems worth mentioning." He refilled Fitzduane's glass.

The effort of holding his glass steady forced Fitzduane to pay reasonable attention. He was almost awake. "And you're going to tell me about them," he said helpfully.

"My friend the prime minister," said Kilmara, "is fucking us around."

"Have you ever considered another line of work? I fail to see the attraction in working for a bent machine politician like our Taoiseach. Delaney is a prick—a bent prick—and he isn't going to get any better."

Kilmara privately agreed with Fitzduane's comment but ignored the interruption. "A good friend of ours in the Mossad—and they're not all such good friends—has told me of a Libya-based hit team, some seventy plus strong, that has unfriendly intentions toward an objective in this country."

"The PLO coming here?" said Fitzduane. "Why? Unless they've been out in the sun too long and want a real rain-drenched holiday to relax in. What has the PLO to do with Ireland?"

"I didn't say PLO," said Kilmara. "There are PLO in the group but as mercenaries, and the objective, if you can believe what the Israelis found on a rather abortive preventive raid, is the U.S. Embassy in Dublin. The timing is put at some time in May."

"How would seventy armed terrorists get into the country," said Fitzduane, "and what has an attack on the U.S. Embassy got to do with me? The embassy is in Dublin. I'm going to be as far away as one could possibly be without falling into the Atlantic. I'm going to be sleeping twelve hours a day and talking to the sea gulls and meditating on higher things and drinking poteen and generally staying as much out of trouble as a human being possibly can."

"Stay with me," said Kilmara, "and I guarantee to get your full attention. We've kicked this thing around since our Mossad friend visited and we heard the news about the Hangman's death—and our conclusions will not make your day. We think this U.S. Embassy thing smacks of the Hangman's game playing, or that of his heirs and successors. It's probably a diversion, and heaven only knows where the real target is. Possibly it won't be in Ireland at all. It could be anywhere, including back in the Middle East. Unfortunately, suspecting it's a diversion doesn't help. The Rangers have been ordered to keep the place secure until the flap is over. That means my ability to deal with any other threat is drastically curtailed. I don't have the manpower to mount a static defense and also maintain strength for other operations."

"I thought the idea was that the Rangers were only to be used as a reaction force, along with certain limited security duties."

"It was and it is—normally," said Kilmara, his voice expressing his frustration, "but I was outvoted on this one. Ireland has a special relationship with Uncle Sam, and my friend the Taoiseach played it perfectly and boxed us in. The Rangers are a disciplined force, and there are times you just can't buck the system."

"So where is all this getting us?"

Kilmara shrugged. "You've got good instincts. If you think the Hangman is out of the picture, I'm tempted to go along with you, but when you're this tired—who the fuck knows? Anyway, it's my business to cover the down side."

Fitzduane yawned. The clock struck two o'clock in the morning. He was so spaced he was floating. It was no time to argue. "What do you want me to do?"

"I've got a radio and other equipment here for you," said Kilmara. "All I want you to do is proceed as normal but with your eyes and ears open. If you detect anything untoward, give me a call—and we'll come running."

"If you're so committed elsewhere, how and with what?"

"I'll think of something," said Kilmara. "It'll probably never happen, but if it does, red tape isn't going to stop me."

But Fitzduane was asleep again. Outside, the storm was abating.

AMBASSADOR NOBLE FELT like a child playing truant as he idled around the hills and lakes of Connemara in his rented Ford Fiesta. It was the first vacation in years in which his pleasure hadn't been diluted with some element of State Department business, and he positively luxuriated in the freedom of traveling without bodyguards. Ireland might have its troubles in the North—and even they were exaggerated and rarely involved foreigners—but the bulk of the island was about as peaceful as could be, he had been assured.

The greatest potential threats to his life were more likely to result from Irish driving habits, an excess of Irish hospitality, and the weather. He would be well advised, he was told, to dress warmly and bring an umbrella. If he planned to fish, he should hire a gillie.

He calculated afterward that his briefing had enhanced the federal deficit by a couple of thousand dollars. He did remember to bring an umbrella. He was managing fine without thermal underwear. He decided the gillie could wait until he arrived at Fitzduane's Island in a few days. He was looking forward to seeing his son and hearing how he was getting on at Draker.

Meanwhile, he was having a ball doing almost nothing at all. No diplomats, no crisis meetings, no telexes, no press. No official dinners or receptions either, he thought as he ate his baked beans out of the can with a spoon and waited for the kettle to boil. And positively no worries about terrorism. He had left them at the office the way all those books on how to succeed said you should.

He looked up at the leaden sky and listened to the rain bounce off his fishing umbrella and thought: Life is bliss.

FITZDUANE SLEPT in and enjoyed a leisurely midafternoon breakfast. The storm had done its worst, but the rain continued as if determined to leave him in no doubt whatsoever that he was back in Ireland.

Kilmara had gone hours before but had left behind a note detailing that day's security procedure. Getting in and out of Kilmara's home without setting off some part of the labyrinth of alarm systems was no easy task, and codes were changed at least daily at irregular times. Fitzduane wondered how Adeline put up with being married to a target. That made her, he supposed, a target herself—and then there were the children. What a life. Was he, Fitzduane, since his encounter with the Hangman, now a target, too? And would he stay at risk? What would that mean for his wife and his children? For the first time it came to Fitzduane that once you were involved with terrorism—on either side—there was really no end to it. It was a permanent state of war.

He was digesting this unpleasant thought when he heard a faint noise coming from the front of the house—a house that was supposed to be empty. It sounded like a door opening and closing. The sound was not repeated.

He was tempted to stay where he was, to ignore what he almost doubted he had heard. He checked the perimeter alarm board—there were monitors in every room—but all seemed secure.

He took the Remington and chambered a round. Moving as silently as he could, he left the kitchen and edged along the corridor to the front hall. He had two doors to choose from. As he deliberated, the door of the living room opened. Fitzduane dropped into a crouch.

Etan stood there.

"Holy shit!" exclaimed Fitzduane.

Etan smiled. "Shane's idea," she said. "The colonel as matchmaker." She looked at the gun. "He's told me quite a bit. Things make more sense now."

Fitzduane realized he was still pointing the gun. He lowered it, replaced the safety catch, and laid it down gently. He felt weak and happy and scared stiff and more than a little stupid. His heart was pounding. He couldn't believe how glad he was to see her. He sat on the floor.

"Hugo, are you all right?" she said anxiously. "For God's sake, say something. You're white as a sheet."

Fitzduane looked up at her, and his pleasure was plain to see. He shook his head. "Cuckoo," he said.

Etan was wearing jeans tucked into half boots and an Aran sweater. He could smell her perfume. She pushed the gun away with her boot and then knelt beside him. "Staying long?" she said. She peeled off her sweater and blouse. She wasn't wearing a bra. Her breasts were firm and full, the nipples pronounced. Her voice had gone husky. She put her hands on his shoulders and pushed. He didn't argue. He lay back.

"Soldier from the war returning. Where have you been? How has he been?" She undid his belt and unzipped him and encircled his organ with her hand. She squeezed hard. "I have a proprietary interest," she said. "My mother told me never to put anything in my mouth if I didn't know where it had been." She teased him with her tongue. "Where has this little man been?" She released her hand and looked. "On second thoughts," she said, "he's not so little." She shucked her boots and wriggled out of her jeans, then lay on her stomach on the carpet. "Do it this way," she said, "nice and slow and deep." She raised her buttocks suggestively and parted her legs. Fitzduane put his hand between them and stroked her where she liked. He ran his lips and tongue along her back and slowly moved down. It was only after she had been moaning and quivering for quite some time that he took her doggie fashion on the floor. Halfway through he turned her and entered her from above. She reached up and sucked his nipples, and he gasped. He drove into her again and again, and their loins became slick.

When it was over, he took her in his arms and just held her. Then he kissed her gently on the forehead. "You know," he said, and there was laughter in his voice, "this has been a year of tough women."

Etan bit his ear and then lay beside him, her head resting on one arm. Her free hand caressed his loins. "Tell me," she said, smiling sweetly, "about Erika."

KILMARA SAT in his office examining yet again the plans of the U.S. Embassy in Dublin and the security arrangements. Every fresh examination made him feel unhappier.

The embassy had been built in the days when a violent protest consisted of a rotten egg or two thrown at the ambassador's car. It seemed to have been designed to facilitate terrorist attacks.

The three-story circular building—plus basements—had a facade consisting mainly of glass hung in a prestressed concrete frame. Offices were positioned around the perimeter of each floor. The core of the building was a floor-to-ceiling rotunda overlooked by the circular corridors. The embassy was located at the apex of a V-shaped junction of two roads, each lined with houses that overlooked the embassy building. Car access to the basement level was by way of a short driveway guarded by a striped pole.

A terrorist was faced with a downright excess of viable choices. The place was so easy to attack that if you didn't know better—and Kilmara unfortunately did—you might think that there must be a snag, or else be put off the idea for reasons of sportsmanship because the target hadn't a chance. Even the sewers—though why any terrorist would choose the sewers when he had such a range of more hygienic options was beyond Kilmara—were not secure.

Kilmara closed the file in disgust. Short of blocking off the access roads—impossible because one was vital for south Dublin traffic— and surrounding the place with a battalion of troops—too expensive considering the state of the nation's finances—full or even adequate security for the embassy was impossible to achieve against a small, well-armed terrorist unit. Against a force of seventy, his efforts would be derisory.

Unless, of course, he got lucky. With a sigh he opened the file again. The saying was true. The harder he worked, the luckier he seemed to get. He wondered if the same principle applied to the other side, and he was not pleased with his conclusion.

The bottom line in this situation meant: one, he had to obey orders; two, out of his full complement of sixty Rangers, roughly a third were assigned to full-time embassy duty, and given that there were three shifts per day, that meant that almost the full command was committed; three, they were operating in exactly the wrong way for a force of this type—tied down and waiting to be attacked rather than staying flexible and keeping the initiative; four, training time was being seriously eroded (to keep to their unusually high standard of marksmanship, Rangers shot for several hours a day at least three days a week and often more); five, his own time was being used up running this screw-up of an operation; six, God knows what else was happening while this was going on.

It was a crock.

FITZDUANE STAYED another night in Kilmara's house and left for home the following afternoon, his body satiated from a night of lovemaking and the long, deep sleep that had followed.

Kilmara had called to say he wouldn't be back and the couple could have the house to themselves. "Couple?" Fitzduane had queried, stroking Etan's nipples with the tips of his fingers.

"Lucky guess," said Kilmara dryly.

Fitzduane laughed. "We're getting married."

"About time," said Kilmara. "I've got to go." He phoned back about two minutes later. "Don't forget what I said," he added. "People in love are dangerous; they forget things."

"I don't feel dangerous," said Fitzduane.

"I'd feel a little better if you did. Check in by radio when you get home. The signal is automatically scrambled. You'll be able to talk freely."

Fitzduane was thoughtful as he replaced the phone. Etan ran her tongue over his penis. "Pay attention," she said. He did.

* * *

THE PILLARS OF HERCULES—better known in more recent times as the Strait of Gibraltar—are a classic naval choke point dominated by the Rock of Gibraltar.

Gibraltar, if one forgets for a moment the slightly paranoid local population of some twenty-eight thousand crammed into a land area the size of a parking lot, consists of surveillance equipment, weaponry, hollowed-out rock, military personnel, and apes in roughly that order.

Despite all this concentration of spies, people, apes, and matériel, it was nonetheless scarcely surprising that the passing through the Strait of Gibraltar of an Italian cattle boat, the *Sabine*, en route from Libya to Ireland to pick up a fresh cargo of live meat for ritual slaughter on return to Tripoli, should be logged but attract no further attention.

The Irish cattle trade with Libya was both known and established. The sight of the *Sabine* was routine. The only change that might have been commented on, but was not, was that the *Sabine* failed this time to refuel in Gibraltar. She had, apparently, braved the bureaucracy and chronic inefficiency of Qaddafi's Libya and bunkered in Tripoli (a practice the experienced ship's master learns not to repeat unless desperate).

An inquirer—if there had been one—would have been told, with a shrug, that it was a matter of an arrangement, and the thumb and forefinger would have been rubbed together. Such an answer would have sufficed.

The *Sabine* left the Pillars of Hercules behind and set a course for Ireland.

Chapter Twenty-four

In the old Land Rover, allowing for a stop in Galway to pick up supplies and eat, they took nearly seven hours to reach the island from Dublin. It rained solidly until early evening, and then they were treated by the weather to such a spectacular display of changing light and mood that Fitzduane forgave all and wondered why he had ever left. It was so bloody beautiful.

His spirits lifted—and then the rain returned in full force as they were approaching the castle, as if to remind them to take nothing for granted.

"This is a fickle fucking country," he muttered to himself while unloading the vehicle. He had been tempted to leave things where they were till morning, but the contents of the four long, heavy boxes and other containers Kilmara had given him were best placed under lock and key as soon as possible.

During the drive he had told Etan much of what had happened. Now he gave Murrough, who was having a drink inside with Etan, a short summary. He had kept his reservations about the Hangman's demise to himself. He didn't want to be unnecessarily alarmist.

Murrough and Oona had lit fires and aired the place, and the heating had been turned on earlier in the day. The castle was warm and comfortable. It felt good to be back.

Murrough was quiet for a while after Fitzduane had finished. Fitzduane refilled their glasses. "You'll have a chance to meet some of these people in a couple of days," he said. "I guess I got carried away during my last week in Bern, when we had one long round of celebrations to see the Hangman off in style. Heini Raufman is still supposed to be convalescing, so I invited him to see how civilized people live, and then somehow Henssen got added to the list—and then young Andreas von Graffenlaub. Andreas needs some distraction. He's bearing up well, but this whole business has been rough on him. His father's death hit him particularly hard."

"Poor lad," said Etan.

"Heini Raufman is the one you call 'the Bear'?" said Murrough.

"You'll see why when you meet him," said Fitzduane.

"It will be nice to have this place full of people," said Etan. She had been eyeing the castle and its furnishings with a definite proprietorial air since they arrived. It was dawning on Fitzduane that there were going to be more changes in his life than he had anticipated. He had to admit that the present decor was overheavy on stuffed animal heads, wall hangings, and medieval weapons. Still, what else would you expect in a castle? He was uneasy about the alternatives Etan might have in mind.

Etan looked at him. "Lace curtains on the windows," she said, grinning, "and flowered wallpaper on the walls."

"Over my dead body," said Fitzduane.

"I think I'd better be leaving," said Murrough, not moving but anxious to bring the conversation back to more serious matters.

Fitzduane knew his man. "What's on your mind, Murrough?" he said.

Murrough took his time speaking. "Those kids from the college, reviving something best long forgotten. What's happened about them? You never said."

"Not an entirely satisfactory outcome," said Fitzduane, "but understandable, I suppose, given the trauma in the college recently. Information on what was going on was supplied to the acting headmaster by the Rangers, working through the police. I gather he was shocked but after reflection chose to believe that it was little more than juvenile high spirits. Above all, he wanted no more scandal. He said he would deal with the matter in his own way at the end of the term, and he'd appreciate if the police would leave it at that, so the police did. It isn't a crime to dress up like the Wolfman and run around in the woods. Anyway, the best efforts of all concerned failed to identify the individuals involved."

"And how about the small matter of our decapitated billy goat and the traces of sacrifice you found?" said Murrough indignantly. "Isn't that a little more than—what did he call it—juvenile high spirits?"

Fitzduane drained his glass. "Indeed," he said, "but there is the matter of proof, and nobody wants to upset the college further. It brings money into the area, and it's had a rough time recently. I think the police felt they couldn't press things."

Murrough digested what had been said. Etan had fallen asleep in front of the fire. He stood up to go. "So it's finished," he said.

Fitzduane looked at the dying embers. His reservations and his conversation with Kilmara seemed remote at this distance. Anyway, May would soon be over. He decided he'd sleep on the problem. "I hope so," he said, "I really do."

AMBASSADOR HARRISON NOBLE FELT that things were going splendidly.

He lay back in his bed and congratulated himself on finding such a comfortable and practical place to stay. It was on the island, it was near his son's school, the woman of the house was a splendid cook, and this man Murrough said he would gillie for him.

Harrison Noble fell asleep within seconds of putting out the light. His sleep was that of a man contented and relaxed and at peace with the world.

DESPITE TAKING their travel sickness pills as instructed, most of the passengers on board the cattle boat *Sabine* were thoroughly ill as they crossed the Bay of Biscay.

The boat rolled unpleasantly without its normal cargo of fourteen hundred heavy cattle and the corresponding load of feed and water. The crew and more than seventy armed men, ammunition, explosives, surface-to-air missiles, and inflatable assault boats did not weigh enough to provide adequate ballast.

The air-conditioning system coped admirably with the smell. The passengers were fully recovered as the boat approached the south of

Ireland. They cleaned and recleaned their weapons and rehearsed the details of the plan.

THE U.S. CULTURAL ATTACHÉ HEADED the crisis team that coordinated security for the embassy when a specific threat was involved. A diplomat largely occupied in his official duties with cultural exchanges, visiting baseball teams, and the arcane queries of scholars and writers might seem an unlikely choice for such a counterterrorist role, but the cultural attaché was also the senior CIA man on the spot and, even more to the point, had experience at the sharp end on several unpleasant occasions in Latin America.

After the last experience, when his unarmored vehicle—a matter of budget cuts—had been sprayed with automatic-weapons fire in San Salvador and his driver killed, he had asked for a posting away from a high-risk zone. He had been sent to Ireland to get his nerve back and play some golf. Both his nerve and his golf had been doing fine until the attack warning had been received.

Now he waited and sweated and drank too much to be good for either his liver or his career and hoped that the extra acoustic and visual monitoring equipment Kilmara had requested would turn up something—or, better still, nothing.

He loathed the waiting, the sense of being a target on a weapons range. He knew too well what happens to targets. His driver in San Salvador had died holding his fingers against the hole in his neck, trying vainly to stop the gushing of arterial blood.

THE WEATHER STILL LOOKED menacing in the morning, but it wasn't actually raining, so Fitzduane and Etan saddled up the horses and ambled around the island.

The sense of fatigue that had dogged Fitzduane since his return seemed to have gone, and the wind in his face as they rode was invigorating.

It was as they were returning that Fitzduane began to experience a feeling of anticipation that was familiar but that at first he could not identify. They had been chatting easily about their future. Now, with the castle in sight again, he lapsed into silence, his mind sifting and sorting a jumble of thoughts and snatches of conversation, trying to identify the source of this unsettling feeling.

He had been too tired, he knew, the last couple of days to think rationally and to listen to his intuition; he had relegated his doubts and feeling of foreboding to the back of his mind. Now he ran through everything that had been said and tried to relate it to what he had either experienced or discovered himself.

The theorizing and the computer assessments aside, Fitzduane was one of the few people involved who actually knew the Hangman. Perhaps *knew* was too strong a word to describe his relationship with the man, but there was no doubt that the time spent in his company had given him some insight into the terrorist's complex character.

The Hangman rarely did anything without a reason, even if his rationale seemed obscure by conventional standards. He was a player of games with a finely balanced tendency toward self-destruction. He was a planner of genius with a useful ability to anticipate the moves of his opponents. He enjoyed teasing the opposition, leaving enough clues to excite his pursuers while at the same time taking steps to see they would always put the pieces together too late. He was a master of feints and deception—a characteristic he shared with Kilmara. He had substantial resources, and he thought on a grandiose scale. Henssen's work with the Nose had suggested he was winding down many of his operations and working toward some final grand slam.

Was it credible that the slaughter in Balac's studio was actually part of some intricate game devised by the man? If so, why? What was the Hangman's overall motivation apart from the satisfaction he seemed to obtain from beating the system? His motives weren't political. He was quite happy to use politically committed people for his own ends, but his constant, specific goal was money. Fitzduane doubted that he wanted money for itself, but rather as an impartial way of rating his performance—and it had the practical advantages of conferring power and freedom.

A consistent theme in the Hangman's behavior—and a jarring counterpoint to his undoubted sense of humor, albeit rather sick humor—was savagery. He seemed to enjoy inflicting pain on society, as if trying to avenge himself for the slights he had undoubtedly received in earlier life.

Revenge was part of his motivation.

But the Hangman was dead. The Bernese weren't amateurs. The entire studio area had been sealed as thoroughly as possible. A body had been found. The autopsy would have been carried out with typical Swiss thoroughness. No error would have been made over the dental records. But were they the Hangman's dental records? The man specialized in switching identities, and obtaining a body would scarcely be a problem for him. Could he have anticipated the possibility of being detected and have turned such an apparent disaster into another misleading dead end?

The trouble was, everybody wanted to believe that the Hangman was dead. They were sick and tired of the whole business; scared, too. The man was unpredictable and dangerous. He could turn on them at any time. Wives and children would be in danger. They would live in a climate of unending fear. No, of course he was dead. Massive resources had been deployed against him. No individual could win against the concentrated might of the forces of law and order.

Like hell.

An image of Balac came into Fitzduane's mind, as sharp and clear as if he were physically present: his eyes gleamed with amusement, and he was smiling.

It was at that moment that Fitzduane knew for certain that it wasn't over—and that the Hangman was very much alive. Fear like pain ran through him, and Pooka whinnied and bucked in alarm. His face went white, and Etan stared at him in consternation. He looked ill, but they were almost back at the castle.

When they rode into the bawn seconds later, they were met by the sight of Christian de Guevain, a Paris-based merchant banker who shared Fitzduane's interest in medieval weaponry—de Guevain's specialty being the longbow—getting out of a taxi festooned with fishing rods and other impedimenta.

He gave a shout of greeting when he saw them, and then his expression changed as he saw Fitzduane's face.

"But you invited me," he said anxiously, "and I wrote to you. Is there a problem?"

Fitzduane smiled. He had forgotten completely about his invitation to his friend.

"No problem," he said. "Or at least you're not it."

He looked at de Guevain's tweed hat and jacket, which were covered with hand-tied flies in profusion. Their brightly colored feathers gave the impression that the Frenchman was covered with miniature tropical birds.

*   *   *

AN EMBASSY'S GROUNDS and building are considered by the host country to be the territory of the country concerned. Translated into security arrangements, that meant that Kilmara's Rangers had to confine their activities to the U.S. Embassy's external perimeter. Internal security remained the responsibility of the U.S. Marines and of State Department security personnel.

Kilmara and his CIA counterpart, the cultural attaché, disliked this artificial division in the deployment of their forces—especially in view of the vulnerability of the location—but neither the U.S. ambassador nor the Irish Department of Foreign Affairs was of a mind to waive the protocols of the Treaty of Vienna governing such arrangements.

The initial breakthrough came when one of the rental agents— previously primed by the police at Kilmara's request—notified them that one of the apartments overlooking the embassy had been let for a short period to four Japanese who were going to be in Ireland for a limited time while looking for a suitable site for an electronics factory. They would like to move in immediately. The substantial advance payment requested by the agent proved to be no problem. References were given to be taken up at a later date.

All the empty apartments overlooking the embassy, and quite a few of the occupied locations, had been bugged in anticipation of some action of this nature. A relay station was set up in the embassy, but the actual monitoring was carried out from Ranger headquarters in Shrewsbury Road.

The acoustic monitoring equipment was state-of-the-art, and the quality of the transmission excellent. Unfortunately, although there were a number of linguists in the Rangers who spoke among them some eighteen foreign languages—including Arabic and Hebrew, both much in demand since Ireland's involvement with the UN force in Lebanon—none of them spoke Japanese.

Then Günther remembered that one of the Marine guards he had been chatting with was a Nisei. It didn't follow, of course, that he spoke Japanese—but he might.

He did.

Listening to the translation, Kilmara started to wonder if maybe he hadn't been too hasty in assuming the whole embassy thing was a blind; it looked as if something were going to happen there after all. Then the link was made with a convention of travel agents booked into the nearby Jury's Hotel for the following day. The travel agents were coming from the Middle East, and there were seventy-two in the party.

Backup units were alerted. Ranger leave was canceled. The next question was when to move in. It looked as if he might have thrown a scare into Fitzduane for nothing. Still, better scared than dead.

Kilmara decided that maybe he was doing too much reacting to events and not enough thinking. He tilted his chair back and set to work on some serious analysis. After half an hour he was glad he had. He called up the rosters on his computer screen and began to do some juggling.

IN THE AFTERNOON the skies abandoned any attempt at neutrality and proceeded to dump a goodly portion of the Atlantic Ocean on the west coast of Ireland.

Etan and Oona went to work out who would sleep where and with whom, and Fitzduane closeted himself in his study to plow his way through a two-month backlog of mail.

There were several communications from Bern of no particular significance except that one correspondent had included a tourist brochure on current and future events in the city. He flipped through it idly, feeling surprisingly nostalgic about the place, when one small item caught his eye. It would normally have interested him about as much as a dissertation on yak hair, but his increasing feeling of unease linked with his current thoughts about the Hangman focused his mind.

The item said that Wednesday, May 20, was Geranium Day—the day chosen that year for all the good people of Bern to festoon their city with that particular flower. A sudden display of crimson.

The timing was too convenient for it to be merely a coincidence, and it fit precisely the Hangman's macabre sense of humor.

He unpacked the radio and called Kilmara. Sound quality was good, but the colonel wasn't available. Fitzduane decided that a message about geraniums passed through an intermediary would only serve to convince Kilmara that he had temporarily gone round the bend.

"Ask him to call me most urgent," he said. "Over and out."

"Affirmative," said Ranger headquarters.

Fitzduane went to help with the bed making. The Bear had phoned from the airport. He had brought his nurse with him—he hoped

Fitzduane wouldn't mind—and Andreas von Graffenlaub had an Israeli girlfriend in tow. They were waiting for Henssen and overnighting in Dublin, then planned to leave early and arrive on the island in time for lunch.

Fitzduane wondered if he had explained that his castle—as castles go—was really quite a small affair. The next unexpected guest was going to have to sleep with the horses.

THE EVENING WAS going splendidly, but try as he might, Fitzduane couldn't get into the right frame of mind to enjoy himself.

He smiled and laughed at the appropriate times, and even made a speech welcoming his guests that was received well enough, but Etan wasn't fooled. His reply that he was probably suffering from some kind of reaction to the whole Swiss affair didn't entirely satisfy her either, but she had Murrough's guest, Harry Noble, on her right to distract her and de Guevain flirting outrageously across the table, so Fitzduane was allowed to sit peacefully for a time, alone with his thoughts.

When dinner had reached the liqueur stage—by which time the fishing tales were growing ever more incredible—Fitzduane excused himself and retired to his study to try Kilmara again. This time he was patched through immediately. He was not reassured by the conversation that followed.

He was still staring into the fire when Etan came in. She sat on the floor in front of the fire and looked up at him.

"Tell me about it," she said.

He did, and this time he held nothing back. Her face was strained and silent when he finished.

FITZDUANE SLEPT fitfully and rose at dawn.

He rode for several hours around the island, trying to see if the landscape itself would yield some clue to the Hangman's intentions. A picture of idyllic peace and harmony greeted his eyes and made him doubt for a time the now-overwhelming feeling of foreboding.

The mist of dawn burned away in the sunlight, and it was shaping up to be a truly spectacular day. The sky was cloudless. The strong westerly had abated to the merest hint of a breeze. Washed by the recent rain, the air was clear and balmy. Insects buzzed, and birdcalls filled the air. Faced with this image of rural tranquillity, Fitzduane found it hard to anticipate what the Hangman could have in mind, and he wondered if he wasn't letting his imagination run away with him.

The obvious target was Draker, and given the Hangman's proclivities, the objective would be kidnapping. God knows—and the Hangman surely did—that the students' families were rich enough to make the game well worth playing.

There was some security now. Discreet lobbying by Kilmara meant that six armed plainclothes policemen had been temporarily assigned to the college. They lived in the main building and should be able to deal with any threat—or at least buy time until help could be summoned. The Achilles' heel of that arrangement was, of course, the length of time it would take to get assistance to the island. The location was isolated—none more so in Ireland—and it would be several hours at best before specialist help could arrive. The local police might get there sooner, but what they could do against terrorist firepower was another matter.

Fitzduane had suggested to Kilmara that the parents, if they were so rich, might be persuaded to finance some extra security. He hadn't been thinking when he made the suggestion. The facts of life were explained to him: If the parents received the slightest hint of danger, all the students would be whipped away back to Mommy and Daddy in Saudi or Dubai or Tokyo faster than a bribe vanishes into a politician's pocket. No students would mean no college, and no college would mean no income for the local community. Without proof to back up these vague theories of a threat, it was not a good suggestion; downright dumb, in fact.

The sea, often so gray and menacing, now presented an image of serenity. The color of the day was a perfect Mediterranean blue—a deceptive ploy, Fitzduane thought, since the temperature of the Atlantic waters, even at this time of year, was only a few degrees above freezing.

"All this peace and harmony is an illusion," he said to Pooka. "But how and when the shit is going to hit the fan is another matter." The horse didn't venture a reply. She went on chewing at a tuft of grass.

Smoke was trickling from the chimney of Murrough's cottage. He distracted Pooka from her snack and cantered toward the house. Murrough leaned over the half door as he drew near, and Fitzduane could smell bacon and eggs. He suddenly felt ravenously hungry.

"You're up bright and early," said Murrough. "What happened? Has Etan slung you out?"

Oona's face appeared over Murrough's shoulder. "Morning, Hugo," she said. "Don't mind the man—he's no manners. Come on in and have some breakfast."

Fitzduane dismounted. "I'm persuaded," he said. "I'll be in in a minute. I just want to pick Murrough's brains for a moment."

Oona grinned and vanished toward the kitchen. "Best of luck," she called over her shoulder.

Murrough opened the bottom half of the door and ambled out into the sunlight. "I must be dreaming," he said. "There's not a cloud in the sky."

"Murrough," said Fitzduane, "last night, when you were bringing me up-to-date on the local gossip, you mentioned that a plane had landed here recently. I didn't pay much heed at the time, but now I'm wondering if I heard you right. Did you mean that a plane landed on the mainland or right here on the island?"

Murrough took a deep breath of morning air and snapped his braces appreciatively. "Oh, not on the mainland," he said. "The feller put it down on this very island, on a stretch of road not far from the college, in fact."

"I didn't think there was room," said Fitzduane, "and the road is bumpy as hell."

"Well," said Murrough, "bumpy or not, the feller did it—several times, in fact. I went up to have a look and talked to the pilot. He was a pleasant enough chap for a foreigner. There were two passengers on board—relatives of a Draker student, he said."

"Remember the student's name?" said Fitzduane.

Murrough shook his head.

"What kind of plane was it?"

"A small enough yoke," said Murrough, "but with two engines. Sort of boxy-shaped. They use the same kind of thing to fly out to the Aran Islands."

"A Britten-Norman Islander," said Fitzduane. "A cross between a flying delivery van and a Jeep. I guess with the right pilot one of those could make it. They only need about four hundred yards of rough runway, sometimes less."

"Why so interested?" said Murrough.

"I'll tell you after we've eaten," answered Fitzduane. "I don't want to spoil your appetite." He followed Murrough into the cottage. Harry Noble was sitting at the pine table with his hands wrapped around a mug of tea.

"Good morning, Mr. Ambassador," said Fitzduane.

Harrison Noble's jaw dropped. "How on earth do you know that?" he said in astonishment.

Fitzduane sat down at the table and watched appreciatively as Oona poured him a cup of tea. "Friends in high places," he said.

Ambassador Noble nodded his head gloomily. He had enjoyed being incognito. Now a bunch of U.S. Embassy protocol officers would probably parachute in. So much for a quiet time fishing.

"I want to share a few thoughts with you," said Fitzduane, "which you may well find not the most cheerful things you've ever heard."

Oona brought the food to the table. "Eat up first," she said. "Worry can wait."

They ate, and then Fitzduane talked.

"Hmm," said the ambassador when he'd finished. "Do you mind if I'm blunt?"

"Not at all," said Fitzduane.

"Lots of gut feeling and not much fact," said the ambassador, "and your law enforcement authorities have been informed of your suspicions. It seems, on the face of it, most unlikely that anything at all will happen. You're probably jumpy because of your recent experiences in Switzerland."

Fitzduane nodded. "A reasonable reaction," he said, "but I run on instinct—and it rarely lets me down."

Murrough went to a cabinet and removed a bolt-action rifle equipped with a high-power telescopic sight. It was a .303 Mark IV Lee-Enfield customized for sniping, a version of the basic weapon of the Irish Army until it was replaced by the FN in the early sixties. He had used one just like it in combat in the Congo. He stripped down the weapon with practiced hands. Noble noticed that he didn't look at what he was doing, but his touch was sure.

"Mr. Noble," said Murrough, "sometimes we don't know how things work even though they do." He indicated Fitzduane. "I've known this man a long time, and I've fought with him—and I've been glad we were on the same side. I've learned it pays to listen to him. It's why I'm alive."

The ambassador looked at Murrough's weather-beaten face for

some little time. He smiled slightly. "Only a fool ignores the advice of an experienced gillie," he said. Murrough grinned.

The ambassador turned to Fitzduane. "Any ideas?" he asked.

"Some," said Fitzduane.

THE BEAR HAD to admit that his initial reaction to Ireland was—to put it mildly—not exactly favorable. The grim weather didn't help, of course, but it merely served to exacerbate his views. Even allowing for the depression induced by a cold wind and a sky the color of lead—it had been warm and sunny in Switzerland when they had left—the most charitable observer of Dublin (all he had seen of the country on that first evening) would have to agree that it was—he searched for the right word—"scruffy."

On the other hand, the city had a vitality and a bounce that were not so apparent in Bern. The streets were full of young people radiating disrespect and energy and a sense of fun, and the whole place reeked of tradition and a volatile and unsettled history. Some of the old buildings were still pocked with bullet marks from the rising against the British in 1916.

Their first evening out was marked by friendly and erratic service, excellent seafood, music that aroused emotions they didn't even know existed—and too much black beer and Irish coffee to drink.

They got to bed in the small hours and didn't breakfast until eight in the morning. The Bear woke up confused and decidedly unsure what a couple of weeks of Ireland was going to do to him. The others said they hadn't had so much fun in years. It was all decidedly un-Swiss.

When they drove onto the island, pausing by the bridge to look down at the Atlantic eating away at the cliffs below, Fitzduane's castle lay ahead of them against a backdrop of blue sky and shimmering ocean.

"Incredible!" said the Bear as they climbed out of the car to greet Fitzduane.

Fitzduane grinned. "You don't know the half of it."

"THE THOUGHT OCCURS to me," said Henssen, "that we don't actually have to do anything even if the Hangman does show up. We start off with two advantages: we're not the target, and we have a castle to hide away in. All we've got to do is drop the portcullis and then sit drinking poteen until the good guys arrive."

The Bear was outraged. "Typical German fence sitter," he said. "Leave a bunch of kids to a ruthless bastard like the Hangman. It's outrageous. You can't mean it."

"You've got a nerve talking about sitting on the fence," said Henssen cheerfully. "What else have the Swiss done for the last five hundred years except wait out the bad times eating Toblerone and then picking over the corpses?"

"Calm down, the pair of you," said Fitzduane. "Nothing may happen at all." The group fell silent. They were seated around the big oak table in the banqueting hall. The centuries-old table was immense. Its age-blackened surface could have accommodated more than three times as many as the twelve who were there now. They all looked at Fitzduane. "It's only a gut feel," he added.

The ambassador spoke. His son, Dick, had joined the group for lunch. The ambassador had no intention of letting him return to the college until this bizarre situation was resolved. A small voice privately wondered if he, the ambassador, could be on the Hangman's list. The head of the U.S. State Department's Office to Combat Terrorism would look good stuffed on the Hangman's wall.

He cleared his throat. "I speak as an outsider," he said, "and to me the evidence is not entirely convincing." There was a murmur of protest from several of the others. The ambassador held up his hand. "But," he continued, "most of the people here know you and seem to trust your instincts, so I say we stick together and do what we can. Better safe than sorry."

He looked around at the group. There were nods of agreement. "The next thing is to decide who does what," he said.

"Easy," said the Bear. "This isn't a situation for a democracy. It's Fitzduane's castle and Fitzduane's island—and he knows the Hangman best. Let him decide what to do."

"Makes sense," said Henssen.

"Looks like you're elected," said the ambassador. There was a chorus of agreement.

Fitzduane rose from the table and went to one of the slit windows set into the outer wall of the banqueting hall. It had been glazed, but the slim window was open, and a breeze off the sea blew in his face.

He could see a ship in the distance. It was a small freighter or a cattle boat—something like that. It was approaching the headland where the college was located. The weather was still superb. He wished he were out on Pooka with the sun warming his body and the wind in his face rather than preparing for what was to come. He went back to the table, and Etan caught his eye and smiled at him; he smiled back.

"There's one thing before we get to the specifics," he said to the group. "I can only tell you what I feel—and I feel that what is to come will be pretty bad." He looked at each face in turn. "Some of us may get killed. Now is the time if anyone wants to leave."

Nobody moved. Fitzduane waited. "Right, people," he said after an interval. "This is what we will do." He glanced at his watch as he spoke.

It was 3:17 P.M.—1517 in military time.

Chapter Twenty-five

ABOARD THE *SABINE*—1523 HOURS

Kadar held the clipboard in his left hand despite the discomfort, as if to convince himself that his hand was still intact. The physical pain was slight, and the wound was healing nicely, but the mental trauma was another matter. The sense of vulnerability induced by having had part of his body torn away remained as an undercurrent during all his waking hours.

The Irishman had been responsible. A shot from Fitzduane's pistol during those last frenetic few seconds in the studio had marred what had been otherwise a near-perfect escape. The round had smashed the third metacarpal bone of his left hand. Splinters protruding from the knuckle were all that had remained of his finger. He had been surprised. There had been no pain at first, and he had been able to follow his prearranged escape routine without difficulty— even managing the zippers and straps and buckles of his wet suit and aqualung with his customary speed.

The pain had hit when he emerged from the concealed chute into the icy green waters of the Aare. He had screamed and retched into the unyielding claustrophobia of his face mask. Just the memory made him feel queasy.

Fitzduane: he should have had that damned Irishman killed at the very beginning instead of letting Erika have her way. But to be truthful, it wasn't entirely Erika's fault. He had liked the man, been intrigued by him. Now he was paying the price. So much for the famed nobler side of one's character. It had cost him a finger.

Kadar looked at the polished brass chronometer on the wall. It was an antique case fitted with a modern mechanism—typical of the care that had gone into the design of the cattle boat.

The vessel was perfect for his purpose. Not only did it attract no attention, but it was clean and comfortable. To his surprise and relief, there was no smell. Evidently modern cattle, even on their way to a ritual throat cutting in Libya, expected—and received—every consideration. The parallels with his own operation did not escape him. There would be plenty of space and fresh air for his hostages. There would be none of the discomfort associated with an airplane hijack— heat and blocked toilets and no room to stretch your legs. No, the *Sabine*, with her excellent air-conditioning system and spacious enclosed cattle pens, seemed to have been purpose-built for a mass kidnapping. It would be equally effective for a mass execution.

Operation Geranium: it was the largest and most ambitious he had mounted. He would finish this phase of his career on a high note. The world's antiterrorist experts would have to do some serious rethinking after his pioneering work became known.

Kadar enjoyed planning, but the period just before an operation when all the preparation was complete was the time he enjoyed most. He savored the sense of a job well done combined with the anticipation of what was to come.

The trouble with most hijacks involving large numbers of hostages was that the terrorists started on the wrong foot and then all too quickly lost the initiative. The first problem was that there were never enough men involved. Even in the confined surroundings of an airplane, half a dozen fanatics had a hard time keeping hundreds of people under guard over an extended period. The most extreme terrorist still needed to eat and sleep and go to the bathroom. His attention wandered. He looked at pretty women when he should be on guard—and then bang! In came the stun grenades and all the other paraphernalia of the authorities, and—lo and behold—there was another martyr for the cause. Pretty fucking futile, in Kadar's opinion. The argument that the publicity alone justified an unsuccessful hijack didn't impress him one small bit.

Another common difficulty was that hijackers, forced to use easy-to-conceal weaponry like pistols and grenades, tended to be under-armed. In contrast, the forces of law and order, galvanized into action by the media and the weapons merchants, had invested in a massive array of antiterrorist gadgetry and weaponry. The scales had never been tilted more heavily against the terrorist. Counterterrorism had become a complete industry.

But even with the manpower and firepower issues left out of it, there still remained a key flaw in terrorist hijack tactics: the initiative, once the initial grab had taken place, passed almost completely to the authorities. The hijackers waited and sweated, and the authorities prevaricated and stonewalled. The only thing the terrorists could do was kill prisoners to demonstrate intent, but even that option was counterbalanced by that unwritten but well-known rule: Once the killing starts the assault forces go in, and too damn bad about the consequences. To make matters worse from a terrorist point of view, experience had shown that a specialist assault force could take out a hijack position with minimal casualties—most of the time. The Egyptians were the exception to that rule.

The final problem with hijacks was that either the terrorists didn't seem to know precisely what they wanted—Kadar, professional and Harvard man that he was, found this hard to swallow, but his research showed it was often the case—or what they demanded was obviously politically unacceptable or impossible. Often it was both.

It had to be admitted that unless you were a publicity hound—and Kadar was profit-oriented first and foremost, though he wasn't averse to a degree of media flirtation and had enjoyed his obituaries immensely—the hijack track record was not good.

"Room for improvement," as a schoolteacher would put it.

In Kadar's view, a fundamentally new approach was required—and Operation Geranium was the result.

FITZDUANE'S CASTLE—1555 HOURS

Fitzduane had phoned the police security detail at Draker College and, for good measure, had also spoken to the acting headmaster.

His concerns had been politely received but with thinly disguised incredulity. He didn't need to be psychic to know that he wasn't getting through. The sun continued to blaze in a cloudless sky. The idea of a serious threat in such an idyllic spot lacked credibility.

Sergeant Tommy Keane from the police station on the mainland had showed up on his bicycle and, after a private discussion with Fitzduane, had reluctantly agreed to stay around for the next few hours. It was too hot for fishing anyway. He'd try to sneak away in the evening. Meanwhile, he might as well keep an eye on what his eccentric friend was up to—and try to keep him out of trouble.

Fitzduane's little army now numbered thirteen. Eleven, including Fitzduane, reassembled in the great hall. Murrough and his wife were on the fighting platform of the tower. Armed with powerful binoculars, they could observe the bridge onto the island and much of the surrounding countryside with ease. Visibility was generally excellent, though a thin heat haze had sprung up and obscured details in the distance.

Fitzduane spoke. "Our first priority is to secure this castle, so I want you all to be thoroughly familiar with the physical layout, hence the guided tour. I'll go through it again now and explain how the defenses—if required—will work."

He turned to a large plan of the castle painted on wood and resting on an easel. It had been made nearly three hundred years earlier, and the colors were faded. His mind wandered for a moment to the many other occasions when Fitzduanes had assembled to ward off a threat. Most of the time they had been able to talk their way out of trouble. Somehow he didn't think that talk would be the answer this day.

"As you can see," he said, "the castle is situated on a low outcrop of rock bordered on two sides by the sea. The sea approach doesn't guarantee security against trained individuals, but any major assault would almost certainly have to be made from the landward side. Even when the tide is out, the rock is steep and covered with seaweed, so maneuvering a body of men on the seaward approaches is well-nigh impossible.

"I'm going to use the term *castle* for the whole walled-in area, but of course, the castle actually consists of several component parts, mostly built at different times. The cornerstone of the castle—and the part that was built first—is the sixty-foot-high square stone tower known as the keep. On the top of the keep is what is called the fighting platform. That is the open area protected by a parapet.

Under the fighting platform are five rooms, access to which is by the circular stone staircase. In all the rooms and on the stairs there are observation and firing points.

"Next to the keep and connected to it at second-floor level is the long rectangular building we are in, which is known as the great house. That was built when things were supposed to be getting more civilized around here but still with an eye on defense. It consists of three floors under a pitched roof. The top floor is this room and the kitchen. Underneath are bedrooms, and under those are stores and utility rooms. The outside wall of the great house is part of the perimeter and is defended by the sea access and the normal fighting points, and it is overlooked by the top stories of the keep. However, there are no battlements here, and the pitched roof is vulnerable to plunging fire.

"The rest of the castle consists of the courtyard area, called the bawn, enclosed by a twenty-foot-high perimeter wall. Battlements run the length of the wall, and under these are the stables, bakery, smithy, and other workshops. The weak point of the perimeter wall is, of course, the main gate, but that is defended by that small square tower, the gatehouse. The gate itself still has a working portcullis."

"What is a portcullis?" asked Andreas von Graffenlaub's Israeli girlfriend.

Fitzduane had learned that her family had been part of Dublin's Jewish community before emigrating to Israel. Her name was Judith Newman, and her looks were a strong argument in favor of making love and not war. She seemed quite unfazed by what was happening. Of course, she of all people would be used to terrorist threats. She came from a kibbutz near the Syrian border.

"It's the iron gate that looks like a grid. It rises and falls vertically. The idea is that it can be dropped in a hurry if any unfriendlies show up. There are spikes set into its base, so it's no fun if you are under it at the wrong time. It used to be operated by a big hand winch, but now there is an electric motor."

"But you can see through it," said Judith. "It's not solid."

"You can indeed see through it," said Fitzduane. "Which was partly the idea. It means you can also shoot through it. I imagine weight was also a consideration. A solid gate of that size would be impractical to raise and lower by hand on a routine basis."

"So the bawn could be swept by fire from outside?"

"The portcullis would stop much of it, because the metal bands are two inches wide with four-inch spacings, but yes, if the wooden gate were destroyed and only the portcullis were left, the bawn would be vulnerable to fire from outside. The solution is to move around on the battlements or to use the tunnel system."

"Tunnels," said the Bear.

"Tunnels," said Fitzduane. "They are one of the reasons the Fitzduanes survived over the centuries. There is a network under the castle."

"You should get into embassy design," said Ambassador Noble dryly.

ABOARD THE *SABINE*—1630 HOURS

The three unit commanders—code-named Malabar, Icarus, and Phantom (courtesy of Baudelaire)—trooped into the room and saluted. Kadar demanded obedience and discouraged familiarity. Insisting upon the details of military discipline helped create and maintain the austere professional atmosphere he preferred.

Two of the unit commanders, Malabar and Icarus, were Arabs; they wore checked keffiyehs and camouflage combat fatigues. The third commander, Phantom—a Sardinian called Giorgio Massana—had already changed into his wet suit.

"At ease," said Kadar. "Be seated."

The captain's quarters of the *Sabine* incorporated a dayroom of adequate size. The three commanders, already laden down with ammunition pouches and other combat equipment, squeezed with difficulty onto the padded bench seat that ran around two sides of the small conference table. They waited expectantly. They had been briefed extensively already, but Kadar, they knew, parted with information the way a python sheds its skin: there always seemed to be something new underneath.

Kadar referred to his clipboard unnecessarily to mask a twinge of pain. His left hand was now gloved, and a prosthetic finger disguised his disfigurement. The details of Operation Geranium had been worked out on a computer and had resulted in enough charts and plans to fill a book, but for now he wanted to cover only a few key points. He felt like a football coach before the big game. He despised speeches before battle, but he had to admit they were effective.

He consulted the chronometer and then spoke. "At 1730, the main staff at the college goes off duty. They leave in a minibus for their homes in and around the village and are always off the island by 1750 at the latest. That leaves behind in the college some fifty-eight students and a small night-duty faculty presence of three or four. The evening meal is served by the students themselves." He smiled. "There is also an armed guard of six men.

"The critical time window for our purposes is the period of daylight from 1750 to 2200 hours. There is still some light after that time but not much, and I consider it expedient to build in a margin. Our objective is to complete the first phase within that time window.

"At 1800 hours it is normal practice for all students and night faculty to gather in the assembly hall for what they call daily review. Accordingly 1800 hours is the pivotal implementation time for our operation. Just prior to that time a number of actions will take place.

"All communication to and from the island will be severed. Telephone and telex lines will be cut. The bridge will be blown up in such a manner as to make it look like an accident. Any radios will be destroyed.

"A small group of students aided by one faculty member, all members of the cult of the Sacrificers"—he smiled again—"will kill the police security guards and will seize the students and faculty members as they are gathered together.

"Elements of Phantom in a Pilatus Britten-Norman Islander, a small twin-engine aircraft with short takeoff and landing properties, will land on the road near the college. Further elements of Phantom Unit will assault Fitzduane's castle and eliminate the occupants.

"With the beachhead secured by Phantom Unit and their young friends, the balance of the assault force, Malabar and Icarus units, will board the high-speed inflatables as rehearsed, land, and take up position as planned. By 1830 hours at the latest, all our forces will be ashore with their objectives secured, and the island will be entirely in our hands—and no one on the mainland will be any the wiser.

"No later than 1900 hours, but with the margin built into the time window as discussed, the Islander aircraft, which is equipped with integral wingtip fuel tanks and long-range underwing fuel tanks giving it a range of fifteen hundred nautical miles, will take off again, carrying two rather special hostages.

"We shall have all night to prepare our positions in the college, with particular emphasis on laying explosives in such a way that it will be quite impossible for the government authorities even to contemplate an assault without guaranteeing the deaths of all the hostages. And all we are asking for is money—a politically quite acceptable commodity to part with and one not in short supply if one's children are involved."

He paused and drank some mineral water. "And of course, the whereabouts of two of the hostages will not even be known. A little extra surprise for our friends. Their father is a key figure in the present Middle East peace talks. He is a friend of the U.S. President. There is no way the Irish will risk the consequences of their deaths. The Irish government will give in, and the parents will pay; the whole exercise will take place out of sight of the world media, so there will be no problem with loss of face for anyone. Our friends in Libya have agreed to act as intermediaries.

"There is a tendency in hostage situations for the authorities to drag out the negotiations in the belief that the kidnappers—us in this case—will not carry out their threats to kill their victims. As a matter of fact, hijackers have a track record of bluffing much and killing little, so the approach of the authorities would seem to be justified. In this case, it is essential that we convince the Irish government and the parents that we are deadly serious. To that end the faculty and ten students—those with less affluent parents and of no political significance, naturally—will be killed immediately. The executions will be photographed and videotaped. Arrangements have been made to radio photographs to our agents so that the parents of the surviving students will be in no doubt from the beginning as to our intent. The video will travel in the Islander, and copies of it will be issued subsequently, if necessary.

"You will note that we are contacting both the parents and the Irish authorities simultaneously. This is to prevent the authorities from endeavoring to resolve matters on their own and to exert the maximum pressure in the shortest possible time. Further, we have made sure that both parents in every case will be informed.

"The protocols regarding details of payments and so on have already been drawn up and are with our intermediaries in Libya. They will supervise our withdrawal from the island on a government-to-government basis. It won't be the first time they have performed such a role. They rather enjoy appearing as honest brokers in these situations.

"When the bridge has been replaced by the Irish authorities—a matter of hours using a military structure—the force will depart from the island in a bus convoy and will travel to Shannon Airport, where a Libyan jet will fly us to safety. The hostages will travel with us. They will fly with us to Libya and be released on arrival"—he paused and smiled enigmatically—"unless, of course, I come up with a more entertaining notion."

Kadar looked at the unit commanders. "Any questions?"

There was silence at first. The commanders were confident, forceful men, but Kadar awed them. He was brilliant, he was violent, and he was unpredictable—but he rewarded results. Experience had shown that blind obedience was the best policy most of the time. Questions were not normally expected, but Kadar seemed to want to talk. He was justifiably enthusiastic, almost euphoric; it was a thorough plan, and all three commanders were convinced it would work.

The commander of Phantom Unit spoke first. "The next couple of hours will be critical. Is there any chance of interference from the Irish Navy or these people that I have heard so much about, the Rangers?"

Kadar was amused. He was conscious that he was showing off a little, but he was enjoying his minor moment of glory. It was no more than his due. It was unarguable: his planning had anticipated everything.

"The Irish have over three thousand kilometers of coastline to guard," he said, "and only four ships to do the entire job. The chance of a naval service ship turning up at the wrong moment is statistically most improbable. However"—he paused for effect—"arrangements have been made to divert the one ship on duty on the Atlantic coast. The primary task of the Irish Navy is fishery protection. An anonymous tip has decoyed the vessel *Eimer* to chase a fleet of Spanish fishing boats fishing illegally off the Kerry coast."

"And the Rangers?" said the Phantom Unit commander.

This time Kadar laughed outright. "They could have been a problem, but they have responded magnificently to a diversion we have prearranged in Dublin." He looked at his men. "They think we are mounting an operation against the American Embassy, and they are defending it in depth."

"So there is nothing to stop us," said the Icarus Unit commander.

"Nothing," said Kadar. He felt a sudden twinge in his hand. His missing finger throbbed. "Nothing."

FITZDUANE'S CASTLE—1645 HOURS

Fitzduane disliked talking about the tunnel system; it was the hidden card in Fitzduane family history. In this case, however, he felt he had no choice but to reveal part of what lay underneath the castle; still, he confined his tour to the upper level. Access in this case was from the ground floor of the tower.

Fitzduane flicked a switch as they passed through the concealed door. A ramp sloped down to a passage with a vaulted roof. He motioned the others to follow him. The passage ran straight to the gatehouse across the bawn. A circular staircase wound its way to the second-floor level. They emerged in the windlass room, from where the portcullis was controlled. Murder holes and firing apertures allowed the guards to control both the entrance below and access to the gate.

He led the group back into the tunnel. "Now you know how to get from the keep to the gatehouse without having your ass shot off. That's the good news. The bad news would be the discovery of that tunnel by the other side. It can be blocked from the keep—a heavy iron door slides into place—but how long that would stand up to high explosives is another matter. Swords and lances were more the thing when this was built."

De Guevain was looking around curiously. "How was the tunnel constructed? From the outside the castle looks as if it were built on a solid block of granite, and the sea is so close. I'd guess we are near to being below sea level."

Fitzduane smiled. "We are below sea level when the tide is in, but there is nothing to worry about. It's the very geology of this location that made my ancestors settle here. What appears to be a solid block of granite is, in fact, more like a doughnut in shape. The possibilities of that were obvious. The family has been digging on and off ever since."

"You, too?" asked the Bear.

"I don't like tunnels." Fitzduane walked on toward a heavy metal-shod door. The key turned silently. "This is the armory." He beckoned the group to enter the room. He switched on the main lights when all were inside.

There were expressions of surprise. Swords, knives, battle-axes,

maces, pikes, bows and arrows, armor, muskets—hand weapons of
every type lined the room from floor to ceiling or stood in racks.

"Incredible!" exclaimed de Guevain. "This collection must be
priceless."

"It used to be bigger," said Fitzduane, "but some of the finer
pieces were sold by my grandfather to ease his later years."

"Where do they come from? And why so many?" asked Henssen.

"A castle is first and foremost a fighting machine," said Fitzduane,
"and most of the weapons you see here belong to the castle's own
armory. Over the centuries techniques and weapons changed, and
the family modernized but without, as you can see, throwing much
away. They were a thrifty lot."

"There's nothing more modern here than a Brown Bess musket,"
said Ambassador Noble. "And though they were fine for Waterloo,
I don't see how they'd rate against the kind of firepower today's
terrorists carry."

Fitzduane nodded. He crossed the room and worked a mechanism. A section of racking slid away to reveal a door. He opened it
and led them through. This room was smaller, though still good-
sized. It was painted white and was brightly lit. Tools, power equipment, and workbenches took up most of one wall. Wooden racks
containing late-nineteenth- and twentieth-century weapons took up
most of another wall, and four long boxes lay open on the floor.
There was a waist-high work surface in the center of the room with a
series of firearms laid out on it.

"Now that's more like it." De Guevain held up an M-16. "Where
did you get this?"

"Vietnam."

"And this?" said Noble, indicating an AK-47 Kalashnikov assault
rifle.

"Lebanon."

"And this?" The Bear held up a long-barreled broom handle
Mauser pistol; a wooden shoulder stock was attached.

Fitzduane laughed. "A bit before my time. That's a souvenir of the
War of Independence—Ireland's independence, that is. It's a relatively unusual nine-millimeter Parabellum version."

"And these?" asked Andreas von Graffenlaub. He was pointing at
one of the open boxes. Fitzduane went over and extracted a weapon,
a short, stocky-looking automatic rifle with the magazine fitted
behind the trigger guard instead of in the traditional in-front posi-

tion. A compact telescopic sight was clipped to a bracket above the receiver.

"I'd better explain," said Fitzduane. He spoke very briefly about Kilmara and the Rangers. He then continued. "So I've got some firepower on loan, though not enough for all of us. This"—he held up the automatic rifle—"is the new Enfield SA-80 automatic rifle that has been adopted by the British Army. It's what they call a bullpup design. Having the magazine behind the trigger guard makes for a thirty percent shorter weapon for the same barrel length; it's easier to maneuver in a confined space." He pointed at the telescopic sight. "And with its four-power magnification sight, you've got one of the most accurate combat assault weapons yet made. Mind you, at nearly eleven pounds fully loaded, it's a heavy bugger for its size, but that pays dividends when you're firing on full auto. You can control this gun.

"In terms of modern weapons, we've got four SA-80 rifles, four nine-millimeter Browning automatic pistols, a Hawk grenade launcher, grenades, and some other equipment, including Claymore directional mines. That sounds impressive until you realize what we may be up against. The opposition will have automatic weapons, too, and there may be far more of them." He didn't add that in the main, they would be younger, fitter, and more recently trained.

There was silence in the room. The sight of the modern weaponry—not some collector's curiosity piece to hang on a wall or to show to friends after dinner—had a chilling effect.

RANGER HEADQUARTERS, DUBLIN—1708 HOURS

Kilmara put down the phone. The red light indicating that the scrambler was active was extinguished. He shrugged. "I've just been talking to the sergeant in charge of the security detail at Draker. It's a beautiful day. All the students are doing whatever students in the middle of nowhere do—and two of his men sat out in the sun too long and have gone bright red."

"Sounds like a rough detail," said Günther. "What about Fitzduane?"

"I was talking to him, too. He remains convinced something is going to happen on the basis of no proof at all. He's organized that

castle of his as if Geronimo were on the prowl—and he now intends
to go over to Draker to give a hand. With our luck these days the
guards on duty there will think some of Fitzduane's people are
terrorists and they'll all shoot each other."

"How many people has he got?"

"Around a dozen, including himself," said Kilmara, "of which no
fewer than nine have some kind of military training. I'm beginning to
wonder if I did the right thing giving him that weaponry."

"You think it's a false alarm," said Günther.

Kilmara stared grumpily at nothing in particular. "That's the trouble. I don't—but that's pure instinct and faith in Fitzduane's vibes.
The evidence says that the action is going to be here in Dublin. My
guts tell me we've got our people watching the wrong mouseholes."

"Despite the Japanese? Or the seventy-two Middle Eastern travel
agents—who the Irish Tourist Board had never heard of until the
agents approached them—flying in tonight?"

"Despite everything," said Kilmara. "I've been thinking. I don't
believe the Hangman gives a fuck about politics. Why would he want
to hit the U.S. Embassy? What's in it for him? He's a bottom-line
man."

"The Hangman's dead," declared Günther.

"Don't talk like a bureaucrat."

Günther grinned. "The rescheduling is finished."

"So what have we got apart from an over-budget overtime bill?"
said Kilmara.

"For starters, we've got far too many people tied up on this
embassy thing. It's ridiculous."

"It's politics, but don't tell me what I know already. I want to
know what kind of unit we can field as a reserve now we've done our
computer games."

"About a dozen," said Günther, "and of course, there is you—
and me."

"That's not so crazy. I'm fed up sitting behind a desk."

"The helicopter situation is not good," reported Günther. "All
the Air Corps machines are assigned to cover the embassy, the
ambassador's residence in Phoenix Park, and the airport, and anyway, they're all going to be grounded at dusk. I wish we had night-
flying capability."

"Road would take five to six hours," mused Kilmara.

"More like six," said Günther, "if we're talking about Fitzduane's

Island. The roads are terrible once you get past Galway, and at that point we'd be driving at night with heavily loaded vehicles."

"And that bridge on to the island is all too easy to cut," said Kilmara. "If we're going to do it, we'll have to do it by air."

He sat in thought for several minutes. On the face of it, his existing deployment was correct. There had been clear evidence of a threat to the U.S. Embassy in Dublin. The arrival of the Japanese—two of whom had already been identified as being associated with militant terrorist groups—confirmed that threat. Monitored conversations indicated that the Japanese were the advance guard and would link up with a substantial group that was flying in late that night under the cover of a convention of travel agents from the Middle East. The Irish Tourist Board, which would normally have been actively involved in such a visit, had merely been informed at the last minute—an irregular procedure—so it really did look as if the terrorist threat were about to become a reality. He could pick up the Japanese now, but he had no line on the weaponry involved, and it made much more sense to wait until that, too, could be identified.

All very fine, but an all-too-predictable response. His instincts screamed "setup," but even if it was a diversion, he knew that the Hangman—if it was indeed him—was sufficiently ruthless to make the diversion a reality in its own right.

Even with the Hangman out of the picture, there were other possible threats to be considered. At all times the Rangers should have a reserve ready to deploy. The root problem at the moment was the way in which the Rangers were being used. Instead of being deployed as a reaction force in the specific antiterrorist role for which they were trained, they had been pushed to the front to handle something that should have been given to the police and the regular army.

Reluctantly he came to a decision. "Günther, there is nothing more we can do for Fitzduane right now except monitor the situation and put the reserve on standby at Baldonnel. Sending them across by road is out. The facts that the Hangman is obsessed with flowers and that Fitzduane has funny feelings are not good enough reasons for me to lose my reserve."

Günther rose to his feet. "Fair enough."

"Hold it," said Kilmara. "I haven't finished. If we do have to move, we'll have to do it very fucking fast—and we may be up against heavier firepower than we're used to. I want the Optica armed and the unit to be in heavy battle order."

"The Milan, too?"

"The whole thing. And I'll command from the Optica."

"And what about me?"

"You like jumping out of airplanes. Why miss a good opportunity?"

"This is a fun job," said Günther as he left the room.

"It changes as you get older," said Kilmara to himself. "Your friends get killed."

FITZDUANE'S CASTLE—1715 HOURS

The heat haze had increased. Murrough handed Fitzduane the binoculars. Fitzduane stared at the distant spot indicated by Murrough for about thirty seconds, then lowered the glasses.

"Hard to tell," he said. "Visibility at that distance isn't so good. All I can make out is a blur; most of it is cut off by the headland. Some kind of freighter, I suppose." He turned toward Murrough. "There have been boats passing in the distance every hour or so all day. What's unusual about this one?"

Murrough took back the binoculars and had another brief look. "The haze has got worse all right. I should have called you earlier. It's hard to be absolutely sure, but I think our friend over there has been stopped for a while."

"How long?"

"About twenty minutes. I can't be certain."

"Which way did it come? Did you get a look at it earlier?"

"From the south," said Murrough. "It was far out and moving slowly. It's a cattle boat, one of those new jobs with the high superstructure and lots of ventilators like mushrooms on the top."

"How big are those things?"

"I don't know exactly. But big enough to hold over a thousand cattle and all their feed. Maybe the boat's stopped to feed the cattle."

Fitzduane lifted the binoculars to his eyes again and commenced a 360-degree sweep. It was the same boat he'd seen earlier in the afternoon. He continued sweeping and stopped with the glasses pointing at the bridge. A station wagon crossed over it onto the island and pulled to the side of the road. Two men got out and looked around. He passed the binoculars to Murrough.

"Fishermen," said Murrough. "I can see fishing rod cases, and they're wearing fishing gear."

"But what do fishermen use ropes for?" said Fitzduane. Retrieving the binoculars, he watched one of the men lower the other below the bridge supports. The man then lowered a bulky package. He opened his fishing rod case and extracted something. When he clipped into place a bulky banana-shaped object, there was no longer any doubt as to what he was holding.

"Christ!" shouted Fitzduane. "He's got an AK-47. I'll bet even money the fuckers are going to blow the bridge."

Murrough brought his sniper's rifle to his shoulder and took aim. The man under the bridge scrambled up the rope, and both men ran for cover. There was a dull explosion and a small puff of dust, and smoke and debris flew into the air. The bridge didn't appear to move.

"They made a balls of it," said Murrough. He choked on his words when the bridge suddenly collapsed at the island end and the whole structure slid down into the sea. The two saboteurs rose from cover and went to review their handiwork. They stood by the cliff edge and looked down. Then one of them turned and began examining the castle through binoculars. Seconds later he gesticulated and brought his AK-47 up to the point of aim. The muzzle faced the keep and winked flame. A burst of automatic fire gouged the ancient stonework.

Fitzduane and Murrough fired at the same time. There was little kick from the SA-80; the weapon was as accurate as promised. Both terrorists died before they hit the submerged debris of the bridge. The spume of the sea turned momentarily pink.

"Show time," said Fitzduane. "Stay here. I'll send someone to relieve you in a couple of minutes; then I want you down in the bawn. We're going to retrieve that station wagon and go calling."

His walkie-talkie crackled. "Get down to the study," said a voice strained with tension.

Fitzduane slung the SA-80 and headed down the circular stairs. The study door was open. Etan was slumped in a chair looking dazed, a bloody cloth pressed to the side of her head. The radio given to him by Kilmara had been smashed into pieces. It was irreparable. Ambassador Noble stood just inside the door with a Browning automatic in one hand and a walkie-talkie in the other. He was ashen gray with shock. He was staring at a figure that lay sprawled on the ground facedown. A knife of an unusual design lay by the dead body's hand.

Fitzduane turned the body onto its back. A grotesque wolf mask stared up at him. The shirt below was matted with blood where several rounds had struck.

Ambassador Noble spoke dully. "I heard Etan scream and saw this dreadful figure strike her and then turn to attack me. He had a knife, so I fired instinctively." As Fitzduane pulled off the mask, Noble fell to his knees. "Oh, my God," he said. "What have I done?" He took his son's body in his arms, and tears streamed down his cheeks.

There was silence in the room. Then Fitzduane spoke. "It's not your fault. There was nothing else you could do."

Harry Noble stared at him blankly. "Dick belonged to this cult you spoke about," he said, his voice flat.

"So it seems. This is the way the Hangman operates. He corrupts and manipulates, and young people are always the easiest to manipulate. I'm sorry." There was nothing else he could say.

Noble bent down by his son again and kissed him, then picked up his Browning and looked at Fitzduane. "I shouldn't have doubted you. Whatever has to be done, let's do it."

Etan sobbed without tears, and Fitzduane held her in his arms. Soon she was quiet. "So it's really going to happen," she said.

"Yes," said Fitzduane.

The Bear stood in the doorway. "The phone is dead," he informed them, "and the electricity is out. We're trying to get the generator going now."

"There's a knack," said Fitzduane. He felt more than heard a faint throbbing sound as the big diesel cut in. The lamp on the study desk came on.

"There are only twelve of us now," said Etan.

"It'll do," said the Bear.

DRAKER COLLEGE—1745 HOURS

Pat Brogan, the sergeant in charge of the security detail at the college, always looked forward to the departure of the staff minibus. There was a rotating element in the catering and cleaning staff that could permit some dangerous person to infiltrate, and in any case they were just more bodies around to keep an eye on. After the bus left, he had only the students and a few known faculty members to consider, and he felt he could relax.

All in all, it was a pretty good assignment, he thought, if a trifle boring. They had comfortable private rooms—not barracks smelling of sweat and socks like up on the border—and a study had been set aside where they could lounge in easy chairs, watching television or making tea or whatever. The college had thoughtfully provided a fridge for milk, which the guards kept well stocked with beer, and it was a cold beer he had in mind as he handed over to the evening shift.

It had been a long, hot, glorious day, and all was well with his world except that his face was brick red from too much sun. He had read somewhere that pale Irish skins were especially vulnerable to the sun: not enough pigmentation or something. Apparently redheads had the worst time. To judge by O'Malley's state, it was all too true.

He snapped the magazine out of his Uzi submachine gun as he entered the rest room and put the weapon in the arms locker. He kept the .38 Smith & Wesson revolver he wore in a Canadian-made pivot shoulder holster. Orders were to be armed at all times, even when off duty, and wearing a handgun was now as routine to him as wearing a shirt.

The television was on, and the chairs were in their accustomed positions facing it. He knew he'd find the three other off-duty guards already comfortably dug in. He hoped they hadn't made too much of a dent in the beer. The hot day had encouraged the stock to shrink as the hours passed. He took a can of beer from the fridge, noting subconsciously that some kind soul seemed to have replenished the drink supply. The unit was practically full.

Normally he would have popped the can immediately and taken a long swallow before going to his chair, which was situated, as befitted his seniority, in the center of the row directly facing the screen. But this time an item on the television caught his attention. Unopened can in hand, he went to his chair.

The smell of beer and some other odor was strong as he approached the row of seats. Some sod has puked, he thought, suddenly annoyed at this breakdown of self-control and discipline. People should be able to draw the line between making life comfortable and being downright careless. He looked to see which stupid fucker was responsible, and froze.

All three guards were sprawled in unnatural positions in their chairs, their faces twisted and distorted in a record of their last agonizing moments. Vomit stained their clothes. The beer can in O'Malley's hand had been twisted into an almost unrecognizable shape in the last few seconds of horror before death won out.

Gripped by fear, Brogan stumbled backward, knocking the television set to the ground in a cascade of sparks and broken glass. A figure with the head of an animal stood in the doorway. Brogan's thoughts went to rumors he had heard when he first came on the job. "Students playing games," he had been told. "Keep an eye on them, but don't make too much of it."

Holy Mother of God, he thought, some games!

"Aren't you curious?" whispered the figure in the doorway. "Professionally curious, I mean. Don't you want to know what killed them?"

The figure moved forward into the room, holding a knife in one hand. Brogan reached for his revolver, but a second figure stood in the doorway with an Ingram submachine gun in its hands. A burst of fire smashed into the wall beside him. The gun made little noise. He could see the bulky silencer fitted to the otherwise compact weapon. His revolver had only just cleared the holster. He dropped it onto the floor and slowly raised his hands. He realized that he had never truly believed there was any threat to the college—nor, it seemed, to judge by the tone of the briefing, had his superiors. Terrorist attacks were a media event, something for the television news. They didn't happen to real people. The figure with the knife spoke again. It had moved around to Brogan's right. It was close.

"We used cyanide. Not terribly original, but you must admit it works, and it's quick, though I'm afraid you can't say it's painless. Injecting the cyanide into unopened beer cans took some practice"— there was amusement in the voice—"but I think you'll agree we mastered the art."

Brogan tried to speak, but his mouth was dry. The figure laughed. "Afraid, aren't you? Afraid of a bunch of kids. That's how you thought of us, wasn't it? Very shortsighted. The average age of our band is nineteen: old enough to vote, to join the army, to kill for our country. Old enough to kill for ourselves. You really should have taken us more seriously. You did find out about us, didn't you? We read your briefing files. Your security was atrocious. You thought only of an external threat and even then did not take that seriously."

"Why didn't you shoot me?"

"You've no imagination," said the figure. It thrust the knife under Brogan's rib cage into the thoracic cavity and watched him drown in his own blood.

Another figure appeared in the doorway. "We got both of them."

"Any noise?" said the figure with the knife. He was pleased that it had all gone so smoothly. They had killed six armed men without a shot being fired against them. The remaining faculty and students had assembled for daily review. The entire college would be theirs in a few minutes. Kadar and his force would arrive to find the job already done. He'd be pleased. He rewarded success on the same scale that he punished failure. And if Dick had done well at the castle on the other end of the island . . .

"None," said the newcomer. "They both drank the tea we brought them."

"Five out of six with cyanide," said the figure with the knife. "Who called it right?" He was referring to the pool they had organized among themselves. There were ten Irish pounds riding on the result.

"I did," said the figure with the Ingram.

Brogan's death throes provided a background to their conversation. His head and torso rose from the ground, and blood gushed from his mouth as he died. The body collapsed.

"Let's take them," said the one with the knife. He removed Brogan's locker key and opened up the arms locker. He loaded an Uzi and put spare clips in his pockets.

FITZDUANE'S CASTLE—1746 HOURS

Fitzduane—no sexist by most standards—had always had the strongest objections to women being put on the firing line. Seeing dead women in a dozen wars, often leaving orphaned children sometimes still being suckled, had hardened these views. In this case, however, more than a third of his little force was female, and that element was not prepared to be placed in a cellar out of danger. He also had to admit that like it or not, he needed the extra manpower: the word *personpower* stuck in his throat.

He compromised on the basis of training and experience. He wasn't entirely happy with the result. Katia Maurer was no problem. As a nurse she had a clear role, and a medical facility was established in one of the empty storerooms in the tunnel complex. The Bear was visibly relieved. Oona was the logical person to take charge of the meals. She knew the castle and the location of all the supplies. She got organized in the kitchens off the great hall.

The Israeli girl, Judith Newman, shot so competently in the target practice they had arranged in the main tunnel (wearing earplugs against the deafening noise), and it was so clear that she wanted a combat role—and had the experience to back it up—that he assigned her along with Murrough, de Guevain, Andreas von Graffenlaub, and Henssen to go with him to Draker.

That left Etan, inexperienced but determined to fight if she had to. The only consoling fact was that under the Bear's expert eye, she had begun to shoot well. Despite the need for combatants, Fitzduane had tried to dissuade her from active involvement. He had pulled her away from the others and had closed the door of his study, and for a few intense minutes he had argued with her. She had waited until he finished, put her arms around his neck, and kissed him gently. Then she had looked into his eyes. "This isn't the Congo," she had said. "I'm not Anne-Marie. It's going to be all right."

Fitzduane had started at the mention of his dead wife's name, and then his arms had tightened around her and he had hugged her to him and held her until called away.

Apart from Tommy Keane, who had relieved Murrough on the fighting platform, the entire party had assembled in the bawn. Everyone's clothes reeked of burned propellant and gun oil from target practice in the tunnel—Fitzduane wanted the existence of their weapons to remain a surprise—and everyone, including Katia Maurer and Oona, he noticed, was armed. He had made them all look at Dick Noble's body. He could see from their expressions that the reality of their predicament was beginning to sink home.

"I don't like splitting our group," said Fitzduane, "but our phones are down and our long-distance radio has been destroyed, and we've got to try to do something about those kids. Several of us here have already had experience of the opposition we're up against, and they are not the kind of people you negotiate with. They don't bluff; they kill. If we don't get to the students before they do, there will be no good ending.

"Draker is too big and sprawling; it's indefensible. My intention now is to head over there and bring the kids and the few faculty members back to the castle, and then hole up until help comes. We can hold out here for an adequate time—that's what a castle is all about—and it's a plan I've already discussed with Colonel Kilmara of the Rangers.

"I don't know what the Hangman's plan is, but I would guess his objective is a mass kidnap for money. Intelligence reports indicate that he has trained a force of seventy or so, and I'd venture that most of them are going to land from that cattle boat at the headland. Some may have come overland as well, I don't know. And there may be a plane involved in this thing. The point is that we are going to be pitted against a superior force with superior training and firepower. That means we don't fuck around. I want no heroics or thoughts about the Geneva Convention. This isn't war. It's a fight for survival. We kill or we get killed—and no prisoners unless I order it. We can't afford the manpower to guard them.

"If possible, I'm not going to use the students in this fight. I'm sure some of them have weapons training, but unfortunately we don't know who we can trust, as our recent tragedy so clearly shows. Besides, whether they are old enough to vote or whatever, I'm fed up with seeing kids who've had no chance to live getting killed. Keep one thing in mind: no strange faces. If the face isn't one of ours, shoot it. If you've any questions, they'll have to wait. Get to your posts. Draker team, mount up. Let's get the fuck out of here."

Fitzduane and de Guevain got into the front of the saboteurs' station wagon, and the other four members of the group squeezed themselves flat in the back. Etan blew Fitzduane a kiss through the window. He almost seemed, she couldn't help noticing, to be smiling. The son of a bitch, she thought. Of course, danger is what this man is used to; putting himself in harm's way is what he does. War is what he is good at.

How will I react to danger? she wondered. The next few hours would tell. The image of the death of red-haired Anne-Marie Fitzduane in the Congo nearly two decades earlier came to her, and it was as clear as if she had been there. Death by decapitation. She imagined the blade cutting into her flesh and the shock and the agony and her blood fountaining, and she felt sick with fear and horror. Would this be her fate? She caressed the wooden stock of the Mauser she had been issued and resolved that it would not. She felt the adrenaline flow, and with it, courage.

Chapter Twenty-six

The frogmen of Phantom Unit had trained in the relatively balmy, if polluted, waters of the Mediterranean. Although they had been warned otherwise, the clear skies and hot sun of that unusual Irish day had lulled them into a false sense of familiarity with their environment. It could almost have been the Mediterranean. The unpleasant reality of the near-freezing temperatures of the Atlantic came as a shock despite the wet suits all four men wore. As the long swim progressed, the cold sapped the energies of the men, and their responses slowed. They would make it, thought Giorgio Massana, Phantom Unit commander, but at a price.

Spare tanks of compressed air and other specialized equipment traveled with them on a battery-powered underwater sled called a SeaMule. The SeaMule was capable of pulling two men in addition to its normal load, but there was a penalty to be paid in terms of battery life, and the lack of physical activity as one was towed meant body warmth drained away faster. Massana allowed only one man to be towed at a time, and then only for brief periods. He had had batteries cut out on him before, and he needed that equipment if he was to get

425

into the castle. There was no way they could pull the SeaMule by themselves.

They had swum from the *Sabine*, which was anchored off the headland. Nearing the coastline they encountered shoals of seaweed dislodged by recent storms, which in turn hid numerous submerged rocks. They had to proceed with the utmost care, and their progress was labored. Maneuvering the SeaMule through this underwater obstacle course was both difficult and exhausting.

It cost them the life of one man. Alonzo, a fellow Sardinian and the best swimmer in the group, was smashed into a kelp-disguised rock when the undertow threw the sled temporarily out of control. There was no discernible noise and little blood, but the skull of the one person in the world whom Massana really cared about was crushed effortlessly as the Atlantic flexed its muscles. They left Alonzo floating semi-invisible in the seaweed. In his black wet suit he already looked like part of the undersea world. The undertow smashed him again and again against the rocks, and brain matter leached from the ripped hood.

They came ashore on seaweed-covered rocks with the gray mass of Fitzduane's castle above them. Near invisible against the rocks in their black suits, they rested for a couple of minutes. As he gathered his strength, Massana wondered why a seaborne assault by a specialized group was necessary against only three or four unarmed civilians who would certainly not be expecting an attack. He had been briefed on the likely presence of a Hugo Fitzduane and two people who worked for him in various capacities and who were sometimes in the castle. A radio report from Draker had warned that there might be some guests. To Massana, such targets were scarcely worthy of his team's special skills. They certainly weren't worth losing Alonzo for. He felt a sudden hatred for Kadar; then his training reasserted itself. He signaled his two companions to move. They unpacked the assault equipment.

Three rubber-coated grapnels trailing ropes hissed from their compressed carbon dioxide–powered launchers and lodged inside the castle defenses. Massana and one other frogman began to climb. The third frogman, a silenced Ingram at the ready, surveyed the keep and battlements, ready to lay down suppressing fire.

Massana reached an aperture in the battlements and vanished from view, closely followed by the second frogman. A hand beckoned.

The third frogman, who would now be covered by the first two, slung his Ingram and began to climb.

Bloodlust rose in him as he relived past kills and anticipated the shedding of more blood in the imminent future. There was nothing so exciting as the taking of human life. He reached the battlements and dropped between two crenellations to land in a crouch on the parapet. He moved to unsling his weapon and at the same time checked his surroundings.

Massana and the second frogman lay in pools of blood to his left. A distinguished-looking man in a fishing jacket with a bloodied sword in his hand stood over them. Too late the third frogman realized that the cuff on the hand he had seen had been dark brown and not black. He almost had the Ingram in firing position when the point of a halberd emerged from his chest.

The Bear looked at the dead frogman. "Any more?" he asked Noble.

Noble stood there with a bloody katana—a Japanese samurai sword from Fitzduane's collection—in his hands, impressed at the power of the weapon and the simplicity with which it killed. "Not for the moment."

The Bear put his foot on the frogman and wrenched the halberd free. It took effort. He had thrust with all his force. He waited for a few moments to get his breath back before he spoke.

"They've got some kind of powered platform down there," he said. "I'd like to check it out, but it would be wiser not to until the others get back."

Noble nodded in agreement. He was staring at his bloodstained hands as if mesmerized. "I've been involved in the antiterrorism business for years," he said, "but it's all been theory. Reports, papers, meetings, seminars—none of them prepares you for this." He gestured toward the crumpled bodies.

"They'd have killed you if you'd hesitated," said the Bear. "Believe me."

"I do."

The Bear looked over in the direction of Draker. "I wonder how Fitzduane and the team are getting on."

ABOARD THE *SABINE*—1806 HOURS

Kadar stood on the "monkey island," the small open deck on the roof of the *Sabine*'s enclosed bridge, which represented the best observation point on the boat, short of climbing the three-legged radio mast rising above him. He was looking through powerful tripod-mounted naval binoculars. He could see the aircraft but not yet hear it. As it flew closer, he made a positive identification. It was the Islander carrying the airborne Phantom Unit—Phantom Air.

Ziegle, his radio operator, who was wearing a Russian back-mounted military radio, confirmed it: "Phantom Air reporting in, sir. They say that the bridge has been blown. The bridge unit seems to be on the way to Draker by vehicle as arranged. They want to know if they should land immediately."

"Any news from Phantom Sea?"

"They reported arriving at the base of the castle," said Ziegle, "but nothing since then. The signal strength was not good. The castle walls may have interrupted further transmission."

Kadar was not overly concerned by the reply. Taking out Fitz-duane's castle was a sideshow. The key was the securing of Draker and the hostages. With the hostages under his control, any other problems were matters of detail.

"Any news from Draker?"

Ziegle clasped his earphones to his ears and bent his head in concentration. His gesture reminded Kadar that however brilliant his planning, his acceptance of Soviet-made radio equipment from the Libyans for interunit communication had been a mistake. Ziegle's heavy back-mounted set was powerful enough, but the smaller radios used by the field units were on the margin of acceptability. Fortunately their short range and poor quality would not matter once they were all positioned in Draker, and for other communications, such as with the authorities, they had the backpack unit and the powerful Japanese-made ship's radio. The error was irritating but not serious.

Ziegle looked up. "Draker is secure. The leader of the Sacrificers reports no casualties on his side. All the guards are dead. Two of the faculty members had to be killed. The remaining faculty and all students are under guard in the assembly hall. They are moving on to the next phase."

Kadar felt a surge of relief, though his face remained impassive. His farsighted decision to use a suborned group of students had paid off. The security people had never expected an attack from within.

Kadar believed that a strong force such as his would probably have succeeded in capturing Draker without internal help, but the risks would have been much greater. Help could have been summoned, and the weak points in the sea landing could have been shown up as fatal. The fact was that while disembarking, the terrorists were vulnerable to even a small force on the cliffs above, and they were even more vulnerable while ascending the tunnel that led from Draker's small jetty to the college buildings at the top. Getting up that tunnel against any sort of armed opposition would have meant, at best, heavy casualties.

The advantages of the sea to land a large force were overwhelming, and his use of the Sacrificers backed up by Phantom Air—an excess of caution, it now seemed—had compensated for the risks.

Ziegle was looking at him.

"Tell the Sacrificers' leader congratulations," said Kadar. "Ask him to confirm that the top end of the tunnel is secure. Tell Phantom Air to circle the island to see if anyone is out there and then to land in ten minutes."

Ziegle spoke into his radio microphone. Kadar watched the Islander bank to starboard and then, at a height of about a thousand feet, commence a slow perusal of the island. "Reconnaissance is seldom wasted," he said to himself, using the old army adage.

"The jetty access tunnel is secured," said Ziegle, "but there is only one man on guard there. Another man is on guard at the main entrance. Sacrificer leader himself needs the other three to guard the hostages. He requests you land reinforcements as soon as possible."

Kadar, feeling at that moment, he thought, more exhilarated than General MacArthur could ever have felt even when he had retaken the Philippines, gave the order to land. At Kadar's signal the waiting terrorists, laden with weapons and explosives, climbed down scrambling nets into inflatable assault boats and headed for shore.

Kadar followed with Ziegle and his personal bodyguard. As they landed on the jetty, they received a message that a figure wearing the black combat gear of Phantom Sea had waved from the keep of Fitzduane's castle. Several bodies had been sighted as well.

So at last Fitzduane was dead. Kadar felt a sense of relief at the news. Although probably by instinct rather than deliberation, Fitzduane had a bad habit of turning up at the wrong moments. News of his death was comforting: it was a good omen for the mission.

THE ROAD TO DRAKER COLLEGE—1806 HOURS

Fitzduane resisted the urge to press the accelerator to the floor. High speed would look suspicious, and anyway the road surface was not in great shape.

He could now guess at some of the elements in the Hangman's plan. In hindsight, making his move just after the staff bus was off the island had been obvious. The landing would be taking place right now. The question was, were the Sacrificers being used as he feared?

Henssen was lying on his back, squeezed between Murrough and the left side of the Volvo station wagon's wheelhousing. He held de Guevain's strung longbow in his hands, and an AK-47 they had found in the car rested between his knees.

He looked out through the rear window. "We've got company. Some kind of small twin-engine plane. Maybe it's the good guys," he added hopefully.

"I wouldn't bet on it," said Fitzduane. "On the basis of the timing, I think we're going to be between a rock and a hard place if we're not careful. Does it look as if it's going to land?"

"Shit!" cried Henssen. The Volvo had hit a pothole, and the AK-47 bounced and crashed back into his balls.

Fitzduane turned his head quickly and saw what had happened. "Silly place to keep a weapon."

"That's a very unfunny remark," said Henssen, rubbing his private parts with his free hand. "The plane is banking by the looks of it. It's probably going to circle until we get out of the way. If it's landing here, we're screwing up its airstrip."

Fitzduane's eyes were fixed on the road ahead. Draker College was coming up fast. He could see a figure by the gate. "I know all the guards by sight. If we see one, then maybe we're in time. If it's something else"—he glanced at de Guevain—"you're on. Think you can do it from eighty meters?"

"We'll know soon enough." De Guevain was wearing a checked keffiyeh that he'd found in the car. Fitzduane was similarly attired.

The Frenchman's manner was withdrawn and focused, and his hands were clasped around the slender shaft of a heavy hunting arrow.

The figure in the animal mask up ahead waved at them with his left hand. His right hand was clasped around the pistol grip of a Uzi submachine gun. Fitzduane slewed the car to a halt, using the hand brake to demonstrate a suitable degree of fishtailing. The rear of the car was seventy-five meters from the Sacrificer.

DRAKER COLLEGE—1809 HOURS

They'd done it, they'd actually done it, the Sacrificer on guard at the main gate was thinking. His father was a Spanish industrialist who had prospered under the Franco regime but now felt it expedient to keep a low profile. He spent more and more time pursuing various business interests—and women—in South America. His younger son, Carlos, was something of a disappointment. The lad lacked the realism necessary to survive in this world, and the machismo. He was, to be frank, an embarrassment. Draker College was an ideal place to put him until something could be worked out. His father did not spend much time thinking about what that solution might be. He was a master practitioner of the "out of sight, out of mind" philosophy, and there were so many more enjoyable distractions.

Carlos's hatred of his father created a void. The camaraderie of the Sacrificers filled that void and gave Carlos a sense of power and self-esteem which, up to that time, he had very obviously lacked. He was impressed by his own daring. Only minutes before he had actually killed two human beings with cyanide. Now he waited for the saboteurs of Phantom Unit who had been assigned to blow the bridge. He didn't know them by sight, but he had been briefed on the make and registration number of their car, and he knew their estimated time of arrival.

The Volvo had stopped just out of easy shouting distance, as if it had hit a rock or had some mechanical trouble. Maybe it had a flat tire; the way it had slewed suggested that. He made a thumbs-up sign to show that they had taken the college successfully and walked forward to give them a hand.

The driver and the passenger got out, and the driver kicked the left rear wheel in irritation. The other man opened the back of the station wagon and peered inside. Carlos could see the tip of what looked like a tire iron. He was torn between going to help and staying at his post as instructed. He cupped his hands to shout that he would like to help but that he was under orders.

The passenger stepped out from behind the car with something in his hands that seemed pointed above Carlos's head. His brain, pre-conditioned to see a spare wheel or a jack, rejected the initial message of his eyes. His brain was still making an attempt to process what he was seeing when the arrow struck the center of his chest, smashing through his ribs and penetrating his lungs. A second arrow followed almost immediately and hit him lower in the abdomen. He collapsed without a sound. He was thinking as he died that the day had gotten colder.

DRAKER COLLEGE—1810 HOURS

De Guevain was temporarily stunned by the consequences of his act. His face lost all its color, and he stood, unmoving, the bow dangling in his hands. Fitzduane tore the bow from his grasp and threw it into the back of the Volvo, then pushed de Guevain roughly into the passenger seat and slammed the door after him. With the tailgate still open, he accelerated the car and roared through the main entrance into the forecourt inside.

The place was deserted. Several cars stood there with their hoods open and engines wrecked.

"Do it very fucking fast," said Fitzduane.

Murrough, who knew the college layout, signaled Andreas to follow. Together they ran around the back of the college to where the jetty tunnel emerged. Murrough, his .303 sniper rifle strapped to his back, had an SA-80 in his hands with the fire selector switched to auto. Andreas carried Fitzduane's pump-action Remington and the Hawk grenade launcher. The Hawk was, essentially, a giant semi-automatic two-handed weapon loaded with twelve 40 mm grenades in a rotary magazine that it could discharge in six seconds. It was heavy and took practice to use accurately, but as a close-assault weapon it was devastating.

They could only hope that the attack force had not yet made it out of the tunnel. It was the one location where they might hold off a superior force. They had been instructed not to fire, if possible, until Fitzduane had secured the hall, where he knew the students normally assembled. "Right now we've got surprise on our side," he had said, "but that's strictly a one-shot deal."

Murrough's heart gave a leap when he saw that the mouth of the jetty tunnel was empty. He was fifteen meters away when two camouflaged figures emerged. He hit the ground, and Kalashnikov fire sliced the air around him. There was a double roar as Andreas's Remington went into action. A hail of fire was returned from the tunnel, which had suddenly filled with men.

Murrough lay on the ground, the fire too intense to permit him to move. A grenade tumbled through the air and blew a garden water butt to pieces beside him, drenching him. Sick at heart, he knew they were too late. They couldn't hold the tunnel.

He felt his legs being pulled, and he slid backward over the gravel path. An accented voice told him to stop being an idiot, and he began to struggle. Stone splinters and earth cut his face; rounds sliced the ground where he had been an instant before. He emerged behind the brick base of a greenhouse. Andreas, panting with the effort, let go of Murrough's ankles. "It seemed like you were glued there," he said.

"I was," said Murrough.

The fire from the tunnel slackened, and four terrorists ran out. Recovering quickly, Murrough dropped two with an SA-80 burst, and Andreas got a third with the Remington. The fourth went to ground in the garden. The firing from the tunnel mouth increased again, and they knew another wave would emerge any moment. There were too many to stop. It was now just a matter of time.

"I think we're out of the surprise business," said Andreas.

"Maybe," said Murrough. He racked his brain to recall what he knew of the garden and tunnel layout. There had to be some way to buy some time.

DRAKER COLLEGE—1813 HOURS

Fitzduane, followed by de Guevain, Henssen, and Judith Newman, headed into the main building toward the assembly hall.

Judith had sprinted back to the dead guard at the gate to relieve him of his Uzi and spare magazines. Her eyes had lit up when she saw the Israeli-made weapon. She had learned to shoot with one on the kibbutz before anyone had gotten around to teaching her to cook or sew, and from her early teens she could outshoot most of her fellow sabras. She caught up with the others as they moved swiftly but cautiously through the long corridors that led to the hall.

Fitzduane had briefed them on what he remembered of the geography of the place. He was far from familiar with much of the Draker College layout, but details of the main public rooms remained in his mind. The assembly hall, which doubled as a theater, had a stage at one end and an L-shaped gallery equipped with an organ at the other. The main doors opened to the right of the stage end. The room, which had two sections of seats divided by a central aisle, could accommodate about two hundred and fifty. There were windows at the second-floor level, and you could see out through some of them to the grounds at the rear. He hoped like hell Murrough and Andreas were not being targeted from a window overhead. He had forgotten to warn them of that particular possibility. There was a second door on the other side of the stage, directly facing the main doors. There were no doors at the rear of the room that he could recall, though stairs led to the gallery from that end and the gallery itself had an exit at the second-floor level.

He guessed he was up against no more than four to six of the Sacrificers. Given the layout of the room, they'd be on the stage, by the doors, and—probably—in the gallery.

He pointed at a small door set into the paneling farther down the corridor. "Henssen and Judith, that's yours," he said. "There's a circular staircase behind it that leads to the gallery. Get up there and move when I do. Remember, take out the opposition fast or we'll have a massacre on our hands." The two nodded and vanished through the paneling.

Fitzduane braced himself outside the main doors with de Guevain, now with some color back in his cheeks, to one side. A burst of fire came from the rear of the college. Fitzduane, carrying his own Browning automatic shotgun loaded with XR-18 ammunition, nodded to de Guevain. Acting as one, they flung open the double doors, sending one guard standing on the inside of the doors sprawling. In the center of the stage, a Sacrificer who had been threatening the rows of students below him swiveled his weapon toward the intruders and died instantly under a blast from Fitzduane's shotgun.

Fitzduane fired a second time at another Sacrificer standing by the facing door. Wheeling around, de Guevain shot the guard they had knocked to the ground as they entered the room.

Judith mounted the circular staircase ahead of Henssen. The sound of firing from the rear of the building came as she was opening the gallery door a crack to take a look. A Sacrificer who had been positioned in the center of the gallery to keep watch over the hostages ran across to the windows to see the cause of the disturbance outside. He turned in alarm at the sound of Fitzduane bursting in below and for a split second stood there uncertain which way to move. Judith shot him three times in the torso while he was making up his mind. Henssen, seeing the body still upright, fired over her shoulder with his AK-47, sending chips of bone flying in a spray of blood out of the corpse's head. The body collapsed against the gallery rail, pouring blood onto the students below.

Outside, the sound of gunfire intensified.

Inside the assembly hall the students stared uncertainly at their rescuers. Many of them still had their hands on top of their heads, as the Sacrificers had instructed. They couldn't adjust immediately to this new development. Most were still in shock. The bodies of the duty faculty lay where they had fallen after execution in front of the stage. The floor was slippery, and the air reeked of blood, cordite, and the smells and sweat of fear.

One body seemed familiar to Fitzduane. The figure was tall and slim, and a ragged line of bullet holes punctured her breasts. Her face still showed the horror of her manner of dying. Her round granny glasses were in her hand, and she lay in a pool of her own blood.

DRAKER COLLEGE—1817 HOURS

Kadar stood on the jetty, frustration eating away at his insides. Most of his unit had been withdrawn from the tunnel, leaving a scratch force to try for a breakout. There was no information as to who was resisting them, but reports from the firing line suggested that the opposition was light. Unfortunately, light or otherwise, it was all too well placed.

He had no intention of leaving his forces in the tunnel, where they were at their most vulnerable. He would accept a delay and try a pincers movement on the opposition. Radio contact with the Sacrificers had been cut, so it seemed as if that particular card had been neutralized somehow. He had tried to raise Phantom Sea in Fitzduane's castle, but again there was nothing but static. Suspicion nibbled at his mind, but he suppressed it. Ropes snaked to the ground as his specially trained climbers led the way up the cliffs. One way or another they would brush this irritation aside—and soon.

He was pleased at his foresight in blowing the bridge. His victims had nowhere to go. It was only a matter of time. He ordered Phantom Air to delay landing until they either broke out of the tunnel or had secured the cliff top.

Whom could he be up against? Kadar paced up and down in frustration. Above him there was a cry as one of the lead climbers lost his footing and hung, for a moment, by his fingernails from a rock. Kadar was almost sorry when his scrabbling feet found safety.

The assault carried on.

DRAKER COLLEGE—1817 HOURS

Many of the students knew Fitzduane by sight from his rambles around the island, and it was this fact that made the difference. Given confidence by the presence of a familiar face who seemed to know exactly what he was doing, the released hostages streamed out of the college toward Fitzduane's castle at a fast jog. Escorted by de Guevain and Henssen, they had two miles to cover in the open, a fact Fitzduane disliked. But they were fit young people used to much longer runs, and the bottom line was that there was no alternative. The college layout would be known to the terrorists, and it was too big and sprawling to be held. Duncleeve, Fitzduane's castle, was home ground. There they had a chance.

A thousand feet up, the pilot and copilot of the Islander spotted the exodus and radioed Kadar for instructions. Seconds later the pilot banked and headed in to scout the road between the running students and Fitzduane's castle. The strip the pilot had landed on before had already been passed by the students. The pilot had no choice but to try to land on an untested spot. The Islander was a rugged aircraft built for poor conditions, so the pilot was confident he could set it down safely. He wasn't so sure he'd ever get it off again, but he knew better than to argue with his commander. He cinched his seat harness tighter and prepared to land.

Inside the college Fitzduane and Judith had moved to a second-floor location that directly overlooked the grounds at the rear and the top entrance of the jetty tunnel. He could see where Murrough and Andreas were pinned down by observing where the fire from the tunnel mouth was focused. The greenhouse the two men were sheltering in was a cascading mass of breaking glass. Fitzduane hoped the two had found some cover from the debris. He could think of more comfortable places to hide.

Thirty yards away a camouflaged figure was crawling along a gravel path to the side and rear of the greenhouse, out of sight of the occupants. He paused and removed two cylindrical objects from a pouch on his belt. Fitzduane imagined he could hear the first grenade pin being pulled and tossed aside. He had the radio in his right hand and was trying to raise Murrough. As the terrorist came to his feet and brought his right arm back to throw, Fitzduane pocketed the radio and lifted the Browning to his shoulder. The firing pin clicked on an empty chamber.

A three-round burst from Judith's Uzi caught the grenade thrower in the back of the head. He pitched forward, the grenade leaving his hand and rolling under a galvanized wheelbarrow. Fitzduane raised his head soon enough after the explosion to see the barrow, perforated like a colander, sail through the air and land in an ornamental pool with a huge splash, sending a shoal of goldfish to a slow death on the stone surround.

Judith was firing single shots into the tunnel entrance. Fitzduane picked up Murrough on the radio. "Are you okay?"

"We're not hit," said Murrough, "though we've a fair few cuts from all the glass. We can't move, though. There's too many of them in the tunnel mouth for us."

"Have you used the Hawk?"

"Not yet," said Murrough. "It's hard to get off a clear shot under this much fire."

"There's a fuel tank to the right of the tunnel entrance," said Fitzduane. "It's aboveground but buried for safety reasons in sand and concrete. A pipe from it runs down the tunnel to the jetty."

"I remember," said Murrough. "It's that bump to the right of the tunnel entrance."

"Roger," said Fitzduane. "Tell Andreas to check his grenade bandolier and look for M433 HEDP rounds."

There was a pause. Judith turned to Fitzduane. "I'm keeping their heads down," she said, "but I don't have the ammunition to keep this up for long." She held up two magazines. "Just these and three in the weapon." She fired again and inserted the next-to-last clip.

"We've found four," said Murrough, "and there are a few other varieties—some labeled M397 and M576."

"Load two of the 397," said Fitzduane, "and then the four HEDP."

There was another pause, and then Murrough answered: "Done."

A figure, grenade in hand, made a run from the tunnel. Now reloaded, Fitzduane and Judith both fired. The figure buckled but with a last effort threw the grenade. Helpless, they watched it land in the greenhouse. A cascade of brown liquid shot up into the air and rained downward.

"Shit," said Murrough. "It landed in some kind of liquid fertilizer tank. We're covered in the stuff."

"That'll teach you," said Fitzduane. "Only a moron would pick a greenhouse to hide out in."

"Get a move on," said Judith.

Fitzduane grinned at her. She had a Swiss sense of humor. She shot like a Swiss, too. "Murrough," he said, "at my command, put the 397s into the tunnel and then put the next four rounds into the tank—and if it works, run like hell to the front. We'll join you there."

"And if it doesn't?" Murrough muttered to himself.

"Ready?" Fitzduane asked Judith.

"Ready."

"Fire!" Fitzduane's automatic Browning boomed repeatedly, and Judith emptied her last magazine in a series of three-round bursts. Fitzduane could see movement in the greenhouse, where Murrough was firing the SA-80 on full automatic.

The fire from the tunnel slackened as the terrorists withered under this surge in the opposition's firepower. Andreas broke cover with the bulky Hawk grenade launcher in his hands. His covering fire slowed as Judith ran out of ammunition and Fitzduane reloaded. The terrorists inside the tunnel raised their heads.

Andreas fired the first two grenades from the Hawk into the entrance. The grenades impacted on the floor, and a small charge in each one flung the projectile back into the air to chest height, where it exploded. Shrapnel raked the confined space, and the sound of screaming echoed out. He turned the Hawk toward the fuel tank and fired the four M433 high-explosive dual-purpose grenades in two seconds, then ran with all his might away from the line of the entrance, with Murrough sprinting behind him.

The first two grenades—capable of penetrating two inches of armor—were partially smothered by the concrete and sand safety cover that was itself blown apart in the process. The third and fourth grenades, their way now cleared, exploded inside the two-thousand-gallon tank, rupturing the container but not immediately setting fire to the contents.

Fuel poured into the tunnel and then blew when it encountered a red-hot grenade fragment. A fireball shot out of the entrance, engulfing the greenhouse that had so recently sheltered Andreas and Murrough.

There was silence from the tunnel mouth except for the crackling of flames. Black smoke billowed upward and stained the sky. At the bottom of the tunnel, and standing well to one side, Kadar felt the touch of a dragon's breath on his face. The men inside were dead, but most of the others had been withdrawn before the explosion.

The lead climbers were approaching the last stage of the ascent to the top of the cliff.

THE ISLAND ROAD—1825 HOURS

The pilot of the Islander took his eyes off the group of students running toward him. They were now spread out in an irregular field more than a hundred yards long. He calculated that he could bring the aircraft to a halt about a quarter of a mile ahead of the leading runners, allowing plenty of time for the Phantom Air team to de-plane and set up blocking positions.

The pilot felt his wheels touch the ground in a near-perfect landing. Ahead of him he saw the runners break to left and right and a Volvo station wagon accelerate from their midst and head straight toward him. Frantically he applied the brakes; the Volvo, bouncing and vibrating at high speed, had eaten up his runway margin in less than seven seconds. The pilot tried to imagine the effect of a head-on crash at a combined speed of more than a hundred miles an hour. He knew that whatever the outcome, after it was over, the respective occupants would be unlikely to take much interest in the matter.

He looked at the patch of bright green boggy ground that bordered the road to his left and then back at the Volvo, now only seconds away from impact. His resolve faltered. Better chicken than dead, he decided, and slid the plane off the road onto the bright green grass. A mere fraction of a second later the Volvo skidded to a tire-burning halt on the other side of the road.

"A draw!" the terrorist pilot said to himself, feeling pleased that the Volvo driver's nerve had cracked only a split second after his. But the pilot's glee didn't last long. The bright green grass was, in fact, algae, he noted, and his aircraft, complete with the entire Phantom Air Unit, sank in twelve feet of scummy brown water.

"Fuck that for a caper," said Fitzduane as he stood on the verge and watched air bubbles make patterns on the green surface. "It's always easier to play a match on your home ground."

Runners streamed past him, and he waved them on toward the castle. De Guevain and Henssen puffed to a halt beside the Volvo.

"You're absolutely crazy," said de Guevain, shaking his head. Sweat streamed off him.

"Crazy but effective," corrected Henssen.

Fitzduane grinned, then opened the tailgate of the Volvo. "You old people," he offered, "need a lift?"

FITZDUANE'S ISLAND—1845 HOURS

The castle portcullis crashed into place as the first of the terrorists reached the top of the cliff. Farther down the road there was a series of scummy plops as the two surviving members of Phantom Air who had escaped from the aircraft pulled themselves out of the algae and started to walk back to the college. Neither was looking forward to Kadar's reception, but there was nowhere else to go.

Chapter Twenty-seven

The director general of the Irish Tourist Board was an urbane-looking silver-haired political appointee in his early fifties. His main operational tools—whatever the issue—were his smile, his connections, and his ability to say virtually nothing endlessly until the opposition was worn down.

In this case the issue was the proposed detention of a group of Middle Eastern travel agents by the Rangers. His aides had assured him that arresting visiting travel agents was unlikely to advance the cause of Irish tourism—and it would look and sound really lousy on television.

"Lousy on television"—the director general reacted to such stimuli like a dog to Pavlov's bell. He salivated, nearly panicked, and demanded an immediate crisis meeting with the commander of the Rangers.

It took Kilmara ninety minutes to get rid of the idiot and his supporting cast. Only then did he return to his desk to find that the informal two-hourly radio check he had agreed upon with Fitzduane during their last call had not been made and that the telephone line

441

seemed to be out of order. A call to the security detail at Draker College proved equally abortive, which was not surprising since all the phones on the island ran off the same cable. He put a call in to the police station at Ballyvonane, the nearest village on the mainland. He knew the station itself would be closed at this time of the evening, but the normal routine was for calls to be transferred to the duty policeman at his home.

The phone was answered on the tenth ring by a noticeably out-of-breath voice. Kilmara was informed by O'Sullivan, the local policeman, that he had just cycled back from the bridge access to Fitzduane's Island after trying to get hold of Sergeant Tommy Keane, who was in turn wanted by the superintendent to answer a small matter to do with an assault on a water bailiff. Kilmara had the feeling that O'Sullivan might expire before the conversation finished. He waited until the policeman's breathing sounded less terminal. "I gather you didn't find the sergeant?" Kilmara finally asked.

"No, Colonel," said O'Sullivan.

"What's this about the bridge access? Why didn't you cross onto the island?"

"Didn't I tell you?" answered the policeman. "The bridge seems to have collapsed. There is nothing there except wreckage. The island is cut off completely."

Kilmara hung up in frustration. It was now nearly 2000 hours. What the hell was happening on that island? The evidence was stacking up that all was not well, but it was still not conclusive. Geranium Day in Bern and severed communications didn't necessarily add up to a combat jump onto Fitzduane's Island. Or did it if you threw in Fitzduane's vibes and the Hangman's track record?

He looked at the paperwork on the Middle Eastern group, which was due to arrive on the last flight from London. The flight had originated in Libya, but there was no direct connection to Ireland. Was it credible that such a group wouldn't at least overnight in London to recharge on Western decadence?

He had a sudden insight that he was approaching the problem the wrong way. The question wasn't whether the travel agents were genuine or otherwise. The question was how to deal with two problems at once, and the answer, from that perspective, was obvious. In a way he had that cretin from the tourist board to thank for pointing it out. It took him twenty-five minutes on the phone to make the arrangements.

He found Günther in the operations room. The German looked up as he entered. He had been trying the direct radio link to Fitzduane, but now he shook his head. "Nothing," he said. "Completely dead."

He followed Kilmara back to his office. Kilmara gestured for him to close the door. "The British owe us a few favors," he said.

Günther raised his eyebrows. "So?"

"I've called one in," said Kilmara. "The Brits aren't too happy, but they'll do it."

"Fuck me," said Günther. "You're getting the British to handle the problem at the stopover in London."

Kilmara nodded. "We can't stand down the embassy security until it's done and we've sorted out our Japanese friends. But it does clear the decks a little and allow us to take a trip with a clear conscience."

"So we drop in on Fitzduane."

"We do," said Kilmara. "Let's move."

BALDONNEL MILITARY AIR BASE OUTSIDE DUBLIN—2045 HOURS

Voices crackled in his headphones. They were being cleared for takeoff. In an ideal world, Kilmara began to think—but then he brushed the thought from his mind. He had spent most of his career working within financial constraints when it came to equipment, and lusting after night-flying helicopters in a cash-strapped economy like Ireland's wasn't going to achieve much right now.

Truth to tell, apart from the helicopter deficiency—the most expensive items on his shopping list by far both to buy and to maintain—the Rangers were well equipped and were as highly trained as he could ever hope. They'd find out soon enough whether it would all come together as planned. This was going to be like no other operation the Rangers had carried out—and it would be their first combat jump as a unit.

Of course, it could all be a false alarm, yet somehow Kilmara knew it wasn't. Something told him that on the other side of Ireland blood had started to flow. Spontaneously his right hand felt for the steel and plastic of the SA-80 clipped into place beside his seat.

He looked out through the transparent Perspex dome of the Optica cockpit at the runway ahead, then glanced behind him to where the two Islander twin-engine light transports waited with their cargoes of Rangers and lethal equipment. The pilot's voice sounded in his earphones. The Optica had been specially silenced so that normal conversation was possible without using the intercom, but external communications made the intercom mandatory.

"We're cleared," the pilot said.

"Final check," ordered Kilmara.

Günther's voice crackled in immediately, followed by that of the commander of the second plane.

Kilmara looked at the pilot. "Let's get airborne."

They took off and headed west into the setting sun.

DRAKER COLLEGE—2045 HOURS

As reversal followed reversal, while outwardly showing scant reaction, Kadar had experienced the full spectrum of emotions from paralyzing fear to a rage so intense that he felt as if his gaze alone would destroy. The news that Fitzduane was, in fact, still alive did nothing to help his mood. Executing the pilot of the Islander had provided the cathartic outlet he needed. A smear of algae on the floor and a head-high blood and brain matter stain on the wall were all that remained of that incompetent.

His mind had adjusted to face the change in developments head-on. He could now see the advantages of the situation. He was confronted with the most satisfying challenge of his professional life and an adversary worthy of his talents. Operation Geranium would succeed, but only after effort and total commitment. It would be a fitting finale to this stage of his career, and to look on the bright side, fatalities on the scale he had suffered meant a much-enhanced bottom line. A reduction of overhead, you might say.

Kadar studied the map and the aerial photographs. He now knew who and what he was up against—and where they were. The island was isolated. Fitzduane's castle was surrounded, and Kadar had the men and the weapons to do the job. That damned Irishman was about to learn some military facts of life.

Lesson one: His medieval castle would prove no match for late-twentieth-century firepower.

FITZDUANE'S CASTLE—2118 HOURS

Fitzduane had let them rest for ten minutes after they made it back to the castle and then put them all to work in an organized frenzy of effort. The terrorists had appeared not long after the portcullis had slammed into place but at first had made no attempt to approach closer than about a thousand meters. Then, as the evening shadows deepened, movement could be detected in brief flashes. The noose was tightening.

When the nearest terrorist was about six hundred meters away, Fitzduane ordered Murrough and Andreas to open fire on single shot. Sporadic sniping then broke out, with no automatic fire being used on either side. The firing died down after about fifteen minutes, with the terrorists in position for an assault in a semicircle around the castle and with their watchers monitoring the sea side. Murrough and Andreas swore they had achieved some hits but couldn't be too precise about the numbers.

Sergeant Tommy Keane was the castle garrison's first fatality. A random sniper round hit him in the center of his forehead while he was peering through an arrow slit in the keep. He died instantly.

Kadar's forces were now dug in around them, just outside normal combat-rifle range, and daylight was fading. The castle defenders had completed most of their preparations, but Fitzduane noticed that his people were getting tired and potentially careless. He called a food break and held a council of war with those not on watch. The mood was somber but determined. Tommy Keane's death had countered any euphoria left after their escape from Draker. The brutal realities of combat were becoming clear: it was kill or be killed, winner take all.

"At the college we had surprise on our side," said Fitzduane. "Now they know where we are and roughly who we are, and the ball is more in their court. We'll have to keep sharp if we're to come out of this in one piece."

"How long do you think we'll have to hold?" asked Henssen.

Fitzduane shrugged. "We had a regular radio check with the Rangers set up. We've missed several in a row now, so that should bring some help in a couple of hours. On the other hand, we're cut off from the mainland, and who knows how much help will arrive? My guess is that it may take some time before the scale of the problem becomes known and adequate reinforcements are thrown in. We may have to hold until morning or even later."

"Not a long time for a siege," said Henssen.

"Long enough when modern weaponry is involved," said Fitzduane. "But let's save conjecture till later. First of all, I want to review our preparations." He turned to the Bear. The Swiss detective's formal training and his personal interest in weaponry made him the natural choice as armorer.

"We've improved our small-arms position," said the Bear, "thanks to the weapons taken from the frogmen and from Draker College. In fact, unless we arm some of the students, we have more weapons than people to use them. Starting with automatic weapons, as of now, we have the four SA-80 rifles, one M-16, one AK-47, five Ingrams, and three Uzis—that's fourteen in all. In conventional rifles, we have Murrough's .303 Lee-Enfield and two .303 deer rifles I found in the armory.

"Moving on to shotguns, we have one Remington pump action— that's the shotgun Hugo brought back from Switzerland—one Browning automatic shotgun, and six double-barrel shotguns." He turned to Fitzduane. "Including a pair of Purdeys, I see," he added, referring to the famous English sporting guns, each individually tailored and costing about as much as a suburban house.

"It's a long story," said Fitzduane, "which will keep."

"That makes a total of eight shotguns," continued the Bear, "although only the Remington and the Browning are of much military use. The next category is handguns. We have seven—four nine-millimeter Brownings, one nine-millimeter Mauser broom handle, a U.S. Army .45 Colt service automatic, and a rather old .45 Webley. Ammunition: moderately healthy if everyone maintains fire discipline and uses either single shot or short bursts; not so good if we all operate on full automatic. In numbers, we have about three thousand rounds of 5.56-millimeter ammunition left, about fifteen hundred of nine-millimeter, over a thousand rounds of assorted shotgun ammunition, and less than two full clips for the AK-47. In terms of other firepower, we have a regular arsenal of antique weapons, including half a dozen muskets, two crossbows in full working order, and Christian's longbow."

"My longbow is not an antique," objected de Guevain.

"Whatever," said the Bear. "The point is that we have a large collection of weapons of limited military value in modern terms, but some of which could prove useful. I've distributed them around the castle to be grabbed in emergencies. The muskets, incidentally, are loaded, so be careful."

"I assume you'll be using a crossbow, Heini," said de Guevain. "The Swiss national weapon wasn't the crossbow, as it happens, but the pike or halberd."

"Let's get back to other firepower," said Fitzduane.

"Well," continued the Bear, "here we have the Hawk forty-millimeter grenade launcher and about thirty grenades of different types. We have a box of conventional hand grenades. We have some C-4 explosives and Claymores we took off the frogmen's raft, and we have some home brew made with weed killer and sugar and diesel oil and other trimmings. Unfortunately we don't have a lot of gasoline, since the castle vehicles run on diesel, but we've siphoned a few gallons from the Volvo to make Molotov cocktails." He looked at Fitzduane. "I used poteen to make up for the gas shortage. I'm afraid I made quite a dent in your reserve stock."

"My whiskey." Fitzduane paled. "You've taken my whiskey and mixed it with gasoline?"

"Hard to tell the difference sometimes," muttered Henssen.

"What about the cannon?" asked de Guevain. "Are we going to give them a try?" He was referring to the two small eighteenth-century cannon that normally stood in the bawn.

"We'll see," said the Bear. "There is only a small stock of black powder, which I'm keeping for the muskets. That means using our weed killer explosive for the cannon—with trial and error being the only way of working out the right load. I can't say I'd like to be the gunner during those tests."

"They'd be ideal for covering the gate," said de Guevain. "We can load them with nails and broken glass and the like to get a shrapnel effect."

"Let's do it," urged Fitzduane. "We'll try a few test shots at one of the outhouses to get the loading right—and use a long fuse."

"And watch out for the recoil," said Henssen, "or your toes will be flattened—or worse."

"This fellow obviously knows what he's talking about," said the Bear. "And I thought you only knew about computers. Consider yourself volunteered."

Henssen raised his eyes to the ceiling. "Why did I open my big mouth?"

"Good question," said de Guevain.

The review continued, covering the placing of the Claymores, distribution of the hand-held radios, food, medical backup, blackening of faces, duty rosters, and the host of matters, major and minor, essential to consider if the castle was to be defended properly.

"Is there any way we haven't thought of so far that we can send for help?" said Harry Noble. The ambassador's face was pale and strained, the shock of his son's death etched on his features. For the moment the heavy work load was keeping him sane. Fitzduane didn't like to think about the private torments the man would face in the future. To have killed your own son; it was a nightmare. The Hangman had much to answer for.

"Fair point," said Fitzduane. "The question is how. We're completely surrounded and now their ship—"

"The *Sabine*," said the Bear.

"The *Sabine*," continued Fitzduane, "is blocking the seaward route." The ship, now that the focus of the Hangman's attention had switched to Fitzduane's castle, had left the point and was less than half a mile offshore from the castle.

There was silence for a few moments. The fact was that sooner or later the Rangers should realize that something was wrong and send help. In contrast, no one present had any illusions about the dangers of trying to break through the Hangman's cordon, let alone getting off the island.

"Something else to think about," said Fitzduane. "We don't want to let the Hangman get hold of a hostage."

Harry Noble nodded. "That's something I hadn't considered. Perhaps we should wait it out."

Fitzduane looked around. From everyone's eyes he could tell there was general agreement to wait, so they moved on to discuss the students. Some were still in shock at what had happened, but a number, refreshed after eating and intrigued by the preparations they had witnessed while filling sandbags and doing other manual work, wanted to join the active defenders. They were now bunked down behind locked doors in a storeroom off the tunnel. They hadn't gone willingly. The protests had been vigorous and had died down only when Fitzduane explained the problem: After the business of the Sacrificers, who could be trusted?

"I don't know about keeping them all locked up," said Andreas. "I appreciate the problem, but I think we're going to have to arm a few of them. We need the manpower. The perimeter is too big to hold for long with what we've got."

There was some agreement with this view. The defenders were stretched thin, and things would get worse after dusk.

"They're not kids," said Judith. "Many of them are about my age."

The Bear smiled.

"Look," continued the Israeli girl, "they know the security problem. Why not let them pick some volunteers? They ought to be able to pick some people who can be trusted—unless you think they've all been suborned."

Fitzduane shook his head. "No, we probably don't have a security problem with the students anymore, but even so I'm reluctant to put them on the firing line. Let's compromise. Let's put them to work picking some volunteers, but let's not use them unless we really have to."

"Makes sense," said the Bear.

Fitzduane looked at Andreas and Judith.

"Fair enough," Andreas agreed.

"Judgment of Solomon," said Judith.

"Let's get on to considering what we're up against," continued Fitzduane, "and the options open to the Hangman."

He looked at Noble, who had been given the job of coordinating everything they knew, including the string of reports from those on watch. The ambassador, de Guevain, and Henssen had then put themselves in the Hangman's shoes to evaluate his options. Both Noble and de Guevain had previous combat experience—de Guevain had been a paratrooper in his earlier years—and Henssen had the greatest knowledge of the Hangman's methods of operation gleaned from his endless hours working with the Nose in Wiesbaden.

"Best estimate," said Noble, "is that we're up against a force of between seventy and eighty hard-core terrorists, to which may be added a small crew from the *Sabine*. I would guess the one motivation they have in common is mercenary, but considering the Hangman's MO, there will be subgroups with their own specific reasons for wanting to strike back at what they see as the establishment.

"The terrorists will have been highly trained in a rather rigid, unquestioning way. They will have been oriented toward a violent assault against ill-prepared opposition with an emphasis on inflicting maximum damage in the shortest possible time; they probably won't have had the kind of systematic, specialist infantry training needed for an assignment like taking this castle. But whatever the weaknesses in the fine points of their training, they will all be highly proficient in basic weapons handling and are undoubtedly fit, committed, and determined.

"Their weapons seem to be typical Eastern bloc stuff apart from the Ingrams carried by the frogmen and the explosives, which are American. They have AK-47 assault rifles, Makarov automatics, plastic explosives, undoubtedly some hand grenades, and probably a few RPG-7 antitank grenade launchers. We've seen no sign of anything heavier so far, but with the *Sabine* freeing them of normal transport constraints, they may have something more lethal in reserve. If they do, I'm afraid we'll find out the hard way. The likely candidates would be heavy machine guns, mortars, rockets of various kinds, or even artillery. Somehow I can't see most of that stuff being available because, on the basis of what the Hangman originally intended to do, what would be the need? But you never know with this fellow. He likes gadgetry, and he likes surprises.

"We can hold out fairly well against small-arms fire and the other light stuff, but the RPG-7s, if they have them, could be a problem. They won't blow a hole through walls this thick, but if they get one through a window, the room inside won't be a lot of fun."

The Bear broke in. "We've used up every sheet and blanket and fertilizer bag and sack in the place, so we've got sandbagged blast shelters in every room and sandbags hanging inside every window and weapons slit. You can pull aside the bags with a rope if need be. We've also sandbagged the floors against blast and built extensive overhead cover."

"What's the range of the RPG-7?" asked Etan.

"Up to five hundred meters, theoretically," said Fitzduane, "but they are normally used at less than half that. To hit something as small as an arrow slit, particularly at night and shooting upward, you'd want to be closer in still. I don't think the RPG-7s are going to be our main problem. We want to worry more about explosive charges placed up close by sapper squads. A few pounds of C-4 in the right place, and the scenery starts changing. Make sure nobody gets in close, and make doubly sure if they are carrying anything like a satchel charge. Another thing: make sure when you drop somebody, he stays dead. For all the hype about hydrostatic shock and exit wounds the size of soup plates, 5.56-millimeter doesn't always have the knockdown power of 7.62-millimeter."

"Or .303," said Murrough.

"So aim for multiple hits if possible," continued Fitzduane. "Three rounds rapid works just fine." He looked at Noble. "I'm sorry, Harry. We're getting off the point."

Noble nodded. "Okay," he said. "We've covered who we are up against and how many, and we've had a quick look at their fire-power. Now the question is, what are they going to do with all this?

"The Hangman, as far as we know—and thanks to our friend's computers"—he pointed to Henssen—"we know a great deal—has never been faced with this sort of problem. Up to now he has always fought on his terms, mostly quick in-and-out actions with much smaller groups of men. His tactics then have been based on deception, surprise, speed, and firepower; they have been characterized by a disregard for human life and, from time to time, a warped sense of humor and a fondness for the bizarre.

"In this case the Hangman has to get hold of at least some hostages, or he has no chips to play with. Unusually for him, because an escape route is one consistent feature of his operations, he seems to have committed himself totally. That mightn't have been his intention—the plane may have been his way out—but it's the situation now, with all that it implies. He and his men have nothing to lose. They are going to be driven by desperation."

"What's to stop him from getting back on the *Sabine* and sailing off into the sunset?" said Andreas.

"Because high seas or not, he knows full well he'll never be allowed to get away. Every antiterrorist force in Europe wants his hide, and I wouldn't put it past the Israelis to swim over; they tend to travel when the incentive is right. No, the Hangman has to get what he came for here, or he hasn't much of a future."

"So what do you think he'll do?" asked Andreas.

"There are various scenarios we've looked at." Fitzduane broke in. "First, it looks as if he's going to wait until dark; that's the most likely explanation as to why he hasn't attacked up till now. Second, he's likely to use massive firepower to keep our heads down. Third, he's going to mount at least two attacks simultaneously, and one or more of them will be a diversion.

"The high ground in this battle is the keep. If he gets that, he commands everything else. On the other hand, a direct assault on the keep could be mounted only by scaling the walls on the seaward side, and that would be suicidal. The other approaches are protected by the curtain walls. He's most likely to try for the gatehouse first, because from there he can mount a protected fire base against the keep and under its cover take us out with explosives or fire. That suggests an attack combining firepower to keep our heads down, a diversionary attack on the curtain walls, and a sapper attack with explosives on the gatehouse. The portcullis would then be blown with explosives, and in they'd pour."

Fitzduane paused. His message was getting home. The analysis was making everybody think more of the totality of the problem and not just about his or her own immediate tasks. Their shortage of manpower to deal with the diverse areas they had to cover became more and more apparent.

"Another possibility is that they'll concentrate on the great hall and use boats to assault from the seaward side. The great hall backs directly onto the sea, and although it has firing slits and windows, it has no battlements. Also, it's lower to scale, and the slate roof could be penetrated.

"Yet another possibility is that they'll use a favorite Middle Eastern weapon—the car bomb. I imagine they can get some of the vehicles at Draker going again. One of those driven at speed against the portcullis and loaded with a few hundred pounds of explosives might make whoever is manning the gatehouse very unhappy."

He smiled. "Right, so much for the crystal ball stuff. Here's the deployment. Harry and Andreas will take the gatehouse with their personal weapons and the Hawk. Heini and Murrough will man the keep's fighting platform and watch the curtain wall facing the lake. Etan and Henssen will watch the curtain wall facing inland and the great hall. Judith, Christian, and I will make up the mobile reserve. Katia and Oona will look after food, first aid, the students, and whatever else is necessary. We'll keep in touch by radio.

"By the way, one thing we don't know is whether they have any night-vision equipment. I would doubt it, given the operation they thought they were mounting, but let's play it safe. Anyway, they have had enough daylight to map the apertures and our defense positions, so we'd better expect to receive accurate incoming fire.

"The good news, of course, is that we do have some night-vision sights for the SA-80s. They'll work up to about six hundred meters. I suggest you fit them immediately and zero them in in the tunnel on a rota basis. Night vision is something they probably won't expect from us—let's not reveal the fact that we have it too early. I'll tell you when.

"We do have floodlights set up for the bawn, the battlements, and the outside perimeter of the castle. We've wired them up on separate circuits, so one shot won't put out the lot, but I don't think they'll last too long in a firefight. The hope is they'll give us an edge when it matters.

"Remember to use the cover we've got and not to fire from the same position for more than a few seconds. Our muzzle flashes will show up in the darkness." He paused for a moment, then clapped his hands. "Let's go to it."

Outside, full darkness was fast descending, and a strong breeze had picked up, sending the clouds scudding across the half-moon. No movement could be detected amid the force that faced them, but each defender knew that the respite would be short-lived.

Those issued the SA-80s switched sights under the Bear's direction from the four-power day and low-light SUSAT sights to the similarly magnified night-vision Kite system and then zeroed in one by one in the tunnel. The compact Kites were a vast improvement over the bulky image intensifiers Fitzduane had first encountered in Vietnam. They carried third-generation tubes resistant to "whiteout" and weighed only a kilogram each.

The magnified picture they presented dispelled any illusions the defenders might have had that the terrorists had somehow vanished. The noose had tightened further.

Working swiftly, the Bear and Christian de Guevain set up the initial experimental charges in the two cannon. The weapons looked sound, but what ravages time had worked to their castings would be determined only by experiment. Using a ramrod made from a mop handle, de Guevain loaded the first charge of weed killer mix and a wad. As an afterthought he inserted one of the ornamental cannon-balls. He then retreated smartly behind a pile of sandbags while the Bear lit a paraffin-soaked rag stuck on the end of a fishing rod and, remaining under cover himself, swung the burning rag to the touchhole that he'd primed with black powder. There was a modest explosion, and the cannonball plopped to the ground about ten meters away.

"It'll scare 'em shitless," said de Guevain.

The Bear handed de Guevain the mop. "Sponge out," he said.

Sponging was an essential part of the procedure if the next gun-
powder charge was not to be prematurely ignited by either the hot
barrel or any remaining particles from the previous firing. "This time
I'm doubling the load—and you can do the honors."

The fourth shot sent the cannonball right through the stone wall of
the storehouse. It came to the Bear that Fitzduane's castle was due
for considerable structural alteration before the night was out.

They increased the charge slightly for the fifth test and used the
shrapnel mix. The results were awe-inspiring. The Bear and de Guevain settled on that formula and went to work making extra pre-
packed charges of both propellant and shrapnel out of rolled-up
newspapers and panty hose. By the time they had finished, darkness
had fallen.

Finally, it was truly night.

AIRBORNE APPROACHING THE WEST OF IRELAND—
2223 HOURS

Kilmara was in continuous radio contact with Ranger headquarters
in Dublin, but there was still no word from Fitzduane, and the
Ranger colonel was becoming increasingly worried. He could understand one or two checks being missed, given the social rather than
military environment in Fitzduane's castle, but the total silence over
such a long period was disturbing. Add in the inability to communicate with the guards at Draker—or, indeed, anyone else on the
island—and the bridge's being down, and it looked like this was
going to be no drill.

Flying in the silenced Optica in darkness was an experience. The
transparent Perspex bubble in which they were encased became
invisible, and one had the sense of being part of the night, of actually
flying without the physical aid of an airplane. It was disorienting.
There was no apparent structure from which to get one's bearings,
no window ledge or solid door. It was both exhilarating and terrify-
ing, but it did make for an outstanding observation platform, and
unlike a helicopter, which spends most of its time trying to shake
itself to pieces, the Optica had no problem with vibration.

He switched on the lightweight Barr and Stroud IR-18 thermal
imager and scanned the countryside below with the zoom lens set at

wide angle. The unit worked on the principle that everything above absolute zero emits some radiation in the electromagnetic spectrum and that some of this is infrared, with contrast resulting from both the relative temperatures and the strength of emission. The resulting television picture was a cross between conventional video black and white and a photographic negative. The system could "see" through mist and fog and normal camouflage. Fortunately, he thought, the human body is an excellent heat source and shows up clearly against most terrain. The unit just might help make some sense of what was going on on the island.

As the Optica flew on, he practiced mostly by spotting cows. On the outskirts of one village he ran across a hot spot he could not identify at first: the shape was horizontal and smaller than a cow, though it was emitting nicely. A check with the zoom revealed a couple hard at it on a blanket, a penumbra of hot air around the central image bearing witness to their dedication.

Kilmara knew that it was theoretically possible to land any of the three aircraft in the flight on the island—all had short takeoff and landing characteristics—but the margin for error was slight even during the day. It was not a viable option at night.

The Rangers were going to have to jump once he had some idea of the local tactical situation. The big question was where. Jumping on top of a hostile force in an age when everyone carried automatic weapons wasn't the best way to boost morale. He had already had the dubious thrill of jumping into enemy fire, and although the tracers looked pretty as they sailed up toward you, it wasn't an experience he longed to repeat.

From their past discussions Kilmara knew that Fitzduane's preferred tactical option would be to hole up in his castle until help came, but he also knew that what one wants and what happens in a combat situation can be very different things. Since the two sides, by definition, have totally opposing objectives, much of combat in reality tends to be a chaotic mess. In this situation the views of the college faculty could have complicated the equation. The action could be concentrated around Draker College.

Kilmara knew that his best chance of finding out what was going on before he committed his small force lay in making radio contact. The long-range transceiver might be out for some reason, but when he came close to the island, he should be able to make contact with Fitzduane's personal radio—if anyone was listening.

A message from Ranger headquarters sounded in his ears. An emergency meeting of the Security Committee of the Cabinet had convened. Right now the primary task of the Rangers, it had been clearly laid down, was to ensure the safety and integrity of the U.S. Embassy in Dublin. No convincing case had been made for any change to those instructions. Colonel Kilmara and the airborne Ranger group were to return to Baldonnel immediately. Kilmara's request for backup army support on standby had been denied.

The Taoiseach's hostility was becoming a problem. Well, fuck him anyway. The pilot looked at Kilmara. He had not acknowledged the radio message, though the routine words had come instinctively to his lips. He had served under the colonel for a considerable period of time. Kilmara pointed at the long-distance radio and drew a finger across his throat. The pilot switched off the unit and grinned. "Doing a Nelson?" he asked.

Kilmara made a face. "I've no ambitions to be a dead hero or to be kissed as I lie there dying," he said into the intercom.

"But Nelson won the battle," said the pilot.

Kilmara raised his eyebrows and went back to looking at cows. On previous operations they had always had the reassuring backup of the regular army. This time it looked as if they'd be on their own.

The black silhouettes of the hills of Connemara showed up on the horizon, and there was the glint of moonlight off a lake below. "ETA twenty-two minutes, Colonel."

The colonel had his eyes closed. "Too many cows," he said.

The pilot checked the firing circuits of the Optica's electronically controlled machine guns and rocket pods. The aircraft had been designed for observation and endurance, but with lightweight armaments it had proved possible to give it some punch.

The firing circuit check light glowed green. All was in order. The Rangers flew on.

FITZDUANE'S ISLAND—2220 HOURS

All preparations had been completed more than twenty minutes earlier, but a glow had lingered longer than expected in the sky, and Kadar wanted the maximum benefit from the cover of darkness. The night still wasn't jet black, but given the near-perfect day and the half-moon, it was as dark now as it was going to get within his time frame, and the increase in cloud cover should provide the needed protection.

Fitzduane's castle had been well enough sited to cope with medieval warfare and even conventional musketry, but it had disadvantages when longer-range weapons were brought into play. Kadar had found several random jumbles of boulders in a semicircle about a thousand meters from the castle, and there he had constructed three sangars, rock-fortified emplacements, to hold his two heavy machine guns and the SAM-7 missile. He was out of normal rifle range but well within the distance appropriate for a heavy sustained-fire weapon. The Russian 12.7 mm DShK 38/46 was effective up to two thousand meters.

Kadar regretted he hadn't brought any specialist night-vision equipment, but he doubted it would prove essential. Firing parameters had been constructed while there was still adequate light, and the basic structure of the castle was clearly outlined against the night sky. His covering fire might not be as accurate as he would have liked, but the volume would make up for it.

Another dull explosion sounded from within the castle courtyard—what the plans he had found in the Draker College library called a bawn—and he again failed to identify its source. It was too loud and resonant for a rifle or shotgun but lacked the acoustic power of a heavier weapon. Perhaps it wasn't an explosion at all but some kind of pile driving or hammering or an attempt to signal. A signal—that was probably it. He smiled to himself. It was a brave attempt, but there was nobody to hear.

He had brought two Powerchutes on the *Sabine* for the primary purpose of providing an escape vehicle in an extreme emergency. A Powerchute would get him off the island to a place where a vehicle, money, and other emergency supplies were concealed. The second unit was a backup.

He knew that in committing the Powerchutes to the battle ahead, he was cutting off his own last retreat, but that didn't matter anymore. This was a fight he was going to win. He didn't want the second-class option. He wanted the exhilaration that makes men the world over attempt the impossible, the thrill that comes from taking the maximum risk: of committing everything or dying.

He gave the signal. The Powerchutes started their engines and moved forward. Each powered parachute consisted of a tricycle framework with a propeller mounted at the rear. Forward momentum and the slipstream from the propeller inflated the parachute canopy. Within a few yards the Powerchutes were airborne and climbing rapidly. The Powerchute was a parachute that could go up as well as down; it could be maneuvered much like a powered hang glider, reach a height of ten thousand feet, fly at fifty kilometers per hour—or descend silently with the engine cut off. Each Powerchute had a maximum payload of 350 pounds, and in this case it was being used to the absolute limit. Each was fully laden with pilot, weapons, grenades, satchel charge, and homemade incendiaries.

Kadar turned to his final surprise. The welders of Malabar Unit had done an excellent job. The big German tractor and the trailer they had found at Draker College had been armored with steel plate—front, back, and sides—thick enough to stop high-velocity rifle bullets. Firing ports had been cut at regular intervals for the crew's automatic rifles, and an explosive charge protruded from a girder at the front.

Kadar had made himself a tank. He spoke into one of the Russian field radios and the tank-tractor's engines burst into life.

"Geranium force," he ordered. "Attack! Attack! Attack!"

The darkness around the castle was rent with streams of fire.

Chapter Twenty-eight

The sandbags covering the arrow slits shook under a burst of heavy-machine-gun fire that raked across the front of the gatehouse. Fitzduane had stipulated that the sandy earth used to fill the bags be well dampened. The sweating students had groaned because the earth was noticeably heavier when wet, but the merit of this precaution now became obvious: the damp earth absorbed even the heavy-machine-gun rounds, and though the sacks themselves were becoming bullet-torn, their contents stayed more or less in place. Their defenses against direct gunfire and the more dangerous problem within the stone confines of the castle—ricochets—were holding. Noble's mental image of the sandbags leaking their contents like a row of egg timers did not seem likely to materialize for some time.

Noble was just thinking that thanks to the castle's thick stone walls, the noise of the gunfire was almost bearable when a double blast sent tremors through the whole structure and temporarily deafened him. He removed a sandbag and peered through a murder hole overlooking the main gate. Two rocket-propelled grenades had blown huge gaps in the wooden gates. As he watched, two more

459

grenades impacted. He hugged the floor while further explosions rent the air only a few meters away from where he lay. Blasts of hot air and red-hot grenade fragments seared through the open murder hole. When the clatter of shrapnel falling to the floor had died down, he snatched a look at the gateway again. The second set of explosions had finished the destruction of the wooden gates and blown the splintered remnants off their hinges. Burning pieces of the gates cast flickers of orange light into the darkness, and the familiar smell of woodsmoke blended with the acrid fumes from the explosives. His initial shock at seeing their defenses torn away so quickly turned to relief when he noticed that the portcullis still stood more or less intact, its grid structure absorbing the shock waves and presenting a difficult target for the hollow-charge missiles.

A camouflaged figure darted out of the darkness and dropped to the ground. A few feet from Noble, Andreas was watching the perimeter through the night sight on his SA-80. The man was clutching a satchel charge. He lay in a slight dip, thinking he was concealed by the darkness while he regained his breath. He was still well over a hundred meters away.

Andreas fought the desire to shoot when the green-gray image of the terrorist showed clear against the orange graticule of the sight. It would be so easy. The temptation was nearly overwhelming, but Fitzduane had given strict orders that the night-vision equipment was to be used only for observation until he gave the word. He wanted the attackers to get cocky, to come closer thinking they were concealed by the darkness. To enter the killing ground.

"Sapper at two o'clock—a hundred and twenty meters," he said to Noble. "You take him." Noble looked toward him uncertainly, hearing the noise but not the words, and Andreas realized he must still be deafened from the blast. He repeated his request, shouting into Noble's ear. Noble nodded and readied his Uzi.

The sapper advanced another twenty meters on his belly and then broke into a run. The heavy machine gun began concentrating its fire on the gatehouse.

The sapper was fifty meters away when Noble, still dazed, fired and missed. The sapper hit the ground. He was now dangerously close, and Andreas was thinking that playing it smart and not using the SA-80s yet might mean not using the SA-80s ever. "Being too clever by half," as the English put it. The sapper showed himself again, and Andreas was about to fire when heavy-machine-gun rounds hitting just above the arrow slit made him duck, granite chips filling the air. He heard Noble's Uzi give a long half-magazine burst. Then the air outside the gatehouse was in flames as the satchel charge blew up, the force of the blast blowing him back from his firing position.

"Got him," said Noble.

Andreas grunted an acknowledgment. His ears were ringing. He thought he heard Noble say something, and then all he could think of was crouching out of harm's way as the heavy machine gun again cut in and methodically traced and retraced its malevolent way across the front of the gatehouse. The damn gun would burn out its barrels soon if it kept up this rate of fire.

There was a pause in its firing as if the gunner had read his mind, and he snatched a look into the darkness again with the SA-80 sight. He could see shapes getting nearer and decided to examine the ground in front of them more methodically. The heavy machine gun was still quiet, and the automatic rifle fire, though intense, was mostly going high.

Fitzduane had been right. The opposition was getting cocky. Whereas earlier, during daylight—and even more recently when the firing had commenced—they had all been nearly invisible under cover, now, confident of the concealing darkness, they had emerged from their positions and were moving forward slowly for an assault.

The death of the sapper did not seem to have deterred them, so something else must be up. He scanned the line of men again. There were no signs of scaling ladders or any other obvious method of gaining access to the castle. He looked deeper into the darkness. The Kite image intensifier was at its limit of operational effectiveness of six hundred meters when he began searching the road that led up to the castle. At first he could detect nothing except a faint impression of slow movement, and then out of the darkness he could see a large black shape with some long object protruding in front of it. He waited while the shape slowly advanced another hundred meters and then, after a further look, passed the SA-80 to Harry Noble.

The ambassador looked where he indicated and then ducked as muzzle flashes stabbed from the armored monolith creeping toward them. "I think we're moving toward the surprise event," he said.

"I hate surprises," said Andreas.

Noble was speaking by hand radio to Fitzduane. He put down the radio and fired several single shots into the darkness toward the spread-out line of advancing terrorists. Andreas watched them dive to the ground and then cautiously rise again when they realized that no one had been hit and the opposition was light.

There was an enormous explosion behind them from the direction of the keep. They both looked at the radio, which remained silent. Noble reached out and picked it up. He was about to press the call button when Fitzduane's voice crackled out of it. "Relax," it said. "That's part of the Bear's war, and he's doing just fine. Now get on with the gate."

Andreas looked at Noble. "Does he mean what I think he means?"

"It's what we planned," said Noble. "He wants us to open the portcullis." He pressed the switch, wondering if they still had power or if they would have to crank it by hand. The old motor whirred, then caught, and the spiked portcullis began to rise from the ground.

"This is crazy," said Andreas. "They'll get in."

"I think that's the whole idea," said Noble.

Andreas felt his bowels go liquid. He could hear Noble inserting a fresh magazine into the pistol grip of the Uzi and the click as the weapon was cocked. Noble indicated the Hawk grenade launcher and the bandolier of 40 mm grenades. "Fléchette rounds," he said, "then armor-piercing explosive."

THE FIGHTING PLATFORM of the keep was the best observation point in the castle. That was fine, except for the fact that it could clearly be seen to be so and as such was likely to attract unwelcome attention.

Apart from the anticipated volume of incoming fire, Fitzduane had been worried about its nature. The top of the keep was a flat, open rectangle with a high crenellated parapet that would tend to concentrate the effect of blast. It could be neutralized with one single mortar round or even a couple of grenades.

Fitzduane's solution led one student to remark that the Fitzduane family motto should be "Dig and Live" and its coat of arms a crossed pick and shovel on a background of sweat-saturated sandbags. A block and tackle were rigged on the platform, and a seemingly unending succession of sandbags and balks of timber and pieces of corrugated iron was hauled up. The result was a fair reproduction of a First World War trench dugout in the sky. The roof was designed to be mortarproof—at least for the first couple of blasts (during which time the occupants, if they had any sense, would bug out to the floor below). As it happened, the construction of the dugout roof made all the difference.

The pilots selected for the Powerchutes, two brothers, Husain and Mohsen, were Iranians and followers of a modified version of the teachings of Hasane Sabbah, who had founded the sect of the Assassins in the Elburz Mountains north of Teheran in the eleventh century. The brothers' early belief in the purity of assassination as a political tool had been tempered by the discovery that the game could work two ways. After an Israeli hit team had whittled their dedicated band of twenty down to just the pair of them, they had added the profit motive to the teachings of Hasane Sabbah. But they still retained enough fanaticism, or were just plain dumb enough, in Kadar's judgment, to be prepared to push their attacks to the absolute limit.

Photographs and drawings of the main features of Fitzduane's castle had been found in several books in the Draker College library, so the brothers had been thoroughly briefed. The plan was for the first Powerchute, flown by Husain, to swoop in and drop a satchel charge on the keep's fighting platform while the second Powerchute, flown by Mohsen, would send its specially weighted charge through the slate roof of the great hall. Both pilots would then drop their incendiaries on the great hall, into the yawning aperture made by the explosion of the weighted satchel charge, thus setting the top floor of the building alight—one guidebook made great reference to "the splendor of the carved oak beams dating from medieval times"—and rendering it uninhabitable. The pilots would then cut their engines and, using only the steerable ramjet parachutes of the Powerchutes, would land on the cleared fighting platform and hold it while their brethren reinforced them by climbing up from below on ropes.

The entire Powerchute attack, Kadar calculated, could be completed in less than ninety seconds. To check this, a rehearsal was carried out on the mock-Gothic keep of Draker College. Using dummy bombs and in daylight, the two brothers clocked in, on their first attempt, at a creditable ninety-four seconds, including a final sweep of the "fighting platform" with automatic rifle fire as they sailed down. They shaved a further five seconds off with practice.

The actual attack did not work out according to plan except that it accelerated the brothers' path to the goal of all followers of Hasane Sabbah killed in the line of duty: Eternal Paradise. But it was close.

The Powerchutes achieved total surprise. With the noise of their engines drowned by a fusillade from the cordon of terrorists, Husain was able to sweep in undetected and release his satchel charge—a webbing satchel containing plastic explosive, shrapnel, and a three-second fuse—exactly over the target. Unfortunately the light of the half-moon as it shone intermittently through the scurrying clouds made visibility difficult, and he didn't see the dugout that had been constructed on the platform.

The bomb glanced off the dugout and slid down toward the slate roof of the great hall. Exploding in a near-perfect imitation of a directional mine, the shrapnel caught the second Powerchute on its approach, which was lower than intended thanks to the fickleness of the Irish wind, in a pattern that would have done credit to a champion skeet shooter.

Mohsen didn't even have time to complain about the Irish climate or to reflect that it might have been a good idea to practice in advance with real explosives or to curse his miscalculating brother seven different ways. He was killed instantly, his body pierced in a dozen places, and his Powerchute carried him across the castle walls to crash minutes later in a ball of flame against the cliffs of the mainland. Inside the dugout, protected by a triple layer of sandbags, the Bear and Murrough were scarcely affected by the explosion except to feel a little sick at the thought that their attackers seemed to have the very weapon they had feared most—a mortar. Expecting a barrage of further rounds now that the gunner had zeroed in on them with the first shot—not so common with a mortar—they headed as one for the circular stairs and took up fresh positions in Fitzduane's bedroom immediately below.

The defenders on the battlements outside scarcely had time to think at all. First a huge black shape sailed by, spraying blood like some vampire celebrating the abolition of garlic, and then automatic-weapons fire from the sky made the point that the first vampire wasn't flying about alone.

Etan, crouched in a sandbag cocoon on the inland-facing battlements, was the first to react. The rapid semiautomatic fire of her Mauser caused Husain to take a raincheck on Paradise and to swerve away violently, abandoning any thoughts of dropping the incendiary on this pass. He banked and climbed to prepare for another run. All Etan could see was a black figure almost invisible against the clouds while the moon was obscured.

"What the fuck is that?" asked Henssen, who was wiping something wet off his face and hoping that it wasn't what he thought it was or, if it was, that it wasn't his. He couldn't feel any pain, but his heart felt as if it were going to pound its way out of his body.

"I don't know," said Etan, "some kind of flying thing, I think. It's like a balloon, but quick."

Fitzduane ran up in a crouching run, holding himself easily as if he'd done this kind of thing many times before—which he had. If nothing else, combat taught you very quickly to make yourself small. Fitzduane was an expert. He seemed to have visibly shrunk.

Etan pointed. Fitzduane, squatting well down behind the parapet and the sandbags, raised his SA-80 and examined the area she had indicated with the night sight. He could see nothing at first, given the Kite's limited field of view—one disadvantage of using a telescopic sight instead of wide-angle binoculars—but a quick pan picked up the image of a light metal frame containing a sitting figure with legs outstretched as if driving a go-cart. A checked keffiyeh was wrapped around its head and mouth, the ends streaming close to a giant propeller enclosed in a circular protective guard like that of a swamp boat. For an instant Fitzduane thought that if the keffiyeh would only stream back another couple of centimeters, the problem might solve itself. Then he looked further and saw the familiar outline of a military ramjet cargo parachute. The metal frame turned to head directly toward him, and he could see stabs of flame. He switched the fire selector of the SA-80 to automatic reluctantly, bearing in mind his own strictures on the subject, and opened fire.

The powered parachute was moving deceptively fast—somewhere in excess of forty kilometers per hour at a guess—and it sailed low over the castle before he could fire a second burst. A small black shape left the metal frame as it passed and landed on the opposite battlements, exploding among the zigzagging double line of sandbags and sending smoke and flames into the air and streams of liquid fire into the bawn below.

The powered parachute came into his line of vision again when it turned and prepared for a further attack. He could see the pilot in profile less than two hundred meters away. He fired again. This time the figure arched and its head sagged. The metal frame with its swamp boat propeller dipped but flew on and vanished into the darkness.

"Holy shit," said Henssen in relief, "but they're an all-singing, all-dancing outfit." He turned toward Etan, who seemed to have sunk out of sight behind the sandbags. "Good for you, Etan," he said. "If it hadn't been for you and your broom handle, we might have been barbecued."

There was a low moan from behind the angle of the sandbags that concealed Etan. The bags were arranged in a double zigzagging line along the battlements to minimize the effects of exploding hand grenades or mortar bombs.

Henssen turned the angle.

Etan lay on her back, her hands gripping her right thigh. Blood, black in the darkness, welled through her fingers.

OUTSIDE FITZDUANE'S CASTLE—2242 HOURS

Abu Rafa, commander of Malabar Unit—the unit responsible for the attack on the gatehouse—could scarcely contain his frustration. In his considered professional opinion, Kadar, who might be brilliant at planning terrorist incidents and kidnaps, was making a mess of a classic but straightforward infantry problem: the capture of a weakly held strongpoint by superior military forces.

The correct solution would have been to attack immediately on landing while the momentum of the initial assault was with them and when daylight would have allowed them to apply their superior firepower to full effect—and to hell with casualties, which wouldn't have been heavy anyway in a sudden, forceful attack.

Bringing up the heavy machine guns, waiting until dark, and using such gadgetry as the Powerchutes and the tank-tractor struck Abu Rafa as a load of pretentious shit. Ironically it reminded him of the warnings of his onetime archenemy, he of the black eyepatch, General Moshe Dayan of Israel. Dayan had become disturbed at the tendency of the Israeli Army after the War of Independence to try for clever tactics instead of forcing home the attack—what he called the "Jewish solution." Most times, Dayan argued, what counted was less *how* you attacked than the spirit and force with which you did it; the intention should be to "exhaust the mission," to keep at it until you succeeded and not fuck around trying to be clever.

Abu Rafa thought that Dayan, may he rot forever in hell, was right, Allah knows. The accursed Israelis had proved it often enough—and unfortunately by combining the best of both approaches.

The Malabar commander's frustration was further exacerbated by the latest developments: the tank-tractor, whose attack should have coincided with the Powerchute assault, had broken down less than five hundred meters from the gatehouse. The fault wasn't serious and would mean only a fifteen-minute delay, but it occurred after the Powerchutes were beyond recall so the benefits of a combined strike had been lost.

The good news was that the defenders' volume of fire was very light and not accurate, except, it appeared, at close range—as the sapper had learned the hard way. Apart from him, there had been no casualties in Malabar. Seeing the weakness of the opposition and fed up with freezing in the chill night air, in what by Irish standards was a comparatively balmy evening, the commandos of Malabar were raring to go.

At first Abu Rafa thought it must be some trick of the light, and then it became clear that what he was seeing was really happening: the portcullis, that much more serious obstacle than the now-destroyed heavy oak gates, was rising. A sally by the defenders? Most unlikely. A trick? They wouldn't dare, given their inferior firepower. No, either they were surrendering or the incoming fire had affected the portcullis mechanism. Or maybe the Sacrificer was still alive and was working inside in their behalf.

Whatever the reason, it was visible proof of which side Allah was backing. Abu Rafa looked at his Russian radio and for a second debated getting Kadar's permission to attack—and then frustration won out.

"Malabar first section," he shouted, "follow me!" With a ferocity that General Dayan himself would have admired, he ran forward, firing from the hip, followed by the shouting, cheering men of the first section, automatic rifles blazing. They stormed through the gateway and were spreading to the left and right to secure the gatehouse and the battlements when Abu Rafa first had the thought that maybe Allah was hedging his bets.

The courtyard was suddenly illuminated by floodlights. Straight ahead of him and on the battlements there were sandbagged emplacements. A burst of fire hit him in the chest, severing ribs and blowing apart his lungs. He saw three of his men disintegrate as a tongue of flame followed by a shattering roar burst forth from an opening in a pile of sandbags.

The last sound he heard before his body was shredded by the second concealed cannon at point-blank range was that of the portcullis slamming shut.

FITZDUANE'S CASTLE—2250 HOURS

Eleven terrorists had gotten in—rather more than had been planned for—before the portcullis was dropped back into place. As a killing ground the bawn was ideal, and for the first few seconds surprise was total. Facing the terrorists were the two cannon manned by the Bear and de Guevain. Fitzduane, Judith Newman, and Henssen fired from the battlements. Noble and Andreas cut off the rear.

Seven terrorists died in the defenders' first hail of fire before the lights were shot out, and two more were caught by fléchette rounds fired from a murder hole by Andreas as they scrabbled at the portcullis and called to their comrades outside.

The two surviving terrorists had gone in the same direction but were now on different levels. One had made it to the battlements about twenty meters from where Etan lay wounded and unconscious, the bleeding now stopped temporarily by a tourniquet that had been applied by Henssen. The other, immediately below, had made it to the cover of the outhouse—the one that had been used as a test target for the cannon—located almost immediately under his comrade's hiding place. He was using the windows and apertures to shoot from, and his short, professional bursts were disconcertingly well placed. The Bear and de Guevain were pinned down. They couldn't get around the front of the cannon to reload without exposing themselves to the crossfire from one of the two terrorist positions.

Andreas had released his loaded fléchette rounds. The next 40 mm grenades in the Hawk were dual-purpose armor-piercing. He checked the ammunition reserve. After he had fired the two in the weapon, he would have two armor-piercing left. Most of the ammunition supply consisted of the standard M406 HE (High Explosive), although there still remained some other specialized rounds for specific applications.

Fitzduane was on the battlements across from the terrorists. The sandbags were now working in the terrorists' favor. The infiltrator on the parapet was well concealed behind the zigzagging fortifications and was well positioned to sweep most of the bawn with fire. More seriously, if he could hold his position, he would be joined by reinforcements climbing up that section of the wall. It was beginning to look to Fitzduane as if his plan to whittle down the opposition in a killing ground might backfire.

Fitzduane spoke into the radio. "Harry, what's that armored tractor of theirs up to?"

"It's halted about five hundred meters away." Noble peered through the night sight. "There are a couple of people working on it, so I guess it broke down. Probably caused by all that weight. I wouldn't count on its staying that way for long. And by the way, we've only got four rounds of armor-piercing left."

"Have you a shot at either of our visitors?"

"Without moving, negative. Want us to give it a try?"

"No," said Fitzduane. "You and Andreas stay where you are and hold that gate. Use the SA-80 on single shot, and see if you can take out the guys working on the tank. We need to buy some time." Fitzduane clicked the radio to another channel. "Check in, Henssen."

"Etan needs help," answered Henssen. "I'm okay."

"You've got a hostile about twenty meters away, gatehouse direction," said Fitzduane.

"I know," said Henssen. "I'm going to take him out."

"No," said Fitzduane. "No crawling around corners yet. Use the Molotov cocktails. I'm sending Judith along to help."

There was the explosion of a grenade from behind the battlement sandbags facing Fitzduane, followed by a burst of AK-47 fire. There was a pause of about thirty seconds, and the routine was repeated.

"I think our visitor is coming my way," said Henssen into the radio. "He's grenading each zig and zag as he comes."

"Give ground," said Fitzduane.

"Why do you think we're still alive?" cried Henssen. "But it's slow pulling Etan. If he rushes us, we're fucked."

"If he rushes you, blow his head off."

"Hugo," said Murrough, "I'm within a whisper of a clear shot. When he next raises his head, I'll get him."

"Jesus," said Fitzduane, "where the hell are you?"

"Top of the keep," said Murrough. "Top of the dugout, in fact."

Judith slid in beside Henssen, smelling of poteen and gasoline from the bag of Molotov cocktails she carried. "Get her out of here," she said to Henssen, who hesitated. "Now!" she whispered urgently. Henssen did as he was told. He crawled away, dragging the unconscious Etan along the gritty stone behind him.

Judith lit two of the Molotov cocktails and tossed them over the angled wall of sandbags, where they burst farther down the battlements. She lit two more and threw them. A line of flame lit up the night, exposing two attackers who were climbing through the crenellations behind where the terrorist was concealed.

Fitzduane and Murrough fired instantly, hitting the same man. Already dead, he collapsed forward into the burning gasoline. The second climber died a second later when Judith took his head off with a burst from her Uzi. The original terrorist, his keffiyeh and camouflage a mass of flame, ran screaming along the battlements toward Judith, a fighting knife in his hand and all caution driven from his body by the intense pain.

There was a double stab of flame from a shotgun, and the burning terrorist was hurled back against the sandbags, his lower body a bloody, wet mass. Katia Maurer reloaded the shotgun and went back to tending Etan. Judith replaced the empty magazine on her Uzi and tried to stop shaking.

Henssen took the lighter from her trembling hands and lit a succession of Molotov cocktails and sent them hurtling down to the base of the battlements. There were screams and cries from below. Through a firing slit figures could be seen retreating into the darkness. One dropped after Murrough fired from the dugout roof. Judith crawled along the battlements and swung two Molotov cocktails tied to a length of electrical wire through the windows of the outhouse below, turning the remaining terrorist's hiding place into a furnace. Seconds passed, and then, with a cry, a burning figure ran out into the combined gunfire of Fitzduane and Judith.

Suddenly, as if by agreement between the two opposing forces, the shooting stopped, and there was almost complete silence. Fitzduane became aware of the sound of the sea and of the wind as it blew across the battlements, and he could hear the hiss as the flames encountered the wetness of body tissue and blood. He could hear the cries of the wounded outside the castle. By the light of the nearly spent Molotov cocktails he could see bodies littering the bawn below, where the Bear and Christian de Guevain had emerged from their sandbag emplacements and were already halfway through loading the cannon.

He became aware of something else, a voice repeating something again and again. It seemed to make no sense; there was no one there. He sat down and shook his head. The voice continued. He could see himself as if he were detached from his body and floating in the darkness. He looked down, and he could see the castle spread out below and fires burning inside it and outside the walls.

Slowly he felt himself being drawn back into the castle, and then the Bear was shaking him gently by the shoulder and talking into the radio, and he could hear the faint sound of suppressed aircraft engines overhead.

ABOVE FITZDUANE'S ISLAND—2305 HOURS

"I don't believe it," said the pilot. "It's nearly the end of the twentieth century, and there is a siege going on that's straight from the Middle Ages."

"Not exactly the Middle Ages," said Kilmara. Two lines of heavy-caliber tracer curved out of the darkness and converged on the castle.

"Green tracer, 12.7-millimeter," said the pilot. He had flown forward air control in Vietnam. "Kind of makes me feel nostalgic. We're out of range at this height, though a few thousand feet lower it'll be no day at the beach. I wonder what else they've got."

"I expect we'll find out," said Kilmara. "Get Ranger HQ on the radio."

The transport twins and their cargoes of Rangers had been left to circle out of sight and earshot over the mainland while the Optica went ahead to do what it was good at: observe. They were flying at five thousand feet above the island for a preliminary reconnaissance while Kilmara tried to establish radio contact with Fitzduane below and to determine the scale and location of what he was up against.

Already he realized that he had underestimated the opposition. The sight of the *Sabine* offshore told him how the Hangman's main force had arrived, and that suggested very strongly that the Dublin operation was a bluff.

The Rangers had nearly been caught off guard completely. As it

was, most of his force was more than two hours away even if it was
released immediately—which he doubted would happen.

FITZDUANE'S CASTLE—2307 HOURS

Sheltered in the storeroom off the main tunnel, the surviving students felt more than heard the initial noises of combat above and
around them. The subsequent sound of cannon fire almost directly
overhead was more immediate and menacing. It brought home the
unpleasant thought that they were not out of danger yet—and that
the defenders of the castle might lose. The prospect of being held
hostage again by people as ruthless as these terrorists accelerated the
process of selecting volunteers to join in the fighting.

There had at first been some resentment at Fitzduane's decision to
keep them unarmed and away from the firing line, but the logic of his
reasoning soon won out. They had to face the unpalatable fact that
the initial threat had come from their own student body—and there
was no guarantee that one or two or more Sacrificers might not be
left. The discussion of how to resolve this dilemma had begun enthusiastically but not very productively. Things changed when the
Swede, Sig Bengtquist, a mathematician and a distant relative of the
Nobel family, started to speak. Up to now he had been silent, but the
notepad he seemed never to be without, even when dragged un-
willingly into some sporting activity, was covered with neat jottings
in his microscopic handwriting.

"There is no foolproof way of ensuring that we do not select a
Sacrificer by accident," he said. "But I think we can establish some
orderly criteria to improve our chances of choosing the right people."

"You've worked out a mathematical formula," said a voice.

"Yes," said another. "We're going to draw the lucky winners out
of a hat or roll dice to see who gets a chance to be shot at."

There was strained laughter. They had decidedly mixed feelings
about experiencing any further the lethal realities of combat. Some
were terrified at the thought. Others were itching for a chance to hit
back and be players and not merely pawns in this game of life and
death. What they had seen earlier in the day—the slaughter in the
college—had left them with no illusions about glory or the supposed
glamour of war.

"Go on, Sig," said the deep baritone voice of Osman Ba, a Sudanese from the northern part of the country and the Swede's best friend. From the contrast in their coloring they were known as "Day and Night." There were nods of agreement from the others. There were about fifty students in the room—representing half as many nationalities—and since there weren't enough chairs, most were sitting on boxes or on rugs on the floor. Empty sandwich plates and glasses were piled next to the door. Several of the students, worn out by the excitement of the day and the post-stress reaction, had fallen asleep. The others all looked tired, but what they were trying to do held their interest, and their eyes, though mostly red-rimmed from strain and fatigue, were keen and alert.

"I have drawn up a matrix," said Sig, "a spread sheet if you're accountancy-minded, cross-referencing all who have volunteered to fight with the criteria. As it happens, this approach produces sixteen names, so we still have to find some way to whittle the list down to the ten names we've been asked for. I would suggest nothing more scientific than reviewing the sixteen names and, after any objections, putting all the remaining ones into a hat and pulling out the first ten."

"Makes sense," said Osman Ba.

"What are these criteria?" asked one of the Mexicans. "I think it's only fair that we should know how these names have been selected."

"Of course," said Sig. "The points are mostly obvious. All additional suggestions are welcome." There was silence in the room before Sig spoke again. They could hear sounds of gunfire and more explosions. The prospect of leaving their safe underground haven was looking less appealing by the minute.

"Not a member of the ski club," said Sig. "All the known Sacrificers were, you will recall."

"That lets me out," said a Polish student, "but it doesn't make me a Sacrificer."

"Eighteen or over," continued Sig, "familiar with weapons, good health and eyesight and no serious physical defects, good reflexes, good English—that seems to be the common language among the existing defenders. Not an only child." The list went on for another dozen points. "And someone we all instinctively trust. Gut feel," he added.

He read out the sixteen names. Three were vetoed. At Sig's suggestion, no reasons were given. The remaining thirteen names were placed in the now-empty bread bin. Three minutes later the chosen ten looked at each other in the knowledge that before dawn one or some or all of them might be wounded, even dead.

Sig was elected leader of the volunteers.

"Why only ten of us, I wonder?" asked Osman Ba. "They could have asked for more. Why not twelve like the apostles?"

"One of the twelve was a traitor," said Sig. "I guess Fitzduane is trying to improve the odds." He was reflecting that his little group was about as multinational as it could be. Would it help that traditional enemies—Russian and Pole, Kuwaiti and Israeli, French and German among them—were now on the same side? Did it make any difference what nationality you were when you were dead?

His mouth was dry, and he swallowed. Osman was doing the same thing, he noticed. That made him feel marginally better.

ABOVE FITZDUANE'S CASTLE—2307 HOURS

"Quite a party," said Kilmara into his helmet microphone.

"About bloody time," answered Fitzduane. The signal strength was good, and though his tone was professionally neutral, the relief in his voice was palpable. "I hope you've brought some friends. The Hangman is here in strength."

"Situation report," said Kilmara.

Fitzduane told him, his summary succinct and almost academic, detailing nothing of the fear and the pain and the gut-churning tension of combat.

"Can you hold?" asked Kilmara. "I'll have to locate my DZ well north of you or the 12.7s won't leave much of us. It could take an hour or longer to link up with you."

"We'll hold," said Fitzduane, "but it's getting hairy. We don't have enough bodies to man the full perimeter properly. We may have to fall back to the keep."

"Very well," said Kilmara. A heat signature blossomed on the IR-18 screen. Reflexes already primed, virtually simultaneously the pilot punched a switch to ripple-fire flares and, banking away from the oncoming missile, put the Optica into a series of violent maneuvers culminating in a steep dive.

"A fucking SAM," said the pilot seconds later when it was

clear that the heat-seeking missile had been successfully decoyed by the intense heat of the flares. "Who would have thought it? A heat-seeking SAM-7 at a guess. Good thing we got away or we'd be fireworks."

"Brace yourself for more fancy flying," said Kilmara. "We're going to have to keep their heads down during the jump." He broke off to bark instructions to the two Ranger transport aircraft, which were preparing for a run to the drop zone. In response, the lead plane peeled off to starboard, leaving the second Islander alone heading toward the DZ. It was out of range of the heavy machine guns, but a SAM-7—what the Russians call a *Strela* or "Arrow"—has a range of up to 4,500 meters, depending on the model, and the slow Islander, low and steady for the drop, would be a tempting target. A possible tactic was to fly very low because a SAM-7 isn't at its best below 150 meters, but there was the small matter of allowing the parachutes time to open. In addition, budget constraints had meant that automatic flare dispensers weren't fitted to the transports, though conventional Very pistols were carried and might be of some help.

Kilmara raised Fitzduane again for a brief discussion of tactics and the disposition of the Hangman's forces. The primary targets would be the missile position and the heavy-machine-gun emplacements. The other threats would have to wait.

Unfortunately they wouldn't. As the Optica prepared for its strafing run and the Ranger transport flew toward the DZ, the Hangman launched another attack on the castle, with the tank spearheading the thrust.

FITZDUANE'S CASTLE—2318 HOURS

The tank was advancing very slowly. The weight of its armor alone was unlikely to account for its pace, nor would there be any tactical reason for advancing at a crawl, so either the machine wasn't working properly or there were more unpleasant surprises in store.

At 150 meters, Andreas opened fire with the Hawk, acutely conscious that he had only four armor-piercing rounds left. A Kalashnikov bullet ricocheted through the arrow slit as he fired the first projectile, and he missed completely. Shaken, he aimed again. When the tank was about 120 meters away, he fired. This time the round punched through the armor plate and exploded. Still the tank came on.

At eighty meters Andreas fired two more armor-piercing rounds. One 40 mm grenade hit the facing armor plate close to where it butted against the side armor. The explosion blew the welding, peeling open the front of the tank like the lid of a sardine can. Still the tank came on, and only then were the slow speed of the vehicle and its resistance to the armor-piercing grenades explained. Behind the steel plate was a second multilayer wall of concrete blocks and sandbags, their sheer physical mass impossible to penetrate with the light weaponry at the defenders' disposal.

The peeled-back armor and the close range did offer some possibilities. Andreas lowered his aim. Perhaps he could knock out a wheel or disable the steering mechanism. His last armor-piercing round seemed to have little effect, but three high-explosive grenades fired in quick succession from less than forty meters at the right front wheel of the armored tractor jammed a steering rod and forced the vehicle marginally out of alignment with the gate.

Still the vehicle came on. Firing was now incessant on all sides. The terrorists sensed that they were close to breaching the castle, and the defenders, casting aside all attempts at restraint, used their night vision–equipped SA-80s and full firepower to devastating effect.

It wasn't enough. Six terrorists died in the hail of accurate automatic rifle fire before the remainder realized what they must be up against and sought physical cover—but then sheer numbers began to tell. A gap in the clouds meant that moonlight illuminated the battleground for a few critical minutes. Windows and firing slits could be seen as black rectangles against the gray mass of the castle walls. Accurate automatic rifle fire kept the defenders pinned down while the tank prepared to advance to point-blank range, where it would detonate the explosives it carried on a boom.

Keeping Fitzduane's castle between it and the SAM-7 position, the Optica screamed low over the sea at near-zero height, causing Murrough on the roof of the dugout to duck as the futuristic-looking aircraft flashed above him before it climbed at the last moment and then banked and dived. The SAM-7 fired a split second before a stream of tracer bullets followed by rockets blew the entire missile crew to pieces and the launcher into the undergrowth.

The SAM-7 had been aimed at the Ranger transport carrying out its low-level drop on the north side of the island. Six Rangers had jumped before the missile, traveling at one and a half times the speed of sound, hit the port engine. The high-explosive head ignited on contact, blasting the engine and wing off the aircraft and setting fire to the fuel tanks. The sky lit up, and the flaming mass, raining debris, knifed its way through the night air and exploded against the hillside, mercifully cutting short the agonies of the pilot and copilot and the remaining two Rangers still aboard. One more Ranger was killed by a piece of red-hot engine cowling as he swung from his parachute.

Five Rangers, including both members of the Milan missile team, reached the ground alive. When they linked up Lieutenant Harty, the unit commander, checked in by radio with Kilmara. Then he spoke into his helmet microphone. "Let's do it, lads," he said. "Time for them to pay the bill."

Spread out in combat formation, faces blackened, heavily laden with weapons, ammunition, and equipment, the unit moved toward the action. The sound of firing, the crump of grenades, the arcing of tracers, and a burning glow indicated with brutal simplicity the location of the battleground.

FITZDUANE'S CASTLE—2338 HOURS

Andreas loaded his last two high-explosive grenades. The noise inside the gatehouse was deafening. Beside him, Harry Noble, reinforced now by the Bear and de Guevain, fired burst after burst at the elusive, threatening figures outside. The terrorists had learned from their earlier casualty rate and now made use of every scrap of cover, including the lumbering shape of the tank. Their fire had increased in accuracy and was backed by the heavy machine guns, which made accurate defensive fire nearly impossible even when a clear target could be made out.

The tank was less than twenty meters away—it was now obvious that the boom with the explosive charge was inside some sort of protective metal casing—when Andreas released his very last grenade. The tank lurched as if it were human. The right wheel and steering rods had been blown away completely. Already veering to the right of the gate before the final grenade hit, the tank now slewed off the road completely and tottered over on its side. Andreas and Noble gave a cheer.

"Down!" shouted the Bear, pushing Andreas to the floor. The entire building rocked as the boom charge exploded. The blast funneled through firing slits and murder holes, throwing Noble, who had reacted a shade too slowly, against the portcullis winding mechanism. The main gear wheel tore open his body in a dozen places, killing him instantly. The Bear glanced through a murder hole. The main force of the blast had been dissipated against the thick walls of the bawn. The portcullis, though twisted and bent and bearing the scars of the earlier RPG-7 assault, was still intact. He checked the castle approach, where the wrecked tank, now reduced to a twisted mass of hot metal, lay to one side. As he watched, thick smoke, billowing from a row of smoke grenades, began to obscure the access road to the portcullis. The temporary lull in the firing from the terrorists in front of the castle ceased, and yet again automatic fire thudded off the castle walls and whined through the firing slits.

A roaring shape, a Land Rover, shot out of the smoke and smashed into the portcullis. The Bear glimpsed a figure jumping from it just before impact, and again he flung Andreas to the floor.

This time the force of the explosion was truly horrific in its immediacy and intensity. The floor heaved and ripped open, revealing the mangled remains of the portcullis below. It was no longer an effective barrier. Dazed and breathless from the blast and unable to respond, the Bear watched helplessly as figures ran through the open gateway.

He heard running footsteps on the stairs outside, and a hand grenade was thrown into the room. The small black object bounced across the floor before the Bear's eyes, coming to a halt less than two meters from him. It seemed to pause before toppling over through the crack in the floor and exploding a split second later.

A camouflage-clad figure, the keffiyeh around his neck wet with blood from a long slash on his right cheek, burst into the room, firing an AK-47. Lying on the floor just behind him and out of sight, de Guevain, who had been reloading, grabbed a cavalry saber and slashed the terrorist across the back of the knees. The terrorist pitched forward, his automatic rifle dropping from his hands. Andreas, also sprawled on the floor, extended his SA-80 with one hand and pressed the muzzle against the terrorist's neck. The three-round burst exploded the man's head and filled the room with a red mist.

A second grenade was lobbed into the room, but in his excitement the terrorist in the doorway had forgotten to pull the pin. The Bear, still shaken but forced into action by the desperate need to survive, seized it, pulled the pin, and threw it back through the doorway.

The terrorist concealed there couldn't run for cover down the narrow circular stairs because of the men behind him. There wasn't time to throw the grenade back into the room. He chose the only option he could think of and dived into the room away from the grenade, rolled, and came up firing. Rounds pumped into Harry Noble's dead body. The grenade exploded at the top of the circular staircase, temporarily blocking access to the room. Andreas shot the terrorist in the stomach before he had time to change his point of aim.

De Guevain ran to the concealed door that led to the tunnel and swung it open. Andreas and the Bear grabbed what extra weapons and ammunition they could and, with a last glance at Harry Noble's body, ran for safety. De Guevain followed, pulling the massive door behind him and ramming home the series of bolts and securing bars. They had bought some time at the cost of yet another life—but the Hangman's forces were now inside the castle.

ABOVE FITZDUANE'S ISLAND—2351 HOURS

The *Sabine* had moved to within five hundred meters of the shore and then had opened fire on the keep with a pair of heavy machine guns. Murrough had been swept off the dugout roof by this concentration of fire from an unexpected quarter, and his body now lay outside the castle walls.

Circling high above the battlefield, his ammunition low, Kilmara had expended the last of his ordnance on this new threat. In two low-level attacks he had put the heavy machine guns out of action and holed the ship below the waterline. The cattle boat, essentially a series of open ramp-linked decks with the engine and crew quarters at the stern, had no bulkheads, and seawater had rushed in through the holes. The *Sabine* was sinking.

The few surviving crew had headed toward land in an inflatable. With the Optica's external weaponry out of ammunition, Kilmara instructed the pilot to fly low. He killed the three survivors with his automatic rifle, using the Kite night sight and shooting through a firing port in the door.

The SAM-7 missile was out of commission, and there was no sign that the terrorists had brought more than one unit, so the Optica was now operating as it had been built to—as a combined observation aircraft and command post. Kilmara's eyes were fixed mainly on the IR viewer screen, with intermittent glances at the flames and tracers and other graphic signs of the intense combat below. Keeping above the effective range of the surviving land-based heavy machine guns, the Optica circled the combat zone, monitoring developments, providing precise enemy position locations for the advancing Rangers, and keeping in touch with Fitzduane, Dublin, and the remaining Ranger transport, which was still circling, ready to drop its force as soon as the heavy machine guns were silenced.

As commander, Kilmara found that the hardest part of any combat situation was the necessity of remaining aloof from the main action while his men fought and, all too often, died. He had a near-overwhelming desire to parachute from his transparent bubble in the sky, but he kept it suppressed and concentrated on what the modern military termed "C3I": command, control, communications, and intelligence. Or, as he had once termed it: "Fucking around with a fiddle while Rome burns."

If only the Rangers on the ground could clear the heavy machine guns out of the way, then he could bring the balance of his force into action. "If only"—a pretty useless phrase in the real world.

Kilmara pressed the radio transmit button to call the Rangers on the ground but after a moment released it without speaking. His men knew full well what to do.

IRONICALLY, CONSIDERING the arrival of the Rangers on the island and the recent news that regular army reinforcements were at last on the way—although they would not arrive for several hours—the situation on the ground had never looked worse. The terrorists were now inside the castle. They had taken the gatehouse and occupied the outhouses and battlements of the bawn. Fitzduane had just made the decision to abandon the great hall and consolidate in the keep and the tunnel below. He hadn't much choice, since the terrorists occupied the floors below the great hall.

Fitzduane's original force had been whittled down to seven effectives, including two middle-aged women who were primarily noncombatants. Several of the seven were wounded, lightly in most cases but with the inevitable toll on energy and stamina. Henssen had lost the use of one arm. Ammunition, given the intensity of the combat, was running low. The grenades and other specialized weaponry had been largely expended.

With great reluctance, Fitzduane deployed the ten student volunteers. At the rate things were going, he'd soon be down to a bunch of teenagers and medieval weaponry.

Chapter Twenty-nine

Kadar's mood had oscillated from one extreme to the other during the last few hours. Now, despite the initial setbacks, he felt euphoric. Victory was imminent, and it was all the sweeter for being the harder won.

He looked around the great hall. The room was impressive, the quality of the woodwork outstanding. How many generations of Fitzduanes had talked and eaten and planned in this very room? What blood had been shed here? What compromises and betrayals had been required for the Fitzduanes to have survived Ireland's turbulent history?

He sat in the padded carved oak chair at the head of the table and rubbed his fingers on its massive, timeworn oaken mass. He could feel the slight undulations that represented the original adz marks. My God, he thought, this banqueting table must have been made before Christopher Columbus sailed for America, before Leonardo da Vinci painted the Mona Lisa, before Louis XIV built Versailles.

"Sir?" said Sabri Sartawi, the commander of Icarus Unit and now the only one of Kadar's senior officers still alive. Kadar was sitting at the head of the table, his eyes closed, his fingers caressing the beeswax-polished wood. There was a smile on his face. Desultory gunfire could be heard around the keep, and from time to time the dull whump of a Molotov cocktail. It was a hell of a time to daydream, but nothing Kadar did surprised Sartawi anymore. The man was obviously insane; still, his insanity was mixed with brilliance. It now looked as if despite everything, they were going to pull it off.

"Sir?" repeated Sartawi more forcefully, and Kadar's eyes snapped open. For a moment Sartawi thought he had gone too far. The eyes blazed with anger.

The moment passed. "Yes?" said Kadar mildly. His fingers were still feeling the patina of the table.

"Situation report, sir," said Sartawi.

"Proceed."

"We've broken through the concealed door in the gatehouse winding room," said Sartawi. "It leads down a circular staircase into a tunnel. We estimate that the tunnel links up with the base of the keep, but we can't be sure because our way is blocked by a heavy steel door."

"Blow it."

"We can't," said Sartawi. "We used up the last of our explosives in the car bomb. We're out of grenades and RPG-7 projectiles, too. We never expected to have to fight this kind of battle. Also, we're very low on ammunition, perhaps one to two magazines per man."

"Are the Powerchute and the LPO-50 ready?" said Kadar. The Powerchute in question was the one that had been flown by that unlucky follower of Hasane Sabah, the Iranian Husain. Although Husain had lost interest in this world after his encounter with the firepower of Fitzduane's SA-80, his dead body had balanced the motorized parachute in such a way that it had made quite a respectable landing on its own—not far from the takeoff point. Kadar had had it moved so that it could take off again out of sight of the defenders in the keep.

"Both are ready," said Sartawi. "And the heavy-machine-gun crews have been briefed."

Kadar was silent for a moment, lost in thought. He pushed back his chair, stood up, and paced up and down the room. He turned to Sartawi. "We have metal-cutting equipment," he said, "the stuff we used to make that armored tractor. Use that on the tunnel door. I'll lay odds that our hostages are on the other side. I want the door open at the same time as the Powerchute attack. Also, I want all this"—he gestured around at the great hall—"set fire to. We'll burn the bastards out."

"What about the Rangers?" asked Sartawi. "A few jumped, I think, before we hit the plane."

"A handful of men two kilometers away isn't likely to affect the outcome," said Kadar. "And by the time they get close enough to join in the fighting, we'll have the castle and the hostages."

I hope you're right, thought Sartawi, but he didn't say anything. He'd heard the Rangers were formidable, but it was true there could be only a few of them—and they would be out in the open against the fortified heavy-machine-gun positions.

Kadar took one last look at the great hall. "Beautiful, isn't it?"

Sartawi issued the orders. Battle-fatigued members of Icarus Unit hauled cans of fuel up the stairs and drenched the floor and timbers of the huge room, then spilled more fuel on the stairs and in the rooms below.

FITZDUANE'S CASTLE—0013 HOURS

There had been a brief lull in the fighting, though sporadic sniping continued. Fitzduane had used the respite to arm and deploy the students and to carry out a quick tour of inspection of his much-diminished perimeter. Everyone was exhausted and hungry and looked it. Food was provided while there was the opportunity. They all knew they had very little time.

Slumped on a sandbag in a corner of what had been his bedroom but was now the main defensive post at the top of the keep—the fighting platform seemed to attract a disproportionate amount of heavy-machine-gun fire—Fitzduane took the mug of coffee and the sandwich that Oona offered him. He didn't really know what to say to her. Only twelve hours ago she had been a contented woman with a husband she adored—and now Murrough was dead. So many dead, and because of him. Would it have been better to have stood aside and let the Hangman have his way? He didn't think so, but when your own immediate world was affected, it was hard to know what was right.

Truth to tell, violence didn't discriminate. The victims of warfare in the main weren't any better or worse than anybody else, whatever the propaganda made out. The North Vietnamese, the South Vietnamese, the Israelis, the Arabs, the police, the terrorists—almost all were fundamentally alike when you really got down to it: ordinary people with wives and mothers like Oona who got caught up with something that got out of control.

Oona finished dispensing coffee and sandwiches to the others in the room before turning back and looking at him. Fitzduane felt the sandwich turn to cardboard in his mouth. He swallowed with difficulty and then tried to say something appropriate, but what words he managed sounded inadequate.

Oona kissed him on the forehead. "Now look, Hugo," she said, "we all have to die, and Murrough died in a good cause, to save other people, and children at that. He died fighting and, may the Lord have mercy on his soul, but he loved to fight."

When Fitzduane took her in his arms, he could feel her sobs, he could hear Murrough talking to him, he could see him, and he knew then that whatever the Hangman might attempt this time, he was going to be stopped.

Oona gently freed herself and wiped the tears from her eyes. "Eat your food and don't worry about Etan," she said. "And then put a stop to the Hangman once and for all."

Fitzduane smiled thinly. "No problem."

Oona hugged him again, then returned to help the others.

As she left, the Bear came into the room and sat down on another sandbag facing Fitzduane. He was puffing slightly. "Castles," he finally managed, "weren't built for people of my dimensions and stature."

"If you wore armor regularly," said Fitzduane, "you got into shape fast enough, and hopping up and down circular stairs was no problem. Also, everyone was smaller in those days."

"Hmph," muttered the Bear. He ate the rest of Fitzduane's sandwich in silence.

"You did an ammunition check?" asked Fitzduane.

"Uh-huh"—the Bear nodded—"another one. You won't be surprised to hear the situation has worsened. I'm impressed at how much we've been able to get through. I guess it's not surprising when you can empty a thirty-round magazine in less than three seconds."

"So how many seconds per man do we have?" said Fitzduane with a tired smile.

"For automatic weapons, less than five. We're better off for shotgun rounds and pistol ammunition, though not by much. We're out of grenades and Molotov cocktails. We've got two Claymores left and plenty of antique weaponry—and food."

"Food?"

"Lots of it. If an army really does fight on its stomach—and who should know better than Napoleon?—we're going to be fine."

"I am glad to hear that," said Fitzduane.

FITZDUANE'S ISLAND—0013 HOURS

If there was one thing in the world—leaving out drink and women—that Ranger Sergeant Geronimo Grady loved more than driving fast cars at somebody else's expense, it was firing the Milan missile at government expense.

At least he was one taxpayer who knew exactly where his money was going, for each missile cost as much as he would earn in two years, and the supporting equipment, such as the computerized simulator that he'd spent so many hours, days, and weeks practicing on, cost more than he was likely to earn in a lifetime. It was a sobering thought, and it added a definite piquancy to his pleasure.

Oddly enough, he had never considered firing the Milan at a real human target. Up to now it had been more like a giant video game, even when he'd fired live missiles in the Glen of Imaal. He wondered how he'd feel as he pressed the firing button knowing that other human beings were about to be obliterated by his action. Given his relentless Ranger training, the briefing on the Hangman, and the basic fact that if he did not eliminate the opposition first, it would be quite delighted to do that small thing to him, he thought he'd feel just fine, but he didn't know. He wouldn't actually know until he'd done it—and that experience was only scant minutes away. His hands felt sweaty, but he couldn't move to wipe them.

Twenty meters ahead of him Lieutenant Harty was about to kill two terrorists posted on the Hangman's perimeter to take out any Rangers who had survived the SAM-7. Grady could have done it—they looked close enough to touch and smell through the gray-green image of his four-power night sight—but it was to be done silently. Harty specialized in such tasks and was equipped accordingly.

The double thunk of the specially built heavy-caliber subsonic weapon was scarcely perceptible in the gusting wind. Grady saw the effect before he heard the noise, and the result was all the more obscene for being rendered bloodless by the limited-color filtered image in his telescopic sight. It was as if the first man's face had suddenly been wiped away and replaced with a dark smear. The second terrorist turned his head in a reflex action toward his dead comrade. The modified Glaser bullet struck him on the cheekbone and blew off the top of his skull.

Grady and his loader ran forward and slid into the captured position. A regular army Milan had a four-man section to direct, load, and fire the missile, but in the Rangers, as always, you did more with less, better and faster. Or you didn't get in, or you died.

It was a natural depression, nearly ideal as a Milan position, though devoid of the top cover that was a basic requirement if you were going after tanks. But there were certainly more than the five meters of clearance that you needed to the rear to avoid toasting yourself in the backblast.

Eighteen kilos of firing post—the unglamorous term applied to the expensive missile-launching setup containing tripod, aiming mechanism, electronic sight, and firing button—were placed in position and carefully leveled. Grady lay down behind the weapon, and twelve kilos of factory-sealed missile were placed in position on the firing post.

Ahead of him, slightly to his right and just under a thousand meters away, were the heavy-machine-gun emplacements pinpointed by the colonel circling in the Optica overhead. Nearly a full kilometer couldn't be considered point-blank, but it was close enough. At that distance Grady could achieve almost one hundred percent accuracy on armored moving targets, at least in training. So the first gun position shouldn't be a problem.

The second position might be harder, since it would have time to locate the Rangers and open fire before he could reload. If they had infrared equipment, the backblast would give him away immediately. Theoretically, since the missile would take perhaps twelve seconds to complete its flight, both emplacements could fire back for vital seconds if they reacted fast enough. On the other hand, if they were concentrating on the castle and didn't have any specialized gear, he might just get that second missile off in time. It was possible to fire up to five missiles a minute under some circumstances, but in this case, if he allowed for reloading and changing the point of aim—not to mention firing in the dark under combat conditions—the minimum time window, assuming two first-time hits, should be estimated at around thirty seconds.

He calculated that in those thirty seconds the Russian-made 12.7 mm heavies could put about six hundred rounds into him, Geronimo Grady, personally. It was an incentive to shoot straight.

It occurred to Grady that he was doing much the same job as Harty had just carried out, though on a larger scale. He tried to cleanse his mind of the images of two human beings being so casually swatted away. He tried not to think what Geronimo Grady would look like after six hundred 12.7 mm rounds had done their worst to him. Then training and discipline took over, primed by a healthy dose of fear. Harty tapped him on the shoulder. "Engage," he said.

FITZDUANE'S ISLAND—0013 HOURS

Five Rangers out of the first stick designated to jump had survived the SAM-7 strike.

While Harty, Grady, and Roche, who was acting as loader, concentrated on setting up the Milan missile position, the balance of the tiny force, Sergeants Quinlan and Hannigan, infiltrated through the terrorists' perimeter defenses and set up a strike position less than a hundred meters from the two heavy-machine-gun positions and well to one side of the Milan's projected line of flight.

The two men had seen the effect of a Milan strike on a number of occasions and had no desire to encounter an errant missile. They comforted themselves with the thought that not only was the Milan under Grady's hand devastatingly accurate, but it was so programmed that if, for example, Grady were hit and lost control, the missile would ground itself and self-destruct instantly. Or should.

It was Quinlan and Hannigan's job to do any required tidying up after the Milan had done its work—to kill any and all survivors and either capture or destroy whatever 12.7s survived the initial attack. To achieve this goal, what they lacked in manpower they compensated for in weaponry.

The term *heavy battle order* meant just that. In the weapons canister attached to his leg by a cord when he jumped, each man had brought with him a Minimi machine gun equipped with Kite image intensifier telescopic sights, ammunition belts in special lightweight containers that could, if required, be clipped directly onto the weapons, spare barrels, reserve ammunition in clips—the Minimi could use either belts or the standard NATO clip found in the SA-80—grenade launchers, 40 mm grenades, hand grenades, Claymore antipersonnel mines, automatic pistols, and fighting knives.

Heavy battle order looked impossible the first time you saw all the gear laid out on the ground, and it felt absolutely impossible the first time you kitted up, but the right candidate and training, training, and more bloody training, thought Quinlan, made all the difference. Now he regarded it as routine not only to be able to carry such a load but, if necessary, to move silently and swiftly and to fight while draped in it all like a Christmas tree.

The most frustrating thing about infiltration, thought Hannigan, was having to bypass all those juicy targets in favor of one designated goal. Quinlan seemed to enjoy the actual business of evasion, but Hannigan always got frustrated at having to exercise such restraint. In this case he couldn't deny the logic of taking out the 12.7s first, but it hurt him particularly to have to remain impotent, with his marvelous collection of tools of destruction unused, while a pair of hostiles chatted in plain sight a couple of stone's throws away before one of them climbed into a strange-looking contraption, started up an engine, and, lo and behold, but wasn't science wonderful, shot off into the sky suspended from a parachute—a device that, up to that moment, Hannigan had always suspected of being used solely for descending.

There was a double click in the radio earpiece built into his helmet. He forgot about flying parachutes, and the unsettling fact that the pilot seemed to have been wearing something unpleasantly like a Russian-made flamethrower, and concentrated on the heavy-machine-gun positions.

Grady was about to do his stuff.

FITZDUANE'S ISLAND—0013 HOURS

He knew he didn't have to fly the Powerchute himself, and he also knew that if he did, he could use it for the purpose for which he had originally included it: to fly to the mainland if things went wrong.

Nonetheless, he thought as he strapped himself in, it just felt right to do the job himself, to show all of them, friend and foe alike, that he was not just a thinker and a planner but a true Renaissance man— scholar and artist and man of action.

"Commander," said Sartawi, after he had checked Kadar's flamethrower and other weaponry—and after he had decided he'd shoot Kadar down if he showed the slightest sign of trying to desert the battle, "I wish you'd reconsider. You are too important to risk." Sartawi was also aware that only Kadar knew the details of how the hostage negotiations were to be conducted.

Kadar grinned. He felt no fear, though the danger was obvious. To risk one's own life was the ultimate sensual thrill. He felt powerful, indestructible.

"Sir," insisted Sartawi, "have you considered the risk from the Ranger aircraft circling above?"

"Sartawi," said Kadar, "I'm making the flight, and I want no more arguments. As for the Ranger aircraft, it is toothless. It has obviously expended all its ammunition or it would be participating in the battle. Now are you clear as to what we are doing?"

Sartawi nodded. "Yes, sir," he said. "The heavy machine guns will keep the top of the keep and designated apertures under fire until you are in position to strike. On your radio command—or as signaled by the first use of the flamethrower—the machine guns will cease fire and you will attack the top of the tower with the flamethrower. You will then land on the dugout and be joined by an assault team currently in position at the base of the tower. Using the flamethrower to clear the way, you will then sweep the tower floor by floor. Simultaneously we shall break through into the tunnel." He paused.

"The machine guns," prompted Kadar.

"Once the keep has been taken," continued Sartawi, "the heavy machine guns and all units now outside the castle will withdraw to within the castle. There, with the hostages captured, we shall negotiate as originally planned. The Rangers will have arrived a little late."

"There you are," said Kadar, "a nice simple plan with a healthy risk-to-reward ratio—and our defenders further distracted by a little heat from the side once the great hall goes up in flames."

Sartawi looked blank. "It's a good plan I'm sure, sir. But risk-to-reward ratio? I'm afraid I don't understand this term."

"Quite," said Kadar unkindly. "Not to worry: you'll understand the result." He gunned his engine, and the backwash from the propeller behind his seat inflated the parachute. The craft rolled forward and was airborne in seconds.

Sartawi resisted the impulse to empty his Kalashnikov into the arrogant bastard. He didn't know what a hard time Ranger Sergeant Martin Hannigan was having resisting a similar impulse, but with Sartawi himself as the target.

THE KEEP OF FITZDUANE'S CASTLE—0023 HOURS

Fitzduane had passed the last of his SA-80 ammunition to Andreas, who seemed to have a talent with the weapon, and was now armed with his Browning 2000 self-loading shotgun, a Browning HiPower 9 mm automatic pistol, and his katana.

Score two out of three for John Browning, he thought. How many people had been killed with weapons designed by Browning? Was a weapons designer a war criminal or merely a technician whose designs were abused? Did it matter a fuck anyway?

His Browning shotgun was no longer its long rib-barreled, elegant self. Faced with the space restrictions of close-quarters combat within the castle confines, he had taken a hacksaw and, feeling like a vandal for desecrating such an integrated design, had sawed the barrel virtually in half. The muzzle now started only two fingers' width beyond the wood-encased tubular magazine that supported it. The resultant weapon looked crude and deadly, and loaded with XR-18 ammunition, it was still effective up to about fifty meters.

He ran through his defenses, trying to work out his strengths and weaknesses—and what the Hangman might do. His perimeter was now confined to the keep itself and the tunnel complex below. The rest of the castle was in enemy hands. The likely points of attack were the steel door into the tunnel, the door between the keep and the great hall, and the top of the keep itself. There was also the risk of penetration at any of the narrow slit windows of the keep, although most would be a tight squeeze even for a very slim man. They could, however, be fired through by an attacker and therefore had to be either blocked up or guarded.

If the attackers got into the tunnel, the defenders could—in extremis—retreat into the keep. On the other hand, since they already held the gatehouse end of the tunnel, if the attackers captured the keep, the Hangman would for all practical purposes have his hostages, even if his men never actually penetrated the tunnel itself—for who outside could tell the difference?

The question of how best to defend the tunnel had been much debated. Finally Fitzduane had decided that since the terrorists would most probably blow the door—something the defenders couldn't really do much about except try to contain the blast—the best solution would be to build another series of defenses in depth in both the tunnel and the rooms to either side. So, using sandbags, furniture, cases of food, and anything else that came to hand, the defenders had constructed a series of funnel-shaped killing grounds, each one of which could be abandoned in turn if the attackers used grenades or otherwise made the position indefensible. In addition, the remaining Claymores had been sited to sweep the killing grounds.

The ability of the defenders to hold the tunnel depended to a significant extent on the weaponry remaining to the terrorists. The defenses were adequate against small-arms fire, but intensive use of grenades and RPG-7s would turn the tide no matter how hard the defenders fought. Fortunately it seemed the terrorists were low in such weaponry since its use, intensive in the early phases of the battle, had now trailed off to virtually nothing.

Fitzduane considered the problem of ammunition shortage. The only solution to that, barring the hope of resupplying from enemy casualties, was to fall back on the antique weapons. Muskets, a blunderbuss, the crossbows, and de Guevain's longbow had all been prepared for use. Pikes and swords and other nonprojectile weapons, down to his set of French kitchen knives, lay at hand.

The student volunteers were an agreeable surprise. They were bright and zealous, concealing their fear under stuck-out chins and other resolute expressions. They were also—in the literal sense—fighting mad. They had seen people they had lived and worked closely with slaughtered, and they wanted revenge. Giving them weapons had turned this desire into an achievable reality. They were determined to get even.

Sadly the stark truth of what they were up against had been brought home to them in the most fundamental way within minutes of their initial briefing. A young Sudanese, Osman something or other—Fitzduane hadn't had time to learn most of their names—had been killed while keeping watch at a murder hole. He had taken a shade too long to check his area, and just as he was about to replace the rope-suspended sandbag that covered the hole, he had been hit in the head and virtually decapitated by a 12.7 mm heavy-machine-gun bullet. Less than two minutes later a blond Polish boy had died the same way. The eight survivors had learned from this fast. They now moved and reacted as if every action in battle were a matter of life and death—which, pretty much, it was.

The radio beside him came to life. "Receiving you," said Fitzduane.

"We're about to take out the 12.7s," Kilmara informed him. "We'll be dropping the second stick—Günther's lot—almost immediately and near the action. It shouldn't be much longer. What's your situation?"

"We're close to the bow and arrow stage," said Fitzduane, "and we're kind of low on arrows."

"Try charm," said Kilmara. "One extra thing: your roof is on fire. I can't see anything yet, but there's a heat buildup like you wouldn't believe on the IR."

"Well, fuck 'em," said Fitzduane. "Now I'm really pissed off. It's my home they're messing with."

"Will the heat be a problem?" said Kilmara. "Can you defend the keep if there's an inferno next door?"

"I think so," said Fitzduane. "Heat rises, and the walls are damned thick. It might get hot in here, but it shouldn't become untenable."

"I'll hold you to that," said Kilmara. "Got to go. It's show time."

THE TUNNEL UNDER THE CASTLE—0023 HOURS

Andreas watched the heavy iron door, which was all that separated the defenders from their attackers, glow cherry red as the oxyacetylene cutting flame bit into it. The door was old—made generations before the invention of modern hardened metals—and the flame was cutting through it effortlessly. Sparks poured into the tunnel, and soon the cutting flame itself could be seen.

The radio wouldn't function underground, so Andreas sent one of the students to inform Fitzduane that things were about to liven up again. The good news was that their use of a torch to break in suggested that the attackers were either very low on, or out of, explosives.

Andreas's main fear was grenades. He tried to think whether he'd taken enough precautions against them. The defenders had prepared their normal sandbag barricades, of course, but they had also made extensive use of chicken wire and fishing net screens, which they could shoot through but which should, while they lasted, deflect any thrown object.

He wondered if the tunnel defense was a strong enough force to hold. The addition of the ten students had seemed like a major boost, but after the two fatalities, and once the runner was subtracted, the net gain was only seven—and four of those were on duty at various locations in the keep. The tunnel force actually numbered just six: Andreas himself, Judith, de Guevain, and three students. Henssen was now unconscious under Katia's care, and Oona was acting as den mother to the noncombatants.

Six amateur defenders against a trained attacking force didn't sound quite enough somehow, though now that he thought of it, he, Lieutenant Andreas von Graffenlaub of the Swiss Army, wasn't exactly an amateur—and these bastards who were trying to break in were already responsible for the deaths of three members of his family.

He switched off the main lights in the tunnel and brought his SA-80 up to the point of aim. A light-colored outline in his image intensifier marked the line of the cutting torch. The door was almost through. The tunnel defenders were about to find out if there was a grenade problem.

The severed door crashed forward onto the stone flags of the tunnel. The sudden noise was followed by absolute silence.

Beside Andreas, Sig Bengtquist licked his lips and tried to swallow. He had no night vision equipment, and all was threatening darkness. "Day and Night": he thought of Osman with a sense of terrible loss and sadness, and then anger and a resolute determination to hit back, to put a stop to this evil, gripped him.

THE MILAN TEAM OUTSIDE FITZDUANE'S CASTLE
—0023 HOURS

The pre-aim mark of the Ranger Milan was aligned with the protruding barrel of the first heavy-machine-gun position. The terrorist gun crew was hidden by the stacked rocks and improvised sandbags of the emplacement, but Grady could imagine the scene inside: the heat from the weapon as belt after belt of ammunition snaked its way through the receiver to be sundered into brass cartridge case, propellant, and projectile. The crew members would be concentrating solely on the mechanics of aiming and operating the weapon, relying on their comrades to secure them from any unexpected attack. They would be tired but exhilarated, infected by the power of the weapon they served. They would be young men with mothers and families and children and dreams, motivated to be here on this island far from their home for reasons Grady would never know or ever really want to know—what difference would it make?

He pressed the firing button, sending a signal to the junction box. From there a powerful current ignited the gas generator at the back of the missile, simultaneously launching the missile and blasting the now-useless launch tube away from the launcher. Once the rocket was free of the launcher, its motor cut in. The missile accelerated up to its maximum velocity of more than nine hundred meters per second, trailing its guidance wire behind it.

With the weight of twelve kilos of missile now free of the firing post, the pre-aim mark was no longer needed, and Grady concentrated on keeping the missile within the "80 mil" circle at the center of the reticule sight on the target. The trick was, in fact, to concentrate on the target, not the missile, since the Milan's tracking computer monitored the missile's position by reading the infrared signals emitted by the missile's rocket motor and sending any fresh guidance instructions along the hair-thin guidance wire.

For the first four hundred meters the missile's flight path was normally erratic, but beyond that distance the missile would follow the instructions transmitted by the wire and could be flown with unjammable accuracy onto the target. In simple terms, where Grady pointed the eight-power sight on the firing post, the missile went. Grady was flying it the way a child flies a model airplane, only at a speed and with a precision and purpose that had little to do with any child.

The missile hit precisely as aimed. Designed for punching through the thick superstrength metal skin of a main battle tank, the warhead achieved its purpose by a savage transfer of kinetic energy rather than conventional explosives. Massive shock waves spread through the rock emplacement, shattering it into lethal fragments and destroying men and weapon in a millisecond.

"Cut!" shouted Grady. His number two, Roche, the loader, activated the quick-release latch that held in position the now-defunct junction box and the other end of the fired missile's guidance wire. A new missile tube was clipped into position in a routine practiced a thousand times; a fresh junction box and guidance wire were connected with the Milan firing post's electronic brain.

Grady traversed to the second heavy-machine-gun emplacement, the tripod mechanism smooth and positive; it was checked automatically by a test 360-degree traverse each time the tripod was set up. Training, training, training, concentrating only on what had to be done: no other thoughts were in his mind.

He could see the second gun firing tracer toward the castle. He aligned the pre-aim mark. This time he could see into the emplacement. Someone was gesticulating. The 12.7 mm stopped firing.

He pressed the firing button. Again his vision was obscured for perhaps half a second while the smoke from the initial ignition dissipated. On still days the smoke could linger for over a second and a half, and an operator would have to steer blind for that time, relying only on skill and experience. Novices tended to try to jerk the missile back on target when it reappeared, but that never worked. You had to keep cool and work smoothly. The Milan liked to be caressed to a kill.

The gun was swiveling toward his position. The high-magnification periscope sight of the Milan showed a gaping muzzle that now seemed to be pointed directly at him. He could see the flames as the heavy weapon fired. The rounds traveled faster than the missile and cracked supersonically over his head. He was unaware of the incoming fire. He was thinking that the flaming muzzle pointed toward him made an excellent point of aim.

There was a small explosion where the muzzle had been, and the target was obscured. His mind simultaneously registered a 40 mm grenade strike, estimated that it was either Hannigan or Quinlan giving him covering fire, registered annoyance that his aiming point had been removed, suddenly understood that he had been within a split second of being killed—and guided the missile home through the smoke and debris of the grenade explosion to the target.

It was another direct hit. "Cut!" he shouted, and again the release mechanism was activated by Roche, the junction box and umbilical wire were released, and a fresh missile was clipped into place.

Quinlan and Hannigan raked the shattered remnants of the heavy-machine-gun positions with 40 mm grenade and machine-gun fire, cutting down the few survivors in seconds.

An intense firefight broke out all around the Rangers. The terrorists, realizing that they had been infiltrated, were trying to wipe out the threat. Automatic fire filled the air, and there was the flash and crack of exploding grenades, the whump of 40 mm projectiles, and the dreadful scything and slashing of Claymores. The highly trained Rangers, though outnumbered, had the advantages of surprise, night-vision telescopic sights, better weaponry, and full ammunition supplies.

Circling above them, Kilmara in the Optica, now able to fly much lower thanks to the elimination of the heavy machine guns, identified pockets of resistance. The IR-18's thermal imager cut through darkness and normal camouflage effortlessly. Body heat given off by exertion and the radiant heat from weaponry made the task easier still. Personal infrared IFF (Identification—Friend or Foe?) transmitters worn by the Rangers enabled him to filter out his own unit. The task was made administratively easier by a coupled computer unit that remembered the situation on the ground at a designated point in time and overlaid coordinates.

The moment the destruction of the Hangman's 12.7s had been confirmed, Kilmara had given the order for the remaining Ranger transport to go in and, this time, drop its cargo of six heavily laden and impatient Rangers within five hundred meters of the outer perimeter of combat. Within minutes the Ranger reinforcements were in action. Günther now took over ground command.

It soon struck Günther that hostile fire was slackening and had been lighter than expected ever since they landed. In the noise and fury and chaos of the firefight it took a few minutes for the significance of this to register, but when with three aimed three-round bursts of his SA-80 he had killed a small group of men with bayonets fixed to their AK-47s, he thought it worth investigating further. He checked the ammunition pouches on the corpses. All were empty. He checked the clips on the AK-47s. These were empty also.

He radioed his suspicions to Kilmara. Seconds later a "Hold fire unless threatened" order was given to the Rangers, and a loudspeaker-enhanced voice boomed a call to surrender from the sky. The command was repeated in French and German and Kilmara's rather basic Arabic.

There was no response. The surrender plea had come too late. As best they could determine, all the terrorists outside the castle were now dead or incapacitated, the fallen all having been given an extra burst as they lay in accordance with normal Ranger procedure in a firefight of making sure that what goes down stays down. Safe prisoner taking was impossible under such circumstances, but the threat of being shot by a wounded fanatic—as experience had shown—was very real.

The battle outside the castle was over.

Chapter Thirty

Sig Bengtquist lay sprawled against some sandbags that had become dislodged in the fight and tried to make sense of it all.

He found it difficult since he was in pain, though the medication given to him by the Ranger medic—a grim figure in his blue-black combat uniform, blackened face, radio-equipped combat helmet, and mass of high tech weaponry—was starting to take effect. He was beginning to feel drowsy. Recent memory and current reality were becoming confused.

He fought the drug. He knew he'd never experience anything like these last few minutes again. The firefight had been more intense, more savage, and more brutal than he had ever imagined. The saving grace was that it had been brief. The carnage in the tunnel had been over in a few terrible minutes, and now the floor and the walls and even the ceiling were streaked with blood and human matter, and shattered bodies littered the ground.

The stench was that of a slaughterhouse.

He remembered the door crashing onto the flagstones after the terrorists had cut through it. It was pitch-dark. The sound had

499

reverberated in his ears for what seemed an eternity, and he had become convinced that under its cover the terrorists were advancing, that even as he cowered in fear, they were only seconds away, the blades of their fighting knives and bayonets ready to cut and slash at his body.

Sig had a horror of knives. Clammy sweat poured off him as he crouched blind and helpless.

"A soldier has three enemies," Fitzduane had said. "Boredom, imagination, and the enemy. Lucky you—you won't have time to be bored. That leaves two: your imagination and the terrorists. Of the two, you'll find your own mind by far the more dangerous, so watch it. A little fear gets the adrenaline going and gives you a fighting edge; that's fine. Too much fear, on the other hand, paralyzes you like a rabbit caught in a car's headlights. That, my friends, gets you—and the comrades who depend on you—killed."

He had smiled reassuringly: "The solution to excessive fear is to keep your mind busy with what has to be done and not what might happen. Think like a professional with a problem to solve and not some kid with his head under the bed sheets. Remember, chances are that there isn't anyone under the bed, but if there is, blow the motherfucker away." He had paused a beat. "This isn't a lecture from the textbooks. I've been there. Believe me, I know."

Think like a professional! Think like a professional! The instruction ran through Sig's mind like a mantra, blocking out the terror that had so nearly overwhelmed him and giving him something very specific to focus on.

He could hear footsteps moving toward him and make out the faint glow of a shielded flashlight. This wasn't his imagination. They were coming, and they seemed to think that they had found an undefended way into the keep; otherwise there would be gunfire and grenades and certainly no flashlight. They believe we would have fired by now if defenders were in place, he thought. He heard voices speaking in whispers, and the intonations suggested relief. "Jesus Christ," he said to himself, "they really do think they have made it."

ANDREAS WATCHED them in his image intensifier as they came through the door. First came a pair of scouts obviously primed for trouble—but with no grenades. And their bayonets were fixed. Could they be short of ammunition as well, or was this their routine when mounting a close assault? Had they fixed bayonets when they closed in on the gatehouse? He thought not, but he couldn't be sure.

The first scout checked out the dummy emplacements and found no one. They had been arranged to look as if they had been abandoned uncompleted, as if it had been decided not to defend the tunnel. The ruse seemed to be working. The first scout signaled his partner, who in turn signaled back through the doorway. Reinforcements started slipping through. They came fast and then crouched on either side of the tunnel ready for the next phase of the assault. Andreas could still see no grenades. Of course, they could have them in ammunition pouches or fatigue pockets, but still, there would normally be some in evidence in this kind of attack. Could the defenders be having some luck for a change? They were going to need it. Eighteen terrorists were now in the tunnel—that seemed to be the entire strength of the assault group—and the scouts were preparing to move forward yet again.

Andreas tapped Judith on the arm. She silently counted to five, giving him time to line up his SA-80 again. The first scout was only a few paces away. He was now beyond the killing ground of the Claymore.

Judith fired the remote switch linked to the Claymore, and seven hundred steel balls were blasted by the directional mine down the tunnel into the advancing terrorists. Floodlights positioned to leave the defenders in darkness flashed on, revealing bloody carnage.

Andreas shot the first terrorist scout through the torso and put a second round through his head. The five surviving terrorists rushed forward, guns blazing, knowing that speed and firepower were now their only defense. There was nowhere for them to hide and no time to flee.

SIG SAW a bayonet slide toward his face and parried it with a desperate swing of his Uzi. Another AK-47 turned toward him, and he saw the muzzle flash and felt a savage blow on his shoulder. He raised the Uzi by the pistol grip and emptied half a magazine into the desperate face in front of him.

Andreas was on the ground, locked in hand-to-hand combat with a terrorist. Judith seized the attacker by the hair, pulled back his head, and cut his throat.

A fighting knife slashed at Sig's thigh, and then the hand wielding the knife was gripped by one of the student volunteers—it was Kagochev, the Russian—and the two went rolling over the sandbags into the bloodstained killing ground. Kagochev was thrown against the wall. As the attacker was about to finish him, an arrow sprouted from the terrorist's chest, and slowly he slid backward. A second arrow hit him as he was falling.

Another terrorist leaped at de Guevain as he was drawing his bow for the third time, and the Frenchman fired at point-blank range, sending the arrow right through the attacker's body to pin him against a storeroom door.

Andreas had the SA-80 in his hands again and was firing aimed shots. As if in slow motion, Sig saw the brass cartridge cases sail through the air to bounce off the wall or the ground. Andreas was moving in a fighting frenzy, shooting every terrorist he could see whether living or dead.

And then his magazine was empty. He ejected it and slapped a fresh one into place. He worked the bolt and fired, and the click of firing pin on empty chamber in the tunnel was like a slap in the face. Andreas stopped and shook his head and looked around.

He and Sig looked at each other and knew the attack was over. There was silence in the tunnel but for the sound of heavy breathing.

Shortly afterward there was a warning shout and a quick exchange of identification, and the first of the Rangers appeared through the door they had been defending.

"Doesn't look as if you really needed us," he said.

Andreas smiled tiredly. "Maybe not," he said, "but it's very good to have you here. I don't think there was much more left in us."

The Ranger glanced around. "There was enough," he said thoughtfully. "There was enough."

ABOVE DUNCLEEVE—THE KEEP OF FITZDUANE'S CASTLE—
0030 HOURS

The infrared heat emissions generated by Kadar's Powerchute would have been picked up by Kilmara's IR-18 scanner in the Optica if he hadn't been so tightly focused on the heavy-machine-gun installations and the infiltrating Rangers. Kadar's second bit of luck was that the Rangers on the ground who did see him take off were keeping radio silence until the Milan opened fire—and at that stage they had other things on their minds.

Kadar was not aware of the precise nature of the Optica's detection equipment, but as an added precaution against visual observation he circled around the front of the castle walls, flying only a few meters above the ground and thus out of sight of the defenders in the keep. He did not gain altitude until he was over the sea.

The castle lay ahead and below him.

Beyond it he could see stabs of orange light and the sudden flash of grenade explosions. The Rangers must have arrived earlier than expected. It was fortunate there were so few of them. He was confident his men could hold at least until he had secured the remaining portion of the castle—and then it really wouldn't matter. When he had the hostages, the tables would be turned.

He noticed with relief that the heavy machine guns were no longer firing. He checked his watch. The plan was working. His men must have ceased fire at the time agreed. He hadn't noticed because he had been flying out to sea at that moment. It reminded him that he was operating more than a minute behind schedule. He tried to check in with Sartawi by radio but received no reply. Sartawi was doubtless otherwise occupied. He tried to raise the small assault group now waiting in hiding at the foot of the keep and received a double microphone click in reply. It wasn't an orthodox acknowledgment, but he understood the circumstances. He was pleased. Things were looking good.

He was not unaware of the hazardous nature of his mission, but even though he had the means to make his escape, he no longer considered such an option. He had heard that war generated its own momentum, and now he knew it was true. His original objective, the capture of the hostages, hadn't changed, but his prime motivation now, regardless of the cost, was to win. He knew he was going to. It wasn't that his forces were stronger or better equipped or for any precise, quantifiable reason. Instead, it had to do with more ephemeral things such as the scale of his vision, the force of his leadership, and his sheer overwhelming willpower. He had always been successful in the end, despite difficulties at times. It had been so since he had started to control his own destiny, and it would remain so.

He tried to imagine how the defenders inside the keep would feel if they knew he was up here armed with a weapon that was virtually irresistible. Would they pray? Would they try to run? Where could they run to? How would they deal with the unbelievable horror of being burned to death—hair on fire, skin shriveling, eyeballs exploding, every nerve ending shrieking and screaming? In the end not a corpse, but a small, black, shrunken heap scarcely recognizable as ever having been human. On top of everything else it was, in Kadar's opinion, an undignified way to go.

Ahead of him the sky turned red with fire as the roof of the great hall fell in and flames and sparks shot up into the night sky. God, but it was an impressive sight—a tribute to his, Kadar's, power and vision and a direct insult to Fitzduane. The castle was the man's home, and it had stood for hundreds of years—and now he, Kadar, was casually destroying it. He wondered if he would have the chance of burning Fitzduane to death—or was Fitzduane dead already? He rather hoped not. He would enjoy looking into his eyes before engulfing him in a stream—what flame gunners called a "rod"—of burning napalm.

He decided to circle again, until the temporary increase in the intensity of the fire from the great hall had subsided. It was always like that when a roof fell in—a sudden flare-up that died down very quickly, a last show of strength before the end.

He would be a couple of minutes late landing on the keep, but that shouldn't really make any difference. The heat from the great hall combined with the intense heavy-machine-gun fire must have rendered the top couple of floors untenable. Certainly he could see no one on the dugout roof now, and there had been reports that it had been manned earlier.

He used the extra time while he circled, and the great hall fire waned, to rerun through his mind the details of his assault plan. The flamethrower was the same Russian LPO-50 model he had used to such good effect at Camp Marighella in Libya. He had brought it not for any military reason—the remotest possibility of the scale of combat that had developed had never occurred to him, even in his most pessimistic evaluations—but to deploy on the hostages in case of intransigence. For this reason he had brought along only three ignition charges—tanks like divers' air bottles containing thickened fuel propelled by pressurizing charges that fired through one-way valves when the trigger was pressed—which permitted just nine seconds of continuous use—not enough for general combat but more than adequate for several very spectacular executions.

The three charges would also, he was sure, be quite enough to turn the tables in the narrow stairs and rooms of the keep. One to two seconds per room should be more than sufficient to incinerate every defender inside. It had been pointed out to him by his instructor that the LPO-50 was, in fact, designed exclusively for outdoor use, for the very good reason that the heat it generated was intense and the oxygen usage quite enormous. Kadar had brushed aside such caveats. He was confident that he could handle the flamethrower, even in the confined space of the keep, without either cooking himself or being asphyxiated. He was a master of the tools of killing.

Initially he had considered flying around the keep and smothering each aperture with napalm, but that would have left him vulnerable to the defenders' fire. There was also the problem that the LPO-50 was bulky and almost impossible to use from the Powerchute without modifying the airframe, since the unit was designed to be worn as a backpack. He had also disliked the idea of being so close to all that flaming oil when the only thing that kept him up was a fragile nylon parachute canopy. He could see his wings melting and himself reliving Icarus's unenviable experience.

He had therefore settled on the simpler plan of landing on the now-deserted roof, breaking through the sandbags to incinerate any defenders below, bringing up reinforcements by rope from the base of the keep, and then blasting his way, room by room, floor by floor, to the hostages. It was a simple, direct plan, and it was going to work because no one can stand and fight when facing a flamethrower. Very soon he would control the keep.

His mind flashed back to those early, vulnerable, happy days in Cuba when he and Whitney were lovers. He had been naive then, naive and ignorant of the reality of the human condition, which is to control or to be used or to die. He remembered Whitney's death; it hadn't been in vain. That terrible episode had made Kadar strong and invulnerable. He recalled his meticulous plotting and execution of his mother and Major Altamir Ventura. There had been so many since then. It had become easier over time. More recently the violence had become an end in itself. It had become a necessity. It was now an exquisite sensual pleasure.

The Hangman prepared to attack. Sixty seconds from making a landing on the keep, his Powerchute engine sputtered and cut out. It was out of fuel—the result of a slow leak caused by one of Etan's rapidly fired broom handle Mauser bullets during the flying machine's previous attack.

Terror and rage suffused Kadar's being. His mood crashed from euphoria to panic. For several seconds he sat in the Powerchute, motionless, incapable of deciding what to do. Then he noticed the craft's forward motion, and his confidence returned. Unlike a helicopter, which went vertical rather quickly when the power was cut off, the Powerchute was a forgiving beast when engineless. It was, after all, no more than a parachute with something like a propeller-equipped lawn mower engine tacked on. The parachute was quite big enough and strong enough to bring both pilot and appendages to the ground in a mild and gentle manner.

Unfortunately for Kadar—given the chute's forward momentum and the way the wind was gusting—the immediate ground was represented by the burning cavern that had been the great hall.

Slowly he sailed nearer and nearer to it until he could feel the heat sear his face. The metal of the Powerchute frame became too hot to touch. The flamethrower was going to explode and douse him with burning napalm. Horror overwhelmed him. He began to shake with fear.

Frantically he tried to free himself of the flamethrower and at the same time to steer away from the conflagration.

The flamethrower had been clipped to the Powerchute frame with D-shaped carabiners—the things climbers use. They were easy to manage and utterly reliable if handled at the right angle, but in this case Kadar had to twist awkwardly back, and the release of each one of the four carabiners in turn was an endless nightmare. His fingers slipped and skidded and became slimy with blood from his scrabbling fingernails. He was physically sick with fear and panic.

He unclipped three of the carabiners, but the fourth evaded his every attempt. The flamethrower remained tied to the Powerchute as if it had a mind of its own and were determined to go down with its owner and burn him to death.

Kadar saw that he was not going to make it if he stayed with the doomed aircraft. He hit the quick-release buckle on his safety harness, balanced himself on the edge of the Powerchute's metal frame, and, timing it as well as he could, threw himself through the air toward the edge of the dugout.

The drifting Powerchute still retained some momentum, which caused him to land hard on a corrugated-iron-reinforced corner of the dugout. The edge of the rusty metal sliced into his torso, and he heard a crack. He felt a terrible pain in his leg, as if his femur were broken. He felt himself sliding, and his hands flailed frantically, trying to find something to grip. He found a makeshift sandbag, but the material, previously slashed by heavy-machine-gun bullets, tore in his hands.

He was screaming—he couldn't stop screaming—and he couldn't see because blood from a slash on his forehead mixed with earth from the sandbag was streaming into his eyes, and he felt a sudden, terrible rush of heat from the flames when the fire in the great hall burned through the metal casing of the abandoned flamethrower, igniting the whole twenty-three-kilo backpack.

He felt himself being gripped by his left arm and pulled forward away from the edge and dumped facedown on the sandbagged center of the roof. He slid his right hand under his body and drew his pistol. The weapon was already cocked with a round in the chamber. He slid the safety catch to the off position.

"Turn around," said Fitzduane, who had decided to reoccupy the top of the keep after the heavy-machine-guns positions had been destroyed. A further incentive had come from a Ranger report of some as-yet-unaccounted-for flying machine that had been seen taking off with a hostile aboard.

The form lying facedown on the sandbags looked familiar, but Fitzduane couldn't bring himself to believe that it was the Hangman, or Balac or Kadar or Whitney or Lodge or whatever he was calling himself these days.

Kadar wiped the blood from his eyes and blinked. He could see. It was still possible. It could be done.

He raised his upper body on his hands, then took most of his weight on one arm and gripped his pistol with the other. He half turned to identify the precise location of his target. His eyes locked on those of his rescuer, and he started in surprise and then burning hatred. Good God! It was his nemesis; it was that damned Irishman. A lust to obliterate Fitzduane swept over him.

Simon Balac! The Hangman! The shock of recognition hit Fitzduane with equal force. He was momentarily stunned. Somehow he had assumed that the Hangman would remain safe in the background, directing operations. He had never expected that the man would put himself in harm's way. He felt a cold, clinical desire to kill, and then an adrenaline rush. It was a combination he hadn't experienced since seeing Anne-Marie slaughtered in the Congo nearly two decades earlier. It was a killing rage. He moved a step toward Kadar.

The Bear, who was out of ammunition and had been delayed while looking for an alternative weapon, was climbing the ladder leading to the roof. He called out to Fitzduane. It was a casual shout of inquiry, but it saved Fitzduane's life. The Irishman turned slightly to acknowledge the Bear as the Hangman rolled and fired.

Fitzduane felt a burning sensation as the round furrowed his cheek. He staggered backward and slipped on a coil of rope. He crashed onto the sandbags as further shots from the Hangman cracked over his head and smashed into the tripod-mounted block and tackle.

With difficulty the Hangman hauled himself upright.

Distracted by his agony, his hands shaking, Kadar made a half turn and fired in the direction of this new arrival. His burst of four shots missed, but the Bear lost his original point of aim, and instead of impacting on the Hangman's torso as intended, the crossbow bolt sank into the Hangman's broken leg at knee height, splintering bone and ripping cartilage. He screamed at the sudden crescendo of pain and emptied his magazine in futile rapid fire in the direction of his tormentor.

The Bear crouched down on the access ladder behind cover and restrung his crossbow and fitted a fresh bolt.

Kadar sobbed in agony and frustration and groped for a fresh magazine for his automatic. There was nothing there. He remembered his fatigues ripping when he landed. The spare clips must have fallen out of his torn cargo pocket. He glanced around and saw one of the magazines on the edge of the roof. As he limped hesitatingly toward it, a second crossbow bolt smashed into his back. It failed to penetrate his Kevlar body armor, but the momentum of the missile threw him forward, and he stumbled onto his knees.

The impact of the roof on his wounded knee and broken leg caused pain so extreme that he felt cocooned in a miasma of pure horror. Beads of sweat broke out on his face, and it was only through the maximum exertion of his formidable willpower that he was able to remain conscious. He fought to stay in control. His nightmare of suffering was worse than anything he had ever known or could have believed possible. His cries echoed into the flame-lit darkness, and tears ran down his cheeks. He tried to crawl toward the magazine. He whimpered.

Fitzduane, blood streaming from his furrowed cheek and momentarily disoriented by his fall, took long seconds to recover. Still somewhat dazed and oblivious of the shotgun strapped to his back, he dragged himself to his feet and with both hands grabbed the heavy coil of rope he had tripped over.

Kadar sensed Fitzduane's approach as he was reloading his automatic. He worked the slide, chambered a round, and cocked the weapon, then turned to shoot the Irishman.

Fitzduane slashed down hard and at an angle with the rope, lacerating Kadar's face and knocking his gun hand to one side. He then dropped the rope and seized Kadar's hand as it moved back toward him. Groggy from his wounds and the near-unendurable pain, Kadar tried to fire but could not; Fitzduane had his thumb inserted between the hammer and the firing pin, and he gripped the slide tightly. Slowly Fitzduane forced the weapon away from where it had been pointed, but he had to remove his thumb as the Hangman twisted the automatic. Kadar fired repeatedly in a frenzy of desperation, but the rounds blasted futilely into the night.

Fitzduane waited until the Hangman's weapon was empty and then butted him in the face with his head, smashing his opponent's nose. As the Hangman reeled and cried out in agony, Fitzduane loosened his grip on the man's arms and drew his fighting knife. He plunged it under the body armor into the terrorist's stomach and twisted and ripped with the blade. A terrible keening moan filled the air.

The Bear came up, another bolt fitted to his crossbow, and fired point-blank at Kadar's threshing, contorted face. The Hangman's head was twisted to one side at the moment of being struck, so the bolt cut through both cheeks, clefting the palate and smashing teeth. His whole body convulsed at the impact, but frenzied, he fought on. Blood and mucus frothed from his lips and bubbled from the holes in his cheeks, and terrible gagging animal sounds came from him. The Bear felt nauseated as he strained to reload his weapon.

Fitzduane withdrew his fighting knife, angled it toward the vitals, and then thrust it hard into Kadar's side and left it there. Without a pause he flicked open the coil of rope, knotted it around the Hangman's neck, and kicked the spasming body over the side of the keep. The rope hissed through the pulley and then snapped taut.

Fitzduane lay down on the roof and looked over the edge. The rope from the block and tackle ended in a shape twisting and turning in the glow of the fire from the great hall. It hung just a few feet from the ground.

Fitzduane hauled himself off the roof and descended the circular stairs to the bawn below. The Bear followed him.

When they reached the courtyard, Fitzduane turned and looked up at the hanging form. A Ranger shone a light on the distorted and bloody head. The crossbow wounds dripped blood and matter. The damage done to the face was extensive. Nonetheless, they could see that it was, without question, the Hangman. The body was still twitching.

Fitzduane looked across at his friend and then back at the Hangman. The killing rage had subsided. What he saw sickened him.

"It must be finished," said the Bear.

The Irishman hesitated for a moment, and then he thought of Rudi and Vreni and Beat von Graffenlaub and Paulus von Beck and of all the pain and bloodshed and horror that this man—this man he had once liked—had been responsible for. He thought of the time he had gone to Draker to tell them of the hanging and how he had stood there in his wool socks talking to a lived-in but still attractive brunette in her mid-thirties who wore granny glasses. He thought of the carnage in Draker when they had gone to rescue the students, and of a blood-smeared body perforated with Uzi fire, one hand still holding her granny glasses. He thought of Ivo and Murrough and Tommy Keane and Dick Noble and of the woman he loved, her thigh pumping blood. He thought that he was tired and that the Bear was right and that this thing must come to an end. He didn't care about the reasons anymore.

The body twitched again and swung slightly on the rope.

Fitzduane slid his automatic shotgun into firing position and released four XR-18 rounds into Kadar's form, smashing the torso completely, ripping the heart from the body, but leaving the head and hands intact.

"Dead?" he said to the Bear.

"I think it is quite probable," said the Bear, going very Swiss and cautious all of a sudden. There was a pulpy mess where Kadar's middle body had been. "Yes," he said, nodding. "Yes, he is very definitely dead."

"Swiss timing," said Fitzduane.

"So it is over," said the Bear. He was looking at Fitzduane with compassion and not a little awe. The business of killing was a tawdry activity, whatever the need, but it was a business, like most human activities, that demanded talent. Fitzduane, sensitive and sympathetic though he was by nature, had a formidable talent for violence, a hard and bloody edge to his character. Here was a decent man who had tried to do a decent thing and who had stumbled into a bloodbath, had participated in that slaughter. What scars would his friend's soul now carry? The Bear sighed quietly. He was weary. He knew that he, too, was tainted.

He shook his head, depressed, then pulled himself together and gave a quiet growl and stared at the remains of the Hangman. Fuck him anyway; he deserved to die. It had to be done.

Fitzduane looked out over the glowing remains of the great hall and beyond the bawn. There were no lines of tracer, no explosions, no screams of pain or sounds of gunfire. Rangers were moving into the sandbagged emplacements on the battlements. Kilmara in his Optica still circled in the sky above.

Fitzduane reached out for his radio. "You still up there?"

"Seems like it," said Kilmara. "It's really quite beautiful from the air, but there's nowhere to pee."

"The Hangman's dead," said Fitzduane.

"Like the last time?" said Kilmara. "Or did you manage a more permanent arrangement?"

"I shot him," said Fitzduane, "and knifed him and the Bear shot him and we hanged him and he's still here—well, most of him. Enough to identify anyway."

"How often did you shoot him?" said Kilmara for no particular reason. Stress reaction was setting in. He suddenly felt very tired.

"Quite a lot," said Fitzduane. "Why don't you come down and take a look?"

"So the fat lady has finished singing," said Kilmara.

"Close," said Fitzduane.

DUNCLEEVE—FITZDUANE'S CASTLE—0300 HOURS

Fitzduane and Kilmara finished their tour of inspection, and then Kilmara was called away to take a radio message from Ranger headquarters in Dublin.

Kilmara was limping but otherwise in good shape. He had sent the
Optica back to refuel an hour ago and had parachuted into the bawn.
It had been a perfect jump, but he had landed on one of the cannon
and twisted his ankle.

The immediate threat seemed to be over, but until the island had
been thoroughly searched by daylight, they couldn't be sure, and it
was prudent to play safe. Accordingly the exhausted defenders and
the only marginally fresher Rangers stood to and manned the full
castle perimeter again but left the territory outside to the dead and
whatever else chose to roam around at that hour of the morning.

Ground transport brought regular army units to the mainland end
of the island road, and a company of troops was sent over by rope
while the engineers set to work building a Bailey bridge. Mortar and
light artillery emplacements were set up to give fire support if
needed. As dawn was breaking, around five in the morning, the first
regular army unit arrived on the island.

Kilmara had been absent longer than expected. He returned looking distinctly annoyed, sat on a sandbag, and poured some whiskey
into the mug of coffee a trooper brought in.

"I've got good news and ridiculous news," he said. "What do you
want to hear first?"

"You choose," said Fitzduane. He was sitting on the floor, his back
resting against the wall. His wounded cheek had been tended to by a
Ranger medic. It appeared quite likely there would be a scar. Etan was
nestled in his arms, half asleep. Without conscious thought he was
stroking her gently, as if seeking reassurance that she was indeed alive.
"I'm too bloody tired. I don't think I've ever been so tired. If this is
what a siege is like, I'm glad I missed out on the Crusades. Imagine
this kind of caper going on for months on end in a temperature like a
furnace while you're wearing the equivalent in metal of half a car body
under a caftan with a cross painted on it for the other side to shoot at.
They must have had iron balls in those days."

"Or died young," said the Bear.

"Start with the good news," said Etan, who was bandaged and in
slight pain but cheerful; she was just glad to be—more or less—
unharmed. The Ranger medic had said the wound wasn't serious and
would heal quickly.

"We've got a prisoner—a guy called Sartawi, one of their unit
commanders," said Kilmara, "and nearly in one piece for a change.
And he's talking. It will make explaining away all these dead bodies a

lot easier if we have the background. All I can say so far is that it's just as well you had your shit together, Hugo; otherwise we really would have been headed for a bad scene. The Hangman didn't intend to leave any survivors. There was a hidden agenda, and Sartawi was in the know. All the students were to go in the exchange. It was the Hangman's idea of a little joke."

"What's the ridiculous news?" asked the Bear.

"We're having a visitor," said Kilmara. "He's flying in by chopper—piloting the damn thing himself—in less than an hour, and he's being tailed by a press helicopter. This is all going to be a media event."

"The little fucker doesn't miss a trick," said Fitzduane. "I take it you tried to put him off?"

"Need you ask?" said Kilmara. "I told both him and his press guy that the time wasn't right, and anyway, the place isn't secure."

"But he didn't believe you," said Fitzduane.

"No," said Kilmara. "He did not."

"Why don't we kill him?" said Fitzduane. "I've had a lot of practice lately."

"On live television," said Etan, "and in front of half the Irish media? And me without my makeup on."

"I'll help," said the Bear, "but who are you talking about?"

"Our Taoiseach," said Fitzduane, "one Joseph Patrick Delaney, the prime minister of this fair land. He screwed us in the Congo, and he's been screwing this country ever since. He's coming here to kiss babies and pin medals on the wounded—and make a short speech saying he did it all himself. He's corrupt and a class-A shit and decidedly not one of our favorite people."

"Oh," said the Bear. "I thought the Rangers were responsible for keeping him safe."

"This is a very mixed-up country," said Kilmara. "I think I'll get drunk."

FITZDUANE'S CASTLE—0623 HOURS

It had started to rain shortly after dawn, and the wounded man lying concealed under the remains of the homemade tank greeted this downturn in the weather with relief. The cold rain soothed his horribly burned body and helped conceal him from the searching soldiers.

The man hadn't been wounded in the tank itself, but near the walls. He had been caught by a Molotov cocktail blast as he prepared to throw a grapnel, and for some seconds before his comrades had beaten out the flames he had been a human torch. By the time he recovered consciousness the comrades who had saved him had been killed. He had found their bodies one by one as he crawled his way to the cover of the tank and temporary safety.

He was within a few seconds of the cooling wreckage of the tank— the journey seemed to have taken hours—when a random burst of automatic-weapons fire smashed into his legs, splintering the bones and destroying any lingering hope that he might have a future. He could, perhaps, surrender, but the best he could hope for would be life as a revoltingly disfigured cripple—and he had no home to go to, no country to go to. The idea of a future in a refugee camp—if he wasn't shot or imprisoned—had no appeal. And he would be penniless. Ironically, for many the whole point of this mission had been to make enough money to give themselves completely new lives. And for a time it had looked as if they might make it.

Well, it was the will of Allah. Now all that remained was to die in the most suitable manner—to die avenging his comrades and so to meet them again in the Gardens of Paradise.

He had lost his AK-47 when he was hit by the gasoline bomb, and that he regretted, for a true soldier never abandons his weapon; but crawling to his steel sanctuary he had found something far more deadly: an RPG-7 rocket launcher. It was loaded, and although there were no spare rockets, he was confident that one would be enough for his purpose. He doubted very much that he would have the opportunity to fire a second time. It would be as Allah willed. Each man had his own destiny, and out of apparent disaster often came good.

The man with the burned body and smashed legs moved his weapon into firing position when he heard the sound of helicopter rotors coming ever closer. The pain was truly terrible, but he embraced it and used it to keep himself conscious for those last few precious seconds.

The helicopter came into range. The RPG-7 was a straightforward point-and-shoot weapon with no sophisticated guidance system, so it was vital that he be accurate.

The helicopter was going to land in front of the castle. Through the 2.5 magnification telescopic sight it looked as if there were only one person inside it, but he must be someone important because soldiers were bracing themselves and an officer was shouting commands.

All eyes were on the helicopter. No one noticed the tip of the RPG-7 pointing out of a slit in the wrecked tank. The helicopter was less than seventy meters away when the dying man fired.

The Taoiseach of Ireland was actually thinking of Kilmara, and the bittersweet irony that the man he had betrayed so long ago was now going to enhance his political reputation through reflected glory, when he saw the 1.7-kilogram rocket-assisted fin-stabilized missile blasting toward him. For an infinitesimal moment he thought his victorious troops were firing some kind of victory salute.

The HEAT warhead cut straight through the Perspex canopy, making two neat, round holes as if for ventilation. There was no explosion. Fitzduane, Kilmara, the Bear, Etan, and the other survivors of the original defenders watched the missile strike—and plow through the cabin harmlessly—with absolute incredulity.

There was a barrage of shots as the firer of the missile was cut down.

Kilmara put down his high-power binoculars. He had been looking directly at the Taoiseach in the approaching helicopter at the precise moment of the free-flight missile's impact.

"Well, I guess we can't win them all," he said slowly as the Taoiseach headed too fast toward a decidedly rough landing. "Too much vodka on the RPG-7 production line, I suppose." His eyes lit up. "Still, that'll teach him to listen to my advice. What a hell of a way to start the day."

"How did you do that?" said the Bear to Fitzduane.

"And without moving your lips," added de Guevain.

"I didn't," said Fitzduane, "though it was tempting."

"Probably a spell," said de Guevain.

"Great television," said Etan. "The bastard will make the news yet again."

"Nonstick politician or not," said Kilmara with some satisfaction, "I think he'll need a fresh pair of pants. Oh, well, his day will come."

The media helicopter had arrived and was obviously torn between wanting to get close-ups of the perforated aircraft and a not unreasonable desire to avoid receiving the same sort of treatment as the Taoiseach. Camera lenses sprouted from open doors and windows.

The pilot—manifestly without combat experience—made a series of quick forays and then darted away. Fitzduane expected this amateur jinking to dislodge one of the cameramen any minute and for a body or two to come flying through the air.

"What's the time?" asked the Bear.

"About six-thirty," said Fitzduane. "Time for all good Irish men and women to be in bed."

"Time for breakfast," said the Bear.

"Typical bloody Swiss," said Fitzduane.

"If everybody minded their own business," said the Duchess in a hoarse growl, "the world would go round a great deal faster than it does."

—LEWIS CARROLL,
Alice in Wonderland

"A Swiss Lewis Carroll is not possible."

—VRENI RUTSCHMAN, Zurich,
March 1981

Author's Note and Acknowledgments

Games of the Hangman is a work of fiction—with all that such a convention implies—but it was inspired by a true event that happened very much as described at the beginning of this book.

I caught the body as it was cut down and felt much as Fitzduane did. Samuel Johnson remarked: "Depend upon it, Sir, when a man knows he is to be hanged in a fortnight, it concentrates his mind wonderfully." To which I might add: so does finding a hanging body.

This book would not have been possible without the help of a great number of people who gave of their time and enthusiasm. It is not the convention to include detailed acknowledgments in a work of fiction, but conventions evolve, and in this case I feel it would be ungracious—not to mention plain unfriendly—to fail to acknowledge the cooperation and assistance I have been rendered. Literally hundreds of people and dozens of organizations were involved—too large a number to mention all individually—but I have included some to represent the many. Certain people, particularly those involved in counterterrorism and certain other military specialties, would prefer not to be mentioned at all for obvious reasons.

Ranks, titles, and positions mentioned were those held at the time of the research.

The list of those organizations and individuals to whom I would like to express my gratitude and appreciation is as follows:

Ireland:
The Irish Army: Captain Peter Byrnes; Commandant Des Ashe; Commandant Martin Egan; Commandant Des Travers; Captain Howard Berney; Sergeant John Rochford of the Infantry Weapons School.
The Irish Police, the Gardai Siochana: Sergeant Vincent Bergin; Superintendent Matt English. Their Forensic Science Laboratory: Dr. Jim Donovan; Dr. Tim Creedon; Mary O'Connor.
The U.S. Embassy: Colonel Haase, Military Attaché; John Dennis, Cultural Attaché; Margo Collins.
RTE, Ireland's national television service: Joe Mulholland, editor of "Today Tonight"; Olivia O'Leary; Pauline O'Brien; Deirdre Younge; Tom McCaughren.
The *Irish Times:* Niall Fallon.
Special tribute to Liz O'Reilly; the Clissmann clan; and Budge and Helmut and Conn and Sandra and Frank and Dieter and Mary in particular.
Tony Gunning and the staff of AIB Clonmel.
Kate Gillespie; Sibylle Knobel; Joe and Christiane Hackbarth; Alan Dooley.

Switzerland:
The Swiss Army: Oberst Stucki; Hauptmann Urs Gerber; Major Stahli; Etienne Reichel; Korporals Thomas Aebersold and J. Hanni.
The Bern Criminal Police: Adjunkt Amherd, Chief of the Kriminalpolizei; Detective Sergeant Heinz Boss.
The Swiss Federal Police: Dr. Peter Huber; Commissaire Jordan.
Der Bund: Christine Kobler, Ulrike Sieber.
Many thanks to: Anne Marie Buess; Eva and Walo von Buren; Jacqueline Vuichard; Luli Fornera; Vreni and Gotz; Ursula Meier; Hans Rudi Gunther; Hanna Trauer; Alfred Waspi; Xavier Koller; Beat and Chloe Hodler; Carmen Schupbach; Mario and Brigitte Volpe; Suzanne Bondallaz-Reiser; Niklaus and Anke von Steiger; Oskar Ludi; Daniel Eckman; J. J. Gauer of the Schweizerhof; Peter Arengo-Jones, John Wicks of the *Financial Times;* W. Mamie; N. Vogel; Vincent Carter; Mario-Michel Affentranger; Rolf Spring; Professor Leupi; Dr. Guido Smezer; Dieter Jordi, Notar; Examining

Magistrate Yester; Dr. Janos Molnar; Professor Ulrich Imhof; Dr. Strasser Yenni; Mr. Studen of the Bürgergemeinde; Dr. George Thorman; Dr. Christophe de Steiger; Marcel Grandjean; Dr. Frei; Isidor J. Mathis of the Bellevue Hotel; Gami Florian of the Aarbergerhof.

Germany:
The Bundeskriminalamt and Wiesbaden: Gitta Wenssen.

Great Britain:
Leonard Holihan of the Arc Institute and Optica; Chris Chadwick of Optica.
Hugh Townsend of Pilatus Britten-Norman Islander.
Pete Flynn of Powerchute.
Geoff Sangster of Royal Ordnance.
Ken Salisbury of Pilkington Defence.
Peter Barnes; Colin White; John Drewry; Chester Wedgewood; Annie Lapper; Pilar Pelaez.

The United States:
The U.S. Army, via Dr. William F. Atwater and Armando Framarini of the Ordnance Museum of the Aberdeen Proving Ground.
Bonnie Carlson, Michael Kaplan, and the staff of Sterling Lord Literistic; Vicki Kriete.
Alan Williams, Publisher; Peter Schneider; and the other personnel of Grove Weidenfeld.
Al Russo and Joe Bradley of Stardate Computer Systems of Brooklyn.
Chris and Jane Carrdus—special thanks; Elliott Erwitt; Denis Martin; John Pritchard; James T. Miley; Jimmy Ziede; Caleb and Barbara Davis; Pat Martin; Donetta De Voe; Ellen and Gerard Coyle; Jim and Jean Edgell; Nomenida Lazaro; Ron Levandusky; Jack Clary; Art Damschen.

Fellow writers: Sam Llewellyn; Mike de Larrabeiti; and Stuart Woods.

It's a long list—but then it's a long book—and the Hugo Fitzduane stories are far from over.
If I'm missing an umlaut or two, I ask my Continental friends to forgive me.
I thank you all.